P9-DXN-491

JK
468
.I 6
C 66
Corson
The armies of ignorance

DATE DUE

Laramie County Community College
Instructional Resources Center
Cheyenne, Wyoming 82001

THE ARMIES OF IGNORANCE

Books By William R. Corson

The Betrayal
Promise or Peril
The Consequences of Failure

THE ARMIES OF IGNORANCE

THE RISE OF THE AMERICAN INTELLIGENCE EMPIRE

WILLIAM R. CORSON

L.C.C.C. LIBRARY

DISCARD

The Dial Press/James Wade
New York

8-12-78 P06 244 WSL (Baker+Taylor)

Excerpt from *Confederate Spy: Rose O'Neale Greenhow* by Nash K. Burger, published by the
K.S. Giniger Company, Inc., in association with Franklin Watts, Inc. Copyright © 1967 by
Nash K. Burger. Reprinted by permission of the publishers.

Published by
The Dial Press/James Wade Books
1 Dag Hammarskjold Plaza
New York, New York 10017

Copyright © 1977 by William R. Corson

All rights reserved. No part of this book may be
reproduced in any form or by any means without the
prior written permission of the Publisher, excepting
brief quotes used in connection with reviews written
specifically for inclusion in a magazine or newspaper.

Manufactured in the United States of America

First printing

Library of Congress Cataloging in Publication Data

Corson, William R.
    The armies of ignorance.

    Includes index,
    Bibliography.
    1. Intelligence service—United States. I. Title.
JK468.I6C66   327'12'0973   77–88822
ISBN 0–8037–0282–5

ACKNOWLEDGMENTS

It is impossible to acknowledge all the assistance, information, encouragement, advice and insights of those who helped me in the research, preparation and writing of this book. For many, their contribution was that of patient teachers explaining the meaning, significance and interplay of persons and political factors in events which had intelligence implications, but which were driven by other than the facts or truth of intelligence. Others contributed, again, by explaining and providing perspective to the intelligence truths of the moment. And finally, others provided assistance by sharing their views about what was right in American intelligence and how that which was wrong might be remedied or otherwise improved to meet our nation's genuine intelligence needs.

The list of persons to whom I owe personal thanks is seemingly endless. Individuals such as Corporal Danny O'Donnell, USMC, and Sergeant Major Harry Manion who taught me how to process and not become swamped by flows of intelligence information; Colonel Henry A. Aplington III, USMC, who shared his skills and experience and helped me to understand the meaning of the bit or piece of intelligence information whose significance was not immediately apparent; Vice Admiral Rufus Taylor, USN, who by personal example and tutelage made clear the necessity to provide one's own analysis and opinion to "higher authority" without fear or favor, and Ambassador Julius C. Holmes who patiently taught me how to deal with and meet the intelligence needs of policy makers. These men and scores of others unhesitatingly communicated the results of their own experience, articulated the hard questions of intelligence and provided the kind of unflinching, effective support one must have to carry out intelligence operations.

These kinds of personal assistance were equally matched by the willingness of participants in some of the activities described in this book to provide their interpretation of the human factors and pressures involved in those events. These persons, such as Bill Harvey, Ray Leddy, Wyn Scott, George Carroll, Wayne Nelson, John Bross, Tom Braden, Chester Cooper, although not well known outside the intelligence community, were most helpful in explaining the intricacies involved in conceiving, planning and executing intelligence activities. Similarly, extended discussions with Fritz Schwarz, Bill Miller and Bill

Bader of the Church Committee staff provided necessary insights in understanding the byplay of knowable events as well as the ambiguities surrounding the unknowable ones which are perhaps lost to history. Special thanks are also due to John Taylor of the National Archives for his great help in locating key documents in the diffuse and widely scattered paper trail of American intelligence. And similarly, to the librarians at the Presidential Libraries for their help in filling gaps in that trail and pointing the way to other collections of papers which give added dimension to their voluminous holdings. To these persons must be added Matthew Stover, Yale '76, who as my research assistant navigated the twists and turns of America's intelligence paper trail, waded through many thousands of pages and documents to isolate the continuing threads in America's intelligence heritage.

To my good friend Justin E. O'Donnell a particular word of thanks for his insights, criticisms and encouragement in trying to make clear the human factor in the overall intelligence process. "OD", as he is known to hundreds in the intelligence community, is an exceptional person whose career as an intelligence professional is living testimony that the successful pursuit of intelligence is not incompatible with the preservation, protection and defense of our Republic and our personal freedoms.

For permission to quote from copyright material I wish to acknowledge the following publishers: Reader's Digest Press for quotations from Harry Rositzke's *The CIA's Secret Operations* (1977); Doubleday Publishing Company for quotations from Jacob Mogelever's *Death To Traitors* (1960); Franklin Watts Inc., for quotations from Nash K. Burger's *Confederate Spy: Rose O'Neale Greenhow* (1967); and the New York Public Library for quotations from the Elizabeth Van Lew papers and diary in its Manuscript and Archives Division.

Although many persons were of assistance in the overall development of this book from its earliest inception to final writing, its errors of omission and responsibility for interpretations are mine alone. These are acknowledged here not as a "cop-out," but rather in simple recognition of the fact that final historical truth about American intelligence is an elusive goal which must be pursued in a series of steps or approximations and which because of faulty memories, destroyed, missing or non-existent documentation and the valid necessity to keep some things secret may still leave the goal beyond our grasp.

To my agent, John Cushman, and editor, Jim Wade, a special kind of thanks for their unflagging support, suggestions and ideas about how best to portray the "long march" of American intelligence from its beginnings and into the uncertain future. Finally, I gratefully acknowledge the patience and understanding of my wife, Judy, and sons, Adam and Zachary, without which it would not have been possible to traverse the odyssey involved in researching and writing this book.

Potomac, Maryland
August, 1977

William R. Corson

This book is respectfully dedicated
to the President and the Vice-President
of the United States of America—
and to my fellow citizens.

In times of change and danger when there is a quicksand of fear under men's reasoning, a sense of continuity with generations gone before can stretch like a lifeline across the scary present.

John Dos Passos
The Ground We Stand On (1941)

CONTENTS

THE ARMIES OF IGNORANCE

CHAPTER 1
CHANGING THE INTELLIGENCE GUARD

In the early days of August 1974, as the nation watched Richard Nixon fall from power, the intelligence community's leaders viewed the events with a sense of foreboding. The Watergate and House Judiciary Committee impeachment hearings had revealed too much about the intelligence community's operations for its comfort; the community's "apolitical, nonpartisan" public relations illusion had been cracked, although not completely shattered. Its leaders knew—or feared—that the Nazi generals' defense at Nuremburg of having "only followed orders" wouldn't wash for them. They knew that the line of approval and authority between their activities and the Oval Office was difficult to confirm. It was a time of considerable soul searching; their dilemma hinged on the fact that although some of their activities might properly be blamed on Nixon and his predecessors, many could not. The intelligence leaders, according to their own lights, had for many years rationalized their interpretations of a presidential nod or an offhand remark as the basis for their illegal activities. On August 9, the rationalizations fell apart, and the thought that they might have to face the music publicly was sobering. Someone had to accept blame, or at least responsibility, if the media, Congress, and the public's desire for retribution were not appeased by Nixon's resignation. The situation went far beyond the outcries which followed such earlier intelligence foul-ups as the Bay of Pigs and U-2 incidents. It was based on the recognition that, as Gerald Ford acceded to the presidency and simultaneously assumed the role of first intelligence officer, he might disavow the intelligence community's leaders and offer them as scapegoats to the potential public wrath.

Gerald Ford had to be brought on board very quickly and become convinced that keeping the seamy side of the intelligence community's activities from public view was truly a matter of national security. There was no way to shy away from or attempt to cover up these matters by keeping President Ford in the dark. There was no time for that approach; instead, Ford had to be "hooked" with a heavy dose of intelligence information, but one which wouldn't provoke his own righteous wrath. The treatment had to be just right. Enough disclosure to justify letting sleeping dogs lie, but not so much to bring about a full presidential reconsideration of actions which had been underway

3

for more than three decades. Quite obviously this does not refer to the intelligence community's routine workings, but rather the current ongoing operations and activities which had previously been expressly approved by the new president's predecessor(s). Although at the time of a new president's accession to office his predecessor's orders and decisions remain in effect, there is a necessity to provide him with sufficient information about them to enable him to decide whether to continue, modify, or withdraw presidential authority for activities previously approved. It should be noted that this situation obtains because the president, as the nation's first intelligence officer, is able to go directly to any element of the intelligence community and issue orders which do not necessarily go through such staff organizations as the National Security Council or the White House staff itself.

To these ends President Ford, shortly after assuming office, was provided with special intelligence briefings by the intelligence community's leaders to help him assume his new intelligence role. However, as subsequent events revealed, he was left woefully unprepared to counter the public revelations of intelligence abuses involving drug testing, political assassinations, wiretapping, domestic surveillance, illegal break-ins, mail intercepts, etc., which began to appear at the end of 1974. These left Ford with the messy chore of making the intelligence community's actions believable and acceptable while exorcising its vices.

There is only one valid generalization which can be drawn from presidential assumptions of intelligence power; that—possibly excepting the unique situation of Richard Nixon—each of the new presidents has come to his role unprepared to take it over. To be sure, none of the presidents has been either stupid or basically uninformed; nonetheless, each did not know all that his predecessors had done, or how they had used the intelligence community. There is no presidential intelligence "turnover" file, nor has there been a full, frank "Dutch Uncle" talk between the outgoing and incoming presidents about the intelligence community's dubious or illegal activities. This lack of communication about intelligence matters between presidents has constituted a void which the intelligence community's hierarchy has been only too willing to fill with their own views, proscriptions, and representations. Consequently, each new president, as best he can, has had to find out the bitter truths for himself. Some have fared better than others in this task, but none has been completely successful in working his will over the intelligence community, or in penetrating all its secrets. Nor has any president, at least from the time of Woodrow Wilson, been immune from the temptation to use one or more elements of the American intelligence community of the moment to carry out extra- or illegal acts in accordance with his own perceptions of national security, or for personal, quasipartisan political purposes.

In the course of American intelligence history until 1945, the turnover from one president to the next has not been that serious a problem. But World War II changed that situation, revealing the president's increasing dependence on intelligence in deciding fundamental issues faced by the United States as the world's preeminent superpower. Since 1945 each new president has been faced with the difficult, complex task of achieving effective control of America's intelligence services, agencies, and subordinate organizations—collectively, the "intelligence community." The term is not altogether satisfactory—it lacks a precise definition—but it has acquired wide usage nonetheless. Today, although there is an organization called the Intelligence Community Staff, there is no intelligence community per se to which it belongs or administers. In this book the term reflects the sum of a sophisticated system of many agencies and extensive activities which have in common only a functional base, not the single, unified structure of a bureaucratic entity. This usage also suggests the autonomy of the members of the intelligence community and their activities. While presidents have had specific problems with individual organizations and/or their leaders, these problems are more usefully seen as problems with the intelligence community as a whole. For example, the presidential resolution of intelligence jurisdictional disputes affects the entire community, not only the conflicting organizations.

When a new president takes office he generally knows little about the true state of affairs in the intelligence community. Similarly, new presidents know little about what the intelligence community has actually done with—or without—the advice and consent of their predecessors. Each president's problems, style, and methods employed in running the intelligence community during his tenure in office are discussed in the following chapters; here the concern is with internal conditions in the intelligence community at the time of a president's accession, what he is told about them, and what exactly is involved in assuming his intelligence role.

Presidential assumptions of intelligence power are similar only in that they have been carried out in secret, and the new president has initially been entirely dependent upon the intelligence community leadership for information about the organizations' sensitive, clandestine, and illegal activities. From the intelligence leaders' point of view, each new president poses a potential threat: a "zero-base" response, wherein all activities might have to be rejustified, or a repudiation of past actions and the possible removal of the intelligence leaders themselves. As a consequence, how and to what extent a new president is invested with power over the intelligence community is a complex exercise. It involves much more than showing the new president how to make a call on the White House–Kremlin hot line or how to insert a plastic card in the "black box" and initiate a nuclear war. It requires making a new president a witting (or partially witting) accomplice to the ongoing questionable and illegal activities of the intelligence community. It matters not that these have been previously approved or tacitly condoned by his predecessor; they must be cleared by the new president if the intelligence network is to continue and those in charge are to remain in charge. But taking the intelligence community's reins is unlike the investiture of the more visible presidential powers. It is not simply assumed, and it is not subject to either legislative checks and balances or public opinion.

At the time of Harry Truman's abrupt accession to the presidency, conditions in the intelligence community were not at all what they seemed. Cooperation and coordination were the official watchwords, but these were declared, not achieved. Cooperation came to mean an endless series of meetings at which previous agreements had to be renegotiated. Nothing was ever final. One day's decision was the basis of the next day's appeal. Coordination was a euphemism for temporary alliances between strange bedfellows to make sure one's own resources weren't usurped by the bureaucratic winner of the moment. Fortunately the war's outcome did not ultimately depend on the outcome of these bureaucratic quarrels; they were mostly waged in Washington, although they frequently spilled over into the overseas theaters.

The wartime busyness of the thousands who toiled in the intelligence community's far-flung vineyards obscured the bitter feelings rife among its leaders and those who ultimately decided national policy. There were fundamental divisions over the role of intelligence in determining national policy and the direction and control of intelligence resources. During the war these divisions had been papered over by ad hoc arrangements designed to coordinate the efforts of the Federal Bureau of Investigation, the Office of Strategic Services, the intelligence services of the army and navy, and so on. These rather elaborate arrangements produced a truce of sorts in the community, periodically breached whenever a change in the bureaucratic turf of one of the organizations was ordered or contemplated.

As vice-president, Truman had acquired little first-hand knowledge about these divisions and the lingering controversies in the intelligence community which they had produced. Not unlike other vice-presidents, Truman was outside the inner circle of presidential advisors, and was not included in their deliberations. This is not surprising; the American system of government doesn't require much from vice-presidents, and regardless of campaign rhetoric, no president has shared his executive responsibilities or authority with his vice-president. It is a ceremonial office with few windows to provide its occupant an accurate view of the government's inner workings. Some vice-presidents have had a better view than others because of their familiarity with the operations of the executive branch. But in Truman's case, the wartime necessities for secrecy screened out evidence of disputes and disagreements in the intelligence community. From where Truman sat everything appeared fine. What intelligence information he received as vice-president was strictly upbeat: it heralded American successes and proclaimed that FDR and the Joint Chiefs of Staff would see the country through to final victory. It was only after Roosevelt's death that the intelligence divisions and disagreements were revealed to Truman—and not by the intelligence leaders themselves.

Because the disputes in the intelligence community serve to define its environment, they are worth describing in some detail. Some may contend that this approach biases a description of the intelligence community, but the plain fact is that these disputes effectively establish the bounds within which the intelligence community carries out its assigned functions. Although these may be mandated by law or presidential order, their execution depends upon acceptance, agreement, and interpretations in the intelligence community's hierarchy and its informal but very real power centers.

On April 12, 1945, the day Truman acceded to the presidency, the fundamental divisions in the intelligence community were manifested by disagreements with the policy of unconditional surrender, the increasing subordination of positive intelligence activities to conventional military operations, and postwar plans for the organization of America's intelligence services. Almost in spite of the war's progress, these disagreements were symptomatic of the true state of affairs in the community.

In the case of the policy of unconditional surrender—which Roosevelt announced with stunning casualness at an impromptu press conference at the Casablanca conference in 1943—the intelligence community's disagreement with it never surfaced. Because none of the intelligence leaders had been involved in developing the policy, no one was exactly sure what it meant. Consequently, each of the intelligence leaders perceived it according to his own understanding, and no formal attempt was made to seek a specific interpretation *or to redirect intelligence operations in support of its supposed objective.*

Those who, like Major General George V. Strong, the army's assistant chief of staff for Intelligence (G-2), favored the policy did so without really understanding its long-range and strategic implications. General Strong and field-command intelligence officers in both the European and Pacific theaters were swayed by the frustrations encountered in trying to overcome enemy forces which were apparently willing to fight to the proverbial last man rather than accept terms which would avoid needless bloodshed. Little thought was given by United States operational intelligence personnel to the idea that the demand for unconditional surrender might be the cause of their enemies' unwillingness to give up. Their views were given added emphasis in the Joint Intelligence Committee estimate, prepared in early March 1945, which suggested that although the military situation indicated that the Axis—especially the German—military capabilities were lessened, there was no valid intelligence to indicate a willingness on the part of Axis field commanders to surrender locally rather than continue fighting. The estimate noted that as long as German and Japanese military command structures remained intact it would be necessary for the Allies to defeat their forces in detail. It concluded that victory over Germany would not be achieved until the end of 1945, and over Japan not sooner than the end of 1947. This was the prevailing intelligence wisdom which Truman inherited on April 12, 1945.

Although some justification did exist for the sanguine views of those faced with the problem of producing intelligence to support active military operations, it was incomplete. They chose to ignore intelligence information acquired by the OSS from its clandestine contacts in Germany's armed forces on the presumption it was a plant or a hoax. Because of their day-to-day preoccupations, the operational intelligence leaders who dominated the Joint Intelligence Committee paid little attention to so-called strategic intelligence. As individuals and as a group they rarely became involved in long-range deliberations about intelligence policy and its relationship to national policy. For them national policy was like Mount Everest—it was God-given and it was there. To appreciate their position one should bear in mind that the production and interpretation of tactical operational intelligence is a continuous, although fleeting, task. Tomorrow's attack, the results from yesterday's patrols, aircraft sorties, and the like are the stuff of their world, reflected in a daily intelligence summary which shows the box score and gives the morning line on the enemy's capabilities. Because of these concerns, the relationship between a policy goal (such as unconditional surrender) and the problems in determining, for example, the location and numbers of enemy defenders at strongpoint X is tenuous at best. Finally, by April 1945, the tactical intelligence empires had grown to such considerable size that—without publicly acknowledging it—its leaders favored unconditional surrender because it ensured continued receipt of the means and men to maintain those empires.

On the other hand, those directly involved with strategic intelligence and covert operations in enemy-held territory were convinced from the onset that FDR's stated policy of unconditional surrender had prolonged the war much longer than necessary. Their arguments fell on deaf ears. Part of this rejection was due to personality conflicts among the mixed bag of America's wartime leaders, but much of it stemmed from the attitudes of America's military high command about resistance movements. Once the Allies had gained the military initiative, the principal commanders—Eisenhower, MacArthur, Marshall, King, and Arnold—viewed resistance movements as marginally effective adjuncts to conventional military operations, rather than as suitable means to bring about the further positive goal of removing the enemy's political and military leadership. The idea of a German field marshall turning over his baton to a partisan leader, or to one of the OSS's "overnight" colonels, was outside their scope of high-level consciousness. Bizarre surrenders did occur later in the war, most notably in Indochina and Manchuria, but in April 1945, America's traditional military leaders were generally correct. But in their orderly, somewhat chivalrous perception of the nature of the war in which they were involved, they overlooked the key problem posed by the policy of unconditional surrender: someone in the enemy camp has to be left alive to indicate acceptance of a peace based on the lack of any terms, and whoever does the accepting has to be able to make it stick, at least until the conquerors are safely in place and able to control the situation. During the period 1943–45 the strategic-intelligence supporters argued that the stubborn pursuit of unconditional surrender to its illogical end would result in there being neither a de jure nor de facto element of the enemy's government left to announce surrender to the people, let alone to the Allied forces.

Unfortunately, the resistance question clouded the disagreement in the intelligence community about how to end the war without a final Armageddon. Those like Allen Dulles, who from his post in Switzerland worked to keep the resistance movement alive in Germany and elsewhere in Europe and thus plan for Hitler's downfall from within, were consistently frustrated by the vagueness of unconditional surrender. In spite of intelligence derived from prisoner interrogations and analysis of enemy propaganda which clearly indicated that the policy's amorphic nature was prolonging the war by stiffening the German and Japanese peoples' will to fight, unconditional surrender was left undefined and uninterpreted. As James P. Warburg, then deputy director of the Overseas Board of the Office of War Information in charge of propaganda, noted in his book *Germany: Bridge or Battleground,* Josef Goebbels used unconditional surrender "to demean the good faith of the Allies" and "to paint the most terrifying picture of what unconditional surrender would mean to each individual German."* In response to this situation, on May 4, 1943, Warburg submitted the following suggestion to Elmer Davis, the director of the Office of War Information, who in turn passed it on with his endorsement to Roosevelt:

MEMORANDUM
TO: Mr. Davis
SUBJECT: State of Mind of German People and the Need for a Statement of American Policy

Even if we discount as possible enemy "plants" the increasingly frequent reports of sagging morale in Germany and the satellite countries, there is sufficient evidence to warrant the following assumptions:

1. The Germans no longer see how they can win the war through decisive military victory. We now have such phrases as Goebbels' "The war in its fourth year has reached its hardest stage and the way out of its trials and sufferings, or even its end, can nowhere be discerned," instead of the former promises of victory.

2. A large number of Germans are more or less openly saying "Let's get it over with." Otherwise, Goebbels would not find it necessary to attack over and over again the idea that there could be another 1918. This indicates that the effectiveness of the "strength through fear" line is beginning to wear off. It will not really lose its power so long as the United Nations fail to define their attitude toward Germany after its unconditional surrender, so long as Goebbels can continue to assure the German people we intend to destroy them utterly and dismember their country.

This is the moment when an authoritative statement—no matter how tough— could be used to prove to many Germans that what they will suffer from defeat, no matter how unpleasant, is actually not as bad as what they will suffer from a continuation of the war. The attached draft has been prepared to illustrate what sort of statement would in our judgment constitute a good propaganda weapon.

*James P. Warburg, *Germany: Bridge or Battleground.* New York: Atheneum, 1954, p. 124.

DRAFT STATEMENT: POLICY TOWARD THE GERMAN PEOPLE

1. The objective of the United States is the unconditional surrender of all our enemies. The United States government will not conclude a peace or armistice, nor will it enter into any negotiations whatever, with the present German government or with any other groups or individuals in Germany.

2. The United Nations have in their possession evidence concerning the crimes committed by officials and agents of the Hitler regime. Persons guilty of such crimes will be suitably punished. The United States will not be a party to any mass reprisals against the German people.

It must be noted, however, that any further execution of hostages or other nationals of the United Nations, whether outside or inside of Germany, must be taken into account. Also that internal disturbances may prevail in Europe at the close of hostilities; and that it will be impossible to guarantee the personal safety of any German national in the liberated countries, even if he be innocent of crime against noncombatants, unless he is a prisoner of war of the United Nations armies.

3. The United States will insist on the restoration of all property looted or stolen from the occupied countries, by whatever means.

4. After the end of hostilities German resources will be held in trust for the German people and order will be maintained in Germany by the United Nations.

5. The United States at the end of the war will aid in feeding the hungry and in general economic rehabilitation. Our first responsibility, however, is to our allies, particularly to those who have been plundered, starved and enslaved by the Nazi regime. The longer the war continues, the less food will be available to the German people.

6. The United Nations are not fighting the German people as a race; we are fighting the Nazi and militarist philosophy of aggression, and all persons in whom that philosophy is embodied. Those German people who support their government which has brought war upon the world must be presumed to adhere to that philosophy. German individuals or groups who repudiate it must prove their repudiation not only by words but by acts.

7. The United States and its allies are working for a world based upon the four freedoms. The German people will be encouraged to reorient their lives toward a faith in freedom under law; and will be invited to take part in the free world of the future when and if they demonstrate that they have accepted their share of its duties and responsibilities, and will forego the use of force or the threat of force in their relations with other nations.*

Warburg's bureaucratic ploy to define unconditional surrender and inferentially to turn it into a "good propaganda weapon" for OWI didn't work. On May 26, 1943, FDR rejected Warburg's suggestion, returning the memo to Elmer Davis with a note saying, "I talked about some further statement to the Italian and German peoples, but we all agree that the matter should be held in abeyance for a short time at least. FDR." FDR's action was not lost on most intelligence leaders. They concluded opposition to unconditional surrender to

*Ibid, p. 125–26.

be a futile exercise, although those involved in intercepting and decoding German and Japanese communications still had serious reservations about its wisdom.

From intercepts of communications among disaffected military leaders in both Germany and Japan, the communications intelligence analysts knew about the existence of loosely organized "peace groups." These leaders—some of whom later become involved in the abortive plot to kill Hitler—recognized that the war had become a no-win proposition for them, and, more importantly, that they were prepared to end the war if given a clear signal concerning the extent of retributive justice the Allies would exact under unconditional surrender. The intelligence was clear; why it was ignored is not. No one who dealt with the production and evaluation of communications intelligence information about unconditional surrender wanted to get involved in another Pearl Harbor brouhaha which would show intelligence was not reaching the president's desk.* Consequently, those totally privy to the American communications intelligence take kept their own council. They stayed deeply hidden in the intelligence community's shadows and left resolution of the disagreement to others.

An interesting aside to the disagreement over unconditional surrender is that it did not produce the blizzard of memoranda which usually follows in the wake of the announcement of a major new national policy. This was due in large measure to the way in which the policy was announced, and the fact that those most immediately involved with its implications in the intelligence

*Once this fact became known to General Marshall, he sent the following memorandum to Roosevelt, dated 12 February 1944:

MEMORANDUM FOR THE PRESIDENT
SUBJECT: "Magic"

I have learned that you seldom see the army summaries of "Magic" material. For a long time, the last two months in particular, I have had our G-2 organization concentrating on a workable presentation on "Magic" for my use as well as for the other officials concerned, particularly yourself. A highly specialized organization is now engaged in the very necessary process of separating the wheat from the chaff and correlating the items with past information in order that I may be able quickly and intelligently to evaluate the importance of the product.

Recently, I have had these summaries bound in a Black Book both for convenience of reading and for greater security in handling. Sometimes two or three of these booklets are gotten out in a single day. I think they contain all of the worthwhile information culled from the tremendous mass of intercepts now available and that are accumulated each twenty-four hours. The recent discovery of the Japanese Army machine code has added a tremendous amount of such material and will continue to give us a great deal from day to day. The problem is how to avoid being buried under the mass of information, and I think the present arrangement satisfactorily meets that difficulty.

I am attaching two of the current booklets which I hope you will glance through in order to familiarize yourself with the manner in which the information is presented. I should like to send these booklets each day direct to the White House and have them delivered to you by Admiral Brown.

community and the military high command had received no prior warning nor participated in its formulation.

Sometimes national policy, especially in the fields of military and foreign affairs, is announced by floating a trial balloon. This method may employ a statement attributed to a "high-level source" or a subcabinet official. If the balloon doesn't fly the contemplated policy is withdrawn or modified before it becomes official. Other methods, such as formal statements issued by the president or secretary of state or defense, or communiqués issued subsequent to a meeting between heads of state or their principal representatives, are also used to announce national policy. Or, as in the case of unconditional surrender, the president can use an informal setting to announce a new national policy. In the absence of prior staffing and preparation this informal method invariably produces problems, because those responsible for implementing national policy are faced with the unwelcome task of changing their organization's direction in midflight.

In the case of unconditional surrender, its announcement at Casablanca caught most of the intelligence community's leaders—as well as most of the conference participants—completely unawares. According to JCS briefing documents which record what General Marshall, Admiral King, and General Arnold discussed with FDR on January 7, 1943, about the forthcoming conference, there is no indication that the subject of unconditional surrender was raised. The future course of the war, the matter of a second front, and the Allied military plans for the rest of 1943 were all considered, but nothing about the war's end. The war's immediate problems were much too pressing to speculate about the form of final victory. The tide of battle had turned, but only barely; all those involved believed that much hard fighting still lay ahead.

The Casablanca conference itself, like most wartime summit conferences, produced more problems than solutions. The Allies revealed themselves as being on the same side, but severely divided about when and how much resources should be allocated to the various fronts. FDR gave the conference its most dramatic moment by announcing unconditional surrender. He did so at an impromptu "coffee break" press conference by saying:

Another point. I think we have all had it in our hearts and our heads before, but I don't think it has been put down on paper by the prime minister and myself, and that is our determination that peace can come to the world only by the total elimination of German and Japanese war power.

Some of you Britishers know the old story—we had a general called U.S. Grant. His name was Ulysses Simpson Grant, but in his and the prime minister's early days he was called "Unconditional Surrender" Grant. The elimination of German, Japanese, and Italian war power means the unconditional surrender by Germany, Italy, or Japan. That means a reasonable assurance of future world peace. It does not mean the destruction of the population of Germany, Italy, and Japan, but it does mean the destruction of the philosophies in those countries which are based on conquest and the subjugation of other people.*

The other United Nations, he added, felt the same way.
Churchill was surprised. He later said to Robert E. Sherwood,

I heard the words unconditional surrender for the first time from the president's lips at the conference. It must be remembered that at that moment no one had a right to proclaim that victory was assured. Therefore, defiance was the note. I would not myself have used these words, but I immediately stood by the president and have frequently defended the decision.**

The apparent spontaneity of FDR's remarks contributed to later disagreement in the Anglo-American intelligence community. At the time, most of its leaders, as well as the military high command, were unaware that prior to the conference FDR had received from James Dunn, the assistant secretary of state, an internal State Department Advisory Group staff paper which had strongly advocated a policy of unconditional surrender.*** After Casablanca the intelligence community leaders found out about Dunn's end-run tactics, and this further exacerbated relations between them and State's policy planners.

As suggested above, there was no formal opposition to the policy of unconditional surrender. William Donovan, director of the OSS, discussed it with FDR in the spring of 1943 and came away with an understanding that it was to be left undefined and uninterpreted. Because unconditional surrender could be taken to mean almost anything, Donovan was convinced this left the door open for his organization to pursue a peace arrangement; the vagueness of unconditional surrender could later be used to justify its terms. Consequently, Donovan advised Allen Dulles to continue his efforts in seeking a surrender agreement with the German generals who had read and believed the handwriting on the wall. Except for Eisenhower, who asked Secretary of State Edward Stettinius to try to modify the unconditional surrender formula, the military high command embraced the formula of unconditional surrender as its own. They firmly believed that events under their control would ultimately dictate the final surrender policy, and not words, regardless of who stated them.

There the matter of unconditional surrender languished until Truman's accession. However, almost immediately thereafter, the onrush of events overtook the military's ability to control them, and Truman was stuck with a policy

*James MacGregor Burns, *Roosevelt: The Soldier of Freedom.* New York: Harcourt Brace Jovanovich, 1970, p. 323.

**Anthony Cave Brown, *Bodyguard of Lies.* New York: Harper & Row, 1975, p. 247.

***See especially, *Department of State Postwar Foreign Policy Preparations.* Department of State Publication 3580, General Foreign Policy Series #15, p. 127.

of no one's real choosing but one which could not be dropped without serious repercussions in any future dealings with the Soviet Union and Great Britain. Both Secretary of War Stimson and General Marshall began to fear that a situation was developing in which there would be no German government or German high command with which to deal.

On April 14, 1945, less than forty-eight hours after Truman assumed office, the American ambassador in London, John G. Winant, called Marshall in Washington on the "X-ray" scrambler telephone to get some advice and report where unconditional surrender was leading. Their conversation illustrates the bottom line of the problems brought about by unconditional surrender, which the intelligence leaders had forecast from the policy's announcement.

Marshall: Yes, Mr. Ambassador, this is General Marshall.

Winant: This is Winant, General. I wanted to talk to you about a matter that has to do with the unconditional surrender terms.

Marshall: Yes.

Winant: You remember that when you were here with the Chiefs of Staff we went over those terms. I am calling you today because I thought that you were the only one whom I could catch at the Pentagon building. I sent over the Military Advisors to the European Advisory Commission to see General Eisenhower and General Smith this past week, and they have returned, and I think you know about the Bern incident.*

Marshall: Yes, the Bern; I know that.

Winant: Just at that time, Sir William Strang, who represents the British on the European Advisory Commission, introduced a paper which suggested that we should be prepared to issue a proclamation to take the place of the unconditional surrender terms, provided there was no German political authority or military authority in Germany to agree to surrender. Unfortunately in that paper Strang did not use, or the British did not use, the phrase "unconditional surrender." They also so changed the unconditional surrender terms as to include other matters on which we had not come to complete agreement. That added to a feeling of distrust on the part of the Russians, and they felt that we meant to change our general policy.

Marshall: That we meant to change our general policy. They, being the Russians?

Winant: Yes, that they thought that the British meant to change their general policy. For that reason I sent a message to the State Department explaining the situation, and I got a reply from them quoting a message to me from the president. It was a single sentence. It read as follows: "I do not wish any document or proposal changing the unconditional surrender terms."

Marshall: I have that.

Winant: In talking with Ambassador Gusev, the Russian ambassador, I had previ-

---

*The Bern incident refers to Allen Dulles' Operation Sunrise, to effect the surrender of the German armies in northern Italy.

ously explained that the United States had no intention of changing the unconditional surrender terms. All military advisors who have been talking with General Eisenhower and General Smith . . .

Marshall: All military authorities who have been talking with General Eisenhower and General Smith . . .

Winant: . . . and with General Smith tell me that they believe that we should get agreement within the European Advisory Commission with the British, the Russians, and the French, that if conditions are such that there is no political or military authority in Germany to accept the responsibility of surrender, we should be in a position to issue a proclamation on which all are agreed, calling for, or rather, declaring an unconditional surrender. The urgency of this matter is from a negotiation point of view, and not from an immediate military operational point of view. If there are changes to be made in the unconditional surrender terms, we want to keep them to a minimum. The details of changes in bringing the unconditional surrender terms document into alignment with a proclamation document I shall forward to the Department of State. I wanted to talk to you only on the changes in substance. One of those changes will be the following: "And Germany having been rendered powerless to continue organized resistance." That is one of the additions that we would make to the preamble. And then there is another substitute change. It's to be added the end of Article I, the following:

"Further resistance to the forces of the United Nations or failure to comply with such requirements or orders will be considered as violations of the laws of war and will be dealt with accordingly." Now it is our idea that this document should be issued by the four governments after consultation with and after attaining the consent of the Soviet supreme command and SHAEF.

Marshall: Are you making a distinction there between the Soviet government and the Soviet supreme command?

Winant: Yes, I am.

Marshall: All right.

Winant: The document should not be issued in our opinion until these two supreme commanders have agreed that the military situation permits. The document calls for "complete defeat." If you issue the document before organized resistance was destroyed, we believe it would have a bad effect on the morale of our troops and the whole . . . on morale at home, and it might also affect war production at home. All three of these. The reactions would be equally true in Great Britain. I want to tell you what my problem is. All I have to date is the president's direction to me, stating: "I do not wish any document or proposal changing the unconditional surrender terms." What I would like to do is to follow the recommendations, the suggestions from SHAEF that I negotiate a proclamation document in line with the unconditional surrender terms already agreed upon which were recommended by the European Advisory Commission and accepted by the three governments. The Russians, the British, and ourselves. Now, we also are instructed to include the French republic and we have got agreement so far as the amendment of unconditional surrender terms are concerned. Therefore, I would negotiate to work out a proclamation calling for the declaring of unconditional surrender with the three governments, namely, the Russians, the British, and the French. I would like permission to do that because I do not want to bring the matter forward until I have clearance from home.

[At this point the circuit broke down and was not reestablished for about an hour.]

Washington: General Marshall has gone and he wanted to know if there was anything further. He said he had gone along to take care of what you had already told him.

Winant: I want to ask one other thing. And I will address them to General Marshall if I may.

Washington: All right. Fine.

Winant: I would also like you to do what you could to expedite agreement on the French zone of occupation in Germany and the Austrian agreement which are before the European Advisory Commission, on zoning and control. We shall forward recommendations and these questions over the weekend. Did the general understand . . .

Washington: He understood perfectly, Mr. Ambassador. He said he got all of that information and we are giving him a copy of it and he said he was leaving and he was going to go to work on the problem right away.

Winant: I understand. I felt that he would be more familiar with it than anyone I could talk with and that more than anyone else he would realize the significance of it.

Washington: Certainly.

Winant: Therefore, I thought it was proper to talk with him.

Washington: Yes sir, he waited here about five minutes but we hadn't any prediction whether it would be five minutes or half an hour before the circuit would be back in.

Winant: Will you thank him for me?

Washington: I will thank him, yes, sir. And that is everything now you have?

Winant: That is right.

Washington: Because he said anything else that you had to just give us and we would take it right up to him.

Winant: All right. Thank you.

Washington: We have that. Thank you very much.*

As Truman's instruction to Ambassador Winant indicated, the new president played out the string of unconditional surrender and the intelligence leaders concluded from his actions that theirs was not to reason "why not?" but rather to use the resources under their control to prove a policy's wisdom. The lesson of unconditional surrender was not lost on intelligence community leaders, who reasoned that they would have no real role in future policy matters in the Truman administration.

*National Archives, Joint Chiefs of Staff, Record Group 218, file dated April 14, 1945.

In fairness to Truman it should be noted that he had no inkling about the intelligence community's disagreement with FDR's policy of unconditional surrender. Truman conceived of the intelligence community as a functioning cog in the overall scheme of things, rather than as a resource to test the efficiency of his and others' ideas. The information Truman received from the intelligence community was severely filtered, and unlike FDR, he chose not to test it himself. This practice reinforced the disagreement with unconditional surrender and promoted the intelligence community leadership's further conclusion that under Truman there would be no court of last resort to deal with unforeseen questions about policy, nor one which challenged the conventional wisdom held by those in the presidential inner circle.

The second disagreement, over the increasing subordination of positive intelligence activities to conventional military operations, was more pragmatically based than the one over unconditional surrender. In this case those who espoused the means, methods, and techniques of espionage, sabotage, and guerrilla resistance argued that these measures were not being properly used. They contended that positive intelligence had a greater rather than lesser capability to accomplish its purposes in an active military environment. Theirs was an argument which had been drowned out by the sounds of the big guns, battles, and saturation bombing. Those most intimately involved believed that the subtleties of unconventional warfare were overlooked in the exercise of increasing American military power.

The intelligence community's leaders, especially those in the OSS and those involved with the Special Operations commando organizations which had come into being during the war, argued to little avail that a few persons strategically placed could do much more than merely acquire information. By April 12, 1945, the disagreement over the role of positive intelligence means and methods raged in every theater of war, especially in the vicious but bloodless one in Washington. Some disagreement was personal, but much of it was based on the military's syndrome of not paying attention to early warnings of problems not yet encountered. In this case it was the problem of the thousands who shed their uniforms, burned their Nazi party cards and lost themselves among the hordes of displaced persons trying to get out of the way of the advancing Allied armies. The positive intelligence advocates argued that as part of the Allied offensive efforts were required to utilize these people— not only to head off a last stand, but also to provide some means to sort out the soon to be occupied population.

In Italy the problems were extremely severe. The military's difficulties in presiding over the quarrels between their hastily organized "military government" apparatus and the Allies' behind-the-lines intelligence organizations reverberated in Washington and London and in Eisenhower's Supreme Command. These quarrels were the precursors of similar ones which were to result from the precipitate end of German military resistance. Those most heavily involved in positive intelligence activities complained to Marshall by word and memo that the Allies' "end game" was poorly conceived and too costly.

Largely because FDR lay dying at Warm Springs, these complaints remained unresolved, and upon his death were not raised anew with Truman.

The third area of disagreement involved the postwar organization of American intelligence. By April 12, 1945, this disagreement had moved from the high ground of intelligence jurisdiction over sources and methods down into the budgetary trenches, where the ability to justify expenditures was based more on one's bureaucratic in-fighting ability than on intelligence results. Since Pearl Harbor, the Treasury doors had been open to intelligence community members. However, as the war moved to its conclusion the Bureau of the Budget, under the leadership of Harold D. Smith, began to scrutinize closely their requests for Fiscal Year 1946, scheduled to begin on July 1, 1945. For many of the intelligence community leaders the experience of truly justifying their budget requests, providing expenditure schedules, etc. came as a great shock. The leaders had grown accustomed to the "cost plus" way of carrying out the United States' wartime intelligence business, and of all the intelligence staffs only J. Edgar Hoover's FBI really knew how to play the budget game. The military services, which had squirreled away funds for unexpected contingencies, were able to take care of most of their intelligence needs by judiciously "reprogramming" money from one area to another, but the military high command used the budget crunch as a means to bring the OSS to heel.

These then were the disagreements which underlay the intelligence community at the time of Truman's accession to office. Their course, and their effect upon Truman's stewardship over the intelligence community, is fully traced in Chapters 5 and 6. For our purposes here, their existence on April 12, 1945, bore heavily on how Truman assumed leadership of the intelligence community, and on what he was not told about America's intelligence secrets.

In the first instance, as Truman details in his memoirs, *Year of Decisions,* FDR's death propelled him into a situation where the pace of problems and the necessity for decision making left little time for contemplation. There also was little time or opportunity for Truman to imitate FDR, who had functioned as his own intelligence officer for the past six years. Continuity of FDR's policies was the name of the immediate exercise, but to do so involved letting Truman know what lay behind the adoption and real meaning of those policies.

The most pressing secret which had to be communicated to Truman was the soon to be tested nuclear device. This secret and the burden it entailed upon those who understood the bomb's military and political implications were severe. Truman had to be told, and the lot fell upon the secretary of war, Henry L. Stimson.* The telling had a sobering effect on both Stimson and Truman, because by mid-April 1945, the reports from Alamogordo indicated that a long shot was soon to become a reality. Hitherto, plans for the bomb as a weapon of war had been put off on the very human grounds that it might not work,

---

*During Truman's service in the Senate, he had been informed by Secretary of War Henry Stimson about a "secret" project being carried out at Oak Ridge, Tennessee, and at Stimson's request agreed not to probe into its purpose and operations.

or might not be necessary to bring the war to an end. None of those most intimately involved wanted the responsibility of recommending the use of the atomic bomb, and by sharing its secret with Truman they were able to shift a portion of their responsibility onto the new president's shoulders.

Truman accepted responsibility for the atomic bomb in good faith. In the first few weeks of his presidency he was feeling his way. The problems were many and diffuse, and he was careful not to challenge the high command and the advisors he had inherited from his predecessor. His style differed substantially from FDR's in that instead of playing one member of his newly inherited administration off against another, he took what was placed on his desk and made his decisions on that basis.

With some notable personal exceptions this approach worked well for Truman the president, but not so well for Truman the intelligence officer. Unlike FDR, who took his intelligence straight and pondered its meaning against optimistic reports and assessments of Allied operations presented by his military commanders, Truman relied on those in charge of military operations to interpret intelligence according to their own judgments. As Truman notes in describing his first full day in office:

Only a little while after Secretary Stettinius left, I met with the military leaders for the first time. It was eleven o'clock when Secretary of War Stimson and Secretary of the Navy Forrestal came in with General George C. Marshall, army chief of staff, Admiral Ernest J. King, chief of Naval Operations, Lieutenant General Barney M. Giles of the air force, and Admiral William D. Leahy, chief of staff to the president. I knew and respected all these men, and it was comforting to know that I would be advised by leaders of such ability and distinction.

In their report to me they were brief and to the point. Germany, they told me, would not be finally overcome for another six months at least. Japan would not be conquered for another year and a half. Their summary covered our far-flung military operations, but there was little detailed examination of our various positions. Everywhere, it appeared, our forces and those of our allies were doing well.*

By this meeting the intelligence die was cast. The military planners' estimate of the situation was accepted by Truman as received. This constitutes no indictment of Truman; the former Captain Truman may have been somewhat in awe of the military leaders he had inherited, and in any case it is a bit too much to have expected him to know the right questions to ask, or how to challenge the premises on which the estimate and briefing were based. Then as now it is difficult for the president to challenge the military and intelligence conventional wisdom placed before him. In this briefing the fatal flaw was not in what was actually set forth, but rather in the selectivity of its presentation. The military leaders presented the worst possible case and did not balance it with intelligence information which suggested the likelihood of a more rapid end to the Axis powers, or the means to achieve such an end.

*Harry S Truman, *Memoirs: Volume One, Year of Decisions.* New York: Doubleday, 1955, p. 12.

There was nothing inherently malevolent in the military leaders' omission of conflicting intelligence information. After being sworn in, Truman made it clear that his intention was to continue FDR's policies; the military leaders believed, quite rightly, that it was not their place to bring those policies into question. However, their error was in assuming that the president's steward-ship over the intelligence community could be discharged on an absentee landlord basis. In this case, the military leaders also believed the president would be better served if differences of opinion and analysis about intelligence information were resolved by them before reaching him. The end-run tactics of those such as Donovan, who had a personal relationship with FDR, and those others who placed their ideas and pet projects in front of FDR through methods outside the military chain of command, had rankled the military leaders throughout the war. FDR encouraged and abetted those tactics be-cause he was at once his own intelligence officer and commander in chief. This was his style, but not Truman's; he preferred a more orderly way of doing business in dealing with questions about the war.

From the moment of the military briefing on April 13, the intelligence community's free spirits and those with information which didn't conform to official cant were denied access to the president. The military leaders coun-tenanced no attempts to provide Truman with independent means to challenge their positions and analyses. Truman was told as much as his military leaders thought he needed to know. Disagreements were not detailed for his considera-tion, nor were the means and methods used in acquiring intelligence laid out for his consideration and/or continued approval. In short, Truman dealt with a final intelligence product which had been carefully screened for his consump-tion, and he assumed stewardship over the intelligence community without really becoming part of the intelligence process.

With the exception of information and intelligence about the atomic bomb, Truman was not made privy to the inner workings and secret arrangements between American and British intelligence leaders. He was not told the full story about sources and methods in connection with the communications intelligence breakthrough achieved through cooperation between the United States and Great Britain. To be sure, he received communications intelligence —i.e., information derived from intercept and codebreaking operations—but this intelligence was highly sanitized before being presented to him. In assess-ing what he was told upon his taking over, it is clear that no serious effort was made to let him know about problems in America's intelligence community.

In the aftermath of FDR's death, the intelligence leaders watched and waited for a signal from Truman to indicate his intentions toward them and their work. It was not long in coming. The April 13 military briefing provided some indication, but not nearly enough to conclude that the in-telligence leaders were no longer welcome at court. Donovan fretted be-cause he couldn't get to see Truman alone. Others, like Rear Admiral R. E. Schuirmann, director of Naval Intelligence, believed it was still possible to articulate their views through the intelligence briefing channels established by FDR. The most significant of these was the president's Map Room. As Truman notes:

A few hours after my first press conference was held [April 17, 1945], I went for the first time to the supersecret Map Room in the White House. Very few of the White House staff had access to this carefully guarded room, and very little was ever said about it. . . .

The Map Room was planned by President Roosevelt and was located on the ground floor of the White House, directly across the hallway from the elevator. Every morning Roosevelt would come down in the elevator from his living quarters and go to this closely guarded room.

It was lined with a map of the world and maps on larger scales of Europe and Asia, on which were outlined the locations of all major military forces in the world. Detailed maps showed the battle lines everywhere, and from the center of the room it was possible to see at a glance the whole military situation. It was an immensely important intelligence center. There had been nothing like it in the First World War. This was the first global war that had ever been fought with fronts on every ocean and every continent.

Changes in the battle situation were immediately marked on the Map Room maps as messages came in from commanders in the field. Messages came constantly throughout the day and night, so that our military picture was always accurate up to the moment. I frequently met our top military leaders in this room and went over in detail the situation on each front.

So accurate and complete was the information that was gathered together here that the Map Room became the very heart of all the military information necessary to conduct this global war. It played an important part in coordinating the decisions of the Allied forces. And certainly it helped me quickly to visualize the world situation and to grasp the basic military strategy.

By a special communications system and by means of special devices set up in this room Churchill and I were able to telephone each other in complete security. These conversations were transcribed and kept as part of the diplomatic record for future reference.*

To understand the intimidating effects of the president's Map Room (or as it is presently called, the White House Command Center) is to understand the psychological basis and aspects of the president's power. There the president is truly king. He has, at his personal disposal, the means to communicate his will as no commander in history has ever enjoyed. It may be likened to sitting in a soundproof science-fiction control booth, where by the nod of one's head legions are made to advance or withdraw. The sense of power is immense and sometimes overwhelming, because it appears to be exercised in a vacuum.

The staffing of the president's Map Room reflected these realities. The persons selected to serve there were chosen on very strict criteria. They were expected not only to transmit complex ideas and items of information to the president, but also to be able to get prompt answers to the president's ques-

*Ibid., p. 51.

tions. FDR's daily intelligence briefing frequently resulted in an extended dialectic exchange between him and the briefer concerning the meaning of the information. This procedure worked well for FDR. He picked his briefers' brains in order to glean their personal insights. He knew that the briefers were thoroughly prepared. After FDR's death, the intelligence personnel who had been required to confront the question "what do you think that means?" were shunted aside in favor of those who merely reported the "facts," repeated their preapproved interpretations and pointed out the positions of friendly and enemy forces.*

This action was the signal the intelligence leaders had feared. It was manifested clearly during Truman's first visit to the Map Room. Unlike FDR, Truman did not go alone. He was accompanied by Marshall, Arnold, and King, who proceeded to brief him concerning immediate events. Truman continued this practice. Sometimes he went to the Map Room with Admiral Leahy, other times with one or more of the Joint Chiefs, but never was it a case of Harry Truman trading ideas with one of his own personally selected troops. From Truman's papers it is obvious that the intelligence he received was more like a comptroller's report relating standings in a sales contest than an explanation of ongoing problems and ambiguous events and information.

The result of these crosscurrents was that Truman assumed titular control over the intelligence community without really knowing what he had inherited. He was not lied to by his military leaders; they were honorable men, but they made an unwarranted judgment about the new president's need to know. Based on Truman's statement that he wished to continue FDR's policies, it was indeed fitting and proper for the military chiefs to indicate how they intended to carry out those policies. But it was not proper to cut Truman off from independent—without fear or favor—intelligence resources before the fact. This access is absolutely essential to a president; not to enable him to play a vicarious James Bond role, but rather as an essential means to measure a given policy's effectiveness and to determine when and how it might be modified or eliminated. Because such access was not available to Truman at the very onset of his presidency, his future problems with the intelligence community were made more severe and, even more importantly, many of the decisions he made in the first several weeks were ones he came to regret.

By January 1953, when Dwight D. Eisenhower became president, the intelligence community had gone through a number of organizations and reorgani-

---

*Colonel Richard Park, who was in charge of Roosevelt's Map Room, commented that "the president's briefings were something to behold. It afforded a rare view into the workings of his mind as he grappled with the conflicting and often ambiguous pieces of information provided by the intelligence services. In many cases the exchanges between the briefers and the president took on the appearance of a Socratian dialogue wherein the search for meaning was carried out in both practical as well as esoteric terms. For all who were involved it was an exceptional opportunity and the president appreciated the fact that his 'young owls,' as he called them, were not afraid when asked to state their own personal interpretations frankly and fully."

zations. The crucial divisions over the proper role of intelligence in making national policy and the ultimate direction and control of intelligence resources still remained unresolved. And there were new disagreements in the intelligence community, running the gamut from personality clashes in its hierarchy to a free-for-all over responsibility for covert operations at home and abroad.

Unlike Truman, Eisenhower, by virtue of his prior wartime service as the Allied supreme commander and head of NATO, had a fairly good grasp of most of the intelligence community's secrets. He knew, for example, how fast and far communication intelligence techniques had improved since the end of World War II, the capabilities and limitations of major American overseas covert operations (and those of the allies with whom the United States cooperated). All of Eisenhower's knowledge about intelligence operations was to a point—not the point of understanding on a personal, experiential basis the murky details of covert operations, but rather the understanding of a high-level military commander who appreciated their costs, supposed benefits, and relevance to the national decision-making process. On the other hand, Eisenhower lacked understanding, either conceptually or practically, about the internal security maneuvers carried out by the intelligence community in the United States. To be sure, Eisenhower understood the role and function of military counterintelligence, but nothing in his background or outlook prepared him to deal with domestic countersubversion.

Eisenhower's problems lay not so much in knowing about disagreements in the intelligence community as in controlling the exuberance of its leaders, who had become policy makers without portfolios. Like Truman, Eisenhower took up his stewardship over the intelligence community at the end of a war. This produced its own unique set of problems because of the "anything goes" justification used by intelligence operators during a period of armed conflict. Thus, it fell to Eisenhower to wind down many activities, and replace those who had helped Truman discharge his intelligence leadership with men of his own choosing. During the period between his election and inauguration, he was extensively briefed by intelligence personnel. At one such briefing in December 1952, during his visit to Korea, he was informed about plans to insert United States agents into China by deliberately having them taken prisoner. He listened without comment; within days after assuming office he canceled the plans.

From the experience of those involved with the Eisenhower intelligence briefings, it is obvious that he used his period as president-elect to test the temperature of the intelligence community's waters. The results were not totally unexpected. There was marked disagreement among the intelligence leaders about which "threat" was the greatest, and who should have the lead responsibility for coping with it. Each element trotted out its own acquired information to support its contention. The military intelligence services added up the battalions of communist forces and cast the threat in terms of more, if not another, armed conflict. The CIA spokesmen focused on the communists' worldwide efforts at conspiracy and subversion. The Atomic Energy Commission's intelligence representatives honed in on America's loss of nuclear monopoly and argued for expansion of their own clandestine service. The State Department lamented the fragility of America's alliances. Justice and the FBI came forth with a litany of woes about internal subversion; the codebreakers provided lyrics to support a view of America encircled by a band of enemies intent on its destruction. All this was designed to show Eisenhower that the need for intelligence and intelligence operations was never greater.

Eisenhower's response was twofold. In the first instance he didn't believe half of what he was told. This was the height of wisdom; he was well aware of the intelligence practitioner's tendency to project the worst possible case as a means to insure that their forecasts included any future outcome. Secondly, he relied on his own experience with military staffs in a manner designed to get just what he thought he needed to know.

No one in the intelligence community was quite sure what it all meant. They had come, said their pieces, were exposed to Eisenhower's considerable personal charm and left unsure not about what they should do, but rather about what they shouldn't do. Eisenhower's technique amounted to control over the intelligence community by illusion. Aside from stopping the plans to infiltrate fake POWs into China, the name of the game was to continue the march, but be prepared for a new set of drum masters. These came in rapid succession in most of the key intelligence posts, save that of J. Edgar Hoover, who was allowed to continue his unchecked direction of the FBI.

In looking back, the temper of the times provides some justification for Eisenhower's tolerance of the intelligence activists. The threats were at least partially real. The question of whether these threats should be confronted by dubious if not outright illegal means was not confronted. Involvement in such disparate activities as illegal break-ins, wiretaps, mail intercepts, infiltration of domestic organizations, manipulation of foreign governments, etc. were given *continued* sanction at the time of Eisenhower's accession without much more than a reminder to keep one's new bosses informed.

The word quickly spread throughout the intelligence community that what was already called the Cold War provided continued justification for measures initiated and carried out during both World War II and the Korean War. Their view was that the mere existence of the Cold War created a de facto, all-embracing, no-time-limit "war powers act" which gave them absolute license to ignore, violate or otherwise abridge anyone's civil, personal, and human rights.

Eisenhower's style was not unlike that of many military commanders of his era. He preferred to deal with the intelligence community on an arm's-length basis which questioned neither its sources nor methods. There is no judgment here; each president has faced the dilemma posed by the intelligence community's capacity for good or evil, and based upon his experience, personal outlook, and the international and domestic situation of the moment has wavered over how much personal control he wanted to have over the intelligence community. Eisenhower started out by knowing many secrets, and he later was acquainted with domestic as well as overseas covert operations. These he accepted as a given and turned over the responsibility for decisions concerning the limits of their illegality to key persons in his administration. In essence, past practice became basic justification, or rather provided a kind of unstated code of what would be acceptable in the future without new approval. The "turnover file of enemies' lists" was accepted as received from those who had kept them in the previous administration. This gave the intelligence community a degree of latitude which, perhaps justified by the Korean War, was too great once the Korean truce was reached.

By John F. Kennedy's accession on January 20, 1961, a truce of sorts had been reached in the intelligence community over the role of intelligence in determining national policy. The military intelligence services were not completely satisfied with their Cold War role. Their leaders resented their junior-partner status in the Dulles brothers' foreign policy firm. However, the rise of the National Security Agency and substantial increases in the army, navy and air force's independent communications intelligence organizations placated them a bit; their near monopoly on communications intelligence information served as a partial check on Dulles' CIA. To be sure, the military high command had no quarrel with the Dulles' Cold War doctrine; nonetheless, the military intelligence practitioners sought a more active role in the policy-making process. They wanted to be treated as coequals in matters which committed their resources rather than as compliant supporters of plans hatched by Allen Dulles' subordinates in the CIA. In most cases Dulles, through his considerable personal talents, prevented outright violations of the truce, and by coopting some key military personnel into the CIA staved off major confrontations between the military and the CIA.

In spite of the uneasy policy truce, in January 1961, there was still a fundamental division concerning the physical direction and control of intelligence resources. The military was reluctant to continue subsidizing the CIA by assigning military personnel to the Agency, a practice long part of the CIA and its predecessor organization, the OSS. However, by the end of the Eisenhower administration there were those in the military intelligence hierarchy who deeply resented the practice's implications insofar as they lost effective control of their personnel and also had to pay for them out of military appropriations.

Although control over military personnel was the paramount consideration, the cost of subsidizing military personnel on duty with the Agency was part of a larger disagreement in the intelligence community over the size and shares of the intelligence budget. This disagreement had festered for the last several years of the Eisenhower administration and by the time of Kennedy's accession had become a major problem. Aside from big-dollar expenditures on satellite photography and hardware for NSA, the military intelligence services' budgets for personnel and operations during the late 1950s were quite austere; during the same period the CIA's budget was more than ample. Then as now, the argument over who got what and how much produced a running battle between the military intelligence services and the CIA. What particularly rankled military intelligence leaders was the fact that the CIA's budget was hidden in the Defense Appropriations Bill and its total amount was considered sacrosanct. The military intelligence leaders complained, and rightly so, that they had to justify down to the last penny every line item while the CIA had to justify nothing. Dulles smiled throughout and occasionally threw the military a bone, especially in "mutually beneficial" research and development money. There the situation rested as the military intelligence services waited to see if JFK would turn out to be a big intelligence spender or continue with Eisenhower's cutbacks in military spending for intelligence purposes.

During the transition period between JFK's election and inauguration, the intelligence money question never came up. The intelligence community's leaders—especially Dulles and his deputy, General Charles Cabell—had other, more important concerns, that is, to insure that control of the intelligence community stayed in the hands of Dulles and his "old boy" network. This was no trivial exercise; it involved convincing JFK that continuity in the intelligence community's hierarchy, as in the FBI, was above and beyond partisan considerations.

Dulles was more than equal to the challenge. He and his cohorts promoted the view of a selfless band of brothers whose personal loyalty to the president was absolute. At the intimate Georgetown dinners with JFK's advisers, the intelligence professionals carefully insinuated the idea that theirs was a different kind of bureaucracy. Dulles' psychological operations worked extremely well. As a particular case in point, Robert Kennedy came to believe that under Dulles the CIA had become a sort of refuge for the freethinkers and liberals who had been driven underground by the McCarthyites. Averell Harriman, for one, was enlisted to vouch for the indispensability of Dulles and his democrats-in-hiding.

Once Dulles' position as director of Central Intelligence (DCI) and director of the Central Intelligence Agency was assured, the intelligence community's hierarchy rallied round the flag and moved to get the hook in JFK. This they did by playing on JFK's almost fatal fascination with the elusive promise of covert operations to provide the communists with a sign of the new president's resolve. The intelligence leaders told JFK what he wanted to hear. The immediate focus was on Laos, Vietnam, and Cuba. Each was pictured as a low-risk, high-payoff, quasi-covert paramilitary operation. Success was assured by the intelligence leaders. The new president received no detailed options which laid out past failures in these areas, with the reasoned misgivings of those who had encountered serious obstacles in opposing communists. All he got from the intelligence spokesmen were promises of cheap, quick victories. The briefings, both intelligence and operational, which occurred produced an almost immediate presidential sign-off which ordered the intelligence leaders to move full speed ahead with all operations.

It was a stacked deck. The conflicting views of those in the intelligence community who advised caution were summarily set aside in favor of those who advocated action without much consideration for what would happen, or the possibility of failure in the operations themselves. There was no effort made to provide JFK with a way out in the event things went wrong in any one of the areas.

The briefing instructions on the Laos, Vietnam, and Cuba covert paramilitary operations indicated a conscious intent on the part of the intelligence leaders not only to place these operations in the most favorable light, but also to marshal the intelligence community's resources in an adversary role. The distinction is subtle but important, because it promoted in the president's mind a form of selective misperception which encouraged the view that his intelligence advisers unanimously favored the proposed operations. In JFK's case, this practice produced rather disastrous personal results and rebounded to the severe disadvantage of the intelligence community's hierarchy. In short, they conned Kennedy and they were caught.

Another measure of the intelligence community hierarchy's duplicity in dealing with Kennedy involved the so-called missile gap. Following Kennedy's nomination, President Eisenhower directed that Kennedy be given briefings concerning the status of military, foreign policy, and intelligence matters.* In the course of these briefings Kennedy was made privy to the Gaither report which, among a wide variety of strategic evaluations, speculated about the future of Soviet missile development. From the various caveats and "on the

*Although, as indicated above, president-elect Eisenhower received a wide variety of intelligence briefings on President Truman's orders, these were not part of a formal presidential transition program *per se*. The briefings, in large measure, were due to Eisenhower's longstanding personal relationships with United States military commanders, and not to Truman's initiatives. Eisenhower resented Truman's inaction on this matter and consequently established a formal presidential transition program to insure that a new administration would be able to take over in smooth fashion. Eisenhower's initiative was followed by passage of the Presidential Transition Act on March 7, 1964. Its purpose was stated to be: "The Congress declares it to be the purpose of this act to promote the orderly transfer of the executive power in connection with the expiration of the term of office of a president and the inauguration of a new president. The national interest requires that transitions in the office of president be accomplished so as to assure continuity in the faithful execution of the laws and in the conduct of the affairs of the federal government, both domestic and foreign. Any disruption occasioned by the transfer of the executive power could produce results detrimental to the safety and well-being of the United States and its people. Accordingly, it is the intent of the Congress that appropriate actions be authorized and taken to avoid or minimize any disruption. In addition to the specific provisions contained in this act directed toward that purpose, it is the intent of the Congress that all officers of the government so conduct the affairs of the government for which they exercise responsibility and authority as (1) to be mindful of problems occasioned by transitions in the office of president, (2) to take appropriate lawful steps to avoid or minimize disruptions that might be occasioned by the transfer of the executive power, and (3) otherwise to promote orderly transitions in the office of president."

other hands" in the report, JFK deduced the existence of and a widening of the missile gap. As is well known, he made effective use of the missile gap in his campaign for the presidency. After his election he repudiated its existence. These two actions reveal the politicization of American intelligence. In point of fact the intelligence leaders allowed the erroneous Gaither report to stand without providing JFK with the valid hard intelligence *in their possession* which completely contradicted the report. Once JFK was installed as president, the intelligence leaders made it quite plain that they had known all along there was no missile gap, but had kept silent over what had become a political issue. The message was not lost on JFK, who concluded that he could count on the intelligence leaders to protect, if not further, his personal political interests.

From subsequent events it is clear that during the transition period, and until several months after the ill-fated Bay of Pigs invasion, JFK did not receive a complete intelligence sources and methods briefing. And then it was less a briefing than a post-mortem report from Robert Kennedy on the Bay of Pigs fiasco and an indictment of some intelligence community leaders for having played fast and loose with the new president and members of his administration.

In connection with the key question of sources and methods, JFK, like his two immediate predecessors, was given final-product intelligence which left unanswered the questions by whom and on what basis the information was actually acquired. This properly is a matter of individual presidential preference; however, in Kennedy's case as in Truman's, the decision was made by Allen Dulles rather than the president himself. Obviously, there is no necessity to burden a president with case officer minutiae; but without adequate understanding of sources and methods, it is impossible for a president to make a decision based solely upon the finished intelligence he receives.

Another feature of JFK's investiture in the intelligence priesthood involved the manner by which he was informed about the intelligence community's efforts in domestic intelligence, internal security, and counterespionage. These were not covered in any real detail. JFK was given a broad overview which pictured these operations as an ongoing series of quiet, effective actions whose results would be reported routinely to the president through the National Security Council's Internal Security Interagency Group. Their necessity was stressed as part of the "big picture" of law enforcement and as an adjunct to American overseas containment of communism. No evaluation was provided to show that most of the actions were a waste of time and money. Also, no mention was made of the patently unlawful activities of the FBI, CIA, or NSA. Kennedy was given a few tidbits to indicate the community's counterintelligence capability in finding out what people were thinking and saying, but beyond the standard reference to the FBI's case files no hint was given the new president concerning the CIA's counterespionage files, the National Security Agency's "watch list," and the like. In this the intelligence leaders played on

JFK's vanity; they believed they could satisfy his curiosity about counterespionage matters with clandestinely acquired information about public personalities instead of with reports from the United States and "friendly" foreign spies and agents who had acquired similar information about American political figures. A big thing was made over source "Marianne," a member of General DeGaulle's personal and political inner circle and who was on the CIA payroll. Although Marianne's information was not very useful in terms of immediate practical intelligence, it provided a personal insight about De-Gaulle which captured JFK's interest.

In today's post-Watergate terminology, the intelligence leaders "stroked" JFK in a way designed to lull him into letting them run the community according to their own perceptions. By itself this is not surprising. The permanent bureaucracy, in or out of the intelligence community, attempts to do the same thing with its transient heads. The turnover at the top in all phases of the executive branch, whether in the Department of Defense or Transportation, breeds a defensive attitude on the part of those who must provide for continuity of operations and who see themselves as the real guardians of the state. In JFK's case, the bureaucracy—especially those in the intelligence community—had mixed feelings about his call "to get the country moving again." To a point they favored a more active role for the intelligence community, but they were unsure about their place in such a move. Hence, as the new, young Camelotians took up their posts, the stroking was extended to those who had assumed key positions in the new administration. The clear message from the intelligence community's leaders to those on the working level who had to deal with the new appointees was "go slow, be careful, because the 25-year-old you slight today may end up in charge of a task force charged to reorganize your operation or disestablish your own personal sandbox tomorrow!"

From the intelligence leaders' point of view the transition from Eisenhower to Kennedy went splendidly. Dulles was particularly pleased because his rule of the CIA had been extended without question of a successor. No JFK watchbird had been placed in the CIA's executive suite to report back on what was being done in the new president's name. Kennedy underwent so many formal and informal briefings that it is hard to point out one which embodied the intelligence community's total approach. All the briefings were designed to ease JFK into his intelligence responsibilities without providing him with the means to challenge the status quo. For a time it appeared to be touch and go, because JFK was receiving warning signals from persons outside the intelligence community's direct control. Some of his young aides, especially Michael Forrestal—the son of former secretary of the navy and the first secretary of defense, James Forrestal—expressed reservations about the glibness with which problems were made to appear insignificant. However, following the briefing of January 25, 1961, at which time Kennedy was given a full dog-and-pony show about the forthcoming Bay of Pigs invasion, Dulles was convinced that the intelligence community's leaders were home free. From reports of the briefing, it was clear that JFK did not demur in the slightest concerning the plans, and Dulles concluded that the president's support would be sufficient to keep the military on board for the duration. Until that time the military had some reservations about the Bay of Pigs. These were essentially tactical in nature, dealing with the poor choice of the landing area, the state of the Cubans' training, command and control procedures, etc. But once the military saw which way the presidential wind was blowing and received assurances from Dulles that they wouldn't be cut out of the action—and presumably the after-action rewards—their reservations disappeared. Nary a voice was raised by the Joint Chiefs of Staff against the operation. Although the Bay of Pigs was an amphibious operation, the views and opinions of the commandant of the Marine Corps, General David M. Shoup, about the CIA's plans were neither sought nor permitted to be placed in front of the president. In passing it is worthwhile to note that in the Bay of Pigs post-mortem (which resulted in Dulles' downfall) the military's earlier reservations about the CIA's lack of professionalism became part of the bill of particulars which provoked Kennedy to say that he wanted "to splinter the CIA into a thousand pieces and scatter it to the winds."

One further aspect about JFK's rites of passage into the intelligence community is worth mentioning: the dossier analysis of JFK which was used to help decide the appropriate thrust for his briefings. How sinister this kind of practice sounds depends largely on one's point of view; there is a practical side in knowing the right way to approach any president with information and/or problems requiring a decision. There is no simple solution to this question. No two presidents' styles are exactly alike, and their preferences and personalities are crucial to the decision-making process. Some presidents prefer a one-page, either-or decision memo; others the full-scale briefing ritual; some an on-the-run verbal summary by a single key aide; and in rare cases a one-to-one presentation by the "technician" who actually must implement the decision once it is approved. An indirect assessment of JFK was made in order not to offend him by the method of presentation, or to trigger subjective, antagonistic response to well established operations and practices in the intelligence community. The intelligence leaders realized that JFK knew he had to have an intelligence service, but they also knew he did not necessarily have to buy the one they were selling.

Among other personality considerations, the indirect assessment of JFK sought to identify in advance how he could be expected to respond when informed about the intelligence community's covert operations. In broad essence, the indirect assessment sought answer to the question, "What sort of a man is he?" Those who worked to find an answer were quite aware that the difference between Kennedy's public and private images was crucial (as it is with most public officials, elected or otherwise). To assist them, CIA psychologists were given access to the quite considerable Kennedy family files, not just those pertaining to JFK himself. Much of the early information about him was not of American origin. It had been provided to the OSS in late 1942 by the British Special Operations Executive MI-5 organization. MI-5, with responsibility for counterintelligence and its long experience in the field, held extensive files on many thousands of Americans. Under the terms of the agreement with the British, the OSS was allowed to copy MI-5's files, and was thus able to achieve a quantum leap in the fields of counterintelligence and counterespionage. Between the MI-5 files and the information which, in consequence of Kennedy's wartime security clearances, had been compiled about him over time by various American intelligence agencies, a profile concerning his expected behavior as first intelligence officer was drawn. Much of the material in these files was extremely personal in nature. This was not the intelligence community's immediate concern. Regardless of one's personal opinion concerning the merit of the intelligence community's making an appraisal of the president as an intelligence leader, there is some justification for those who know the particular and peculiar demands associated with intelligence decisions to understand his strengths and weaknesses in that role. It is quite true by virtue of a person's election that the people, in essence, give their stamp of approval of a man's fitness to serve as president. The electoral process provides considerable scrutiny of a potential president's health, finances, and positions on issues, as well as his political philosophy. Nonetheless, this process is imperfect as a means to predict a president's subsequent performance in such varied roles as chief executive, commander in chief of the armed forces, and especially as first intelligence officer. There is no easy way to know in advance how a president will respond to the temptations to use intelligence resources for partisan purposes, or to use secret intelligence means to achieve controversial, if not illegal, ends. The intelligence community's dilemma over these questions has been profound; it is difficult to say no to a sitting president.

The intimidating power of the American presidency compels an absolute, unquestioned obedience on the part of underlings which is scarcely equaled in despotic societies. Early on in their careers, the intelligence community leaders learned that while individual presidents might publicly proclaim their desire to have some "no-men" in their band of advisors, such a role—if one is naive enough to believe such a statement—has indeed been lonely and quite unrewarding. Since Franklin Roosevelt, there has always been a place for a "court jester" in the White House, but hardly any room for a truly skilled devil's advocate. As a consequence, the intelligence leaders have adopted the protective coloration of total obedience to the president while pursuing their own ends and visions. Or there has been apparent harmony, and final resolution of the dilemma has been deferred until the next president takes office.

In the case of JFK, the intelligence community resolved its dilemma by not laying out the seamy specifics of their operations. The intelligence leaders relied instead on JFK's disinterestedness with detail. The briefings, with the exception of the one about the Bay of Pigs, were painted with an extremely broad brush. This was done not so much to cover up particular operations as it was to avoid directing JFK's attention to specific aspects concerning the costs, personnel, and cover stories for the operations. Each briefer was advised that it was his responsibility to respond to JFK's questions, but not to raise questions.

In sum, the intelligence community leaders acted on the assumption that it was not their place (or in their self-interest) to provide JFK with the questions he needed to ask if he were to understand fully what the troops in his newly acquired intelligence empire were actually doing. The broad facts were presented in a carefully chosen way which suggested that their meaning was self-evident. This device played on the normal human reaction which deters a person from asking what might appear to be a stupid question, or to acknowledge that he didn't know something which someone in his position should be expected to know. The technique works exceptionally well in dealing with the circulating elites of Washington politics, where possession of before-the-fact information is the coin of the realm.

Some months later, in discussing the period of the initial intelligence briefings with Robert Kennedy, he commented that at the time their problem was knowing the right questions to ask and a failure on his and the president's part to recognize the full span of the intelligence community leaders' interests.

The abrupt accession of Lyndon Johnson to the presidency gave the intelligence leaders no time to ease him into his role as first intelligence officer. By nightfall on November 22, 1963, President Johnson was in the center of a maelstrom as each of the intelligence agencies rushed to feed information into the White House in partial explanation of what happened and why in Dallas. It was a time of incredible confusion. The usual quiet efficiency of the Pentagon and White House command centers was upset by the presence of many officials who normally would have been kept informed by aides or printed material. These persons seized on messages as they were decrypted almost the way J. P. Morgan would rip a stock quotation out of his personal office ticker. Thus, the orderly flow of intelligence information about the assassination was broken and disjointed as the far-flung outposts of the intelligence community attempted to respond to the crisis. The hourly intelligence summaries and spot reports painted a picture of panic not unlike that at the time of Pearl Harbor. Because everything reported was assumed to bear on the assassination, there was scant effort spent on determining which items were truly relevant. The situation was further aggravated by the worldwide Red Alert which had been ordered while *Air Force One* was in flight back to Washington; this literally blew the intelligence and military's most sophisticated communication circuits.

The crisis atmosphere prevailed for several days as a frantic search for what might lie behind JFK's assassination was sought. The situation led to such inadvertent disclosures to Johnson as, "We got this from our tap on so and so," or "Our man in the Mafia, Vietnam's Presidential Palace, the Kremlin, Havana, etc. says . . . etc." Taken together these bits and pieces of basically raw, unevaluated information provided Johnson with a sources-and-methods briefing unlike any those of his predecessors had received. Also, they indicated to Johnson that the games each of the intelligence agencies had been playing in the field of domestic intelligence were far more extensive than had been commonly supposed by him or anyone on the White House staff.

In the course of sorting out the kaleidoscope of events and correcting much of the information which had been passed to him, it became obvious to the new president that many of his inherited intelligence crisis managers were less able than he or Kennedy had thought. After the immediate crisis had passed, the intelligence leaders tried to cover their tracks, but it was too late. For those at the top of the intelligence community in Washington, the first few days after JFK's death were a nightmare. For example, somehow the intelligence community lost track of key Soviet leaders, whose absence was considered as a clear signal of imminent nuclear war. This lack of information was primarily responsible for initiating the worldwide Red Alert. Although this procedure has a human, go—no-go feature, it failed to stop the machines which sent the order because the "human" with the responsibility was overcome with grief over Kennedy's death. So much for "fail safe" provisions during times of unexpected crisis.

Khrushchev's appearance the next day at the United States embassy in Moscow, after an all-night train ride from the Black Sea, allayed some fears. His presence made headlines, but the alert continued for several more days, during which war by intelligence accident was a real danger. Only in the course of the intelligence post-mortem was it discovered that key Kremlin personnel hadn't been lost or out of Moscow, but that the regular reports of their movements and whereabouts had been submerged by the communications tidal wave which had inundated Washington. As the fear of war and further assassinations of American officials receded, the intelligence community's leaders found themselves in a new and uncomfortable position.

The new president began to probe deeply into the intelligence community's sources and methods. He wanted to know what marching orders had been given to the intelligence community's legions, especially with respect to Castro. This curiosity was based on a CIA report he was shown during the crisis period which highlighted Castro's remarks warning reprisals against American officials for trying to kill him. As a consequence, Johnson was told about the several years' efforts to kill, or get someone to kill, Castro. This information led Johnson to make his posthumously quoted remark that "Those guys were running their own Murder Incorporated in the Caribbean."

In the course of conducting his own intelligence evaluation Johnson rapped many knuckles and took his own independent measure of the community's leaders. Today it is not possible to detail the full extent of what Johnson was told; this information is only available in its entirety on the tapes located in the Johnson Memorial Library in Austin, Texas. These tapes, many of which contain information provided Johnson by persons outside of the normal chain of command and/or the intelligence leaders' control, have not been transcribed and are still under lock and key. Nonetheless, CIA, JCS, and FBI files clearly set forth that information about illegal and extralegal activities, which has entered the public domain as a consequence of recent Congressional investigations and revelations, was at least partially covered by the intelligence leaders.

These files reflect the manner in which a presidential briefing is put together. Depending on the topic and the rank or status of the briefer, the file might contain a briefing aide de memoire, institutions concerning the extent of information to be provided, or the briefer's verbatim remarks. Normally briefing papers are not read to the president. The emphasis is on eye contact and the conveyance of a few major points which can be explained in a brief and concise manner. Aside from the daily pins-on-the-map kind of presentations, those made by key officials who are not briefers per se, but who would lay out, for example, the mail-intercept program, are backed up by a "Black Book" which includes all the necessary background and detailed specifics about the program. Filling these books, keeping them current and finding enough time to study them is a major activity of those who must brief the president about the intelligence community's many enterprises.

In spite of the intelligence community's rear-guard attempt to orchestrate the flow of information about its activities, Johnson knew how to get what he wanted. His techniques were simple; sometimes he would turn on the charm and others his temper. Usually these worked well enough, but his most effective technique was one whereby he would "outdumb" those he believed were trying to hold something back or deceive him. He would pretend not to understand what he was being told and thereby force the official to go into greater detail and reveal the missing links in what was being provided. Another effective LBJ technique involved bringing a lower-level member of the intelligence community in to the White House for a special "prebriefing" on a topic scheduled later for a formal briefing. Under this procedure the individual prebriefer was sworn to secrecy as one of the president's own, and was persuaded to divulge what the president would *not* be told about the topic at the formal briefing. By this means Johnson came to know how far he could trust his intelligence leaders and perhaps even more importantly, how much they really knew about what was actually going on in their organizations.

Johnson's deep probing set the intelligence community leaders completely off balance. Their first conclusion was that one of their peers had broken the gentleman's agreement which held that criticism of one by the other to the president should not be personal or based on specific foul-ups. The intelligence leaders never discovered the source of the "leaks." Although orders were issued in the military intelligence services and the CIA prohibiting "unauthorized transmission of information to the White House," nothing much came of the effort. Similarly, little notice was given to the small cadre of relatively obscure members of the intelligence community who resigned from their own agencies and quietly took up positions working for, or in, the White House.

These persons gave Johnson an edge in dealing with the intelligence community. It didn't hold throughout his presidency, but it did help him in gaining a semblance of initial control over some of the community's activities.

Once the first briefings had been completed and the Warren Commission established, Johnson gave a flickering green light to the intelligence leaders: its legions were to continue the march. One significant caveat was added: "Thou shalt not contemplate, engage in or otherwise abet plots involving political assassination." Johnson believed quite strongly this was a no-win proposition which almost certainly generated counterproductive aftereffects, if not reprisals. Other practices, like the mail-intercept program, break-ins, and surveillance for political purposes—as well as political "destabilization" and the use of third-country counterespionage resources for non–American-attributable operations—were allowed to continue. Thus operations of extremely dubious legality were authorized only very indirectly by Johnson. He acknowledged his awareness of the illegal practices like a sphinx, leaving their advocates to draw their own conclusions about his approbation or lack thereof. Those involved felt some trepidation; although Johnson had not said no, they came away with the clear impression that in the event their activities went awry they would be offered up as sacrificial goats. This fear, plus the belief that up there—somewhere—was a personal agent of Johnson's looking over their shoulders, served to curb some of the more outrageous practices and operations. It also helped to force the intelligence leaders to learn more about the actual operations of their agencies. The lesson of John McCone being fired for not knowing what was going on in the CIA with respect to the Castro "hit" was not lost on the other intelligence leaders.

Johnson brought the intelligence community under some real, if not permanent, presidential control. His personal style was much more effective than if he had overly relied on executive orders, presidential directives, and the like to make his will known. Unlike his predecessors, Johnson had a superb grasp of the fact that the informal centers of power in the intelligence community, as well as the rest of the federal government, were of much greater consequence than the transient formal ones shown on an organization chart.

The national traumas associated with the assassination of John Kennedy served to mute the intelligence community's current disagreements. In November 1963, these included jurisdictional disputes between the military services and the CIA over who had the lead in positive intelligence operations in Southeast Asia. There was also an argument between NSA, the military communications intelligence organizations, and the CIA about whether the CIA should continue with, or expand, its communications intelligence activities. A peripheral disagreement involved control over the satellite photo program and how its take should be disseminated. These matters reached Johnson's desk, but he made little effort to resolve the disagreements. Instead, he pursued a policy of watchful waiting which was designed to take the measure of those engaged in the bureaucratic in-fighting. It was a shrewdly designed ploy. There were those in the intelligence community who fretted over Johnson's apparent indecision. Others held back, awaiting some signal from the White House. Still others made their own moves without presidential sanction, and these were the persons who later came to the fore as members of Johnson's own team. Johnson used the bureaucratic disagreements in the intelligence community as a test to determine the essential toughness and extent of its ambitions. As a consequence, although Johnson kept many of Kennedy's inner circle of "best and brightest" White House advisers, he did carry out a major housecleaning in the intelligence community.

Richard Nixon's accession to the role of first intelligence officer in January 1969 differed substantially from those of his predecessors. Although in 1960, due to President Eisenhower's initiative, the presidential transition had been formalized, the intelligence turnover was still informal in 1969. To be sure, candidate Nixon as well as president-elect Nixon had received military and foreign affairs briefings during the period between his nomination and inauguration, but these were pallid affairs. As a matter of fact and record, Nixon was systematically deceived about the war's progress. This was less due to malevolence on anyone's part than to the self-deception which had, over the course of the Vietnam War, become institutionalized under the "light at the end of the tunnel" rubric. In the last half of 1968 truth in high places, especially about the war and its domestic fallout, was an extremely scarce commodity. Nixon kept his own counsel throughout the presidential transition. Many of the intelligence players of the moment had either forgotten or never knew the extent of Richard Nixon's considerable knowledge about the community's most precious secrets.

As vice-president, Nixon had been a member of the National Security Council. This membership did not automatically give him access to details concerning the intelligence community's sources and methods, let alone those associated with specific operations. The National Security Council, then as now, was a deliberative, policy-oriented organization, not one concerned with operations details. During the Eisenhower administration, minutes of National Security Council meetings and the recollections of participants clearly indicate that the ugly side of intelligence operations were not explicitly discussed. Nonetheless, as a consequence of Eisenhower's illnesses in 1956 and 1957, it became necessary to tell Vice-President Nixon what the intelligence community was actually doing. "Acting" President Nixon was an apt and eager pupil.

The intelligence leaders, especially Allen Dulles, moved quickly to bring Nixon into the intelligence fraternity. The initial plan was very simple. It was based upon an appeal to Nixon's vicarious interests in the supposedly romantic side of spying; that is, case reports of derring-do directed against communist enemies. The approach worked to a degree; however, the case reports, some of which were described by E. Howard Hunt and others temporarily in from the cold, only served to whet Nixon's appetite. As a result, he probed deeply into the intelligence community's inner sanctum of secrets, finding out, for example, about mail intercepts, false documentation methods and techniques, special communications techniques, and penetrations of enemy intelligence services, as well as the military's and CIA's sub-rosa relationships with other nation's intelligence services. These—especially those with the Israeli intelligence service, which provided a domestic not-for-attribution capability—were of particular interest. Nixon's show of interest was greeted with some initial misgivings, but they soon gave way to the conclusion that "he's one of us." Few details escaped Nixon's attention. He seemed especially fascinated with esoteric pieces of technology which were under development by the CIA and its captive organizations, including the Advanced Research Projects Agency in the Department of Defense. The briefers who described the plastic "isolation room" bubble in the United States embassy in Moscow found him courteous, thoughtful, and incisive in his questions about how it actually worked, the complications in constructing such a device, and its other potential applications. After being told about the CIA's experiments in subliminal suggestion in an Alexandria movie theater—in which viewers were admonished to buy popcorn and who instead lined up at the drinking fountain because the suggestion made them thirsty—he remarked that such a technique might be politically useful, but not if the viewers were given a subliminal command to "vote for X" and then ended up looking for a name on the ballot which began with the letters "For." His comments were worth a laugh, and the intelligence scientists went back to their laboratories content in the belief that their efforts were appreciated by the acting president.

On a personal note, as one of the many who briefed Nixon on specific operations, I came away impressed with his grasp of the reverse chain of reasoning one must use in going back from an observable but not understood fact in order to place it in its proper context to give it meaning. The operation in question involved tracing a leak of classified information back to the source. In this case, as in most cases of this type, the problem was one of too many possibilities; any one of several hundred persons who had had access to the information could have passed it along, and many of these persons had since been scattered all over the world. Nixon remarked, "And when everyone is suspect the culprit is safe in the crowd." He paid close attention to the fact that the number of suspects made physical and other means of surveillance impractical, and also negated confrontation or accusative questioning. In the course of our discussion he showed a clear understanding of the inherent difficulties encountered in the search for a hidden motive, especially when an act of betrayal results in no apparent gain or immediate pleasure. He seemed to file away the fact that the case was broken by the discovery of a seemingly unrelated event which when unraveled identified the source of the leak. Although homosexual activities on the part of one of the culprits led to their unmasking, Nixon noted, "It's too easy to go after the queers—they're too obvious a target and the opposition uses them as a red herring to divert our people from those who really run things." Some ten years later in Vietnam, after briefing Nixon about one small corner of the war, he reminded me of our previous meeting and indicated that the human element in security was the one variable which could never finally be quantified.

Nixon made it clear to those who briefed him how important he considered them and their efforts to the national interest. Nixon made many personal converts during this period among the intelligence community's operational personnel. He did so not by transparent flattery and ego feeding, but by a sincere seeking after the ideas and understandings of the intelligence community's future leaders. He appealed to the intelligence practitioner's pride and sense of craftsmanship. In retrospect one might see this as some kind of Machiavellian deception, but I think not. It seems more a case of innate curiosity on Nixon's part, much like a child who wants to know what lies behind a magician's illusions. Technique and detail were Nixon's interests. Matters such as how to open and reseal a letter without leaving any marks, or how to detect, remove, or install a bug and maintain a surveillance of a subject, are of interest to many outside the intelligence profession, and the case can be made that Nixon wanted to acquire some grasp about how effective and reliable these techniques actually were.

As a result of his premature investiture, he made many friends throughout the intelligence community. Through the remainder of his term as vice-president he was considered to be a friend at court, and was provided with a considerable amount of inside information through informal channels. Furthermore, between 1961 and 1969 Nixon maintained personal relations with key individuals in the intelligence community, as well as with those he identified as comers. This enabled him to remain abreast of events in the sub-rosa programs and know about the controversies encountered by Kennedy and Johnson in their dealings with the community.

Nixon's extended personal contacts with intelligence operators and detailed understanding about the intelligence community's practices and problems served him extremely well when he finally became president. Before his inauguration Nixon was given intelligence information of extremely dubious worth. This was not fateful to his subsequent stewardship over the intelligence community because once ensconced in the Oval Office he knew how to find out where the bones were buried and who placed them in their unmarked graves.

In view of Nixon's subsequent fall, it is ironic to note that of all the presidents who preceded him he was the best qualified to become the nation's first intelligence officer. Perhaps he knew too much. Leaving aside his prior knowledge about the intelligence community and its secrets, it is of more than passing consequence to take note of the manner in which he assumed his presidential intelligence leadership role. The reason behind the approach Nixon adopted was not immediately apparent to his crop of White House aides. For most of them, including Haldeman and Ehrlichman, this was their first look into the intelligence community, and the presentations of the DIA,

CIA, NSC, etc. were a sight for them to behold. No one present at those series of briefings tumbled to the fact that what they were shown was a mirrorlike illusion from which the subsurface reality had been carefully shielded. It was like viewing an X-rated movie which had been cleaned up to make it suitable for family viewing. Those who later came to the intelligence community's leaders to resolve the problems of White House leaks and political protest over the war were totally unaware of Nixon's inside knowledge of the community's most secret methods and sources. In a very real sense, Nixon used his own staff as a cut-out to conceal contact between himself and key persons in the intelligence community's clandestine organizations.

Given the sievelike nature of the Nixon White House and the inexperience of his principal aides, this was a wise move, but only so long as Nixon was able to act as his own intelligence officer. From the organizational arrangements in the White House which followed Nixon's accession it is clear that he delegated control over the intelligence community in such a way that his aides were instructed to treat it as one bureaucracy among many. Because much of the intelligence community's final product is a result of the bureaucratic practices of gathering, sorting, and transmitting information, Nixon's initial decision made sense. It also enabled him not to waste time and thought on intelligence information which had only peripheral interest to him in the concrete decision-making process. He felt much better served by a one-on-one meeting with an individual he had known from his vice-presidential days, or by a particular report relayed to him through his own net of "watchbirds."

The smoothness of Nixon's takeover muted most of the intelligence community's major disagreements. It was made clear that there was money enough for all, and room for everyone in Vietnam. Further, Nixon gave the intelligence community's paper warriors sufficient leave to pursue their games of estimate one-upsmanship. It kept everyone busy and happy over the prospect that intelligence would make policy rather than simply conform to it.

Like Johnson, Nixon had an excellent appreciation of the intelligence community's informal power centers and the importance of individuals who were in, but not completely a part of, its bureaucracy. These persons are called "true believers." They accept the intelligence community's bureaucratic structure as a necessary nuisance, but do not feel constrained by it. For many of these persons, intelligence is a way of life, not just a way of earning a living.

In sum, Nixon took charge of the intelligence community without the appearance of much fuss and feathers. His approach to those who were bureaucratically oriented appeared to be businesslike, in support of their managerial (as opposed to operational) outlook. Without overstating the situation, a clear perception of business as usual was conveyed, and those who dealt in intelligence "facts" were left none the wiser about the intelligence community's "black" activities—and the new president's knowledge of them. Nixon's original tactic was well chosen. It prevented the disagreements which had emerged in the last year of the Johnson administration from flaring up and diverting him from his other presidential responsibilities. As these increased there was less reliance on the personal intelligence information report. The word was passed to "put it in writing." This became accepted procedure in the Nixon White House, and the special, out-of-the-ordinary channel intelligence reports became part of the steadily increasing paper flow of information reaching the president.

It should be noted that the illegal acts which Nixon knew about from his previous experience contributed to his final downfall.* Nixon failed to realize in 1969 that these acts had, in the twelve to thirteen intervening years, achieved a dynamism of their own and were no longer truly amenable to one man's control. This fact was not conveyed by Nixon's secret support in the intelligence community; it was ignored by those who had become complacent about their ability to manage activities which had grown so much during the period. Few in 1969 recognized the genuine diseconomies of scale in their operations, and this lack of understanding caused Nixon to think it was possible to add more tasks to those underway without running the risk of disclosure or failure. The point is that there is an upper total limit of clandestine activities which can be carried out by any organization, regardless of its size.

From Truman to Ford, each presidential assumption of power over the intelligence community has been different; no two have been exactly alike. However, each of them can be seen as reasonable precursors of a president's subsequent stewardship over the intelligence community. They contained the seeds of difficulty and conflict, especially those conflicts involved in the president's ensuring that his decisions are based on reality, not the personal conceptions of the intelligence community's rotating, quasi-permanent elite. The assumptions of presidential intelligence power give us, at the onset, benchmarks from which it is possible to measure the intelligence community's evolution as a bureaucratic organism, and the conflicts between the intelligence community's hierarchy, the president, the Congress, and the people themselves.

---

*It is worth noting that Nixon, responding to interrogatories submitted to him by the Senate's Select Committee to Study Governmental Operations with Respect to Intelligence Activities, denied receiving information about the intelligence community's illegal activities "while president." However, in response to Interrogatory 9, which read:

> Please state whether, while vice-president or president, you received information that, at any time prior to your administration, an agency or employee of the United States government, acting without a warrant, conducted any of the activities referred to in Interrogatories 1 (mail intercepts), 2 (electronic intercepts), 3 (telephone intercepts), 4 (break-ins).

Nixon replied, "I remember learning on various occasions that during administrations prior to mine, agencies or employees of the United States government, acting presumably without a warrant, conducted wiretaps, surreptitious or unauthorized entries, and intercepts of voice and nonvoice communications." So much for what Nixon knew and when he knew it. See: U. S. Senate, Select Committee to Study Governmental Operations with Respect to Intelligence Activities. "Supplementary Detailed Staff Reports on Foreign and Military Intelligence, Book IV." Washington: U. S. Government Printing Office, April 23, 1976, p. 149.

CHAPTER 2

AMERICA'S
INTELLIGENCE HERITAGE

To understand contemporary events in America's intelligence community and the actions of those who have directed its operations in the so-called modern period (that is, since the end of World War II in 1945), it is necessary to look to the past.

Prior to the outbreak of World War II in September 1939, America's intelligence heritage can best be seen in terms of the records of individuals: how they responded to and carried out the many roles of the intelligence officer/-spy/agent on their country's behalf—rather than by the institutional history of the early, essentially makeshift wartime intelligence organizations which faded out of existence once the various wars ended. Also important is the attitude of these operatives toward the political/military leader of the moment and his attitude toward them and their work. Just as the attitudes of people involved in intelligence toward their vocation (or in some cases, avocation) is important, there is a personal factor in the overall equation which often determines the success or failure of intelligence operations and activities. The records and accomplishments of these individuals constitutes a tradition of sorts which, although lacking formal rituals and symbols, has implicitly and explicitly been handed down from one generation of intelligence practitioners to the next and, even today, remains intimately involved in resolving the modern American dilemma over the proper role for and type of control over intelligence operations, activities, and personnel.

The exploits of those who, during the "prehistory" of today's institutionalized intelligence system, served the United States in intelligence roles show the principal early themes of American intelligence. In addition, they identify the strange, oftentimes paranoiac political reactions and responses which America's espionage activities had apparently induced in the body politic both during and after wartime. Although these themes do not completely forecast the final form and structure of our present intelligence system, they reveal the character of American intelligence and tell us much about the motivations of Americans who choose and have chosen the intelligence profession as their own.

It may seem a bit bizarre to speak about the character of American intelligence, but no more so than to speak of the character of American jurisprudence, government, or people. In each of these areas the American experience has been different from other nations'. To be sure, in all areas of our national life we have borrowed a bit here and there from other nations' experiences and techniques; yet the results have been uniquely and distinctly American in their character. This applies equally well in describing the character of American intelligence. It is a mistake to assume because the tradecraft, mechanical techniques, and the like are employed by two nations, governments, entities, organizations, or individuals that their characters are the same. For example, it does not follow that because the United States and the Soviet Union both conduct elections to select their leaders that the character of their governments are the same. In this sense, the character of American intelligence refers not to the *form* of intelligence, but rather to the *substance* which lies behind the motivations of those who carry out the intelligence function. These people are key; their approach has formed the character of American intelligence. In so doing they have had a long and influential, if little known, history.

Richard Rowan wrote in his encyclopedic history of intelligence, *Secret Service,* "Spies and speculators for thirty-three centuries have exerted more influence on history than on historians." In America's two centuries, the same can be said, with the added caveat that its intelligence practitioners are unique in the annals of intelligence. Their uniqueness derives in part from the fact that, as a class, their motivations for becoming spies were patriotic. This is not to say that other countries have not had individual spies who were similarly inspired; but in terms of number no other nation's intelligence service has had so many so highly motivated. Also, unlike the experience of other nations (with the possible exception of England since World War I), the American patriotic spy has been consistently drawn from elements in our society which may be classified as "establishment." That is, from elements who believed in property rights, principles of law, and the notion of élites based on accomplishment rather than accidents of birth. In essence, the American patriotic spy is comparable in terms of attitudes, origins, and background with America's founding fathers, who by most standards of measure don't fit any revolutionary profile.

Every war in American history includes examples of the use and performance of spies. The wartime exploits of the American patriotic spy reflect mastery of the intelligence craft's techniques and practices and, perhaps more significantly, an ability on their part to engage in essentially immoral activities in pursuit of moral objectives and for most to remain untainted by their sordid experiences. Their performances in defending the nation during war are in keeping with American ideals and beliefs. But there is a dark side to the character of American intelligence, revealed by the willingness on the part of those persons who have become imbued with the intelligence practitioners' ethos to continue to use their techniques during periods of peace for purposes inconsistent with United States law. This conflict between good and evil, once the clear and present dangers of war are past, in the use of intelligence practices to maintain domestic tranquility is by no means new or original to the American scene. It has been waged for centuries with various justifications. Monarchs, emperors, and victorious men-at-arms have consistently used intelligence resources and personnel at their disposal to maintain their own personal versions of internal and national security by spying on their own subjects, political rivals, and members of their immediate entourages. Although such practices are not new, their place in American intelligence is scarcely justified.

It is not our purpose here to idealize America's intelligence heritage as conveyed by the performance of the patriotic spy, nor to condemn those persons who have chosen the intelligence way of life and have participated and used the techniques and methods of intelligence for illegal purposes. It is left for the reader to ponder and decide whether the United States can have the good of intelligence without its evil. We seek perspective in this matter not only to understand our historical past and present, but also to face the challenges posed by an uncertain future.

A digression about this kind of historical statement is in order. It is necessarily somewhat exclusive in nature, but not to blur the historical record and the contemporary issues associated with that record. These are best understood and resolved when one has a reasonable perspective about that which has gone on before. How such perspective and knowledge about the past is acquired is important because the process itself influences our responses to historical and contemporary information.

Each of us has his/her own historical sense. It is derived from a variety of formal and informal sources and it plays a subtle, but powerful role in determining how we perceive past and present events and personages. The formal sources include exposure to historical events in connection with one's secular and/or religious education. No one who has grown up in America has been able to avoid completely some exposure to various aspects of American history, or to keep all the yesterdays clear and separate in his/her mind. Because of this, the past has a way of intruding on the present; how we remember or understand the past shapes our responses to the future. In this regard, "hard" historical sources which accurately reflect past realities are rarely seen as final either by historians or plain people. Historical revisionism and myth-debunking by historians have their counterpart in ordinary human behavior, where in the normal course of aging one can gain added insights, reinforce one's personal biases and prejudices, or perhaps acquire hitherto unknown information about oneself and others which calls into question previously held beliefs. Witness the remarkable effect of the television adaptation of Alex Haley's *Roots* on the attitudes and outlooks of countless Black Americans who really knew very little about the institution and practices of slavery. Sometimes unwanted or unsought information produces traumas of a sort when cherished beliefs, like those about personal and national heroes, are revealed to be false.

The comment of the newsboy who confronted "Shoeless" Joe Jackson of the 1919 Black Sox with the plea, "Say it isn't so, Joe!" has its modern parallel in the hearts and minds of those who say to themselves that the media drove Richard Nixon from office, that John Kennedy was a saint, or that evil acts carried out by the CIA, FBI, et al. in pursuit of good causes are really not evil at all.

History, especially in its idealized form, is a powerful conditioning factor. I don't mean simple knowledge of dates, places and names, but rather what we think we know or have been led to believe happened, and under what circumstances. Beyond formal historical sources and such quasiformal ones as the media (particularly motion pictures and television), each of our historical senses has been further influenced by informal sources, namely, family, friends, and associates.

Today, for example, members of my generation frequently find themselves trying to convey to their children through admonition, homilies, and personal experiences the meaning of the Great Depression. In most cases it appears to be a futile exercise, but in the event there is another major depression one can be certain that these informal oral histories will be recollected by those seeking to understand their individual present and as a means to fathom the future. This is not to say that our view about the past is correct, but simply that it becomes part of our children's historical sense concerning those events. Sometimes the view of history handed down from the old to the young creates a delayed reaction which may be triggered by a contemporary experience or event. Such a reaction leaves one with the feeling of having been there before, almost in the way an actual event is sometimes foretold in a dream. This kind of metaphysical transference can play tricks upon one's appreciation and attitudes about contemporary events, especially when they involve something traumatic in nature. For instance, in the ghastly aftermath of the assassination of John F. Kennedy it was not uncommon to hear the sophisticated as well as the more superstitious refer to some prophecy of doom or retribution told to them in their childhood. And the historians helped by pointing out the eerie coincidences between the Lincoln and Kennedy assassinations.

Modern living produces a situation where it is relatively rare to find a family with more than two generations living together. This weakens the informal transfer and development of historical sense which has formerly been provided to children from their grandparents and, in many homes, their great-grandparents. Because my own grandparents were part of our household and lived into their nineties, I was nurtured on the stories of their youth, when the West was still "wild" and the Civil War a personal experience. It's one thing to read stories about Wild Bill Hickok and another to hear, from one's own grandmother (who was a young widow at the time of Wild Bill's heyday and observed him in Dodge City and Abilene), that he was a queer who rarely took a bath. These stories, like others told to children about the "old country," Ellis Island, racial and religious discrimination, political corruption, and so on become part of one's emotional and intellectual baggage and influence the development of one's historical sense. Though the extent of this influence is impossible to measure, its effect is very real.

For our purposes, the term "historical sense" has relevance in attempting to explain how the American intelligence system came into being and subsequently evolved. Admittedly, most Americans' historical sense about intelligence and intelligence operations is less accurate or developed than that about the right to vote, or who and what it took to carry out the industrial revolution in America. In the latter, the conflict between historical myths and realities is less severe because the problems involved seem behind us. But not so with intelligence; it, like other areas where the process of perfecting our national institutions while simultaneously preserving our individual freedoms are involved, remains to be resolved. The reader is advised not to trust his/her historical sense about intelligence too far. What follows in this and subsequent chapters is an attempt to add to the historical sense about American intelligence in order to help one make a better-informed judgment about its present state, and to establish a basis on which to accept or reject the plans and paths national leaders intend for it in the future.

The exploits of America's patriotic spies from the Revolutionary War up to World War I are presented in Chapter 10, "An Afterword." The transition from the prehistorical period of individual performances in intelligence to that of an institutionalized system generally begins during World War I. To be sure, the transition sputtered and faltered thereafter; but World War I set the United States on an intelligence course from which there has been no turning back. How that transition was effected lies in the performance of individuals who, in spite of official disinterest prior to World War I, became intelligence professionals and were imbued with the intelligence ethos—or as some might say, were bitten by the intelligence "bug." These early professionals, unlike the large number of wartime patriotic spies, constituted a small band of brothers. Their motives were much the same as those of the wartime patriotic spies; their continuing commitment to intelligence involved a forward outlook which reflected the necessity to prepare for war during times of peace. It also reflected an almost evangelical belief on their part in the power of intelligence to either avert war or determine its final outcome. One of these intelligence professionals, who was during this era of official intelligence neglect a "true believer," left a lasting mark on American intelligence and may be looked upon as a prime example of the intelligence professional's contribution to the American intelligence heritage. That person was Major General Ralph H. Van Deman, U. S. Army.

Van Deman was no ordinary man. He was born in Ohio in 1865, and upon graduating from Harvard in 1889 he spent a year in law school before changing course to pursue a career in medicine. He served briefly as an army surgeon, then attended the infantry and cavalry school at Fort Leavenworth. His extensive education and maturity made him a logical candidate for intelligence work. In July 1897, Van Deman opted for intelligence and was assigned to the Mapping Section of the Military Intelligence Division (MID) because of his promise and enthusiasm. At the time, duty in mapping and reconnaissance, like that in the OSS and CIA's clandestine services in the hot and cold wars of later years, was where the intelligence action was supposed to be—if not the opportunity for medals, promotion, and recognition. But Van Deman was considered by his superiors to be too valuable at headquarters to be sent on secret missions or to get into combat during the Spanish-American War. Even then, knowledge of high-level deliberations was an effective bar to the individual who preferred the challenges of the "field" to the supposed rewards of being close to the seat of power. In one such instance Van Deman, who had volunteered to go on secret missions, lost out to his friend, Lieutenant Andrew S. Rowan. Rowan was ordered by the Chief of the MID, Major Arthur L. Wagner, to deliver the legendary "message to Garcia," the Cuban insurgent leader. Also, Major Wagner sent Lieutenant Henry H. Whitney, rather than Van Deman, on a secret mission to Puerto Rico and points elsewhere in the Caribbean, disguised as a deck hand on a British merchant ship to check out the local defenses and make contact with insurgent groups. (See Chapter 10, "An Afterword.")

These decisions of Major Wagner's which left Van Deman in Washington, and the fact that he had missed "his" war, rankled him more than he was initially willing to admit. Although Major Wagner did order Van Deman to Cuba for the clean-up period of the hostilities, in April 1899 he opted out of intelligence and was assigned to the Philippines as an aide to Major General R. P. Hughes. He remained in that job for two years. This was Van Deman's period in the wilderness, during which he suffered many personal doubts about his future and whether he ought to stay in the army.

However, in July 1901, after being promoted to captain, Van Deman was reassigned to Manila, where his intelligence past caught up with him. Van Deman, Lt. Col. Joseph T. Dickman, and Captain John R. M. Taylor were given the job by General Arthur MacArthur to establish a Military Information Division of the Philippines. This job set Van Deman firmly on the intelligence road. His *Memoirs** indicate an almost metaphysical conversion and commitment to intelligence as a consequence of his experience in Manila. The organization he created, the Manila MID, was an outgrowth of a Bureau of Insurgent Records which had been established in 1889, "for the purpose of collating and translating insurgent documents and records."**

Under Van Deman, who acceded to the top job in short order, the Manila

---

*Ralph H. Van Deman, *Memoirs,* unpublished manuscript, several copies of which are located in various army libraries including those of the Army War College, Carlisle, Pennsylvania, and the Army Intelligence Center at Fort Holabird, Md. Part I, pp. 5–8.

**Department of the Army, Letter, Office of the Adjutant General, "Statement of Military Service, Ralph Henry Van Deman 0–362," Washington, April 26, 1973.

MID became a surprisingly modern intelligence organization. It included elements which covered the entire spectrum of intelligence operations, from such overt ones as collecting information about the Philippines' lines of communications, agriculture, sociology and the like to covert ones involving the use of paramilitary forces and counterguerrilla terrorists. The Manila MID experience was a heady one for the thirty-five-year-old Captain Van Deman. Not only had he seen what could be accomplished with a coordinated intelligence system, he had run it.

In the fall of 1902, Van Deman returned to the United States, where for the next several years he was "seasoned" with troop duty and by attendance in the first class of the Army War College in Washington. Van Deman had been identified as a "comer" by General MacArthur, but it was considered unwise to bury him in intelligence before he had been given the opportunity to come to the attention of other high-ranking officers who made the preselections of Army officers destined for higher responsibility. In June 1906, he was sent with Captain Alexander Coxe on a covert mission to map the lines of communications leading into and out of Peking, China. Returning to Washington in March 1907, Van Deman was rewarded for this mission by being assigned Chief of the Map Section of the Military Information Division. Shortly thereafter, in June 1907, Van Deman became involved in the bureaucratic squabble which resulted in the merging of the MID into a new War College Division. This squabble put the fledgling War Department intelligence organization into eight years of limbo, during which period Van Deman bided his time, returned to the Manila MID and carried out various covert missions in the Far East.

Returning to Washington in July 1915, for duty with the War College Division, Van Deman found the state of American intelligence appalling. Despite the fact that war had been raging in Europe for nine months and U.S. military and naval observers were sending in reports about it, no system existed to present war information to the general staff, subordinate elements of the War Department, or to the national government's leaders. Upon reporting, Van Deman found a table "piled high" with information reports from the Pershing expedition in Mexico which were not even being filed. In short, the entire War Department intelligence effort amounted to a dead-letter mail drop which did nothing with reports which had been acquired at considerable personal danger and sacrifice by persons in the various operational areas.

Van Deman took a close look at the situation and, though a relatively junior officer in the Washington military political hierarchy (he was a major by this time), took the unprecedented step of forwarding his findings to the Chief of Staff in a "Historical Sketch" memo which said in part:

... the most necessary and essential kind of information, the information without which no war plan can be made that is worth the paper it is written on, does not come in of its own accord or a matter of routine. It must be actively sought, traced out and proved out.

To sum up the whole matter in a single sentence, we are no better prepared, insofar as organization for intelligence duties in the field are concerned, than we were the day the General Staff was created, and as far as military information is concerned we are not so well prepared since much of the information on hand at that time has not since been corrected or added to and is now so old as to be practically worthless.*

The significance of Van Deman's "Historical Sketch" is hard to contemplate in terms of his position in the military hierarchy; it was roughly equivalent to Luther's indictment of the Church. The immediate official response was silence. To acknowledge its arguments was to acknowledge one's own failures. Consequently, nothing was done to remedy the failures and deficiencies Van Deman had so accurately delineated. However, undaunted by the bureaucratic nonresponse to his charges, Van Deman—with the tacit but completely disavowable support of the Chief of the War College Division, Brigadier General Joseph E. Kuhn—went ahead on his own to repair those deficiencies.

For the next year, Major Van Deman became an intelligence "outlaw" who operated without any semblance of legal authority in an attempt to create an intelligence organization if one should be needed in the event the United States entered the war. With the help of friends in and outside the government, Van Deman created an invisible intelligence organization which, if it had been discovered, would have produced apoplexy in the Wilson White House and long stretches in Leavenworth for all those involved.

To protect Van Deman from inadvertent disclosure about his intelligence "volunteers," General Kuhn informed the Chief of Staff on April 11, 1917 (a week after the American declaration of war) that:

As matter of fact, the Intelligence section (under the direction of Major Van Deman) has been engaged in secret intelligence work for the past year in close cooperation with the various secret service organizations of the various departments of the civil branch of the government—the State Department, the Department of Justice, the Treasury Department, etc. This work has necessarily been accomplished with practically no funds and with such a limited personnel as to make effective work of any kind almost an impossibility. The officer personnel has consisted of a single General Staff officer and one retired officer as assistant.**

With United States entry into World War I, Van Deman considered it more imperative than ever to establish an independent military intelligence branch and capability. Despite the previous failure of his historical sketch to awaken the Chief of Staff to the need for coordinated intelligence, the combination of war and General Kuhn's encouragement convinced Van Deman to take his

*Ralph H. Van Deman, "Historical Sketch," memo to Chief of Staff, March 2, 1916. 32 pp.

**War Department, Memo for the Chief of Staff, "Organization for Intelligence Work," April 11, 1917.

case directly to the Chief of Staff, General Hugh Scott. Van Deman entreated Scott on three separate occasions, but the Chief of Staff was of the anti-intelligence school of thought and denied each request. Van Deman noted:

He could see no reason for the United States Army to have any such thing as a military information service and that, if as explained, the British and French armies had such organizations and were receiving the necessary information concerning the enemy there was no reason why we should not say to them "Here, we are now ready for service— we would be pleased if you hand over to us all the necessary information concerning the enemy which your intelligence services have obtained." No amount of talking or argument could change the Chief of Staff's opinion and after two or three such interviews he became exasperated and ordered the writer [Van Deman] to cease his efforts with the organization of a military information service.*

Further, in the course of these confrontations Scott ordered Van Deman not to leapfrog him and plead with the Secretary of War, Newton D. Baker, for a separate intelligence organization.

Disillusioned but not shaken from his belief in intelligence as the nation's first line of defense, Van Deman resolved to reach Secretary Baker without violating the letter of General Scott's order. He thereupon approached two friends of Baker's, who presented the secretary with the case for expanded American intelligence activities. On April 30, 1917, Baker called Van Deman into his office and heard him out. Three days later Van Deman was a lieutenant colonel and orders were issued on May 11, 1917, directing the establishment of a Military Intelligence Section under Van Deman's leadership. It was a brilliant personal victory for Van Deman; the confusion of war provided the necessary distraction from any consideration of his previous illegal activities. Striking while the iron was hot and when uncertainty of the war's outcome was still very real in official quarters, he also persuaded the Secretary of War to obtain a congressional appropriation of $1 million for "Contingencies— Military Intelligence Section." Thus, Van Deman, who had a framework of ideas concerning what needed to be done with intelligence, legitimized his earlier illegal activities, gained authority to employ civilians as needed, formalized the basis of his previous clandestine relations with persons in other government agencies, and got the money he needed to operate with shortly after the war began.

In breathing life into his now legitimate organization, Van Deman maintained his freedom of action by preparing a memo for the Chief of Staff, signed by General Kuhn, which said in part: "We have never even attempted in any previous war to carry out the duties which must now be undertaken. It would be inadvisable to attempt to prescribe fixed rules."** However, in this same

*Van Deman, *Memoirs,* pp. 30–31.

**War Department, Memorandum for the Chief of Staff, "Proper Organization of a Military Intelligence Section, General Staff," May 11, 1917.

memo Van Deman indicated that the new section would have an Administration Branch to manage intelligence collection, an Information Branch to handle espionage and counterespionage, and a Censorship Branch. Again recognizing the need to legitimize actions carried out both before and after the fact of official cognizance, he followed his organizational memorandum with one which contained an extremely clear statement of what national-level intelligence would and should entail. In this memo, Van Deman introduced to intelligence usage the terms "negative" intelligence—that is, actions designed to deny intelligence to the enemy, and "positive" intelligence—the use of all available intelligence sources and methods to gather information needed by our forces. The memorandum also outlined the need for a coordinated intelligence apparatus among the various U.S. military and civilian agencies, as well as with friendly foreign agencies. On the key issue of intelligence coordination/control, Van Deman argued that because the intelligence information required was military in nature and since the War Department General Staff was the primary organization charged to operate on a broad military spectrum, its Military Intelligence Section should be given the intelligence coordination function and responsibility. In the high-level discussions which followed, Van Deman's argument prevailed. Although the various military and civilian agencies carried out specific intelligence operations in support of their assigned missions, these were coordinated by Van Deman, whose ideas served as the basis of how American intelligence was managed during the war.

Before looking at Van Deman's organizational legacy to American intelligence, it is essential to go beyond the intricate maneuverings which were required to create the Military Intelligence Section to include the attitudinal problems which also complicated Van Deman's choice of intelligence practices. There were both conceptual and practical problems once the reluctant decision was made to commence a truly national-level intelligence organization. Writing after the war, Van Deman's successor, Brigadier General Marlborough Churchill, described these by saying:

The field assigned to Military Intelligence in the War Department is so broad that there is a tendency on the part of officers either to have only a very hazy idea of its scope, or to understand but one phase of intelligence work and to disregard the many other phases. . . . For example, if an officer has served with combat troops in France, he is likely to think only of combat intelligence. . . . On the other hand, if an officer has been unfortunate enough to remain during the war on duty in the United States, he is very likely to think of Military Intelligence only as a bureau of investigation, or sort of military secret police . . . [while both of these play their parts, there is additionally] the duty of maintaining complete foreign map collection and complete terrain handbooks covering areas in which we are likely to carry on military operations. . . . The other major function which has been assigned to MID consists of playing the part in our Government Information Service [of obtaining] data on foreign armies. . . .*

*Marlborough Churchill, "The Military Intelligence Division, General Staff," *Journal of the United States Artillery,* Vol 52, #4, April 1920, pp. 293–295.

In successfully resolving these problems, Van Deman, as head of the Military Intelligence Division (MID), created a stateside intelligence organization which at the time of the armistice (November 11, 1918) employed 282 officers, 29 sergeants and nearly 1,000 civilians in a network "which was not only of paramount value to the War Department but covered the world in furnishing information to the State Department, the Department of Justice and other government departments, bureaus and war boards."* By today's bloated standards this was a modest organization; however, what is even more incredible in the Van Deman–led expansion of the MID is that there were never more than six officers of the regular service on duty in it any one time. This fact raises the further question of whence came the Van Deman intelligence disciples who followed his lead. Some, like John Foster Dulles (who came from private law practice) were early converts. A more interesting insight into Van Deman's recruiting practices and ability to attract particularly talented people is seen in the case of Herbert O. Yardley. Yardley's recruitment to MID devolved from the authority Van Deman had been given by Secretary of War Newton Baker to appoint "qualified" civilians as commissioned officers of the National Army. According to Yardley, a State Department code clerk when war was declared, he was convinced that America must establish a cryptographic bureau like those of the European countries to gather information from enemy communications. However, then as now, Yardley was faced with the problem of knowing to whom in the government he should present his "better" idea. A Signal Corps officer helped by saying, "Have you seen Major Van Deman?" "No, who is he?" "He isn't much of anything right now, but he will be heard from. He's the father of military intelligence in the Army. He can use you. Go see him." Yardley went and Van Deman did need him, commissioning him a first lieutenant and placing him in charge of Codes and Ciphers (MI-8) of the MID.**

---

*Peyton C. March, *The Nation at War*. New York: Doubleday, Doran & Co., 1932, p. 226.

**Herbert O. Yardley, *The American Black Chamber*. London: Faber & Faber, 1931, pp. 34–35. Yardley stayed in Washington with MI-8 for most of the war, and then in August 1918, went to England to examine British code and cipher practices. Next he joined Van Deman's security forces at the Versailles peace talks, where his genius kept American dispatches from leaking out and also deciphered those of other nations. By April 1919 he was back in America, hoping to receive funding to make MI-8 an ongoing peacetime bureau. Finding money was no easy matter for military agencies in postwar Washington, as Yardley discovered:

> My estimate for an efficient Cipher Bureau called for one hundred thousand dollars per annum. The State Department agreed to turn over to Military Intelligence forty thousand dollars per annum out of special funds, provided the Navy Department was entirely excluded, for they refused to share their secrets with the Navy. This left a deficit of sixty thousand dollars which Military intelligence managed to obtain from Congress after taking some of the leaders into their confidence. (p. 166)

Although Yardley assumed that the $60,000 came from Congress on an official basis, the actual amount of funds provided by the Congress was considerably less, with the deficit being made up

Yardley's cryptographic bureau soon proved its worth. Under his leader-ship, MI-8 developed codes for use by the U. S. government which remained unbroken by the enemy throughout the war. Yardley also placed mobile radio intercept stations on the Mexican border to keep track of German attempts to establish a clandestine radio station in that country. Another important success of MI-8 was detecting the secret writing used by German agents, which led to the only death sentence for espionage adjudged in the U.S. during World War I. It was later commuted.*

Another facet of Van Deman's contributions involved his organization of the intelligence information gathering and presentation function. In this area Van Deman, due to years of intelligence experience, was aware of the fact that the best intelligence is of no value unless it is collected, analyzed and dis-seminated promptly. He systematized the intelligence background information on hand in the War Department and established procedures to handle the increasing flow of reports coming in from the American Expeditionary Force (AEF), Allied governments, and MID agents in Europe, the United States, and elsewhere in the world. Coordination was effected with the new Aviation Corps, and priority was given to the dissemination of intelligence to its con-sumers in the War Department and back to the AEF. Also, briefing maps were maintained by Van Deman's organization in both the Capitol and the White House.**

Taken together, Van Deman's organizational contributions created a com-plete intelligence system which coordinated all available assets at the national level. Van Deman centralized the services and functions of the forebearers of a number of modern organizations: the Army Map Service (now the Defense Map Service), the attaché system, the Intelligence Command, the Army Secu-rity Agency, the National Security Agency, the Defense Investigative Agency,

---

by "Friends of Congress," who as civilians also had a deep and abiding interest in the Black Chamber's operations.

The upshot of these maneuvers was housed at 141 East 37 Street in New York City, far from the prying eyes of Washington. There Yardley and a staff of civilians solved more than 45,000 cryptograms between 1919 and 1929. Through the cooperation of the State Department and the major telegraph companies, the so-called Black Chamber received and solved encoded messages from over twenty nations, including China, England, Germany, France, Spain, Cuba, Mexico, Japan, and the Soviet Union.

The American Black Chamber's brilliant work came to a close with Hoover's accession to the presidency in 1929. The theme of the Hoover administration was morality, and when Secretary of State Henry L. Stimson discovered what his department was financing, he made his famous "Gentlemen do not read each other's mail" remark and dissolved the Black Chamber. Thereafter, MI-8's files were given to the Signal Corps, and the State Department lost its best intelligence source. Yardley drifted off to write books and play poker, and although he lived until 1958, he never again worked with codes for the American government. He did, however, spend two years during World War II breaking Japanese codes for Chiang Kai-shek.

*Van Deman, *Memoirs,* pp. 62–63.

**Ibid.,* pp. 39 and 58.

the Industrial Security Organization, the U.S. Army Intelligence Center and school, and the tactical intelligence organization within the Army.

Although by themselves these contributions are enough to earn Van Deman the title "Father of American Military Intelligence," there was more to his career than simply the display of organizational/management genius. This other side involved Van Deman's perception and actions in dealing with the intelligence profession's age-old security problem. Before Van Deman's appointment as Chief of the MID, a controversy was underway between the Secret Service (Treasury) and the Bureau of Investigation (Justice) about which organizations should hold jurisdictional sway over internal security investigations and matters. Almost coincident with Van Deman's appointment, a civilian volunteer "internal security" vigilante-type organization, the American Protective League (APL), had come into being, thereby complicating his handling of the problems of intelligence and military security.

On one level, to insure security within the army, Van Deman developed a system of "silent watchers" to report on irregularities. Although most War Department officials, including Van Deman, deplored the necessity to spy on their own forces, no one could be certain how effective, if at all, German subversion was in the armed forces. In retrospect, it turned out not to have been a very serious problem.* Van Deman also instituted an alert guard system for War Department offices, ID card systems, and a variety of other steps to enhance security to include passport control, port and industrial security organizations, and a system of central files in Washington to support the total security program. Subordinate offices of the MID, manned by mobilized police officers, were established in eight U.S. cities to carry out personnel security investigations. And to facilitate the AEF's internal security, a force of fifty sergeants, French-speaking specialists in intelligence and security, were recruited and designated by Van Deman as the Corps of Intelligence Police (CIP), the predecessor organization of the Counterintelligence Corps (CIC).**

All these actions were to the good and eminently required by the military situation. But like others before and after him, Van Deman became ensnared in the dilemmas and jurisdictional battles involved in the gray and often overlapping problem areas of internal-domestic, military, and national security. Although each of these areas appears clear and separable in the abstract, on a practical level they rarely are. Jurisdictional delimitations work to a point in resolving the problems, but these have usually failed in the end because of the personal egos of those involved and the real difficulty in turning over an investigation or a security responsibility to another organization once an operation is underway.

In Van Deman's case, he looked upon the problems of internal-domestic, military, and national security as a coherent whole which would only be really

*Ibid., Part I, p. 56.

**War Department, Memorandum for the Chief of Staff, "Intelligence Service," August 11, 1917.

solved under a centralized direction which coordinated and controlled the components of an overall security system. It was an idea whose time did not come in Van Deman's lifetime, and during his tenure as Chief of the MID it brought him into bitter personal conflict with those in the internal security arena who also favored centralized direction, but only of a single organization —theirs. To understand and place this theme of Van Deman's career in perspective it is necessary to backtrack to the controversy between the Secret Service (Treasury) and the Bureau of Investigation (Justice) and the further role of the American Protective League. (For background to the pre–Van Deman involvement in the controversy, see Chapter 10, "An Afterword.")

The congruence of security problems caused by World War I, the Secret Service, the Bureau of Investigation, and the APL impinged on Van Deman's ability to build, operate and maintain an intelligence system capable of meeting the nation's need for military and political intelligence. In consequence, Van Deman could no more ignore the "negative" intelligence activities of the civilian agencies flailing about in the United States in their search for subversives and spies among the population at large than those of actual enemy agents identified by his and other Allied intelligence agencies.

Unfortunately, the two years of spy scares preceding America's entry into the war had produced a chaotic situation in terms of creating any kind of effective counterespionage response. The APL produced a horde of jungle beaters who, with the idea of "every man a counterespionage agent," had made the task of detecting and/or catching actual enemy agents well nigh impossible. Under these conditions Van Deman, the intelligence professional, was bound to come into conflict with the politically motivated amateurs.

The scene was set for conflict; Van Deman was drawn into it by the Attorney General's report to the House and Senate on December 4, 1917, in which he described the Justice Department's position on internal security by saying:

. . . the department encourages the organization of various local volunteer citizens' committees for the purpose of being on the lookout for disloyal or enemy activities and the presentation of such matters to the proper officials. These volunteer associations have rendered very great assistance.

One of them in particular, which is nationwide in scope and which is known as the American Protective League, has proven to be invaluable, and constitutes a most important auxiliary and reserve for the Bureau of Investigation. . . . Its members are not officers or agents of the department and do not attempt to take any decisive action in any matter, except through the regular officers of the department.

Although Attorney General Gregory claimed the APL did "not attempt to take any decisive action in any matter, except through the regular officers of the department," the opposite was true and Gregory knew it. Chicago APL "Captain" Thomas Gowenlock stated his group's most valuable work as "breaking up activities of labor agitators and anarchists."* In pursuit of this dubious national security goal, League units wiretapped, infiltrated IWW, socialist, and union groups, posed as fund raisers, broke up peaceful meetings, roughed-up speakers, and made illegal arrests. Like the undercover FBI agents of recent times who infiltrated Black activist and antiwar groups, APL infiltrators often overplayed their roles, became a group's most radical members, then provoked acts of violence which otherwise would not have occurred.

The American Protective League's illegal methods were rationalized by the claim, supported by government officials such as Secretary of State Robert Lansing and newspapers such as the *New York Times,* that the IWW and socialists were financed with German funds.** In fact (which went unreported by the *New York Times*), government audits and detailed investigations of the IWW and other groups uncovered no evidence of funding from Germany. The true rationale for the illegal raids rested with the public's government-induced sense of paranoia, the APL's support of and dependence upon reactionary businessmen for its membership and financing, and the reasoning expressed by U.S. Attorney for St. Paul, Alfred Jacques, who said:

I thought it a good idea to keep these IWW aliens so busy defending prosecutions for failure to register that they would not have time to plot against the industrial interests . . .***

The APL antilabor push was directed from a central clearing house for reports on the IWW in Chicago. The office was run by William C. Fitts, an assistant to Attorney General Gregory. With the support of this office and elements of Van Deman's MID, federal law was subverted and ignored as troops were illegally dispatched to deal with labor-industry disputes. According to the nation's statutes, federal troops could only be called out to the states by the governor, after presidential approval had been granted. However, during World War I, state militias often responded to calls from mayors; when the state militias found themselves in a precarious position, emergency calls for help were sent to the nearest commander of federal troops to come quickly to avoid a "massacre." Once federal troops entered the scene under this kind of situation, military intelligence officers compounded the outrage by asking the War Department not to withdraw the federal forces because the IWW was believed to be active. The presence of federal troops in these kinds of "emergency" situations gave MID operatives an excuse to meddle in civilian affairs. Although Van Deman was professionally dismayed by the massing of federal troops upon the appearance of a picket sign or a few union organizers, he was reluctant to interfere with the rights of commanders to respond to what might

*Thomas Gowenlock, *Soldiers of Darkness.* New York: Doubleday, 1937, p. 41.

**See esp., *New York Times,* September 6, 1917, pp. 1:8 and 2:1.

***Jacques to Gregory, January 15, 1918, File 187415, Record Group, National Archives.

be a serious situation. The problem of security was a real one. Sabotage had already been experienced and there were some concrete examples of espionage against the United States even before the country went to war.

The combined work of the APL and MID stilled the alleged IWW and socialist threats, but with hundred of thousands of agents in the field eager to enforce "patriotism," the League needed a new focus for its energies. The new target was draft evaders. Both Gregory and Secretary of War Baker asked for assistance in rounding up men who failed to report for their physical examinations. A bounty of $50 was offered for the delivery of each evader. Bureau of Investigation agents were forbidden to collect the reward, but APL members or state and local authorities were eligible.

In the spring of 1918, the APL declared open season on all draft evaders, deserters, and delinquent enlistees—"slackers," as they were collectively known. In return for a promise from the Justice Department that they would have sole jurisdiction over slackers, APL members pledged to forego the $50 per man bounty. On April 15, however, Gregory authorized "expense reimbursements" of up to $50 per slacker to law enforcement personnel, in effect renewing the bounty-hunting incentive. Slacker raiding became the APL's principal wartime role. Of the three million investigations conducted by the APL for the government during World War I, over two million were associated with the Selective Service System.

Many of the APL's investigations resulted from mass raids carried out in conjunction with the Bureau of Investigation, police, and the army in major cities. Raids would often last for several days. Any man of military age who could not produce his draft card was held for questioning. In an atmosphere of guilty until proven innocent, men were often held for hours and sometimes days as their draft status was tracked down through a confused liaison with the Selective Service. For the first time in history, thousands of average citizens with no overtly suspicious characteristics were subjected to the American intelligence agencies' repressive tactics. Protests poured into the Justice Department, not only from socialists and Wobblies, but from outraged families with "patriotic" names like Adams and Washington.

Public protest was compounded by the official treatment of conscientious objectors. COs with legitimate deferrals were herded into camps, pestered, and even sadistically attacked by soldiers and other law-enforcement personnel. Some COs were sentenced to jail: one socialist received a life sentence for following his conscience.

Secretary of War Baker, a former pacifist, defused the conscientious objector issue by putting COs to work at government-owned farms, but furor over the slacker raids died hard. Gregory had to order an investigation of his subordinates' methods. John Lord O'Brian conducted the investigation.

As early as 1917, Attorney General Gregory had begun searching for a means with which to control the vastly expanded manpower placed under his command by the war. He created a War Emergency Division to enforce all war-related legislation and to keep a rein on the Bureau of Investigation and the Justice Department's proliferation of agents and volunteers.

To coordinate the War Emergency Division, Gregory chose John Lord O'Brian, a progressive Republican lawyer from a respected Buffalo, New York, law firm. Born in Buffalo in 1874, O'Brian had attended Harvard before returning home to practice law, later serving briefly as a United States Attorney in New York. He returned to private practice in Buffalo following World War I, but was in Washington again as Assistant Attorney General from 1929 to 1933. Franklin Roosevelt consulted O'Brian on internal security matters prior to World War II, and O'Brian's recommendations against a volunteer force of civilian counterespionage fanatics prevented a repetition of World War I's domestic confusion. He then served as general counsel to the Office of Production Management, Supply Priorities, and Allocation Board, and was a member of the War Production Board through 1944. He came back to Washington in 1951–52 to serve on the National Advisory Board on Mobilization Policy. It should also be noted that before World War I O'Brian brought into his firm a young lawyer named William J. Donovan, head of the Office of Strategic Services in World War II. (See Chapters 3, 4, and 5 for a discussion of William J. Donovan and his role in America's intelligence community.)

The coincidence that O'Brian and Donovan knew each other and were professionally associated should not be dismissed lightly. Both men exerted strong influence on American intelligence policy during World Wars I and II and the Korean War. Individuals and their interrelationships with one another have had a strong effect on the development of America's intelligence heritage and the intelligence community itself. As intelligence operations expanded rapidly into the mid-twentieth century, these personal relationships came to form a powerful and unofficial intelligence net of influences and alliances which operated in and outside official government channels.

In the mid-1950s, O'Brian became a member of Covington and Burling, one of Washington's largest and most prestigious law firms. He died in Washington on April 10, 1973, at the age of 98.

It was O'Brian more than Gregory who maneuvered the Justice Department into control of domestic intelligence. Of all the players in the game, he was the only real match for the wily Colonel Van Deman. When O'Brian arrived in Washington, the APL had already finished most of its destruction of the IWW, and Van Deman was courting an APL national director, Albert Briggs, to bring the League into close partnership with MID. Van Deman offered a commission to Daniel Frey, another APL national director, and arranged for a joint MID/APL office to be created in the War Department. MID officers were assigned to local APL chapters to supervise league investigations into the activities of private citizens of interest to Van Deman.

O'Brian called Briggs, Frey, and Victor Elting, the third APL national director, into his office when he arrived at the Justice Department. He was aware of the League's past problems, and started his reorganization at Justice by separating the Bureau of Investigation from the APL, thereby taking control over the APL without interference from Bruce Bielaski, the chief of the Bureau of Investigation. O'Brian emphasized to the directors that the League was purely voluntary, with no federal power to arrest. Its only responsibility was to gather information and supply it to the Justice Department. The three men accepted O'Brian's order, but when they passed it along to the APL membership they met stiff resistance. The rank and file had been enjoying their assumed federal powers, and were loath to abandon them, especially when local Bureau of Investigation and MID agents continued to encourage APL excesses despite O'Brian's orders.

The APL's continued violations of the law provoked Secret Service Chief William J. Flynn to resign in January 1918, and Secretary of the Treasury William McAdoo, in response, correctly publicized the danger of the League to the government. But McAdoo undercut his argument by demanding a central intelligence bureau headed by Flynn. Despite the merits of this position, it was widely interpreted as an attempted grab for political power via control of the nation's intelligence agencies.

Gregory was too preoccupied with consolidating the APL to bother with McAdoo's latest outburst. In continuing his policy of growth by absorption, Gregory was negotiating the takeover of the American Defense Society (ADS). The ADS had been formed with the support of Theodore Roosevelt and other wealthy Republicans in 1914 to pursue war preparedness. Roosevelt served as the organization's honorary president; former Attorney General Charles J. Bonaparte was honorary vice-president. ADS opposed German business in America, the employment of Germans, and the teaching of the German language in the schools. An offshoot organization, the American Vigilance Patrol, was formed in 1917 to stop seditious oratory. The ADS even scared veteran MID officer Nicholas Biddle, who wrote Van Deman:

We are to have another Secret Service Organization . . . the power of these volunteer organizations is tremendous, and it would seem to me advisable that some steps be taken either to curb or control their activities.*

Van Deman responded to Biddle's letter by suggesting to Bielaski that ADS be brought under Justice Department control. Roosevelt objected because he felt such an alliance would be too restrictive. The ex-president, in something of a flip-flop, announced his support for McAdoo's central intelligence bureau plan. A meeting was scheduled for January 28, 1918, between the ADS and APL directors, but before it could take place, the Justice Department obtained a conviction against ADS members for making false espionage charges. The verdict publicly discredited ADS, and its influence in the intelligence-organization control battle died out. The Justice Department had in this instance used

---

*Biddle to Van Deman. October 29, 1917. File 10261, Record Group, National Archives.

its power to eliminate a rival for intelligence control with prodding from Van Deman, who provided the evidence for the ADS conviction.

Meanwhile, McAdoo's plan was about to be finally buried through the combined efforts of Van Deman and O'Brian. The two men saw that it would be expedient to combine their influence in the intelligence battle to sink their major competitor. Their plan called for O'Brian to write an unofficial letter to each of the intelligence services requesting a meeting, ostensibly for Van Deman to express his fear of the threat posed by spies infiltrating from Mexico. It also called for Van Deman to display the communications intelligence intercepts made by Yardley and his crew to "prove" the threat's existence. At the meeting, the various representatives agreed to continue their sessions on a weekly basis at the Justice Department. All except the Treasury Department's Secret Service representative agreed to attend. This situation lasted several weeks, until O'Brian went to the Treasury Department in an effort to reach an understanding. He invited McAdoo's representative to the next weekly meeting at the Justice Department.

This meeting took place on March 6, 1918. Representatives of MID, ONI, State, Labor, Justice, Treasury and the Bureau of Investigation met to resolve McAdoo's complaints. Two plans were proposed: (1) a central bureau of intelligence with a director appointed by and responsible to the president (McAdoo's plan); and (2) a clearing house without a central bureau to compare reports and assign investigations. Although there was genuine substance to each proposal, the real issue underlying the two was how large the APL's authority would be in domestic intelligence, and the future role of the Secret Service. O'Brian and Bielaski allowed the MID and ONI representatives to sink the central intelligence option. All the agencies, except the Secret Service, feared that any central bureau would upset the control relationships they had worked so hard to establish with the APL. The Secret Service was also the only group without a good working relationship with the APL. The military representatives, in foretaste of similar battles to come, made the point that MID was already serving as a clearing house because it received, indexed, and classified reports from all the intelligence bureaus. Like all good bureaucrats, they saw no need to change the status quo unless it would be in their self-interest. The only obvious beneficiary of a new plan would be McAdoo and his Secret Service. The central intelligence proposal was shelved for forty years, when the Central Intelligence Agency was sanctioned in language very similar to McAdoo's.

With the Secret Service out of the picture, O'Brian and Van Deman squared off to fight the final battle for domestic control of intelligence. As the situation stood, O'Brian held a trump card because his War Emergency Division controlled the APL, and legally MID could only investigate civilians through its APL liaison and ties. By late April, however, a demand for military control over all espionage and sabotage violations became audible across the country. The spy paranoia which had been encouraged by government officials and the press led individuals to criticize the Justice Department and President Wilson for being "soft" on espionage. Citizens wrote their Congressmen to ask that the military be given more authority. Assistant Attorney General Warren wrote Gregory, "One man shot after court martial is worth a hundred arrests by this Department."* Former President William Howard Taft recommended the establishment of a firing squad to deal with traitors and spies.

This almost fanatic embrace of militarism to "save" the country scared O'Brian, not because of its obvious threat to civil liberties but because it left the domestic intelligence field open to Van Deman. O'Brian recognized that the only way to insure and maintain his power through the APL's dominance was to attack MID and the move for military control, but Van Deman was already several steps ahead in what had become a desperate game with implications far beyond the ambitions and egos of those concerned. Through Frey's office in the War Department and the Bureau of Intelligence's War Intelligence Board, MID had established close ties with local APL chapters.** Many Leaguers preferred to work with MID because the army intelligence officers encouraged them to use broad powers while the Justice Department was attempting to put a lid on League excesses. The militarist cause was also aided by 1918's being an election year. Public opinion wanted a crackdown on the alleged spies, and politicians wanted the votes of the public.

O'Brian swung into action, using his talents as a top-drawer lawyer to construct a case against broader military jurisdiction which would carry political weight. Gregory assisted by starting a propaganda campaign in support of the APL. The Attorney General called in his chits with the press corps and had them pen articles describing the League as tough and successful against espionage and sabotage and inferentially promoting the idea that if the APL civilian vigilantes were so good at protecting the nation from spies, the army

*Warren to Gregory. January 11, 1918, File 9–5–395, Record Group 60, National Archives.

**The War Intelligence Board was used to coordinate APL assistance to the various domestic intelligence services. Its membership was as follows:

Chairman: Hinton G. Clabaugh, Division Superintendent, Bureau of Investigation, Department of Justice
Members: Colonel Carl Reichman, Military Intelligence Officer, Central Department, War Department.
Major T.B. Crockett, Military Intelligence Officer
Lieutenant Edwin L. Reed, Aide for Information, 9th, 10th, and 11th Naval Districts
General James E. Stuart, Post Office Inspector in Charge
Colonel L.G. Nutt, Supervising Agent, Internal Revenue Service
H.R. Landis, Inspector in Charge, Immigration Service
John J. Bradley, U.S. Marshal
Charles Howe Bradley, Special Agent in Charge, Treasury Dept.
David S. Groh, Special Agent in Charge, Plant Protection Division, War Department
John H. Winterbotham, Chairman, Chicago Division, American Protective League
Robert A. Gunn, Chief, Chicago Division, American Protective League.
[See Emerson Hough, *The Web*. Chicago: Reilly and Lee, 1919, p. 487.]

should keep its nose out of the action. In fairness to O'Brian, who was confused but not an unthinking zealot, he also took these actions in a rather belated attempt to debunk the spy scare and call the country back to its moral heritage. This took considerable courage at a time when delay in making pronouncements about principles was the more expedient course of action. In April he released a report from American fire insurers which showed that there had been "substantially no fire losses" related to sabotage during the previous year. He sent a memorandum to Gregory and Wilson urging that the president make a speech to cool the national frenzy for irrational repression, saying:

This war is one for American principle and for the sanctity of long-recognized standards raised by international law. Any act of such oppression directed toward an enemy alien is an act which discredits the good name of America and its motives in this war.*

Gregory, whose political ambitions exceeded his talent and grasp, was also coming to realize the sham of the spy scare. Although he publicly defended the APL as part of his bureaucratic power base, in private he wrote:

There is quite a deal of hysteria in the country about German spies. If you will kindly box up and send me from one to a dozen I will pay you very handsomely for your trouble. We are looking for them constantly, but it is a little difficult to shoot them until they have been found.**

The state of the nation bordered on panic. On April 18, Senator George Chamberlain's Committee on Military Affairs opened hearings on a bill to extend military jurisdiction to the country at large. To testify in this search for a man on a white horse, he called in representatives of all the intelligence agencies. The effectiveness of the Justice Department in dealing with subversives, and O'Brian's contentions, were on trial. Showing the same solidarity with Justice and the APL they had in March when McAdoo and the Secret Service were shot down, the MID and ONI representatives refused to find fault with the Justice Department. In this, the MID and ONI were less coconspirators than an a capella choir singing the song of bureaucratic solidarity in the face of Congressional curiosity. The hearings produced some headlines to scare people, but after Gregory and Wilson responded to O'Brian's memo by writing public statements against the bill, Senator Chamberlain was forced to withdraw it on April 23. Thus Congress, or at least those in league with Senator Chamberlain, was foiled in its attempt to turn the country over to the military in whatever form.

In the aftermath of this Constitutional crisis which went largely unnoticed, the Justice Department held onto civilian jurisdiction; however, MID retained

---

*O'Brian to Gregory and Wilson. Undated, File 190470m Record Group 60, National Archives.

**Gregory to T.V. Taylor, April 15, 1918, Gregory Papers, Library of Congress, Box 1.

the power to conduct civilian investigations through the APL. From this point forward, MID officers began to recruit additional civilians independent of the APL, because they distrusted the loyalties and abilities of many League members. Colonel Carl Reichmann, an MID representative on the War Intelligence Board, wrote Van Deman to request permission to establish a separate corps of informants. Van Deman noted that the request was against regulations (i.e., illegal), but approved it nonetheless. He urged Reichmann to keep his actions secret from the APL. Colonel Van Deman warned of "the unnatural jealousy of the League in retaining and maintaining the powers and privileges which it has arrogated to itself and the prestige which it has secured."*

Although it made good sense for Van Deman to move away from an overly dependent relationship with the APL, the approval of secret groups such as those proposed by Reichmann proved to be his downfall in his battle with O'Brian. Consistent with Van Deman's orders, recruitment of secret MID civilian agents continued throughout May, especially in the West and the Midwest, but by mid-June the operation had come to O'Brian's attention. A second revelation was the Pablo Waberski case. Waberski was a German native masquerading as a Russian. He was employed by Kurt Jancke, head of German intelligence in Mexico City. Jancke dispatched two men to accompany Waberski from Mexico into the United States, where Waberski was to conduct espionage and sabotage activities. On February 1, 1918, the trio entered the United States at Nogales, Arizona. Waberski was arrested by military police, but his companions were not. One was a British Secret Service agent, the other one of Van Deman's MID agents. Armed with these facts, O'Brian asked Secretary Baker to keep MID out of the Justice Department's jurisdiction. O'Brian and Van Deman had successfully eliminated Secret Service competition in domestic intelligence; now O'Brian wanted to eliminate MID's competition as well. As he saw it, Van Deman had violated the spirit of cooperation by organizing secret units to compete with the Bureau of Investigation's sanctioned APL. Earlier O'Brian had turned his back on MID improprieties, but he now cited the Waberski case as evidence of Van Deman's threat to American civil liberties. Waberski, based on illegally acquired wiretap information, was probably guilty of intended espionage; but under existing statutes he had committed no military crime, and it was illegal for Van Deman to hold him incommunicado in a military stockade—where, incidentally, Waberski died before he could be brought to trial. These events revealed MID to be more of a competitor than ally, and O'Brian invoked laws that he had conveniently ignored previously to defeat his opponent. Together with Gregory, he protested to Secretary of War Baker.

Van Deman's activities were grounds for court martial, but rather than lose a valuable man, Baker transferred him to the European war zone where such

*Van Deman to Reichmann. May 15, 1918. File 9684. Record Group 165, National Archives.

activities would be legitimate. He then appointed Lieutenant Colonel Marlborough Churchill as Chief of the MID.*

Van Deman, taking his banishment from Washington with characteristic good humor, went to Europe as a replacement for the very able AEF G-2, Colonel Dennis Nolan. In Europe, Van Deman visited the Intelligence School at Langres, France, and units in the line, to prepare himself to replace Colonel Nolan. But the war ended first, and Van Deman was assigned by General Pershing to serve as senior American intelligence officer and Chief of Allied Counterintelligence for the Paris Peace Commission. During the ten months he held this post, Van Deman, who had always had a disinclination toward the political left, developed an abiding hatred of Bolshevism. This was enhanced by his seeing circulars appealing to American forces to mutiny. Van Deman traced their origin to an American Communist living in a part of Germany not occupied by the Allies. This appeal, and others like it circulating at the time in the AEF, were intended to create dissent between officers and their troops and between Regular Army and temporary officers.** A measure of Van Deman's far-sightedness is shown in his proposal to create an internationally backed League of Nations intelligence agency. He wrote to Colonel Churchill that nobody he talked with:

seems to be impressed with the necessity for having such a service. . . . How under the sun they expect to function without it, I can't imagine and am sure they will have to come to it in the end. Just now, however, they seem to have exceedingly vague ideas of what the organization of the League is going to be.***

Returning to Washington in August 1919, Van Deman served briefly as deputy to Churchill in the MID, then returned to the Philippines in March 1920 as Commander of the 31st Infantry and Post of Manila. He remained in this position until April 1923, except for a three-month stint of detached service with the British Army in India "for observation and study." He served with the National Guard for several years, first in Washington in the Militia

---

*Lieutenant Colonel Marlborough Churchill had no background in intelligence. Born in 1878, his father had been professor of sacred rhetoric at the Andover Theological Seminary. Churchill received his preparatory education at the Phillips Academy and went on to Harvard College, from which he graduated in 1900. After a year as an English instructor, he abandoned his father's profession and took a commission as a second lieutenant. The next fifteen years saw him in assorted artillery assignments, including a stint as editor of the Army's *Field Artillery Journal.* Then from January 1916 to June 1917, Churchill was an official observer with the French Army. He followed up with service on General Pershing's staff in Europe, returning in May 1918 to take over from Van Deman at MID. Despite his inexperience, Churchill guided the Military Intelligence Division through four difficult years and, based upon the organizational groundwork laid by Van Deman, firmly established G-2 as a functional section of the army.

**Van Deman, *Memoirs,* Part III, p. 8.

***Ibid.,* Part III, pp. 19–20.

Bureau, then as an instructor with the 159th Infantry Brigade in Berkeley, California. Promoted to Brigadier General in October 1927, he assumed command of the 6th Brigade. The last two years of his active duty were spent on the West Coast, at Fort Rosecrans in San Diego and as Commanding General, 3rd Infantry Division at Fort Lewis. He was promoted to Major General in May 1929. After thirty-eight years service, in September 1929, General Van Deman retired in San Diego. Though a private citizen, he remained a very active counterintelligence and counterespionage leader, operative, and "adviser" to the intelligence community. (See Chapter 3 for a discussion of General Van Deman's "second career" in intelligence.)

Returning to the internal security/intelligence situation at the time of Van Deman's transfer to Europe, membership lists from the MID's volunteer corps were turned over to O'Brian by Colonel Churchill. Churchill continued to allow MID agents to pursue civilians under the guise of slacker raiding, but the operation shrank and became less well coordinated. With Van Deman off in Europe, O'Brian held sway over the intelligence community; however, O'Brian's and the Justice Department's real problem was that they were not in control of the American Protective League.

By mid-1918 the APL was too large and had been created from too many separate organizations for anyone to control its operations completely. Individual APL chapters tended to throw their allegiance to whomever gave them the most power (or money). Frequently this was a local businessman, police chief, or MID officer, not the Justice Department. Orders from O'Brian, Frey, and Briggs in Washington were routinely disobeyed or ignored. For the remainder of the war, various segments of the APL abused their position through illegal wiretaps, arrests, harrassments, violations of personal records, and general disregard of civil liberties. The Justice Department lacked the money and manpower to control the APL, or to do without it.

The vast APL organization had taken on a life of its own. When the war ended there was a small percentage of Leaguers who wanted to continue their crusades, and those tried to make the APL a permanent part of the American scene. After the armistice, Briggs, Bielaski, and O'Brian told League chapters to disband. The War Department told MID to suspend domestic operations. Despite these official orders, certain APL groups reestablished themselves as vigilance committees, and MID officers stayed at work, contacting former Leaguers for information and keeping the secret network alive. Van Deman made contact with them upon his return from Europe.

The leader of the move to keep the APL alive was Thomas Crockett, a former Briggs assistant who was a member of the War Intelligence Board and MID Chief in Chicago. He appealed his orders to demobilize, and contacted other APL offices around the country to coordinate a search for radicals. Other military intelligence officers rallied to Crockett's side, but the War Department cut MID back to 103 officers and gave it three peacetime missions: (1) to disseminate information to the press; (2) to maintain military morale; and (3) to decode messages. Crockett, with some encouragement by Van Deman, continued his fight, claiming that strikes were being organized by the IWW and Bolshevists, and asking for files on radicals, labor organizers, conscientious objectors, draft evaders, and propagandists. His crusade ended on January 24, 1919, when the Military Intelligence Division reiterated its order for all civilian investigations to cease and for MID personnel to confine their activities to military reservations. The order did leave the loophole that MID officers were allowed to receive information from civilians. This encouraged MID officers to maintain their APL ties. Although O'Brian ordered all APL files sent to Washington, many ended up in the hands of MID and ultimately in Van Deman's. Some bureaus, such as Crockett's Chicago branch of the APL, voted to burn their records rather than turn them over to Washington.

The armistice had been signed, but there was no peace treaty, and the country was still on the lookout for conspirators and conspiracies. Despite the official orders, ex-APL members formed law-enforcment leagues and MID agents operated independently to infiltrate unions and other alleged radical groups. Of the thousands of arrests and convictions under the Espionage and Sedition Acts, many had been for dissent, but not one for active spying. O'Brian remained in the Justice Department to clean up loose ends, but both Bielaski and Gregory left.

President Wilson appointed William E. Allen, an O' Brian assistant, to take over the head job in the Bureau of Investigation. For his new Attorney General he wanted Alexander Mitchell Palmer, the Alien Property Custodian. Palmer was a Quaker and a reformer who left his profession as a Pennsylvania lawyer and corporation director to serve as a Democratic Congressman from 1909 to 1915. As Alien Property Custodian, he had been appointed in the fall of 1917 to acquire the records of property owned in the United States by German citizens and their allies. He was allowed to seize property and assets he deemed dangerous to the nation for the war's duration. His office expanded from one room and one clerk in 1917 to 550 people and an entire building in 1919. The APL assisted Palmer in his search for alien property, and in his first year of operation he attached over $700 million worth. Palmer received additional investigative assistance from the special bureau he created headed by Francis P. Garvan.

Palmer was young, progressive, and a good campaigner, which made him attractive to Wilson as the Democrats looked toward the 1920 presidential election. His appointment as Attorney General was announced in March 1919. O'Brian counselled Palmer to avoid the reconstitution of the APL, and on April 3, Palmer issued a statement similar to MID's earlier position, explaining that the Justice Department could not sanction private investigators, but would welcome outside information of relevance to the department. Meanwhile, Marlborough Churchill urged the use of old APL files by MID and told Crockett he could ask ex-APLers for specific information.

O'Brian continued his strong influence on Justice Department policy until he left on April 30. He denied requests of public officials and politicians to use APL files; released all but 150 aliens convicted during the war; saw the APL disbanded and the Bureau of Investigation reduced to prewar staffing levels; and reviewed all prosecutions under the Espionage Act, convincing Wilson to pardon three men and commute the sentences of 102 others. O'Brian also kept Palmer from supporting a peacetime antisedition act, and blocked efforts by the Bureau of Immigration to use the Bureau of Investigation to help obtain deportations of members of the IWW and suspected anarchists.

When O'Brian returned to Buffalo, Palmer became the dominant personality in the Justice Department. In short order, the department was again challenged by a perceived radical threat. A group of letter bombs was sent to several cabinet members and other prominent politicians. The press and much of the nation jumped to the conclusion that the IWW and communists were behind the crime. Soldiers, sailors, and APL veterans responded by raiding socialist papers and breaking up left-wing May Day celebrations. Palmer did not involve his department in these illegal acts; neither did he condemn or control the vigilante efforts.

Emerson Hough added to the antialien feeling with publication of *The Web*, an official history of the American Protective League. The book promoted selective immigration, deportation of those deemed un-American, denaturalization of disloyal citizens and anarchists, elimination of alien labor and German goods, and an end to the teaching of the German language in the schools.

On May 28, Major Crockett reentered the antialien battle by contacting old APL chiefs to request any information they could recall concerning alien, labor, and radical activity in their regions. Also in May, Palmer appointed William J. Flynn, the ex-Secret Service Chief, as his new Bureau of Investigation director. He was confirmed on July 1, and Palmer's old intelligence chief, Francis P. Garvan, became assistant director.

Attorney General Palmer's moderate stance changed markedly on June 2, 1919, when his house was bombed. Within days he approached Congress with a request for $500,000 to fight radicals. The *Washington Post* urged the reconstitution of the APL to help stop the bombings.* MID Chief Marlborough Churchill also requested a half million dollars from Congress with which to investigate radicals. State politicians perceived the political profit to be gained in hunting Reds, and many organized semiofficial anti-Red squads. The New York State Senate organized its own secret service and dispatched them to raid radical headquarters throughout the state, including those of the socialist party and the IWW. The Red Scare was on.

On August 1, 1919, a rising young star in the Justice Department's Bureau of Investigation, John Edgar Hoover, was placed in charge of a newly formed Anti-Radical Division. By 1920, Hoover was calling it the General Intelligence Division (GID). Over one-third of the Bureau of Investigation's agents were

---

*The *Washington Post*, June 3, 1919.

assigned to his command. He instructed them to turn in any radical information they could find, hearsay or otherwise, to Washington. Hoover's men took a special interest in radical publications, raiding publishing houses and personal libraries. In a few years, Hoover's offices contained the best library of radical and subversive literature in the world, most of it stolen. Through his agents and infiltrators in radical organizations, he produced a card file which included by the end of 1921 more than 500,000 names of individuals, many of them aliens. GID published a weekly intelligence report on domestic security and distributed it to selected government officials.

The Department of Labor assisted Hoover by passing on the names of alien radicals whom they thought might deserve deportation. Private individuals and companies, local, state and military authorities, and APL veterans all contributed information on radicals as requested by the Bureau of Investigation. Federal troops came into frequent use as domestic inflation spurred increased strikes. MID operatives followed closely after the troops, reopening branch offices and reestablishing APL contacts.

Throughout this growing crisis, President Wilson had been preoccupied with obtaining a peace settlement; after he suffered a stroke in September, he paid even less attention to domestic affairs. Secretary of War Baker took an active role in strikebreaking by sanctioning the use of federal troops on the basis of state rather than presidential authorization. MID and Bureau of Investigation agents posed as radicals, stirred up strikes and then used the presence of troops as an excuse to impose martial penalties. Together with local police and private detectives hired by industry, they intimidated workers, threatened aliens with deportation and forced them back to work.

O'Brian had promoted caution in dealing with radicals, and had maintained the confidentiality of APL files; but official Washington now took a different attitude. Churchill defended MID's harsh actions. He was convinced of a Bolshevist threat and recommended training for officers in how to handle "radical rebel groups." Palmer allowed APL files to be released for use by politicians and law-enforcement groups. As to the methods of the Bureau of Investigation, he commented:

If some of my agents out in the field . . . were a little rough and unkind, or short and curt, with these alien agitators . . . I think it might well be overlooked.

Daniel Frey, the former APL director and MID liaison officer, made an anti-Red speech in October, calling for the registration of all aliens. He believed they should all be forced to learn English and become citizens, and that all foreign publications should be banned from the United States.

In November, Hoover recalled APL veterans to duty, enlisted new volunteers, and recruited local police. The GID planned raids on aliens and the offices of foreign organizations in over a dozen major cities. Briggs responded to a request from Churchill by sending a complete list of former APL chiefs and their addresses to MID headquarters. The domestic wartime intelligence community was thus reconstituted with Palmer, Hoover, and Churchill in charge.

The big push came in a series of raids during January 1920. Hoover deployed men in 33 cities. Undercover agents called membership meetings of alien and labor organizations for January 2, and raided the meetings after the recruits had arrived. Over the course of the winter more than 4,000 suspected alien radicals were imprisoned. As civil libertarians began to criticize the tactics of the Justice Department and MID, Hoover and Churchill combed their files to discover relationships between their critics and suspected radicals. These alleged ties were used as an excuse to badger the intelligence community's critics. O'Brian issued a public statement against the Bureau of Investigation's terrorist tactics, but Palmer was building up the issue of a Red Menace to further his political ambitions, and no longer heeded O'Brian's advice. Churchill wrote an article in April 1920, noting that he believed in the subordination of military to civilian authority in peacetime, but that the use of MID was necessary to support troops in disturbed areas. He cited the confusion in domestic intelligence:

Theoretically, the civilian investigational agencies, the Department of Justice and the Secret Service of the Treasury, should find out everything there is to know and tell us. Practically, they are presently working under almost insuperable difficulties which tend to complicate the situation and make almost impossible the normal relation between civil and military authority.*

After the January raids, interest in Red baiting began to trail off. Palmer had pursued his repressive policies too far, and the public was shocked to read of innocent families molested in their homes in the middle of the night by Justice Department operatives. It became quite evident that the intelligence community had not done its homework. There had been no accurate intelligence relative to the radical alien threat. Palmer's program was revealed as a politically motivated expedient. The Democrats lost the presidential election to Harding, and Palmer left office with Wilson in 1921.

William J. Burns replaced Flynn as Bureau of Investigation director. He used government agents as well as members of his private detective firm to watch radicals, but received no support for his program from Attorney General Harry M. Daugherty, who was too busy pursuing his corrupt role in the Teapot Dome scandal. J. Edgar Hoover continued with his private surveillance program and issued weekly intelligence summaries outlining the disposition of radicals, but his actions were low key and went largely unnoticed. In 1924, in the wake of the Teapot Dome revelations, Daugherty was replaced as Attorney

*Marlborough Churchill, *Journal of the United States Artillery,* "The Military Intelligence Division, General Staff," April 1920, p.313.

General by Harlan Fisk Stone; Hoover was selected to replace Burns.

Although Hoover had been in the thick of earlier Bureau of Investigation repressive tactics, he survived Stone's purge of the "Ohio Gang" in the Justice Department. Several stories exist to explain Hoover's survival and subsequent appointment by Stone to head the Justice Department Bureau of Investigation's successor organization, the Federal Bureau of Investigation. One contends that Hoover, the complete bureaucrat, represented himself as an apolitical individual who merely carried out the orders of his superiors based on the assumption of their responsibility in investigatory matters and greater understanding of the "big picture." Maybe yes, maybe no. Another alleges that William J. Donovan, who had been brought into Justice by Stone to serve as the Assistant Attorney General in charge of the Criminal Justice Division, perhaps with prodding from his mentor and friend John O'Brian, cautioned Stone against appointing Hoover to the top investigative job. Further, this story contends Hoover responded by making it clear to Stone that there was enough in his files to effectively sink the Republican Party in the upcoming presidential election. Others, at some later date, may confirm or reject this latter explanation. However, two additional items tend to support it. One, Hoover's later animosity toward Donovan went well beyond their publicized arguments over intelligence turf during World War II with Hoover "leaking" some very damaging personal information about Donovan to President Eisenhower in 1952–3 when Donovan was under serious consideration for appointment as the Director of the CIA. The other, that when Stone ordered an end to all wiretapping and instructed the Bureau of Investigation to confine its investigations to violations of the law, Hoover nodded his head in obeisance, but continued secret civilian surveillance through the assistance of people like Van Deman, and organized tight personal control over the bureau's remaining 300 agents. It is difficult if not impossible to believe that Stone did not know that his orders to Hoover were being routinely violated, because Donovan and O'Brian informed him to that effect.

One last domestic intelligence failure should be mentioned. This was in connection with the Bonus March on Washington in July 1932, when a largely peaceful demonstration by World War I veterans turned into a violent attack by federal troops. Some government authorities, particularly Army Chief of Staff General Douglas MacArthur and J. Edgar Hoover, who supplied MacArthur with intelligence, wrongly believed the bonus marchers to be part of a new communist-inspired conspiracy against the United States.

The marchers were, in fact, largely middle class and well behaved. They staged a series of peaceful demonstrations and camped out in abandoned federal buildings and on the Anacostia mud flats. Their numbers included very few communists, and these had only a rudimentary organization. The group boasted a rigorous internal police force which bordered on being fascist in character. Ironically, the majority philosophy of the protestors was very close to that of General MacArthur, who feared and attacked them.

Violence was almost averted by the actions of District of Columbia Police Chief Pelham Glassford and President Herbert Hoover, but events combined with stubborn personalities and the District of Columbia's confusing federal/ local jurisdiction subverted their efforts. When the marchers first arrived, Glassford and Hoover arranged for them to be supplied with food and shelter, and protected their right to protest. However, when the protestors were asked to vacate federal buildings which they occupied illegally, scattered violence erupted. Glassford briefly lost control of the situation, and the District Commissioners, known as the "Three Blind Men," took the opportunity to ask President Hoover for the intercession of federal troops.

Hoover was reluctant to send in troops, and refused to do so without Chief Glassford's recommendation. Even though he had not, the commissioners assured Hoover that Glassford endorsed the action. The president then issued an order for troops to move the protestors back to the Anacostia flats where the government had given them permission to camp. The operation was to be under Glassford's command.

Meanwhile, MacArthur had been preparing for war. He had called up reserves, tanks, and artillery from installations near Washington. In addition, he had asked J. Edgar Hoover to infiltrate the marchers' ranks and provide him with intelligence. Hoover's men reported that there were very few communists and that the marchers were remarkably well-behaved. This was not what the FBI Director nor MacArthur wanted to hear. Despite the reports of his own agents, Hoover told MacArthur that there were many dangerous communists among the Bonus Army and that they were inciting the group to violence.

This false intelligence, coupled with the fact that the D.C. commissioners were acting without Chief Glassford's knowledge, gave MacArthur room to move. The chief of staff took personal command of the troops and had his men start driving the protesters out of the buildings at bayonet point. When Glassford heard what was happening, he resigned and declined to challenge MacArthur. President Hoover was shocked when he learned that MacArthur was pursuing unarmed men with fixed bayonets, and dispatched a messenger to remind the general that he was to stop at the Anacostia River Bridge. The message reached MacArthur, as did another in later years, but the egocentric chief of staff ignored the three orders from his commander-in-chief, burned down the campground on the flats and ran the protestors out of town.

Glassford, Hoover, and much of the public were outraged. In his defense, MacArthur and Secretary of War Patrick J. Hurley cited the need to destroy the Red menace of the marchers. As it happened, at the time of MacArthur's raid the handful of communists associated with the bonus marchers had been meeting in a church in another part of the city in an attempt to resolve their own differences. The few communists from whom MacArthur might have "saved" the capital escaped his wrath.

Once again, accurate intelligence prepared by responsible intelligence personnel without political and philosophical axes to grind had been used by intelligence leaders for a repressive overreaction. The wrong was compounded by the failure of the chain of command to function properly because of the personal animosities between President Hoover and General MacArthur and the D.C. commissioners and Chief Glassford. Further problems resulted when the president chose to defend MacArthur in the interest of executive branch solidarity, and instead dragged himself into public disfavor along with the chief of staff.*

The threads to America's intelligence heritage may be likened to a series of lines of varying thickness moving through time, sometimes on parallel tracks, sometimes converging, running in concert and then splitting off into divergent directions. Some threads fade out and reappear at a later date because external events reactivate them.

One purpose has been to show the persistence of some of these threads in order to put in perspective contemporary events and actions taken by and on behalf of the modern intelligence community. There has been no attempt to draw direct analogies between the historical past and the modern period in American intelligence. While analogies of varying closeness do in fact exist, it is first necessary to see how other Americans responded to what were perceived as unique and extraordinary situations and circumstances. Nor do we cite the good and bad of American intelligence simply to show its persistent problems, but rather to give the reader a frame of reference of historical precedent with which to aid his/her judgment of the merit and justifications of those who in modern times have grappled with these same problems.

There is much in America's early intelligence history for which we as a people have ample reason to be proud. There is also much which dispels myths about our essential sense of fair play, law-abiding, and the degree of public support for the government and the principles on which it operates during times of crisis. The latter goes well beyond Tom Paine's ideas about "summer patriots" to include recognition that from the Revolutionary War through World War I, those who were willing to risk their "lives, honor, and purse" have been a consistent minority of the population. This early history shows the dynamics and challenges of intelligence work. The theme of the American patriotic spy is based on the large number of Americans who opted to become spies for their country, a situation unique in the thirty-three-century history of espionage. No other nation can make a similar claim. Each of those described herein, and thousands more who made a similar choice, tell us something about Americans as a people and about the intelligence profession's demands, challenges, rewards, or lack thereof.

Similarly, the conflicts between presidents, Congress, and the intelligence

*For more on the Bonus March see esp., Donald J. Lisio, *The President and Protest: Hoover, Conspiracy and the Bonus Riot.* Columbia, Missouri: University of Missouri Press, 1974.

professionals of the time—and with the Constitution and the law—point out the difficulties in reconciling the practices of intelligence within the framework of a democratic society. These conflicts presage the broad social questions implied in the need for secrecy in intelligence and the weakness of our system of checks and balances in meeting that need while preserving our basic civil liberties.

One additional conclusion from this early history of American intelligence stands out: the role of the individual. One man or woman often did make a difference, and perhaps that fact was the subjective basis for their choice to labor in America's intelligence vineyards, knowing their efforts would likely be unheralded and scarcely rewarded. Also, as attempts were made to coordinate the efforts of an increasing number of individuals, it became clear that conventional theories—past and present—of government organizational form, structure, and management were inadequate to produce a systematized intelligence system which could continue after the crises of the moment were passed and the dominant personalities of the period vanished from the scene. The record indicates that we survived the feast-or-famine attitude about intelligence, but just barely; and this survival was due to the next generation of patriotic spies who rallied around the "cloak and dagger."

Many of the intelligence leaders and their mentors were exceptional people; but no John Marshall emerged to set the intelligence community on a consistent course of evolution which enabled successive leaders to anticipate fully the changing demands of intelligence as America moved from revolution to civil war to world war. Nevertheless, the ad hoc, generally war-induced, responses did produce a form of social Darwinism which narrowed or provided indications about how and by whom the nation's intelligence effort can and should be directed and controlled.

It should also be noted there is no body of law which deals with the problems of intelligence. Certainly the Constitution exists to affirm basic rights and to circumscribe the government's actions; however, these provisions have proven inadequate to square the rights and proscriptions of government with the demands of intelligence for secrecy, and with the problem of maintaining internal and national security while forces within and outside the body politic use the protection of those rights. This legislative gap, which derives in part from Congress' unwillingness or inability to challenge successfully the executive, has produced a double void. On the one hand, the Supreme Court has been unable to test the constitutionality of Congressional attempts to circumscribe presidential actions taken under "executive privilege" because there have been none. On the other, it has produced a situation where subordinate elements of the executive branch have, in responding to presidential orders, or raised eyebrows, or grunts, have operated in a nether world where the legality of their actions have never been adequately tested in the courts.

It should be possible for us to look objectively at intelligence in the modern era not as a series of unique or aberrant events and responses, but rather as a continuation of that heritage which was borne out of the actions, frustrations, beliefs, and responses of those who pursued the elusive goals of intelligence since the Revolutionary War.

Epilogue

Before we leave this phase of American intelligence, there is a necessity to identify a phenomenon of that era—beginning with the World War I period —which emerged as part of our continuing intelligence heritage. Let us call it the "intelligence subculture." Beginning with World War I, a highly select band of brothers came into existence who maintained a continuing interest and personal involvement with intelligence, both directly and indirectly, in subsequent years. These persons became intelligence professionals of a much different stripe than those who chose to carry out the lonely, often boring tasks of collection, evaluation, and dissemination of intelligence information during America's peacetime intervals. They were among the first to recognize that intelligence and control of the process which produced it was the *sine qua non* of America's future dominance of the international environment.

As such, their approach to intelligence was based both on the nation's security needs and on the application of intelligence in business ventures, both domestic and international. The early group with this understanding about the applications of intelligence in other than a strict national security context also recognized that real political power was more realistically based on effective control of the nation's intelligence apparatuses than on the simple holding of titular or elected office. To this end, they also concluded that an "in and out" approach to government service, combined with an effort to preselect career types who could be counted upon to provide them with intelligence information on a personal basis during their "out" periods, was sufficient to maintain effective control, and could be used to get answers to specific questions which were beyond their civilian capacity to obtain. For example, the "take" from America's Black Chamber was routinely disseminated to key members of America's financial and legal community who by virtue of their previous service were members of the intelligence community's subculture.

These practices, and the attitudes of those who lived them in word and deed, were never set forth as an articulated, fully reasoned concept. However, they did guide and direct the actions of those people who, recognizing the enormous potential of intelligence in determining the future of another country or controlling the world monetary system, did so from the period following World War I.

The people who understood these features of intelligence may be considered as the founders of America's ex-intelligence personnel fraternity. A fraternity, as we shall see in later chapters, which has facilitated and encouraged the government's intelligence agencies to multiply their extralegal and illegal activities and which has generally rendered any investigation of these activities futile and unproductive. Although it is not possible to identify definitively the intelligence subculture's founder, the most likely candidate is Robert Lansing, who served as Woodrow Wilson's Secretary of State. Lansing, who used MID and Secret Service agents to obtain secret information, longed for direct control over his own agents; therefore, in 1916 he created a Bureau of Secret Intelligence in the State Department. The Bureau was headed by a Chief Special Agent who drew his salary from a confidential account controlled by the Secretary. The funds for this came partially from private "benefactors" who recognized the limited value of the information available from the APL zealots and who were willing to pay for quality information which could be acquired if the operatives had the imprimatur of the Secretary of State on their credentials. To increase the Bureau's secrecy, the Chief Special Agent paid the operatives by personal check out of a slush fund account established by Lansing from "contributions" received from friends and business associates. Under Lansing, the ostensible purpose of the Bureau was to advise the Secretary on intelligence and security. However, based on the open checkbook nature of the Bureau's operation, it was able to recruit the best agents money could buy. As a measure of the value of money in the intelligence business, this group provided the letter from German Ambassador Von Bernstorff which Lansing quoted from selectively to create the impression that the German government was funding pacifist organizations in America. After Lansing's departure from State, the Chief Special Agent and his staff became passport investigators rather than the next Secretary's secret intelligence force.

After leaving office Lansing retained a lively interest in intelligence matters, impressing their importance on and recruiting as pledges in the subculture his nephews by marriage, John Foster and Allen Welsh Dulles; the latter, in his "inside" intelligence career as Director of the CIA, also ran a special personal net of agents.

Another of the intelligence subculture's founding fathers was John Lord O'Brian, whose exploits in the Justice Department during World War I have been described. Beyond these activities, O'Brian, the perennial advisor on intelligence and internal security matters to presidents from Wilson to Kennedy, was an able recruiter to the intelligence cause, William J. Donovan being the foremost example. Others of like persuasion were similarly recruited by O'Brian, first to his law firm and thence into key intelligence positions in succeeding national administrations.

The final founding father was Grayson M. P. Murphy, whose background and secret mission in South America for President Theodore Roosevelt is described Chapter 10. Murphy, who went on to become a very wealthy New York financier, participated in the intelligence subculture's development by using his position as head of the International Red Cross to provide cover for an unofficial network of agents which operated in Europe following World War I. Around 1920 there was a blending, if not merging, of the Lansing-Dulles/O'Brian-Donovan/Murphy chapters of the subculture which enabled these three elements to operate a rather effective international intelligence operation.

During the interwar period, the intelligence subculture's leaders maintained an intelligence capability which, once war came again, was useful in the wartime expansion of the American intelligence community. Following the end of World War II, it was further expanded by including in the fraternity many new members who had completed their pledge training in the OSS, military intelligence, and the FBI.

CHAPTER 3

COUNTDOWN
TO PEARL HARBOR

In the years before the Japanese attack at Pearl Harbor, the state of America's intelligence services reflected the nation's isolationist mood. One opinion offered in Congress during this period was that he who looks for trouble finds it; that is, "the nations best prepared were the ones which got into that [First World] war first."* However, as a major war in Europe came closer to reality, a reasonable consensus began to build for increased military preparedness. The measures taken were in keeping with the isolationist mood. They were designed to improve and upgrade the quality of military hardware, but strictly for defensive purposes.

The United States was belligerently neutral; even the modest increases in ships and planes would not have been approved by a Congress determined to avoid entanglement in a foreign war. Although wars were underway in Spain and China, Congress, by word and deed, acted as if neither existed or had any implications for the United States. It was a time not so much of innocence as of self-inflicted blindness which held that by seeing no evil its reality could be denied. Congress' idea of isolationism went far beyond avoiding foreign wars; there was the pretense that the United States had no real interests elsewhere in the world. Our economic dependence upon and interdependence with other nations was silently assumed as a historical, almost God-given natural order which was neither discussed nor questioned. Except for the fact that our export policy allowed for sale on a cash basis of material and equipment, neutrality dictated an arm's-length approach to potential and actual belligerents. This approach had its effect on intelligence activities. United States military attachés and diplomats who were gathering information about the Spanish Civil War, the undeclared Sino-Japanese war, and the war preparations elsewhere in Europe and Asia found that their reports were treated with Olympian disdain by most government officials outside those in the intelligence community itself. There seemed to be an unstated official attitude that because there were always going to be foreign quarrels and wars, there was no need to know more about them than the simple fact of their occurrence. Nor was there much

*81st Congress Record, p. 6138, June 22, 1937.

to be learned about American defense problems through studying the way other nations were fighting and readying their people and forces for war. Thus isolationism was reinforced by the corollary idea of "Fortress America," which held that our national intelligence needs could and should be met by limited passive observation.

In fairness to those most directly involved—Congress, President Roosevelt and key members of his administration, the Military High Command and those who could be considered "in" intelligence at the time—it should be noted that no one or any element of these groups fully anticipated or recognized until it was almost upon us, the reality of total war and the sheer magnitude of its intelligence aspects and requirements.*

During the uneasy years between President Roosevelt's inauguration on March 23, 1933, and the outbreak of World War II in Europe, on September 3, 1939, America's separate intelligence services constituted a small group of people informally bound together in pursuit of a common function. Largely because of fiscal austerity, interservice rivalry among the intelligence services was minimal. The intelligence services' relative poverty forced aside rivalries and made for good personal relations among its various members; this led to the informal sharing of ideas, viewpoints, and information of mutual interest. As a group, their solidarity was further heightened by the professional stigma attached to one's being in intelligence. This had nothing to do with the seamy and immoral sides of intelligence operations, but to a kind of put-down which held, "poor old Jones, he'll never get his star (ambassadorship, assistant director's chair, etc.)—intelligence, you know!" It didn't seem to bother those who had opted for intelligence careers. They were content with the personal rewards involved in dealing with the different and unfamiliar problems of intelligence as well as living in other than a conventional military environment. Or, in the case of the civilian agencies, an individual's interest in an intelligence career was increased by the lack of routine and by not having to meet arrest quotas or socialize for the sake of socializing.

---

*A word of caution about the term "intelligence" is in order. Too often it is used synonymously or interchangeably with "information." This is inaccurate and quite misleading. Information until, and unless, it has been analyzed and evaluated remains nothing more than a fact. Information may be interesting, amusing, or hitherto unknown to the person receiving it, but by and in itself it is inappropriate to call it intelligence. The three terms "intelligence," "intelligence information" and "information" need to remain distinct. Intelligence by itself refers to the meaning of, or a conclusion about, persons, events, and circumstances which is derived from analysis and/or logic. Intelligence information consists of facts bearing on a previously identified problem or situation, the significance of which has not been completely established. And information is made of raw facts whose relationship to other phenomena has yet to be considered or established. Similarly, the methods involved in acquiring information and/or intelligence information by any means and turning it into intelligence constitute the intelligence process or cycle. The distinctions between these terms are important to remember, because the hazards in blindly making the semantic leap from information to intelligence, or assuming they are one and the same, has been a root cause in most of America's and other nations' misadventures.

The kinds of conditions which prevailed in the intelligence services during the 1930s enabled those who opted to work in the field to gain a kind of scholarly perspective about intelligence. There was a lack of urgency, or even harrassment, from the various headquarters to get this or that piece of information on a rigid time schedule. Consequently, it was possible to gather information in an orderly way and to analyze and report it in terms of a coherent whole.

By mid-1938, the intelligence professionals were severely frustrated by America's policy of neutrality and congressional stinginess. Both at home and abroad, each of the intelligence services was being required to do more and more with scant increases in funds and staff, and results of their efforts—in their view—were being kept from the public for reasons which didn't make sense. Their discomfort was not with secrecy for secrecy's sake, but with the fact that the reality of the world and domestic situation required more active, positive intelligence measures, not fewer. It also was a time during which domestic and foreign intelligence operations dovetailed in a curious way to suggest the need for more formal relationships between the intelligence organizations and some kind of central direction.

The means by which the prewar intelligence leaders were able to force changes in the neutrality policy, and gain support as well actual increases in money and personnel for intelligence purposes, is illustrated in the case of Leon G. Turrou. It was an unprecedented case with legal, domestic-security, foreign-policy, and intelligence implications which are still quite pertinent today. It began, without mention of Turrou's name or any public stir, in the spring of 1935. Major Truman Smith, Military Attaché in Berlin, found out that Captain Wilhelm Canaris, the Chief of the Abwehr (the intelligence service of the German High Command) had violated orders from Hitler which forbade him from sending *V-Männer* (agents) to the United States. Although incomplete and largely based on "pillow talk" between one of Smith's subordinates and a woman employed by the Abwehr, it suggested the existence of a Nazi espionage net operating out of New York City. There wasn't much to go on except the knowledge that Canaris had established a *Kriegsorganization* (war organization, or KO) in New York City, that it was using German merchant flag vessels to transmit intelligence information from the U.S. to Germany, and that it was being run by other than diplomatically accredited personnel.

Major Smith's information was conveyed to Major Joe N. Dalton, the acting adjutant general and G-2 of the Army's Second Corps area at Governors Island. In this post Major Dalton had neither the resources or mandate to do much about potential espionage rings. But when he received Smith's information he enlisted the aid of U.S. customs officials, who agreed to look for any suspicious activity that might bear on the movement of military information to Germany. At this time neither Dalton nor Smith had a name or face to match the identity of the Abwehr KO in New York.

There the matter rested until the evening of September 27, 1935. At Pier 84, where the German liner *Europa* was berthed, Morris Josephs, a customs guard, observed a heated conversation between a smooth-shaven man wearing a dark hat and one of the ship's stewards. His suspicions aroused, Josephs stopped the man as he was about to leave and searched him. In the man's pockets Josephs found negatives of films and a packet of letters in German. Josephs took the man into custody, removed him to the Customs House and notified John W. Roberts, the supervisory customs agent, about his actions. Roberts, who had been previously informed by Major Dalton about the suspected spy courier arrangement with German flag vessels, conducted his preliminary interrogation of the suspect; he then called his contact in Army Intelligence, Major Stanley Grogan, to let him know that they might have netted a German spy.

The next day, the man, a German national whose name was William Lonkowski, was further questioned by Roberts in the presence of Grogan, who was in civilian clothes and remained unidentified to the suspect. The interrogation was classic in its execution. Roberts, the customs agent, was made to appear as a rather obtuse, bureaucratic cop only interested in smugglers; what appeared to be the material taken from Lonkowski the night before was left in plain sight during the interrogation in order to make him think that his captors were unaware of its contents. Emboldened by the apparent pedestrian nature of his captors, Lonkowski denied he was in the employ of the German government and tried to pass himself off as a self-styled piano tuner and an aviation magazine correspondent. According to the prearranged decision between Grogan and Roberts, Roberts ostensibly bought Lonkowski's story and asked him to return three days later for further examination. Behind this arrangement was an important fact and a difficult decision. Major Grogan and his staff, with assistance from Naval Intelligence personnel, had firmly identified the photographs' subject—the plans for a new Curtiss experimental scout bomber being developed for the Navy at the Curtiss plant in Buffalo, New York. The plans carried an "X" designation to indicate it was an experimental aircraft. This designation by itself did not establish the plans as "defense secrets" as we use the term today. Later, Curtiss officials testified that the plans were "confidential." At the time, however, this had little standing or meaning at law. Obviously the plans had defense implications, but in 1935, before such items were stamped "Top Secret," "Secret," or "Confidential" in accordance with presidential orders, the connection between work carried out by industry for the government and official secrets was somewhat tenuous. As a result, Major Dalton, who was apprehensive over what might occur if the matter were turned over to the New York City police authorities, took the biggest gamble of his career and asked Roberts to release Lonkowski in hopes he would lead them to other members of the suspected spy ring.*

*Lonkowski escaped to Germany, but other members of his spy ring were convicted. See the *New York Times,* 3 December 1938, p. 1.

It should be noted that in 1935 jurisdiction over espionage matters was a tangled web in which no government agency had overall responsibility. The vagueness of the Espionage Act of 1917 was such that it was barely enforceable, being directed more toward prosecuting Americans for acting against their country than against agents of a foreign power. Because Lonkowski was a foreign national and not a member of the United States armed forces, Dalton put himself out on a bureaucratically indefensible limb by intervening in the matter at all. Nevertheless, Dalton caused Lonkowski to be released and ordered Grogan and his men to mount a round-the-clock surveillance of his movements. Short-handed though Dalton's counterintelligence forces were, they kept Lonkowski under surveillance. A day later, in the early morning hours of September 29, 1935, in a car driven by Dr. Ignatz Theodor Griebl, an army medical reserve officer and leader in the American Nazi movement, Lonkowski fled to Canada and thence back to Germany, where he subsequently surfaced as a key intelligence official in the Reich's air ministry.

Acting on Major Dalton's orders, the army agents made no attempt to stop Lonkowski. Their intent was to let Lonkowski return to his lair, and once he sailed for Germany, Major Smith was alerted to pick up his trail. Today, some forty years later, it's difficult to comprehend the sheer courage of Dalton's and Grogan's actions. It took a great deal of guts for them to act on the basis of their beliefs and break the rules. They were—and there is no pejorative connotation to the term—among the first of America's "cold warriors" at a time when simple consideration of war was thought by many to be anti-American, if not self-serving on the part of those in the armed forces.

Major Dalton reasoned quite properly that Dr. Griebl might lead to others whose relationships to the spy ring and assignments were as yet unknown. Also, by focusing on Dr. Griebl, Major Dalton lessened the chance of causing a bureaucratic flap if his actions became known to the politically motivated members of the army's general staff, because the army did have some jurisdictional basis in carrying out an investigation of Dr. Griebl. Fortunately, Major Dalton never had to play the bureaucratic game of justifying his actions. He soon realized, from the stake-out of Dr. Griebl's office at 56 East Eighty-seventh Street and the surveillance of his comings and goings and those of his after-office-hours visitors, that he and his men had stumbled on something bigger than they had originally imagined. To meet his personnel needs to follow up on the leads derived from the surveillance, Major Dalton turned to "friends" in the intelligence community.

Among these was Leon G. Turrou who, since 1929, had been a special agent in the FBI's New York City field office. Because of the important role of Turrou in the spy ring case and its subsequent results, a word is in order about the man himself and his shadowy past. Turrou was born in Poland in 1895, several months after his father had died in Paris. His mother died three months after his birth. He was adopted by neighbors who took him to Cairo and Alexandria, where he attended school for a short time. At the age of seven his foster parents took him to China. When he was about eleven years old, his foster mother died and his foster father took him to Odessa and thence to Warsaw. His foster father fought with the Imperial Russian Army during the Russo-Japanese War, after which he took him back to China. Soon afterward the foster father, an importer, remarried; and eighteen months later, he died, and Turrou was shipped to England. There followed about two years in Berlin and London, after which he came to the United States, earning a meager living by washing dishes and translating. In 1915, Turrou left the United States for Paris, finally joining the Russian Imperial Army. When the war ended he returned to the United States, eked out a living as a translator for the anti-Communist Russian-language newspaper *Slovo,* and eventually joined the U.S. Marines. Later he returned to the Soviet Union as a translator with the Hoover Relief Commission. He worked for a time for department stores, eventually drifted into the postal service and from there into the Federal Bureau of Investigation. Today it is hard to conceive of someone with Turrou's background becoming an FBI agent. But in 1929, the after-shocks of Attorney General Palmer's "Red scares" in the early 1920s were still being felt by those in and outside the government. Turrou possessed respectable "anti-Communist" credentials as well as first-hand knowledge and experience in the Soviet Union. These credentials must also have been accompanied by some talent because, in 1938, at $4,600 a year he was the highest paid special agent in the FBI's New York field office.

Dalton trusted Turrou completely. Theirs was a curious friendship. Aside from the fact that both had served in the trenches during World War I—Turrou in Russia's Imperial Army and Dalton in the U.S. Army—and both worked together in Moscow with Herbert Hoover's European Recovery Administration, they were very different kinds of people. Turrou, the cosmopolitan turned cop, and Dalton, the straight-line soldier turned intelligence officer, are a most pertinent example of the seemingly incongruous personal relationships found in the intelligence trade. In spite of their personality differences, they both shared a genuine repugnance toward totalitarianism long before the term gained currency, and were deeply devoted to the preservation of American liberties. Without undue emphasis it should be remembered that in the mid-1930s those who raised questions or tried to draw attention to either Nazi or Soviet excesses were often considered pariahs in their own country.

Notwithstanding the curious chemistry of their relationship, Dalton and Turrou, with other friends in the Office of Naval Intelligence, were able slowly but surely to unravel the details of Dr. Griebl's secret life. Early on in the investigation it became clear that Dr. Griebl was running a spy ring. This was grist for Dalton and Turrou's mill, but the elements of proof involving an overt act, or plans of a conspiracy, remained beyond their grasp.

The investigation continued in a quasi-official manner. There were insufficient funds and not enough people, but Dalton and Turrou pressed on. Also, the jurisdictional considerations mentioned above gave them some pause and caused them to be reluctant about using illegal means to get the evidence they needed. Today this sounds almost anachronistic—if not ludicrous in terms of what has recently taken place in the name of national security—but in the mid–1930s these were real constraints. Dalton and Turrou were more than willing to evade regulations or keep their superiors in the dark about what they were doing, but they pulled back from breaking the law. However, as the evidence began to mount, it was decided—without making the decision a matter of record, or seeking approval of an official request—to initiate a limited mail-cover operation designed to find out the overseas addresses to which Dr. Griebl and his clandestine associates were sending letters and packages. This they did by relying on a member of the "old boys" network of former comrades in the American Expeditionary Force who happened to be in the U.S. Postal Service. Times were simpler then. It was easy for Dalton to go to former Sergeant Paul Fogarty, the postal inspector in charge of overseas mail in New York, and get him to allow one of the army's men to copy down the names and addresses of the persons to whom Griebl et al. were sending letters and packages. The initial results were disappointing. Most of the addresses were in Germany, and upon checking with Major Smith were found to be cover names. This gave the military attachés and Dalton's men little to go on. However, late in 1937 the name Mrs. Jessie Wallace Jordan, residing at 1 Kinlock Street, Dundee, Scotland, popped up out of the mail-cover operation. Although nothing had been sent from Dr. Griebl to Mrs. Jordan, the mail cover showed that she had received correspondence from three of the doctor's nocturnal guests, and no obvious connection existed between them and the mysterious Mrs. Jordan.*

Based on this information, the need-to-know circle was expanded to include Colonel Sherman Miles, then military attaché in Great Britain. It was not an easy decision. Both Dalton and Turrou had serious reservations about Miles, who was looked upon as a "social" officer—that is, one who had elected the military to give the impression of doing something "worthwhile." Miles, who later became the army's G–2, was not all that bad, but Dalton and Turrou's fears about Miles the soldier/politician were not completely unfounded. Miles, like many of his ilk and background, were apolitical chameleons who could applaud the wisdom of a Hoover or Roosevelt regardless of the merits of their arguments. But Dalton and Turrou reasoned that one had to make do with who and what was available. On this kind of fateful consideration, Dalton suggested—again very informally and well outside of channels—that Miles contact Sir Vernon Kell, the head of Britain's Secret Service, to see whether his organization might be interested in the contents of Mrs. Jordan's mail. This was Dalton's second major gamble. He accepted the risk based upon the belief that Miles, who had become a real Anglophile, might play the game to demon-

---

*Mrs. Jordan was involved in the spy ring and had been arrested for espionage activities in Scotland. See the *New York Times,* 17 May 1938, p. 2.

strate his own savoir faire and engage in a personal no-risk operation which might make him a hero. Dalton's instincts were correct. He knew his man and his ambitions. As a result, Miles contacted Sir Vernon and brought him up to date on the activities of Dr. Griebl and his friends and their correspondence with persons in Germany and with Mrs. Jordan. All this was carried out very informally between Miles and Kell. They shared the same club in London and their discussions were carried out on the kind of basis which characterizes elliptical conversations between two persons who know that what their peers and superiors don't know can't hurt them. On an official basis there was no way Miles could have made an official request for a mail intercept of Mrs. Jordan's correspondence. It would have blown the entire operation and produced reverberations from Whitehall to the White House.

Sir Vernon, acting on Miles's information about Lonkowski, Dr. Griebl, and the suspected members of the spy ring, initiated an investigation which established that Mrs. Jordan was more than a postal drop. Her activities included photographing as well as sketching British military installations and trafficking in defense information. As a consequence, Mrs. Jordan's mail to and from the United States and Germany was intercepted and copied. The take from the operation revealed a great deal about the operations of Dr. Griebl's spy ring as well as Nazi activities in England and the United States. However, in spite of the incriminating evidence that Sir Vernon turned over to Colonel Miles, its use in an American trial was questionable. Kell's information gave Dalton and Turrou's forces the advantage they needed. It specified the who as well as the what, when, and where of the spy ring's activities. At this time Major Dalton and Turrou decided to go official and bring the FBI into the case on a formal basis. Turrou's superior, Reed Vetterili, was ecstatic. No real questions were asked about how the army had learned so much, and Vetterili informed J. Edgar Hoover that they had the chance to shoot some Nazi spies in a barrel. Hoover, who immediately saw the potential in "smashing" a spy ring, gave his complete blessing. On February 26, 1938, FBI agents from the New York field office arrested Guenther Gustave Rumrich, a former sergeant in the U.S. Army who had deserted in 1935, Erich Glaser, an army private, and Miss Johanna Hoffman, a hairdresser on the *Europa*. * The arrests, with promises of more to come, were carried out with the kind of flair Hoover exploited in capturing John Dillinger and Baby Face Nelson. The news of the arrests hit the media as well as the government like a bolt out of the blue. It was a headline-grabbing event which added to the then already considerable reputation of the FBI as an all-seeing, omniscient organization. At the time of their arrest no hint was dropped that the three spies had been identified in connection with the Griebl investigation, or from information derived from the British mail-intercept program. In the crush of events it was scarcely noticed

---

*Rumrich, Glaser, and Hoffman were all indicted and convicted of espionage. See the *New York Times,* 1 December 1938, p. 1 and 3 December 1938, p. 1.

that Mrs. Jordan had been arrested by the British Secret Service in Scotland on March 2, 1938, on espionage charges which were left unspecified because of Britain's Official Secrets Act.

Thus began the longest and one of the most bizarre peacetime spy cases in American history. Before it was ended eighteen persons, of whom only four were subject to United States jurisdiction, were indicted by a federal grand jury on charges of spying for Hitler's Reich. The case quite literally had something for everyone. It involved everything from an aborted attempt to kidnap an army colonel to establishing a femme fatale in a Washington salon to entice secrets from amorous and indiscreet government officials. Material witnesses mysteriously escaped to Germany, J. Edgar Hoover clashed with U.S. Attorney Lamar Hardy over his handling of the case, the State Department wanted to drop the whole matter, the interventionists in Congress were up in arms over the state of our security, and President Roosevelt, who was trying to pursue an even-handed policy with respect to Germany, was presented with a major foreign policy flap which wouldn't go away.

The indictments indirectly revealed that Germany's military intelligence service had made some deep penetrations of America's security, but left unanswered some serious questions about other spy rings in the United States which had been detected in the course of the investigation. The investigation itself was not particularly unique save for the fact that it had been carried out at all. Today the names of the culprits, and the way details about their nefarious schemes and some of their bungled, comic-opera antics were found out, are only footnotes to history. For our purposes, though, the actions of Leon G. Turrou throughout the case illustrate how intelligence leaders are able to use their resources in pursuit of a legitimate intelligence objective to force political change and gain bureaucratic advantage.

Turrou, based on his earlier association with Major Dalton, had gotten involved with the case before the FBI was formally called in. After the initial arrests, Turrou, the ranking special agent in New York, was placed in overall charge of the investigation. In this role Turrou became the visible element of the intelligence community's leaders' attempt to make their case for more authority and means to carry out positive intelligence and counterespionage missions. Turrou was more than equal to the task. In addition to getting confessions from the arrested spies, Turrou was able to "double" several of those involved and enlist them to return to Germany and spy for the United States. Interestingly, the confessions were easily acquired by Turrou without benefit of any "rubber hose" interrogation techniques. Turrou knew much about each person's secret existence, and playing on the caught spy's compulsion to talk, it was simple for him to convince them that their best hope lay in being fully cooperative.

Turrou, acting on the advice and direction of J. Edgar Hoover (whose views about expanding United States intelligence forces were supported by Colonel E. R. W. McCabe, the army's G-2, and Rear Admiral Ralston S. Holmes,

Director of Naval Intelligence), played as much to the press as he worked in support of the U.S. attorney. This produced a conflict of sorts in Washington when Attorney General Homer Cummings attempted to gag Hoover and Turrou. Cummings knew a trial could not possibly be avoided, but he wanted the case to stay in the courts and not become part of a political debate over counterespionage and American relations with Germany. Cummings was successful to a point. Hoover curbed his tongue; Turrou, however, was not to be denied.

On June 20, 1938, when the grand jury handed down its indictments, it appeared that Cummings had succeeded in his attempt to keep knowledge about spy activities confined to what was contained in the charges. It was believed this would be enough to satisfy the public's curiosity, and since the spy ring had been "smashed" the broader issues would be mooted. Cummings' plan almost worked. However, at 4:30 PM on June 20, Turrou submitted his resignation from the FBI, effective at 5:00 PM. The Turrou resignation caught Cummings and President Roosevelt completely unawares, and when it was disclosed that at 5:15 PM Turrou had signed a contract with the *New York Post* to do a series of articles about spy activities in the United States, the gauntlet was cast down. The issue went above and beyond the trial itself. Turrou's action forced President Roosevelt to acknowledge the necessity of doing something more to deal with deficiencies in the nation's intelligence services.

During the evening of June 20, after a series of frantic and heated phone calls between Harry Hopkins and J. Edgar Hoover, Attorney General Cummings, and U.S. Attorney Lamar Hardy, it was clear that Turrou had additional information which, if published by the *New York Post*, would precipitate a major domestic and international crisis. Therefore, it was decided to meet Turrou's challenge head on by coming out in favor of more money and men for intelligence purposes and acknowledging the seriousness of the spy threat. By preempting Turrou's presumed argument and simultaneously seeking an injunction to prevent the articles' publication, President Roosevelt bought some much-needed time in the hopes of quieting the issue and dissuading the intelligence leaders from "leaking" or going public with other damaging information. Hopkins was furious over the entire episode. He railed at Hoover that FBI agents and intelligence personnel should only do what they were told and keep their mouths shut, but his fury was to no avail. J. Edgar Hoover, ever the perfect bureaucrat, covered his backside by voiding the previous acceptance of Turrou's resignation and backdating a letter which dismissed him from the FBI "with prejudice." This deprived Turrou of pay for his accumulated leave and retirement benefits; nonetheless, Hopkins' suspicions remained that Hoover and Turrou had been league throughout.

Aside from the question about Hoover's relationship with and public rebuking of Turrou, one has to wonder about the success and/or sources of support involved in Turrou's wartime comeback as an intelligence officer in the face of President Roosevelt's statement concerning his lack of "patriotism and ethics." Although it breaks the narrative of events somewhat, it is necessary to outline Turrou's subsequent career because it reflects the continuity of purpose and actions of key intelligence personnel as they move in and out of the intelligence community's various organizations.

Following Turrou's resignation from the FBI in 1938, he busied himself for the next four years with lecturing, writing articles about the Nazi spy menace, and a book entitled *Nazi Spies in America* which in turn was made into the film *Confessions of a Nazi Spy*. During this period he remained in touch with his friends in the intelligence community and became associated with a private investigating firm which carried out "contract" investigations on their behalf. However, following the sudden death of his wife, in early 1942, Turrou left the cover of the quasi-"proprietary" investigating firm and enlisted as a private in the U.S. Army. At the time of his enlistment he claimed to be 42, when in fact he was actually 47. Strangely enough, in spite of the recruiting sergeant's advice and refusal to enlist him, a waiver came through and he was accepted. After basic training, Turrou was appointed a first lieutenant in the Corps of Military Police.

Turrou's subsequent wartime career was not without note. In turn he served as the Chief Investigator and Assistant Director of the Army's Criminal Investigation Division (CID) in North Africa and on December 12, 1944, was personally ordered by General Eisenhower to report to his Chief of Staff, General Walter Bedell Smith, to take charge of CID operations in the European and African theaters. In this role Turrou worked closely with those in charge of the OSS's "X-2," Counterespionage Division, as well as with those in the positive side of military intelligence. These tasks would have been enough to keep most intelligence professionals fully occupied, yet Eisenhower and Smith gave Turrou an even more important "additional" duty, naming him the Operations Chief of CROWCASS (Central Repository of War Criminals and Security Suspects). Under Turrou, CROWCASS, which was headquartered at 53 rue des Matheninas in Paris, operated on two distinct levels: (1) to catalog war crimes and the location of war criminals; and (2) to recruit former Nazis to serve as U.S. intelligence agents and sources. CROWCASS had more authority than is commonly supposed. Almost in anticipation of the Nuremburg Trials and the Allied Military Government's de-Nazification program, CROWCASS decided disputes concerning alleged Nazis and war crimes activities and "extradited" many of those involved to the country offering the severest penalty. In addition, Eisenhower provided Turrou with fulfillment of the intelligence officer's "impossible dream," namely unlimited funds and unquestioned authority to requisition selected military personnel from any U.S. military organization in the European theater for duty with CROWCASS as well as to hire, with no questions asked, indigenous personnel in the occupied areas. With this kind of power it was not difficult to recruit former Nazis, especially former members of the SS, as well as persons in Nazi-occupied countries who had been collaborators.

During the CROWCASS operation, Turrou frequently came into conflict with the Soviets, and this experience reinforced his earlier antipathy for the communists. As such Turrou, who had easy access to Walter Bedell Smith and indirectly to Eisenhower, was one of the Cold War's first spokesmen. On July 1, 1946, CROWCASS was officially closed down and its records—less those which dealt with the new U.S. intelligence assets—were shipped to Berlin and incorporated in the Allies' document center.

Shortly thereafter Turrou was discharged and took up residence in Paris. How active he was in actually running the network of agents which resulted from the CROWCASS operation is a matter of speculation. However, it is known that during the postwar turbulence in America's intelligence commu-nity and especially during Walter Bedell Smith's term as U.S. Ambassador in Moscow and subsequent tenure as the Director of Central Intelligence, the CROWCASS assets were a key ingredient in U.S. intelligence operations carried out in Western Europe.

Although Turrou was more visible than most intelligence professionals—albeit only periodically and fleetingly—his "active" career apparently came to an end on June 19, 1961. On that date, at the age of 66, he was awarded the Medal of the City of Paris by Julien Tardieu, President of the Paris Municipal Council. The honor was conferred for "important contributions" to French-American relations. Almost as a final footnote to Turrou's long and varied career in intelligence, it was reported that he was President of the Inter-Allied Federation of Reserve Officers, an organization long suspected of having other than social interests.

At President Roosevelt's press conference on June 24, 1938, it was obvious that Turrou had achieved the objective of forcing the administration to take a more positive stand in favor of expanding the intelligence services. *The New York Times* report of the press conference revealed the extent of President Roosevelt's capitulation to the intelligence services and, by his demeanor, recognition that his sway over those in actual control of intelligence sources and methods had not been and was likely never to be complete.

Because of its signal importance, *The New York Times* report of the press conference is presented below:

WASHINGTON, June 24—President Roosevelt disclosed today that he favors larger appropriations for the Army and Navy intelligence services for the expansion of counterespionage activities within the United States. He made the statement as he expressed the government's official concern over the attempted sale by a former Federal Bureau of Investigation agent of information concerning German espionage in the United States.

On the more official aspects of the disclosures of German spy activities in the United States the President withheld comment. Asked whether he thought more money should be provided for each branch of the services for "counterespionage" work, Mr. Roosevelt remarked, after a moment's hesitation, that the answer would depend on a definition of counterespionage activities.

Saying that he understood the term to mean running down foreign spies in the United States, he said that on that basis he was entirely in favor of increasing appropriations of both departments. In calling for more funds for the Army and Navy Intelligence Corps, however, the President wanted it clearly understood he would not sanction espionage by American agents abroad.

In language and demeanor that reflected disappointment and chagrin, President Roosevelt questioned the patriotism and ethics underlying the former FBI agent's attempted sale of German spy information unearthed in his official capacity.

Dismissing all legal considerations, the President brought within the range of his indictment the newspaper syndicate publishers who had contracted to buy the series of stories based on the investigations of the resigned agent. He first said the seriousness of the question went directly to the relations between government employees and the press, but promptly corrected his statement on recalling only a single syndicate was involved.

At no time did the President mention the names of the contracting parties, but there was no doubt among the 150 newspapermen present at his press conference this morning that he had in mind Leon G. Turrou, recently resigned Department of Justice investigator who was chiefly responsible for a New York grand jury indictment of German nationals engaging in espionage activities in this country.

President Roosevelt was asked whether he had any comment to make on the disclosures in the FBI inquiry. He sat silently considering the question, obviously aware of the significance that would be attached to his reply, and after a long pause he answered in the affirmative.

The President said the issues involved in the attempted sale and purchase of the information developed by the FBI agent was frankly one of patriotism and ethics combined. He said that, as he understood the facts, a government employee in pursuance of his regular duties had unearthed a great deal of information relating to foreign spies in this country.

He did not minimize the seriousness of the disclosures and noted that they obviously called for criminal action by the Department of Justice. President Roosevelt then commented in substance as follows:

The former Justice Department investigator, having obtained all the details on which the presentation to the grand jury would be based, and before the trial on its indictments had begun, resigned from the government and within fifteen minutes signed a specific contract, it was stated. The result was to jeopardize a criminal prosecution by the Federal Government in a serious case involving the national defense.

There was no question here of legality of the acts of either the agent or the syndicate publisher, the comment continued. The matter was entirely one of patriotism and ethics. But for an ex-government agent and a newspaper publisher to undertake to disseminate information of the kind involved in the Federal investigation was to invite official concern as well as the question of motive.

President Roosevelt was reluctant to discuss the government's attitude toward the part of the Reich government in the espionage activities credited to it in the grand jury investigation.

Asked if he had been supplied with advance information on the nature of Ambassador Wilson's visit to the German foreign office in Berlin today and whether he had called to protest on behalf of the United States against the espionage disclosures, the President said he had not received any State Department dispatches since Saturday having been occupied in the signing of bills and other official business.

The grave manner in which Mr. Roosevelt approached the subject of the contemplated sale of the investigator's information was in striking contrast with his general demeanor up to that time. He had been laughing long and loudly at attempts of reporters to get him to commit himself on the Candidacy of Governor Lehman of New York for the United States Senate and to comment on reports that Senator Wagner would seek the Governorship.

Rarely does President Roosevelt speak as slowly as he did today on the subject of the espionage disclosures. In much less time than that discussion required, he told of plans to visit Mr. and Mrs. Eugene Dupont next Sunday night on his trip to the West Coast and his hope of being able to see the final intercollegiate regatta races at Poughkeepsie Monday, all of which he outlined in some detail.

Although President Roosevelt was compelled to acknowledge the need and press for enlarging the intelligence services, he came away from the confrontation with half a loaf in that the *New York Post*—without acknowledging the validity of the suit brought by U.S. Attorney Hardy to enjoin it from publishing the Turrou articles—agreed to withhold publication pending completion of the spy trials. The *Post* announced its decision on June 24, 1938, by saying:

The *New York Post* is postponing publication of special articles by Leon G. Turrou, former G-Man, on Nazi spy activity until after the trial of the four defendants now under arrest, and the completion of the Grand Jury investigation.

The *Post* believes that nothing in this series of articles would have, in any way, interfered with the course of justice. But it desires to avoid setting a precedent which might handicap the government in guarding itself against other spy activities.

The purpose of these articles was to awaken the American public to the danger of spies and the necessity of enlarging the FBI, as well as the intelligence services of the Army and Navy. This was in line with the presumed purpose of the government in indicting foreign officials not in this country.

It is not certain how far the administration was prepared to go to halt publication of Turrou's articles, and it is equally uncertain whether Turrou had any real intent in this regard beyond using the threat of the articles to force President Roosevelt to move quickly in seeking more money and manpower for intelligence purposes. The *New York Post* statement, which Turrou helped to write, suggests that Turrou was more interested in the mission of enhancing the intelligence community than in truth for truth's sake. There is no final answer to the question, and it should be noted that the articles were not published after the trial was completed.* This may have simply been an

---

*The trial, which resulted in the convictions of the arrested spies, had an interesting aftermath. It involved Guenther Gustave Rumrich, the sergeant who had deserted from the U.S. Army, who

editorial judgment at the time, but because the changes and expansion of the intelligence services did occur during the course of the trial it appears that Turrou, and whomever else was ultimately involved, decided it was not to their advantage to let it be known how much the government knew and didn't know about espionage activities.

The changes pledged by President Roosevelt came quickly. Some add-ons were placed on the current appropriations bill, and other funds were quietly "reprogrammed" from other departments to pay for the expanded intelligence effort. Once the presidential decision had been made, the budget sleight-of-hand was a simple pencil exercise. Then, as now, there was enough slack in the budget and sufficient ambiguity about "general" and "miscellaneous" line items to use funds with considerable discretion. It mattered not to the intelligence leaders if unspent funds—due for return to the Treasury's general fund —for training the Civilian Conservation Corps' "tree planters" were used to pay agents and grease the gears of secret operations. The intelligence community was off to the races. Military Intelligence Division (G-2) of the Army and Naval Intelligence reserve officers were quietly queried and, where agreeable, received orders for active duty. The number of military attachés was increased, and as a consequence of information developed in the spy-ring case the military and FBI turned some of their attentions south of the border, where both German and Japanese agents were active.

The build-up of military intelligence was orderly. The leaders, especially Rear Admiral Charles E. Courtney, Director of Naval Communications, and Major W. O. Reeder, Officer in Charge of the Army's Signal Service,* were

---

pleaded guilty and became the government's chief witness. Rumrich's testimony, although rambling and sometimes even humorous, made it clear that the spy ring was a creation of the Reich's intelligence service and that he had been recruited to serve it. As mentioned, Hitler had forbade Canaris to dispatch agents to the United States for the Fuehrer wanted no complications with Roosevelt and the unpredictable Yankees. Canaris had announced his total compliance with the order; but in March 1938, roughly three weeks after he had taken office, Joachim Von Ribbentrop, who had replaced Foreign Minister Von Neurath as nominal architect of the Reich's foreign policy, learned that Rumrich had been recruited by Canaris' Abwehr-KO in New York City, had been arrested and confessed his guilt. From Von Ribbentrop's point of view, here was a magnificent opportunity to bring the high-flying Canaris to heel. Von Ribbentrop proposed a deal: either Canaris cease the recruitment of foreign office personnel, or Hitler would be informed that the Abwehr had both disobeyed a direct order and proven itself to be a cabal of idiots. Von Ribbentrop apparently believed that he held the winning cards, but the wily Canaris was not disposed to throw in his hand. Instead, he confronted the Fuehrer and somehow convinced him that the fallen Mr. Rumrich had not been an Abwehr agent at all. The end result was that Von Ribbentrop's bluster yielded nothing: Canaris continued to recruit and train foreign office personnel for service in the Americas. Sometimes he told Von Ribbentrop who these agents were; sometimes he did not. (For the history of this bizarre event, see Ladislas Farago, *The Game of the Foxes,* New York: McKay, 1971, pp. 74–75.)

*On December 10, 1944, the Military Intelligence Service assumed operational control over the Signal Intelligence Service, leaving the Signal Corps to carry on the administrative functions. This so-called dual control lasted until September 15, 1945, when the Signal Security Agency was

cautious in the expansion of their communications intelligence organizations. Their caution had two bases: qualified persons in the area of communications and crypto-intelligence were few, and breaches of security which would reveal their illegal activities had to be avoided. These had a long history and, in spite of Mr. Stimson's oft-quoted remark that "Gentlemen don't read other's mail," were very much a part of the communications intelligence environment. Although one may assume some earlier illegal activities in connection with communications intelligence, it is generally conceded that these began on an organized basis in the autumn of 1916, when a very small group of self-trained cryptanalysts, sponsored and supported by "Colonel" George Fabyan,* operated the Riverbank Laboratories at Geneva, Illinois. Riverbank, through Colonel Fabyan, initiated and established an unofficial or, at most, quasiofficial relationship with the authorities in Washington so that it received copies of cryptographic messages obtained by various and entirely surreptitious means from telegraph and cable offices in Washington and elsewhere in the United States.

The Riverbank connection served the nation well during World War I in breaking diplomatic codes, and for several years thereafter by also providing free training of military cryptanalysts during a period in which there was no money available for that purpose. It was followed in 1921 by an even more obscure connection which established a "Cipher Bureau" (MI-8) office in New York City whose source of funds is a secret which went to the grave with John Foster Dulles—also known as Major Dulles, Military Intelligence Reserve— and his few close associates in Military Intelligence and the State Department who handled the "private" funds. By mid-1938 the Cipher Bureau had gone through several reorganizations designed to cope with the increasing volume of intercepts and/or surreptitiously acquired cables.

The communications intelligence organizations, like other members of the community, welcomed Roosevelt's initiative to put more money into intelligence. The budgetary restrictions during the 1929–38 period particularly hampered research and development in the field of cryptographic devices and machines. Of the former, two types were in use: the M-94, a cylindrical cipher device consisting of twenty-five rotating discs, adopted by the United States Army in 1921; and the M-138, a flat-strip cipher device, adopted as standard equipment by the army in August 1934. Studies were made in the Signal Intelligence Service of several of the hand-operated cipher machines offered by the Swedish inventor Boris Hagelin. Of these, the C-36 was given most consideration, and in a much improved model (C-38) was later put into use as the

---

reorganized under the Assistant Chief of Staff, G-2, as the Army Security Agency. Funds for the Army Security Agency, however, continued to come from the Signal Corps.

*"Colonel" Fabyan's rank derived from an honorary title conferred by the governor of Illinois for his participation as a member of the Peace Commission which negotiated the Treaty of Portsmouth, which terminated the Russo-Japanese War in 1905.

M-209. Not only did lack of funds greatly retard the actual development of cryptographic equipment in this period, but it also prevented adequate procurement and distribution of approved equipment. The development of one machine, Converter M-134-A, which was initiated in 1932, could not be completed until 1937, despite the fact that it gave promise of providing adequate security.

Therefore, much of the newly available money went into the development of the hardware required to handle more sophisticated codes.* The additional money helped some, but then, as now, the development of crypto equipment is difficult to hurry. Actually it is physically and psychologically impossible to develop, procure and put into widespread use a new piece of crypto equipment in much less than five years. Among other reasons, this time factor accounts for the extraordinary precautions taken to prevent enciphering and deciphering equipment from falling into an enemy's hands. However, the greater constraint on the expansion of American communications intelligence organizations was the procurement of personnel technically qualified to carry on the work.

Soon after the spy-ring case was broken, the military intelligence services and the FBI began to face similar constraints in their ability to get qualified people. This was largely attributable to Civil Service hiring and military personnel procurement regulations. The military intelligence services had initial recourse to those in the reserve, but this pool of personnel was insufficient to meet their needs. The spy-ring investigation revealed the necessity to get a broad mix of people with qualifications in a variety of fields. This was easier said than done in 1938–39. Government pay, although certain, was not high enough to induce those with the necessary talents to join the intelligence community in its undeclared war.

J. Edgar Hoover, who sought to control the intelligence community as well as the FBI, came out of the starting blocks very quickly in the race for people. At Hoover's behest, Senator Key Pittman (D., Nevada) called for a separate group of agents in the FBI who would specialize in counterespionage work. These agents were to be specially trained linguists and understand international law in order to cope with the cunning men at the head of foreign intelligence services. Although Hoover's ploy to create a de facto counterespionage corps within the FBI did not succeed, increased appropriations did

*The reader should note that a code is based on arbitrary substitutions in which the substitutions are listed in a code book by the encoder. Sometimes a word is substituted for another word or idea as, for example, "Olympic," in 1945 the code word for the invasion of the Japanese home island of Kyushu. Or a code can be based on the substitution of an arbitrary group of numerals for a word. Cipher, on the other hand, differs from code in that it is constructed upon a systematic method in which one letter or group of letters or numbers represents another letter or group according to some prearranged pattern. Also, when code is used to transmit information it is frequently placed inside an extra covering of cipher—i.e., the code itself is further enciphered to prevent its being "broken" by a cryptanalyst.

allow him to hire 150 additional special agents among which several score were earmarked for counterespionage service in the United States and Latin America.* Hoover was further thwarted in his plans to be the top man in the espionage business by President Roosevelt who, on June 26, 1939, in an attempt to keep peace in the intelligence services, issued a directive to all federal departments and agencies which ruled on the matter of investigative turf without placing any single person or organization in overall charge. It read as follows:

> It is my desire that the investigation of all espionage, counterespionage, and sabotage matters be controlled and handled by the Federal Bureau of Investigation of the Department of Justice, the Military Intelligence Division of the War Department, and the Office of Naval Intelligence of the Navy Department. The directors of these three agencies are to function as a committee to coordinate their activities.
>
> No investigations should be conducted by any investigative agency of the Government into matters involving actually or potentially any espionage, counterespionage, or sabotage, except by the three agencies mentioned above.
>
> I shall be glad if you will instruct the heads of all other investigative agencies than the three named, to refer immediately to the nearest office of the Federal Bureau of Investigation any data, information, or material that may come to their notice bearing directly or indirectly on espionage, counterespionage, or sabotage.

In the several months prior to issuance of this directive an attempt was made by President Roosevelt to bring about coordination of the investigative and intelligence efforts of the FBI, the Customs Service, the Secret Service, and the intelligence units of the State, War and Navy Departments. His efforts were unsuccessful. Each of the organizations guarded their prerogatives most jealously and while tacitly endorsing "coordination" held steadfast in their view that each was an equal among equals. President Roosevelt chose not to do battle with all the agencies, yet by this directive he opted for the principle of unified action among the major organizations rather than centralizing direction and control over all the intelligence services. It was generally acceptable to the FBI and the military intelligence services, and served as a precedent they would later use to oppose attempts at centralization of their activities.

It is not clear how serious Roosevelt's desire was in 1938 to coordinate and centralize control of the intelligence agencies. The intelligence community's

---

*On September 14, 1939, a "high administration" official (J. Edgar Hoover) revealed that for more than a year FBI agents had been receiving intensive training in the techniques of uncovering espionage, sabotage, and subversive activities. The special schools, located in Washington and the Maryland countryside, which met in units of thirty men each, were personally conducted by J. Edgar Hoover. Assignments to the special training were arranged by summoning the specially designated persons to Washington from the various field offices, after which they returned to their home offices, provided on-the-job training to other agents and from there, as overseas activities were expanded, were posted to Latin America and elsewhere. (See *The New York Times,* September 15, 1939.)

internal parochial opposition was based largely on jurisdictional questions; however, the external opposition was perhaps an even greater consideration. It was manifested in two arguments: that the internal security threat was minimal, and that centralization would lead to establishment of a "secret police" organization. In spite of what was revealed in the course of the spy-ring trial and what else was known as a consequence of the various offshoot investigations, it appears that some elements of the military other than its intelligence services wanted to play down the espionage threat; they made use of "friends" in the press to promote their ideas. During the course of the trial several articles were written by Hanson Baldwin of *The New York Times* to reflect these views, as well as by the "Editorial Board" of the quasiofficial *Army-Navy Journal.* These articles had a curious effect. They didn't stop the build-up of the intelligence community but they did prevent centralization of its control.

In November 1938, at President Roosevelt's direction, a series of meetings was held between representatives of the FBI, the Customs Service, the Secret Service, and the intelligence organizations of the State, War, and Navy Departments to devise a method to achieve better coordination and recommend a plan for the overall control of intelligence activities. When asked about these meetings, President Roosevelt became quite testy because it was obvious to him from reporters' questions that the intelligence people were "leaking" details about the meetings to the press. And in the sequence of events which occur in government when its secrets get loose, the ad hoc intelligence task force was terminated. This took place on December 3, 1938, two days after an editorial appeared in *The New York Times* which read in part:

> The fact is that the peacetime spy in America has scant "pickings." There are few real secrets, military or otherwise, here or elsewhere. With such complicated instruments as anti-aircraft fire control directors being sold to other nations, with destroyers being built from American plans in Brazilian yards, with American aircraft sold all over the world, the spy's role is limited. Much of his time, as the Rumrich testimony has shown, is spent in a desperate search for the obvious. There are, of course, exceptions to this rule, but relatively few high-ranking military officials regard espionage as a serious problem.
>
> Nor is there any need to set up another Government agency equipped for counterespionage work and restricted to such activities. Modest increases in the budgets available to the intelligence section of the Army's general staff and the Office of Naval Intelligence may be warranted. But a civilian agency of the Government already has the problem well in hand, and the creation of any super-espionage military agency is both unnecessary and undesireable. It is alien to American tradition, and no glorified "OGPU" secret police is needed or wanted here.

The ostensible peace which followed the June 26 presidential directive didn't last very long. Both the Military Intelligence Division and the Office of Naval Intelligence began to enlist the aid of local law-enforcement officials in carrying out their investigations. In part they were correct in their actions, because there was no way to know in advance where and to whom else an investigation of someone in the armed forces or of a civilian employee of the War or Navy Departments would lead. This often resulted in a situation where civilians outside the jurisdiction of the military came under its scrutiny, and in order to carry out the necessary surveillance measures the assistance of local law-enforcement officials was sought. This relationship in turn produced reciprocal requests between local law-enforcement officials and the military, especially in parts of the country where major military installations were located. Consequently, Hoover moved to stop the military from picking up on investigations initiated by local law-enforcement officials. The military had no grounds on which to object and as a result, on September 6, 1939, a presidential statement was issued to further define the investigatory ground rules. It read as follows:

The Attorney General has been requested by me to instruct the Federal Bureau of Investigation of the Department of Justice to take charge of investigative work in matters relating to espionage, sabotage, and violations of the neutrality regulations.

This task must be conducted in a comprehensive and effective manner on a national basis, and all information must be carefully sifted out and correlated in order to avoid confusion and irresponsibility.

To this end I request all police officers, sheriffs, and all other law enforcement officers in the United States promptly to turn over to the nearest representative of the Federal Bureau of Investigation any information obtained by them relating to espionage, counterespionage, sabotage, subversive activities and violations of the neutrality laws.

These two presidential actions were and are a continuing source of controversy in the intelligence community. Hoover took the statement of September 6 to mean he had been given de facto overall charge of counterespionage, espionage, and sabotage investigations; however, the military intelligence services took the view which held that the June 26 action was directive in nature, i.e. legally binding until rescinded, and consequently they continued to carry out investigations under its authority. The military's only concession to the September 6 statement was to pass information they had acquired from law-enforcement officials to the FBI, or ask those officials to do so. The military's action was taken less in deference to President Roosevelt's request than to the fact that it legitimately had more investigations based on military security problems than it could readily handle. And although these documents are still cited as authority to carry out loosely defined national security or self-defined subversive cases, they have been inadequate to keep the various intelligence agencies confined to their own backyards or to prevent their violating other laws in conducting their investigations. The result is that more often than not investigatory illegalities and excesses by one or another agency have resulted in the Justice Department's inability to successfully prosecute persons who have engaged in espionage and sabotage.

The personnel problem continued to bedevil the intelligence services throughout 1938. The self-protective actions of the entire federal bureaucracy, the Civil Service Commission, and the Civil Service committees in Congress stood in the way of removing or waiving regulations in connection with the recruiting, selecting, testing, promoting, transferring, reinstating, and removing of persons in confidential intelligence positions. The intelligence leaders believed their organizations could not possibly use the competitive public advertising method to get the people they needed. To be sure, overt recruitment was used to get additional FBI agents, but it was not feasible to use similar procedures to get people whose job descriptions and places of assignment couldn't be disclosed. Various subterfuges were used to get around the Civil Service regulations, but these were essentially reserved for use in special cases where the benefit of having a "nonperson" on an intelligence service's confidential roles clearly outweighed the risk of a lawsuit if the individual were killed in a line of duty which had to be officially disavowed.

The personnel impasse remained unresolved until September 21, 1939, when President Roosevelt signed Executive Order Number 8257, which authorized the Civil Service Commission "to permit an immediate appointment without regard to the competitive requirements of Civil Service rules in any case in which it appears that a public exigency exists which is directly connected with the neutrality of the United States, or the preparedness program of the Federal government." Several other changes in the rules were made following issuance of this executive order, but these were simply designed to further streamline and speed up the procedures by which "highly confidential positions in the State, War and Navy Departments" were actually filled.

With Executive Order 8257 in hand, and a growing awareness in the White House and among some key members of the Congress about the effectiveness and consequences of Hitler's *Blitzkrieg* victories, the intelligence leaders put their expansion plans into high gear. Almost in anticipation of passage of the War Powers Act, counterespionage and espionage operations in pursuit of intelligence information and activities directed against the German, Italian, and Japanese intelligence operations in neutral countries were stepped up. Few questions were asked by policy makers about who and how intelligence information was acquired. For example, in this period J. Edgar Hoover was regularly reporting information concerning Nazi agents in Argentina to Assistant Secretary of State Adolph A. Berle, Jr.* Since no formal military or naval agreement for mutual defense or exchange of intelligence information was ever reached between Washington and Buenos Aires prior to 1946, it is obvious, based on the volume and content of reports made by Hoover to Berle, that he had a rather large net of "unofficial" G-men operating in Argentina. The unofficial "official" attitude about these kinds of activities was to pay lip service to FDR's statement that American agents would not carry espionage activities abroad, but to go ahead and "For God's sake don't get caught!"

Naturally some of the expansion of covert intelligence operations occurred

*See National Archives, Record Group 319, Box 176, File 383.2, Argentina through 2–16–43.

as a result of increasing the number of military and naval attachés, but too many of them in an embassy would be too conspicuous. Similarly, the number of legal attachés who also were FBI agents could not be too greatly increased without drawing undue attention to their presence. Because the military, naval, and legal attachés held diplomatic cover, they were less involved in active covert operations than their peers whose cover was provided by private corporations, foundations, and the like.

By the summer of 1939, the flow of intelligence information into Washington had increased substantially. Out of the far-flung uncoordinated nets of military agents, attachés, and FBI agents and the "take" from illegal communication intercepts,* threats to the peace emerged in a host of areas. Obviously, the threat in Europe was the greatest, but there were others closer to home. One such threat grew out of the situation in Brazil, where on May 11, 1938, members of the *Integralistas* (or Greenshirts, the Brazilian Fascist Party) attacked the residence of President Getulio Vargas and narrowly missed assassinating him. For the next year the Brazilian situation went from bad to worse. ONI's agents were particularly alarmed because of the danger of sabotage against U.S. destroyers being built in Brazilian shipyards. At this time a rivalry of sorts existed between navy and army agents because ONI had allocated a considerable amount of its unvouchered funds to its overseas agents to buy counterespionage and pay locally recruited indigenous intelligence sources/operators, whereas the army was using its funds in the United States.**

The intelligence information acquired in Brazil from all sources set off alarm bells in Washington. General Marshall, fearing that another *Integralistas* coup might succeed and bring a pro-Nazi government to power in Rio De Janeiro, ordered the formulation of a contingency plan called "Operation Pot of Gold." This scheme was designed to move 50,000 U.S. troops to various strategic areas of Brazil in order to "destabilize" such a government and eliminate the *Inte-*

---

*Since June 1934, persons within the United States had been prohibited by statute from intercepting any wire or radio communication and making use of information contained therein, unless authorized by the sender. Exceptions were provided with respect to any radio communication, broadcast, or transmission by amateurs or others for the use of the general public, or relating to ships in distress. These exceptions did not, however, permit military officers to intercept communications in the performance of their official duties. (See Section 605, Communications Act of 1934, as amended.)

Under the First War Powers Act of 1941 (Public Law 354, 77th Congress, approved on December 18, 1941), communications by wire or radio between the United States and foreign countries, at the discretion of the president and under rules and regulations prescribed by him, were made subject to interception and examination. No wartime or other legislative authority, however, was conferred with respect to the interception of wire or radio communications within the United States.

**See National Archives, Record Group 165, 2610–2–38CD, #5750, Box 1956, Major Henry A. Barber, Jr., to ACofS, G-2, August 26, 1939.

gralistas. * Today, after the experience of Vietnam and other interventionist adventures, such an idea doesn't seem to be very extraordinary, but in 1939 its mere contemplation was incredible. Incredible not because the United States hadn't sent in troops elsewhere in South America—in Haiti and Nicaragua in the 1920s and '30s—but because of the size of the operation envisaged. At the time, even if the *Integralistas* had welcomed the U.S. forces with open arms, the navy could not have moved 50,000 troops and their equipment into the area. This is one of the early significant examples of the potential stampede effect of intelligence information (which hasn't been turned into intelligence) on decision makers. Fortunately, it never became necessary to pursue the "Pot of Gold" to the end of those early decision makers' rainbow.

Once general hostilities began in Europe in September 1939, America's imperfect and uncoordinated intelligence system broke down. This occurred not because of a shortage of intelligence information and reports, but rather because they were not digested, properly evaluated or disseminated widely enough so that those with planning responsibilities could carry out their functions. The lack of coordination was everywhere apparent. It stemmed primarily from the fact that the previously discounted intelligence estimates about Germany's increased military capabilities had been proven correct. This, coupled with the confirming reality of Germany's intentions, produced a crisis of confidence in administration circles which in turn caused Harry Hopkins and others to take the intelligence services to task on the grounds of failing to argue their conclusions and analyses more forcefully. It was an absurd indictment, but one which would be heard again in the aftermath of Pearl Harbor. Although the intelligence services had been expanded in size and function, the results of their efforts rarely reached a decision maker in a useable form.

On September 9, 1939, Rear Admiral Walter S. Anderson, the director of Naval Intelligence, by memorandum to Acting Secretary of the Navy Charles Edison, strongly urged formation of an intelligence "council" made up of leaders in the intelligence services in order to make sure that President Roosevelt be informed about their intelligence operations and the "take" from these operations. Admiral Anderson believed that such a council was essential to make strategic sense out of the massive volume of intelligence information which was being generated. His arguments fell on deaf ears. Edison was too timid to push for such an idea, and there were those in the army and navy hierarchies who were determined not to let the intelligence services interfere with what they presumed to be the prerogatives of high command. Admiral Anderson was personally dismayed by the prejudice against intelligence, as were those in the intelligence services who tried to cope with the increasing flow of intelligence information their organizations were acquiring. Quite liter-

*United States Army in World War II Series, Stetson Conn and Byron Fairchild, *The Western Hemisphere: The Framework of Hemisphere Defense,* Washington, D.C., 1960, pp. 32–33, 33n.

ally thousands of reports with indications about when, how, and where the Axis powers would strike next went unheeded. In short, what little organization existed attempted to cope with the flood of intelligence information, and except for sticking pins in a map literally ceased to function.

Between the end of organized Polish resistance in about mid-October 1939, and May 10, 1940, when the Germans ended the *Sitzkrieg* (phony war) and invaded Holland, Belgium, and Luxembourg, the American intelligence situation deteriorated even further. Several themes began to emerge. First, the members of President Roosevelt's high command—composed of the president, Secretary of War Harry Woodring, Chief of Naval Operations Harold "Betty" Stark and Army Chief of Staff George Marshall—were hopelessly at odds over the meaning of events, and what actions, if any, should be taken to counter them. With the exception of Marshall, they convinced themselves that an expansion of the war could be avoided. Peace the wish became the father to their thought, and most unfortunately gave substance to an attitude in the intelligence community that it was unwise to be a bearer of bad news, or a "warmonger." Second, almost as a corollary to the first, the antiintelligence outlook within the upper reaches of the military hierarchy began to harden. Many senior officers in both the army and the navy who had achieved their rank and position by going along with policy to get ahead were deeply resentful, and even fearful, of the intellectuals and specialists who felt at home trying to put the many intelligence pieces into a coherent whole. The third theme was a bit more subtle: it involved a growing sense of uneasiness on the part of the intelligence professionals that they were getting in over their individual and collective heads. This was principally due to the fact that the line between their covert and overt operations had become increasingly difficult to maintain. The pressure of events created a situation whereby one action led to another, with each one requiring a greater emphasis on extraordinary and in many cases clearly illegal means.

By May 1940, a de facto clandestine collection system had evolved in the military intelligence services and the FBI in response to their expanded, although barely acknowledged, responsibilities. One element of this system— and perhaps the most important, because it involved both domestic and foreign operations—was run by the U.S. Navy. It was established in early May and headed by a rotund civilian named Wallace Phillips out of an unobtrusive office in New York City. Details surrounding its initial "charter" are even today vague and inconclusive. On the one hand it's clear that Rear Admiral Anderson approved creation of the clandestine collection programs carried out by Phillips' New York office and its worldwide net of operatives and "observers," but unclear who else in the navy's hierarchy was actually aware of its real function. The necessity for such an operation was based on the fact that the navy's overseas overt intelligence operations were becoming increasingly jeopardized because of requirements for information which could only be met by resorting to clandestine and/or illegal operations. Apparently, the decision to run this operation out of New York was based on the need to maintain a plausible denial cover story and to keep its existence secret from prying eyes in the Roosevelt administration. Various subterfuges were used to "sanitize" intelligence information acquired by Phillips' agents, which enabled the operation to remain undetected for more than a year. By today's standards Phillips' operation, which never numbered more than 150 persons, was quite small. However, in 1940 it represented a significant clandestine effort.

During this same general period, the army's clandestine thrust was more domestically oriented. Fallout from the spy-ring case suggested the need to counter subversive activity, especially insofar as it was directed against persons involved in the preparedness program, war plans, and communications activities. It was a wild time. The investigatory jurisdictional squabbles contributed to the confusion, but these were less significant than the fact that the German's successful invasion of Holland, Belgium, and Luxembourg had conclusively demonstrated the effectiveness of so-called fifth column tactics.

The army's Military Intelligence Division, especially its Corps of Intelligence Police (CIP),* was almost beside itself. Everywhere it looked it found vulnerabilities; defense plants, U.S. ports and harbors, military installations,

---

*The Corps of Intelligence Police came into being in 1917. Like other intelligence organizations, it barely maintained its existence in the period between the two world wars. Until 1929, despite the efforts of MID to get official permission for the CIP to collect information on domestic radicals and subversives, such collection was pro forma prohibited by the chief of staff. There was a bit of illegal snooping, but it didn't amount to much. By 1932, however, the bonus marchers were moving on Washington and the CIP was formally authorized a "domestic" role. In June and July 1932, when the bonus marchers were ensconced on the Anacostia flats—in what by any standards was one of the most peaceful demonstrations in American history—Army Chief of Staff General Douglas MacArthur gave the CIP a green light to infiltrate their encampment and provide him with information about the veterans' plans. The CIP agents proved capable of "furnishing information which was obtainable in no other way, because of their ability to associate with the veterans in terms of equality." (See Bruce W. Bidwell, *History of the Military Intelligence Division,* Department of the Army General Staff, 8 Parts, Department of the Army, Washington, D.C., 1961, Part 8, pp. 1–21, 1–25; this study was originally classified "Secret" and was declassified in 1973.) Following the events of 1932, the CIP continued to function in a similar, albeit low-key fashion, largely because of the personnel limitations forced upon it. By 1940, however, the effects of the war in Europe and the spy-ring case of 1938 were manifested in an expansion of the CIP. Its personnel authorization was increased from 40 to 50 in 1938, to 188 in 1940; in 1941 regular army officers were authorized for the first time. In 1940 two reserve officers detailed to counterintelligence were sent to the FBI school at Quantico, Virginia, and then were made part of a new CIP training school in Chicago. Along with mobilized FBI and Treasury agents, they formed its first faculty. About the same time, a former narcotics agent, then the district supervisor in New York for the Bureau of Narcotics and a reserve infantry major, was mobilized. In June 1941 this man was assigned as the first chief of newly reorganized CIP. He was Major Garland H. Williams, who headed the CIP for approximately 18 months, then headed on to the OSS. By the end of 1941, the CIP had reached a strength of 400 and was authorized 1,000. On January 1, 1942, the name of the organization was changed from CIP to CIC—Counter Intelligence Corps. (See U.S. Army, *The Founding of the Army's First Counter Intelligence Organizations,* U.S. Army Intelligence Command, n.p., 1967, unpaged.)

were barely protected and, more importantly, the evidences of Nazi and communist subversion began to increase at an alarming rate. Although increases in personnel had been authorized and were being filled as rapidly as possible, these were inadequate to meet the expanding needs. The desperate—or what was perceived to be desperate—nature of the counterintelligence situation caused the army to turn for additional support to one of its former own— Major General Ralph H. Van Deman, U.S. Army Retired.

Van Deman, whose active military career was described in Chapter 2, is widely considered to be the father of American military intelligence (see Allen W. Dulles, *The Craft of Intelligence,* p.41). However, he also was much more. Upon his retirement in September 1929 at the age of 65, after 38 years of service, Van Deman took up residence in San Diego and subsequently embarked on a second career in intelligence. His detractors, even today, say it might have been better for all concerned if Van Deman had taken up shuffleboard rather than pursuing his obsession with the security of the United States. Opinions are divided over Van Deman, the retired major general and self-designated military cum civilian counterintelligence specialist. Notwithstanding these conflicting opinions, Van Deman, because of his personal predilections, filled a gap in our immediate prewar and wartime counterintelligence activities.

As an interesting case in point, in late 1938 the Soviet Intourist representative in Los Angeles, Mikhail Gorin, sent a suit to the dry cleaners. Unfortunately for him, he had forgotten to check its pockets; in a coat pocket, the delivery man found an envelope containing a fifty-dollar bill and several sheets of paper with notes which referred to Japanese espionage activities on the West Coast. Thereupon the delivery man returned to the dry cleaning shop and showed the material to his boss, who sent him to the Hollywood police station. There—lacking a photostatic copier—the documents were laboriously copied by hand. In the meantime, the highly agitated Comrade and Mrs. Gorin arrived at the dry cleaners. The manager tried to calm them, although he managed to warn the delivery man at the police station to return to the store as if all were normal. He did, and Gorin received the originals and his fifty-dollar bill back.

The Hollywood police, however, sent the copies to the chief of the Los Angeles Police Department's Intelligence Bureau, Captain William F. "Red" Hynes. Hynes, who had served under General Van Deman in Military Intelligence during World War I, showed the documents to Van Deman, who immediately called Captain Ellis M. Zacharias, USN, then the 11th Naval District's Intelligence Officer. Zacharias found the documents to be copies of papers from his own office. This information enabled Zacharias to locate and plug his leak—a civilian contract navy investigator, Hatfis Salich. Unfortunately, the operation wasn't a complete success for Van Deman and Zacharias, because while Gorin was out on $50,000 bail following his and Salich's conviction on espionage charges, he "disappeared" and made his way back to the Soviet Union by ship.*

The Gorin case reveals much about the role of personal, informal relationships among former and present members of the intelligence community in handling extraordinary situations and, indirectly, the counterintelligence challenge faced by the United States prior to Pearl Harbor. Both factors are well exemplified in General Van Deman's second secret career in intelligence. Van Deman had retired in September 1929, at which time the state of America's intelligence services had reached a nadir. Beyond the obvious problems caused by a lack of money and personnel for intelligence duty, there was an attitude of national complacency which held that some kind of millennium had occurred in the games nations play to gain advantage in trade as well as in war. This pre–stock market crash, pre–Great Depression euphoria made consideration of intelligence an almost extraneous effort. But Van Deman, the intelligence professional, didn't share these ideas; and upon his retirement he began a secret project designed to fill the void in America's counterespionage, counterintelligence capability.

To Van Deman the problem of security—even in peacetime—was a real one. His earlier experience had convinced him that America faced a major subversive threat, especially from the communist left. To resolve this problem he turned to a procedure he had developed during World War I when the dozens of organizations devoted to running down German spies were consolidated under a single umbrella organization, the American Protective League.** The

---

*Ellis M. Zacharias, *Secret Missions*. New York: G.P. Putnam's Sons, 1946, pp. 203.–205. Gorin and Salich were both found guilty of espionage. See *The New York Times*, 21 March 1939, p. 10.

**The American Protective League, which assisted the Justice Department and military intelligence in the investigation of "unAmerican activities" and in the mass round-up of 50,000 persons to discover draft evaders. These so-called slacker raids of 1918 involved warrantless arrests without sufficient probable cause to believe that crime had been or was about to be committed. (See Joan M. Jensen, "The American Protective League," Ph.D. thesis, UCLA, 1962, 128 pp., and FBI Intelligence Division memorandum, "An Analysis of FBI Domestic Security Intelligence Investigations," 10/28/75.).

The American Protective League also contributed to the pressures which resulted in nearly 2,000 prosecutions for disloyal utterances and activities during World War I, a policy described by John Lord O'Brian, Attorney General Gregory's Special Assistant, as one of "wholesale repression and restraint of public opinion." (Zechariah Chafee, *Free Speech in the United States*, Cambridge: Harvard University Press, 1941, p. 69.)

Shortly after the war the Justice Department and the Bureau of Investigation (as the FBI was then known) jointly planned the notorious "Palmer Raids," named for Attorney General A. Mitchell Palmer, who ordered the overnight round-up and detention of some aliens subject to deportation. (William Preston, *Aliens and Dissenters*, Cambridge: Harvard University Press, 1963, chs. 7–8. Stanley Coben, *A. Mitchell Palmer: Politician*, New York: Columbia University Press, 1963, chs. 11–12.)

See also, Joan M. Jensen, *The Price of Vigilance*, Chicago: Rand McNally, 1968. One FBI official recalled later, "There were probably seven or eight such active organizations operating at full force during war days and it was not an uncommon experience for an agent of this Bureau

organization, which in 1919 numbered more than 100,000 members, had long ceased to function, but from its rolls Van Deman reconstituted a cadre of unpaid antisubversive "agents." It is unclear whether he similarly began with a nucleus from the voluminous Military Intelligence Division files developed by the American Protective League and the Corps of Intelligence Police during, prior, and after World War I; what is known is that Van Deman did, in connection with his private counterintelligence project, develop card files with more than 100,000 entries concerning individuals he believed to be communists, communist sympathizers, or neo-Nazis.

In a 1971 article, *The New York Times* alleged that Van Deman was supported in his project by the army, the navy, the FBI, and various local police organizations.

Moreover, the general ran a nationwide network of informants, each identified only by a coded number, who reported great volumes of raw information to him. The files show that some information could have come only from agents who infiltrated the Communist Party, labor unions, church groups and other organizations.*

In addition to the card file information, the files also contained photographs of many individuals who were the subject of Van Deman's "research," and an extensive library of material (books, newspapers, magazines) produced by or about communists in the United States.**

---

to call upon an individual in the course of his investigation, to find out that six or seven other government agencies had been around to interview the party about the same matter." (Memorandum of F. X. O'Donnell; Subject: Operations During World War I, 10/4/38.)

* *The New York Times,* September 7, 1971. Although the *Times* article alleges that when Van Deman began his private operation in 1929 the army supported him by providing two civilian employees, filing cabinets and working materials, there is no valid evidence to support that contention.

**A personal note; as a young boy, I first met General Van Deman in Washington, D.C., in 1933. My father, who at the time was a special assistant to Jesse Jones, the head of the Reconstruction Finance Corporation, and who had served under Van Deman during the Paris Peace Commission, introduced us by saying, "Son, I want you to meet the most intelligent man I have ever known." Van Deman was most impressive. He was not stern in his appearance, but his eyes were quite compelling. As we sat at the table in the Willard Hotel's "Peacock Walk," my father and the general reminisced about their time in Paris where Van Deman had served as General Pershing's senior intelligence officer and Chief of Allied Counterintelligence. Their conversation ranged over a wide number of topics. Much of their discussion was well over my head, but one topic remains fresh in my mind. This had to do with the United States' contemplated recognition of the Soviet Union. Van Deman ventured it seemed unlikely that it could be prevented. Both men agreed recognition meant future trouble. When we parted, General Van Deman said, "Ray, keep in contact, and if you come to San Diego stay with us."

The incident remained a boyhood memory until September 1941, when my father lay dying in the Hines Veterans Administration Hospital outside Chicago. During our last conversation, my father reminded me about General Van Deman by saying, "War is soon to come and when it's your turn to go let General Van Deman know." Shortly thereafter my father died. We received a letter of condolence from Van Deman which included an offer to be of personal help. The war

Apparently Van Deman made no particular effort to keep secret the fact that he was collecting information on communists. A colleague on the San Diego Harbor Commission said that the general had been warning of a communist menace since the early 1930s, that "mysterious people would be reporting to him on communist activities at all hours," and that Van Deman "had a picture file, front and side, of every known communist."*

To see Van Deman's place in the pre–Pearl Harbor intelligence activities it's necessary to digress from our narrative and trace the outlines of his controversial subversives file project. There is no hard evidence to suggest that he began the project with the blessing of any person in an official government role. However, there is evidence that, from the beginning of his retirement, he was informally called upon for information and assistance by intelligence chiefs of both the army and the navy and, until his death in 1952, by J. Edgar Hoover, whom he curiously referred to in correspondence as "My dear Colonel Hoover." Also, the Van Deman files clearly bespeak a sharing and exchange of information between himself and selected members of the intelligence services, as well as some "private" organizations and persons who have been active in combatting the so-called Red menace.

In December 1941, Van Deman became an intelligence "advisor" to the War

---

came, I made my own way into the marines, and thought little about General Van Deman. As a young lieutenant, between the end of World War II and the start of the Korean War, my own researches into the history of American intelligence resulted in a kind of personal rediscovery which connected the Van Deman I had once met with the Van Deman whose 38-year career in intelligence was unparalleled in American history. Upon my mother's urging, I contacted General Van Deman in San Diego just prior to the Korean War. We met several times under circumstances which were almost Socratic. His mind and memory even at the age of 84 were remarkable. Our talks covered the entire spectrum of the intelligence profession and he imparted a complete conception of intelligence which, as he said, was "possible to visualize, but perhaps impossible to achieve." In view of the controversy which ensued after his death over the card file project, his further statement that "counterespionage is the scalpel an intelligence officer must learn how, and be able, to use with great care if the efforts to gather information are to produce intelligence truth," is pertinent 26 years later. Van Deman may have been, as some have said, simply an anticommunist zealot, but I think not. Both his careers reflect the incredible difficulties in dealing with, and balancing the human and legal factors involved in using intelligence and its procedures to preserve, protect, and defend our liberties without destroying them in the process.

Finally, Van Deman—ever the intelligence officer—left me with a conundrum which after 27 years remains unresolved. It involved my stated disbelief that the activities surrounding his card file project could have been carried out without the financial assistance of others. His reply was equally disarming and bemusing. In essence he said, "I have never personally accepted a penny to carry out this work; however, others have had need for funds to do what is necessary" and he asked, "Do you have any quarrel with the idea that private citizens should not make funds available to those able and willing to carry out the work required to keep us free?" We left it there with his gentle admonition, "Your father understood this and there is no reason you should not." My thoughts jumped to my father's relationship with Jesse Jones and the Houston Endowment, but Van Deman, in a sphinxlike pronouncement, said, "Your future lies with those in the active forces, but never fear, there are those in reserve who will help in their own silent ways."

*San Diego Union, January 2, 1972, p. 2.

Department. The details of his service are lost in the shadowy world of counterespionage. Indicative of his contribution to the war effort, however, he was awarded the Legion of Merit in mid-1946 (at age 81) for "accumulation and evaluation of confidential intelligence information" during the period between December 1941 and May 1946. His efforts were of "the highest importance and have materially assisted the war effort." In acknowledging the award, Van Deman provided some clues as to what his "contributions" were: "I appreciated receiving this citation, because it shows that the War Department had appreciated the fine intelligence work carried on by civilian volunteers at their own expense during the war period." He said the work was of "material aid to the army, navy, marines and FBI."*

On January 22, 1952, Van Deman died quietly at his San Diego home. He was 86. But this was not the end of the project. With characteristic thoroughness he had made arrangements to allow others to continue his work. Most of his files were turned over to the army by his widow on the day following his death. The remaining files, which were apparently only pertinent to California, were given to a nonprofit educational agency called the San Diego Research Library (SDRL) which had been set up for that purpose. The chief of the library was a San Diego attorney, civic leader, and longtime associate of Van Deman's, George Fisher. Fisher, who had a distinguished combat record in both World War I and II and who was a retired major general in the California National Guard, continued the work begun by Van Deman for the next ten years.**

Van Deman's file project, which some say earned him the added sobriquet "the Father of American Surveillance," is more than a legacy from the naive past when counterespionage and counterintelligence were considered unnecessary and unimportant. Rather, it is a statement of the essential difficulty the United States faces in attempting to balance national security with the rights of individual citizens. To Van Deman's credit, he never used his information about "subversives" to light the way for witch hunters. During his lifetime, various government agencies both provided information to Van Deman and also checked his files to determine if someone they were investigating might have communist connections. After his death, this practice was continued by the SDRL, with Fisher and his associates performing records checks for state and local officials. In February 1962, the California Adjutant General seized the records of the SDRL, claiming they were the property of the state. In a successful law suit, the SDRL won back the files as a private research collection put together by Van Deman. The issue of the propriety of checking citizens against these files had been raised, and the SDRL could no longer engage in the practice.

For the years following Van Deman's death, his files were used by the army

*San Diego Tribune, July 20, 1946, p. 10.

**San Diego Union, February 26, 1962, p. 1.

to check individuals being considered for positions of responsibility which required granting a security clearance. This practice, based on executive orders and the individual's authorization to allow government investigators to verify his/her background information, was completely proper. However, in early 1971 the existence of the army-held portion of the Van Deman files came to the attention of a United States Senate Internal Security Subcommittee headed by Senator Sam J. Ervin, Jr. The subcommittee was investigating alleged army spying on civilians. Although the Department of Defense apparently conceded that it was inappropriate to use the Van Deman information in the conduct of its personnel security investigations, the larger question of what to do with the files was not finally resolved.* As was revealed in subsequent Congressional hearings, the Van Deman files were sometimes used in connection with the domestic antiwar surveillance activities ordered by Lyndon Johnson (CONUS) which were carried out by the army and other intelligence agencies. Today, it is claimed by the army that the Van Deman files have been "secured," but there is no assurance that they are not—along with the material developed in the late '60s and '70s—quietly stored in one of the government's data banks, waiting to be used by those who have yet to learn the differences between espionage, subversion, and legitimate political dissent.

With the British evacuation of Dunkirk on May 29, 1940, and the fall of France on June 14, America's intelligence services found themselves in a race against time. The build-up became a little less orderly and the method of informally sharing intelligence information was revealed to be inadequate as they faced the twin problems of expanding their organizations and coping with the increased flow of intelligence information they were generating. A further complication occurred on July 10 and 11, 1940, on which dates Henry L. Stimson and Frank L. Knox respectively were sworn in as Secretary of War and Secretary of the Navy. Both of these appointments were viewed as mixed blessings by the intelligence community. On the one hand, Stimson and Knox were considered to be activists who would help to accelerate the preparedness program and insure an increased flow of money and men into the armed services. On the other hand Stimson, by virtue of his earlier announced aversion to clandestine covert activities, was feared likely to call a halt to such activities already underway if he found out about them. It was also feared that Knox, because of his outgoing, city-desk manner, might be indiscreet with information about the intelligence services' illegal clandestine activities.

Fortunately, the press of business and the rancor in the media and Congress

---

*Although the army turned over copies of the Van Deman files to the Senate's Internal Security Subcommittee in 1970, the index which identified the general's agents and sources was declared —according to military sources—to have disappeared from the army's files at its intelligence center at Fort Holabird, Maryland.

which surrounded their confirmation hearings diverted Stimson and Knox's attention from any consideration about what the intelligence services were actually doing in the clandestine areas. However, during the period between their appointment by President Roosevelt on June 20 and their subsequent confirmation by the Senate both men's assistance was sought by the intelligence professionals in order to help them bring some order out of the intelligence informational chaos. Let us try to describe the thread of events and "conspiracies within conspiracies" which affected the outcome of the intelligence professionals' problems, and in turn how they operated during World War II.

These events and how they converged in the summer of 1940 to produce a desired but altogether unforeseen outcome indicate the intelligence professionals' limitations in changing national policy to conform with their views about what should be done. A strict chronological narrative of events is misleading because, although event B might follow event A, their subsequent influence on the final outcome need not necessarily have been sequential. With this in mind, let us back up to April 1940 when Sir William Stephenson, "the man called Intrepid,"* traveled to America on a secret mission "to establish relations on the highest possible level between the British Secret Intelligence Service organization and the U.S. Federal Bureau of Investigation."**

As H. Montgomery Hyde notes in describing Stephenson's meeting with J. Edgar Hoover in connection with his mission,

Hoover listened with polite attention as Stephenson explained the purpose of his visit. Then he spoke out frankly. He told his caller that, while he himself would welcome the idea of working with British Intelligence, he was under a strict injunction from the State Department to refrain from collaborating with the British in any way which might conceivably be interpreted as infringing or compromising United States neutrality in the European struggle, and he made it clear that he would not be prepared to contravene this policy without a direct order from the White House. Further, he stipulated that, even if President Roosevelt could be persuaded to agree to the principle of collaboration between the FBI and the British S.I.S., this collaboration should be effected initially by a personal liaison between Stephenson and himself, and that no

---

*William Stevenson, *A Man Called Intrepid:The Secret War.* New York: Harcourt Brace Jovanovich, 1976. This book, which details the World War II exploits of Sir William S. Stephenson, who headed Britain's Secret Intelligence Services' U.S.-based "British Security Coordination" office in New York City, provides a sometimes one-sided view about the collaboration between U.S. and British intelligence agencies.

**H. Montgomery Hyde, *Room 3603: The Story of the British Intelligence Center in New York During World War II,* Farrar, Straus, & Co.: 1962, p. 24. This book was published with the approval and concurrence of British intelligence officials as a means to counter the threat posed to British and U.S. intelligence operations by the escape of Kim Philby to the Soviet Union. Much of its discussion is duplicated in *A Man Called Intrepid.* However, taken together the two books, coupled with recently declassified U.S. intelligence documents, provide a reasonably complete statement about what actually occurred during the U.S.-U.K. wartime intelligence alliance.

other United States Government Department, including the Department of State, should be informed of it.*

To get Roosevelt's ratification of the agreement, Stephenson and Hoover enlisted the aid of one of the president's confidential advisors, Ernest Cuneo. Roosevelt's approval was soon forthcoming. Hyde further notes,

That such an agreement was reached at all was a remarkable indication of the President's clarity of vision, while the fact that it had to be kept secret even from the State Department provided a striking illustration of the strength of American neutrality at this period. It was all the more courageous of Franklin Roosevelt to act as he did, since he was in the last year of his presidential term and he had necessarily to behave with particular circumspection if he was to run again successfully for election.**

This little-known incident, which remained hidden from public view until the publication of Hyde's *Room 3603* in 1962, was more than a "courageous act." It was a clear violation of the law. Seen today, President Roosevelt's transgression is rationalized in terms of a president's higher conception of national security or interest. Maybe so, but what nags is what happened to FDR's approval of the Stephenson-Hoover agreement, which he gave, in writing, to Hoover. Roosevelt's papers are silent on this point and the Hoover "files" seem to have been shredded or otherwise disappeared. The fact of the agreement is not in dispute, but one has to wonder why and in what words FDR chose to deliver to J. Edgar Hoover an ultimate piece of blackmail which if made public could have been used as the successful basis for the president's impeachment.

The next set of events occurred from May to mid-June. Stephenson, who had returned in May to report upon the agreement with J. Edgar Hoover on or about the night of May 25, met with Prime Minister Winston Churchill, who ordered him back to the United States to run the British side of the secret intelligence and special operations involved under the agreement's terms. Shortly after Stephenson's arrival in New York on May 29, in connection with one of his additional duties he contacted William J. Donovan to enlist his aid on behalf of Churchill's request to Roosevelt for destroyers, as well as light naval craft, first-line aircraft (including flying boats), and military equipment and supplies.***

At the time (although he was generally aware of Stephenson's quasiofficial and longstanding personal relationship with the British Secret Intelligence Service), Donovan had no idea about Stephenson's secret intelligence agreement with Hoover. Donovan was supportive of Churchill's request and he

---

*Ibid. p. 26.

**Ibid., p. 27

***Ibid., p. 35

arranged a meeting with Knox and Stimson at which both he and Stephenson were present.* This meeting, which took place in Washington several days after Roosevelt's appointment of Stimson and Knox, concerned Churchill's request and produced a suggestion by Stephenson that Donovan visit Britain to verify the necessity of the requirements and to evaluate the British capacity to hold out. It should be noted that at the time of this meeting that although both Stimson and Knox had been appointed by President Roosevelt neither had yet been confirmed by the Senate, and it was far from certain that Roosevelt might not be forced to withdraw their names.

The confirmation battle over Stimson and Knox caused some consternation among the United States' intelligence professionals, and probably with Stephenson as well. Each had their own purposes which appeared to be better served if Stimson and Knox were allowed to quietly replace Secretary of War Harry Woodring and the Acting Secretary of the Navy Charles Edison without being compelled to be too explicit about what actions, beyond those taken in the name of United States preparedness, they favored in helping or working with the British. The fear, then as now, was based on the fact that Stimson and Knox, who had been briefed by the intelligence professionals as well as operational types in preparation for their confirmation hearings, might in a fit of candor reveal more than they should. Later they would learn how to dissemble and respond to Congressional inquiries with the appropriate degree of ambiguity; however, until they had a full commitment to keep the administration's secrets from Congress—as well as from the press—it was a risky situation. And no one in the intelligence community was completely sure that the antiwar elements in Congress did not have information about their illegal activities which could be trotted out to embarrass them and burn Stimson and Knox.

The next set of events followed after the Stephenson, Donovan, Stimson, Knox meeting. As noted, the intelligence professionals had their own plans for Knox and Stimson; however, they also had no knowledge about the Stephenson-Hoover agreement. If they had, it's likely they would have pursued a different course in dealing with both men. Word about this meeting was informally passed several days after its occurrence by the Secretary of the Navy's aide, Captain M. L. Deyo, USN, to Captain D. W. Knox, USN (Retired),** who in turn discussed its implications with Rear Admiral Ander-

---

Ibid., p. 36

**Captain Dudley Wright Knox, USN (Ret)—no relation to Navy Secretary Frank Knox—who served as principal deputy to the various Directors of Naval Intelligence from the early 1920s to the time of his second retirement in 1946, was one of the most influential leaders in American intelligence throughout that period. He was a historian in his outlook and a bureaucratic "string saver" who knew where all the secrets were hidden as well as who had something to gain or lose if they were exposed. In his deputy role, Knox provided a kind of continuity in the evolution of United States Naval Intelligence activities and thinking which enabled him to influence events and policy in quiet but altogether effective ways. Because of Knox's careful selection of trained naval

son, the Director of Naval Intelligence. Captain Knox and Admiral Anderson were a bit puzzled about the nature and purposes of the meeting. Donovan's relationship to Stimson and Knox was clear in their minds, but Stephenson's role was not immediately apparent. Admiral Anderson, who had served as the United States Naval Attaché in England during 1934–36, was generally aware of Stephenson's in-and-out relationship with the British SIS, but he was not sure what his real mission was at this time. Discreet inquiries at both the Department of State and to Captain Daniel Callaghan, USN, Roosevelt's Naval Aide, did not answer the question, except to confirm that Stephenson had been traveling to and from the United States and England in recent months and was presently installed as a "Passport Control Officer" in New York City—a title consistently used by the British SIS in providing cover to its overseas agents. Coming up with a dry hole in trying to figure out if Stephenson was on special intelligence mission, they shrugged it off and assumed his purpose was simply to argue for the military aid Britain so desperately needed. Based upon this slightly flawed premise, Admiral Anderson and Captain Knox's conclusions were several. One, Secretaries Stimson's and Knox's avowed support of the Neutrality Act during their confirmation hearings, which required Britain to pay for arms on a cash and carry basis, was more apparent than real. Two, the intelligence services might be able to "piggyback" the need to resolve their situation on an ostensible consideration of Churchill's request for military assistance.

As a result, in the immediate period following Secretary-designate Knox's appearance before the Senate's Naval Affairs Committee on July 1, 1940, Admiral Anderson made the subtle suggestion that the secretary or some "independent" observer undertake a mission to Britain to resolve the differing intelligence interpretations about the war. Admiral Anderson was careful in not going too far, nor in letting on that he knew about Stephenson's suggestion for a similar visit in conjunction with Churchill's request for military equipment and assistance. Tempers were short in official Washington in the summer of 1940. The Selective Service debate had given new life to the isolationists' cause and rekindled talk about "merchants of death" and the absurd idea of "pulling England's chestnuts out of the fire." In fact, "contingency planning," in the future event that military equipment for Britain might have to be transported on United States flag vessels and convoyed by United States Navy ships, was carried out under conditions of secrecy which were designed more to avoid political embarrassment than to maintain military security. These attitudes, coupled with the fall of France, required Admiral Anderson and his cohorts to walk a fine line in dealing with Frank Knox—and they knew it. However, by appealing to Knox's well-known penchant as the editor-publisher

intelligence officers for duty at the White House—who continuously and informally reported back to him—he was rarely surprised by policy shifts in presidential administrations from Harding through Roosevelt. Also, his contacts throughout the rest of the government were legion.

of the *Chicago Daily News* to "get the story and get it straight!" they made it appear that the conflicting analyses and reports from all the intelligence services were producing unnecessary confusion in the administration—which they were—and that it was possible for him to find out the real situation.

As a consequence of Admiral Anderson's suggestions and his personal observations, which were reinforced by the conflicting and almost aimless discussions espoused in Cabinet meetings, Secretary-designate Knox became convinced of the necessity to do something about the chaotic intelligence situation.

From review of the DNI files of those fateful days in early July 1940, it's clear that the intelligence situation had captured Knox's attention. This is not to say that the earlier suggestion of Stephenson's about aid to Britain did not influence his thinking, but rather that the entire idea of aid to Britain was so explosive that using it as the basis of a mission was considered unwise.

The idea that Knox might go to Britain on the kind of intelligence mission envisaged by Anderson and his colleagues was considered and rejected on the grounds that the pressure of his duties wouldn't permit his absence, that such a trip would set off additional whistles and bells in the antiwar, anti-Britain, America First forces who were opposing his and Stimson's appointments, and provoke an additional internecine quarrel in the administration's hierarchy. Secretary Stimson was amenable to the idea—after a period of soft-sell convincing by Brigadier General Sherman Miles, then the army's Assistant Chief of Staff, G-2, who was a personal favorite of the secretary's—but Stimson and Knox couldn't immediately settle on a candidate for the task. John McCloy, the soon to be named Assistant Secretary of War, was considered by the Knox-Stimson "search committee" and rejected for basically the same reasons as Knox. Others, including Bernard Baruch and Fiorello LaGuardia, were considered, but they were rejected as not being competent for the task, or likely to produce political complications in the forthcoming presidential election. In spite of Knox's, and to a lesser degree Stimson's, acceptance of the idea, each of the factors had to be carefully weighed because not only did the idea have to be sold to President Roosevelt and his Secretary of State, but the person selected had to be competent to complete the chore and not likely to create an extraneous political issue by the fact of the mission, or by his personal position in life, in or out of the government.

It was not an easy selection; fortunately, a combination of circumstances facilitated its successful outcome. The first was the presence, at the moment of decision, of William Joseph Donovan, who was in Washington testifying before the Senate's Military Affairs Committee on behalf of the Selective Service Bill. The second was Donovan, the man, himself. Both were important: the first because those in the press and Congress advocating that Britain "sue for peace" were becoming more and more outspoken in their insistence that America keep an arm's length away from the war and especially avoid any action which might indicate that the United States was taking sides. The situation argued the necessity to get on with the mission in a hurry. Second, Donovan, at the age of fifty-seven, was the right man to do the job.

Donovan's life and career are set forth in Corey Ford's *Donovan of the OSS,* but for present purposes it's worthwhile to describe those features of his background which bore on selecting him for the mission. In the first instance he was personally well-known to all the key "players" but one, Secretary of State Cordell Hull. Donovan and Hull knew one another, but there was no particular personal rapport between the two men. On the other hand, Knox and Donovan had both been long active in Republican politics. Both had run for office and lost, Knox as the Republican nominee for vice-president in 1936 and Donovan for governor of New York in 1932. In the course of their campaigning they had done many favors for each other and many other members of the GOP. As such, both men had a good supply of personal due notes to call, if partisan political opposition developed over the mission and its expected (or hoped for) consequences. Similarly Stimson, who had been Secretary of War under President Taft nearly thirty years before, was an old friend of Donovan's, and along with Knox had consulted with him prior to accepting Roosevelt's invitation to join the cabinet. In the controversy over their appointment and prior to their confirmation hearings, Donovan had spoken out publicly in favor of appointing Stimson and Knox to the Roosevelt cabinet. Finally, Donovan and Roosevelt were old friends from Columbia University's Law School, where they had been classmates together. As a measure of Roosevelt's esteem for Donovan, he had told Frank Knox at the end of 1939 (at which time FDR initially invited Knox to join his cabinet), "Frankly I should like to have him [Donovan] in the cabinet, not only for his own ability, but also to repair in a sense the very great injustice done him by Herbert Hoover."* In this letter Roosevelt referred to the fact that it was assumed Herbert Hoover, for whom Donovan had campaigned actively in the 1928 presidential election, would name Donovan attorney general. However, as Hyde indicates, "Donovan's appointment was blocked by 'dry' elements in the Republican party, to whom the idea of a member of a community with such 'wet' interests as the Catholic Irish-American community was obnoxious."**

The other side of the Donovan coin was equally compelling. His service as the commander of the famous "Fighting 69th" in World War I had earned him the Congressional Medal of Honor. He clearly was no "cookie pusher," nor someone who could be easily deceived by the facts of a military situation. His legal training and military experience constituted clear credentials of his ability to measure the state of a situation and render an accurate report. As a private citizen, Donovan had periodically left his lucrative law practice in the 1930s

*ed., Elliott Roosevelt, *The Roosevelt Letters* 1952, Vol III, p. 297.

**Hyde, *op. cit.,* p. 34.

to tour the battlefronts during the Italian invasion of Ethiopia and the Spanish Civil War. As a result of these forays, Donovan was an accepted and articulate spokesman who had tried to warn his fellow citizens about the rise and danger of the Fascist powers.

Obviously, from the intelligence leaders' point of view Donovan was the man. Following a late-night dinner with Knox at the Willard Hotel on July 11, 1940, Donovan agreed to undertake the mission if President Roosevelt would buy the idea. The precise record of what happened following Knox and Donovan's meeting is a bit unclear. Whether Knox discussed the matter with others besides those in his immediate entourage before going to Roosevelt is not possible to establish.* However, what is clear in the rapid sequence of events following their meeting is that Knox broached the idea to President Roosevelt of sending Donovan on an intelligence fact-finding mission to Britain rather than one directly concerned with Churchill's military-equipment request. Roosevelt readily and almost immediately accepted the idea as his own. The result was, as the "War Report of the OSS" laconically noted, "he [Donovan] was immediately called to the White House where he conferred with the President and the Secretaries of State, War and Navy. He was asked if he would go to England to study the methods and effectiveness of Germany's fifth-column activities in Europe. In addition, the President wished him to observe how the British were standing up at a time when their fortunes were at their lowest ebb and they faced Germany alone. Donovan agreed to undertake the mission, and other departments of the government asked him to obtain specific information on other subjects."**

This hurriedly called, impromptu meeting turned out as the intelligence leaders had hoped. Its apparent spontaneity and the mission's laundry list of stated purposes did not arouse Secretary of State Cordell Hull's suspicions that the intelligence services were attempting to move into and take over some of his areas of responsibility. Also, the intelligence services' keen interest in the mission's outcome was partially obscured by President Roosevelt's suggestion

*From review of the Director of Naval Intelligence's files concerning these events, it's not clear whether Secretary Knox's previous discussions with Secretary Stimson about the contemplated mission included mention of Donovan's name. Nonetheless, both were agreed to the mission's necessity and the kind of qualifications the individual finally selected should possess.

**War Report Office of Strategic Services (OSS), History Project, Strategic Services Unit, Office of the Assistant Secretary of War, War Department, Washington, D.C. 1949. Hereinafter cited as "War Report." Note: The "War Report" has been commercially republished in two versions. The first, entitled *The Secret War Report of the OSS,* edited and with an introduction by Anthony Cave Brown, by the Berkeley Publishing Corporation, New York, 1976, is an abridged version of the report which includes additions and commentaries by Mr. Brown. The second is *War Report of the OSS,* with a new introduction by Kermit Roosevelt, published by Walker & Company, New York, 1976. The Walker version, although an exact copy, only includes Volume I of the original War Report, which covers the history of the Coordinator of Information (COI) and the headquarters history of the OSS. Neither the Berkeley nor Walker versions include the exhibits mentioned in the War Report text.

that before Donovan depart, he check with the other cabinet members concerning what information they might desire about the present situation. On the surface the Donovan mission appeared to be a simple fact-finding operation rather than one designed to facilitate the intelligence plan already envisaged —though not completely worked out—in Roosevelt's mind. Unknown to Knox, Donovan, and the others at the meeting, the partial fix was already in for an enlargement of intelligence activities as a consequence of Roosevelt's secret agreement, which sanctioned a "marriage" between the FBI and British intelligence. At the time of the Donovan mission, it was one of the unseen forces which would affect the mission and in turn come to bear in resolving how the United States intelligence services would actually operate in wartime and how each would stake out and attempt to maintain their individual pieces of the intelligence domain.

In the several days following the decision to send Donovan to England, the leaders of the intelligence community, most notably Admiral Anderson and General Miles, made ready their forces. There was no intent on their part to "brainwash" Donovan, but rather to make sure that he received a straightforward presentation and that Ambassador Joseph Kennedy not be given an opportunity to prevent the attachés from providing him, without fear or favor, the facts of the situation, or to keep Donovan from talking with key persons in Britain's intelligence services. To these ends cable instructions were sent to England on two levels. One, by way of the State Department from Secretary Hull to Ambassador Kennedy informing him about the visit, clearly indicated that this was not to be a protocol trip. That is, Kennedy was not made responsible for arranging Donovan's meetings, with other persons, or laying on an embassy briefing for him. In rather blunt terms Ambassador Kennedy was told he had no responsibilities in connection with the mission and that Donovan would make his own way in contacting persons suggested by the president and the cabinet members concerned. It wasn't the first time an American ambassador had been cut out of an operation with intelligence overtones, nor would it be the last. However, at this time, because of Kennedy's gloomy estimation of England's fortunes and his views about the inevitability of Germany's success, it was decided that the less Kennedy knew about the mission the better.

The second set of instructions went by way of the navy's "back channels" —a way of communicating outside of normal navy and diplomatic circuits. These cables, drafted jointly by Admiral Anderson and General Miles, directed their respective attachés in London, Captain Alan G. Kirk and Brigadier General Raymond E. Lee, to go all out in helping Donovan. Kirk, Lee, and their respective staffs were expected to provide Donovan with the key information they held as well as to arrange secret meetings with British intelligence leaders. Anderson and Miles were well prepared to orchestrate the Donovan mission. Both, prior to assuming command of navy and army intelligence, had previously served in London as the senior naval and military attachés. As a consequence, they had personal relationships with the key people in the British system and knew which ones really had something to offer Donovan. Donovan, who was not without personal resources of his own in England, was informed shortly before his departure on July 14 that after his arrival in London he would be contacted by Captain Kirk and General Lee, who would provide him with "confidential" assistance in carrying out his mission. The circumstances surrounding the Donovan mission sound a bit cloak and daggerish, but actually they were not. The problems of the mission were political, stemming from the antiwar opposition and the less well known bureaucratic struggle over the role of intelligence in the national decision-making process.

At the time of Donovan's departure for London by way of Lisbon it was assumed that his mission could be accomplished in a few days. This assumption was hardly realistic. However, based on the presumed necessity to maintain the mission's thin cover that Donovan was traveling to London on "private business," Captain Kirk received an order directing him to complete the briefings as soon as possible. Kirk was not too happy with these instructions. He knew that an explanation of the situation's enormous complexity and its outcome's dependence on intelligence was not amenable to a typical once-over-lightly "high level" briefing. But Kirk was a good sailor and he tried his best to hurry the proceedings along. But Donovan was not about to be hurried, and the "few days" were extended to two and a half weeks as he dug deeper and deeper into the overall problem.

Donovan's time was well spent. He came to London a well-intentioned amateur strategist and left with an understanding about intelligence and those who had chosen its challenges which would stand him in good stead in the difficult years ahead. Kirk and Lee laid out the facts of the "friendly" as well as the "enemy" situation. In addition to their briefings and those of their staff members,* Kirk also brought Commander Roscoe H. Hillenkoetter, USN (later the first Director of the CIA), the naval attaché in Paris, to London to provide Donovan with an up-to-date assessment about Germany's long-range intentions and the effectiveness of their "softening up" of the French people. Hillenkoetter's part of the briefings was extremely important because it gave added confirmation to the thesis taking shape in Donovan's mind about the stages and procedures involved in the Nazi's successful fifth-column activities.** From these officers Donovan got a balanced picture about the future

---

*Captain Kirk's London staff included: Commander N. R. Hitchcock, USN; Commander V. Bailey, USN (Ret); Lieutenant Commander W.B. Ammon, USN; Lieutenant Commander J.N. Opie III, USN; and Lieutenant F.X. Forest, USN, who also was accredited as assistant naval attaché in Paris, Rome and the Hague.

**Donovan's briefings by British and U.S. intelligence personnel on the Nazi's fifth-column tactics carried out in connection with their blitz conquests of Poland, Norway, Belgium, Luxemburg, and France, together with the impressions of the veteran foreign correspondent of Secretary Knox's *Chicago Daily News,* Edgar Ansel Mowrer, who had personally observed the fall of France, were used as the basis of a series of four articles which appeared in late August 1940 under the joint

course of events. As Kirk and Lee told him, the British had suffered a defeat on the continent, but due to the successful—almost miraculous—evacuation from Dunkirk its army was intact. In response to Donovan's queries about the British losses of equipment, Kirk and Lee offered a view which was almost heretical: it was less important than originally supposed. They argued that the equipment, essentially tanks and artillery, which had been lost was inadequate to stand up to the Germans, and that the Battle for Britain would be decided in the air. These were heady conclusions. On the one hand, they implied that Hitler's early good fortune was a blessing in disguise in that it was now possible to rearm Britain's forces with newer and better equipment which could enable them to compete more effectively in the future. On the other hand, they suggested that Hitler's "Operation Sea Lion," which called for the amphibious invasion of England and plans for which had been acquired by a joint U.S.-British covert operation, was more a symbolic than real threat . . . *if* the Nazis failed to achieve total air superiority.

At this stage of the briefings Donovan became convinced of the professionalism of the U.S. personnel involved. In response to Donovan's question about the Nazis' capability to achieve the necessary air superiority, Captain Kirk laid all the cards on the table. He indicated without rancor, or any attempt to hide their internal disagreements, that the American attachés and "observers" were equally divided on the question whether the Royal Air Force could in fact stand up to the Germans. Kirk stated there was no certainty involved in the situation and that the outcome would be decided by imponderables beyond anyone's capacity to specify. In response to a direct question from Donovan, Kirk stated that if he had to wager the outcome he would bet against the British, but his heart told him that the "better" wager was in favor of supporting the young men of the RAF, whose attitudes exemplified intangibles which the best intelligence officer ignored at his own peril. This kind of candor made a deep and distinct impression on Donovan. It suggested the existence of a body of men who could be counted upon to take the decision maker to the point where political intuition needed to be blended with an honest appreciation of what had already happened and what was likely to happen next.

Obviously there were some very big ifs involved in Kirk and Lee's conclusions. Nonetheless, Donovan came away convinced that their analyses had

---

byline of Donovan and Mowrer. Secretary Knox wrote an introduction to these articles which said in part: "They are designed to make Americans fully conscious of methods used by the totalitarian powers, so that, if or when such methods are used here, they will instantly be recognized for what they are and their effect nullified. I regard defense against possible enemy propaganda as second only to defense against enemy armaments."

The articles were disseminated by the three leading American news agencies and widely distributed in pamphlet form. On balance, the articles did little at the time to alter the nation's antiwar sentiments; however, due to the counterpropaganda they produced from some hitherto unknown American Nazi supporters, the FBI and the military intelligence services were able to add some key persons to their target list of subversives.

been properly based on an interpretation of the available intelligence information. Every judgment they made was supported with hard facts which had been at least doubly corroborated. The Americans indicated the scope of their own collection effort and their special relationships with the British intelligence services and its leaders. These elements of the briefing constituted a rather daring admission, because the military and naval attachés revealed that they had been operating outside their defined areas of responsibility and behind the back of the U.S. ambassador, Joseph Kennedy. As Donald McLachlan notes,

The Naval Attaché serves two masters: his Ambassador and the Director of Naval Intelligence. His loyalties are placed in that order, because his first duty in a foreign capital is clearly to serve the mission of which he is a member. He must advise its head on naval matters, keep him informed of anything important that he learns through his professional and social contacts, cooperate with Chancery and other attachés, and play his part in the representative social role of the diplomatic team.*

By their admissions, Kirk and Lee and the members of their staffs were confessed heretics who had violated their positions of trust and, by their very words, were being disloyal—or responding to higher conceptions of loyalty in talking with Donovan without letting the ambassador know about their meetings. Whether they agreed with or opposed Ambassador Kennedy's ideas matters not, nor that they had received orders from "headquarters" to give Donovan a special briefing; they had violated a trust and they knew it. Donovan recognized the significance of their admissions, but remained noncommittal. His reaction to the intelligence analyses and how Kirk and Lee's people were actually operating was typical Donovan. He was the tough trial lawyer about to take on a client and before he did, he wanted to know what other skeletons might be lurking in the closet they had referred to, but only barely described. As a result, he asked Kirk and Lee to set up meetings with British intelligence leaders they believed "could add to his understanding" and would be able to discuss how they were organized to deal with their problems. Kirk was completely charmed by Donovan. He saw through the disingenuousness of Donovan's request, and understood that Donovan required more ammunition than the small band of American intelligence brothers had provided to carry the day in the brutal bureaucratic environment of Washington and the White House.

A variety of meetings were arranged. Unknown to Kirk and Lee, these were facilitated by Sir William Stephenson, who in response to a query from the head of the British Secret Intelligence Service, Sir Stewart Menzies, about the visit's purpose replied that Donovan should be given a frank appreciation of the situation as well as how Britain's intelligence services were organized and

*Donald McLachlan, *Room 39, a Study in Naval Intelligence,* New York: Atheneum, 1968, pp. 182–83.

actually operating in support of and with the military services. As a consequence of this exchange, the meetings went well beyond the normal protocol interaction between the Americans and British in connection with official visits by American intelligence authorities.

Although at the time of these meetings with British intelligence leaders (as well as with operational personnel in the commando organizations) Donovan was not completely "initiated" into the inner circle of Britain's SIS, he was given a rather complete picture of the workings of the British military, air, and naval intelligence organizations and their interactions with the separate independent British Counter-Intelligence Security Service. In the course of the meetings enough information about military-originated cloak and dagger operations was provided to enable Donovan to surmise the specifics of the SIS's command and control over clandestine operations.

The British intelligence leaders were careful not to overstate their case. Without directly informing Donovan about their "Ultra" capability,* they made clear their confidence to anticipate Hitler's moves in connection with the upcoming air battle for Britain. This was more than a typical "stiff upper lip" British approach in the face of adversity; it involved laying out the plusses and minuses of the situation and providing an evaluation in terms of valid intelligence acquired by human, mechanical, and electronic means. Donovan understood this kind of plain talk and came away convinced that the Americans had correctly estimated that Hitler's success was far from certain. And that, although time was short, the opportunity for the United States to provide the British with additional support to stem the Nazi tide had not passed.

Among the many meetings Donovan held with British intelligence personnel both high and low, those with General Beaumont-Nesbitt, the head of Military Intelligence, and Admiral John Godfrey, the Director of Naval Intelligence, were probably the most significant in the long run. They were carried out informally, as discussions between the parties rather than as in a briefing, strictly conveying information. After his return to the United States later that month, Donovan thanked Admiral Godfrey in a personal letter by saying, "I shall always remember most gratefully your many courtesies and kindnesses

---

*"Ultra," which Winston Churchill described as "my most secret source," refers to Britain's wartime ability in intercepting and breaking Germany's cipher systems. The story of Britain's successful cryptanalytic "attack" against Germany which enabled Churchill, Roosevelt and their top commanders to know virtually all German intentions before they were carried out (in some cases these Allied leaders were reading Hitler's orders before German generals in the field) is fully described in F.W. Winterbotham's *The Ultra Secret,* Harper and Row, 1974. Winterbotham, who was in charge of the security and dissemination of Ultra intelligence, lays out how Ultra occurred; how it functioned; the secrets it revealed; and how its existence was kept from the Germans. It is a chilling story which needs to be read in its entirety by those who think that the maintenance of communcations security is a simple or trivial exercise. It also clearly sets forth the blending of human and mechanical means to acquire valid intelligence on which the fate of a nation and its people may depend.

to me. Certainly you aided me in getting a perspective that I could not have had otherwise."*

General Beaumont-Nesbitt was able to talk with Donovan as one soldier to another, and bring him up to date not only with information about the changes in warfare occasioned by Hitler's new tactics, but more importantly on the new intelligence challenges and opportunities these tactics had created. Beaumont-Nesbitt discussed, for example, the vulnerabilities of Hitler's forces in terms of their dependence on key items of equipment to maintain their mobility. The point was made that the use of new complex war machines had changed earlier-held ideas about economic warfare in numerous new ways the British were fast learning to realize. These points were not lost on Donovan, who had first-hand knowledge concerning the U.S. Navy's difficulty in upgrading its ships with existing new technology. The term "bottleneck" was not yet in vogue; however, in subsequent discussions with Sir Desmond Morton, the Director of Britain's Industrial Intelligence Centre, it was apparent to Donovan that modern warfare had added more dimensions to intelligence than America's political and military leaders supposed.

Donovan's talks with Admiral Godfrey were perhaps more compelling, because they gave shape to the conception of American intelligence which Donovan later espoused and embraced. Among other items which tended to reinforce what Donovan had been told by the Americans, the most important, for the moment, was Godfrey's statement of position calling for full collaboration in intelligence matters with America and the establishment of direct, full-scale, two-way liaison between the intelligence services. Godfrey's overture was not lightly made and, although it had been agreed to in advance by Churchill, its actual extension reflected a measured judgment on Godfrey's part concerning Donovan the man, as opposed to simply the role of presidential emissary. If Donovan had reacted with suspicion or skepticism that Godfrey was using intelligence collaboration as a ploy to bring America into the war, his subsequent report to Roosevelt would likely kill any chance to get the war material and equipment the British so desperately needed. This kind of collaboration, aside from that agreed to between Hoover and Stephenson, was fraught with political peril.

From a consideration of Donovan's later intelligence exploits it doesn't appear that he needed much convincing; but the results of Donovan's first intelligence mission do suggest that a conversion of sorts into the intelligence "faith" did take place. On the eve of his departure, as a result of Admiral Godfrey and others' efforts, McLachlan reports,

Donovan went back convinced and enthusiastic; he spent his last evening in England with Godfrey at his home, Braddocks in Sevenoaks, where they sat up talking till the small hours.

*McLachlan, *op. cit.*, p. 227.

That the evening was fruitful was shown in a private note sent to Vice Admiral Tom Phillips, addressed from Braddocks and dated 2 August 1940: "I have just had three hours with Donovan and attach a precis of what he told me regarding his intentions on returning to USA." This was marked on 4 August to the First Sea Lord and First Lord, and on the same day Pound commented "This is very satisfactory." Churchill merely wrote three days later "Seen."*

Donovan returned to America on August 4, 1940, and the next morning reported to Secretary Knox. As word about his comments began to percolate its way through the navy's hierarchy, alarm bells were sounded out of fear that Kirk's and Lee's candor might produce an administration "flap," if not one in Congress. What probably prevented that outcome was Donovan's failure to file a written "trip report"; instead he gave Knox an oral briefing concerning what he had learned and concluded.

On August 9, Donovan and Knox journeyed to the summer White House at Hyde Park to report the mission's results. From there, Donovan and Knox accompanied President Roosevelt and Secretary of Commerce Harry Hopkins by train to Portsmouth, New Hampshire. There is no transcript of the several discussions between the principals which took place on their overnight train ride. The first involved all four men, during which Donovan reported essentially what he had told Knox a few days earlier concerning his assessment of Britain's staying power. The second, after Roosevelt retired, dealt with the problem of Ambassador Kennedy and the questions about the feasibility and methods, as well as the actual capability, of the United States to provide the requested weapons and equipment. The last, between Donovan and Hopkins —which continued until daybreak—is a conversation lost to history. Its specifics are probably not too important; it is reasonable to conclude that Hopkins used the opportunity to test and measure Donovan's sincerity of purpose and to make a judgment about whether to bring him into the inner circle of power. Although Donovan had some access to President Roosevelt as a result of their personal relationship and through the agency of Knox and Stimson, this was insufficient to guarantee him membership in the inner circle of actual political power over which Harry Hopkins presided in the name of the president. There is no way to assay Hopkins' total judgment about Donovan. Hopkins' own lines into the intelligence community confirmed the face value of Donovan's sincerity of purpose, though at the same time they confirmed the political pitfalls in tampering with existing relationships in the administration among those both in and out of the intelligence community. This is not to say that Hopkins didn't consider Donovan useful and effective; but in August 1940, Hopkins probably concluded that Donovan's ideas about intelligence were still ahead of their time.

From subsequent events and internal navy memoranda it is possible to infer

*McLachlan, *op. cit.,* p. 226.

what in essence Donovan told Roosevelt. The most accurate statement is probably McLachlan's, which summarizes the information contained in Admiral Godfrey's precis of his conversation with Donovan. McLachlan indicated that

Donovan urged the appointment of a "sensible Ambassador," who would go back and forth across the Atlantic and keep the two countries in touch; someone who could detect ways of making concessions without condescension, while insisting on and explaining prickly matters of sovereignty and protocol. Together with numerous requests for various weapons Donovan took back the suggestion of full collaboration in intelligence and access for the British to U.S. consular officers' reports, especially from French ports and North Africa. He recommended direct liaison between Godfrey and the American DNI, as well as the stating of direct and secret communications through special signal systems.*

In the American intelligence community's prolonged evaluation following the Donovan mission, the leaders were less than satisfied with the outcome. Some changes were made, but these were more cosmetic than real. The Royal Air Force's success in the Battle of Britain took some urgency out of the situation. The crisis past was sufficient reason for administration officials outside the intelligence community to direct their attention elsewhere. Some policies, like lend lease, which enabled Britain to get the war material it needed without having to pay for it on a cash and carry basis, were effected, but Donovan's suggestions about intelligence and intelligence cooperation with Britain were put on the back burner.

The intelligence professionals' hopes for an increased appreciation of the need for and utilization of intelligence in the decision-making process became a casualty to the single-mindedness exemplified in the slogan, "we must be the Great Arsenal of Democracy." Preparedness and defense became ends in themselves, and those who strove so mightily to get America "ready" paid little attention to those able to answer the implied question: "What are we actually getting ready to do?" For example, in spite of the intelligence analyses derived from the aborted fate of Hitler's Operation Sea Lion, thousands and thousands of precious man hours were spent in planning and preparing America's eastern coastal defense to repel a German amphibious invasion.

As a consequence of these planning fiascos and the almost myopic concern of the War Department "planners" with the physical problems of mobilization, the intelligence professionals regrouped and tried to get their organizations in shape to anticipate the next crisis. They operated alone and their analyses were neither welcomed nor accepted in the so-called war planning process.** The Donovan mission did result in some expanded relations be-

*McLachlan, op. cit., p. 227.

**See Julius Augustus Furer, Administration of the Navy Department in World War II. Washington: U.S. Government Printing Office, 1959, pp. 119–20. Furer notes: "The process of evaluating

tween the American and British intelligence services in England and elsewhere in Europe. And although the direct collaboration advocated by Admiral Godfrey and Donovan wasn't officially authorized, the two elements came to trust each other more and work together in a variety of ways. Elsewhere in America's intelligence community, especially in its communication intelligence organizations, the word was passed to get on with the job at all possible speed. The intelligence professionals' sense of urgency produced some increased activity, but it also produced problems in the form of personnel turbulence as the few people with extensive experience had to be shifted about to plug the holes, or direct the staffing and operations of the new and expanded organizations.

The next crisis was not long in coming. It arose almost immediately after FDR's reelection on November 2, 1940, out of a request from Churchill that U.S. Navy ships be provided to convoy British merchant ships across the Atlantic. Unlike the Battle of Britain, which the British fought alone, the United States was asked to join in the Battle of the Atlantic. The seriousness of Churchill's request was set forth in his letter to Roosevelt indicating that in the five weeks prior to November 3, British merchant ship losses reached a total of 420,300 tons.* Churchill's letter compelled Roosevelt's attention; however, it should be noted that this same information had been provided by Admiral Anderson's people in ONI to the Secretary of the Navy in the somewhat naive hope that it would reach the president.

Churchill's request prompted Roosevelt to call on Donovan once again to find out the facts. This time the situation was a bit different. Like a player in a poker game, Roosevelt had already contributed his ante in the form of lend lease, the destroyers for bases deal, etc.; now he was being called upon to add to the pot in order to protect the investment and commitment he had made to Britain's survival. The "risk-benefit" analysis of such an additional action was infinitely more complex than the earlier ones because once taken it would be difficult, if not impossible, for Roosevelt to fold his hand. No one among Roosevelt's advisers, including Knox, Stimson, and Hull, were sure how, or if, they should proceed. The navy line on this question, which essentially reflected the opinion of the Director of the War Plans Division, Rear Admiral Richmond K. Turner, held that "We'll do what we're told, but the responsibility for the decision if it goes awry won't be on our hands or heads." In spite

---

and disseminating the information contained in Intelligence reports came in for investigation and some criticism by the Joint Congressional Committee that inquired into the attack on Pearl Harbor. It was brought out during the hearings that the Director of Naval Intelligence had authority to disseminate technical, statistical, and similar information received by his Office, but that he had no authority to evaluate certain aspects of military intelligence such as developing the enemy's intentions, nor to disseminate such information and its evaluation. These were responsibilities of the War Plans Division."

*The Second World War, Sir Winston S. Churchill, 6 vols., Boston; Houghton Mifflin, 1948–53. Vol. II, p. 495.

of the "cover your backside" aspect of this view it did have some merit. At the time, the navy was going flat out in order to get the fleet prepared, and consequently its leaders were sorely pressed to undertake the magnitude of operation the convoy situation required. The navy's intelligence leaders, based upon their educated guess that Britain's communication intelligence organizations had a capability in hand which made the convoy task less dangerous than supposed, did not completely share the official wisdom. But they weren't asked, nor were their analyses of the seemingly uncanny successes of the Royal Navy considered in preparation of the "Convoy Position Papers."

Once Roosevelt gave his approval for a second Donovan mission, its preparations were carried out differently than the first. This time the stakes were considerably higher and the potential as well as real influence of Donovan on the decision-making process was acknowledged by many others besides Knox, Stimson, and the intelligence leaders. As a consequence, the military planners, especially Admiral Turner and Major General George V. Strong, head of the army's War Plans Division, became directly involved in the preparations; Roosevelt had asked Donovan, in addition to reporting on the convoy issue, to "make a strategic appreciation from an economic, political and military standpoint of the Mediterranean area."* Their involvement produced some heated debate over how the mission should be run and who should control it.

Fortunately the military planners' obstructionism didn't overly get in the way of the intelligence leaders in briefing Donovan for the mission. This occurred basically because Sir William Stephenson was, unknown to the military planners, directly involved, and was able to provide Donovan with information the American intelligence leaders were forbidden to reveal: namely, communications intelligence acquired by American intercept programs. Stephenson, who believed that Donovan's assignment constituted a genuine need-to-know clearance, added substantially to what American personnel were allowed to provide. Also, during this period Major Frederick D. Sharp, General Miles' secret liaison officer with Stephenson, kept him informed about what Donovan was and was not being told.

In London, the American intelligence staffs were tasked by Knox and Stimson not only to provide Donovan with their estimates of the situation, as they had done previously, but also to try to keep the British honest. It was believed the British might engage in a hard sell on this trip and that Donovan, where necessary, might need some countervailing arguments as well as some devil's advocate back-up support. American intelligence leaders simultaneously looked with favor and some hesitation on Donovan's mission as a two-edged sword which could be used to cut red tape but also, if they weren't careful, could create additional problems between themselves and the military planners. Both views proved to be correct.

In particular, the intelligence leaders of the U.S. Navy felt some trepidation

*War Report, *op. cit.,* p. 6.

over the mission. On the one hand, they had already concluded that the decision to convoy British merchant ships was forthcoming. On the other, they worried that the earlier rejection of the British offer for intelligence collaboration might result in their taking a tougher bargaining position which would seek to put the United States in a subordinate rather than partnership role. Their fear was that if Donovan was convinced too readily by the British arguments for convoy protection it might lead to the establishment of unacceptable conditions relevant to the sharing of intelligence information, especially from communications intercepts, control of the convoys, and the debriefing of British merchant ship masters and their crews by the U.S. Navy.

Because Donovan was presumed by Stephenson to be the most significant independent voice on these matters with access to President Roosevelt's ear, he alerted Menzies to the even greater importance of this mission than the earlier one. As Hyde notes in quoting a message drafted by Stephenson:

> Donovan exercises controlling influence over Knox, strong influence over Stimson, friendly advisory influence over President and Hull. . . . Being a Republican, a Catholic and of Irish descent, he has following of the strongest opposition to the Administration. It was Donovan who was responsible for getting us the destroyers, the bomb sight and other urgent requirements. . . . There is no doubt that we can achieve infinitely more through Donovan than through any other individual. . . . He is very receptive and should be made fully aware of our requirements and deficiencies and can be trusted to represent our needs in the right quarters and in the right way in the U.S.A.*

There probably was some verbal overkill in this message; however, it and other ones from Stephenson to Menzies produced the desired result of making sure that Donovan was given full and complete access to Britain's intelligence secrets.

Although it is only incidental to the fact and results of Donovan's second mission, the failure of its cover plan revealed how ill-prepared America was in carrying out a clandestine covert operation. During the preparations for the mission there was considerable disagreement between the War and Navy Department planners and the intelligence leaders about how the mission should be covered; that is, kept secret. All were agreed of the necessity not to draw attention to Donovan and the mission, but beyond that they got bogged down in specifics. Half a dozen proposals were considered, ranging from using a navy plane to transport Donovan to having him affect a physical disguise. The final plan, which was adopted over the intelligence leaders' and Donovan's opposition, called for him to travel incognito by commercial aircraft, pick up some War Department "observers" along the way and stay underground throughout. The intent was good, but the execution and the lack of real security in working out the details of false passports, roundabout routing, and

*Hyde, *op. cit.,* p. 44.

turning what had originally been a single-agent mission into a group-travel junket left a great deal to be desired. Too many knew about the cover plan, and once blown it was obvious that too much unofficial discussion had taken place with persons who had no genuine need to know, or no reason not to pass along gossip from one to the other.

On December 6, Donovan, traveling under the name "Donald Williams," departed from Baltimore by Pan Am clipper to London via New York, Bermuda, and Lisbon. Unfortunately, his departure and identity was established by the press, who noted that Donald Williams' baggage bore the initials "WJD" and reported "close friends" in Washington confirmed that Donovan intended to visit points in Africa, Greece, and Spain. So much for Donovan's cover. The State Department confirmed that Donovan was headed over the Atlantic on another mission, but insisted that the department knew nothing of its purpose.

How and by whom the press was alerted to Donovan's departure produced some ill feelings and accusations among those involved in planning the mission. Because the intelligence leaders and Donovan had opposed the cover plan, both were suspect. Nothing was proven, but the incident produced some additional enmity between General Strong and Donovan which was to carry over in their later relationships. As an aside to this rhubarb over Donovan's blown cover, the military planners were unable to make a clear connection between Donovan and the two passengers who boarded the plane with him in Baltimore. These men, who apparently knew Donovan, were a Monsieur Desgarges, who only much later was identified as a former French intelligence officer, and a "Mr. O'Connell," who in fact was Sir William Stephenson.

By the following day, December 7, when Donovan departed New York for Bermuda, the cat was out of the bag about "Donovan and his party" which had picked up, in addition to Desgarges and Stephenson, five U.S. Army officers. These five included Lieutenant Colonel Vernon S. Prichard, Lieutenant Colonel John C. Kennedy, Major Riley F. Ennis, Captain Bruce C. Clarke and Captain Rudolph E. Smysyer Jr. Colonel Prichard, the group's leader, as part of the original cover plan refused to discuss the purpose or destination of his group, or to allow photographs. The attempt to dissociate Prichard et al. from Donovan might have held together if the clipper had left on schedule, but due to bad weather its departure for Lisbon was delayed until December 14, by which date the cover plan had been completely exposed.

The delay was also important because it gave Stephenson a protracted opportunity to further presell Donovan on the merits of the British case and to lay out the potential vistas resulting from additional collaboration with the British on operational and intelligence matters. Although Stevenson on Stephenson in *A Man Called Intrepid* is silent on whether Stephenson told Donovan at this time about the relationship between the British SIS and the FBI, it is reasonable to infer from reports of Donovan's subsequent discussion with American intelligence personnel in London and upon his return to Washington that he did in fact become aware of its existence sometime during the period of the mission. This is mentioned here because the question of "when did Donovan know and how did he know" about the British SIS–FBI relationship bore heavily on the outcome of the battle described later in this chapter over the establishment of the Coordinator of Information's Office in mid-1941.

Finally, the Donovan mission reached London on December 15, 1940. Colonel Prichard and his group of stalwarts dispersed in accordance with their instructions to measure the actual state of the British forces. Although they were not technically a part of the Donovan mission, the military planners had inserted them into the overall equation as a means to counter Donovan's expected rose-colored outlook about the British forces. The military planners feared that the high-level treatment of Donovan was likely to produce false conclusions which would result in further diversions of military equipment to Britain at a time when it was, in their opinion, more urgently needed in the United States. One has to remember that in December 1940, the U.S. Army was smarting over the appearance of newsreel coverage which showed the new conscript army being trained with corn brooms on their shoulders in place of rifles. Also, it was intended to find out if the British, contrary to their earlier assurances, were playing fair in their stated willingness to share results of their research and development in radar, fire-control equipment, etc. The Prichard group achieved their purposes. Their report confirmed that the British Army's morale was indeed good, and training and regrouping was well underway in spite of equipment shortages. In fact, it was noted that the British Armored Division, which had left their tanks behind at Dunkirk, was carrying out training and maneuvers with five vintage tanks which had been resurrected from the British museum. On the minus side, Captain Bruce C. Clarke discovered, as a result of a cocktail party conversational slip by a British major in the Royal Engineers, that the British were developing in Scotland an advanced-type landing craft—a fact which British authorities had neglected to mention to the American attachés. Taken together, the Prichard group's report constituted a limited endorsement of Britain's feasibility as an ally. Its contents also raised the question which would be heard many times later during the war: in the planning of operations the British would be accused by Americans of being willing to supply the general if the United States would supply the troops.

Turning back to Donovan, Stephenson's advice to Menzies was completely heeded. Although Donovan was no Disraeli, the British rolled out the red carpet. Captain Kirk and General Lee met Donovan at the London train station, but the British picked up the protocol ball and whisked him and Stephenson away to the first of many high-level meetings. From thereon the American intelligence staffs were left on the outside looking in. Although Donovan kept Kirk and Lee generally informed about who he was seeing, there was little sharing of content of his various conversations and visits to secret intelligence installations. Beyond giving him access to intelligence information of the most sensitive nature, the British intelligence leaders treated Donovan as an equal.

In the next several days Donovan, who previously had correctly prophesied Britain's victory in the air battle for Britain, became convinced they would win the war. This conclusion, which Donovan publicly announced in London, went a bit beyond what his British intelligence hosts intended. They had wanted Donovan to come away with an accurate assessment of their confidence in winning, but they did not want him to conclude that the ultimate victory could be achieved easily, quickly, or without substantial American assistance. From Captain Kirk's reports to Admiral Anderson at the time of the Donovan mission, the British line was designed to avoid complicating the request for convoy support and additional military equipment with one for American combat intervention. The exception to this line was voiced, understandably, by Churchill, who told Donovan—as he had similarly been belaboring Roosevelt for the past year—about the necessity for the free world (meaning the United States and the United Kingdom) to exterminate the Nazi vermin. In their meeting on December 18, Churchill's rhetoric was, then as always, impressive, but Donovan was careful not to exceed his charter. Both men tacitly shared the view that the request for convoy assistance might turn into a pregnancy which couldn't later be aborted; however, Donovan was convinced that this was insufficient reason not to provide it.

In the week following Donovan's meeting with Churchill, the briefings and discussions with Menzies and the other intelligence leaders were even more intense. The full potential of the British Ultra capability was explained, and its significance was made clear to Donovan by inspecting the devastation of Coventry after having been told about Churchill's decision not to suggest to the Germans that the British knew of their planned air attack by taking extraordinary precautions to protect the population. This kind of a communications intelligence cause-and-effect briefing fulfilled two basic purposes. It convinced Donovan completely about the role of intelligence in modern warfare, and dramatically illustrated the lengths to which one must be prepared to go in order to maintain secrecy about sources and methods. By telling Donovan much more than he really needed to know to carry out his basic mission, the British intelligence leaders not only "hooked" Donovan on intelligence, but more importantly inflicted upon him the intelligence brotherhood's own version of Cassandra's curse, which imposes a vow of silence on those who gather and hold intelligence which flies in the face of public misrepresentation of events by persons in political office. Thus Donovan, soon to become a leader in America's intelligence community, became constrained from offering countervailing arguments to the questions "to what end and what purpose," by the intelligence community's concern for the sanctity of its sources and methods.

On December 26, under a brilliantly executed deception plan which left German agents, who had been attempting to keep Donovan under surveillance, guessing "which taxicab is carrying Donovan?" he literally vanished from London. The United States government reported him on a "private trip," but beyond that they were unable to say much more. For the next month, Donovan and his personal escort, Brigadier Vivian Dykes, one of the Assistant Secretaries to the War Cabinet who had been selected by Churchill and Menzies, went to war. No efforts were spared by Admiral Cunningham, Commander of Britain's Mediterranean Fleet, and General Wavell, Commander of British Land Forces in the area, to show Donovan how they were fighting the Nazi and Italian forces. As part of the Churchill-Menzies-Stephenson plan, Donovan was given much more than a cook's tour of the battlefronts. In addition to detailed briefings, he was informed about, and at each stop along the way observed, everything from antisubmarine operations to the posting of the famed long-range desert patrols—how the British forces were tying intelligence into their operations. This was crucial to Donovan's understanding and would later serve as the base of his arguments in the American controversy over how intelligence acquired by one agency or means could and should be shared among its various consumers. Donovan's extended reconnaissance required him to learn and remember a great deal. It was too risky for him to take or keep notes, especially about how British sources were getting intelligence from areas occupied by the Germans and Italians. However, Donovan, who was blessed with an incredible memory, did keep it all straight with a personally designed list of seemingly unrelated "cue" words which he later used in discussions with American intelligence leaders. For example, the cue words "dog trot" were used to trigger his remembrances about the command and control, operational techniques and procedures used by the long-range desert patrols. It was a good method and one which would be later employed in the training of OSS agents.

The truly incredible aspect of Donovan's second mission—from his arrival in London on December 15 to January 30, 1941, when he surfaced in Athens—is difficult to convey. It was the historically unprecedented act of opening one nation's most sensitive intelligence secrets to a foreigner—and a civilian with only limited authority at that. The significance of this action is not immediately apparent, but suffice to say that Donovan personally came to know more about Britain's intelligence operations than all but the few at the very top of its various intelligence services. At Churchill and Menzies' behest Donovan was given a detailed overview about what went on in the British intelligence services' compartments and labyrinths; an overview, one might add, which was so unique that no president of the United States or director of Central Intelligence has received a similar one about American intelligence operations. From Donovan's subsequent behavior we may conclude there was considerable method in Churchill and Menzies' apparent madness. It involved burdening Donovan with the ability to know what Britain was capable of doing and how to penetrate the mazes in America's intelligence community should the opportunity arise.

Turning back to the actual mission on January 30, Donovan appeared in

Athens whence he flew the next day to Istanbul. Preceding Donovan's departure there had been an exchange of cables between Churchill and Roosevelt commending Donovan for his "fine work" in the Middle East and suggesting an extension of his tour to include Bulgaria, Yugoslavia, and other countries in the area.* Churchill's request was greeted with some misgivings in Washington's intelligence circles. Donovan had been out of touch too long and American intelligence leaders were worried that the extension of his mission might delay them in finding out what he had learned, or agreed to support. Although Roosevelt agreed to let Donovan continue on, a bargain of sorts was struck with Admiral Anderson to allow U.S. Naval attachés "access" to Donovan in connection with the rest of his itinerary after he had seen the Bulgarian leaders in Sofia and the pro-German regent in Yugoslavia. Admiral Anderson really didn't expect his attachés to completely "debrief" Donovan in advance of his return to the United States; however, it was hoped that they could gain some forewarning about what to expect, especially on the critical issue of convoy protection and Hitler's timetable for the subjugation of the Balkans. Thus, Donovan arrived in Istanbul accompanied by Brigadier Dykes in a fighter bomber piloted by Lord Forbes, the British air attaché at the Athens legation and also senior air intelligence officer with the Royal Air Force's Middle East command. There they were met by the U.S. Naval Attaché to Turkey, Commander Richard B. Tuggle, who stayed with Donovan for the next week and then passed him along to the attaché at the next stop on the tour. Commander Tuggle's reports of his conversations with Donovan helped to clear the air at least somewhat about the convoy problem. They indicated confirmation of the navy's earlier guess that it could count on some sophisticated British communications intelligence back-up to offset their dependence on the inadequate ASDIC system used to detect submarines, and on British willingness to play fair and square on the convoy command and control problem as well as in the debriefing process. Beyond this Donovan kept his own counsel, but Tuggle's preliminary information was enough to enable naval intelligence leaders to move ahead with their own preparations. One of these, which would have great significance in the months ahead, was to order Captain Kirk back from London to replace Admiral Anderson as Director of Naval Intelligence. In the anticipated battle over intelligence it was correctly assumed by naval intelligence leaders that Kirk, who had a high degree of personal rapport with Donovan, could represent the navy's interests more effectively than Admiral Anderson.

For the next six weeks Donovan continued his peripatetic wanderings throughout the Middle East, with a side trip to London where Churchill presented him to the king. During this overt phase of his mission Donovan was careful to avoid making any statement about the United States' intentions, except for reminding the various political leaders that it was his impression

*Churchill, *op. cit.*, Vol. III, p. 24.

Hitler's side was the losing one. His message in these meetings was less a call to get on board with the British—and perhaps later the Americans—than one designed to raise doubts about the German and Italians' long-range staying power. It was a remarkable tour de diplomacy, an exercise in psychological warfare which enabled Donovan to promote not only the idea of the Axis' inevitable defeat, but also his views about the importance of the Mediterranean in World War II. According to Wayne Nelson, who authored that portion of the War Report dealing with Donovan's mission:

Donovan felt that many people were prone to think of the Mediterranean as an East-West channel for shipping. He believed it should be thought of primarily as a no-man's land between Europe and Africa, two great forces, or potential forces, facing each other from the North and South. Germany controlled either directly or indirectly most of the northern "battle line" of this front on the Continent of Europe. It was imperative in Donovan's view for the British—or the British and the Americans—to control the southern front along the Mediterranean shore of Africa."*

On March 18, 1941, Donovan returned to the United States. He had traveled in excess of 25,000 miles, talked with hundreds of persons on all levels, and acquired an unparalleled grasp of the war's realities and its challenges. Unfortunately, he knew too much; as with his first mission, there was to be no completely happy ending to this one either. On the morning of March 19, in the company of Secretary Knox, he briefed President Roosevelt in the presence of Harry Hopkins for little more than an hour. This period of time was totally inadequate to convey the full meaning and significance of what he had learned on the mission. But then as now, the White House palace guard—in this case in the person of Hopkins—acted to hoard the precious commodity known as the "president's time" for their own purposes. The impact of Donovan's conclusions and recommendations was thus greatly lessened. As a result, Donovan's shortened remarks were later damned with faint praise by others in the administration, and his ideas were put down on the spurious grounds of his being overly pro-British. It was a bum rap, and although Donovan was permitted to take to the air waves in a coast-to-coast radio speech to describe in highly sanitized terms what he had seen and concluded, the administration ascribed no real urgency to his recommendations. To be sure, the decision on convoy protection assistance was soon forthcoming, but scant credence was given to Donovan's recommendation that the United States go all out to give the British the means to attack and knock Italy out of the war.

The reasons for Roosevelt's lukewarm endorsement of his package was particularly lost on Donovan, who had become a pawn in a private game being played between Roosevelt and Churchill over how and by whom the Nazis would finally be brought to heel. This game turned on something known to

---

*War Report, *op. cit.*, p. 6n.

Churchill and communicated to Donovan and Roosevelt; valid intelligence information which confirmed Hitler's intention to attack the Soviet Union after he had consolidated his southern flank by taking over the Balkans. But at the time this was not made known to American intelligence leaders and military planners. DNI files make clear that during Donovan's briefing of Roosevelt the question of Germany's intentions was confined to the Balkans, rather than dealing with the expected subsequent attack on the Soviet Union. Although Donovan knew that Roosevelt knew, like any good intelligence officer he refrained from raising the contents of Churchill's secret intelligence in front of Secretaries Knox and Hopkins because determination of their "need to know" was not his to make. The option to raise the question of Germany versus the Soviet Union was Roosevelt's, but he chose not to do so. However, as in most elliptical intelligence discussions carried out in front of persons without a need to know, Roosevelt conveyed a signal to Donovan by mentioning that his naval aide, Captain Daniel Callaghan—whom Donovan knew to be the White House staffer entrusted with the responsibility for final decrypting and handling of sensitive intelligence information which carried the instruction "For the President's Eyes Only"—was about to be replaced by Captain John R. Beardall, USN. Donovan received Roosevelt's subtle signal "loud and clear," and in War and Navy Department debriefings which followed in the next several weeks steered clear of any mention about what Hitler was expected to do after he gained control in the Balkans.

One can only speculate about Roosevelt's motives in this matter. On the one hand, he might have distrusted Churchill's intelligence about the impending German attack, or considered it a ploy to lever the United States into providing even more support so that the British could go take the offensive against the Italians and Germans in the Middle East. On the other hand, he might have seen it, as some did after the fact, as the means to bleed the Germans to the point where they would be compelled to end the war and simultaneously weaken the Soviets. Regardless of Roosevelt's motives, one of the effects of not considering the implications of Germany's potential attack on the Soviet Union was added delay in getting the American intelligence house in order.

Although approval of convoy protection came out of the Donovan mission, the earlier and restated recommendation for full British-American intelligence collaboration was put on hold. There were so many crosscurrents involved in this decision that it's hard to pin down which one actually prevented acceptance of the idea. To be sure, the potential German attack on the Soviet Union had some bearing on the issue, but internal War and Navy Department memoranda and Hoover's animosity toward Stephenson for making secret contact with United States military intelligence services suggest that further relations with the British intelligence services were not welcome.

Following Donovan's partial put-down by administration leaders, events rapidly began to confirm his analysis of the Balkan situation. In swift order, beginning on April 6, Hitler went on the attack and the Balkan nations began to fall. Some who derived a perverse "I told you so" sense of satisfaction pointed to the fall of Greece as refutation of Donovan's stated thesis about the capability and determination of the British, and also of the Greek army's fighting ability. The arguments waxed and waned in Roosevelt's administration about what would happen next, and during this time the intelligence leaders backed off from entering the fray. It was not the time for them to either provide intelligence or advance its acceptance as a means to answer the questions. There matters rested for the next several months, during which time Donovan kept a low profile, standing up only occasionally to repeat his views about British determination and that the "moral force in wars, in the long run, is stronger than any machine."

By early June, Donovan was convinced that the intelligence he had received from Churchill et al. assaying Hitler's intent to turn his forces against the Soviet Union was correct. Also, following Roosevelt's March 25 announcement that the U.S. Navy would provide convoy protection to British merchant ships, Donovan had been receiving dismaying reports from Stephenson and some American intelligence leaders, especially Captain Kirk (by then Director of Naval Intelligence), about the difficulties involved in working out the details of the necessary intelligence cooperation between American and British authorities. It was a case of the same old story—operational types like Admiral Turner blocked successful interaction between British and U.S. Naval Intelligence, and the British liaison group in Washington and the intelligence personnel were constantly thwarted by the fact that no single voice in either the War or Navy Departments could speak with authority. Because the convoy problem involved more than the navy's role in providing ships—it also meant security of military equipment in transit from arsenals and defense plants, security during loading and preparations for departure—almost every element of the American intelligence community was in the act. And no one was in overall charge. The result was much more than a case of bureaucratic confusion; it was a counterintelligence nightmare which was compounded by the fact that the FBI, the army's Counter Intelligence Corps, the navy's counterintelligence equivalent, the Bureau of Customs, and others were all involved in counterintelligence operations without telling each other what their agents were doing.

The British were particularly distressed by all this confusion. Not only did they find it difficult to carry out convoy planning preparations, but more important, the lack of someone in charge and the obvious inept security arrangements caused them to fear for the convoys' safety. As a passing note, the British fears about the lack of security were not unfounded; after the war, during his confirmation hearings held in Executive Session with the Senate's Foreign Relations Committee, Dean Acheson stated: "During the war, documents of the greatest security, which were prepared in the War Department and were sent over to the War Production Board, we now discover in the captured files of the German Secret Service. How they got there—every single effort of the FBI and everything else has been put on this, and no results have come up."*

Donovan's concern about the sorry state of affairs arising out of the inability, or unwillingness, of the American intelligence community to cooperate with the British was quite real. He had tried twice to convince Roosevelt of the necessity for full and completely integrated intelligence collaboration, but with little success. Now this lack of intelligence collaboration threatened the safety of operations involving American ships and personnel, but to make the case he needed a plan beyond his earlier exhortations. In trying to formulate one, he directed the question "What needs to be done?" to Commander Ian Fleming, who at the time was a key officer in British Naval Intelligence and was in Washington trying to sort out the confusion over the convoy problems. In response, Fleming wrote and privately delivered a memorandum to Donovan with his thoughts on the subject.

The memorandum read as follows:

In accordance with your request, the following suggestions concerned with the obtaining of intelligence through United States sources and the cooperation of U.S. intelligence services with our own are submitted privately.

Admiral Godfrey, Director of Naval Intelligence, has seen these suggestions and concurs generally in them.

A copy of this memorandum will also be shown to Admiral Danckwerts [Head of the British Liaison Mission].

It is requested that no action may be taken on any of these suggestions referring to the SIS without prior consultation with Mr. Stephenson or without the full concurrence of his chief.

The State Department to send a circular telegram to all their diplomatic and consular posts in Axis or Axis-occupied territories, requesting information on the following subjects:

(a) State of morale (military, official, and citizen).

(b) Bomb damage (especially locality, effect on production percentage of unexploded bombs, value of new bombs).

(c) Suggested bombing targets with reasons.

(d) Health of the people and army (nutrition, hygiene, epidemics, efficiency of particular medicines, etc.).

(e) Rumours current.

(f) Efficiency of British propaganda (number of listeners, quality of reception, etc.).

(g) Military, naval, air, economic and industrial intelligence of a specific nature.

(h) Efficiency of civilian defense (fire-fighting, shelters, number of gas masks, etc).

(i) Prestige of the Party and popularity of individual Party members.

(j) Prestige of the Services and popularity of individual officers.

*Executive Sessions of the Senate Foreign Relations Committee (Historical Series), Volume II, Eighty-first Congress, First and Second Sessions, 1949–50, U. S. Government Printing Office (1976), p. 10.

(k) The main sentiments or emotions to be met with (e.g., war weariness, fear of America, hatred of Russia, etc.).

(i) Any further remarks, including observations of an apparently trivial nature.*

Beyond this laundry list of strategic intelligence requirements, Fleming further suggested that agents be selected from the existing American military intelligence services to constitute the cadre of an American SIS which would initially be trained by the British SIS. In describing the type and qualifications of these agents Fleming said, "These U.S. officers must have trained powers of observation, analysis and evaluation; absolute discretion, sobriety, devotion to duty; languages and wide experience, and be aged about 40 to 50." Also, the American SIS "should be under the protection of a strong government department and it should be insured by every means possible against political interference or control. It should be constituted for the duration of the war only. It could be associated with, but in no way controlled by, the FBI." Fleming concluded:

It is for consideration whether supreme power over the U.S. SIS should not be vested in the President, assisted by an executive committee of three non-political persons, divorced from all other duties. This committee might consist of one member from the Army, one from the Navy, and one member from business or industry.

How strongly Fleming's memo influenced Donovan's subsequent actions is hard to say. Its arguments were ones Donovan could and had previously embraced—although not to the same extent. However, the chaos in the American intelligence community was more likely the probable cause that stimulated Donovan to try one more time to get Roosevelt to act and bring some order out of that chaos. Whatever the combination of initiating factors, on June 10, 1941, after some heated and lengthy discussions with Ben Cohen and Tommy Corcoran about the intelligence situation and the preparation of several drafts, Donovan submitted a memorandum to President Roosevelt with a call to action. It read as follows:

Memorandum of Establishment of Service of Strategic Information

Strategy, without information upon which it can rely, is helpless. Likewise, information is useless unless it is intelligently directed to the strategic purpose. Modern warfare depends upon the economic base—on the supply of raw materials, on the capacity and performance of the industrial plant, on the scope of agricultural production and upon the character and efficacy of communications. Strategic reserves will determine the strength of the attack and the resistance of the defense. Steel and gasoline constitute these reserves as much as do men and powder. The width and depth of terrain occupied by the present day army exacts an equally wide and deep network of operative lines.

*McLachlan, *op. cit.,* pp. 232–34.

The "depth of strategy" depends on the "depth of armament."

The commitment of all resources of a nation, moral as well as material, constitute what is called total war. To anticipate enemy intention as to the mobilization and employment of these forces is a difficult task. General von Bernhardi says, "We must try, by correctly foreseeing what is coming, to anticipate developments and thereby to gain an advantage which our opponents cannot overcome on the field of battle. That is what the future expects us to do."

Although we are facing imminent peril, we are lacking in effective service for analyzing, comprehending, and appraising such information as we might obtain, (or in some cases have obtained), relative to the intention of potential enemies and the limit of the economic and military resources of those enemies. Our mechanism of collecting information is inadequate. It is true we have intelligence units in the Army and the Navy. We can assume that through these units our fighting services can obtain technical information in time of peace, have available immediate operational information in time of war, and on certain occasions obtain "spot" news as to enemy movements. But these services cannot, out of the very nature of things, obtain that accurate, comprehensive, long-range information without which no strategic board can plan for the future. And we have arrived at the moment when there must be plans laid down for the spring of 1942.

We have, scattered throughout the various departments of our government, documents and memoranda concerning military and naval and air and economic potentials of the Axis which, if gathered together and studied in detail by carefully selected trained minds, with a knowledge both of the related languages and techniques, would yield valuable and often decisive results.

Critical analysis of this information is as presently important for our supply program as if we were actually engaged in armed conflict. It is unimaginable that Germany would engage in a $7 billion supply program without first studying in detail the productive capacity of her actual and potential enemies. It is because she does exactly this that she displays such a mastery in the secrecy, timing and effectiveness of her attacks.

Even if we participate to no greater extent than we do now, it is essential that we set up a central enemy intelligence organization which would itself collect either directly or through existing departments of government, at home and abroad, pertinent information concerning potential enemies, the character and strength of their armed forces, their internal economic organization, their principal channels of supply, the morale of their troops and their people and their relations with their neighbors or allies.

For example, in the economic field there are many weapons that can be used against the enemy. But in our government these weapons are distributed through several different departments. How and when to use them is of vital interest not only to the Commander-in-Chief but to each of the departments concerned. All departments should have the same information upon which economic warfare could be determined.

To analyze and interpret such information by applying to it not only the experience of Army and Naval officers, but also of specialized trained research officials in the relative scientific fields, (including technological, economic, financial and psychological scholars) is of determining influence in modern warfare.

Such analysis and interpretation must be done with immediacy and speedily transmitted to the intelligence services of those departments which, in some cases, would have been supplying the essential raw materials of information.

But there is another element in modern warfare, and that is the psychological attack against the moral and spiritual defenses of a nation. In this attack the most powerful weapon is radio. The use of radio as a weapon, though effectively employed by Germany, is still to be perfected. But this perfection can be realized only by planning, and planning is dependent upon accurate information. From this information action could be carried out by appropriate agencies.

The mechanism of this service to the various departments should be under the direction of a Coordinator of Strategic Information who would be responsible directly to the President. This Coordinator could be assisted by an advisory panel consisting of the Director of FBI, the Directors of the Army and Navy Intelligence Service, with corresponding officials from other governmental departments principally concerned.

Much of the personnel would be drawn from the Army and Navy as well as other departments of the government. The proposed centralized unit will neither displace nor encroach upon the FBI, Army and Navy Intelligence, or any other department of the government.

The basic purpose of this Service of Strategic Information is to constitute a means by which the President, as Commander-in-Chief, and his Strategic Board would have available accurate and complete enemy intelligence reports upon which military operational decisions could be based.

In response to Donovan's memo, Roosevelt named a committee of Cabinet members including Stimson, Knox, and Attorney General Jackson to review the memo and recommend a plan of action. This was a typical bureaucratic response which ended by dividing and not deciding. Once the principals passed the Donovan memo on to their subordinates for comment, the bureaucratic in-fighting became intense. Although it is somewhat inaccurate to say that the army and navy opposed Donovan's concept, there were enough key persons in both services who felt threatened by its implications to attack it and Donovan personally. The intelligence leaders again stayed discreetly out of the squabble, having been neither asked to comment or discuss how the plan, if adopted, should be implemented. In the forefront of opposition to Donovan's plan was J. Edgar Hoover. He had little objection to receiving what others might provide, but he was adamantly opposed to the reciprocity of information implied in Donovan's memo, or anything which suggested someone other than he be given authority to direct or otherwise control the FBI's intelligence-gathering assets.

The attitudes of Hoover and the military leaders produced an impasse over the Donovan memo. However, on June 22, when after achieving total tactical and strategic surprise and knocking out most of the Soviet air force on the ground, Hitler invaded the Soviet Union, it was an entirely new ball game. There is nothing like crisis to compel American political leaders to end their procrastination on questions which should be decided on their merit or logic, but rarely are. In this case, the German attack, with its lightning speed and astounding success, indicated a situation in which the problems of intelligence could not be resolved by an on-again, off-again "cooperation" with the British intelligence services. Almost for the first time since the war had started did those who had downplayed the importance of intelligence come to realize that they were flying blind in the face of a very real disaster. Their acceptance of this view was not based on some latter-day conversion to the ideas embodied in Donovan's reports and memos, but rather on the self-evident fact that if Hitler acquired control over the physical, mineral, and petroleum resources of the Soviet Union it would be well-nigh impossible to stop him anyplace this side of the Rio Grande.

The chaotic intelligence situation was forcefully demonstrated by the fact that the British, even with their Ultra capability, were unable to provide an accurate assessment of the German forces' progress. The United States had no trained military eyes in the Soviet Union, having long since given up on placing military attachés there, and therefore Roosevelt and his advisors were reduced to listening to German claims of success to know how the war was actually proceeding. All these facts came together to force consideration of America's intelligence situation. As a consequence, Roosevelt declared the bureaucratic paper war over Donovan's memo ended, and directed him to draft a Military Order embodying its basic proposals and recommendations. Without conceding final defeat, the military obstructionists bided their time and awaited their chance to have at Donovan's Military Order draft. He didn't make them wait too long; on June 25 his handiwork was circulated for "comment" among the State, War, and Navy Departments. The draft read as follows:

Military Order
Designating a Coordinator of Strategic Information

By virtue of the authority vested in me as President of the United States and as Commander-in-Chief of the Army and Navy of the United States, it is ordered as follows:

1. There is hereby established the position of Coordinator of Defense Intelligence, with authority to collect and analyze information and data, military or otherwise, which may bear upon national defense strategy; to interpret and correlate such strategic information and data, and to make it available to the President and to such other officials as the President may determine; and to carry out, when requested by the President, such supplementary activities as may facilitate the securing of strategic information not now available to the Government.

2. The several departments and agencies of the Government shall make available to the Coordinator of Strategic Information such information and data relating to national defense strategy as the Coordinator, with the approval of the President, may from time to time request.

3. The Coordinator of Strategic Information may appoint such committees, consisting of appropriate representatives of the various departments and agencies of the Government, as he may deem necessary to assist him in the performance of his functions.

4. The Coordinator of Strategic Information shall perform these duties and responsibilities, which include those of a military character, under the direction and supervi-

sion of the President as Commander-in-Chief of the Army and Navy of the United States.

5. Within the limits of such funds as may be allocated to the Coordinator of Strategic Information by the President, the Coordinator may employ necessary personnel and make provisions for the necessary supplies, facilities, and services.

6. William J. Donovan, United States Army, is hereby designated as Coordinator of Strategic Information.

This draft Military Order produced even more opposition, especially from the army, than had the earlier memorandum. Wisely, Donovan decided to divide and conquer; the draft, which was almost completely military in nature, left J. Edgar Hoover content in the belief that his domain was intact. Both the army and navy objected to the draft because it appeared to usurp some of their basic functions. There was wry humor in these objections because, as the intelligence leaders noted to one another, the army and navy's intelligence divisions, which had been treated like unwanted stepchildren by the "planners and commanders," were now considered too important to be given over to Donovan's foster home for intelligence personnel. It was a time during which many egos were bruised and unfortunately, although he was totally circumspect throughout, a great deal of personal enmity was directed toward Donovan by military leaders who were unsure of their own futures.

The final draft of July 11 reflected acceptance of the military leaders' opposition. It deleted the reference to "Coordinator of Defense Intelligence" and substituted the ambiguous but benign term "Coordinator of Information." Also, William J. Donovan lost all reference to a relationship with the United States Army. The issue was further complicated by not calling the order either an Executive or Military Order. It read as follows:

Designating a Coordinator of Information

By virtue of the authority vested in me as President of the United States and as Commander in Chief of the Army and Navy of the United States, it is ordered as follows:

1. There is hereby established the position of Coordinator of Information, with authority to collect and analyze all information and data, which may bear upon national security; to correlate such information and data, and to make such information and data available to the President and to such departments and officials of the Government as the President may determine; and to carry out, when requested by the President, such supplementary activities as may facilitate the securing of information important for national security not now available to the Government.

2. The several departments and agencies of the Government shall make available to the Coordinator of Information all and any such information and data relating to national security as the Coordinator, with the approval of the President, may from time to time request.

3. The Coordinator of Information may appoint such committees, consisting

of appropriate representatives of the various departments and agencies of the Government, as he may deem necessary to assist him in the performance of his functions.

4. Nothing in the duties and responsibilities of the Coordinator of Information shall in any way interfere with or impair the duties and responsibilities of the regular military and naval advisers of the President as Commander in Chief of the Army and Navy.

5. Within the limits of such funds as may be allocated to the Coordinator of Information by the President, the Coordinator may employ necessary personnel and make provision for the necessary supplies, facilities, and services.

6. William J. Donovan is hereby designated as Coordinator of Information.

(Signed) Franklin D. Roosevelt

J. Edgar Hoover referred to the July 11 designation of Coordinator of Information as "Roosevelt's folly," and made it clear to Sir William Stephenson that nothing therein altered their prior arrangement, and that he, Hoover, was still the single point of contact between the American and British intelligence services. Hoover made it clear that if the informal liaison Stephenson had established with the army and navy included passing any information about FBI operations and/or those of the British Security Coordination office, their relationship would be ended. Stephenson agreed; he had no other alternative. However, unknown to Hoover, during the period between June 10, when Donovan submitted his initial memo, and July 11, when he was designated Coordinator of Information, Admiral Godfrey, the British Director of Naval Intelligence, had met with President Roosevelt and was able to get his tacit approval to begin the kind of intelligence collaboration previously advocated by Donovan. Although the collaboration which resulted fell short of that envisioned by Ian Fleming between the British SIS and an American SIS, it did have the salutary effect of increasing the number of American intelligence personnel in England more than sixfold. Protocol prevented giving these additional officers the diplomatic status of attaché; consequently they were sent to England as "observers." Once there, the observers were easily integrated into the British system, taking up desks in the offices of both the British Naval and Military Intelligence organizations. The results of this collaboration were outstanding and the officers concerned proved apt pupils. In Washington, however, the lingering animosity of the military planners/commanders toward Donovan prevented Captain Kirk and General Miles from colocating British personnel in American offices. In spite of this, an increasing amount of intelligence information did begin to flow between the British mission in Washington and American intelligence services. The separation of personnel made for a lot of running back and forth, but it was better than the chaotic situation which had preceded it.

Meanwhile Donovan, who had his designation as Coordinator of Information and not much else, was faced with the horrendous chore of putting together a new, unwanted, neither-fish-nor-fowl organization. Since the advent of the New Deal, this has become a not uncommon feature in government; but it's never easy, and in the case of the Coordinator of Information's office the difficulties were much more severe than, for example, those associated with the WPA. New organizations do not spring up full blown out of the bureaucratic womb complete with people, office space, and all the things needed to carry out their mission. People, which are the most difficult to get, must be begged, borrowed, and stolen from other departments and agencies, and the Civil Service must be cajoled, if not conned, into granting "clearances" and exemptions to the government's hiring procedures.

Donovan was more than equal to the challenge of breathing life into the Coordinator of Information's office. His basic approach, which today stands almost as a classic model in how to create a new government agency, was premised on the need to get the right people for key positions—without regard for their political predilections or party registrations—delegate authority to them, and thereby force positive decisions on their part. Coupled with this latter feature, Donovan avoided interposing committee reviews between himself and his line operators. The mix of people Donovan personally recruited in the first several months of the OCI's operations reflected the breadth of vision set forth in his June 10 memorandum. Those who became committed to sharing Donovan's dream included: Robert E. Sherwood, the noted playwright, who agreed to take on the job of organizing and directing the COI's propaganda functions; Archibald MacLeish, Librarian of Congress, who agreed to the establishment of a research organization called the Division of Special Information in the library and detailed persons from the library's staff to work for the COI;* Elmo Roper, the pollster, who agreed to take on the

---

*Illustrative of the nonbureaucratic ways in which Donovan negotiated with elements in the government to gain their assistance for the COI is the agreement with Archibald MacLeish. Donovan neither sought the "advice and consent" of the Congress, nor informed that separate and equal branch of government about the agreement. Their agreement read as follows:

Coordinator of Information
Washington, D.C.

July 30, 1941

Mr. Archibald MacLeish
Library of Congress
Washington, D.C.

Dear Mr. MacLeish:

There is outlined below the services which it is my understanding the Library of Congress will furnish to the Office of Coordinator of Information.

The Library of Congress agrees to set up a division to be known as the Division of Special Information which will undertake the services hereinafter specified. The Office of the Coordinator of Information will constitute the sole client of the Division and the Division's sole function will be to furnish the information requested by the Coordinator. The reference material and information prepared or held in the custody of the Division will be available

task of planning the COI's organization and overseeing its internal management; Thomas G. Earley, Secretary of the Civil Aeronautics Board, who with his knowledge of the bureaucratic ways and pitfalls in Washington was per-

only to the Office of the Coordinator except as permission is specifically given for other uses by the Coordinator or his authorized representative.

The Library of Congress, through the Division of Special Information, undertakes to perform the following functions:

1. To index all available relevant material in the field of foreign affairs. This index shall be both regional and functional, and shall include such cross-indexing as will serve to coordinate it with indexes and files of designated government agencies. The indexes shall include at least the following:

(a) A panel of experts and consultants within and outside the government, together with their appropriate fields. Full use shall be made of the Civil Service Commission Roster in this connection. It would be desirable to have the data appearing in the panel include the information which the Coordinator's personnel officer would require in the selection and engagement of personnel.

(b) Books, articles, documents, and special collections in libraries throughout the country.

(c) Research in progress within and outside the government.

(d) Existing memoranda, indexes and manuscripts within and outside the government.

(e) Maps.

2. The Division of Special Information will undertake to prepare memoranda concerning probable and possible problems of a strategic character which may arise in foreign affairs. It will also build up biographical data on key men in public and military affairs in foreign nations. Care will be taken to see that this does not duplicate existing biographies in other government agencies. The selection of and priority accorded to subjects shall be approved by the Office of the Coordinator.

3. The Division of Special Information will set up and maintain an index of policy declarations in the defense and international fields made by the President, Congress and responsible members of the Executive. Such declarations of policy as may be relevant may be included in an appendix to each memorandum.

4. The Division of Special Information will undertake the preparation of background materials, as follows:

(a) In connection with its indexing, it will endeavor to locate existing background materials within and outside the government.

(b) It will prepare comprehensive memoranda related to problems likely to emerge in the order of precedence determined by the Coordinator.

(c) It will organize reference files which will include articles, clippings, etc., from American and foreign periodicals, releases from governments in exile, propaganda material, foreign material, etc.

5. Members of the staff of the Division of Special Information shall prepare specific memoranda analyzing specific problems as requested by the Coordinator or his representative.

It is agreed that the approval of both the Coordinator, or his representative, and the Librarian, or his representative, shall be a prerequisite for appointments. The Chief of the Division of Research and Analysis in the Office of the Coordinator of Information will forward to the Librarian of Congress, with my approval, recommendations for all appointments of a professional grade.

The Division of Special Information shall be organized into such regional and functional sections as the Coordinator or his representative shall approve. The reports and other informational materials from these sections shall be submitted for final analysis to a Board of Analysts reporting directly to the Coordinator.

suaded to assume responsibility for the COI's administrative functions; Dr. James Phinney Baxter III, the historian and President of Williams College, who was lured from academe to head the COI's Research and Analysis Branch

---

The Board of Analysts will draw upon all sources of information in and out of the government for its purposes, calling on the Division of Special Information for help with a wide range of problems. To facilitate the submission of such problems, one member of the Board of Analysts will act as Director of Research for the Division of Special Information. The administrative direction of the Division of Special Information, in so far as matters of personnel, equipment, and usual administrative routines are concerned, will be placed in the hands of an officer of the Library, who will be requested to assume these additional burdens.

The effect of the scheme of organization outlined above will be to place in the Division of Special Information in the Library of Congress, as the heads of sections of that Division, specialists in the various geographic areas, having a very high degree of competence—having, in fact, the highest degree of competence provided by American scholarship. These specialists, although reporting to the Coordinator of Information through the Board of Analysts, will actually possess special qualifications not represented on the Board and will therefore, from time to time, appear before the Board and sit with it in its deliberations.

Major items of furniture including desks, files, chairs, tables, typewriters, and a mimeograph machine are to be procured by the Office of the Coordinator and loaned to the Library without expense to the latter. All other items of supplies are to be procured by the Library and are to be a charge upon the amount specified for contingencies. The Library of Congress shall provide for photostating at cost, and this shall be charged to the contingency item. The Library of Congress shall provide for telephone service at cost, and this shall be charged to the contingency item.

Costs of any structural alterations or construction which may be necessary for the Division of Special Information will be borne by the Office of the Coordinator of Information. Where duplicate reference books, maps, atlases, etc., are required for the use of the Division of Special Information in quantities which the Library cannot supply without injury to its services to the Congress, etc., funds for purchase will be supplied by the Office of the Coordinator.

As payment for the above outlined services, it is understood between us that an initial sum of $75,000 will be transferred to the Library forthwith for expenditure prior to September 30, 1941. The Library will be free to make commitments on an annual basis prior to the end of the first quarter, i.e., September 30, 1941, in general accord with the schedules accompanying the estimate for appropriations which was submitted by your organization to the Bureau of the Budget on July 27, 1941.

It is obvious that in an operation of this nature and the articulation of the Division of Special Information with the Office of the Coordinator of Information now being evolved, a number of changes undoubtedly will be required, as experience indicates. Moreover, because of the nature of the undertaking, I am presuming that in the progress of our work it may be desirable to have the Coordinator's office absorb certain personnel and their functions now provided for in your budget. In such event, it is assumed an appropriate financial adjustment will be made in the amount available to the Library.

We both realize, I believe, that the earlier stages of gathering and indexing the information sought, will require a larger staff than probably will be needed after the division has accumulated the data already known to be available. It is also recognized that it is impractical at this time to set the duration of the period during which the Division of Special Information will render the services outlined. When the time comes to make advisable adjustments, I feel confident that we can count upon an understanding of the mutual nature of the problem.

I cannot write such a letter as this without simultaneously expressing my personal appreciation for your willingness to provide the services outlined and the individual cooperative spirit you and your staff have indicated in this joint undertaking.

with the promise that he and the scholars whom Baxter was expected to recruit would in no way be constrained in their research by previously determined conclusions, or administration cant.

Donovan's lieutenants only needed to be pointed in the right direction; each was a self-starter and moved ahead at a speed which left the bureaucracy amazed. While the actions of his key subordinates were underway, Donovan, who recognized the crippling effects of trying to achieve "bureaucratic coordination" while carrying out new and unfamiliar work, moved to get his own personal coordinator. On August 13, Donovan wrote to Secretary Knox requesting the temporary detachment of James Roosevelt, then a reserve major on active duty with the marines, to COI. By August 23, James Roosevelt was the COI's liaison officer, and in this role—without excessive use of his father's name—made it clear to the various departments that to get along with the White House they had better go along with Donovan and the COI.

James Roosevelt's liaison efforts opened many doors and produced the kind of cooperation with the intelligence services Donovan so urgently needed. For example, liaison between the navy and COI was initially established under the Administrative Branch of ONI, and Commander R. E. Webb was appointed administrative liaison officer to COI. Webb came to be known as Donovan's "dog robber" who could be counted upon to come up with a crypto machine, a PT-boat or an unmarked car to meet the COI's esoteric and exotic requirements. In September 1941, Lt. Commander A. D. Chandler became the navy-COI operations liaison officer, and by October 6 he had located eleven naval and two marine corps officers who, after late-night interviews with Donovan, were detached by Captain Kirk to serve with COI. In late October, after Chandler had been selected for a clandestine operation, he was replaced by Lt. Commander Riheldaffer, USNR, and the navy's liaison with COI/OSS was placed under the Special Intelligence Section, where it remained throughout the war. Riheldaffer, who became known as Donovan's one-man "press gang," was one of the silent heroes of World War II. At Donovan's request he was able to find and recruit from the navy and marines whomever COI/OSS needed, whether they happened to have formerly been a member of the Detroit "Purple Gang," or a second-generation German-American who was serving on an oiler in the South Pacific and whose grandparents were living near Peenemunde.

If the above outline is in accord with your interpretation of our agreement, will you kindly sign the copy enclosed herewith and return to me.

Very truly yours,
/s/ William J. Donovan
William J. Donovan
Coordinator of Information

Accepted and Approved
/s/ A. MacLeish
Librarian

During the early months that Donovan was breathing life into the COI, he avoided moving into the secret intelligence field. His first priority was to establish some regularity and an analytical method to handle the flow of intelligence information and turn it into usable intelligence. Some, like Wayne Nelson, believed that this decision was based on Donovan's view that providing finished intelligence in a usable form for policy makers was initially more important than dealing with secret intelligence operations. Nonetheless, in order to insure the military services' cooperation with the COI, Donovan did move to get into the secret intelligence business. This was a much more tricky operation than that of interposing COI into the intelligence information flow and process. As such, it required Donovan to convince the military intelligence leaders and their operational mentors that their secret intelligence activities were better carried out under the COI's ambiguous charter which allowed Donovan "to carry out, when requested by the President, [such] supplementary activities," and that they were individually and collectively vulnerable to disclosure about their services' previous secret activities which had been carried out without the White House's knowledge or approval.

In bringing the military services' unauthorized, clandestine, and illegal intelligence activities under the protection of the COI's "charter," Donovan displayed all the strategems of a trial lawyer. Armed with information provided him by Stephenson and favorably disposed persons in the army and navy's intelligence services, he confronted General Marshall and Admiral Stark with the facts about the sub-rosa illegal activities underway in their respective services. He was quick to add that while these activities were necessary and worthwhile they were scarcely defensible—in public or at the White House— by persons in the military's high command. It was a classic confrontation. Neither Marshall nor Stark were aware of the full extent of these activities, but they were sensitive to Donovan's arguments that it would be wiser on their part to get them out of the military's direct line of responsibility and accountability.

As a consequence of these and others discussions in the military hierarchy, on September 5 the army capitulated to Donovan's arguments in a memorandum from General Miles to General Marshall. It read as follows:

Memorandum for the Chief of Staff

Subject: Undercover Intelligence Service.

1. The military and naval intelligence services have gone into the field of undercover intelligence to a limited extent. In view of the appointment of the Coordinator of Information and the work which it is understood the President desires him to undertake, it is believed that the undercover intelligence of the two services should be consolidated under the Coordinator of Information. The reasons for this are that an undercover intelligence service is much more effective if under one head rather than three, and that a civilian agency, such as the Coordinator of Information, has distinct

advantages over any military or naval agency in the administration of such a service.

2. In the event or the immediate prospect of any military or naval operations by United States forces in any part of the world, however, the armed forces should have full power to organize and operate such undercover intelligence services as they may deem necessary.

3. The Coordinator of Information has indicated in conference that he is prepared to assume the responsibilities indicated in Par. 1 above.

4. A memorandum similar to this is being submitted to the Chief of Naval Operations by the Director of Naval Intelligence.

5. *Action recommended.*

That the Secretary of War approve the recommendations contained in Pars. 1 and 2, above, so far as the War Department is concerned.

Sep. 6, 1941
APPROVED

By Order of the Secretary of War
      G. C. MARSHALL   /s/SHERMAN MILES
        Chief of Staff

                                    SHERMAN MILES
        by /s/ W. B. SMITH   Brigadier General, U. S. Army
    Col., G. S. C., Sec. W. D. G. S.   Acting Assistant Chief of Staff, G-2.
    NOTED—CHIEF OF STAFF   Noted by Sec. War 9/9/41
             W.B.S.   E.H.B.

The navy, hoping to retain control over the operations run in New York by Wallace Phillips, held out a while longer. However, Donovan was finally able to convince Captain Kirk and Admiral Stark that their greater course of wisdom lay in giving over their secret intelligence operations to COI by the simple expedient of having Vincent Astor tell them it was costing too much. Astor's remarks were made with the clear implication that unless the navy accepted Donovan's "offer," it might be necessary for him to bring the navy's secret operations to the attention of President Roosevelt. As a result, a memorandum similar to the one Miles sent to Marshall was sent from Captain Kirk to Admiral Stark; and on October 10, Donovan acknowledged their acceptance of his terms by sending a memorandum to the White House indicating that COI had assumed responsibility for the military services' secret intelligence operations:

Coordinator of Information
Washington, D.C.

Memorandum for The President.

From: The Coordinator of Information.

By joint action of the Military and Naval Intelligence Services there was consolidated under the Coordinator of Information the undercover intelligence of the two services. In their memorandum the reasons stated for the action are:

1. That such a service is much more effective under one head rather than three, and

2. A civilian agency has distinct advantages over any military or naval agency in the administration of such a service.

This consolidation has been approved by the Secretary of War and the Secretary of the Navy.

In making this consolidation effective, it is necessary to do the following:

1. Send to a given country a man who is essentially an organizer. The function of this man would be to set up agents of information who would be able to supply him with information:

    (a) During the period that our diplomatic corps is accredited to that country; and

    (b) To be in a position to continue sending reports in event diplomatic relations are severed.

Vital considerations in making this plan effective are security and communications. Therefore, it will be necessary for our representative to have:

    (a) Status for his protection;

    (b) Use of the diplomatic pouch;

    (c) Establishment of a line of communications, both by radio and other means, that will endure after the particular country has been closed to us diplomatically.

As a concrete illustration of what can be done, we are now planning to deal with a very present problem in North Africa by setting up at once a wireless station in Tangier and having stationed there an assistant Naval or Military Attache who can unify the activities of the Vice-Consuls in North Africa and stimulate efforts in the selection of local agents of information.

/s/ W. J. Donovan

Because the navy's secret intelligence operations were basically carried out by civilian employees, it was simpler to fold them into the COI's organization than were those carried out by the army, which included a mix of civilians and military personnel. From the onset Donovan made it clear to the military services that he was the man in charge. For example, in an October 12 memorandum to Phillips he said:

I have gone over your memorandum. The set-up you have does not conform in all respects to what I have in mind.

FIRST: I want you to be in charge of intelligence as distinct from operations. The operations I will have headed up separately. The functions are distinct.

SECOND: The Planning Committee must stem from the Coordinator. On it will be not only yourself and such other administrative officers who would naturally be placed there, but I would want on it too those representing an outside perspective.

THIRD: Communications must be entirely separate.

FOURTH: Codes likewise separate.

While operations and intelligence are distinct I would want you, in sending intelligence officers, at the same time to take over the additional function of setting up those individuals in the particular countries, who would be used subsequently under the operations officer.

As to the individuals you named, I know most of them and would want to discuss them with you.

WJD

Although some military leaders in the War and Navy Departments were miffed over Donovan's tactics in gaining control of their undercover intelligence operations, they were also relieved by the fact that those operations would continue and be paid for out of Donovan's unvouchered funds.* As both General Miles and Captain Kirk knew, their organizations' prior undercover activities had been carried out on, at best, very shaky legal grounds, and they held further fears that Congress and/or the White House might inadvertently discover that although unvouchered funds had paid for some of these activities public funds had also been spent on other than intended purposes.

By mid-October 1941 Donovan had his basic structure in place. Intelligence information began to flow from the various intelligence organizations into and through COI to the White House and thence back to its natural consumers; plans were underway to expand overseas operations. It was a hectic time, during which the COI's expansion resulted in Donovan's rapidly increasing band's having to take up fleeting residence in half a dozen locations in Washington. In spite of the fact that if one missed a day at work it might take two to find out where the office had been moved, no one seemed to unduly mind the confusion. Donovan's spirit kindled in most the same kind of zeal which imbued the early New Dealers. Their shared attitude reflected Donovan's belief that it was important and challenging work and they plunged into it wholeheartedly.

---

*As Kermit Roosevelt notes, one of the undercover intelligence operations was "The North African Operation which had begun before the existence of COI, and was under the direction of Robert D. Murphy, who had been chargé d'affaires in Vichy and was subsequently ambassador to Belgium and Japan. It derived from the conclusion of the Weygand-Murphy Accord in February 1941, under which the U.S. had agreed to send certain essential materials and supplies to North Africa on condition that they be used there and not reshipped to Europe, where they might benefit the Axis. It was understood also that the U.S. would send to French North Africa certain officials to see that this proviso was not disregarded. In the spring of 1941, twelve control officers were selected by G-2, State Department and ONI. They were dispatched in the summer of 1941 to be stationed in Casablanca, Algiers, Oran, Tunis and Rabat. The career officers already in these cities did not know the real purpose of the control officers, however, and the new group was actually responsible to Murphy in Algiers. . . . When he [Donovan] was instructed to consolidate the undercover intelligence of Army G-2, Office of Naval Intelligence and COI in October of 1941, he already had a plan prepared. Its principal feature was the dispatch of a COI representative to Tangier who would unify the activities of the Vice Consuls and 'stimulate' their efforts. This representative would be supported by additional COI personnel. He would also establish a clandestine radio network which could continue to operate in the event of a break in diplomatic relations." (See Walker version of the "War Report," pp. viii–ix.) Also, see Chapter 4, "The World War II Struggle for Intelligence Control," for a discussion about how Donovan actually implemented his North African plan.

A fallout effect from COI's early effectiveness in energizing the government's intelligence process was that it revealed deficiencies in the separate organizations' procedures. As the War Report notes:

The policy of cloaking in vagueness the true purposes of COI in the authorizing order of 11 July was beginning to boomerang as operations got under way and inevitably COI began to come into real or imagined conflict with other departments and agencies. Donovan's memorandum to the President of 21 October remarked, "while originally we both considered it advisable to have no directive in writing, it now seems necessary to do so to avoid misunderstanding with other departments."*

Although the bureaucratic inertia Donovan encountered was bothersome and produced unnecessary delays, it did not deter him from pressing ahead to get an organized intelligence system in place. Donovan's sense of urgency was contagious. It permeated the COI staff; as its members went forward to do battle in the government's bureaucratic fiefdoms, the results were often remarkable. Donovan's principal deputy, Edward Buxton,** was particularly adept around the conference table through his judicious use of "Why not?," which compelled his opponents to remove the red tape surrounding clearance of persons, acquisitions of space, materials, etc. During those last fateful months before Pearl Harbor, Donovan acted throughout as if he knew, or had reason to believe, that war was soon to come. And when it did, on December 7, 1941, Donovan had in place the cadre of an intelligence organization*** which, in addition to its wartime exploits of derring-do, was to become the catalyst as well as the inhibitor in the subsequent wartime evolution of America's loose confederation of intelligence services and interests into an intelligence community, although one still without effective central direction.

*War Report, *op. cit.,* p. 15.

**Buxton, a New England business and newspaper executive, had an outstanding record in World War I. He became assistant coordinator in the spring of 1942; with the establishment of OSS he became assistant director, in which position he remained until July 1945, when he resigned because of ill health.

***In addition to the key persons already mentioned, Donovan secured the services of William D. Whitney, a former Rhodes Scholar and New York lawyer, to represent COI in London and to maintain liaison with the British intelligence services there. Also, Donovan persuaded Atherton Richards, a business executive, to take charge of the COI's Visual Presentation Branch.

CHAPTER 4

THE WORLD WAR II STRUGGLE FOR INTELLIGENCE CONTROL

On Sunday morning, December 7, 1941, Japanese aircraft attacked American military and naval installations at Pearl Harbor, Hawaii. In the surprise engagement which lasted approximately two hours, 19 ships were sunk or disabled; about 150 planes were destroyed; 2,335 soldiers and sailors were killed, and 68 civilians perished. In rapid order the Japanese seized Guam (December 13) and Wake Island (December 22). Manila and Cavite fell to the Japanese on January 2. After a seige of more than three months Bataan collapsed (April 19) and American forces withdrew to Corregidor Island, where 11,500 surrendered (May 6) to the Japanese. Each of these tragic events underscored the ineffectiveness of America's intelligence efforts.

Although the disaster at Pearl Harbor and those that followed constituted serious military reverses, they did produce some salutary effects on a national level. Overnight the nation became unified, and the isolationists who had opposed America's involvement in the wars in Europe and Asia had no choice: they rushed to the defense of their country. The resolution of President Roosevelt's question—how to aid the Allies, whose survival was essential to the survival of America—was effectively mooted by the Japanese surprise attack on Pearl Harbor and by Hitler's subsequent declaration of war on the United States on December 11, 1941.*

---

*Theories abound to explain Hitler's declaration of war on the United States; however, none adequately explains why Hitler precipitously abandoned his plan to keep America neutral as long as possible. (See especially United States Office of the United States Chief Counsel for Prosecution of Axis Criminality: Volume V, Nazi Conspiracy and Aggression, Washington 1946–1948.) Some vaguely suggest conspiracies in Washington, London, and Berlin, yet no definitive hard intelligence exists to support these views, or that Hitler himself felt compelled to aid the Japanese because by attacking Pearl Harbor Japan had in effect nullified the mutual support provisions in the Tripartite Pact between Germany, Italy, and Japan which was signed at Berlin on September 27, 1940, or that Hitler felt overly threatened and/or angered by British and American successes in the Battle of the Atlantic.

Perhaps the most bizarre unofficial "explanation" for Hitler's action is included in an apocryphal, unsubsantiated story which alleges that at the moment of Pearl Harbor, Colonel "Bertie" McCormick, publisher of the *Chicago Tribune,* who was in London after a meeting with Hitler, was carrying a letter from the Fuehrer to President Roosevelt which included a warning about

Once the aftershocks from both the Japanese and Hitler's actions had been absorbed, the isolationists who had immediately rallied round the flag began to suspect that errors and blunders were not responsible for these actions; rather, they were due to some malevolent conspiracy hatched by President Roosevelt which had been aided and abetted by the military high command and its intelligence organizations. Like conspiracy theories concerning other wars and national tragedies (such as presidential assassinations) the one about the origins of the Pacific War and Hitler's war declaration was fed by incomplete, partial, and ambiguous answers to unanswerable questions, and the willingness of those who cannot accept the idea of their personal culpability in matters of national importance to believe the worst about their public officials.

Even today, after investigations have been carried out, both secretly and openly, by seven different boards within the military services during and after hostilities, the Joint Congressional Committee on the Investigation of the Pearl Harbor Attack* and the effluvia from wartime reminiscences and memoirs of

---

the contemplated Japanese attack. The story further alleges that McCormick was delayed in his departure from England by unidentified high-level British officials who had knowledge about the letter and the Japanese plans for the attack. Although no hard evidence exists to support this story, approaches have, over the years, been made to American intelligence officials by nondescript individuals—known in the intelligence trade as "paper mills"—attempting to peddle a copy of the purported Hitler letter. None of these approaches has resulted in anything positive, though the story reappears from time to time and as such is part of the conspiracy folklore concerning the start of World War II.

*United States Congress, Pearl Harbor Attack, Hearings Before the Joint Committee on the Investigation of the Pearl Harbor Attack, 79th Congress, 2nd Session, Public Document #79716, Washington, 1946, 39 volumes. The committee began its work early in September 1945, with secret hearings, but between November 15, 1945, and May 31, 1946, open hearings were conducted in the course of which some 15,000 pages of testimony were taken and a total of 183 exhibits received, incident to an examination of 43 witnesses. In July 1946 the committee put out a final report of 580 pages containing its findings, conclusions, and recommendations. The report was accompanied by a set of 39 volumes of testimony and exhibits. The report was really not a single report: there was one by the majority (signed by six Democratic and two Republican members), and one by the minority (signed by two Republican members). The minority report was not nearly as long as that of the majority, but it brought into focus certain troublesome points which still form the subject of acrimonious discussions and writings by those who believe the attack was "engineered" by President Roosevelt and that certain authorities in Washington were as culpable as the principal commanders in the army and navy in Hawaii. It is an interesting fact that both the majority and minority reports contain glowing tributes to the role played by Communications Intelligence (COMINT) before and during World War II. The minority report on this matter is particularly revealing; it says:

"Through the Army and Navy intelligence services extensive information was secured respecting Japanese war plans and designs, by intercepted and decoded Japanese secret messages, which indicated the growing danger of war and increasingly after November 26 the imminence of a Japanese attack.

"With extraordinary skill, zeal, and watchfulness the intelligence services of the Army Signal Corps and Navy Office of Naval Communications broke Japanese codes and intercepted messages between the Japanese Government and its spies and agents and ambassadors in all parts of the

those most intimately involved, the debate concerning a conspiracy or lack thereof still rages. Our purpose here is not to try to resolve the conspiracy debate or give final answer to its basic questions: Why were the capital ships anchored at Pearl Harbor at a time of crisis?; Why, if MAGIC intercepts of Japanese diplomatic codes and their decryptions were used properly, were the commanders at Hawaii not better informed?; Why did General Marshall refuse to use the scrambler telephone to warn the commanders at Hawaii in time?; Why was General Marshall horseback riding through the Virginia countryside when the final part of the critical Japanese fourteen-part message was expected? As suggested above, these questions and related ones which have been raised concerning President Roosevelt's complicity and/or duplicity defy final answer. Nonetheless, although it will not satisfy the conspiracy buffs and theorists, it is possible to examine the methods and especially the attitudes in the intelligence community and the military/political high command concerning the handling of the intelligence information acquired prior to and after the attack at Pearl Harbor. In this regard, procedure which dervies from organizational theory is more important than personality.

In what follows there is no attempt to redo any of the Pearl Harbor investigations mentioned above, but rather to provide an abbreviated description how the Pearl Harbor case study is used in training intelligence officers to handle, evaluate, and interpret intelligence information, especially that derived as a result of communication intercepts and cryptanalysis. And I use the case study description to underscore the structural and procedural deficiencies in the intelligence community which were revealed by the Pearl Harbor attack and which, since that time, have been left largely unremedied in the course of the intelligence community's development.

The methodological approach used in the Pearl Harbor case study, or in similar ones derived from such intelligence postmortems as those following the Berlin airlift crisis, the North Korean attack, the Tet offensive in Vietnam and the seizure of the U.S.S. *Pueblo,* is based on the observable fact of the event, from which the intelligence officer is expected to reason backward and forward in an attempt to isolate the hitherto previously known intelligence information bearing on the event, to analyze and evaluate how it was treated, and to place the event in its political, military, and historical context.

In carrying out the Pearl Harbor case study, the individual intelligence officer is initially provided with almost all the intelligence information which was available as a whole in the intelligence community in the twelve to thirteen

---

world and supplied the high authorities in Washington reliable secret information respecting Japanese designs, decisions, and operations at home, in the United States, and in other countries. Although there were delays in the translations of many intercepts, the intelligence services had furnished to those high authorities a large number of Japanese messages which clearly indicated the growing resolve of the Japanese Government on war before December 7, 1941." (See: The 79th Congress, 2nd Session, Senate Document #244; Washington: Government Printing Office, 1946, p. 514.)

months preceding the attack, and that which was acquired generally in the several months thereafter. The intelligence information provided is segregated by source or means as well as by the acquiring agency; that is, information acquired by electronic means, cryptanalysis, etc., and by human means, both covertly and overtly collected by the various agencies. Also, one is given analyses, if any, made of the intelligence information at the time of its acquisition and a trace of the intelligence information and/or its analysis as set forth in logs, "buck slips," and the like, of its handling and dissemination. At each step both backward and forward along the trail, the individual intelligence officer is cautioned not to turn to any of the after-the-fact testimony given by the principals during the various investigations as a means to support his personal evaluation of the intelligence information and the events themselves. The idea being, of course, for the case study intelligence officer to first identify what actually happened before grappling with its whys and wherefores. From personal experience it is a humbling exercise not only to carry out an intelligence case study, but also to provide "tutorial" direction to others with a similar charge, because it forces one to put aside any preconceptions or biases in favor of one theory or another.

The sheer volume of intelligence information from all sources considered in the Pearl Harbor case study defies easy summary. The two basic streams of intelligence information, those from electronic and human sources, may be likened to two rivers starting from a truncated mountain with one (the electronic) rushing down the mountain's steep side and ending up in a stagnant pool, and the other meandering down its gentle slope and emptying into the sea, where its meaning and character become lost as it merges with other extraneous streams of information. The intelligence information considered in the Pearl Harbor case study suggests a curious set of mosaics. One mosaic portrays the Japanese military forces fully occupied by the war with China and reluctant, if not unable, to expand their operations. Another shows severe limitations on Japanese war production capabilities, especially with regard to the production of aircraft. Another gives the clear impression of a studied, measured approach on the part of the Japanese in the buliding of the so-called East Asian Coprosperity Sphere, with each acquisition being carefully digested before the next is considered. And a mosaic which lacks any consistent clue to the existence of an anti-American propaganda campaign. In fact the domestic fallout from cultural exchanges such as the visit to Japan by the University of Chicago's baseball team suggests exactly the opposite. Confusingly, the mosaic derived from diplomatic intelligence information reports suggests less a worsening of diplomatic relations than a move toward defining the precise features of the disputes between the United States and Japan. One sees in it, perhaps consistent with the dynamics of diplomacy, a slow, almost reluctant process on both sides to agree about what they disagree. Finally, the human intelligence information from the Western hemisphere, collected primarily by the FBI and the military intelligence services, especially with respect to Japanese espionage activities in Mexico and California, raises questions which hang suspended in the air concerning whether the Japanese actions were taken in response to American ones rather than vice versa.

Occasionally, as one constructs these mosaics a bit or piece emerges which doesn't seem to fit anywhere. Some of these are seen in the "think piece" reports from the military officers studying the Japanese language and who, unlike the military attachés, lived with Japanese families and were part of an indigenous academic subculture. Several make mention of a fatal kind of determinism on the part of Japanese academics, who viewed Japanese-American relations as being on some kind of a collision course beyond their or anyone else's ability to alter. Others, especially the more junior military attachés, suggest a curiously uneven state of morale among Japanese junior officers. Most of them were seen to be unquestioning in support of their nation's policies; however, aside from professional admiration of Germany's military successes, there is a thread of disquietude among these officers concerning Hitler's claims about a master race.

Finally, after the Pearl Harbor case study intelligence officer completes his backward-forward trace of the human intelligence information, he is required to answer the questions, "What, if any, predictive elements does the information contain and what conclusions other than those contained in the analyses made at the time are valid?" To the first, the consensus of those who have carried out the study is that the human intelligence information, by itself, is sufficiently ambiguous to rob it of any real predictive capability. For every positive item pointing toward the attack at Pearl Harbor there is an equally compelling one to suggest either no attack or one much more likely to take place elsewhere in Asia. On the other hand, one negative item or lack of intelligence information—namely, that American intelligence in late November 1941 was no longer able to locate a good part of the Japanese battle fleet —leaves one with the view that negative intelligence was an inadequate indicator for the intelligence community leaders to use to resolve the ambiguities concerning potential Japanese attack intentions. For various reasons the warning implied by loss of the Japanese battle fleet's location were not taken seriously; the most important reason being that those who dealt with this information believed that a Japanese attack on Pearl Harbor was inherently improbable.

To the second question, the consensus conclusions are a bit more fundamental. They include a judgment that the human stream of intelligence information was, by objective standards, not altogether inadequate. The reports did contain enough intelligence information to provide the basis of a more precisely directed collection effort; however, there was little or no follow-up or feedback to the collection elements by those with a responsibility for analyzing the intelligence information and turning it into valid intelligence. What is seen is a process of reasoning, paradoxically, from a base of intelligence information which was at once too large and too small. Also, a clear dichotomy of attitudes emerges from the analyses prepared at the time between one school of thought, which looked upon intelligence as simply facts, and another, which saw it as the basis for action or decision, preventive or otherwise. This conflict was fundamental to the intelligence failure then, and is even more fundamental today. Finally, one concludes that the human intelligence information did not merge, as some analysts have suggested, to produce an unacceptable signal-to-noise ratio: i.e., due to the volume of intelligence information on hand the relationship between relevant intelligence information to that incidental or peripheral to the fact (the attack itself) prevented hearing the correct signal. Rather, the streams themselves, because they were not aggregated, produced a cacophony of signals. In other words, the Pearl Harbor case study shows a second or multiple order of signal-to-noise ratios in which the individual streams of intelligence information produced their own internal signal-to-noise ratios. The distinction is subtle, but nonetheless important. Each of the human stream signals—those from the various collection efforts (economic, political, military) were clear; however, because they were not necessarily or immediately reinforcing the others, the resultant effect was the production of noise from each of the stream's signals.

In answer to the implied question, "Didn't the intelligence services or their leaders get together back in Washington to resolve the discrepancies or apparent contradictions between the intelligence information their organizations had acquired?," the evidence clearly indicates that they did not. To be sure, there was some "reading" of other agency reports, such as that carried out by low-level military officers of their sister services' reports, or those in the State Department, but no reproduction or organized lateral dissemination in pursuit of a synthesized analysis of the intelligence information acquired and held by the various organizations was carried out. In essence, the intelligence "liaison" of the time between the intelligence community's individual organizations served to worsen rather than enhance their leader's ability to know what else one's own organization needed to know in order to more effectively direct its own resources.

Turning to the electronic stream of intelligence information acquired during this period, the conclusions were much the same. However, one conclusion identifies the principal culprits for the intelligence failure at Pearl Harbor and thereafter: the almost completely total divorcement of the electronic streams from the human streams of intelligence information, and the concentric compression involved in handling the electronic stream (i.e., the more pertinent the information, the fewer the number of people who actually saw it) were an open invitation to disaster. As revealed by the Joint Congressional Committee's attempt to trace the flow of MAGIC intercepts emanating from Tokyo to Washington and elsewhere, through the decrypting and translating process to their delivery to President Roosevelt, Secretary Knox, Secretary Stimson, General Marshall and Admiral Stark, these men did know prior to the attack that the Japanese intended to break off negotiations. However, neither the intercepts nor other intelligence information gives clear indication concerning any intended Japanese target. As a consequence, although the Congressional inquiry was designed to discover why the Japanese were successful in their attack on Pearl Harbor and to pin clear responsibility for the intelligence failure, it did neither.

For those with an interest in tracing the evidentiary chain for themselves —to find out who delivered the MAGIC intercepts to President Roosevelt and the others, their reported reaction to its contents, as well as their testimony taken in the course of the Joint Committee hearings—an edited version with analysis is set forth in Roberta Wohlstetter's *Pearl Harbor: Warning and Decision* and Hans Louis Trefousse's *What Happened at Pearl Harbor.* * In these books, as in the Joint Congressional Hearings and Reports, the questions "What did we know and when did we know it?" are answered, but they leave the question unanswered of why the intelligence leaders were unable or unwilling to argue the case for additional intelligence information more forcefully, and/or to take some precautions based on the intelligence which they did have.

Wohlstetter comes closest among those who have written about Pearl Harbor to answering the latter question in terms of organizational weaknesses in both the intelligence services and the military/political high command. However, although her thesis is partially correct, it does not completely demonstrate that the key organizational weakness was one stemming from the handling of intelligence information once it had been received in Washington and delivered to the principals. The trace of the electronic stream of intelligence information—mainly MAGIC intercepts—especially demonstrates why army and navy forces in Hawaii were surprised by the Japanese attack. It clearly demonstrates three conclusions: (1) that too few people were permitted access to the MAGIC information to enable them to activate our defenses; (2) that because MAGIC information was not evaluated (i.e., turned into valid intelligence) by those most intimately involved in its production before it was turned over to the principals, it was not adequate to serve as the basis to preempt the Japanese, regardless of where they might choose to strike; and (3) that none of the MAGIC information was used to direct other covert and overt means of collection to seek its corroboration or refutation.

Each of these conclusions requires some amplification because they constitute a legacy carried into and through World War II, which still constitutes a trilemma yet to be fully resolved. In the first place, because communications intelligence information based upon successful codebreaking was then, as now, invested with the Churchillian "most secret source" accolade, it was held too closely by those in the inner circle. In consequence, the persons with a responsibility for implementing decisions in preparation for whatever decision might be made were kept in the dark until it was too late. This kind of high-level "I've

*Roberta Wohlstetter, *Pearl Harbor: Warning and Decision.* Stanford University Press, 1962.
Hans Louis Trefousse, *What Happened at Pearl Harbor?* College & University Press, 1958.

got a secret" game played at the time of Pearl Harbor—and at the time of other "surprise" occurrences—produced fateful consequences. It led to a kind of waiting for the shoe to drop without letting anyone else in the house know that there was an intruder undressing in the attic. Ironically, even if President Roosevelt, General Marshall, and Secretaries Knox and Stimson had been agreed that the fourteenth part of the important MAGIC intercept did in their judgment signal a sneak attack, it is unlikely that dissemination of that kind of information would have made much difference unless it were accompanied by an unequivocal order to man all battle stations. Warnings, oblique or otherwise, based on intelligence—regardless of source—have a long and consistent record of being ignored by their recipients. And at the time of Pearl Harbor, because diplomatic relations between the United States and Japan had deteriorated so sharply, it appeared to many that Japanese military preparations seemed more like a normal course of action, rather than one in preparation for a surprise attack.

In connection with our second conclusion, even if one gives President Roosevelt and other American leaders the benefit of the doubt in not hollering "wolf" to their military commanders, or in not broadening the need-to-know access circle for MAGIC information, they are culpable in failing to do what was necessary to turn it into valid intelligence. For example, the Pearl Harbor case study makes it apparent that after President Roosevelt and the other principals received MAGIC information, none of them challenged the information on the grounds that it *might* be part of a deception plan. They accepted the information as a given and neither sought to prove or disprove its contents. The reasons for this behavior—or sin of official omission—which has become almost institutionalized in the past three decades are not too obscure. On the one hand, no president has been willing to acknowledge to the individual with the best understanding of an either-or intelligence-related conflict that he doesn't understand the meaning of the intelligence information placed in front of him. On the other, the system of personal advisors which has grown up around the presidency since Roosevelt is designed to diffuse and lessen the necessity to make a choice based upon intelligence.

In the Pearl Harbor case study, the incredible aspect of this anti-intelligence bias in the presidential decision-making process is that not one of the navy's communication intelligence specialists, who for several years had handled the decrypting and translating of Japanese intercepts and who had extensive experience in Japan, was ever asked by FDR or others in his inner circle his opinion as to the information's meaning or validity. Maybe these naval officers who had spent their adult lives mastering the complexities of cryptanalysis, linguistics and understanding the Japanese national and political psyche would have copped out and told President Roosevelt what they thought he wanted to hear; but I think not. The question, of course, must remain moot. However, the president who fails to try to get the best answer, without fear or favor, from whomever is the best source runs the same danger as did Roosevelt, Truman, and Johnson when they sat on, or tried personally to intuit the meaning of, intelligence information which was at odds with their desires to avoid conflict.

We cite the Pearl Harbor case study because it provides a point of departure for events in the intelligence community during World War II. Although the organizational deficiencies were almost immediately recognized in the aftermath of Pearl Harbor and during the course of the subsequent Japanese successes, there was a strange reluctance on the part of those in charge of America's military forces to remedy them. Instead, the onrush of events paradoxically conspired with the phenomena of bureaucratic inertia to produce a further institutionalization of these deficiencies in a variety of organizational forms which made a virtue of the apparent contradiction between intelligence in support of operations and in policy development, and which also left unresolved the key question of intelligence control for both purposes.

In describing the status of army intelligence in the aftermath of Pearl Harbor, General Eisenhower, who had been appointed Chief of the Operations Division (successor to the War Plans Division) of the War Department General Staff in March 1942, made the following observation:

> In the first winter of the war these accumulated and glaring deficiencies were serious handicaps. Initially the Intelligence Division could not even develop a clear plan of its own organization nor could it classify the type of information it deemed essential in determining the purposes and capabilities of our enemies. The chief of the Division could do little more than come to the planning and operating sections of the staff and in a rather pitiful way ask if there was anything he could do for us.*

Although Eisenhower's postwar statement confirmed the obvious, the actions taken at the time by him and others to remedy the "glaring deficiencies" failed in their stated purposes. One such important action, taken in early 1942, involved a reorganization within the War Department which called for a restructuring of the Military Intelligence Division (MID) as a means to correct the lack of continuity between collection, evaluation, and dissemination of intelligence information which was revealed by the Pearl Harbor intelligence "failure." In describing this response, army historians noted:

> The new organization was announced to the army in Circular #59. As it affected the army its changes were far reaching and fundamental. The most striking feature of the proposed reorganization was the distinction between operating and staff functions. The latter were to be retained by the general staff division, but the former were to be placed in operating agencies. This entailed the separation of the larger part of the organization of each staff division from the small policy-making group who performed truly staff functions. The policy groups would remain in the General Staff as a small policy-making and advisory staff divorced from the operating functions of their organizations. By ruthlessly regrouping many old offices and functions and integrating them

*Dwight D. Eisenhower, *Crusade in Europe*. New York: Doubleday, 1948, p. 32.

into the new organization, smoother functioning was expected.

The language of the Circular did not make clear distinction between the [old policy-making] Military Intelligence Division and the [newly created operating] Military Intelligence Service. From the present point of vantage the intentions of the Circular seem clear. This distinction, however, was not made clear until Circular 5–2, September 1944, was issued, although some progress had been made in the July 1942 revision of AR 10–15. Circular #59 charged the Military Intelligence Division, G-2, "with those duties of the War Department General Staff relating to the collection, evaluation and dissemination of military information." The Military Intelligence Service was established "under the direction of the Assistant Chief of Staff, Military Intelligence Division, War Department General Staff . . . [to] operate and administer the service of the collection, compilation and dissemination of military intelligence." Here was a verbal paradox. In the vocabulary of G-2, intelligence is based upon the evaluation of information. Information is the raw product from which intelligence is produced. Military Intelligence Division was charged then, with duties relating to the evaluation and dissemination of information while Military Intelligence Service was not charged with the evaluation but with the dissemination of intelligence.*

In the staffing which preceded issuance of Circular #59, the then army's G-2, Brigadier General Sherman Miles, argued to no avail that the "verbal paradox" contained in the MID and MIS statements of mission would produce more rather than less intelligence chaos. He pointed out that dissemination of intelligence information, or raw information without evaluation and analysis, was worse than no dissemination at all. It was a losing argument. Generals Marshall, Eisenhower, and Strong all looked on Miles as being weak and ineffective, and thought his objections were based on some kind of bureaucratic ploy designed to establish a before-the-fact alibi rather than on Circular #59's functional flaws. As a consequence of his opposition, General Miles was relieved as G-2 and was replaced by Major General George V. Strong, whom Eisenhower described as a "senior officer possessed of a keen mind, a driving energy, and ruthless ambition."** Overlooked in Strong's appointment was his obdurate obstructionism in the pre–Pearl Harbor period to the kind of intelligence organization intended, but not achieved, because of the kind of thinking which produced the verbal paradox in Circular #59.

General Strong soon came to regret that he managed to stuff Circular #59 down General Miles's throat. As G-2, with the responsibility for implementing its provisions, General Strong indicated his dissatisfaction with the reorganization within three months and offered an alternate structure to General Marshall.*** Without the approval of General Marshall, and in belated recogni-

---

*U.S. Army Military Intelligence Division, "A History of the Military Intelligence Division, 7 December 1941–2 September 1945." Typescript, 1946, pp. 12–13. Copies of this study bear the marking "Secret"; however, it was declassified by the Office of the Secretary of Defense in 1976.

**Eisenhower, *op. cit.*, p. 37. For further evidence of Miles' weak character, see Wohlstetter, op. cit., p. 289.

***Military Intelligence Division History, *op. cit.*, p. 19.

tion of General Miles's earlier objections, General Strong proceeded on his own to bring the evaluation and dissemination functions together under the MID's umbrella, in an organization which he designated the Evaluation and Dissemination Branch. Although Strong came to reject his earlier idea of a separate MIS, he retained the organization and attempted to make it responsive to his personal ideas concerning the proper thrust, direction, and scope of the army's intelligence collection effort. It is not necessary to detail all the internal reorganizations of army intelligence which followed in General Strong's wake; these, which did not essentially change the intelligence structure, are less important than the dominant personality of General Strong. Strong, who presided over the burgeoning expansion of the army's wartime intelligence organization during his tenure as G-2 (which lasted until February 7, 1944), engaged in a series of running disputes with William Donovan and other intelligence community leaders which effectively blocked creation of a systematic, institutionalized central intelligence service, or one in which the army's separate intelligence service would continue to operate under other than his direct control.

While these perturbations were underway in the army, the navy was experiencing its own strong reaction to the events at Pearl Harbor. Fortunately, personnel in the Office of Naval Intelligence (ONI) came through the search for scapegoats relatively unscathed. During the post–Pearl Harbor investigations, ONI's basic organizational structure was judged sound. In the spring of 1942, Admiral Stark, who had a limited view of the role of intelligence, was replaced as Chief of Naval Operations by Admiral Ernest King, who was given the additional post of Commander in Chief, U.S. Fleets. ONI's leaders were now able to get on with the task of meeting the navy's wartime intelligence needs as well as participating in the bureaucratic struggle over intelligence.

Before describing how ONI's leaders fought the Washington wartime bureaucratic struggle over intelligence domains and hegemony over the intelligence community as a whole, mention needs to be made about the navy's development of its intelligence training organization. As noted in the previous chapter, prewar expansion of the military intelligence services was hampered by a variety of circumstances; however, from a conceptual standpoint perhaps the most important was the difficulty of taking intelligence doctrine (i.e., the evaluated experience of persons acquired over a long period of time) and translating it into a foreshortened form which could be used to train intelligence officers for duty on an operational level. With the onset of the war there was not enough time to employ the leisurely prewar apprentice approach. The task of developing a short-term substitute fell upon the competent shoulders of the Deputy Director of Naval Intelligence, Rear Admiral Ellis M. Zacharias, who later described the problem by saying:

Training of personnel was our primary problem, since we had only an inadequate intelligence school chiefly concerned with the preparation of officers for investigating duties, known as "gumshoe" activities, among those in a belittling mood. Complaints heard in the field offices decided me to make training my number-one project. Radical changes had to be made, and I took it upon myself to make them immediately.

The old school was abolished and two new schools were created: one in Frederick, Md., called the Basic Intelligence School, to introduce newcomers to the elementary principles and techniques of intelligence; and another, the Advanced Intelligence School in New York, to train intelligence officers on an operational level. This second school grew out of the realization that Naval Intelligence in war has somewhat different tasks from those of Army Intelligence. The elements of ground combat and the problems it raises are largely nonexistent in naval warfare, so that what the Army calls its combat intelligence has but limited application in the Navy. What we needed was operational intelligence, an activity between strategy and tactics providing in intelligence everything a commander might need to take his ships into combat or to conduct amphibious warfare. The immense mobility of our fleets and the wise expanse of our watery battlefield necessitated a broadening of intelligence work, too; and we felt that our operational intelligence would take all these factors into consideration. We planned to train hundreds of operational intelligence officers by driving them through a hard curriculum compressed into a comparatively short time. We actually trained a thousand—and as I now look back upon this project and the demands which soon poured in upon us, I feel that we were not disappointed in our expectations. My faith in Lieutenant John Mathis, USNR, who headed this school, was well founded. His legal mind, pleasant personality, and keen investigative abilities gave me confidence. Ably assisted by an outstanding faculty of men high in the educational field, such as Lieutenant Richard W. Hatch, Lieutenant Garrett Mattingly, and others, the success of this undertaking was assured.*

Admiral Zacharias' words bear repeating here because, as one of America's foremost intelligence leaders, he put his finger on the important gray area in the intelligence spectrum: "operational intelligence, an activity between strategy and tactics," which forces consideration and synthesis of the real distinctions between an enemy's capabilities and intentions and one's own. Too often in the past these distinctions have been kept separate or overlooked, and have led national leaders to act or not act in a manner which has subsequently been dubbed an intelligence "failure." The point is that "flash points" of potential hostilities during an ostensible period of peace and the existence of optional targets or objectives during war require a different intelligence outlook than that concerned with the nitty-gritty problems of tactical intelligence and the large ones associated with grand strategy.

The navy, almost in anticipation of hostilities, had, in late October 1941, replaced Captain Alan Kirk as Director of Naval Intelligence (DNI) by Rear Admiral T.S. Wilkinson. Kirk, who had fulfilled his mission in facilitating the navy's cooperation with Donovan during the battle over creation of the COI in the summer of 1941, was posted back to London where, after the war began, he assumed the post as Chief of Staff to the U.S. Naval Headquarters in

*Zacharias, *op. cit.*, pp. 296–97.

London. Wilkinson's appointment as DNI was less based on an intelligence background than on the recognition that in the Washington scheme of things rank, especially one's date of flag or general officer rank, determined who among the designees to an interservice or interagency committee would end up in the chair. By naming Wilkinson as DNI, the navy insured that their man would control whatever joint organization was created; due to the navy's custom of promoting a captain (the equivalent rank of an army colonel) to the rank of rear admiral with two stars and the army's practice of promoting a colonel first to the rank of brigadier general (one star) and then to major general (two stars), the navy's flag officer or admiral would effectively outrank his army peer. Also, the navy, in assessing who was available for joint intelligence activities from among the army's general officers, knew that there was no one who outranked Admiral Wilkinson. On such rather mundane considerations then, as now, the bureaucratic squabbles over intelligence turned.

As suggested in the previous chapter, the creation of Donovan's COI was a force in the on-again, off-again movement toward coordination of American intelligence activities. And almost in response to the progress Donovan had made to that end during COI's brief existence, the military moved to check his efforts. This took form in the creation of a Joint Army and Navy Intelligence Committee on December 3, 1941.* The dubious authority for this apparent bureaucratic volte face on the part of the military services was derived from the largely moribund Joint Army and Navy Board, which had been organized in 1903 to make recommendations to the Secretaries of War and Navy on matters involving cooperation between the two armed services.** However,

---

*Military Intelligence Division History, op. cit, pp. 88–89.

**This agency was first established in 1903 by voluntary agreement between the Secretary of War and the Secretary of the Navy. It never had a legislative basis. The board was described in its original charter as advisory to the two secretaries, and its recommendations became effective only upon their approval and promulgation. In some cases the approval of the president was also required. The board originally consisted of four high-ranking officers of the army and four from the navy. The membership was later specified to be: from the army, the Chief of Staff, the Deputy Chief of Staff and the Assistant Chief of Staff for War Plans; from the navy, the Chief of Naval Operations, the Assistant Chief of Naval Operations, and the Director of War Plans Division. Although the composition of the Joint Board varied over the years, the principles upon which it was founded remained the same, except for a period of interruption; it was suspended by President Wilson in 1914 and reestablished at the end of World War I in 1919. In the period from 1919 onwards there were no major changes in the organization of the board until President Roosevelt's order in July 1939, which placed the Joint Board, the Joint Economy Board, the Aeronautical Board, and the Army-Navy Munitions Board under the direction and supervision of the president as commander in chief of the army and the navy. Since 1942, the Joint Board was in effect replaced in the planning and conduct of joint operations by the Joint Chiefs of Staff; it was finally abolished by the creation of the Department of Defense in 1947. The weaknesses of the Joint Board were to a large extent implicit in its precept and organization. First, it was purely an advisory body with no authority to order coordination in either of the two services. Its advice was only put into effect upon the orders of the two secretaries, who were not members of the board. Thus responsibility for giving advice was divorced from the capacity for action. Secondly, it lacked a permanent

with the outbreak of hostilities the original idea of checking Donovan was overtaken by the necessity of engaging in some kind of broader joint action, if for no other reason than to create a forum where each intelligence service could get some idea about what the others were doing.

Thus, almost in begrudging acceptance of the idea that the entire nation was at war—and in which victory was by no means assured—the Joint Intelligence Committee was organized under the Joint Chiefs of Staff:

> This Committee, known also as JIC, was a continuation and enlargement of the Joint Board Committee of the same name which had been authorized in 1941. It received no charter from the Joint Chiefs of Staff until May 1943, but it was given a directive and was reorganized early in March 1942. Even before this, on February 11, 1942, a Combined Chiefs of Staff paper had defined the duties and membership of the Joint Intelligence Committee. Its primary functions throughout the war period were to furnish intelligence in various forms to other agencies of the Joint Chiefs of Staff and represent it on the Combined Intelligence Committee.
>
> As originally constituted, the Joint Intelligence Committee was composed of the directors of the Intelligence Services of the Army and the Navy and representatives of the State Department, the Board of Economic Warfare (later the Foreign Economic Administration) and the Coordinator of Information (later the Director of Strategic Services). The charter of May 1943 added the Director of the Intelligence Staff of the Army Air Forces. This membership remained unchanged throughout the remainder of the war.
>
> The Joint Intelligence Committee was assisted by a full-time subcommittee and some ten or more specialized subcommittees. The permanent working staff was organized by the Committee early in 1942 as the Joint Intelligence Subcommittee (JISC). Its status was formalized in the Charter of the Committee on May 1943. Two months later, the Joint Intelligence Subcommittee was renamed the Joint Intelligence Staff (JIS). The latter agency was given a charter by the Joint Chiefs of Staff in May 1944 and operated under it throughout the remainder of the war.*

At the JIC's first meeting on March 5, 1942, the tone was set for the kind of high-level bureaucratic wrangling which would characterize the Washington intelligence community's wartime activities. The JIC members present included Rear Admiral T.S. Wilkinson, Director of Naval Intelligence, in the chair; Brigadier General Raymond E. Lee, Assistant Chief of Staff, G-2; Adolf A. Berle, Assistant Secretary of State; Colonel William J. Donovan, Coordinator of Information; Charles B. Rayner (in behalf of Colonel R. B. Lord), Chief

---

working staff, making it difficult to deal adequately with the issues and problems which came before the board. (See: U.S. Navy Department Report to War and Navy Departments and Postwar Organization for National Security, October 22, 1945; 79th Congress, 1st Session: Senate Committee on Naval Affairs; Washington: United States Government Printing Office, 1945, pp. 57–58. Also known as the "Eberstadt Report.")

*General Services Administration, National Archives and Record Service, the National Archives. Federal Records of World War II: Military Agencies (vol. 2). Washington: U.S. Government Printing Office, 1951, p. 9.

of Operations, Board of Economic Warfare. Also present were Captain J.V. Ogan, USN (Ret.) and Colonel Louis J. Fortier, U.S. Army, the senior members of the Joint Intelligence Subcommittee (JISC).

At the onset, Admiral Wilkinson made it clear to all present that although the JIC lacked a formal charter it was to serve as a gatekeeper through which all papers prepared by the JISC and the Combined Intelligence Committee (CIC)* would pass for approval before being forwarded to the U.S. Joint Chiefs of Staff or the Combined Chiefs of Staff and the Combined Staff Planners. This approach gave the military intelligence leaders something of a partial handle on Donovan and his rapidly expanding COI organization. The idea was to interpose the *negative* authority of the JIC—its ability to prevent ideas calling for positive intelligence operations from being forwarded from Donovan to the Joint Chiefs of Staff. It was believed by the military intelligence leaders that this procedure would curb Donovan's freewheeling tendencies. Their scheme worked only to a limited extent, due in part to Donovan's continued "out of channels" access to President Roosevelt and his relationship with British intelligence authorities which enabled him to operate in areas outside the immediate jurisdiction of the American military authorities. Also, the JIC became a captive of its own bureaucratic impulses by proliferating a myriad of subcommittees of its own subcommittee, all of which ended up talking about the need for intelligence rather than serving as the mechanism to provide intelligence of any real value to its creating organization, the Joint Chiefs of Staff.

In commenting on the first several years of the JIC's operations, former ambassador Julius C. Holmes, who served as its Executive Secretary and later, in London, as General Eisenhower's political advisor, noted the JIC was based on the false premise that coordination by itself was sufficient to meet the very different functional requirements for intelligence in each of the different services and to provide efficient allocation of intelligence means to fulfill those requirements. Holmes added, "the military intelligence leaders all looked on Donovan like the fox in the hen house who was intent on usurping their 'hens' in pursuit of intelligence for someone's organization other than their own. The conflict of interest was apparent from the very beginning when one of the

*"Eberstadt Report", *op. cit.,* p. 4. Provision for the Combined Intelligence Committee (CIC) was made in the agreement to create the Combined Chiefs of Staff, but it does not appear to have met before May 1942. Its working subcommittee, however, known first as the Combined Intelligence Subcommittee (CISC) and from August 1943 as the Combined Intelligence Staff (CIS) met as early as February 19, 1942. This subcommittee was composed of the Joint Intelligence Subcommittee, later the Joint Intelligence Staff, and the British Joint Intelligence Committee in Washington. The Combined Intelligence Committee consisted of the Joint Intelligence Committee and representatives of the British Joint Intelligence Subcommittee in London. Both the Combined Intelligence Committee and the Combined Intelligence Staff continued throughout the war. The former was responsible for collecting and disseminating military intelligence for the use of the Combined Chiefs of Staff and the Combined Staff Planners.

members was called upon in his other role as the director of an intelligence organization to order his organization to get some information for use by the JIC."

The JIC situation was not without irony. As it proliferated during the course of the war, its stated mission functions* became less and less significant due to the independent authority of the military high command over the war's politics and the logistical problems associated with those politics. Also, like other bureaucratic "paper mills" which turn out studies of dubious value at the drop of an informal comment or an overzealous interpretation of its charter, by the end of July 1942, the JIC and its principal subcommittee had been tried and found wanting in the decision-making process.

At the JIC's twenty-fourth meeting on July 30, 1942, Captain H.C. Train, USN, Director of Naval Intelligence, stated that Rear Admiral C.M. Cooke, Chairman of the Joint U.S. Staff Planners, had remarked to him, informally and unofficially, that the planners regarded with concern the volume of papers produced by the JIC, and had suggested that they be limited to two categories: (a) subjects pertinent to plans in the process of formulation and (b) matters of interest in the immediate future. General discussion among the JIC members brought out that the committee was without any clear indication of what plans were under consideration by the planners, what specific information they desired, or what were their general fields of interest. In response, the JIC directed its subcommittee to prepare a memorandum to the Joint Chiefs of Staff along lines dictated by the chairman (at this time Major General Strong), indicating the nature of the unofficial suggestion of the planners, the existing lack of information as to subjects of immediate interest, and the committee's policy with regard to papers on its own initiative.

Mention is made here of this rather obscure event in the bureaucratic history of American intelligence in World War II because it reveals the systemic, almost innate failure of the United States to translate an acknowledged "need for intelligence" into a meaningful organizational response. In the first place, the initial creation of the JIC in response to the perceived threat to its members' "territory" was conceptually flawed because the individual members had much more to gain than lose by a more complete interchange of information and the establishment of an arrangement whereby the more specialized and/or

---

*"1. The Mission of the Joint U.S. Intelligence Committee is to prepare such special information and intelligence studies as may be required by higher authorities, or as may be indicated by the situation, and to prepare daily joint summaries.

2. The Joint U.S. Intelligence Committee should present the considered, composite convictions of that committee and should be primarily factual. In their studies and deliberations preliminary to committee conclusion, it is intended that members of the committee should present their individual views regarding the matter under consideration.

3. When higher authority has reached a decision or has issued a directive, the committee will be guided accordingly." (See: The National Archives, Record Group 218, Records of the United States Joint Chiefs of Staff, CCS 334, 3–11–42.)

competent means available to each could acquire intelligence information which fell between their respective areas of special interest, but which was required by both parties to carry out their missions. Secondly, once the Axis powers' advances had crested, many intelligence questions and answers were no longer amenable to the deliberate consideration of bodies so far removed from direct contact with the enemy. The intelligence needs of America's combat commanders became more fluid, requiring a shift away from the more measured methods of a contemplative staff organization like the JIC. To be sure, there was a role for the JIC to play; however, the Joint Chiefs of Staff, which was supposed to provide it with direction and had the authority to compel field commanders to gather strategic and other intelligence information in support of future *planned* operations, failed to do so. Similarly, the JIC members who also headed their respective intelligence organizations did not, in these latter roles, order their organizations to turn over all the intelligence information acquired by sources under their control to the JIC.

Within a month after the JIC had commenced operations, Donovan became convinced of its uselessness in meeting the intelligence needs of either the JCS, President Roosevelt, or the newly formed American combat commands. Donovan personally stopped attending the weekly JIC meetings, although he continued to send a string of personal deputies to represent the COI's interest, and others to the JISC to keep tabs on the "studies" it prepared. But Donovan was not one to remain frustrated that his vision of a central intelligence organization had been thwarted. Realistically he reasoned that the onset of hostilities had created additional requirements for the kinds of "operational" intelligence mentioned by Admiral Zacharias, and a legitimate raison d'être for an expanded series of secret intelligence operations as well as for broader kinds of strategic political/military intelligence. Also, from his observations of British combat forces, he knew the value of an organization which spanned these areas of intelligence interest and which could interact directly with combat commanders. His ideas were not new or unique, but to implement them it was bureaucratically necessary to redefine the role of the COI and tie the changed organization into the war at other than the White House level. He had to place it within the spawn of alphabet-soup information agencies, all of which had some, however secondary, role in the actual conduct of the war.

To these ends Donovan tried to turn COI into a line organization under the JCS, as well as into a staff service–oriented organization designed to provide special studies and analyses which were outside the scope and capabilities of the intelligence community's individual members. With respect to the latter, Donovan early on became convinced that the institutional parochialism in the JIC and JISC was an effective bar to the production of meaningful and useful intelligence studies. Consequently, Donovan's Research and Analysis (R&A) Staff under the direction of Dr. William Langer, the distinguished Coolidge Professor of History at Harvard, began to "hustle" for work outside the JIC framework. This took the form of special studies—on such topics as the organization, routes, and capabilities of the Turkish railway system and ports and harbor information in North Africa—carried out for the army's G-2, the navy's ONI, the recently independent A-2 (Air Intelligence Division of the Army Air Forces), the State Department, and others. Because these were separate studies prepared for the individual intelligence organizations rather than for the JCS, Donovan was able to get away with the bureaucratic sleight-of-hand which in effect bypassed the JIC. From Dr. Langer's memos, it is obvious that there was little reluctance on the part of individual intelligence leaders to operate outside the control of the JIC, or any inclination on Donovan's part to disrupt these relationships by disseminating the studies to other than the requesting intelligence organization.

Although Donovan's Current Intelligence Staff did provide substantial inputs of intelligence information to the JIC for basic background studies and its "JIC Weekly Summary," his method of keeping the COI's (later OSS's) Research and Analysis Staff generally outside the constraints posed in producing intelligence by "interagency committee" worked well throughout the war. As a consequence, R&A became the most respected part of the entire OSS operation and was considered important enough to be transferred intact to the State Department at the end of the war. However, in the early, confused days of the war, before R&A had completely proven itself, there were conflicts over some of the special studies. The most important of these was between COI and the Board of Economic Warfare (BEW) over the former's production of a bomb-target selection and analysis for A-2 in connection with preparations for General Doolittle's raid on the Japanese home islands on April 18, 1942.

This early disagreement over who was responsible for air-target analysis was an ominous harbinger of things to come later in the war and thereafter. A careful review of the original COI R&A target analysis for the Doolittle raid and for other target analyses it carried out throughout the war shows that Donovan, Langer, and their analysts (one of whom was Walt Whitman Rostow) accurately anticipated the argument between the proponents of "surgical strike" bombing and those favoring saturation, total destruction aerial bombardment. In abbreviated form, although the COI/BEW disagreement was initially cast in terms of each organization's jurisdiction as well as some personal recriminations between Donovan and Colonel R.B. Lord, the head of BEW's operations divisions, the Doolittle target analysis partially raised the surgical versus destruction bombing issue. Donovan's people contended that the Doolittle raid had primarily a psychological result rather than one designed to accomplish much in the way of significant physical destruction. Later on in the war, other COI R&A target-selection analyses concluded, much to the dissatisfaction of the "big bomber" adherents, that precision bombing raids designed to produce bottlenecks in German war production represented a better use of available air power than the saturation raids of Dresden and Hamburg. In reading these analyses, most of which, for extremely vague reasons, still remain classified, one is struck by the insight of those involved in identifying, at the height of the war and years before the postwar's so-called Strategic Bombing Survey had been ordered, that the big bomber raids were not adversely effecting German war production, or the German people's will to continue the war. For example, one handwritten memo to Dr. Langer, which was affixed to a December 1943 analysis of the bombing designed to knock out German tank production and signed only with the initial "H," noted: "We should argue more forcefully against this waste of air power. Decentralization has enabled the Nazis not only to continue their tank production on schedule, but also, while we have been attempting to bomb the 'big' factory targets out of existence, to increase it in step-by-step fashion. Also, we ought to crank in some of the MO information coming in from the field (see encl msg from Bern) in our arguments. If these conclusions are valid it looks like the hard-working Germans will keep right on working because they're still eating better than anyone else in Europe. Calvin suggested we might make our point by getting the British to lay on a few one- or two-plane raids against those optic targets we talked about last week. Let me know what you think."

The importance of R&A's pioneering work in air-target selection and analysis is significant not only in terms of the World War II experience, but in terms of the methodology that organization developed to deal with the complexities of aerial targeting problems. This methodology, although not precisely set forth at the time as doctrine, has subsequently come to form the base of a "General Theory of Aerial and Missile Targeting" which today is used as a common language among the dozen or so organizations involved in this phase of intelligence. As such, this methodology, which parallels the kind of "input-output" analysis developed by Professor Wassily Leontief to describe a nation's economy, serves as a suitable vehicle for the intelligence organizations to decide whether, for example, Moscow or Leningrad is the best target and who should be given the responsibility for taking it out.

There is no need here to detail all the activities carried out by the COI/OSS's Research and Analysis Branch. As the War Report notes:

R&A engaged in a search for facts. Trained researchers were brought to the service of the Government to probe out, or deduce, the elusive but necessary fact or set of facts . . . it applied to existing facts analytic and interpretive skills theretofore not employed for intelligence purposes. Economists, geographers, political scientists and historians were enlisted in its service. Thus R&A developed new techniques for determining the intentions and capabilities of other nations . . . and operated in an intelligence area previously little developed by the United States—the complex field of economic, political and geographic relationships. The collection of great stores of source material and the analytic employment of such material furnished a rounded background of intelligence, primarily employed for military operations, but holding manifold peacetime possibilities for the strengthening of America's knowledge of foreign affairs and contributing to the future security of the United States.*

*War Report, op. cit., pp. 167–68.

Given the accuracy of the War Report's statement about the role of R&A and the correctness of Donovan's view that its activities did "represent substantial progress made toward the *ultimate intelligence target, a thorough knowledge of the other great powers' capabilities and intentions* [italics added], on which the strategic decisions of this nation will be based,"* one needs also to answer the question, "Why did R&A succeed?" Admittedly, this question bears a corollary, "Why have the R&A's postwar successor organizations and the intelligence community itself failed?" This latter question is answered in succeeding chapters. At this point, it is feasible to look at the R&A experience somewhat in isolation, not simply as the only way that the broader analytical tasks of intelligence should be carried out, but rather to determine what, if any, unique features were exhibited in the R&A experience and whether its success was based strictly on the personalities and abilities of those involved, or the environmental conditions and situations created by the war.

As a consequence of what is called "total war"—war which is as much economic, social, and political as it is strictly military in nature—the R&A approach to analytical intelligence was one whose time had come. Donovan, as a result of his missions for President Roosevelt, recognized this consequence long before others in America's political, military, and intelligence hierarchies, and he acted on this recognition by organizing the Library of Congress' Division of Special Information and the R&A branch to collect and collate the intelligence information which was scattered throughout the government in libraries, universities, newspaper morgues, private collections, etc. This process was more than a simple "literature search," or an amassing of data ad infinitum and ad nauseum, but rather one systematically designed to acquire intelligence information which could be employed analytically in pursuit of Donovan's "ultimate intelligence target." This merits added emphasis because Donovan committed intelligence heresy by also saying that the R&A branch pursued a thorough knowledge of "intentions" in addition to "capabilities." Since Donovan's time it has become an article of faith—and printed doctrine —in the intelligenc community that its members must not concern themselves with intentions, for that is the route which leads to Congressional investigations and presidential wrath if one's analytical judgment is proven wrong by the unpredicted behavior of the United States' friends and foes. Thus we may say that the R&A experience was unique in the sense that the kinds of intelligence information it sought encompassed both pragmatic (capabilities) and interpretive (intentions) criteria.

Before discussing Donovan's vision of a broadened concept of analytical intelligence, something must be said about the organizational evolution of the R&A branch, first in COI and later under the OSS. This evolution proceeded in a series of uneven steps with the search for function becoming the prime ingredient of change. As the War Report notes:

*Ibid., .p. 179.

Like COI/OSS itself, the functions of R&A were defined in practice rather than by fiat. It was primarily a service so conceived that it could be of value to many agencies but subject to no one. It served the operating branches of the OSS, but it did most of its work for various agencies of the JCS, State Department, the armed services, and others. And in its work for the latter agencies R&A found its greatest significance.*

This quest for definition initially began with the establishment of the Division of Special Information (DSI) in the Library of Congress pursuant to the agreement between Donovan and MacLeish. This action was roughly paralleled by the similar organization of the R&A branch on July 31, 1941, under the direction of Dr. James P. Baxter III, president of Williams College.

DSI, which began actual operations toward the end of August 1941, was initially organized to carry out basic research on a regional basis** and to assemble intelligence information to support that research. Almost immediately thereafter, in recognition of the vastness such a collection effort involved, Donovan separated the collation function from the DSI and in early September created the Central Information Division to handle central filing, registry, and editing of reports. In connection with the CID's activities, a system of cross-indexing was also established which made it possible to retrieve intelligence information once it had been filed and/or used in the preparation of studies. In passing, Donovan's early attempt to build an institutional "memory" in COI reflected his experience with the military intelligence services; they had practiced a policy of "file and forget" intelligence reports, and each new problem or crisis required a frantic search or a "rediscovery" of what was already known.

Although Donovan and MacLeish had originally thought the DSI would be organized on functional lines (e.g., economic, geographic, and psychological) as well as on a regional basis, when COI's R&A branch was established the

*War Report, op. cit., p. 167.

**Ibid., p. 52. Eight regional sections were specifically provided for:
(1) The British Empire Section, covering the United Kingdom, the self-governing dominions (excluding the Union of South Africa, which fell within the jurisdiction of the Mediterranean/Africa Section), India, and the dependencies.
(2) The Western Europe Section, responsible for the Low Countries, France, and the Iberian Peninsula.
(3) The Central Europe Section, concerned with the Greater Reich, Italy, Slovakia, Poland, and Hungary.
(4) The Eastern Europe Section, covering the USSR, Finland, the Baltic states, and the Balkans, including Greece.
(5) The Mediterranean Section, renamed the Africa Section in May 1942, which focussed upon North Africa but was eventually responsible for all of Africa except Egypt, as well as the Atlantic Islands.
(6) The Near East Section, covering the Arab countries, Turkey, and Iran.
(7) The Far East Section, covering Japan and Japanese-occupied areas, China, the Philippines, and Netherlands East Indies.
(8) The Latin America Section, including Central and South America.

functional research responsibilities were given to it rather than DSI. The results of this artificial separation of basic area and functional research were not unpredictable. Basic area research obviously has a role to play in the production of finished intelligence, but its thrust must be relevant to the functions or dynamics of the phenomenon, region, country, or system being examined. As a consequence, after the establishment of the OSS on June 13, 1942, and the obvious weakness in trying to carry out analytical intelligence research on parallel and physically separate tracks, DSI was wholly withdrawn from the library and folded into the R&A branch, wherein its basic area research was combined with functional research and analysis. This action on Donovan's part represented the first serious attempt in American intelligence to establish an integrated interdisciplinary approach to the tasks of analytical intelligence. It attempted to take the meticulous research results of area specialists and historians and combine them with the functional analysis of economists, political scientists, geographers, psychologists, and the like. In consummating this marriage of academic disciplines, Donovan also created a Board of Analysts under the chairmanship of R&A Chief Baxter (subsequently replaced by Langer in early 1942), to serve as the final arbiter on matters concerning the processing, analysis, and dissemination of R&A-produced intelligence studies. Although the board never fully served the purpose for which it was created, it did in fact break significant new ground in making the interdisciplinary approach to analytical intelligence research work by resolving and keeping peace in the academic pecking order among the various academic disciplines represented on the R&A staff. This was an important accomplishment; the board had to make sure that the economists, historians, psychologists, and military professionals interacted as equals with one another and that each was held responsible for making a particular input to the overall intelligence production process. To do this, the board had to make sure that the final intelligence product did not allow one academic discipline's bias to effect the final result, or cloak a study's conclusions with so many caveats that the decision maker was unable to use its analysis. Fortunately, both the board and the R&A branch did not also have to integrate the inputs of those we today call "intelligence scientists"—those with a specialty in nuclear physics, electronics, radar, etc.—into the "what does it mean" analytical intelligence procedure. To be sure, physical scientists did play a role in the R&A's overall efforts, but in the main they were left out of the interpretive and conclusion phase of the analysis.

In January 1943, the R&A branch was reorganized into the structure which remained substantially unchanged until October 1945, when the OSS was transferred intact to the Department of State. This reorganization resulted in the creation of four principal divisions, regional in responsibility, but with functional subdivisions.

They were designated Europe-Africa, Far East, USSR and Latin America, each comprising Economics, Political and Geographic subdivisions. The former Economics Division staff was distributed among the various Economics Subdivisions; personnel of the former DSI sections were taken into the Political subdivisions; and the Geographic Division manned the Geographic Subdivisions. The Psychology Division was abolished and the greater part of its personnel was transferred to the Planning Staff.

A current intelligence staff continued the preparation of periodic intelligence summaries and was responsible for problems related to the collection and dissemination of information on the immediate situation. It worked closely with the regional divisions.

To support the work of the regional divisions, CID, the "library" of Branch documentation was maintained intact, as was the Interdepartmental Committee for the Acquisition of Foreign Publications (IDC). A new functional division, the Map Division, was created of personnel from the Cartographic Section of the former Geographic Division.

By war's end, R&A and its divisions produced approximately 3,000 studies, ranging from brief papers on specific topics like the minimum amount of sabotage required to render a factory inoperative as an alternative to its elimination by aerial bombardment, to massive studies such as the study of Southern Germany, made for military government purposes, which included 1,500 pages of text and 804 maps. In carrying out its studies, R&A broke new ground in the development of the analytical intelligence process. In addition to varied techniques "involving both inductive reasoning, from fragmentary particulars to the general, and the deductive application of broad principles to determine what specific steps a general situation would demand," Dr. Langer's staff achieved a synthesis of intelligence information derived from observable facts (such as the number of locomotives in a railway system) and that from agents reporting on the state of morale among its employees. From this kind of synthesis, R&A was in turn able to estimate the vulnerabilities involved in a given situation plus the capabilities and intentions of its directors. This was a major breakthrough because it provided policy and decision makers with intelligence which told them not only about the enemy's intentions, but also the likelihood of their success. The significance of this kind of combined capabilities and intentions analysis lies in the fact that capability analysis by itself often leads to adoption of the wrong counteraction or a "worst possible case" response, which in turn frequently produces more problems than the original one under consideration. For example, if capability analysis confirms that Country X is able to produce a nuclear weapon, the corresponding tendency is to conclude that it will. To Dr. Langer's credit, the R&A intelligence product went beyond that kind of simplistic reasoning and measured capabilities in terms of observable intentions; that is, the progress in pursuit of an assumed objective in the Axis' war councils. In this example, the actual R&A analysis about German, and to a lesser extent Japanese, efforts to develop an atomic bomb were given short shrift in the strategic decisions which surrounded the United States' decision to use the atomic bomb. To be sure, FDR's decision to develop the atomic bomb predated the emergence of R&A's analytical intelligence capability; however, later in the war, when R&A analyses demonstrated that the Axis lacked the excess resources to build an atomic bomb and continue with their ongoing research and development programs in the fields of rocketry, jet aircraft, etc., and that the Axis political and military leaders—not only Hitler and Tojo—had rejected the feasibility of such an effort, they were not accepted by U.S. policy makers. One prophetic R&A analysis concluded, "If we fail to detonate an atomic weapon beyond the tests contemplated at Station—, the Axis will never develop a similar capability if this war lasts until the 21st century."

Although this analysis and others on the same topic (if stated in less dramatic terms) were further confirmed after the war by Operations "Paper Clip" and "Alsos," they are mentioned here not as a measure of R&A's infallibility or omniscience, but as an example of how Donovan viewed intelligence: as that "on which the strategic decisions of this nation will be based." Whatever the validity of intelligence and the accuracy of its analysis, once it gets into the hands of policy and decision makers it is of little worth if not acted upon. Notwithstanding the almost endemic rejection of intelligence which doesn't conform to already held, subjective beliefs, it should be emphasized that R&A's succesful synthesis of capabilities and intentions analysis constitutes a truly unique aspect of that organization's performance, and is one which has failed to be duplicated in each of the postwar attempts to organize the intelligence community on a national, centrally controlled basis.

Opinions differ over whether the R&A's twin focus on capabilities and intentions analysis was due to the personalities of Donovan, Langer, and the R&A staff—most of whom were acknowledged to be genuine experts—or a fluid situation in the intelligence community at a time when there was room and opportunity to try the uncomfortable and unfamiliar. To be sure, the personalities of those involved were strong, as was their previously acquired expertise; nonetheless, it appears that R&A's successes were generally due to the lack of ideological bias in the analytical process developed by Donovan, Langer, and others. Intelligence purity—i.e., intelligence derived solely from supposedly objective sources and facts—did not dominate the R&A's analytical procedure; rather, the "take" as well as the after-action reports from covert operations were integrated into the R&A analyses. Also, Donovan made the operational side of OSS quite responsive to the needs of R&A by ordering his agents in the field not only to disrupt, disorganize, and destroy the enemy, but also to search out the elusive and obscure bits of intelligence information on which the ultimate accuracy of analytical intelligence's product frequently depends. In short, Donovan established a free flow of communication between those involved with analysis and those in covert operations which enabled both to do their jobs better, and in the process neither compromised the efforts of the other.

From a personal appraisal of R&A studies carried out for policy purposes (rather than those in direct support of covert or military operations), a theme emerges which rejects the monolith theory of one's enemy. Instead of perceiving an indivisible enemy as the totality of its society, economy, military, political system, etc., the rather unique view that the enemy's intelligence targets can and should be attacked selectively was favored. This theme goes well beyond Donovan's statements about a centralized interdisciplinary approach to include acceptance of an intelligence gestalt. This idea implied a role for analytical intelligence in peace as well as war, designed to facilitate accomplishment of Donovan's "ultimate intelligence target."

Finally, although R&A looked tidy enough on paper, something must be said about the style Donovan and Langer imparted to its activities. Interviews with academics who served in R&A show that many look back on their stint as one which included "the best years of their intellectual lives." Although the R&A staff's output was prodigious, its quality remained high throughout the war and remarkably free of the jargon which accompanies much of today's "option analysis." One reason for this high quality was Donovan and Langer's direction, which proceeded on the basic tenet that one should guard against the insinuation of any preconceptions in solving the various tasks of analytical intelligence. The R&A staff was warned against trying to cast their analyses in terms of the comfortable and familiar, or to rely on what had been previously written by themselves or others about a problem or issue. Dr. Langer commented, "The reason this approach worked as well as it did was based largely on the individual researcher's ability to observe the results of his efforts, especially in those areas where his recommendations to do nothing, stop ineffective actions, or change their direction were heeded." This atmosphere, perhaps more than the wartime urgency of the tasks, the glamor of the OSS, and the personalities of its leaders, created a bond between the R&A staff and the rest of those in OSS which made both elements believe in the organization and the importance of each individual's work and contribution.

Donovan's successes and unique contributions in solving the tasks of analytical intelligence were not matched by his efforts in the fields of "secret intelligence"—intelligence infiltration and penetration, sabotage and subversion activities, and guerrilla or commando operations. Conceptually, Donovan looked on these fields "as separate and distinct functions requiring different techniques and training . . . related and interdependent, each preparing for and assisting the others as successive phases of a continuing process . . . to pave the way for the regular armed forces."* Donovan was essentially correct; however, his conception failed, not because it was tried and found wanting, but because the intelligence community's institutional rigidities and the personalities and biases of the United States' political, military, and intelligence leaders conspired to prevent its full and complete testing. Although the conspiracy was neither criminally malevolent nor explicitly intended by those most intimately involved, the results were the same as if it had been.

*War Report, *op. cit.,* p. 70.

As shown in the previous chapter, the military services and the FBI had engaged in secret intelligence activities prior to World War II. In the main, these activities were essentially concerned with espionage, the acquiring of intelligence information by other than overt means or sources (such as those associated with country-to-country official liaison arrangements), and not with offensive activities like subversion and sabotage. Thus there existed a precedent, albeit one not officially sanctioned by the United States government, for the recruitment and exploitation of secret sources and methods. And largely because of their fear that their prewar secret intelligence activities would be exposed, the military services in the fall of 1941 had acquiesced to Donovan's power play and agreed to turn over these activities, as well as their intelligence resources, to the control of Donovan's COI to exploit those resources as he saw fit.

The war brought de facto governmental acceptance of illegal secret intelligence activities, and the military services and the FBI moved quickly to try to regain control over them. This reaction was altogether understandable in terms of the intelligence leaders' perceptions of the necessity to meet the burgeoning intelligence needs of their particular services. Their feeling was that they could not possibly meet their parent service's "unlimited" secret intelligence needs if the limited resources were shared or if the total needs of the intelligence community as a whole were somehow "prioritized" by Donovan. The problem also differed from the analytical intelligence task confronted by Donovan because secret intelligence "assets," unlike area specialists, historians, and economists, are not readily located, quickly recruited, or easily trained.

Donovan, who understood, at least abstractly, this fact about the personnel difficulties involved in secret intelligence better than most, moved in late December 1941 to gain presidential authorization for creation of a 5,000-man commando-type organization. In a memorandum to President Roosevelt on December 22, 1941, Donovan specifically recommended:

1. That as an essential part of any strategic plan, there be recognized the need of sowing the dragon's teeth in those territories from which we must withdraw and in which the enemy will place his army; for example, the Azores or North Africa. That the aid of native chiefs be obtained, the loyalty of the inhabitants be cultivated; Fifth Columnists organized and placed, demolition material cached; and guerrilla bands of bold and daring men organized and installed.

2. That there be organized now, in the United States, a guerrilla corps, independent and separate from the Army and Navy and imbued with a maximum of the offensive and imaginative spirit. This force should, of course, be created along disciplined military lines, analogous to the British Commando principle, a statement of which I sent you recently.*

*War Report, *op. cit.,* p. 72.

On the surface, Donovan's memorandum made sense, but it and its presentation to President Roosevelt contained some fundamental flaws. The first was the memorandum's timing. It could not have come at much worse a time. The military's command and control system was in a shambles and the Joint Chiefs of Staff had yet to be convened, much less organized. All over the world American forces were firing and falling back; actions were underway to repatriate Americans from Japan, Germany, and Italy and to place Japanese-Americans in internment camps. The second flaw was that Donovan's call for commandos put the cart before the horse in his own conceptual sequence in the development of secret intelligence. Rather than first moving to expand and build a secret intelligence organization's capabilities to carry out "infiltration and preparation" missions, he advocated creation of a "guerrilla corps" to carry out the functions whose existence depends on the former. Further, strictly from a bureaucratic point of view, the memo was fatally flawed in calling for a guerrilla corps "independent and separate from the Army and the Navy." For Donovan to think, even with FDR's endorsement, that such an organization could be brought to pass in the face of the military's obvious objections was, charitably, an act of lunacy on his part.

The events following in the wake of Donovan's memo revealed each of these flaws. More to the point, each contributed to a conspiracy which resulted in the failure to develop a meaningful secret intelligence apparatus. Internal bureaucratic conditions were thus created which prevented COI/OSS from ever achieving its intended purpose: developing into a systematic, institutionalized central intelligence service. The first event in the sequence involved President Roosevelt's reply to Donovan, dated the following day, in which he said, "I want you to take this up with Mr. Churchill [who was then staying at the White House] and find out whom we should work with in England toward this end."* How much Roosevelt's endorsement of Donovan's memo was due to its logic and how much was a concession of the moment to Churchill's presence is difficult to judge. Churchill had seen the memo and spoken of "preparing for the liberation of the captive nations . . . to enable the conquered populations to revolt . . . to release the fangs of rebellion."** Each of these three men, in his own way, had different and quite distinct ideas about secret intelligence: whether it was a means, an end in itself, or a function whose existence did not depend on war for justification.

Armed with Roosevelt's "approval," Donovan moved quickly to expand his initial toehold by attempting to gain a monopoly over the expanded "potential market" for the full spectrum of secret intelligence activities, from espionage to subversion and sabotage. As luck would have it, at the time of Roosevelt's partial go-ahead, Donovan's Chief of Operations of Special Activities, Lt.Col. Robert A. Solborg (who had come to COI from the Army's G-2 in mid-

*War Report, op. cit., p. 72.
**Stevenson, op. cit., p. 303.

October) was in England, studying the British Special Operations Executive (MI-6) methods and organization.

Solborg was something of a tragic figure, or more properly a victim in a bureaucratic game he only barely understood. He had come to COI upon the suggestion and recommendation of Major M. Preston Goodfellow, who had become G-2 liaison officer with COI in August 1941. Goodfellow, whose liaison responsibilities included making sure that G-2 personnel found places in COI to protect the army's interests, didn't know Solborg personally; however, following the military's acceptance of COI's lead role in secret intelligence, a search was made of army personnel who might appeal to Donovan. Solborg had been on an undercover assignment in North Africa in 1940–41 and looked to be a likely candidate. Unfortunately, Solborg's clandestine assignment implied more performance than it actually included; but because he had recent field experience and sufficient rank he was tapped by Donovan to become the COI's Chief of Operations of Special Activities. Almost immediately after assuming his post, Solborg began to grate on Donovan. This was partly due to their differing personalities, but mostly it was due to Solborg's unasked for advocacy of combining Secret Intelligence and Special Operations under one organizational head, namely his own. Solborg, arguing for the single-head approach largely on the basis of his limited experience in North Africa, was out of step with Donovan, whose ideas were based on the recognition that for COI to move ahead in this overall area it was necessary for its organization to parallel its British counterpart. This is not to say that Solborg's idea was wrong, but rather that it was inconsistent with the political realities of the moment which called for an immediate cooperation with the British in a common war effort. The War Report notes:

> Their [British] SIS and SOE were completely separate organizations under different cabinet ministers. In the course of discussions with Stephenson in connection with the plan for North Africa, Donovan had been apprised of the high degree of rivalry and, on occasion, jealousy between the two British agencies. Consequently, he realized that it would be impractical to have one branch of COI to deal with both SIS and SOE.*

In response to Solborg's proposal—which was paralleled by a similar one from Wallace Phillips, which Donovan had rejected out of hand—both Solborg and Phillips were sent to England to see the political light. Solborg was dazzled by what Colin Gubbins, the head of SOE, and his band of commandos, saboteurs, and "thugs" showed him. It was a show perhaps unrivalled throughout wartime American-British relations; the intrinsic "glamor" of sabotage, the *machismo* of silent killing, and all the rest were sold to Solborg along with the idea that secret intelligence and special operations were discrete

---

*War Report, *op. cit.,* p. 73. For a further discussion of Solborg's tragic career, see R. Harris Smith, *OSS.* New York: Dell, 1973, pp. 47–52.

functions and never—or hardly ever—the twain should meet. The demonstrations of special operations techniques were almost too exhilarating for Solborg, but fortunately the British demurred in granting his request to become an active participant in the "training" they had him observe. He was given "honorary" commando status, a swagger stick, and a black beret. His British hosts were not about to let him break his neck making a dark-of-the-night parachute jump before he had carried their intended message back to Washington.

Upon Solborg's return from England in early January 1942, he recommended, in a January 13 memorandum to Donovan, that a separate Special Operations Branch be established in COI's Special Activities. Solborg's apparent turnabout satisfied Donovan because it gave the "independent expert"— just back from the front—imprimatur to what he had intended to do all along. However, once Solborg's mentors in the army began to consider what a separate special operations organization in COI might mean to their own plans for commando organizations and operations, Solborg, for reasons lost in the labyrinth of unrecorded, after-hours conversations at the Fort Meyer officer's club bar, strangely recanted and reasserted his earlier advocacy of a single head for Secret Intelligence and Special Operations. Donovan was furious. The Solborg affair threatened a bureaucratic firestorm which might negate the earlier agreement between the military and Donovan over secret intelligence and create yet another committee to deal with the entire spectrum of secret intelligence activities. As a result, after damning him with faint praise for carrying out a "difficult" liaison assignment, Donovan took line control—command of special activities—away from Solborg, who was left with little more than his title. On January 23, 1942, the task of organizing and directing the Special Operations Branch was given to Major Goodfellow, who took on this task in addition to his liaison duties with G-2.

Goodfellow, a Brooklyn newspaper publisher and former Hearst executive, was more bureaucratically adroit than Solborg, the straight-line soldier, erstwhile secret agent. In the week or so which followed, Goodfellow managed to cut Solborg off from the paper flow as well as the personnel dickers between himself and the lame-duck G-2, Brigadier General Sherman Miles. Goodfellow's tactic is not uncommon in either business or government. It basically turned on organizing the Special Operations Branch around Solborg and placing him in a "turkey farm" limbo from which he neither knew or was able to influence the new organization's rapid evolution. Expectedly, Solborg complained to Donovan that he was being "left out of things," with the result that in February he was sent to Portugal to take charge of the three-man COI office in Lisbon.

With Solborg safely out of the way, Donovan and Goodfellow pushed ahead with the separation of Special Activities into SA/G (Special Activities/Goodfellow), also known as the Special Operations Branch, and SA/B (Special Activities/Bruce), under the direction of David K. E. Bruce, which was known as the Secret Intelligence Branch. With these organizational ducks in a row, Donovan was in a position to change the COI liaison with British intelligence to one based on functional lines, which could be used to carry out joint secret intelligence as well as secret operations.

While these internal perturbations were occurring in COI, others, with far-reaching consequence for the future of American secret intelligence operations, were taking place in the military. The most important was the creation of the United States Joint Chiefs of Staff which followed in the wake of Churchill's visit to Washington in December 1941. Churchill's visit had a twofold purpose: to convince Roosevelt of his "victory program" which included acceptance of the idea "Germany first" (that is, the primary objective of the European fight) and to work out the details of cooperation between United States, British, Dutch, and Australian air, ground, and naval contingents. To these ends Churchill and the British chiefs of staff held meetings with Roosevelt and American military leaders. These meetings in turn led to adoption of a series of agreements between the American, British, Dutch, and Australian governments known as the ABDA agreements. Although at the time there existed in the United States an organization known as the Combined Chiefs of Staff, its existence was on paper, a quasicoordinating body rather than an operational entity. Because the ABDA agreements involved operational considerations and decisions—such as the appointment on December 29, 1941, of Field Marshall Wavell as Supreme Commander of all Allied Forces in the ABDA—reference to the American military leaders was made by simply identifying them as the U.S. Chiefs of Staff.

This semantic byplay reflects the fact that at the time of these crucial American-British discussions the United States did not have a single organization with real authority or responsibility for coordinating the efforts of the army and navy in prosecuting the war. The organizational vacuum made attempts to regularize British-American military cooperation much more difficult. From minutes of the series of meetings between the U.S. Chiefs of Staff and the British Chiefs of Staff in January 1942, one realizes that Pearl Harbor had been insufficient to eliminate interservice rivalry. In the course of the meetings, the British tactfully suggested that the word "combined" be applied to collaboration between two or more nations, and the word "joint" to interservice collaboration in one nation. Fortunately, this suggestion was adopted without too much extraneous discussion. Thus, on January 14, 1942, a document setting up the Combined Chiefs of Staff and naming two subcommittees, the Combined Staff Planners and the Combined Intelligence Committee, was approved in principle. Provision was also made for a Combined Secretariat. The term "Combined Chiefs of Staff" was defined as the U.S. Chiefs of Staff and the British Chiefs of Staff. The first meeting of the Combined Chiefs of Staff was held on January 23. The paper describing their organization and responsibilities was considered at this meeting; it was approved at their fourth meeting, on February 10. It was then submitted to President Roosevelt and

Prime Minister Churchill for approval. Roosevelt approved the paper on April 21; there is no record in the Joint Chiefs of Staff records indicating Churchill's approval.*

Notwithstanding the gap in JCS's files, the basic agreement reflected Churchill's unparalleled skills in playing the "committee game." In this regard, the agreement made sure that no strategic decisions would be made without full and complete British involvement in the entire policy-decision process and, as American production of war materiel increased, that its allocation would be in accord with British-American strategic objectives. The agreement established that the Combined Chiefs of Staff were to formulate and execute plans and policies concerning:

(1) The strategic conduct of the war.
(2) The broad program of war requirements, based on approved strategic policy.
(3) The allocation of munition resources based on strategic needs and the availability of means of transportation.
(4) The requirements for overseas transportation for the fighting services of the United Nations, based on approved strategic priority.**

Because the British military leaders, who were able to speak with one voice, almost always seemed to win more than they lost in the meetings between the British Chiefs of Staff and the U.S. Chiefs of Staff, General Marshall, after more than a month of these meetings, finally decided to formally convene the U.S. Chiefs of Staff as a group before they met with the British. Incredibly, the first such meeting was not convened until February 9, 1942, by which date the die had already been cast on many aspects concerning the future conduct of the war. At this meeting, almost in passing, the U.S. Chiefs of Staff agreed —or rather no one present objected—to call themselves the Joint Chiefs of Staff; General Marshall assumed the chair and Brigadier General Walter B. Smith, formerly Secretary of the War Department's general staff, was named United States Secretary for the Combined Chiefs of Staff and also Secretary for the existing Joint Board and a number of other joint army-navy boards and agencies. The functions and duties of the Joint Board and all other agencies previously established by the War and Navy Departments to insure coordination in strategic planning and in military operations were absorbed by the Joint Chiefs of Staff.***

All this in retrospect seems very logical: the Joint Chiefs of Staff came into existence to serve as the United States' representatives on the Combined Chiefs of Staff and to carry out and expand the work presumably performed by the Joint Board. In this latter function the JCS reported directly to Roosevelt as

*Eberstadt Report, *op. cit.*, pp. 58–59.

**Ibid., p. 60.

***Ibid., p. 61.

commander-in-chief, and thence became the instrument through which the president coordinated strategic phases of the wartime military effort. One might question the absence of the Secretaries of War and the Navy at the creation of the JCS, but in those days the issue of "civilian control" over the military had yet to become a major problem or a public concern.

So much for the creation of the JCS and its arrogation of powers from the service secretaries which came out of its first meeting. It is important to note that "the President never approved any charter for the Joint Chiefs of Staff nor was legislative or executive action ever taken to formalize their creation or continued existence, unless the powers implied in the paper creating the Combined Chiefs of Staff and the approval of that paper by the President can be construed as a quasi-legal basis for their existence."* As a consequence, the lack of a specific charter for the JCS produced a situation which enabled it, under Marshall's direction, not only to fill a vacuum in the strategic conduct of the war, but also to become an almost preeminent force in the wartime bureaucratic struggles over intelligence, industrial production, national priorities—and therefore, the shape of the postwar world. One might also conclude that the birth of the "military-industrial complex" President Eisenhower warned about in his farewell address may properly be dated from the JCS's first meeting.

Once the JCS came into existence, Donovan realized that COI's relationships with the military services and other agencies, both directly and peripherally involved in secret intelligence activities, had to be changed. The JCS's de facto control over personnel and material resources made it necessary to place the COI in the JCS chain of command and authority. Moreover, Donovan also realized that secret intelligence activities and secret operations neither could nor should be carried out in an active theater of war without the concurrence and support of the area commanders, and that these activities and operations should be closely coordinated with conventional military operations.** How-

---

Ibid., p. 60.

**Donovan defined these terms by saying, "*Secret intelligence* operations are differentiated in two respects from the normal functions of the intelligence services of the Army and Navy: first, as to scope of activity, and second, as to informational objectives. Secret intelligence is able to place under scrutiny geographic areas where military and naval intelligence are debarred or handicapped by considerations of policy. Moreover, whereas the intelligence services of combat organizations are primarily concerned with the disposition, strength, effectiveness and intentions of the opposing armed forces, Secret Intelligence has as its field the collection, evaluation and dissemination of military, economic and political information shedding light on the condition and intentions of opposing governments. In a global, totalitarian war, intelligence must be global and totalitarian. *Special Operations* is authorized and directed as a part of psychological warfare to formulate, initiate, and make effective operations designed to harass, confuse, disrupt, deceive, intimidate, frighten, injure and, if possible, destroy the enemy, its allies and sympathizers. Such operations will be made to conform to the requirements of the American Military Command for the Area or respective areas in which they are conducted. They may take the form of offensive or defensive measures. These operations may be direct, indirect, or under cover. They may or may not involve

ever, unlike the earlier battle over formation of the COI, this problem was more complex because the issues about the collection, analysis, and dissemination of intelligence information had since become enmeshed with the issue of propaganda as well as secret intelligence.

In the months which followed creation of the JCS, Donovan argued unsuccessfully with Roosevelt for COI to be made a supporting agency of the JCS, and that foreign propaganda carried out by the COI's Foreign Information Service branch (FIS) be closely knit "with the intelligence and the physically subversive activities of the Army and Navy." While Roosevelt dawdled, the bureaucratic battle over propaganda raged. Elmer Davis, head of the Office of War Information (OWI), was arrayed in clear opposition to Donovan and to a lesser degree with Robert Sherwood, the head of FIS. Also, although Sherwood shared most of Donovan's ideas about propaganda, he balked at the idea of bringing FIS under JCS authority because he felt that such a limitation on its activities would effectively nullify the entire effort. All three were strong-willed men. Their quarrel was an ancient one; it turned on their differing perceptions concerning the functions, purposes, and definition of propaganda as well as on bureaucratic questions. Donovan clearly looked on propaganda as an instrument of modern war, whereas Davis considered its proper function simply the dissemination of facts to friend and foe alike. In its barest form, their dispute was one concerning how the United States could engage in propaganda designed to disorganize, mislead, and deceive its enemies and keep those activities separate from the government's efforts to keep the American people properly informed about the war. Donovan believed there was no conflict in operating both systems on parallel tracks and in using truth as well as artful lies to deal with foreign propaganda. However Davis, who completely disdained the black arts of propaganda as well as use of the term itself, believed that truth, or rather "war information"—partially censored on grounds of military necessity and security—was sufficient to counter the enemy's propaganda activities.

Although American-originated propaganda directed toward Axis countries and occupied territories, especially that delivered by radio, was the touchstone

---

physical action and may be conceived with a view to affecting the mind or body. In the accomplishment of the foregoing it may be necessary or advisable, among other things: To corrupt and control enemy organizations and enemy dominated agencies; to fabricate propaganda, rumor and news, and to disseminate the same, whether true or false; to promote or incite resistance, revolution, and sabotage of all kinds; to recruit, train, equip, supply, organize, direct, and deal with groups and individuals; to employ or cause to be employed arms and lethal weapons and instrumentalities of whatsoever kind; and generally to formulate, supervise, implement and conduct against the enemy and its adherents special forms of subversive warfare; and to make the same effective through the control, operation, or use of such facilities as may be neccessary therewith."
(See: Memorandum; From: Director of Strategic Services to Joint Psychological Warfare Committee, Subj: Response to J.P.W.C. 45/D., dated October 24, 1942, forwarded on October 31, 1942 and included as an Enclosure to SECRET, J.P.W.C. 45/1, informational memorandum dated November 2, 1942.)

of the Donovan-Davis dispute, it was only one aspect of the broader question concerning the role and control over the entire gamut of psychological warfare activities which had become an integral part of modern total war. These activities, which had been successfully demonstrated by Hitler's fifth-column, preinvasion softening-up tactics, were ones the American military similarly wanted to use and control for their own purposes. Thus, the psychological warfare and propaganda dispute hinged for its resolution on consolidation of the government's information services and on the issuance of an order which would legitimize COI's activities in these areas and place it under the JCS as a supporting agency.

Some of the difficulties surrounding the argument stemmed from Donovan's earlier, partially successful advocacy of an integrated intelligence information effort. At the time of the battle over establishing COI, little thought was given to psychological warfare and propaganda during actual hostilities, and once war did come it became difficult to separate the functions of promoting the Allies' positions while attacking those of their enemies. Looming large in Roosevelt's reluctance to resolve the issues surfaced by the Donovan-Davis dispute over propaganda was the obvious political hazard in allowing Donovan to have a free hand in the general field of propaganda because of possible partisan political consequences. It was one thing for Roosevelt to turn Donovan loose to use propaganda to deceive the enemy, but quite another to run the risk of charges that his administration was similarly deceiving, however unintentionally, the American people for partisan purposes.

Donovan gave the psychological warfare issue a full shot. He nagged Roosevelt in memos, arguing for retention of FIS under COI and clear authority to carry out a broad spectrum of activities; he argued equally vociferously for placing COI under the JCS. Similarly, he lobbied his case with Roosevelt's advisers, most notably "Judge" Sam Rosenman, to the same effect. Nonetheless, all of Donovan's efforts were to little avail. The logic of Donovan's position, as with so many about intelligence when it comes into conflict with politics, was no match for subjectively perceived political conditions and the obdurate obstructionism of "those who did not know exactly what should be done, but at least thought they knew what someone else should be prevented from doing."

Although Donovan only admitted to his closest associates his disappointment and frustration in attempting to work with and for Roosevelt, the battles over psychological warfare and getting the COI placed under the JCS took something out of him. Donovan, who hitherto had successfully circumvented his opposition in getting COI established and in picking up the secret intelligence functions from the military services, fell victim to his own tactics. For example, Harold D. Smith, the Director of the Budget, with continual easy access to Roosevelt, was able to raise the kinds of doubts about Donovan's activities which caused delays and called into question the informal decisions FDR had already made in authorizing those activities. To wit: on February 28, 1942, Smith wrote to Roosevelt:

The Coordinator's activities have developed to such an extent that a letter or order defining the area of activity assigned to his office is becoming increasingly necessary. If you believe such a definition to be desirable, I will be glad to prepare a draft of the necessary order or letter.*

Donovan was a match for most of his bureaucratic opponents, but Smith and his budgeteers were too much. Theirs were the voices of the bookkeeper's conscience, ones with visions of an orderly set of numbers which would lead to an acceptable cost-benefit analysis of expenditures on secret intelligence, psychological warfare, and propaganda activities. Another point of view about the antagonists in this battle was voiced to me many years later by James Dunn, at the time Assistant Secretary of State, who in response to the question, "Why did Donovan lose control over the foreign propaganda function?" replied that "although Budget Director Smith's actions were important, Donovan lost because he cared too much about COI, the organization he had breathed life into, and because he really never was much of a 'main chance' gambler." Dunn added, "Besides, the political overtones about propaganda, when it came down to push or shove for FDR, the fact that Elmer Davis put himself and OWI on the line was the tipping factor. Davis made it clear that if Donovan retained control over foreign propaganda he would quit—and not go quietly, whereas Donovan made no similar threat."

On June 8, any lingering doubts Donovan may have had about his influence on intelligence policy were resolved by Roosevelt's decision to separate FIS from COI. The decision itself, although an intelligence disaster of the first order, was not so important in terms of its overall effect on America's positive intelligence efforts during World War II as was the manner in which it reached Donovan. Not unlike the cuckolded husband who is the last to know, Donovan only learned after the executive order had been approved that Roosevelt had reversed his earlier decision giving him "the responsibility of planning, initiating, developing and executing a program of psychological and political warfare, including subversive activities; of encouraging and stimulating the support and assistance of allied nations and people of occupied territories; and of disseminating information outside the Western Hemisphere."** And further, the OWI was going to be established along the lines proposed by Elmer Davis and the Bureau of the Budget. The order assigned the FIS branch of COI to OWI and left Nelson Rockefeller's Coordinator of Inter-American Affairs (CIAA) office undisturbed to promote "Good Neighbor" policies in the Western Hemisphere, avoiding any actions to let the Latin Americans know that the Nazis were doing evil things, there or elsewhere.

In one last, futile effort, after learning from his own White House sources that he had been done in by Davis, Smith, Hopkins et al., Donovan, also on

*War Report, *op. cit.*, p. 21.

**Ibid., p. 20.

June 8, asked Roosevelt, if the FIS was to be taken away from COI, that "at the same time there be issued an order concerning our relationship with the Joint Chiefs of Staff." Prophetically, Donovan added:

It is curious to note that at the very moment when the British are beginning to come to centralization of the various activities we already have under one tent, we have many theorists who, because of a false logic, are seeking to break up our own efficient centralization. The separation of our foreign service is the beginning, and I do hope for the sake of the war effort, you will not permit it to go farther. I say this frankly because you know that if you feel my usefulness here is ended you have only to tell me so. I know very well that with the assistance of men of brains and character who have been with me, we have built up a real wartime service for you. I would not want to see it broken up without calling it to your attention. . . . Whatever your decision is, we will implement it loyally and efficiently.*

Beyond the accuracy of Donovan's prophecy and his pledge of fealty, his memorandum reveals a great deal about how the bureaucratic game of intelligence was played then, as now. In the first instance, Donovan knew when he wrote the June 8 memo to Roosevelt that the decision had already been made to strip COI of its FIS organization, but that the promulgation of the order and the full extent of its terms would not be announced for several days. And more importantly Donovan knew that FDR knew that he knew. His statement, "I would not want to see it broken up without calling it to your attention" underscores the grim fact that Roosevelt's determination of a fundamental change and adoption of a new intelligence policy had been made without Donovan's being a party to the discussions surrounding the decision. Again, James Dunn: "There was a strange reluctance on FDR's part in these and other matters to meet face to face with strong advocates of positions which involved their own organizations. FDR had trouble saying no, and he preferred to discuss questions like the one about OWI/OSS with those he thought were disinterested in the outcome." Dunn agreed this kind of practice was nonsensical and dangerous. He concluded by saying, "There's no accounting for presidents, they all become a little mad and because of the office's constraints and frustration tend to look on intelligence, or whatever, as their own private model railroad which they can run as they personally and petulantly see fit."

Almost immediately after submitting his memo, Donovan, Goodfellow, and Bruce departed for London to work out the arrangements and agreements between the COI's SA/G and the British SOE. At the time of their departure none of the three knew whether going on their mission made any sense because, besides the loss of FIS, they didn't know what was planned for the rest of COI. They were a melancholy group; however, Donovan had an "Irish Grandmother's hunch" which he mentioned before their departure to his personal

*Ibid., p. 26.

assistant, Stella Frankfurter (the sister of the Supreme Court justice) that COI would be rechartered under the JCS because General Marshall favored such an approach. But in the looking-glass environment of FDR's wartime White House no one could ever risk making book on what might emerge from it under the guise of a national "intelligence policy."

Shortly after the group's arrival in London, William D. Whitney, who represented COI and carried out liaison duties with the British intelligence services, informed Donovan that Roosevelt had, with the issuance of the executive order which took FIS out of the COI and transferred it to the OWI, simultaneously issued a military order establishing the Office of Strategic Services (OSS) under the JCS.

It read as follows:

MILITARY ORDER

Office of Strategic Services

By virtue of the authority vested in me as President of the United States and as Commander-in-Chief of the Army and Navy of the United States, it is ordered as follows:

1. The Office of the Coordinator of Information, established by Order of July 11, 1941, exclusive of the foreign information activities transferred to the Office of War Information by Executive Order of June 13, 1942, shall hereafter be known as the Office of Strategic Services, and is hereby transferred to the jurisdiction of the United States Joint Chiefs of Staff.

2. The Office of Strategic Services shall perform the following duties:

a. Collect and analyze such strategic information as may be required by the United States Joint Chiefs of Staff.

b. Plan and operate such special services as may be directed by the United States Joint Chiefs of Staff.

3. At the head of the Office of Strategic Services shall be a Director of Strategic Services who shall be appointed by the President and who shall perform his duties under the direction and supervision of the United States Joint Chiefs of Staff.

4. William J. Donovan is hereby appointed as Director of Strategic Services.

5. The Order of July 11, 1941, is hereby revoked.

Franklin D. Roosevelt
Commander-in-Chief

The White House
June 13, 1942.

Thus armed with new authority, and perhaps some unwarranted optimism about the future of the newly established OSS under the JCS, Donovan moved ahead quickly to nail down the details of the agreements between OSS and the British Special Operations Executive (SOE) organization. The discussions, which took place generally during the period June 16–24, between OSS and SOE leaders were amiable throughout and in one sense may be described as a global version of the Parker Brothers' game of "Monopoly," wherein the two teams divided up control of the world between themselves and made arrangements for "joint tenancy" in some countries with one or the other acting as the landlord/coordinator for a wide range of subversive secret activities. Because the resulting agreements represent a unique model of how an "intelligence treaty" between two nations' intelligence organizations can and should be negotiated, they are worthy of close consideration, not only due to their international flavor, but also for the principles they illustrate about how intelligence coordination can properly be achieved.

As a first and essential step, Sir Charles Hambro provided Donovan with the SOE position in a paper entitled: "Notes on Collaboration between British and United States SOE." It read as follows:

OBJECT

1. The object of these notes is to lay down the principles on which such collaboration must be based, the reasons behind these principles and the machinery by which they might be effected.

PRINCIPLES

2. *COOPERATION AT HQ LONDON/WASHINGTON*

This is dependent on close liaison resulting in a common policy and is essential if we are to avoid crossing lines either in policy or in the supply of materials.

This liaison could be effected by a British liaison section working alongside Colonel Donovan's headquarters and a similar American liaison section working alongside S.O.E. headquarters, London. The duties of this liaison section would be:

(a) To represent the views of their respective headquarters on all policy matters so that a common policy for every theatre can be decided on.

(b) To discuss with the H.Q. to which they have been accredited cases of dispute in the field which have been referred to that H.Q.

(c) To exchange information and to keep their headquarters fully informed on matters of interest.

(d) To co-ordinate the production, demand and supply of equipment from British and U.S. sources.

(e) To exchange both operational and technical intelligence, and information on methods of training.

Such a liaison section could consist of one head liaison officer (who would be a high-level representative charged with executive functions supported by requisite staff).

3. *COOPERATION IN THE FIELD*

It is essential to avoid the situation where there will be two completely independent organizations working in the field, with all the consequent dangers of crossing of lines, competition for agents and material etc., and inviting attempts by foreign governments, or groups with whom both organizations would be dealing, to play one off against the other.

In some cases the problem could be dealt with by assigning the given region exclusively either to the American or British organization and the organization which agrees to stay out represented at most only by a liaison officer and small staff.

There will, however, be very few of these simple cases and in most areas the position will be that whilst an area be in predominantly a British or American sphere of influence, both countries will have some interests inside it and will need to establish some representation and possibly a system of agents.

It is suggested that the general principles to be adopted in such cases should be:

(a) Each area should be defined as being either a British or American area.

(b) Inside a British area it will be agreed that the control and direction should be British and that the policy should be laid down and all instruction to the Mission or Missions in that area should be issued from London. In an American area the same procedure would apply as regards Washington.

(c) In the field in a British area there would be a British Mission, the head of which would be controller for the whole area and who would look for his direction and instructions to London. There could, if the Americans so wished in the same territory, be an American Mission and its head at those headquarters would work under the direction and control of the British controller. The head of the American Mission could report direct to Washington on any matter he wished with a copy to the American liaison mission in London, but he would receive his instruction from London and through the British controller and would only act on communications received direct from Washington with the agreement and consent of the British controller. In an American territory the same principles would apply with the roles reversed.

(d) In the event of a difference of opinion arising between the British or American controller and the head of the British or American Mission inside his territory which could not be settled locally, the issue would be referred to London or Washington respectively, and it would be the responsibility of the headquarters in question to settle it with the liaison mission attached to it.

Even these rather general principles may not be able to be applied strictly in all cases and it may be necessary to make exceptions in certain countries to meet special requirements.

The importance of these "notes" cannot be overstressed. Once Donovan accepted their basic criteria they enabled all the participants to proceed with an exceedingly difficult and complex task within a framework of agreed-upon rules which recognized each side's national interests and the necessity to work together for these as well as their common wartime interests. In terms of the bloated size of today's international delegations which are convened to deliberate and debate matters of much less consequence and complexity, the size of the British SOE and American OSS staff contingents which negotiated the agreements was minuscule. At the first meeting, which took place in the morning and evening of June 16, the OSS was represented by Colonel Goodfellow and Colonel Garland Williams, a former narcotics inspector from New York and recruit to the OSS from the army's Counter-Intelligence Corps, and the British SOE by a Colonel Taylor and Mr. Keswick. Notably, neither Donovan or Colin Gubbins, head of the British SOE, believed it necessary for them to attend the meeting. Instead, both leaders were content and confident to let their subordinates negotiate and commit their organizations to actions within the spirit and framework of the "notes." Although these commitments were not final until approved by Donovan and Gubbins, it is worthy of note that with the exception of North Africa, which was basically resolved in favor of the American position (see below), none of them required any substantial modification in fact or principle before their final approval by Donovan and Gubbins.

In the course of their conversations, the participants quite literally reviewed the world and divided it up in terms of how their organizations, separately and jointly, would carry out subversive and special operations. Their conclusions for each area reflected not only existing and projected military activities, but more significantly the political realities associated with the past, present, and future fates of those areas once victory over the Axis powers had been achieved. The following conclusions were arrived at:

1. *India*

It was agreed that India should be regarded as a British area where all operations would be carried out by the British mission, with control being exercised from London. The American S.O. would have the right to send out a liaison mission to be attached to the British mission for liaison purposes, but not for operational purposes.

2. *China*

It was agreed that this area, of which the headquarters would be at Chungking, and which covers the whole of China, including Japanese-occupied China, Manchuria, and Korea, should be regarded as an American sphere of influence. The American mission would be established at Chungking and would direct all S.O.E. activities in this area. It would be controlled from Washington. The existing British mission at Chungking would be reduced and would be turned into a liaison mission attached to the American mission. The British liaison mission, in addition to its liaison duties, would render any assistance which it could to the American mission, but only at the latter's request and under the latter's control.

3. *Australia*

It was agreed that British S.O.E. would have no responsibility for and would take no action in the area covered by General MacArthur's command and that of the American Naval Command in the Southwestern Pacific. This area would be considered as covering New Guinea, and the islands of the East Indian archipelago up to and including Java and Borneo. It would be for the American S.O. to make its own arrangements with the Intelligence Service Division which already exists in Australia under General MacArthur's control. British S.O.E. would continue to give any assistance asked for to this mission.

4. *Southeast Asia*

It was agreed that Burma, Siam, Indo-China, Malaya, and Sumatra should be regarded as a no-man's land which could be worked into as convenient by the British

S.O.E. mission in India, the American S.O. mission in China, and ISD in Australia. Line crossing inside this area would have to be avoided by close liaison between these three missions.

5. *East Africa*

It was agreed that the area covered by the British S.O.E. mission which already exists with headquarters at Durban, charged with working into Madagascar and Portuguese East Africa, should be regarded as a British area. American S.O. would have the right to have a liaison mission attached to the British mission at Durban.

6. *West Africa—Frawest and Neucols*

Whilst it was agreed that the area covered by these two existing British S.O.E. missions, namely, the West African colonies from the southern boundary of Morocco to the boundary of South-West Africa with Portuguese West Africa should be, for the time being, regarded as predominantly a British sphere, it was recognized that the American S.O. had a very definite interest in this area, since if any military action on a large scale were to be undertaken by the United Nations in West Africa, such action would predominantly be the responsibility of American military authorities. The American S.O. therefore consider that they must place themselves in a position to be able to carry out S.O.E. services for the American Command if such a situation should arise. The following procedure was accordingly agreed upon:

American S.O. would establish missions corresponding to our Frawest and Neucols missions. The programs of these American missions would be worked out in as much detail as possible between Washington and London. Copies of this agreed programme would then be sent to the heads of the American missions and the heads of the British missions with clear instruction in both cases that the execution of this programme by the American missions would be discussed step by step with the heads of the British missions and no action taken until agreement had been reached with them. If such agreement could not be arrived at, the point at issue would be referred to headquarters to be settled between London and Washington, and until decision was given no action would be taken by the American missions. It was contemplated that the programme which would be worked out between London and Washington for these American missions would be essentially preparatory in character, consisting of the placing of American representatives at appropriate points, the establishment of dumps of materials, collection of information and operational intelligence, and the working out of plans against appropriate targets.

7. *Atlantic Islands*

It was agreed that these islands comprising the Azores, Madeira, the Canaries, and the Cape Verde Islands should be regarded as an American sphere and operated by an American mission controlled from Washington. The British S.O.E. would have the right to attach liaison officers to the American organization.

8. *Balkans and the Middle East*

It was agreed that in view of the fact that all Military Commands in these areas were British Commands, that the principal political authority was the British Minister of State at Cairo, and the whole of the territory other than Turkey within which and from which operations could take place or be based, was wholly or partially under the British S.O.E., with its headquarters at Cairo, this should be regarded as predominantly a British area. At the same time it was appreciated that there were many ways in which the American S.O. could be of great assistance in this area. It could call upon resources in regard to equipment, materials and possibly personnel which were not available to the British S.O.E., and in certain areas, for example, Turkey and Iran, American personnel could, in some respects, operate more easily than British personnel.

The British representatives stressed the extreme complexity of the situation, with particular regard to the fact that S.O.E. have to work in this area with a number of Allied Governments and foreign freedom movements or resistance groups, and emphasized the delicacy of the political situation in various occupied or semi-occupied countries, and the necessity of any S.O.E. organization conforming to the policy of the local authorities, such as the Minister of State, the local Military Commanders, and the local diplomatic representatives. They were accordingly of the opinion that if line crossing, confusion and friction with local authorities was to be avoided, it was especially essential that in this area there should be unity of control in the field and unity of direction from a single headquarters. They accordingly suggested that the set-up should be as follows:

The controller of the existing British S.O.E. mission would be regarded as being in charge of all S.O.E. operations in that area and would be responsible for all S.O.E. activity to the local authorities, particularly the S.O.E. Sub-Committee of the Minister of State's War Council, and to headquarters in London. An American S.O. mission should be set up in Cairo with the object of providing such assistance as it could to the British S.O.E. and of contributing to the British S.O.E. services which would only be available from the American side. The form and extent of the organization of the American mission and also the scope and character of its activities would be discussed and settled by the Head of the American mission with the British controller under whom he would be working. In the event of failure to reach agreement the issue would be referred to headquarters to be settled between London and Washington. In the meantime, the views of the Controller would prevail. The Head of the American mission would communicate direct with Washington on any matter he pleased, but it would be clearly laid down that as regards any action the American mission would look to the Controller for direction and instructions and would take no action except with his approval.

The substantial effect of this arrangement would be that there would be a single S.O.E. machine in the area, at the head of which would be the present Controller, but that under him there would be two organizations, namely the existing British S.O.E. organization covering the whole area of the mission, and a small American organization which would be fitted in by the Controller into the general programme wherever it could help.

9. *Western Europe*

It was agreed that collaboration between the British and American S.O.E.s in the Western European area (which should be considered as covering Scandinavia and the Baltic area, the Low Countries, France, Switzerland, Germany, Italy, Poland and Czechoslovakia) would have to be arranged in two stages.

On the British side it was appreciated that as there will at some future date, be a very large American force based on Great Britain with the task of carrying out military operations in Western Europe, there must eventually be a complete American S.O.

attached to this American Command to carry out S.O.E. services for it in those areas in Western Europe which have been allocated to American forces. Once these areas were known it would be easy to apply the principle that all S.O.E. activities within the area allocated to the American Command would be carried on by the American S.O., the latter taking over from British S.O.E. any field organization which the British S.O.E. might, in the meantime, have established in territories eventually placed under American command.

It was recognized firstly that this division of military force was still some way off; secondly that it would be some months before the American S.O. would be in a position to operate as an independent organization attached to the American Command; and thirdly, that not only would some interim arrangement have to be come to regarding activities by the American S.O. in Western Europe pending the drawing of the lines of demarcation, but even when the areas of the British and American Commands have been determined there would remain countries unaffected by these invasion plans in which both the British and American S.O.E.s might wish to operate. To cover the interim period referred to above before any area could be allocated to the American S.O. as their exclusive territory, it was suggested that the following procedure should be adopted. An American mission would be set up in London with two main functions. The first would be the preparation of an American S.O. organization for attachment to the American Military Command in Great Britain, and the British S.O.E. would only be involved to the extent to which it could give assistance particularly in matters of training to its American counterpart. The second function would be the setting up of at least embryonic American field forces in the countries likely to be effected by the re-invasion of Europe, namely Norway, the Low Countries and France. The American representatives felt that it would be impossible for them to refrain from taking action at all in the way of infiltration or recruitment of agents until the American sphere of military operations was decided. At the same time they recognized that since the British S.O.E. had organized and were operating field forces in all those areas to a very considerable extent already, it would be inviting trouble for time to come in building up an independent American field force which would very likely cross lines with existing machinery. It was accordingly agreed that during the interim period the American mission would establish and operate agents in the field only in collaboration and under the general direction of the British S.O.E. headquarters. Agents recruited locally by an American representative would be sent instructions only with their knowledge and approval. All American agents in the field in the area in question would be operated by the American S.O. mission in London and not from Washington.

As regards those countries which would not be effected by any division of military force between the British and American Commands e.g., Germany, Switzerland, Italy, Poland and Czechoslovakia, it is suggested by the British S.O.E. that special regional arrangements should be worked out in each case, providing for the exact machinery of collaboration required to ensure that the two organizations did not cross lines. It is for instance obvious that the Poles and the Czechs should not be encouraged to play the British and American S.O.E. off against each other.

10. *North Africa and the Iberian Peninsula*

As the ideas put forward by the British and American representatives regarding collaboration in these areas were completely at variance it was consequently felt that they should refer the proposals to their principals. These were:

The British S.O.E. representatives suggested that North Africa be regarded, at least for the present, as a territory which should be operated from London and they outlined an arrangement by which a combined British-American organization would be operated under a British S.O.E. officer with headquarters at Gibraltar. The factors which the British S.O.E. had principally in mind in making this suggestion were that:

(a) Gibraltar is the natural base for S.O.E. operations in North Africa. It would be the point at which all stores would have to be assembled for distribution in North Africa and it is the site of the S.O.E. W/T [wireless/telegraph] Station which would eventually operate all agent's W/Ts in North Africa and would provide the main line channel to London in the event of other lines failing. As an S.O.E. headquarters at Gibraltar would be dealing with British authorities in that fortress such dealings would be facilitated if a British S.O.E. officer was in charge.

(b) At the present state London is perhaps a better operational for dealing with North Africa than Washington from the point of view of distance and facilities for the consultation of interested parties.

(c) It is desireable that Madrid, which has a direct interest in the North African picture through Spanish Morocco and an indirect interest in the French North African situation, should be kept in step. As the dominating factor in Madrid as regards S.O.E. work is the British Naval Attache, there would be certain advantages in having a man in charge at Gibraltar who had close relations with him.

(d) British S.O.E. were prepared to supply their best available man in the person of Colonel Clarke who had been dealing with this area for a long time, who would be persona grata at Gibraltar, Tangier and Madrid, and who enjoys special relations with the British Naval Attache in Madrid and with the American S.O.E. staff in Lisbon and North Africa.

British S.O.E. suggested that, if their ideas were acceptable to their American colleagues, they would propose that the whole area of the Iberian peninsula and North Africa should be grouped together as a single mission to be operated under the control of London. The exact relationship of American to British personnel at Lisbon, Gibraltar, and Tangier would have to be worked out in the course of further discussion, the guiding principle being the necessity for a certain minimum degree of unity of control in the field and direction from a single headquarters.

The American representatives expressed the view that the North African areas should be regarded as a predominantly American sphere in which a combined American and British organization would operate under the control of Washington. The main factors which they had in mind in making this proposal were that:

(a) Any approaches to French authorities in North Africa would almost certainly have to be made through American channels.

(b) Any military operations which it might be decided to carry out in North Africa would almost certainly be the responsibility of the United States authorities and the command would be American.

(c) All discussions with French authorities in North Africa were intimately bound up with the economic policy to be adopted towards North Africa by the United Nations. This was predominantly a matter for Washington's decision and it was absolutely essential to coordinate any political military negotiations in North Africa with the policy of the Bureau of Economic Warfare in Washington. This could obviously be done most effectively if control of the S.O.E. organization engaged in these negotiations was in Washington also.

The American representatives therefore proposed that an American mission should be set up with headquarters at Gibraltar and they indicated they would like to send a new and senior officer to be head of this mission. They thought that the Iberian peninsula should be separated from North Africa and that special arrangements should be made for Anglo-American collaboration in that area.

Although because of changes in strategy and the unexpected early successes against Italian forces in North Africa, these "territorial imperative" divisions and agreements did not hold completely through the war, they were important in providing a network base on which a spectrum of World War II and postwar secret intelligence organization and secret operations were built. Also, in spite of frictions which developed between OSS personnel in its various SO "missions," and those of the British SOE over the latter's reluctance to let some of the former operate on their own, the Americans, by being "on station," established contacts of their own and gained knowledge about the composition, organization, and membership of indigenous personnel involved in the British secret intelligence and SOE networks. This latter fact is often overlooked in works on this phase of OSS operations; it was crucial in the postwar evolution of American overseas secret intelligence activities, especially in those areas where, as British influence ended, the CIA and others moved in and took over many of the wartime British secret intelligence "assets."

Notwithstanding the SOE agreements' evolutions during World War II and their long-term derived benefits to the American intelligence community, at the time Donovan thought it essential that OSS become rapidly involved in an expanded series of secret intelligence and secret operations in order to maintain control over these kinds of activities. Donovan was keenly aware that precedent and on-going activities were powerful arguments in maintaining an individual organization's authority. It should also be noted that while Goodfellow was negotiating the SOE agreements, Donovan and Bruce were similarly engaged in expanding OSS interaction with the British SIS. These negotiations led to a partial rerun of the Solborg imbroglio because William Whitney believed that OSS's secret intelligence and secret operations relations in England should be combined under a single organization and single direction, namely his. Donovan attempted to get Whitney's agreement that the political realities in England mandated separate though parallel OSS organizations for secret intelligence and secret operations, but with no success. Whitney was unable to grasp that OSS was moving from a liaison relationship to one of active participant in actual operations. As a result, because they could not agree to disagree about the changed situation, Donovan replaced Whitney with David Bruce, who was placed in London in overall charge of OSS operations in the European theater. In this post Bruce walked a bureaucratic tightrope between the British SIS and SOE organizations and maintained enough of the fiction that the OSS was similarly split to enable activities in both areas to be planned and carried out.

Before describing other features of the SOE agreements, it is worthwhile to put the British split between secret intelligence and secret operations in some additional perspective. As mentioned, one reason for this split was the fact that each organization was under the direction and control of a different cabinet officer. There was a more fundamental reason: the differing methods and objectives of secret intelligence and secret operations create considerable justification for keeping them separate. Both secret intelligence and secret operations include covert activities; however, once a secret operation like the sabotage destruction of a power plant occurs, it becomes known to the enemy and those involved must be prepared to "head for the hills." On the other hand, secret intelligence sources and agents are expected to remain in place and undetected. They are required to ferret out the enemy's secrets by penetration and compromise techniques as well as to engage in counterintelligence activities designed to protect their own identity. Conceptually, the idea of blending secret intelligence and secret operations is attractive on the surface; in practice, both the British and later American experience suggest, given the mental outlook associated with persons who work in each field, that placing the two under a single direction is untenable.

Following acceptance of the territorial divisions, the "conversations" produced additional conclusions about the training of American subversive agents, research and development, and the funding and outfitting of secret operations. Training was especially important because although some training of OSS personnel had been underway for several months, primarily at the SOE's training school at Toronto, there was an urgent necessity to expand the program to take care of the greater numbers required by the agreements, and also to provide advanced training in the more sophisticated techniques of subversion and sabotage. To these ends Donovan and Goodfellow asked "that a large number of American officers be permitted to attend the various specialized training schools in Great Britain, and particularly that American SO officers be detailed for short periods of time to the various operational stations and offices in England. This will not only serve as a means of training for the individuals concerned, but will be a most powerful factor in insuring unity of doctrine and effort in the future operations of the two national SO organizations."

The research and development side of the SOE-OSS agreements also reflected Britain's longer experience in the field. For many years the British SOE had been actively involved in the research and development of the so-called special devices used in sabotage, espionage, and surveillance, and those used by agents for lethal purposes. As such, the British contribution enabled the OSS to make a quantum leap into the field of "dirty tricks." The agreement called for Donovan to send personnel of his choosing to the British SOE Research and Development Station IX, located in the British countryside, to participate in its work and to gain information about the state of subversion and sabotage. Further, because OSS did not as yet have a similar organization of their own, the British agreed to effect liaison with Dr. James Conant's wartime science and technology organization, which was aiding and conducting research for OSS. To complete the circle, the agreement also reaffirmed the assignment of Major Freeth and Mr. Billinghurst from the British SOE to the OSS for the purpose of facilitating the expanded production in the United States of "off the shelf" items which were in the SOE inventory. This latter fact represented a necessary and worthwhile concession because it enabled the British, who had the greater experience in the field, to concentrate the efforts of the extremely limited number of qualified personnel on research tasks and let the Americans work on the complex and difficult task of mass producing special devices which hitherto had been custom made or hand tooled in Station IX's laboratories and shops.

Once the agreements had established when and what was to be done and how the expanded demand for special devices was to be met, the participants had to resolve the prosaic but thorny question of the terms and mechanics of payment. Then as now, the question involved much more than putting a simple inclusive price tag on secret operations. On the British side, funds drawn from the British Treasury for SOE expenditures were charged to the secret vote; that is, they were approved by Parliament without its knowing their amount or intended purposes. From secret vote funds, SOE paid the salaries of their officers and operational expenditures for ordnance, special devices, bribes, etc.; however, SOE personnel on detached duty from the military services were paid from the open votes of the service departments. On the American side, the question was more complicated because with the creation of OSS it appeared that the previous method of financing COI's special activities out of block grants from President Roosevelt's secret fund would no longer apply. Goodfellow ventured the opinion that since OSS was now a part of the Joint Chiefs of Staff, grants would be forthcoming from military appropriations in the nature of confidential funds; but on this point neither he nor Donovan was certain. Personnel costs did not pose any problem because all OSS personnel would draw their pay from the service departments' authorizations. Therefore, because ordnance was the big item in the overall cost spectrum of special operations, the participants agreed:

The Office of Strategic Services and the Special Operations Executive both produce ordnance which will be used in practically every case for similar operations, if not in respect of joint operations that resources should be pooled wherever possible and machinery set up—

(a) To determine jointly the types and quantities which each organization should produce.

(b) The allocation of such production to the various operational centres.

(c) As regards the question of finance in respect of such production, it was agreed that each side should finance their own production and that whilst detailed records should be kept of the destinations of all issues, there will be no payments, or financial obligations as between the two organizations or their respective Governments.

Although the agreements were modified somewhat during the war, taken together they constitute a reasonably prescient legacy in the postwar evolution of America's activities in the fields of secret intelligence and secret operations. The British provided the base from which the wartime OSS was able to apprentice its personnel; while there were frictions and contretemps between both parties, these were less important than the fact that "Special Activities" were legitimized, if not institutionalized, in the minds of those who would come to dominate America's postwar intelligence community. Donovan, who advocated, once the war was over, the end of OSS's special activities, never fully appreciated their effect on the thinking of those in OSS and the rest of the American intelligence community. For many, the special wartime activities became ends in themselves rather than one of many means available to produce valid intelligence, or keep a potential enemy off balance.

Upon his return from London in late June 1942, Donovan found himself caught up in a "new period of uncertainty as to the future of the OSS under the Joint Chiefs of Staff." However, pending resolution of its relationship, Donovan moved quickly to expand OSS's special activities and get additional agents into the field. To these ends, the Special Intelligence Branch (SA/B) under David Bruce established branch offices or advanced operational bases in London, Chungking, Lisbon, Cairo, and Lagos. From these bases, agents were dispatched into enemy, enemy-occupied, and neutral countries to observe and personally report on matters of military and naval interest, and obtain and transmit economic, political, and psychological intelligence material. Additionally, Bruce's agents were authorized to purchase information and, when sent to enemy and enemy-occupied countries, to contact and use the resources of organized native subversive and resistance elements. By September 1942, this group of agents numbered approximately 250, all but three of whom were civilians. They were in place in Egypt, China, the Near East, the entire African continent, Palestine, Portugal, Saudi Arabia, Spain, Sweden, Switzerland, Syria, Turkey, Afghanistan, Liberia, Vichy France, Yugoslavia, Greece, India, Ceylon, Norway, and Rumania.

Similarly, the Special Operations Branch (SA/G), under the direction of Colonel Ellery Huntington, had established base stations in England for Western and Central Europe, Egypt for Africa and the Near East, Chungking for Asia, Australia for East Indian and Pacific Islands; and American training schools in the Catoctin area (north of Frederick, Maryland), two others west of Quantico, Virginia, and one across the Potomac from Quantico, all on National Park tracts. Unlike the civilian flavor of SA/B, by September 1942 all of the 260 personnel/agents assigned to SA/G were from the military services. Their mission, as established in the SOE agreements, was to "carry out sabotage and subversive operations and to support and organize guerrilla and revolutionary movements in occupied countries."

With SA/B and SA/G agents in place, an extensive recruiting and training program and some first-step operations underway, Donovan was ready to do battle with the JCS about the OSS's future. In early 1942, the JCS established a Joint Psychological Warfare Committee (JPWC) to plan for psychological warfare. For the next several months confusion reigned supreme as other agencies, such as Nelson Rockefeller's Coordinator of Inter-American Affairs (CIAA), Henry Wallace's Board of Economic Warfare (BEW), Elmer Davis' newly chartered Office of War Information (OWI), and the State Department tried to stake out their claims to a place in the psywar operations. Finally, because these agencies were outside the JCS's immediate authority, a new JPWC was reorganized by JCS Order #68 on June 21, 1942, with a membership of general and flag officers representing G-2, ONI, War Department General Staff and Commander in Chief, U.S. Fleet. Donovan was named chairman. The major responsibilities of the new JPWC were:

. . . to initiate and develop plans for psychological warfare in conjunction with appropriate agencies of the JCS and the State Department or other existing governmental agencies; to coordinate psychological warfare activities of other United States Government agencies, and to collaborate with interested nations to bring psychological warfare in accord with strategy approved by the JCS; to designate the executive to implement and approve psychological warfare plans; and to submit such plans to the JCS through the Joint Staff Planners (JSP). A Joint Psychological Warfare Sub-Committee was simultaneously established as a working committee for the JPWC; and Donovan established within OSS a Supporting Committee on Psychological Warfare.

To provide for the coordination of the psychological warfare activities of other existing governmental agencies JCS Order #68 also provided for a Joint Psychological Warfare Advisory Committee (JPWAC), under the chairmanship of Donovan to include representatives of OWI, BEW, CIAA and State Department.*

All this was easier ordered than done. The proliferation and deliberations of these committees produced a bureaucratic nightmare which took on the appearance of a political satire written by Jonathan Swift. For example, the JPWAC commented in a memorandum to its parent committee on July 18, "Since propaganda is an essential part of psychological warfare it is obvious that the JPWC in following its directive to 'initiate, formulate and develop plans for psychological warfare in connection with other U.S. government agencies,' finds itself deprived of one of the essential tools for conducting this type of warfare."** While this "big end" versus "little end" argument about how to crack the psywar egg without a propaganda hammer was going on, the JCS further added to Donovan's woes by giving the JPWC responsibility for the administration of OSS, in an August 15 directive which said in part:

*War Report, *op. cit.,* p. 98.

**Ibid, p. 99.

All plans for projects to be undertaken by the Office of Strategic Services will be submitted to the Joint U.S. Chiefs of Staff through the Joint Psychological Warfare Committee for approval. The Joint Psychological Warfare Committee will refer such papers as it deems necessary to the Joint Staff Planners prior to submission to the Joint U.S. Chiefs of Staff. The Joint Psychological Warfare Committee will take final action on all internal administrative plans pertaining to the Office of Strategic Services which do not involve military or naval personnel or military or naval equipment.*

The resulting chaos from this directive was predictable. Projects moved up, down, and sideways from one to another echelon for reconsideration, revision, and resubmission. Fortunately for Donovan, OSS operations were not brought to a complete halt by the convoluted approval procedure due to a June 22 interim order issued by Brigadier General W.B. Smith, Secretary of the JCS, which said,

Pending the issuance of specific instruction as to its functions, the Joint Chiefs of Staff desire that the Office of Strategic Services continue the duties and activities of such Branches and Divisions of the former Office of the Coordinator of Information as have not been transferred to the Office of War Information.

This order is designed solely to clarify the relation of the Office of Strategic Services to other government agencies, to facilitate the transaction of current operations, and to make possible the continuance of existing contracts and services.**

Donovan construed General Smith's interim order quite broadly. Operations were "continued" in the sense that add-ons to existing ones were considered not to be new projects, and the British SOE agreements were given "contract" status.

Final though partial resolution of the psychological warfare committee mess was achieved on December 23, upon issuance of JCS/155/4/D "which constituted the first definitive charter for OSS. By this directive the JPWC was abolished and OSS was designated as the agency of the JCS charged (outside the Western Hemisphere) in general with 'the planning, development, coordination, and execution of the military program for psychological warfare,'*** and with 'the compilation of such political, psychological, sociological and

Ibid., p. 99.

**Ibid.,* p. 97.

***The term "psychological warfare," like so many bandied about in the field of intelligence, is one whose etymological trace reflects bureaucratic biases and which suggests an almost elastic perversion of language designed to prevent acceptance and responsibility for its implications. Definition of terms is never easy in government, especially when it results in changed responsibilities and authority, and the problem of defining psychological warfare was one which was never solved in World War II. Although many persons and organizations carried out what they presumed to be legitimate psychological warfare functions, they did so without a formal acceptance of its precise meaning. In this case, Donovan's OSS Supporting Committee labored for six months to come up with an acceptable definition of psychological warfare. It was finally approved by the JPWC on September 7, 1942; however, that organization failed to forward it to the JCS for

economic information as may be required by military operation'. . . . OSS was authorized to operate in the fields of sabotage, espionage and counterespionage in enemy-occupied or controlled territory and foreign nationality groups in the United States. It provided for a Planning Group to be set up in OSS consisting of one member from State, two appointed by the Chief of Staff, two by the Commander in Chief, U.S. Fleet and Chief of Naval Operations and four members, including the Chairman, appointed by the Director of OSS. It stipulated that OSS psychological warfare plans be submitted to the JCS through the JSP. In the field of intelligence it placed OSS on a par with MIS and ONI."* Donovan was reasonably content with the half a loaf contained in the JCS directive. It gave OSS a workable charter, established a straight-line command chain between the JCS and OSS for operational matters, and left the problem of how propaganda was to be integrated into military operations to be fought out between the JCS and Elmer Davis' OWI.

In the seven months of pushing and hauling between Roosevelt's order establishing OSS and the issuance of JCS/155/4/D, the tipping factor in the latter action was principally the contributions OSS made to Operation Torch, the Allied invasion of North Africa in November 1942. These contributions included production of the intelligence required for a major amphibious operation, "black lists" of hostile personnel in the area, agent reports about the population's morale, and, most important from the standpoint of "selling" the OSS to the JCS as a going concern, its clandestine, secret intelligence radio network which had been in operation in the area since March 1942.** This network gave General Eisenhower secret intelligence of inestimable value and contributed directly to the invasion's success. As a result, almost all of the bickering which had surrounded the bureaucratic struggle was swept away by the demonstrable record of OSS in meeting the operational needs of Eisenhower and his combat commanders. In response to Eisenhower's fulsome endorsement of OSS, the JCS designated General McNarney and Admiral Horne to inquire fully into OSS and make recommendations as to its functions. Their report served as the basis for JCS/155/4/D.

---

approval as a doctrine statement. This definition of psychological warfare, which became an underlying assumption justifying many activities of dubious merit, stated that it is "the coordination and use of all means, including moral and physical, by which the end is to be attained—other than those of recognized military operations, but including the psychological exploitation of the result of those recognized military actions—which tend to destroy the will of the enemy to achieve victory and to damage his political or economic capacity to do so; which tend to deprive the enemy of the support, assistance or sympathy of his allies or associates or of neutrals, or to prevent his acquisition of such support, assistance or sympathy; or which tend to create, maintain, or increase the will to victory of our own people and allies and to acquire, maintain, or increase the support, assistance and sympathy of neutrals." (*Ibid.*, p. 99.)

*Ibid., p. 105.

**The network included: MIDWAY (key station) at Tangier, YANKEE at Algiers, LINCOLN at Casablanca, FRANKLIN at Oran, and PILGRIM at Tunis.

Thus fortified with JCS legitimacy and Eisenhower's endorsement, Donovan and the OSS were off to the races. Some haggling over the materiel aspects of the SOE agreements ensued, but these were of little overall consequence. In the main, OSS got the people they needed and, in spite of Donovan's untidy way of doing business, the Bureau of the Budget cooperated by making the necessary funds available. This is not to say, however, that the people, money, and materiel problems of OSS were all solved easily and simply, or to Donovan's complete satisfaction; but rather, that in terms of the United States' difficulties in fighting a world war on the land, sea, and air and keeping the United Nations' forces supplied, that the OSS got its fair share of the resources required to carry out its various missions.

One of these missions logically followed the creation of a secret intelligence organization to operate in enemy, enemy-occupied, and neutral countries outside the Western Hemisphere; namely, counterespionage. As the War Report notes:

Counter-espionage is a distinct and independent intelligence function. It embraces not only the protection of the intelligence interests of the government it serves, but, by control and manipulation of the intelligence operations of other nations, it performs a dynamic function in discerning their plans and intentions, as well as in deceiving them.*

Although G-2 and ONI were carrying out some secret intelligence activities prior to the war, neither organization had a counterespionage capability worthy of the name. Their activities, like those of the FBI in the United States, were essentially involved with domestic-security counterintelligence functions such as the protection of military bases, war plants, clearance of personnel to handle classified material, and detection of enemy espionage. This latter function is obviously part of counterespionage; however, unless it is blended with such positive aspects as penetration of foreign intelligence services, running double agents, etc., the simple detection of enemy espionage by itself is not properly called counterespionage.

As such, the development of a counterespionage organization and capability for OSS represented a much more formidable task than that associated with either analytical intelligence or secret intelligence per se, because to be successful a counterespionage organization requires a vast body of records and files on foreign intelligence personnel, agents, informants, government officials, businessmen, and other nations' intelligence organizations as well as "skilled personnel familiar with the intricate techniques of counter-espionage by which the intelligence efforts of other nations may be controlled and directed."** In mid-1942, at the time the SOE agreements were negotiated and secret intelligence collaboration was further expanded with the British SIS, the United

*Ibid., p. 188.
**Ibid., p. 188.

States had neither the kind of records required nor personnel trained in counterespionage techniques. However, due to the fact that the United States would be carrying out secret intelligence and special operations separately as well as jointly with the British, it became necessary to establish a counterespionage organization in OSS for the protection of those activities and to deal with the foreign intelligence organizations they might involve. As a consequence, in November 1942, Donovan sent James R. Murphy, his principal special assistant, to London to work out arrangements with the British counterespionage organizations, MI-6(V) and MI-5, to establish a London liaison unit of the projected OSS counterespionage organization, and to negotiate an agreement similar to the one worked out with the British SOE. The British proved most helpful. They allowed OSS personnel to duplicate their extensive counterespionage records, which had been acquired over many decades and which contained, in addition to information about enemy and neutral countries' intelligence organizations and related personnel, a substantial amount of information about American citizens, politicians, and diplomats. Also, as in the case of special operations, the British agreed to train American personnel to use these records and to mount counterespionage operations:

The proposed arrangement envisioned the establishment of a civilian CE [counterespionage] organization with OSS—in short, an American entity similar to MI-6(V) and MI-5, the British services for overseas and home security respectively, both of which were civilian services only nominally under military control. . . . At the time it was intended that the new CE unit to be established within OSS should become the exclusive link between British and American CE services. FBI, however, had long maintained a close and cordial liaison with the British security services, particularly MI-5, in the interests of American security in the Western Hemisphere. It was therefore agreed that FBI, in view of its jurisdiction over CE in the Western Hemisphere, could continue its independent liaison with the British services insofar as exchange of CE information to that area was concerned.*

On June 15, 1943, after some internal bickering between the key players in the OSS's fields of special activities, General Order #13 was revised to create the CE Branch (X-2) of the Intelligence Services of OSS. Although X-2 headquarters and its overseas field offices, in carrying out their missions throughout the war, never achieved the notoriety and publicity achieved by OSS's secret intelligence and special operations organizations, X-2 made a unique contribution to the war effort. Also, like those individuals involved in secret intelligence and special operations, X-2 personnel underwent a rigorous form of on-the-job training which enabled them to compress in a few years much of the experience so necessary to successful performance in the demanding field of counterespionage. Because it bears so heavily on the postwar evolution of the American intelligence community, one power given to Murphy's X-2 needs special emphasis; that of "vetting" the agents recruited for service with OSS's secret

*Ibid., p. 190.

intelligence organizations. For example, when secret intelligence personnel located in any one of the enemy, enemy-occupied, or neutral countries wanted to hire or otherwise recruit an indigenous agent, the individual first had to be approved by X-2. This procedure produced considerable friction between those in X-2 and secret intelligence because, when the former organization and/or one of its station chiefs disapproved a potential agent, those up to and including the head of Secret Intelligence were not told why. The reasons behind this seemingly autocratic procedure were based on the fact that X-2 personnel, besides having control over the counterespionage field, were specially indoctrinated, or more properly "cleared," for access to the most sensitive crypto and surveillance intelligence available to American and British authorities. That is, of all those involved in OSS's special activities, only those in X-2 had a presumed need to know about everything which was known about foreign secret sources and methods. James Murphy did not abuse his authority in these matters, although he, Donovan, and Sir William Stephenson never wavered in their determination to keep X-2's counterespionage authority above and beyond that of secret intelligence and special operations. For example, while Allen Dulles was Donovan's "man in Berne," Dulles tried to ignore an X-2 disapproval of an agent he wanted to hire; the prospective agent was "terminated with prejudice" by X-2 and British counterespionage assets. In passing, Murphy received a most remarkable accolade from his opposite numbers in Britain's MI-6(V) and MI-5 organizations: "Jimmy Murphy was the best intelligence officer in the entire American effort."

At war's end, although X-2 was still very much a part of OSS, it had garnered enough experience and had sufficient momentum to become an almost autonomous entity in the American intelligence community. It didn't do so immediately; how X-2 and its personnel fared in the postwar struggle over American intelligence is described in the following chapter.

Paradoxically, too much and too little has been written about the OSS's wartime activities. The War Report gives a fair account of what happened and interesting detail concerning its organizational evolution—especially in identifying the "cut and try" approach taken by Donovan in trying to create a systematic intelligence system—but leaves unanswered how Donovan's concept concerning the "ultimate intelligence target" can or should be fully implemented in meeting the disparate needs of the nation's intelligence consumers, and still be faithful to the Constitution's provisions which guarantee privacy and freedom of expression. R. Harris Smith's *OSS: The Secret History of America's First Central Intelligence Agency** chronicles that history in terms of the "revolutionary" personalities of those involved, but leaves unanswered the question of whether OSS was a unique historical aberration in America's fitful, ambivalent progress toward creation of an institutionalized, centrally

*R. Harris Smith, *OSS: The Secret History of America's First Central Intelligence Agency.* University of California Press, 1972.

controlled intelligence system. In one sense, the question may be asked if Donovan et al. were progenitors of the counterrevolutionaries who took over once the intelligence barricades had been breached, or whether those who followed, many of whom were "foot soldiers" in OSS and other intelligence organizations, concluded from their wartime experience that intelligence simply was a suitable means to personal political power as well as one able to promote the abstract but equally pragmatic notion of national interest. There may be no final answers to these questions and those they imply; however, neither the War Report, Smith's work, nor more dramatic tales of derring-do provide an adequate basis to measure the OSS and its personnel's effect on American intelligence, or establish whether the wartime record of OSS and the other American intelligence agencies illustrates any unique principles. Unfortunately, this institutional effect has been muted by the personality conflicts, as well as the individual personalities, between those most intimately involved, the intrinsic nature of the intelligence process itself, and uncertainties about the necessity and place of intelligence and intelligence operations in arriving at policy decisions.

Besides the personality conflicts previously mentioned, one other deserves mention; not so much as an example of personality conflict per se, but rather as corollary evidence of the personal infallibility theory of intelligence embodied in the actions of General Douglas MacArthur, who created his own intelligence organization, interpreted its results and acted upon his own analysis. MacArthur was an individual of such unique proportions that it is difficult to categorize him. Like other strong-willed people in military history, he produces ambivalent reactions among those who knew him, served under him or have attempted to chronicle his illustrious record. Nonetheless, during World War II, MacArthur the commander was also his own intelligence officer, and this in spite of the fact that he had a half-dozen or so intelligence organizations under his control which taken together had more personnel than any two elements of the intelligence community including the FBI, G-2, ONI, or OSS.*

Although MacArthur allowed Major General Charles Willoughby to serve as

---

*For example, the Allied Intelligence Bureau, composed of combined Allied forces in the Pacific Command Zone of General Douglas MacArthur, was established at Brisbane, Australia, on July 6, 1942, under the auspices of his intelligence staff, headed by Major General Charles A. Willoughby. The bureau was directly headed by Colonel C.G. Roberts, an Australian, with Lieutenant Allison Ind, an American, as his deputy. The principal structural units included a British Special Operations ("sabotage and silent killing") group, a British radio monitoring outfit, the Netherlands Indies Forces Intelligence Service, an Australian propaganda group, and the Australian "Coast Watchers." According to MacArthur's records, which Willoughby has cited:

> ... the history of the AIB is a secret, little publicized but highly important chapter in the story of the Southwest Pacific. From the Solomons to Borneo, from Java to the Philippines, a small adventurous group of carefully trained specialists spread a network of observers and operatives behind the enemy lines well in advance of our main body. . . . Operating in almost total isolation and normally without hope of outside support, every expedition was carried out in the face of great personal risk. If discovered by the enemy, the small parties were doomed to almost certain capture and probable death. In that event those who

his G-2 and personal confidante, there never was any question about the fact that MacArthur presided over the intelligence process in his Southwest Pacific command much like an omniscient judge or as some said, "The Oracle of Delphi."

Whatever MacArthur's personal style or idiosyncrasies, he did understand the importance of intelligence to the military commander, and most significantly the frequent necessity to act or decide on the basis of incomplete intelligence information. This was his real strength, and also one of his weaknesses—as later events in Korea in 1950 would demonstrate. Some in Washington complained that MacArthur took unwarranted flights of fancy over the gaps in intelligence available to him; however, as General Willoughby noted in commenting on why OSS personnel were kept out of MacArthur's theater command, theirs was a requirement for intelligence from the moment of Pearl Harbor, and by the time OSS was really able to function MacArthur's mix of British, Australian, and Dutch intelligence organizations had the situation under full control. Willoughby's caveat was not completely accurate, but there is a modicum of truth in his view that by the time Donovan's OSS got untracked in its struggle to be placed under the JCS, the personnel available to OSS would not have added much in the way of additional intelligence capabilities.

Besides the military intelligence services and OSS, and the minor players such as BEW, OWI, CIAA, Treasury, etc., who scratched around at the margin for crumbs from the overseas wartime intelligence banquet table, the overseas actions of one other member of the intelligence community deserve some mention. The FBI, under the direction of J. Edgar Hoover, was able to grab off the lion's share of authority for intelligence and counterespionage operations in the Western Hemisphere. The bureaucratic backing and filling which preceded this outcome was typical of the way in which a kind of "equal but separate" doctrine was invoked by the major players to prevent the emergence of a truly central intelligence organization. In recapitulation, on December 9, 1941, President Roosevelt had ordered Donovan to coordinate activities of the various North American intelligence agencies. However, "as Donovan undertook this work, objection arose from the FBI, which had been made

---

died quickly were fortunate. . . . Jungle wise "coastwatchers," with tiny radio transmitter-receiver outfits, remained behind as the Japanese invasion swept forward. . . . From these few fearless men a powerful network of sea, air and ground spotters was developed until finally it became impossible for the enemy to make a single major move on the surface or in the sky without intelligence reports being flashed in advance to Allied forces. . . . At the conclusion of the desperate Guadalcanal campaign, Admiral Halsey publicly stated that it was probable that the allies could not have retained their hard-won initiative on Guadalcanal Island had it not been for the consistent advance radio warnings by AIB agents of impending air attacks.

(See Charles A. Willoughby and John Chamberlain, *MacArthur 1941–1951.* New York: McGraw-Hill, 1954, pp. 145–46; and Allison Ind, *Allied Intelligence Bureau.* New York: David McKay, 1954, pp. 10–11.)

responsible for all intelligence in the Western Hemisphere." The War Report further notes:

".... On 23 December a Presidential Directive reaffirmed the authority of the FBI, and Donovan was so informed. The matter caused some discussion since the instructions to Donovan of 9 December and the 23 December Directive were obviously in conflict. On 30 December the President sent a memorandum to the Attorney General, Sumner Welles, Donovan, MID and ONI:

> On December 23rd, without examination, I signed a confidential directive . . . I believe that this directive interferes with work already being conducted by other agencies. In view of this, please meet together and straighten out this whole program and let me have whatever is necessary by way of an amended directive.

The discussion which followed culminated in a meeting at the Attorney General's office on 6 January 1942, wherein the directive of 23 December 1941 was agreed to with only minor changes; COI's representatives might operate in the Western Hemisphere (exclusive of the United States itself) only after informing FBI; but even then they would not be allowed to operate under cover."*

In the main, the OSS adhered to the spirit and letter of Roosevelt's clarifying directive. Its obedience was due not so much to an unwillingness to challenge Hoover on the grounds that what the FBI could do in South America OSS could do better, but rather on the more prosaic grounds that in Donovan's view the real intelligence was elsewhere in the world, especially in those theaters of operations where military activity was underway or contemplated. Although in some of the puffery written about the FBI it has been made to appear that the FBI was the only American intelligence force in South and Central America during World War II, this is far from correct. The military intelligence services, through their military and naval attachés and Department of the Army and Navy "civilian" employees, had a fair share of the intelligence and counterespionage action. This situation came about, almost in spite of J. Edgar Hoover's claims of total authority, due to the fact at the local field-operational level FBI and military intelligence personnel willingly cooperated with each other and did not seek Washington (Hoover) approval for their joint efforts except in unusual cases which involved actions with diplomatic overtones and for which the embassy and/or the State Department had a before-hand, genuine need-to-know requirement concerning the facts of a projected operation. The military, especially because of their attachés' diplomatic status, kept their contributions to the FBI's Western Hemisphere field operations low key. Hoover remained happy throughout. He was content in the belief that he had no real long-term rivals in his plan to dominate America's postwar foreign intelligence apparatus. To be sure, although Hoover recognized that the military intelligence services would have foreign intelligence

---

*War Report, *op. cit.,* p. 17.

interests in the postwar period, he was equally convinced that the organization which had an in-place counterespionage operation and organization at the end of the war would pick up most, if not all, the major foreign intelligence responsibilities. At the time James Murphy negotiated agreements with the British MI-6(V) and MI-5, Hoover didn't feel particularly threatened by these agreements because he maintained control over the Western Hemisphere and was of the opinion that the OSS would quickly pass from America's intelligence scene once the war ended. Hoover's assumptions in these matters were not completely in error.

In terms of the FBI's performance in the Western Hemisphere, it is not exaggerating to say that its personnel, with some notable assists from military intelligence personnel, successfully penetrated each of the area's indigenous intelligence services, many of their law-enforcement agencies, and also carried out some exceptionally complex and effective positive counterespionage operations against Axis intelligence organizations operating therein. Some of the FBI's operations, such as kidnapping undercover Nazi agents in Brazil, Argentina, and Chile and incarcerating them in the United States Canal Zone, took on comic opera proportions; nevertheless, it was good training and experience for the FBI agents who went on to bigger things in America's postwar counterespionage organizations.

There is no attempt here to chronicle the wartime exploits of individuals and the intelligence organizations in which they served. Although many of these intelligence activities and the personnel involved were quite noteworthy in terms of the effects they had on the enemy, they are more important in terms of the large number of persons in all the intelligence services and agencies, variously estimated at between 75,000 and 100,000, who worked in intelligence and became imbued with the intelligence officer's ethos and outlook. Also, the wartime personnel expansion created a situation where in Schumpeter's parlance the intelligence services and agencies became "going concerns"; that is, their raison d'être was clearly established in the minds of American political and military leaders. Similarly, as the wartime exploits of America's spies in baggy pants entered the public domain, and the ripple effect of the returned intelligence officer's "war stories" began to spread from dinner tables to American Legion beer halls and beyond, intelligence and its dirty practices achieved a kind of respectability they had never enjoyed in America's prior history. This ideological and subjective acceptance of intelligence in the political and military scheme of things by America's leaders and the public at large, however, did not extend immediately to agreement by those in and out of the intelligence community of how the United States' intelligence effort should be organized, controlled and directed.

As we have shown, only intermittent progress was made throughout the war in the centralization of intelligence activities. Partly this was due to the committee approach adopted by the JCS, which attempted to meet the military's disparate needs for specific intelligence in support of military operations; but because these needs also required support from intelligence agencies outside the JCS's command, it floundered badly in integrating intelligence into the overall national decision-making process, especially with respect to the organization of postwar political relationships. But primarily the thrust toward centralization of intelligence was blunted and diverted because the necessity for such an approach was lost in the partially correct, oft-stated views, "We won the war without centralizing intelligence, didn't we?" and, "Who needs it?" or that, "Centralization (one organization in real control) of intelligence is all right in theory, but just won't work in practice." Although each of these positions implied the rejoinder, "Yes, but!," men like Donovan who argued for genuine centralization of America's loosely confederated intelligence community found no real audience for their arguments in the highest councils of military and political power.

Our description of the wartime struggle over intelligence may be likened to a chess game; the opening moves of the principals and their organizations were characterized by confusion and faltering steps toward the matching of intelligence functions with organizations and personnel. The middle part of the game was characterized by some intramural guerrilla warfare between the intelligence services and agencies, but these conflicts were of less significance than the overall expansion of the intelligence community itself caused by the war and the concomitant acceptance of the intelligence community as a viable, continuing entity in the quest for personal and political power. With these aspects in mind, the endgame in our metaphor began not at the time of the German or Japanese surrender, but when the war's end came into clear sight. Although it is not possible to date precisely when this revelation occurred—because of the imponderables surrounding the atomic bomb's feasiblity and the existence, as late as April 1945, of a JCS worst-possible-case estimate which visualized the war lasting until the end of 1947—it is safe to say that by mid-to-late summer 1944 there were no lingering doubts about the war's final outcome. And by that time the politics of the war and its aftermath were preoccupying the intentions of many who were part of the intelligence community and various political power hierarchies.

Two moves in the endgame are illustrative of the way in which it was played. The first occurred in September 1944, at which time Thomas E. Dewey, governor of New York and the Republican candidate for president, was challenging FDR's bid for an unprecedented fourth term. Sometime early in the month, Rear Admiral Hewlett Thebaud, the Director of Naval Intelligence, and/or Major General Clayton Bissell, the Army G-2, who were responsible for Joint Security Control in the JCS, informed General Marshall that a person or persons unknown had provided Governor Dewey with MAGIC intercept information which had been acquired prior to Pearl Harbor and which called into serious question the motives and actions of President Roosevelt at the time of the attack and thereafter. General Marshall could not ignore the content and implications of the Thebaud/Bissell information (both officers signed the memorandum transmitting the information to Marshall; however, it is not clear from official records whether it came from G-2 or ONI sources), because if either the Japanese or Germans became aware of the MAGIC successes, they would both change their code machinery and make the Allies' remaining military tasks much more formidable. As a consequence, General Marshall established his own "plumbers" task force, whose identification in the investigation which followed is simply shown as "Members A through F." Their actual identities may never be revealed; however, from what is known about the contents of General Marshall's papers (which are to remain sealed until 1985 or later), the A through F Task Force did confirm the fact of the leak and identified the possible sources from which it could have emanated. In the extremely oblique references to the A through F Task Force found in the Pearl Harbor case study documents, one comes away with the impression that once the possible sources were identified General Marshall, and by this time Admiral King, did not go all out to expose this early "Deep Throat" in the Roosevelt administration or the armed services.

Whether Marshall knew or even suspected who of those named on the task force lists of "possible" and "possible/likely" suspects was actually responsible for passing the information to Governor Dewey is probably lost to history. An individual's motives for such behavior are difficult to categorize, or easily explain, especially when all of the persons on the suspect list were aware of the MAGIC information's sensitivity and its ability to save American lives. Consequently, faced with the possible calamitous effect of Dewey's injecting this material into the presidential campaign, General Marshall and Admiral King took the unprecedented step, without informing President Roosevelt of their action or the information on which it was based, of writing to Governor Dewey as a means to preempt such an outcome.

The Marshall-Dewey correspondence in this matter is of singular importance in understanding how intelligence information may be used to thwart the intentions of a sitting president, promote another's political fortunes or ambitions, and alter the future course of national events. When the letters were written, their contents were known only to a select few; during the Joint Congressional Committee's closed hearings in September 1945 about Pearl Harbor, certain members of the committee placed great pressure on General Marshall to force him to reveal their contents. This came about as a result of a *Life* magazine story by John Chamberlain in its September 24, 1945, issue, which described the episode in some detail and which indicated that *Life* either had copies of or had seen the letters. Marshall argued that the letters should not be placed in the closed hearing's transcript; but when the committee held public hearings in early December, he was forced to reveal their contents. Thus the letters came into the public domain the very day that General Marshall was forced to place them in evidence.

The disclosure of the contents of the Marshall-Dewey correspondence produced such a sensation that *Life* printed the whole of it in its issue of December 17, 1945, with the following introduction:

During the 1944 election campaign General George C. Marshall wrote two letters to Republican Candidate Thomas E. Dewey, telling him that Army cryptographers had broken the Japanese "Ultra" code. This fact was first revealed in a story by *Life* editor John Chamberlain, which appeared in *Life,* September 24. Marshall's purpose, Chamberlain wrote, was to forestall Dewey's revelation of that fact in a possible attack on the Roosevelt administration's Japanese policy before Pearl Harbor. The actual text of the letters remained secret until last week, when General Marshall appeared before the Congressional Committee investigating Pearl Harbor and made the letters public. They appear below.

When he finished reading the first two paragraphs of the first letter, Governor Dewey stopped because as the Chamberlain article reported, "the letter might possibly contain material which had already come from other sources, and that anyway, a candidate for President was in no position to make blind promises." General Marshall sent the letter back again with an introduction which relieved the governor of binding conditions. This time Dewey read the letter and after much thought and discussion decided not to make use during the campaign of any information he previously had.

First Letter

TOP SECRET
(FOR MR. DEWEY's EYES ONLY)

25 September 1944

My Dear Governor:

I am writing you without the knowledge of any other person except Admiral King (who concurs) because we are approaching a grave dilemma in the political reactions of Congress regarding Pearl Harbor.

What I have to tell you below is of such a highly secret nature that I feel compelled to ask you either to accept it on the basis of not communicating its contents to any other person and returning the letter or not reading any further and returning the letter to the bearer.

I should have preferred to talk to you in person but I could not devise a method that would not be subject to press and radio reactions as to why the Chief of Staff of the Army would be seeking an interview with you at this particular moment. Therefore, I have turned to the method of this letter, to be delivered by hand to you by Colonel Carter Clarke, who incidentally has charge of the most secret documents of the War and Navy Departments.

In brief, the military dilemma resulting from Congressional political battles of the political campaign is this:

The most vital evidence in the Pearl Harbor matter consists of our intercepts of the Japanese diplomatic communications. Over a period of years our cryptograph people analyzed the character of the machine the Japanese were using for encoding their diplomatic messages. Based on this, a corresponding machine was built by us which deciphers their messages.

Therefore, we possessed a wealth of information regarding their moves in the Pacific, which in turn was furnished the State Department—rather than, as is popularly supposed, the State Department providing us with information—but which unfortunately made no reference whatever to intentions toward Hawaii until the last message before Dec. 7, which did not reach our hands until the following day, Dec. 8.

Now the point to the present dilemma is that we have gone ahead with this business of deciphering their codes until we possess other codes, German as well as Japanese, but our main basis of information regarding Hitler's intentions in Europe is Baron Oshima's message from Berlin reporting his interviews with Hitler and other officials to the Japanese Government. These are still in the codes involved in the Pearl Harbor events.

To explain further the critical nature of this setup which would be wiped out almost in an instant if the least suspicion were aroused regarding it, the Battle of the Coral Sea was based on deciphered messages and therefore our few ships were in the right place at the right time. Further, we were able to concentrate our limited forces to meet their advances on Midway when otherwise we almost certainly would have been some 3,000 miles out of place.

We had full information of the strength of their forces in that advance and also of the smaller force directed against the Aleutians which finally landed troops on Attu and Kiska.

Operations in the Pacific are largely guided by the information we obtain of Japanese deployments. We know their strength in various garrisons, the rations and other stores continuing available to them and what is of vast importance, we check their fleet movements and the movements of their convoys.

The heavy losses reported from time to time which they sustain by reason of our submarine action largely results from the fact that we know the sailing dates and the routes of their convoys and can notify our submarines to lie in wait at the proper point.

The current raids by Admiral Halsey's carrier forces on Japanese shipping in Manila Bay and elsewhere are largely based in timing on the known movements on Japanese convoys, two of which were caught, as anticipated, in his destructive attacks.

You will understand from the foregoing the utter tragic consequences if the present political debates regarding Pearl Harbor disclose to the enemy, German or Jap, any suspicion of the vital sources of information we now possess.

The Roberts report on Pearl Harbor had to have withdrawn from it all reference to this highly secret matter, therefore in portions it necessarily appeared incomplete. The same reason which dictated that course is even more important today because our sources have been greatly elaborated.

As a further example of the delicacy of the situation, some of Donovan's people (the OSS), without telling us, instituted a secret search of the Japanese Embassy offices in Portugal. As a result the entire military attaché Japanese code all over the world was changed, and though this occurred over a year ago, we have not yet been able to break the new code and have thus lost this invaluable information source, particularly regarding the European situation.

A recent speech in Congress by Representative Harness would clearly suggest to the Japanese that we have been reading their codes though Mr. Harness and the American public would probably not draw any such conclusion.

The conduct of General Eisenhower's campaign and all our operations in the Pacific are closely related in conception and timing to the information we secretly obtain through these intercepted codes. They contribute greatly to the victory and tremendously to the saving of American lives, both in the conduct of current operations and in looking toward the early termination of the war.

I am representing this matter to you, for your secret information, in the hope that you may see your way clear to avoid the tragic results with which we are now threatened in the present political campaign. I might add that the recent action in Congress in requiring Army and Navy investigations for action before certain dates has compelled me to bring back General Gerow, whose troops are fighting at Trier, to testify here while Germans are counter-attacking his forces there. This, however, is a very minor matter compared to the loss of our code information.

Please return this letter by bearer. I will hold it in my secret file subject to your reference should you so desire.

Faithfully yours,
G.C. Marshall

Second Letter

TOP SECRET
(FOR MR. DEWEY'S EYES ONLY)

27 September 1944

My Dear Governor:

Colonel Clarke, my messenger to you of yesterday, September 26, has reported the result of his delivery of my letter dated Sept. 25. As I understand him you (A) were unwilling to commit yourself to any agreement regarding "not communicating its contents to any other person" in view of the fact that you felt you already knew certain of the things probably already referred to in the letters, as suggested to by seeing the word "cryptograph," and (B) you could not feel that such a letter as this to a Presidential candidate could have been addressed to you by an officer in my position without the knowledge of the President.

As to (A) above I am quite willing to have you read what comes hereafter with the understanding that you are bound not to communicate to any other person any portions on which you do not now have or later receive factual knowledge from some other source than myself. As to (B) above you have my word that neither the Secretary of War nor the President has any intimation whatsoever that such a letter has been addressed to you or that the preparation or sending of such a communication was being considered.

I assure you that the only persons who saw or know of the existence of either this letter or my letter to you dated Sept. 25 are Admiral King, seven key officers responsible for security of military communications, and my secretary who typed these letters.

I am trying my best to make plain to you that this letter is being addressed solely to you on my initiative, Admiral King having been consulted only after the letter was drafted, and I am persisting in the matter because the military hazards involved are so serious that I feel some action is necessary to protect the interests of our armed forces.

[The second letter then repeated substantially the text of the first letter except for the first two paragraphs.]

Life failed to note that the last two sentences in the penultimate paragraph of the first letter, beginning "I might add . . ." and "This, however, is . . ." were omitted from that paragraph in the second letter, but there is no explanation for the omission. Perhaps it was simply for the sake of brevity, but this seems improbable. Also, according to Colonel Clarke, the letters which had been prepared for General Marshall's signature did not meet with whole-hearted approval and that the general himself modified them.

There are three brief final footnotes to the Marshall-Dewey correspondence episode. One, it is a fact that Governor Dewey acceded to General Marshall's request—he made no use whatever of the vital secret information during the campaign or after it. Two, General Marshall never told President Roosevelt of the letters to Dewey; in his words, "The President died without knowing of it." And three, the Joint Congressional Committee and/or the Congress itself pulled back from any attempt to find out who had leaked the MAGIC information to Governor Dewey, or who provided information about the episode to John Chamberlain, or why.

Although the culprits in this egregious breach of trust and violation of national security were not found out, the action by itself underscores the potentially disruptive political power of those in the intelligence community if they disagree with national policy, or if they believe that they and/or their organizations are threatened by the contemplated actions of elected and appointed officials.

The second end move in the intelligence community's chess game began on October 31, 1944, on which date President Roosevelt asked Donovan for his ideas concerning the organization of America's intelligence community in the postwar period. In response, on November 18, 1944, Donovan provided Roosevelt with a memorandum summarizing his views about a central intelligence authority and a draft directive to achieve that end. They read as follows:

Top Secret.

18 November 1944

MEMORANDUM FOR THE PRESIDENT:

Pursuant to your note of 31 October 1944 I have given consideration to the organization of an intelligence service for the post-war period.

In the early days of the war, when the demands upon intelligence services were mainly in and for military operations, the OSS was placed under the direction of the JCS.

Once our enemies are defeated the demand will be equally pressing for information that will aid us in solving the problems of peace.

This will require two things:

1. That intelligence control be returned to the supervision of the President.

2. The establishment of a central authority reporting directly to you, with responsibility to frame intelligence objectives and to collect and coordinate the intelligence material required by the Executive Branch in planning and carrying out national policy and strategy.

I attach in the form of a draft directive (Tab A) the means by which I think this could be realized without difficulty or loss of time. You will note that coordination and centralization are placed at the policy level but operational intelligence (that pertaining primarily to Department action) remains within the existing agencies concerned. The creation of a central authority thus would not conflict with or limit necessary intelligence functions within the Army, Navy, Department of State and other agencies.

In accordance with your wish, this is set up as a permanent long-range plan. But you may want to consider whether this (or part of it) should be done now, by executive or legislative action. There are common-sense reasons why you may desire to lay the keel of the ship at once.

The immediate revision and coordination of our present intelligence system would effect substantial economies and aid in the more efficient and speedy termination of the war.

Information important to the national defense, being gathered now by certain Departments and agencies, is not being used to full advantage in the war. Coordination at the strategy level would prevent waste, and avoid the present confusion that leads to waste and unnecessary duplication.

Though in the midst of war, we are also in a period of transition which, before we are aware, will take us into the tumult of rehabilitation. An adequate and orderly intelligence system will contribute to informed decisions.

We have now in the Government the trained and specialized personnel needed for the task. This talent should not be dispersed.

William J. Donovan
Director

SUBSTANTIVE AUTHORITY NECESSARY IN ESTABLISHMENT OF A CENTRAL INTELLIGENCE SERVICE

In order to coordinate and centralize the policies and actions of the Government relating to intelligence:

1. There is established in the Executive Office of the President a central intelligence service, to be known as the . . . . at the head of which shall be a Director appointed by the President. The Director shall discharge and perform his functions and duties under the direction and supervision of the President. Subject to the approval of the President, the Director may exercise his powers, authorities and duties through such officials or agencies and in such manner as he may determine.

2. There is established in the . . . . an Advisory Board consisting of the Secretary of State, Secretary of the Treasury, the Secretary of War, Attorney General, the Secretary of the Navy, and such other members as the President may subsequently appoint. The Board shall advise and assist the Director with respect to the formulation of basic policies and plans of the . . . .

3. Subject to the direction and control of the President, and with any necessary advice and assistance from the other Departments and agencies of the Government, the . . . . shall perform the following functions and duties:

(1) Coordination of the functions of all intelligence agencies of the Government, and the establishment of such policies and objectives as will assure the integration of national intelligence efforts;

(b) Collection either directly or through existing Government Departments and agencies, of pertinent information, including military, economic, political and scientific, concerning the capabilities, intentions and activities of foreign nations, with particular reference to the effect such matters may have upon the national security, policies and interests of the United States;

(c) Final evaluation, synthesis and dissemination within the Government of the intelligence required to enable the Government to determine policies with respect to national planning and security in peace and war, and the advancement of broad national policy;

(d) Procurement, training and supervision of its intelligence personnel;

(e) Subversive operations abroad;

(f) Determination of policies for and coordination of facilities essential to the collection of information under subparagraph "(b)" hereof; and

(g) Such other functions and duties relating to intelligence as the President from time to time may direct.

4. The . . . . shall have no police or law-enforcement functions, either at home or abroad.

5. Subject to Paragraph 3 hereof, existing intelligence agencies within the Government shall collect, evaluate, synthesize and disseminate departmental operating intelligence, herein defined as intelligence required by such agencies in the actual performance of their functions and duties.

6. The Director shall be authorized to call upon Departments and agencies of the Government to furnish appropriate specialists for such supervisory and functional positions within the . . . . as may be required.

7. All Government Departments and agencies shall make available to the Director such intelligence material as the Director, with the approval of the President, from time to time may request.

8. The . . . . shall operate under an independent budget.

9. In time of war or unlimited national emergency, all programs of the . . . . in areas of actual or projected military operations shall be coordinated with military plans and shall be subject to the approval of the Joint Chiefs of Staff. Parts of such programs which are to be executed in a theater of military operations shall be subject to the control of the Theater Commander.

10. Within the limits of such funds as may be made available to . . . . the Director may employ necessary personnel and make provision for necessary supplies, facilities and services. The Director shall be assigned, upon the approval of the President, such military and naval personnel as may be required in the performance of the functions and duties of the . . . . The Director may provide for the internal organization and management of the . . . . in such manner as he may determine.

The substance of Donovan's recommendations, which later came to be embodied in the National Security Act of 1947 and in the establishment of the Central Intelligence Agency, are less important than what occurred once the memo and draft directive began to make the rounds in the intelligence community. In the first instance, Donovan sent the original to Roosevelt along with copies to his Chief of Staff, Fleet Admiral William Leahy; the Secretary of War, Henry Stimson; Secretary of State Edward Stettinius; the Secretary of the

Navy, James Forrestal; General Marshall, Chief of Staff of the Army; and Admiral King, Chief of Naval Operations. As a result of this initial distribution, and in anticipation of Roosevelt's likely call for additional comment on Donovan's proposal, the JCS on November 25, 1944, issued JCS 1181, which reproduced the memo and draft directive and distributed copies to key persons in the War and Navy Department's intelligence services as well as to the Joint Intelligence Committee with a request to that organization to prepare its comments and recommendations on the documents in the form of a report to the JCS. In addition, copies of JCS 1181 and the action memo to the JIC were sent to key persons in other interested agencies. These included the Secretary of State, Director of OSS, Director of FBI, and Administrator, Foreign Economic Assistance Administration.

This was normal staff procedure; however, as word about the memo and draft directive's contents began to seep down into the military intelligence services and into the other "interested agencies," opposition to Donovan's ideas hardened. None of those with a personal stake in the outcome had any inkling which way Roosevelt was inclined. The evidence available to them from their own White House sources merely indicated that FDR had read the Donovan memo and draft directive, mentally filed its recommendations away and had made no decision about when and if to issue it at some later date. Unlike the Marshall-Dewey episode, in the Donovan central intelligence dispute the number of players inclined one way or the other were numerous, if not equally divided.

There matters rested until February 9, 1945, when a signed article by Walter Trohan published in the now defunct *Washington Times-Herald* and the *Chicago Tribune* included word for word the contents of Donovan's memo and draft directive as reproduced in JCS 1181, with the exception of one sentence which was omitted and with certain editorial changes in the original Donovan documents. This was shattering enough; however, when on February 11 a second article by Trohan was published in these same papers which included the word-for-word contents of the January 1, 1945, JIC's 239/5 report and recommendations concerning the Donovan memo and draft directive (except for page 1, the transmittal page), the controversy in the military about a central intelligence authority under civilian control was completely out in the open.

Once the Trohan stories appeared, the JCS, especially General Marshall, was furious because the finger of suspicion was immediately pointed in the ·direction of the Pentagon. This security leak, although not as immediately serious as the MAGIC intercept situation, indicated that resolution of other vexatious problems in the postwar period were likely to be made much more difficult due to the public disclosure of the military's disagreement over the centralization of intelligence authority under civilian control. General Marshall added in the memo to General Bissell, the army G-2 and co-chairman of the JCS's Joint Security Control Office, which ordered an investigation of the leak, "try to nail this matter down with all possible speed. If we don't, it's likely there will be other similar attempts on more important questions."

A hasty search was initiated by the Joint Security Control office to find the source of the leak. The result was that all copies of JCS 1181 and the JIC 239/5 report in military custody were located and properly accounted for. Each copy of the documents was numbered sequentially in the distribution list, which included, in addition to military organizations such as the Office of Naval Intelligence, the other interested agencies mentioned above. The investigators' problem was quite formidable because since issuance of the more crucial document, JIC 239/5, on January 1, 1945, it had been read by quite a few Washington officials, any one of whom might have taken it upon himself to leak it, either because he sympathized with Donovan or its views and wanted to publicize them or because he disagreed with them and wanted to discredit them. In spite of their inability to resolve the ambiguities surrounding the motive, or to identify who had given the JCS documents to Trohan, the in-house investigation by the JCS counterintelligence personnel was quite thorough. It included, in addition to a paper-trail search and questioning of each recipient of the documents, an extensive interrogation of the mimeograph operator, a PFC, and the document control clerk, a corporal who was responsible for the distribution and document control log, to determine whether any "bootleg" copies had been made, but with no success. Likewise, because the JCS lacked investigative jurisdiction, when General Marshall asked the other interested agencies to mount a similar search to see if any of their copies of the documents were missing, they all reported negatively. However, on the basis of an informant's tip that the Trohan leaker was in the OSS, when a follow-up inquiry was made by the JCS to the OSS's Deputy Director, Edward Buxton, concerning its internal distribution of the JCS documents, he refused to provide the investigators with the names of the persons or the offices which had received the copies. One other tip suggested that the source of the leak was Henry Wallace, the former vice-president who had also been the head of the Board of Economic Warfare during Roosevelt's third term and was then the Secretary of Commerce. However, General Marshall ordered the investigators to stay away from Wallace.

The Joint Security Control's counterintelligence report of February 20 concluded, "We'll never know for sure who was responsible for the leak. Trohan has been chummy with J. Edgar Hoover for some time; however, based on the OSS unwillingness to identify those with access to our reproductions of the Donovan memo and draft directive, or to let us see their copies, we're inclined to think there is someone in the second echelon of Donovan's organization who gave Trohan the information with the idea of forcing the argument out into the open to forestall letting the military have the final say in the intelligence organization question."

The tempest over the Trohan stories caused a considerable flap in the intelligence community, but it subsided rather quickly because President Roosevelt, who was in Yalta at the time, was unavailable for immediate comment. However, at his March 2 press conference on the day after he had reported to the Congress on the outcome of the Yalta deliberations, FDR was questioned about the Trohan stories and his plans for the postwar organization of the government's intelligence community. Roosevelt, obviously exhausted from the ordeal of his 14,000-mile trip and disenchanted by Churchill and Stalin's intransigence about the postwar world, fended off the reporters' questions with some difficulty by referring to his hopes for the United Nations without really addressing himself to their questions about America's postwar intelligence needs. Following the press conference, Roosevelt, who apparently had only given brief consideration to the Donovan proposals when they were initially submitted, asked Assistant Secretary of State James Dunn to take a closer look at them and get an outside opinion and/or provide an alternative which would, in effect, place responsibility for intelligence and all that the term might imply under the State Department rather than leave it to the military or the JCS.*

FDR's order to Dunn marked a partial interregnum in the World War II struggle for intelligence control. It also was seen as a signal to the other interested agencies and persons that while Donovan had had the first shot at the intelligence community door prize, others were probably going to get a chance to advance themselves, their plans, and their organizations. Thus by March 30, when Roosevelt travelled by train to Warm Springs for two to three weeks of rest, each of the players in the struggle for intelligence control and those in their immediate entourage entered a kind of final preparation phase in which it was assumed that upon the president's return, responsibility for and distribution of the postwar intelligence pie would be decided. However, on April 12, 1945, Roosevelt died without deciding who or how intelligence should be organized; none of his ostensible intelligence "team" players were

---

*Also, on March 2, 1945, Harold D. Stone, the Director of the Budget, sent a memorandum to President Roosevelt indicating his concern over the intelligence question. It read as follows:

> I notice that at your press conference today some questions were asked about the organization of intelligence in government. Since I have occasion to be concerned about incomplete and ex parte reports being sent to the White House by advocates, I want you to know that the Bureau of the Budget has been making a comprehensive study of all of the intelligence activities. I hope you will ship to us for consideration anything that comes in on this subject.
>
> There seems to be a tug-of-war going on between some of the agencies, which we faced in connection with the Budget. Furthermore, while you were away several additional rumors were set in circulation concerning what might be done.
>
> Since we informed all contenders that nothing would be done prior to a comprehensive study, I hope you will help us hold the fort and not permit anyone to take your time prematurely in connection with this matter.
>
> (signed) H.D.S.
> Director

P.S. See leaks on proposed Orders, attached.

sure whether the new captain, Harry Truman, would want them or their ideas for his team and its subsequent organization.

With the death of President Roosevelt, although the war itself would end in four more months, the wartime intelligence struggle for intelligence control took on a new dimension and direction. It acquired additional internal momentum because whatever ideas and predilections Roosevelt had for the future became irrelevant once he died. How President Truman arbitrated and presided over the intelligence struggle and how it was simultaneously waged in connection with other postwar political struggles is set forth in the next two chapters.

CHAPTER 5

TRUMAN AND THE INTELLIGENCE COMMUNITY: PART I

At the time of Harry Truman's abrupt accession to power, few in the intelligence community's leadership had even partially considered the prospect that he would be serving as the final arbiter in their long-running struggle to gain intelligence control. Their view, based largely on the furor both in and out of government over Donovan's ideas on postwar intelligence, was that Roosevelt had concluded that the time to resolve the issue of intelligence control and centralization and the form of postwar intelligence organization was close at hand, and would be decided before hostilities ended. One cannot be completely certain how accurate their view of Roosevelt's intentions actually was; what is certain is that at the time of his death a variety of postwar intelligence organization plans had been spawned, which paradoxically widened as well as narrowed the issues concerning intelligence functions, organization, and control.

In addition to the Donovan proposal previously described, one drawn up by John Franklin Carter, in response to Roosevelt's order to Assistant Secretary of State James Dunn to get an outside opinion or alternative plan, deserves careful attention. Carter, a radio producer and commentator, transmitted his ideas on intelligence to Roosevelt on March 27, 1945. According to Dunn, FDR seemed favorably disposed toward Carter's ideas, but remarked "I had better let the military take a crack at this before we decide anything, or there'll be another leak." As a result, almost as his last act as titular head of the intelligence community, FDR passed the Carter memorandum to his chief of staff, Fleet Admiral William D. Leahy, on March 29, with the instructions, "To read and tell me what you think. FDR."

Carter's plan offers the remarkable insight of a Washington "insider" who was unencumbered by bureaucratic loyalties or the mandate of implied conclusions when a presidential commission is ordered to study a problem and make recommendations. In this case, both Roosevelt and Dunn had confidence in Carter's judgment and common sense about intelligence as well as in his personal integrity to tell the president what he actually thought rather than what he or others might think the president wanted to hear. As such, Carter's ideas were much more dangerous in the eyes of the intelligence community leaders than those of Donovan, because Carter had nothing personally to gain or lose if his plan were accepted by Roosevelt. The Carter plan read as follows:

General Principles

The method proposed is designed to create a system of foreign political intelligence for the guidance of the secretary of state and the president during the period of postwar readjustment and the subsequent peace.

This system must be simple, economical and impossible to "penetrate" by foreign intelligence systems, if it is to meet the anticipated tests of congressional criticism and national economy. It must also be "law-proof" in the sense that none of its operations if revealed would constitute an infringement of the rights of American citizens or overt acts against friendly governments.

The technique proposed is to assimilate to the regular framework of the federal government's current intelligence operations and to conserve the results of wartime intelligence operations both as an economy and as common sense.

Broadly speaking this technique assumes that during the concluding phases of the war and during the period of occupation of Germany and Japan, the wartime intelligence services—OSS, G-2, ONI, Air Intelligence, FBI—will continue to operate, probably with diminishing intensity, and that the system of foreign political intelligence will gradually take over their functions.

It is also assumed that all of these wartime intelligence systems will be continued in restricted form, in conformity with the technical responsibilities of the services and nothing in this plan should be construed as an argument to abandon or supplant those services, whether separate or coordinated.

I Base Operations

A) *Personnel Files.* The personnel files and personal security data already assembled at great cost by G-2, ONI, FBI, etc., should be kept intact at the end of the war and should be concentrated in a single file for the use of all interested government departments. Jurisdiction over these files should be vested in either the Visa and Passport Division of the State Department or in some appropirate agency, perhaps in the Federal Archives. Use of these files in checking both foreign and American nationals, in relation to intelligence reports, will be invaluable.

B) *Research and Analysis.* The Research and Analysis Division of the OSS and corresponding bureaus of other federal agencies should be concentrated as a permanent joint division of the Library of Congress for the special use of interested federal agencies. These files should be kept current as far as is possible; they will in any event constitute a valuable source of tested data on foreign countries and peoples.

C) *Foreign Demography.* All data gathered by the government on foreign demography—i.e., population pressures, population movements, settlement and migration—should be concentrated in a special division of the Census Bureau. To this division should be referred all foreign demographic material seized in Germany and Japan.

D) *Cultural Relations.* The State Department Division of Cultural Relations, working in liaison with the Bureau of Education, the Library of Congress and private insitutions such as the Carnegie Institute, the Rockefeller Institute, the various boards of foreign business, etc., should assemble and collate current data on foreign educational systems, with special reference to curricula, in order to keep a constant check on tendencies which might produce another Hitler Youth, etc., etc.

E) *Foreign Economic Conditions.* The Bureau of Foreign and Domestic Commerce and such elements of F.E.A., Lend-Lease, UNRRA as survive, should in coordination with Treasury maintain a constant check on foreign economic conditions, in order to be aware of major dislocations of a character which would breed social unrest and political upheaval.

F) *Technological Intelligence.* The federal organization which takes over the work of the O.S.R.D. and similar research and scientific organizations of the war agencies should be required to maintain contact through all appropriate means with scientific and technological developments in every part of the world, working in conjunction with and perhaps as part of the Patent Office, or the Bureau of Standards. In this way, the government should be continuously informed of any important changes in the techno-logical environment and any new discoveries which would substantially affect world economy or world security. A special Division of Technical Intelligence might appro-priately be organized under the Secret Security Intelligence Service (outlined in II-I below), in order to keep touch with efforts by I.G. Farben, Mitsui and similar Axis enterprises to preserve their organization and objectives after the collapse of Germany and Japan.

This base organization is designed to conserve the legitimate values which can be salvaged from the wartime investment in the above-mentioned data, in such a form as to be currently useful to the State Department in time of peace and to give advance warning of developments which endanger world peace or complicate American foreign relations.

G) *Basis for Organization and Operation of the Secret Security Intelligence Service.* It is suggested that the Secret Security Intelligence Service may properly be considered to be a part of the operation and responsibility of the Office of Special Political Affairs, this for both domestic and foreign activity. This office has already within its structure a Division of International Security Affairs, which division is charged with the formula-tion and coordination of policy and action regarding all security phases of the proposed United Nations Organization, and relevant security aspects of United States foreign policy generally. This division is also charged with liaison, within the scope of its jurisdiction, with international organizations and agencies and with other federal de-partments and agencies.

II Foreign Operations

A) *Diplomatic Control.* The American ambassador in any foreign country shall *ex officio* be responsible for *all* American intelligence operations in that country. To implement that responsibility, in each U.S. diplomatic mission there should be assigned a Foreign Service officer specially trained to coordinate these intelligence operations and to advise the ambassador.

B) *Foreign Intelligence Officers.* It is recommended that by executive order or by amendment to the Foreign Service Act, the president be authorized to transfer to the Foreign Service the necessary number of Army, Navy and Marine Corps officers without competitive examination. The officers transferred should be selected from the trained interrogators and operatives of G-2, CIC, ONI, etc., etc., and, for South America, from the FBI.

C) *Foreign Intelligence Training.* The State Department School should institute a special section of Foreign Intelligence. All students should take a general course in this section; those who so desire and are approved should take a special course in Foreign Intelligence. This section should also be charged with supervision of questionnaires and with rating the work of Foreign Intelligence officers.

D) *Visa and Passport Control.* All applicants for visas and passports should, so far as is practical either as a general rule or in connection with a particular country, be checked with the general security data on U.S. and foreign nationals. Broadly speaking, the administration of both visa and passport control should be entrusted to Foreign Intelligence officers who could legitimately interview and question the applicants without infringing their personal rights or liberties.

E) *State Department Dispatch Agents.* Foreign Intelligence officers should be assigned as U.S. dispatch agents at the principal ports of entry, including airports, in order to question individual arrivals and departures.

F) *Division of Foreign Political Information.* A special section should be set up in the State Department to coordinate these operations and to select certain private citizens who may from time to time be encouraged to visit specified foreign countries in order to obtain an insight into current developments. This division should maintain constant contact with the various private American institutions which normally maintain foreign representatives—newspapers, other publications, business corporations, labor organizations, missionary and educational bodies—so that it is currently informed of their foreign personnel and is in a position to suggest that such and such an individual be sent on legitimate private business to such and such a country.

G) *Every U.S. Citizen an Intelligence Officer.* The purpose of the above is to create a system in which every U.S. citizen who travels abroad and, within limits, every foreign national who enters the U.S. or has business with our diplomatic and consular missions abroad, is a source of political intelligence to the Department of State. In this way, there would be no "secrecy" to penetrate by foreign intelligence services, no direct cost to the Treasury of the U.S., and intelligence would tend to follow the real spread of American and foreign business and travels, including of course study abroad. The reports obtained by skilled interrogators dealing with the travelling public would be evaluated against the general files and information of the department. The personnel files, now existing or supplmented, would be used to check the qualifications and reliability of the individual as an observer rather than his political loyalties.

H) *Transfers.* In administering this system, care should be taken to maintain a system of regular transfers and reassignments, to prevent Foreign Intelligence officers from becoming stale. Emphasis should be placed on concise and useful reporting rather than on volume.

I) *Secret Security Intelligence.* The Secret Intelligence Service of the OSS, plus such elements of ONI, G-2 and FBI as are qualified, should be reorganized and constituted as a Secret Security Intelligence Service. The SSI should have as its permanent mission the task of detecting and reporting to the president any developments which threaten the security of the world. During the immediate postwar period the SSI should aid in tracing war criminals, etc., both as implementing the will of the United Nations and as a practical course of training and development. This mission is justified historically by the fact that any threat to world peace is a threat to the United States. Diplomatically, it would be justified by the fact of our responsibility, as member of the World Security Council, to be informed from our own sources of any threat to world security. The director of the SSI should be *ex officio* the appropriate assistant secretary of state charged with intelligence, who should select a deputy who would be a permanent official removable at the will of the president. Members of the SSI should be specially selected and trained and should have access to all the information available to the government required to discharge their mission under the obligations taken by the United States at Dumbarton Oaks, Yalta, and San Francisco.

III Domestic Operations

The State Department has a legitimate interest in maintaining a constant organized check on (a) the operations of foreign political intelligence inside the U.S. and (b) the political tendencies on the part of the American people themselves. This is a problem of considerable difficulty and great delicacy. The following suggestions are offered with diffidence and are subject to radical criticism.

A) *Foreign Intelligence in U.S.* The Liaison Section of the State Department should cooperate fully with the FBI in maintaining a constant check on foreign intelligence and propaganda, including propagandized U.S. citizens, inside the U.S. Data so obtained would be of value, not only to Congressional Committees on Foreign Relations, but to the operations of our diplomacy abroad, without infringement of American statutes. Prosecution under the Registration of Foreign Agents Act would be preferable to prosecution under espionage acts. The Division of Current Political Information should be charged with evaluating the data obtained by the FBI in this field.

B) *State Department Liaison with State Governments.* The secretary of state is charged with responsibility for maintaining relations between the federal government and the state governments. Subject to congressional approval it is suggested that a Foreign Intelligence officer be assigned as State Department liaison officer with the secretary of state of each of the 48 states. These officers, to begin with, should be selected from competent Army, Navy, Marine, etc. intelligence officers and should, so far as possible, be citizens of the state to which they are assigned. This would be popular as aid to veterans, with a small patronage angle, and could be justified by reference to the current brand of phony federalism, as a long overdue recognition of the basic role of the states in our government. These liaison officers, working in cooperation with the FBI, and the Bureau of Immigration and Naturalization (i.e., the Department of Justice), could keep the State Department currently informed on political trends inside the U.S. This would be desirable because state legislatures are peculiarly vulnerable to outside influences and would be a logical obejective of foreign intelligence services seeking to operate in the U.S.

C) *State Department Liaison with Federal Agencies.* Foreign Intelligence officers should be assigned to act as liaison with other federal bureaus or departments. A special liaison staff of Foreign Intelligence officers, under high-ranking State Department officials, should be assigned to work with the Senate and House Committees on Foreign Affairs.

D) *Secret Security Intelligence.* The SSI could also legitimately be employed without reference to our national boundaries to aid in keeping a check on foreign political intrigues and propaganda calculated to endanger world security. Such activity would appear to be a reasonable precaution, in order to avoid the possible diplomatic embarrassment which would follow revelation by other members of the United Nations that our territory might actually be used as a base of operations by foreign interests seeking to endanger world security.

Carter's ideas constituted pretty heady stuff in the arguments about intelligence. They added a significant new dimension to the intelligence control argument by identifying the thrust of the postwar intelligence effort in terms of a "system of foreign political intelligence for the guidance of the secretary of state and the president." This emphasis on civilian control and especially on the reassertion of the secretary of state's primacy in intelligence activities which impinged on American foreign policy was perceived as a direct threat to the military's postwar plans for their intelligence services. As a result, the military was prompt in registering their opposition to the Carter proposal. On April 3, 1945, Major General Clayton Bissell, the army's G-2, in a memo to the JCS's executive secretary, Brigadier General A. J. McFarland, dammed Carter's ideas with faint praise by saying, "While portions of the discussion are timely, the paper is not sufficiently developed to merit serious consideration by the president. However, the paper throws light on the need for study of similar problems at the departmental level." He added, "The entire discussion shows a complete lack of awareness of the scope of military and naval intelligence. The concept of military and naval intelligence as limited to strictly technical matters is contrary to precedent and falls far short of the actual intelligence needs of the secretaries of war and the navy. . . . It fails to provide for the overall supervision and coordination of these activities by the secretaries of state, war, and navy." Finally Bissell, whose own sources in the White House had suggested that an intelligence organization decision was imminent and unfavorable to the army, concluded, "While the plan is not in suitable form for consideration by the president or by members of his cabinet, it does highlight the current need for studies on postwar coordination of intelligence at the departmental level. It is suggested that an appropriate action might be for the president to charge the State, War and Navy Coordinating Committee with initiating a study of postwar intelligence coordination."

All these were familiar enough arguments in the battle for intelligence control. For years, whenever it looked like one of the members of the intelligence community was about to be named "leader," the others, especially the military services, would cry "foul" and call for an interdepartmental review to prevent such an outcome. In this case, Bissell's call to charge the State, War and Navy Coordinating Committee with carrying out a study of postwar intelligence coordination was absurd because, since the creation of the JCS and its arrogation of powers, the service secretaries and the secretary of state had lost any real semblance of line control over the intelligence operations undertaken during the course of the war and over the actions of military and civilian personnel presumptively under their command. Nevertheless, buried in General Bissell's detailed comments on the Carter report was one which was relatively new, and which would be argued forcefully in the years ahead as justification for preventing effective presidential control over foreign intelligence activities under other than internal intelligence community auspices. Namely, Bissell's statement about "diplomatic control" which held that "control of all intelligence activities in foreign countries by the ambassador would be impracticable. He would be incapable of fully representing interests of the War and Navy Departments and control of secret intelligence might compromise his position." Without anticipating the future designation of American ambassadors as the "chiefs of mission" (i.e., in charge of *all* American personnel and activities in a foreign country, ordered by President Eisenhower and reaffirmed by President Kennedy), and the intrinsic merits or lack thereof of General Bissell's contention about diplomatic control, the intelligence community's real fear (which had largely remained unstated until the Bissell memo) was one based on an ambassador's potential to communicate directly with the president. Then as now, what the president doesn't know, or what the intelligence community decides he needs to know, is the key to retaining de facto control over intelligence operations carried out under broad mission-type orders, or implied and delegated authority.

How, if at all, Roosevelt would have resolved the postwar intelligence organization and function questions can only be a matter for speculation.* However, in an interview, James Dunn offered his personal opinion, based upon extended discussions with Roosevelt about the problems of intelligence, that the most likely outcome was one which blended the Donovan and Carter approaches and placed the State Department in the premier position in the intelligence community's hierarchy. As American intelligence activities had expanded during the war, FDR had become keenly aware of his lack of personal "eyes and ears" in the intelligence community. Dunn said, "President Roosevelt was angered and fearful over the implications of the Donovan story as it appeared in the press because it signalled the exercise of a power able to thwart and defy the legitimate interests of the president in seeking an answer to a controversial question." He further stated that "This was also the sense and concern of those of us most intimately involved with the problems raised by the leak of the Donovan and JCS memo while President Roosevelt was at Warm Springs, and once he died the intelligence community leaders moved to delay any action or decision until the power centers around President Truman had stabilized and it was known who would have access to him on such matters."

---

*Further evidence concerning Roosevelt's intentions about a postwar centralized intelligence service is contained in a memorandum from him to Donovan dated April 5, 1945. Written just a week before his death, Roosevelt said:

> Apropos of your memorandum of November 18, 1944, relative to the establishment of a central intelligence service, I should appreciate your calling together the chiefs of the foreign intelligence *and internal security units* in the various executive agencies, so that a consensus can be secured. [Emphasis added.]

> It appears to me that all of the ten executive departments, as well as the Foreign Economic Administration, and the Federal Communications Commission have a direct interest in the proposed venture. They should all be asked to contribute their suggestion to the proposed centralized intelligence service.

Truman's assumption of titular control over the intelligence community was abrupt. There was no orderly transition in the sense of his having had any real before-the-fact knowledge about controversies in the Roosevelt administration concerning present and future military plans, as well as ones in America's wartime intelligence community. And in the first several weeks of Truman's presidency the military leaders kept him reasonably isolated from conflicting opinions and/or options to deal with these problems. Nevertheless, in response to a direct question from Truman on April 13 about "outstanding undecided issues," Admiral Leahy replied, "intelligence." Thereafter, Leahy reviewed the status of the Donovan report, the JCS position, the Carter plan, etc., and left Truman to ponder the problem. To Leahy's credit he did not advocate one proposal or approach in favor of the other. For him it was the president's decision to make; however, Leahy also made it clear that he stood ready to provide him with advice if it was requested.

In the rush of events during the first week of Truman's presidency, it seemed to those most concerned that the intelligence issue had been put on the back burner. However, unknown to the intelligence community leaders and General Marshall and Admiral King (with whom Leahy discussed his conversation with Truman about the intelligence issue), Truman had also discussed the issue with his budget director, Harold D. Smith, and asked him for his advice concerning the need for a quick decision which delineated the merits and deficiencies of the proposals offered to his predecessor. Smith's reply to Truman was soon forthcoming. In an April 20 "Memorandum for the President, Subject: Intelligence," Smith wrote:

The government must have much stronger and more effective intelligence facilities in the postwar period than we have ever had before in peacetime. Recognition of this need is widespread, and had led to the formulation of a number of proposals, of which those of the Joint Chiefs of Staff and the Office of Strategic Services have been most publicized. There is, in some quarters, strong support of the notion that early approval of these or similar proposals is vital to the fulfillment of our emerging international obligations. This impatience may result in recommendations to you to take action which may be premature.

I do not believe that such early action is either necessary or desirable. In making this statement, I question neither the sincerity of the supporters for immediate action, nor do I doubt the very real need for stronger postwar intelligence facilities than the government possessed in prewar days.

Rather, my belief comes from considerable knowledge of the present intelligence programs of the government. This knowledge has been gained from intensive work undertaken by my staff during the past three years. At the request of General McNarney, then deputy chief of staff, intensive study of G-2 was conducted in 1942, and recommendations offered which resulted in some simplification of G-2 organization and some improvement in its relationship with the Federal Bureau of Investigation. In 1943, at the request of Admiral Horne, vice-chief of naval operations, a similar study was conducted in the Office of Naval Intelligence. In the same year, studies were made in the Foreign Broadcast Intelligence Service and in the Radio Intelligence Division of the Federal Communications Commission. Early in 1944, bureau staff participated in a study of G-2 conducted under a board which included Assistant Secretary McCloy, General McNarney, and others. The study resulted in a strengthening of G-2 through a complete reorganization. These studies have necessitated observations in a number of other agencies, including the State Department, Office of Strategic Services, Foreign Economic Administration, Bureau of Foreign and Domestic Commerce, Office of War Information and others. In addition, some study has been made of intelligence services of other countries.

These studies, which directed principally to the immediate improvement of effectiveness in operations, provided extensive insight into the objectives, organization, and the extent of coordination—or lack of it—characteristic of intelligence programs. The studies have furnished a firm basis for the development, in a study I have initiated as one of many dealing with the reconversion of the governmental structure to a peacetime footing, of guideposts for postwar intelligence organization and coordination. This study will take into full account the proposals of the Joint Chiefs of Staff, the Office of Strategic Services, and others.

Facilities currently available for the production of intelligence are extensive and not well coordinated. A principal reason for the lack of coordination which now exists is hasty or competitive action—often unavoidably hasty—taken in the past. In my judgment, well considered and objective action is badly needed from this time forward.

I am confident that we know what is going on in this area, what the problems are, and some of the past mistakes which should not be repeated in whatever plans may be made for the future. It is my hope that you may utilize the bureau's experience and government-wide viewpoint to help you evaluate such proposals as may be made to you. I shall forward specific recommendations from time to time as our work progresses.

To this memorandum Smith appended in his own hand, "I hope to have a chance to speak to you about this next week. HDS."

The Smith memo did not signal the start of an entirely new ball game in the intelligence controversy; however, from the intelligence community leaders' point of view, it did indicate the unwanted presence of a new player in the old game—and more importantly one who apparently had easy access to the president's ear. The next straw in the wind occurred following a May 4 meeting between Smith and Truman, at which time Smith was ordered to carry out a study of "all the agencies and services engaged in intelligence work,"* and to place a hold on any requests for additional unvouchered funds for foreign covert intelligence operations from the president's fund. This was quickly perceived by the intelligence community leaders as a clear signal concerning the new president's attitudes about secret intelligence. To those in the military intelligence services it also indicated the necessity and desirability to get an arm's length away from further involvement in questionable secret intelligence practices and the additional opportunity to disavow and curtail, if not eliminate, Donovan's OSS from the postwar intelligence equation.

*Truman, *Memoirs, op. cit.,* p. 226.

The opportunity arose shortly thereafter in connection with the budget proceedings for fiscal year 1946, due to begin on July 1, 1945. At the time, due to the recent surrender of Germany and Truman's actions in ordering major cuts in the rest of the federal budget in anticipation of the war's end, military appropriations received their first really hard look from Congress since the start of the war. Although OSS appropriations in the previous years were not particularly high relative to the size of its organization and in comparison with total military appropriations, spending to continue OSS's little-known (at the time) activities were singled out by the House's Military Appropriations Committee for close scrutiny. The JCS was not unwilling to offer the OSS up to the congressional budget cutters, but it was a tricky matter to carry off because of possible cuts in other military appropriations. Also, in view of Harold Smith's order from Truman to study the intelligence situation, the intelligence community leaders feared that if too close a look were taken at what OSS had actually accomplished during World War II, a similar look might be taken at the military intelligence services. The situation was not without irony in that the military intelligence leaders who had been playing at undercutting Donovan and the OSS needed to keep him and it in existence at least until the final act of the intelligence organizational drama had been played out.

The flavor of this tragicomedy is conveyed in a transcript of a telephone conversation between John Pugh, staff director of the House Military Appropriations Committee, and Brigadier General A. J. McFarland, executive secretary of the JCS, on May 21, 1945. The substance of their conversation was as follows:

Pugh:	The committee is interested in information on OWI and OSS. They are winding up the hearings and are going to mark up the bill tomorrow. Mr. Taber says the press has repeated stories that MacArthur and Nimitz don't want any part of this agency in their areas. The committee wanted to have Marshall come down. He said it was not his baby. Admiral Leahy was down here to the ceremonies. I spoke to him and he said "Johnny, I shouldn't come down there, I am too close to the president." Then the committee said try and get a dispatch sent out to Nimitz and MacArthur telling them of this story and ask them if it is true, and get us a reply in here tommorow morning. I called General _____ and Admiral Allen of the navy. They have been doing a little negotiating and it was suggested that perhaps the Joint Chiefs of Staff might send somebody down here to clear up this picture for them.
McFarland:	I thought you wanted to get a dispatch off to MacArthur and Nimitz. Who is responsible for the articles?
P.:	That would be perfectly appropriate. I have never seen the articles. Mr. Taber said he saw several articles in the press to the effect that MacArthur and Nimitz don't want the OSS in their theaters. I can't tell you who is responsible. I am taking Taber's word for all that.
McF.:	It's like an anonymous story. That makes it difficult. I don't see any way of getting the facts without asking MacArthur and Nimitz.

P.: Taber says if I don't get this information he is going to get up on the floor and say that the War Department and Joint Chiefs of Staff don't deny them and he assumes they are true. That isn't fair either. It seems to me to be fair to those two officers they should be given the opportunity to express themselves.

McF.: You are in effect asking me for a statement from the Joint Chiefs of Staff on the press reports that Nimitz and MacArthur do not desire the services of the OSS.

P.: I don't know as we want it so much from the Joint Chiefs of Staff unless they can speak for those two officers.

McF.: You want verification of the reports alleged in the press that these officers do not want the OSS in their theaters. The committee wants the truth of the matter: are these reports true or not.

P.: That's right, General. They are meeting tomorrow morning to mark up that bill and want the information by that time. When you get the word I would like for you to communicate it to Mr. Cannon, chairman of the Appropriations Committee of the House.

In a belated attempt to get some statements from the field about the OSS into the record, the JCS sent a book message to Generals Eisenhower (Europe), McNarney (Italy) and Wedemeyer (China/Burma) on May 22 which said:

Question as to relative value of Office of Strategic Services to theater commanders has arisen before House Appropriations Committee in connection with this consideration of OSS budget estimates for fiscal year 1946. Your views requested urgently.

Eisenhower, ever the diplomat, replied:

1. When the Office of Strategic Services was first established, the military services were not any better prepared to utilize services than it was to render the type of service ultimately required. However, its value in this theater has been so great that there should be no thought of its elimination as an activity.

2. Future value of the Office of Strategic Services in the European theater appears to be high but is subject to certain contingencies. Valuable assistance in the prosecution of the war was effected by OSS by successful short-range operations on the entire front where they obtained tactical intelligence and accomplished local sabotage. Strategic operations had the same objects as the tactical but were executed deeper within enemy territory. They were not consistently effective but had some sporadic successes of great importance. Also OSS performed admirably in helping to organize resistance groups in France, Belgium, Holland, Denmark, and Norway, and in assisting to supply them.

3. In the future OSS will function as an intelligence/information-gathering agency and as a counterespionage organization. It is expected that a net utilizing high-grade personnel will feed back a wide range of intelligence and information to the theater commander through the tight control of the intelligence staff. Complete control by the theater commander of OSS activities within his theater or based on his theater is regarded as an essential prerequisite of efficient and smooth operations. Since the

development of an intelligence organization is a long-term project the future usefulness of OSS can be judged only on results obtained. Its success will depend in large measure on the provision for postwar activities of the same high class and reliable personnel as OSS had available during the war. If suitable personnel is made available and if theater commander controls are maintained it is considered that the value of OSS in the European theater will continue to be high.

General McNarney hedged, saying:

Office of Strategic Services activities in this theater reference your WX 86161 have been to carry out special operations and to provide secret intelligence.

These activities contributed greatly to the success of our operations in Italy and could not have been performed effectively in the absence of trained personnel and facilities.

OSS personnel did an outstanding job in directing and coordinating partisan activities and their facilities were indispensable in the negotiations culminating in the German surrender in Italy.

So long as the situation in Italy, Austria, and the Balkans remains unstable, it is essential to continue the secret intelligence activities of OSS in this theater.

Special operations, however, are no longer required and accordingly the OSS staff in Mediterranean theater of operations can be reduced, on the basis of a rough estimate to approximately 20% in 1946 of its average MTO strength for the fiscal year 1945. Recommend that Office of Strategic Services be provided with sufficient funds in the fiscal year 1946 to continue their reduced activities in Mediterranean theater and to permit trained OSS personnel to be redeployed to the Pacific.

General Wedemeyer, who believed that hard fighting against Japanese forces in both China and the Japanese home islands still lay ahead, was more inclined to give the OSS a positive endorsement:

Inasmuch as OSS and Navy Group China are the only American organizations in this theater trained and capable of carrying out demolitions, commando operations and clandestine intelligence activity, it is considered that the potential value of OSS to this theater is high. OSS was subordinated to a minor role in China previously due to the provisions of the SACO agreement* and the relatively few OSS personnel in the theater.

Presently authorized for OSS is a strength of 2,000 United States personnel in this

*In early 1943, after several months' negotiations and with President Roosevelt's verbal approval, Donovan and Secretary Knox signed a secret technical agreement with the Chinese government. This pact created a joint secret service, the Sino-American Cooperation Organization (SACO), under the directorship of Chinese general Tai Li, who operated under the title director, Bureau of Investigations and Statistics, but who was actually the chief of a combined secret police and intelligence organization said to control over 300,000 agents throughout China and in every foreign nation where Chinese communities existed—from Bangkok to San Francisco. Rear Admiral Milton "Mary" Miles, USN, was deputy director as well as Far Eastern chief of OSS and commander of Navy Group/China. SACO was to engage in guerrilla training, espionage, sabotage, and radio interception. The Chinese agreed to supply manpower and facilities, while arms and equipment would come from the United States. (See: R. Harris Smith, *op. cit.*, pp. 245, 251–2, and Milton Miles, *A Different Kind of War.* New York: Doubleday, 1967.)

theater and this number is being approached rapidly. When OSS reaches authorized strength and its efforts are closely integrated with offensive operations intended, I feel certain their approved projects will materially assist theater in its assigned mission.

OSS is now training 20 commando groups and intelligence teams and will furnish United States personnel to these units as advisors. These groups and others already trained are to be charged with responsible missions in direct support of contemplated future plans.

Because the contemplated future strategy in the Pacific involved the invasion of the Japanese home islands and included a converging of the forces under General MacArthur's and Admiral Nimitz's commands, a separate book message was sent to both commanders seeking their confirmation or rejection about statements attributed to them concerning the role of the OSS in the Pacific war:

House Appropriations Committee, now considering Office of Strategic Services budget estimate for fiscal year 1946, has taken cognizance of statements in Washington press to effect that neither General MacArthur nor Admiral Nimitz desires the services of OSS in the Pacific war. Committee requests immediate statment from Joint Chiefs of Staff as to truth or falsity of reports. Urgently request information as to whether or not you desire the services of the OSS in the Pacific war.

Admiral Nimitz was not particularly enamored of the OSS; however, he left the door slightly open for its participation in the Pacific war, but only if the JCS and Donovan told him what they actually planned to do. In essence Nimitz didn't say yes and didn't say no; he also was not willing to give Donovan's "cowboys" an unrestricted visa to operate in the Pacific theater. On the other hand, MacArthur replied in his typical Olympian style:

No statement has emanated from this headquarters nor so far as known from this area in comment on OSS. Any items that may have appeared in the press along this line must be regarded as speculative conjecture.
The OSS has not up to the present time operated within this area, I know little of its methods, have no control of its agencies, and consequently have no plans for its future employment.

The results of these mixed reviews of the OSS and its effectiveness were packaged by the JCS and forwarded to Clarence Cannon, chairman of the Committee on Military Appropriations, with an appended contribution by Admiral Leahy:

The Joint Chiefs of Staff are not in a position to offer any detailed statement as to the appropriations required to support the organization during the coming year. It appears, however, that with the termination of hostilities in Europe, the requirements for the next fiscal year could be appreciably less than those for the past year.

Leahy's comments didn't completely satisfy Chairman Cannon and his committee staff who, although inclined to cut the OSS budget, wanted to avoid any later charges that they had failed to provide "our boys" with what they needed to defeat the Japanese.

The situation produced by this maneuvering was not unlike a labor-management wage-contract negotiation. Cannon wanted the military to specify in advance how much of a cut in the OSS budget they would accept and the military wanted to hear his offer first. This kind of collective bargaining between Congress and the military has not been uncommon in America's annual battles of the budget; however, because this situation was further complicated by the questions concerning the future of the OSS, the pressures were more intense. Neither side seemed willing to make initial concessions; both were afraid that the impasse might leak into the press and call their individual and separate motives into serious question. As a result, on May 28, Major General George J. Richards, the budget officer for the War Department, telephoned McFarland to see if there was some way to resolve the problem and get all parties off the hook.

The substance of the Richards-McFarland conversation was as follows:

Richards: I am up here in a committee meeting and am talking low on this phone. They called me upstairs and showed me a synopsis of the letter Admiral Leahy sent them. The synopsis indicates that that outfit will be employed only to a very limited extent, apparently, in the future. They are willing to let it rock along until September. Then they feel some other disposition should be made of it at that time and that it should definitely operate under your people—

McFarland: They do now.

R.:   but with money appropriated to you, or that it should operate under money appropriated to the War Department. They apparently do not feel like appropriating money direct to it any more.

McF.:   There is an additional letter from General Eisenhower which was sent Mr. Cannon this morning. It should be considered by the committee in its decision. It is a little more favorable than the Pacific commanders and indicates the extent to which General Eisenhower envisages its use in Europe.

R.:   Why don't you and someone else, perhaps a navy man, come up and sit down with possibly Mr. Cannon or the clerk of the committee and run over the whole thing? Could you do that sometime today?

McF.:   I wouldn't want to do it without the sanction of the Chiefs. What would be the object?

R.:   To go over the whole thing with them as to how this thing should be operated in the future.

McF.:   But I have no authority to act for the Joint Chiefs of Staff.

R.:   Well who has? They always come to me and—

McF.:   Unless the Chiefs of Staff have agreed previously no individual can voice their views because sometimes they do not agree. If the committee has a

R.:   proposition to make to the Joint Chiefs of Staff I suggest that they should submit it in writing and let the Chiefs give their own views.

R.:   How long would it take to get some action?

McF.:   I can get it very promptly. The SWNCC [State-War-Navy Coordinating Committee] often speaks of having a representative of the Joint Chiefs of Staff. We don't know at any time what the Chiefs will agree on when there is a disagreement. If I went up there I would have to bring back to the Chiefs what the committee has said. It would be better if the committee sent a concrete proposition, let me circulate it, and get an agreed decision from the Chiefs.

R.:   According to the committee's way of doing things that is cumbersome.

McF.:   Unfortunately it is, but when you have a number of people on the same level, equally authoritative, and sometimes with difference of opinion, the only way to get an agreed opinion is to let them look at it and compose any differences among themselves. I am sure that if the committee will make a concrete proposition, I can assure that the Joint Chiefs of Staff will take early action.

R.:   If you get something by 2:00 o'clock this afternoon could you get an answer back by 11:00 o'clock tomorrow?

McF.:   I am not sure I can do it that fast but I will try. There is nobody authorized to speak for the Chiefs. It is like who speaks for the Congress.

R.:   The Speaker of the House, and Speaker [sic] of the Senate.

McF.:   They can speak for Congress where Congress has declared its policy but nobody can give a definite answer for them on a proposal that is not an agreed policy. No one can give an answer on a proposed bill, everyone is entitled to his vote; and it is only after the votes are counted that we can determine what is the consensus. If you will get me that by 2:00 o'clock I will guarantee fast action and there is a possibility I can get it by 11:00 o'clock tomorrow morning.

The result of this byplay and government by telephone left all parties to the dispute with their egos and empires reasonably intact. The OSS's fiscal 1946 budget request of $45 million, which Donovan acknowledged to contain a $5 million cushion for contingencies, was cut by the Appropriation Committee to $38 million. This latter figure was accepted by all concerned. It represented the rate of OSS's actual expenditures in fiscal 1945 and as such signalled business as usual—at least for a while longer.

Although the outcome of the budget and continued existence of the OSS flap was welcomed by Donovan and his subalterns, it constituted a less than satisfactory one for the military intelligence services' leaders. General Richards' comments about appropriations being made to the War Department for OSS suggested that the service secretaries might become able to control appropriations for intelligence purposes. To be sure, in 1945 the Budget Office of the War and Navy Department still had a role to play in the military appropriations and budget process; however, it was more a technical one than one which questioned and evaluated the merit of operational activities and programs.

For the next several months, as a result of OSS's getting a second life and the apparent necessity to get ready for the invasion of the Japanese home islands, the intelligence organization questions drifted back into a state of semilimbo. Harold Smith and his cohorts at the Bureau of the Budget continued work on their intelligence study while the rest of the intelligence community either went ahead with the task of sorting out friends and foes in Europe, or trying to figure out what constituted sensible intelligence requirements for the Pacific war. This latter task received a great deal of consideration, especially insofar as it involved a veritable discovery of the area's geography and the potential problems associated with the deployment of Japanese forces in China, Manchuria, the Soviet Far East, and Korea. These problems appeared quite formidable, and as members of the intelligence community took up the task it quickly became obvious that the intelligence which had supported MacArthur's and Nimitz's island-hopping strategy was grossly inadequate if American activity in the Pacific should extend to the Asian mainland, either separately or in conjunction with the planned invasion of the Japanese home islands.

This gap in intelligence information produced a variety of responses, but because of MacArthur's and Nimitz's control in the Pacific, little was produced in the way of valid intelligence. In one sense it was almost as if there were a new war, and the United States had to start all over again. One example of the kinds of hijinks which were contemplated, and the Alphonse-and-Gaston protocols which someone outside MacArthur's and Nimitz's commands had to employ, is found in a request from General Wedemeyer to the War Department. In his request Wedemeyer—although he had a perfect right to do so—did not go directly to the JCS for approval in order to avoid creating a situation where General Marshall would be called upon to issue an order to MacArthur or Nimitz, directing their cooperation in Wedemeyer's plan. Wedemeyer, who had served in the rarefied atmosphere of the Plans Division in the War Department and in the JCS under Marshall, was quite aware that the relationship between the JCS and MacArthur was like that between the president and the Senate, wherein the JCS might advise but MacArthur reserved his right to consent; and that throughout the war, the JCS had done little more than suggest a plan to MacArthur for his consideration.

Wedemeyer forwarded his request to the War Department on June 2, 1945:

A plan for the landing of U.S.-trained Korean intelligence teams in Korea from bases in Okinawa has been put before China theater with the request that it be sponsored and presented by the theater to the Pacific area commanders for their approval. Penetration from within China is being undertaken by this theater.

If successful subject plan will produce intelligence desired by China theater. However, since the base area, Okinawa, is outside this theater, and therefore not within the jurisdiction of the commanding general, United States Forces, China Theater, it is believed that OSS, an agency of the Joint Chiefs of Staff, should present the project to them for approval and thereafter the War and Navy Departments will present it to MacArthur and Nimitz for implementation. I concur in operations by Pacific forces to obtain intelligence from Korea with the understanding that such intelligence will be made available to me. If, upon further examination, it is found that the operation must be based in China, this theater will, after approval by the Joint Chiefs of Staff, reconsider its decision not to sponsor the project in the light of the then existing situation.

Although Wedemeyer's request was not formally approved by the JCS, Admiral Nimitz, on the basis of informal communications from Admiral King, did order special reconnaissance units into Korea as well as increased aerial reconnaissance flights over the area. After the war the results of these missions were shown to have grossly overestimated Japanese troop strength in Korea by several hundred percent, and as Admiral Layton, Pacific Fleet intelligence officer, noted, "These missions illustrated in an ominous way the lack of an effective secret intelligence organization in the Pacific theater." Various other special operations schemes were hatched, contemplated and prepared for in the summer of 1945, but nothing of any substance (aside from a few espionage/commando operations in Southeast China carried out by OSS personnel) materialized. Four years later, at an intelligence conference in Tokyo, Major General Willoughby, MacArthur's G-2, described the American intelligence posture in the summer of 1945, as preparations for the invasion of the Japanese home islands were underway: "At the time, due to our lack of reliable secret intelligence information concerning the state of the Japanese people's morale, the actual condition of their armed forces on the ground, etc., the thrust of our intelligence effort was essentially one which may be likened to that in support of an assault on a fortified position."

Meanwhile, as the intelligence community was scratching its collective head about how to proceed in the war against Japan, other events had occurred which would moot the Japanese invasion's intelligence questions, and would also have profound effects on the future of American intelligence and indeed of the entire world. Briefly, these began with the preparations for and the departure of President Truman aboard the U.S.S. *Augusta* for the Potsdam Conference on July 7, 1945. The subsequent activities and agreements made at Potsdam have been thoroughly reported by Truman and other participants, and have also been made the subject of much scholarly analysis, political polemics, and partisan accusations. For our purposes it is noteworthy to recall that on July 16, while Truman was at Potsdam, he was informed that at Alamogordo, New Mexico, the United States had carried out the first successful test of a nucelar device, thus demonstrating the feasibility of an atomic weapon. This information, relayed to Truman on July 17 by Secretary of War Stimson, suggested—although no one was completely sure—that the previous plans and estimates concerning the war against Japan might be in error.

According to Truman, "On July 24 I casually mentioned to Stalin that we had a new weapon of unusual destructive force. The Russian premier showed no special interest. All he said was that he was glad to hear of it and hoped we would make 'good use of it against the Japanese.' "*

There is no need here to detail the events after the test: the problems associated with assembling the weapons for delivery, Truman's comment to Stalin, and his decision on the same day, July 24, to use the atomic bomb against Japan. Based on what is known about the circumstances surrounding Truman's decision it is clear that it was arrived at quickly, but not necessarily without giving adequate consideration to the facts which were known at the time. With hindsight some have questioned Truman's decision; however, most of these "what if" scenarios imply a prescience and appreciation of the total impact of nuclear weapons which was beyond the ken of those directly involved. There are controversies even today concerning the cost/benefits of the atomic assault of Japan, especially over the military classification assigned to the targets. One fact is indisputable: Truman's August 6 statement, released in Washington by Secretary Stimson (in anticipation of Truman's arrival the next day), signalled the start of the atomic age in matters of warfare and intelligence: "Sixteen hours ago an American airplane dropped one bomb on Hiroshima, Japan, and destroyed its usefulness to the enemy. That bomb had more power than 20,000 tons of TNT. It had more than two thousand times the blast power of the British Grand Slam, which is the largest bomb ever used in the history of warfare."

Three days later, at 11:02 A.M., another B-29 dropped a second atomic bomb, this time on the industrial section of Nagasaki. It totally destroyed 1.5 square miles of the city, killed 39,000 persons, and injured 25,000 more. On August 10, the Japanese government requested that it be permitted to surrender under the terms of the Potsdam declaration of July 26, which it had previously ignored.

Lurking behind these events were ramifications which produced a quantum leap in America's intelligence requirements, but which were scarcely appreciated at the time by most political, military, and intelligence leaders. Much has been written about the extreme secrecy which surrounded the development of the atomic bomb. In the main these accounts are correct. Secrecy, in the sense that the Axis intelligence services never found out for sure about the extent of American progress or the basic thrust of the scientific effort, was fairly complete. Similarly, American intelligence attacks against Axis nuclear

*Truman, op. cit., p. 416. "The army plan envisaged an amphibious landing in the fall of 1945 on the island of Kyushu, the southernmost of the Japanese home islands. This would be accomplished by our Sixth Army, under the command of General Walter Krueger. The first landing would then be followed approximately four months later by a second great invasion, which would be carried out by our Eighth and Tenth Armies, followed by the First Army transferred from Europe, all of which would go ashore in the Kanto plains area near Tokyo. In all, it had been estimated that it would require until the late fall of 1946 to bring Japan to her knees."

developments—essentially carried out under the direction of the army's G-2, Major General George V. Strong, and a special section of the OSS's X-2 organization—indicated that neither Germany nor Japan was doing much to develop an atomic weapon.

Unfortunately, however, American intelligence, counterintelligence, and counterespionage activities did not go far enough. Several years later it was conclusively established that almost everything of importance which had occurred in connection with the Manhattan project during the period 1943–1947 had been passed to Gaik Ovakimian, the head of Soviet intelligence in the United States, by the British diplomat and Soviet spy, Donald MacLean.* The upshot of the MacLean penetration and other subsequent events goes well beyond the fact that they enabled the Soviets to produce an atomic bomb more quickly than if they had to rely on only their own experience; it includes the important fact that the success of the initial atomic test would not have reached Stalin, given the difficulties and length of time associated with the transmission of intelligence via the MacLean-Ovakimian–internal Soviet intelligence system, until about August 15. Thus in his "casual" remark to Stalin on July 24, Truman, like other presidents since, stumbled badly because of an intelligence gap which was only identified after it was too late.

Once the Japanese had surrendered, the American intelligence effort in the Pacific took an entirely different direction. Like the situation in Europe following V-E Day, American intelligence resources were directed to roll-up Japanese military, political, and economic records, locate war criminals, assist in surrender negotiations, interrogate Japanese authorities, investigate atrocity allegations, etc. Each of these activities was extremely time consuming, and became increasingly difficult for intelligence personnel to carry out due to the demobilization program, which by January 1946 was discharging military personnel at the rate of more than 25,000 per day. This latter fact, more than any other, prevented the wartime intelligence organizations from exploiting the intelligence bonanza achieved by the abrupt Japanese surrender, and their leaders from bringing about a centralized intelligence system, regardless of where and under whom it might be directed.

While the intelligence community was in disarray and its leaders unsure from one day to the next how many "troops" were left in their shrinking commands, Harold Smith went about the task of studying the intelligence system and laying the groundwork for restructuring it in accordance with Truman's marching order, which said "This country wanted no Gestapo under any guise or for any reason."

To these ends, on August 23, 1945, a time when most of those in the Washington intelligence community's hierarchy were still suffering from their V-J Day euphoria, Smith sent Donovan a memo requesting information about

---

*See Anthony Cave Brown and C. B. MacDonald, editors, *The Secret History of the Atomic Bomb.* New York: Dell, 1977, p. xiv.

how soon and how many OSS personnel would be separated from the organization. Implied in Smith's "the war is over" memo was that the fate of the OSS, like that of the War Manpower Commission, the Office of Civilian Defense, and other wartime agencies, was already sealed; it should be prepared to go out of business on a moment's notice.

Donovan, more in sorrow than in anger, replied to Smith on August 25:

My dear Mr. Smith:

In answer to your communication of August 23, 1945, in reference to further reduction of personnel, we are working under what is in effect a liquidation budget. Within its provisions we have taken steps to terminate many of our operational (as distinct from intelligence) activities and to reduce the remaining parts to a size consistent with present obligations in the Far East, in the occupation of Germany and Austria, and in the maintenance of missions in the Middle East and on the Asiatic and European continents.

As our liquidation proceeds it will become increasingly difficult to exercise our functions so that we have found it necessary to set up a liquidating committee with procedures and controls to provide for the gradual elimination of our services in step with the orderly reduction of personnel.

It is our estimate, however, with the strictest economy of manpower and of funds the effectiveness of OSS as a war agency will end as of January 1, or at the latest February 1, 1946, at which time liquidation should be completed. At that point I wish to return to private life. Therefore, in considering the disposition to be made of the assets created by OSS, I speak as a private citizen concerned with the future of his country.

In our government today there is no permanent agency to take over the functions which OSS will have then ceased to perform. These functions, while carried on as incident to the war, are in reality essential in the effective discharge by this nation of its responsibilities in the organization and maintenance of the peace.

Since last November, I have pointed out the immediate necessity of setting up such an agency to take over valuable assets created by OSS. Among these assets was establishment for the first time in our nation's history of a foreign secret intelligence service which reported information as seen through American eyes. As an integral and inseparable part of this service there is a group of specialists to analyze and evaluate the material for presentation to those who determine national policy.

It is not easy to set up a modern intelligence system. It is more difficult to do so in time of peace than in time of war.

It is important therefore that it be done before the War Agency has disappeared so that profit may be made of its experience and "know how" in deciding how the new agency may best be constituted.

I have already submitted a plan for the establishment of a centralized system. However, the discussion of that proposal indicated the need of an agreement upon certain fundamental principles before a detailed plan is formulated. If those concerned could agree upon the principles within which such a system should be established, acceptance of a common plan would be more easily achieved.

Accordingly, I attach a statement of principles, the soundness of which I believe has been established by study and by practical experience.

Sincerely,
William J. Donovan
Director

Enclosure:

Principles—The Soundness of Which It Is Believed Has Been Established by Our Own Experience and a First-Hand Study of the Systems of Other Nations—Which Should Govern the Establishment of a Centralized United States Foreign Intelligence System.

The formulation of national policy both in its political and military aspects is influenced and determined by knowledge (or ignorance) of the aims, capabilities, intentions, and policies of other nations.

All major powers except the United States have had for a long time past permanent worldwide intelligence services, reporting directly to the highest echelons of their governments. Prior to the present war, the United States had no foreign secret intelligence service. It never has had and does not now have a coordinated intelligence system.

The defects and dangers of this situation have been generally recognized. Adherence to the following would remedy this defect in peace as well as war so that American policy could be based upon information obtained through its own sources on foreign intentions, capabilities, and developments as seen and interpreted by Americans.

1. That each department of government should have its own intelligence bureau for the collection and processing of such informational material as it finds necessary in the actual performance of its functions and duties. Such a bureau should be under the sole control of the department head and should not be encroached upon or impaired by the functions granted any other governmental intelligence agency. Because secret intelligence covers all fields and because of possible embarrassment, no executive department should be permitted to engage in secret intelligence but in a proper case call upon the central agency for service.

2. That in addition to the intelligence unit for each department there should be established a national centralized foreign intelligence agency which should have the authority:

A. To serve all departments of the government.

B. To procure and obtain political, economic, psychological, sociological, military, and other information which may bear upon the national interest and which has been collected by the different governmental departments or agencies.

C. To collect when necessary supplemental information either at its own instance or at the request of any governmental department by open or secret means from other and various sources.

D. To integrate, analyze, process and disseminate, to authorized governmental agencies and officials, intelligence in the form of strategic interpretive studies.

3. That such an agency should be prohibited from carrying on clandestine activities within the United States and should be forbidden the exercise of any police functions either at home or abroad.

4. That since the nature of its work requires it to have status it should be independent of any department of the government (since it is obliged to serve all and must be free of the natural bias of an operating department). It should be under a director, appointed

by the president, and be administered under presidential direction, or in the event of a general manager being appointed, should be established in the executive office of the president, under his direction.

5. That subject to the approval of the president or the general manager, the policy of such a service should be determined by the director with the advice and assistance of a board on which the secretaries of state, war, navy and treasury should be represented.

6. That this agency, as the sole agency for secret intelligence, should be authorized, in the foreign field only, to carry on services such as espionage, counterespionage, and those special operations (including morale and psychological) designed to anticipate and counter any attempted penetration and subversion of our national security by enemy action.

7. That such a service should have an independent budget granted directly by the Congress.

8. That it should be authorized to have its own system of codes and should be furnished facilities by departments of government proper and necessary for the performance of its duties.

9. That such a service should include in its staff specialists (within governmental departments, civil and military, and in private life) professionally trained in analysis of information and possessing a high degree of linguistic, regional, or functional competence, to analyze, coordinate and evaluate incoming information, to make special intelligence reports, and to provide guidance for the collecting branches of the agency.

10. That in time of war or unlimited national emergency, all programs of such agency in areas of actual and projected military operations shall be coordinated with military plans, and shall be subject to the approval of the Joint Chiefs of Staff, or if there be a consolidation of the armed services, under the supreme commander. Parts of such programs which are to be executed in the theater of military operations shall be subject to control of the military commander.

There is multiple irony reflected both in the fact and content of Donovan's letter to Smith. On one hand, it accurately foreshadowed much of the shape of the intelligence system which finally emerged in the postwar period and indirectly identified the problems which continue to plague its operations in terms of the explicit powers required to make such a system work as an integrated whole, but which have never been fully conferred on the director of Central Intelligence. On another, by virtue of its being addressed to Smith, it underscored the topsy-turvy relationships which occur in the national government following an abrupt transfer of presidential power due to assassination, death, or resignation. In this case, as in the others, the "money men," by virtue of their near monopoly over the information and control of government expenditures, are able to dictate the actions of those with newly assigned operational responsibilities (that is, the members of the new president's team, or those "lame duck" holdovers from the previous administration). This latter group's actual power, although often initially reasserted by a president who abruptly accedes to the office, is quite fleeting; while these persons may be from the same political party or hold the same political persuasion, more often than not they lack the personal relationship with the new president on which the successful exercise of operational authority in behalf of the president is based.

Apropos of these painful political facts of life, from the time Truman came to power on April 12, 1945, and the demise of the OSS on October 1 of that year, Donovan never saw Truman alone, nor was he able to speak with him about the postwar intelligence situation. Donovan attempted to see Truman, but was rebuffed by both the military leaders and the members of Truman's Missouri palace guard. Such a situation is not uncommon at a time of abrupt presidential change; nevertheless, in Donovan's case Truman's behavior reflects badly on those who give lip service to the apolitical nature of intelligence and then act to cut themselves off from information and advice which might challenge their own partisan, narrow-minded views, or come into conflict with the views of those who fear intelligence practitioners like Donovan because of their own personal inadequacies and temerity. According to one of his closest associates, James Murphy, Donovan didn't expect to become a member of Truman's inner circle, but he greatly regretted the fact that his and the entire OSS experience was dismissed out of hand by Truman without any opportunity for a fair hearing in the discussions of America's postwar intelligence needs. Finally, the Donovan letter—in spite of its obvious implications to all the other members of the intelligence community—was not circulated outside of Harold Smith's small circle of assistants for comment, recommendations, analysis, rebuttal, etc. This is not say that Smith and/or his latter-day successors do not have a role to play in the policy, organization, and decision-making process in the executive branch, but rather that at this critical juncture in history the fate of American intelligence was decided on too narrow a basis of wisdom, experience or understanding about the United States' total intelligence needs. And even more importantly, this flawed decision produced a gap in the intelligence information available to national leaders in the postwar period which in turn led to irrational responses in dealing with international problems and crises. That is, the lack of valid intelligence in hand during that period effectively prevented American leaders from making logically based discriminations among problems and resulted in a loss of necessary perspective in crisis situations.

At the time Donovan sent his reply to Smith he recognized it to be an improperly directed mea culpa. Donovan, who had labored so long and hard in the cause of creating an effective intelligence system for the United States, was angry. Angry that the progress made since 1940 was going to be lost by default. Angry that Truman had turned his back on the intelligence leaders and instead had allowed Smith to short-circuit the decision process by giving him the sole authority and power to define the policy options.

Backtracking a bit, there is another brief sequence of events which is important in our consideration of the Donovan-Smith letter. As mentioned, Donovan and the other intelligence leaders were aware of Truman's charge to Smith to study the intelligence system and, due to their prior experience with Smith and his principal assistants, were aware of the latters' predilection for coordination over effective control. However, none of the intelligence leaders, except perhaps J. Edgar Hoover, was prepared for the disarray which V-J Day produced in the government's decision-making process. Prior to August 10, they believed that they would have a chance to rebut or otherwise modify Smith's expected views on intelligence insofar as these related to organization, roles, missions, and control over the community. But V-J Day knocked their assumptions into a cocked hat and produced a vacuum in the decision-making process into which Smith flowed.

Donovan was alert and sensitive to these implications and because, through his own sources, he had prior knowledge that the Smith letter was coming he acted to preempt Smith's ploy by publicizing OSS's hitherto unheralded contribution to the war effort. To this end, Donovan ordered John Shaheen, then a navy commander on duty with OSS, to mount a preemptive counterattack against the expected attempt of Smith to dismantle and abolish the OSS. In response, Shaheen asked Donovan, "Could your secretary get me a list of writers in OSS who happen to be in Washington?" Almost immediately thereafter, the publicity blitz moved into high gear. Quoting Tom Braden,

For weeks, a series of sensational stories dominated the newspapers and magazines hailing the exploits of OSS's secret war. As Shaheen and his assistants scoured the files, had the facts declassified, fed them to "writers in OSS who happened to be in Washington," and as they fed them in turn to eager journalists, OSS parachutists returning from their hitherto secret war and expecting to hear the usual jibes about "Oh So Social" suddenly found themselves figures of glamor.*

Journalists like Joseph Loftus, Bess Furman, Tillman Durdin, and Arthur Krock spread the word about OSS, neatly making the point that under Donovan it had blended the talents of persons from all walks of life in such a way that the resulting organization had been able to carry out all the tasks in the intelligence spectrum, from analysis to sabotage, in an outstanding fashion. The entire publicity campaign constituted a good try; but given the public's attention span and the general lack of prior understanding about the intelligence organization problem there wasn't enough time to create the kind of public opinion necessary to prevent precipitate action by a president on a matter essentially under his purview.

One result of the OSS publicity campaign was that Harold Smith's attitude against Donovan hardened even more than previously, and he urged Truman to abolish OSS promptly. Smith was aware that public clamor in favor of keeping OSS could cause a congressional or public examination of the ques-

---

*Tom Braden, "The Birth of the CIA." *American Heritage,* February 1977, vol. 28, #2, p. 7.

tions set forth in Donovan's earlier memorandum to Roosevelt; this might serve to foreclose Truman's options to deal with the OSS and the intelligence community on his own (or on Smith's) terms. Not unreluctantly, on or about September 13, Truman gave Smith the green light to abolish OSS.

The task was accomplished with the kind of secrecy and dispatch those in bureaucracy aspire to but rarely achieve. Drafting the presidential executive order which administered the coup de grace to the OSS fell initially to Smith's assistant, Donald Stone, who after several iterations with Smith and his deputy, Wayne Coy, produced the final version of Presidential Executive Order 9621, "Termination of the Office of Strategic Services and Disposition of Its Functions." It read as follows:

By virtue of the authority vested in me by the Constitution and Statutes, including Title I of the First War Powers Act of 1941, and as President of the United States and Commander in Chief of the Army and the Navy, it is hereby ordered as follows:

1. There are transferred to and consolidated in an Interim Research and Intelligence Service, which is hereby established in the Department of State, (a) the functions of the Research and Analysis Branch and of the Presentation Branch of the Office of Strategic Services (provided for by the Military Order of June 13, 1942), excluding such functions performed within the countries of Germany and Austria, and (b) those other functions of the Office of Strategic Services (hereinafter referred to as the Office) which related to the functions of the said Branches transferred by this paragraph. The functions of the Director of Strategic Services and of the United States Joint Chiefs of Staff relating to the functions transferred to the Service by this paragraph are transferred to the Secretary of State. The personnel, property, and records of the said Branches, except such thereof as is located in Germany and Austria, and so much of the other personnel, property, and records of the Office and of the funds of the Office as the Director of the Bureau of the Budget shall determine to relate primarily to the functions transferred by this paragraph are transferred to the said Service. Military personnel now on duty in connection with the activities transferred by this paragraph may, subject to applicable law and to the extent mutually agreeable to the Secretary of State and to the Secretary of War or the Secretary of the Navy, as the case may be, continue on such duty in the Department of State.

2. The Interim Research and Intelligence Service shall be abolished as of the close of business December 31, 1945, and the Secretary of State shall provide for winding up its affairs. Pending such abolition, (a) the Secretary of State may transfer from the said Service to such agencies of the Department of State as he shall designate any function of the Service, (b) the Secretary may curtail the activities carried on by the Service, (c) the head of the Service, who shall be designated by the Secretary, shall be responsible to the Secretary or to such other officer of the Department of State as the Secretary shall direct, and (d) the Service shall, except as otherwise provided in this order, be administered as an organizational entity in the Department of State.

3. All functions of the Office not transferred by paragraph 1 of this order, together with all personnel, records, property, and funds of the Office not so transferred, are transferred to the Department of War; and the Office, including the office of the Director of Strategic Services, is terminated. The functions of the Director of Strategic

Services and of the United States Joint Chiefs of Staff, relating to the functions transferred by this paragraph, are transferred to the Secretary of War. Naval personnel on duty with the Office in connection with the activities transferred by this paragraph may, subject to applicable law and to the extent mutually agreeable to the Secretary of War and the Secretary of the Navy, continue on such duty in the Department of War. The Secretary of War shall, whenever he deems it compatible with the national interest, discontinue any activity transferred by this paragraph and wind up all affairs relating thereto.

4. Such further measures and dispositions as may be determined by the Director of the Bureau of the Budget to be necessary to effectuate the transfer or redistribution of functions provided for in this order shall be carried out in such manner as the Director may direct and by such agencies as he may designate.

5. All provisions of prior orders of the President which are in conflict with this order are amended accordingly.

6. This order shall, except as otherwise specifically provided, be effective as of the opening of business October 1, 1945.

Harry S Truman
September 20, 1945

In conjunction with the executive order, Donald Stone also produced President Truman's "thank you, don't call us we'll call you" farewell letter to Donovan for his service as director of the OSS. It should be noted that Stone, who had a high personal regard for Donovan's ability, did not share the coolness he was ordered to convey; however, because "orders are orders," he wrote what Truman said to say. In White House staff parlance, these "donkey letters" are oftentimes too effusive and fulsome in their praise of an appointed official's performance, or lack thereof; this letter is unique in the annals of such presidential correspondence, especially in its tone and in its almost begrudging acknowledgement of Donovan's distinguished and lengthy contribution to the development of America's intelligence effort.

The White House
Washington
September 20, 1945

My dear General Donovan:

I appreciate very much the work which you and your staff undertook beginning prior to the Japanese surrender, to liquidate those wartime activities of the Office of Strategic Services which will not be needed in time of peace.

Timely steps should also be taken to conserve those resources and skills developed within your organization which are vital to our peacetime purposes.

Accordingly, I have today directed, by Executive Order, that the activities of the Research and Analysis Branch and the Presentation Branch of the Office of Strategic Services be transferred to the State Department. This transfer, which is effective as of October 1, 1945, represents the beginning of the development of a coordinated system of foreign intelligence within the permanent framework of the Government.

Consistent with the foregoing, the Executive Order provides for the transfer of the remaining activities of the Office of Strategic Services to the War Department; for the abolition of of the Office of Strategic Services; and for the continued orderly liquidation of some of the activities of the Office without interrupting other services of a military nature the need for which will continue for some time.

I want to take this occasion to thank you for the capable leadership you have brought to a vital wartime activity in your capacity as Director of Strategic Services. You may well find satisfaction in the achievements of the Office and take pride in your own contribution to them. These are in themselves large rewards. Great additional reward for your efforts should lie in the knowledge that the peacetime intelligence services of the Government are being erected on the foundation of the facilities and resources mobilized through the Office of Strategic Services during the war.

Sincerely yours,
Harry Truman

The final footnote to this sorry display of presidential bad manners and short-sightedness in ignoring, for all practical purposes, the OSS's potential contribution to America's future intelligence needs is seen in how the entire situation was handled. Executive Order 9621 was not made available for comment to the Joint Chiefs of Staff, the leaders of the intelligence services, or Donovan prior to Truman's signing it on September 20. At the least, the time schedule should have been considered by those most intimately involved in the intelligence process and by the recipients of the OSS's subordinate elements; the secretary of state and war should have been compelled to come up with a plan concerning their utilization within those departments.* Additionally, after Truman signed both the executive order and the letter, he instructed Director Smith to deliver them to Donovan. Smith remonstrated, saying that he felt Truman ought to invite Donovan to the White House and tell him about the decision personally, but to no avail. In turn, Smith, who didn't want to personally bear the order and letter to Donovan, passed the buck to Donald Stone. Stone, who felt much the same way about Truman's evasion, recalls Smith's saying, "the president doesn't want to do it and I don't want't to do it, but because I can, I'm ordering you to do it," or words to that effect. Stone added, "When I delivered the documents, Donovan took it with

* Although Truman's behavior toward Donovan upon becoming president is probably best explained by the attitudes of the military advisers he inherited and who reasoned that Donovan might be an unsettling factor as they "broke in" a new president, his actions at the time OSS was abolished are less clearly based. Truman could become quite angry, especially when he felt that someone was treating the presidency lightly, but he was rarely petty. This is not to say that there wasn't someone else—other than the military leaders who had no foreknowledge about the OSS abolishment decision—in the White House who bore a personal grudge against Donovan and poisoned Truman toward him. The happy conclusion to the Truman "thank you" letter episode is found in the fact that once Truman realized the import of the unique contribution Donovan had made to the American intelligence effort, he made amends; on July 11, 1946, in a White House ceremony, he bestowed the Distinguished Service Medal on Donovan for that contribution.

a kind of stoic grace. He knew it was coming, but he gave no outward indication of the personal hurt he felt by the manner in which he was informed."

With Donovan out of the way and the leaders of the Washington intelligence community's hierarchy overwhelmed by the problem of redistributing their diminishing intelligence assets in a marginally effective attempt to meet the burgeoning intelligence requirements arising out of the military occupations in Europe and Asia, Smith pressed on with his intelligence reorganization plans. Regardless of one's opinions concerning the wisdom of Smith's plans for postwar intelligence, he did possess a remarkable sense of timing in proposing his "better idea." On September 20, coincident with placing the executive order and letter to Donovan in front of Truman for his signature, Smith also delivered his study of intelligence dated the same day. It made a neat package, which also included a letter to Secretary of State James Byrnes directing him to assume the leadership in developing an integrated governmentwide intelligence program through the creation of interdepartmental committees to coordinate the intelligence operations within the departments.* As Donald Stone recalled, "We definitely had President Truman's attention, and presentation of the study in connection with the distasteful business of abolishing OSS amounted to striking while the iron was hot." Psychologically the Smith package also provided Truman with a convenient rationalization which enabled him to lift the intelligence problem off his desk and pass it to someone else; in this case Brynes. Truman, in spite of public protes-

---

* Letter to Secretary Byrnes concerning the development of a foreign intelligence program, September 20, 1945. Public Papers of the President of the United States, Harry S Truman, April 12 to December 31, 1945. Washington: U. S. Government Printing Office, 1961, p. 331.

My dear Mr. Secretary:

I have today signed an Executive Order which provides for the transfer to the State Department of the functions, personnel, and other resources of the Research and Analysis Branch and the Presentation Branch of the Office of Strategic Services. The order also transfers the remaining activities of the Office of Strategic Services to the War Department and abolishes that Office. These changes become effective October 1, 1945.

The above transfer to the State Department will provide you with resources which we have agreed you will need in the development of our foreign policy, and will assure that pertinent experience accumulated during the war will be preserved and used in meeting the problems of the peace. Those readjustments and reductions which are required in order to gear the transferred activities and resources into State Department operations should be made as soon as practicable.

I particularly desire that you take the lead in developing a comprehensive and coordinated foreign intelligence program for all Federal agencies concerned with that type of activity. This should be done through the creation of an interdepartmental group, heading up under the State Department, which would formulate plans for my approval. This procedure will permit the planning of complete coverage of the foreign intelligence field and assigning and controlling of operations in such manner that the needs of both the individual agencies and the Government as a whole will be met with maximum effectiveness.

Sincerely yours,
Harry S Truman

tations of confidence, was not above "sticking it" to Jimmy as a means of keeping him in line and making the point that he, Truman, was president and not Byrnes, who still hadn't figured out how he lost the vice-presidential lottery run by Franklin Roosevelt and Jim Farley in 1944.

The Smith plan, like others previously detailed, is important not only in terms of what eventually resulted, but also in terms of setting forth quite eloquently the discredited doctrine of separation of intelligence functions from their operational necessities; therefore its contents are set forth fully below. Also, the reader who might be inclined to skip over the Smith plan is reminded that Truman carefully read it in its entirety, as well as annotating it. Because Truman came to the intelligence problem almost as a functional illiterate, the Smith plan became the benchmark of his understanding of the intelligence organization control problem; and, more importantly, he adopted its basic conclusions without further question, and transmitted them to those dealing with the problem as the president's "desires" as to how these matters were to be resolved. Much of what Smith wrote was begged, borrowed, or lifted from the studies previously mentioned, although its basic conclusions reflected Smith's own views. Smith pulled back from laying blame for the prewar and wartime inadequacies of national intelligence organizations and their operations at the door of the White House or with the president himself. Thus, by indirection, he gives credence to the view about the semiautonomous state of the intelligence community in the body politic without ever really explaining how this situation came to pass and who allowed it to continue.

Parts of the Smith plan are footnoted because these underscore some essential truths as well as some present-day misconceptions concerning the efficacy of coordination as a substitute for effective line control and direction of intelligence operations. One further element subsumed in the Smith plan deserves prior mention; the policy implications of decisions and actions taken at a level below the White House. There is no criticism implied here because, at the time Smith wrote his plan for intelligence, no one at his level in government fully understood the implications to policy caused by the presence of thousands of Americans in the occupied countries, any more than our leaders understood the implications of total war before Pearl Harbor. It was only later that Truman and his successors came to understand that while they might propose policy in the White House, the thousands of military and civilian personnel ostensibly under their command in more than a hundred foreign countries could and did effectively dispose of those policy decisions in accordance with their own perceptions of America's national interest and their own views about national security. Like Robert E. Lee, Truman and those who have followed him can only issue orders and hope. The Smith plan, which embodied a part of that hope, read as follows:

Report on the Intelligence and Security
Activities of the Government

Bureau of the Budget
September 20, 1945

The purpose of this report is to discuss and propose a plan for the organization of our foreign intelligence and security intelligence activities in the postwar period. It results from studies by the staff of the Bureau of the Budget conducted throughout the war.

The war has occasioned a hasty and unplanned development and expansion to tremendous proportions of the foreign intelligence activities of the government. No one believes they can continue on the same scale in the postwar period. On the other hand, no one believes that we can safely permit our foreign intelligence activities to revert to the equally unplanned basis that existed in the prewar period.

At the outset, it is necessary to be clear about the meanings of "intelligence" and "security intelligence" as used in this report. Foreign intelligence has to do with our knowledge about foreign peoples—their resources, capabilities and intentions. It includes all that is significant about particular countries or areas, which may have a bearing on our relations with and policies toward them and on their relations with and policies toward the United States. In point of time it encompasses the future, insofar as that is possible, as well as the present and the past. It embraces what we need to know about foreign peoples, countries, and conditions in order that our relations with them may be conducted in such a manner as to give the maximum protection to and furtherance of our national interests.

Security intelligence (or counterintelligence) includes our knowledge about activities directed from within or without the United States which are inimical to our internal security. The purpose of security intelligence is to be aware of all unfriendly or hostile persons, movements, and ideologies which constitute a threat or a potential threat in order that steps may be taken to safeguard against them when they become threatening. Security intelligence is thus simply a special kind of total intelligence.

The reasons for treating security intelligence as a separate but special category of intelligence are brought out further later in the report.

Situation Prior to Pearl Harbor

In 1939 the principal source of information about foreign peoples, places or affairs was the State Department missions abroad. Through Reorganization Plan No. II, the information-gathering activities of the Commerce and Agriculture Departments had been coordinated by the State Department. Some personnel from other agencies were assigned to the Foreign Service as attachés, and matters of reporting were coordinated between the State Department and the department involved, as for example, Commerce (Bureau of Foreign and Domestic Commerce), Interior (Bureau of Mines), Agriculture (Bureau of Foreign Agricultural Relations) and others. Communication was through State Department facilities. The military and naval attachés, of which there were then less than a score, enjoyed slightly greater freedom of direct reporting to their agencies.

Compared to current information-gathering activities abroad, our activities in 1939 were indeed modest. They did, however, produce a volume of reports containing a wealth of useful and reliable information. But the conversion of this information into intelligence was hampered by a number of causes, including some basic weaknesses in our structure in Washington. The most significant of these weaknesses from the standpoint of future planning are discussed in the following order:

1. The inadequacy of the intelligence facilities in the departments.
2. The lack of coordination of intelligence among departments.
3. The overemphasis on security intelligence at the expense of more basic intelligence.
4. The lack of central facilities to serve the president or top-level groups.

Inadequacy of Intelligence Facilities in the Departments

The principal weakness of our prewar situation lay in the lack of adequate central facilities in the various departments in Washington to direct the selectivity of reporting, to gear the reporting to actual operational needs, or, equally as important, to evaluate the incoming material and distill out the significant trends. This had several effects which should be noted in planning for the future organization of our intelligence activities.

Failure to determine needs. One of the principal results of the inadequate or totally lacking intelligence facilities in the departments was the failure to determine what the requirements for intelligence were. As a result the facilities that were available for reporting information were not well utilized.

In the War and Navy Departments, standing instructions for reporting were in the form of index guides merely cataloging and assigning file numbers to all conceivable subjects without any selectivity.

In the State Department directives on which the missions based their reporting were prepared in any office of the department as current problems arose and in some agencies outside the department.

Difficulty in recognizing trends. Another of the results of inadequate central facilities in the departments was the difficulty in recognizing trends. In the State Department, for example, reports flowed directly to groups already burdened with the heavy responsibilities of forming policy and initiating action, where, after being read, they were filed in a central file along with the administrative papers of the department. Some of these groups built up staffs of analysts to extract the incoming information. In general, however, the result of this method of handling the flow of foreign information was that the department in Washington dealt almost solely with current news. The cumulative effect of these bits of current news was apparent only insofar as the report itself pointed out the trend, or as the action or policy-making officers followed the trends personally.

Departments such as Commerce and Agriculture did have staffs to analyze or accumulate incoming information. With these resources they produced foreign intelligence which was principally of use to those bodies of the public which they served. Comparatively little attention was given, however, to the necessity of being able to recast their data on short notice for use by other governmental agencies, especially in time of emergency.

In the War and Navy Departments some small central facilities existed, but their inability to recognize significant trends was hampered by a number of reasons, of which their hyperconcern with defensive or security intelligence will be discussed later.

Lack of overall perspective. Another result of the lack of adequate central facilities was that no group was organized to analyze reports from the point of view of a department as a whole. In the State Department, for example, where no central facilities existed, the action-taking or policy-forming officers tended to concern themselves primarily with information pertinent to the geographic area or, in a few cases, subject field (as commercial treaties, communications, etc.) for which they were responsible as operating officials. In addition much of the reporting concerned current events and developments. In the War and Navy Departments, research techniques were not utilized to analyze information and the central staffs were reduced to such a level as to make impossible the handling of any volume of significant material except to distribute it in the form in which it came in.

Lack of Coordination of Intelligence

The lack of any central intelligence activity in the State Department and the provision of only small staffs in the armed services limited coordination of intelligence among these departments practically to the single feature of mutual exchange of individual reports. As late as 1942 some of this exchange was still being handled through formal letters in which the secretary of state "had the honor of transmitting" to the secretary of war the attached report. The result was that on matters involving more than one of the departments, no means existed to provide for a pooling of all available intelligence. Pearl Harbor, simply as one example, is less a failure of any one department than of the inadequacy of our total intelligence operation. The recent publication of white papers, showing that all the information necessary to evaluate the situation was in our files, only confirms the fact that we did not have sufficient facilities to convert that information into intelligence, nor sufficient means for bringing it into play in all the places where it could have been used.

Predilection for Security Intelligence

In addition to being inadequate and poorly organized, the facilities existing in the War and Navy Departments, and to some extent in the State Department, were principally engrossed with intelligence of a defensive or security nature concerning dangerous or hostile individuals who, actually or potentially, might be engaged in espionage, sabotage, or subversion. Had this been recognized, and had plans been made to build a governmentwide program for security purposes around other resources already existing, and separated (except at the very top level) from the operations designed to produce more basic intelligence, one of the weaknesses of our subsequent and present basic intelligence program might have been avoided.

The predilection in an agency for securing intelligence concerning "undesirable" individuals weakens the securing of more fundamental intelligence by that agency. At a time when the armed services might have been accumulating (through the organized reserve and other available sources) the mass of information soon to be needed to fight a global war, they were using most of the limited personnel available in creating and maintaining a large file of undesirable individuals. Similarly, in the development of the reserves, the tendency was to secure officers whose interests or skills were those needed to support a program of this sort of intelligence. The importance of this kind of intelligence loomed so large (at the expense of real military intelligence) that the service intelligence agencies resisted successfully all attempts of forward-looking officers to transfer negative or defensive intelligence operations to such offices as that of the provost marshal general. Further, in July 1939, when it was clear that war in Europe was inevitable, the armed forces plan for intelligence was to obtain, through a presidential letter, the creation of an interdepartmental committee, including the FBI. The purpose of this committee was to intensify investigations of individuals potentially or actually engaged in espionage, sabotage, or subversion. The committee was, until the creation of the Coordinator of Information in July 1941, the only interdepartmental mechanism for mobilizing our intelligence services to meet the responsibilities which in a few short years were to be thrust upon us. As a further reflection of the extent to which the emphasis on security intelligence had inhibited even an awareness of our lack of real positive intelligence, the armed forces viewed this committee as being all that was necessary, and aided by the State Department fought the idea of a Coordinator of Information from the moment the plan was discussed.*

Lack of Central Facilities to Serve the President

Even if the departments had organized the strongest facilities possible for their own purposes, the resultant total operation could still have been deficient with respect to intelligence needed at the very top of the government. On matters involving the bringing together of information in all departments to throw light on determinations affecting our total national policy, our intelligence results were not adequate.

It is significant that when the president's needs for objective and penetrating analysis of the then threatening foreign scene became acute, he was forced to rely on individuals acting as special observers and reporting directly to him. This is not to imply that many of the operating officials in the government were not aware of what was happening or of its significance to us, nor that the State Department and armed services did not have informed opinions from which to advise the president. The point is that the president should not have been forced to rely solely on such opinions, no matter how informed they might be. Rather he should have been able, in addition, to have access to the facts, carefully analyzed and so presented that his own conclusions could be drawn. Some means for coordinating intelligence itself, as well as the judgments of the responsible advisers, is necessary. With such coordination decisions on matters of high national policy can be made not alone on the basis of the opinions of the operating officials, no

---

*Smith's observations concerning the United States' prewar intelligence weaknesses, although generally correct, beg the real issue: namely, that United States intelligence personnel, like any government officials, are bound by the law to take and implement national policy as it is given to them by the president and/or Congress and the Neutrality Act made doing what the situation fully called for extremely difficult, if not outright illegal. As Smith notes, the information available to national leaders was not wholly inadequate; however, he fails to mention that the inadequacy of the evaluation process was due as much to the reluctance of those in Washington outside the intelligence community to order the gathering of follow-up information (which could only be acquired by illegal means) as it was to the lack of facilities to evaluate, synthesize, and transmit that information for use by the president and his advisers. Also, throughout the immediate prewar period those in the American intelligence community who were involved in clandestine surveillance—tapping telephones, interecepting cables and mail, carrying out black-bag jobs, kidnapping those who were "Nazi symps," etc.—lived in constant fear that someone in the media or Congress might acquire their carefully "sanitized" reports about the results and information derived from those illegal activities. It was an Orwellian time, for many in the intelligence services acted—largely on the bases of their own personal convictions about the evils of totalitarianism—on the dictum expressed by Charles Dickens in *Pickwick Papers:* "If that's the law then the law is mad."

matter how well informed, nor on information alone, no matter how reliable, but on all available intelligence fully evaluated and properly presented.

Wartime Expansion and Present Status

In the latter stages of our preparation for national defense and the early stages of the war, a vast expansion of the functions of government in international matters was undertaken. Lend-lease, expanded activities in South America, export control and later economic warfare, alien property control, freezing and foreign funds control, psychological warfare, all signalized the development of facilities to produce quickly the kind of intelligence necessary to conduct the operation concerned.

Officials in the State Department, acting largely on their own initiative because of the department's lack of central facilities, stimulated the creation of operations in such agencies as FCC.

The air force, lacking facilities of its own, finding the MIS deficient, and having no central source to which to refer, was forced to canvass the government in search of information to assist in the selection of bombing targets.

Other large projects to obtain information on weather, terrain, medical and sanitary conditions, food and crops, habits, etc., were initiated. CAA, Public Health, Coast and Geodetic Survey, the Antitrust Division of Justice, PAW, the Weather Bureau and many others all contributed their share as sources of information.

Travellers, officials of companies with foreign plants or business, scientists, refugees, university staffs, libraries, the vast body of the public with information useful to our growing needs was tapped.

Our wartime development was thus characterized by tremendous expansion of informational and intelligence activities in many of the normal agencies of government, as well as by creation of large operations in the new war agencies themselves.

This expansion, however, took place primarily in the collection of information. The many new sources mentioned above were tapped by many different agencies. A mass of raw information flooded in and, through liaison arrangements, fanned out in multiple copies to the many agencies. The expansion that took place was not in accordance with any governmentwide plan. The weaknesses of our prewar pattern were therefore carried into our wartime organization. In addition, the lack of a total plan and of any authoritative mechanism for coordinating the operations of the many agencies involved, has become a problem of such magnitude that it has become of equal priority as the other weaknesses in demanding a solution.

Successful postwar intelligence will not be achieved without first considering the needs of the many departments concerned, nor without finding ways to coordinate their activities to the end that maximum result is achieved with the minimum of expense and effort. This need to achieve a well-integrated governmentwide intelligence program is urgent and goes beyond the problem of merely disposing of duplication. Almost four years of war have revealed the tremendous resources of information that exist in the government and among our nationals. Only by the fullest utilization of our entire resources, not only for the collection of information but for its analysis, tabulation, assembly into useful forms, can our intelligence achieve the quality of performance which will be vital to our future security and position in international affairs.

Conclusions

We must provide for a more adequate intelligence operation than we have ever had before. The very brief analysis given above points to the lessons which must be taken into account in planning for the future organization of the government's intelligence activities.

There are four major conclusions pointing to the need for early action and two of secondary or longer-range import. Each conclusion is discussed below.

More Widespread Understanding of Intelligence

Some of the difficulty of achieving needed improvement in our intelligence operations in the past has been the relative newness of intelligence as a function of government and the absence of a common understanding even of what intelligence is. To some, "intelligence" is a tainted word identified solely with espionage and intrigue. To others it is identified as a kind of information of military or wartime use solely. Still others think of it as applicable only to high strategic or national security questions. Such misunderstanding has caused many of those whose active participation is vital to the development of more adequate intelligence operations in the future to feel that it is a subject of no concern to them and to view with trepidation proposals looking toward a strong postwar program.

Our needs for foreign intelligence have broadened beyond the point where they can be met by the activities of a single intelligence agency. Nor do they fall into simple, mutually exclusive subject categories such as "military," "naval," "economic," and "political" which permit easy assignment of responsibilities among a few intelligence agencies. Nor are they limited to special or "secret" kinds of foreign information.

Rather, they rest on the necessity for understanding fully foreign events, to know all the facts which motivate foreign nations and peoples, and to have readily accessible in usable form a mass of factual information to assist in the shaping of intelligent policy and action at all levels where decision is made or influenced, or where action is taken. They will be met, therefore, only by concerted and widespread activities which utilize to the fullest the tremendous resources existing within the government and among our nationals.

It may well be that the spread of common understanding as to what intelligence is, what purpose it can serve, and how the intelligence operation relates to the action-taking or policy-forming operations, will contribute as much to the accomplishment of a more effective total intelligence program for the government as the prescribing of specific organizational panaceas.

Intelligence Facilities at the Departmental Level

It is commonly accepted that our intelligence operations have not been on a par with those of other nations. This has given rise to a considerable number of proposals for the creation of a single super-intelligence organization not connected with any of the departments. The difficulty with such proposals is that they are based on a limited view of what intelligence is and on a misunderstanding as to the role an intelligence operation must play.

There might be some justification for such extreme centralization if all policy and action affecting our foreign relations and our national defense or national interests were centered at the top of the government and if intelligence were merely the tapping of special sources to report and interpret current developments.

These matters are not so centralized. Our foreign policy, for example, is not made up alone of considered announcements dealing with high-level matters. It is made every day in the thousand and one actions and decisions that are taken at all levels. The intelligence needed to assist wise decisions and support informed action must produce a knowledge and understanding of all the factors involved. Further, it must be at hand. Extreme centralization of the intelligence operation is no more workable than would be centralizing in one agency of the job of producing all statistics for the government. The intelligence operation is handmaiden to the action-taking and policy-determining groups. It must be sensitive to their needs. It must have handy the mass of original documents and material on which its studies are based. While it may secure much assistance from others outside it must be responsible to the place of decision. A department which will be held responsible for its decisions and actions must in turn be able to hold accountable to it the operation which produces intelligence on which those decisions and action will, in part, be based.

The principal foreign intelligence operations of the government therefore should be viewed as being organized at all places where decisions are made and action taken, namely at the departmental, or lower level.

Separation of Security Intelligence Activities

The emphasis in the prewar period on intelligence related to the activities of hostile or undesirable individuals has already been commented upon. It is a conclusion of our studies that the organization of our future intelligence programs should provide for the separation of security intelligence operations from those engaged in producing the more basic categories of intelligence.

The collection and evaluation of security intelligence (sometimes referred to less descriptively as "counterintelligence") requires the use of skills and a point of view not desirable in the production of other forms of intelligence. If we are to make proper judgments as to where our interests lie and what we can do to further them in the postwar period, we will need to have intelligence which gets at fundamentals and is not colored by a point of view that attempts to segregate peoples simply into friendly or hostile categories. It has been said that before the war Germany had more "friends" in this country than did England. Certainly German intelligence, following the speeches and actions of many of our "prominent persons," could easily so conclude. And yet we went to war. In our evaluation of foreign affairs we should take every precaution against being similarly misled. Our relations with Russia, Argentina, Spain, and China need to be viewed in terms of the points at which our interests coincide or clash as nations and peoples, and not solely in terms of whether the "leaders" in these countries are "friendly" or "hostile."

This does not imply that we will not need to organize facilities to follow the activities of unfriendly individuals, at home as well as abroad, nor to conduct programs to counter their activities. Nor is it intended to imply that some significant intelligence will not be developed as a result of those programs.

It does imply, however, that within the departments having responsibilities for producing both security intelligence and basic foreign intelligence, the two operations should be separated. When both are large, for example, they should not be under the same head. Further, a framework for the development and coordination of such security intelligence activities with the internal security programs which they serve should be provided apart from that whose purpose it will be to develop the basic intelligence essential to our future foreign programs and international responsibilities.

Coordination of Intelligence and Security Operations

To the weaknesses of our prewar activities, the expansion of these activities due to the war has added the weakness of lack of coordination of intelligence operations. The same lack of an overall plan that characterized the expansion of our general intelligence activities is responsible also in the security intelligence field for a failure to build around existing programs and resources, for a piecemeal legislative program and for overlapping responsibilities and duplication in operations.

The most obvious result of this lack of coordination is the tremendous wastage of money and effort. Possibly of even greater importance, however, is the fact that the uncoordinated competitive programs of the various agencies dilute the few available skilled personnel and result at times in no one of the agencies having on hand the full background of information of value to the subject under analysis. Another effect of great significance is the false sense of authenticity frequently created by repetitive reporting of the same information. This arises from the fact that in the absence of a governmentwide operational plan, each agency engages to receive all available raw material directly. This has been responsible for interviewing of the same private individuals by as many as twelve different departments or units of departments. It is also responsible for the "liaison officer" and the "round table" at which each agency, by reading all the incoming material, can secure copies for itself and issue reports paralleling those of other agencies.

This overlap cannot be corrected by assigning responsibilities by kinds of intelligence, as "economic," "military," "naval," "political," etc. It can only be solved by assigning operating responsibilities. In each case the agency of greatest competence, ease of accomplishment, or primary interest should be designated as the agency to be responsible for a specific operation, but with the proviso that the operation be conducted so as to safeguard the interests of any or all agencies. Thus, while it might be the most feasible arrangement to have the FCC monitor certain radio messages of interest to other agencies, it is inappropriate for that agency to attempt, as it did at one time, to create an extensive intelligence organization to analyze such material.

The principal agencies presently engaging in intelligence activities have made efforts to improve coordination. In the absence of any authoritative machinery to accomplish the development of operating plans by which all the agencies would be bound, such attempts have resulted only in "ad hoc" arrangements.

The Joint Intelligence Committee, composed of representatives from State, FEA, OSS, MIS (War Department), ONI (Navy Department), and A-2 (Army Air Forces) represents the most important of such arrangements. A quotation from a paper prepared by the Joint Intelligence Committee paints the best picture of its inability to coordinate operations.

> The Joint Intelligence Committee's mission, however, is confined to the Joint Chiefs of Staff organization, is not binding even on those departments represented by the Joint Chiefs of Staff, and lacks clear administrative authority to coordinate the intelligence activities of its member agencies. During the war a series of expedients such as the Joint Intelligence Publishing Board, the Joint Topographical Committee, the Joint Intelligence Collection Agencies and others have, with

more or less success, relieved various situations where lack of coordination was most conspicuous. However, there does not exist any agency which can state authoritatively which intelligence subjects are, at any given time, of most importance to the interest of the United States; or is responsible for seeing that important gaps in intelligence are filled.

Study of our experience during the war has shown that without an authoritative coordinating mechanism acting in the interest of the government as a whole, the responsibility of a department for the conduct of an intelligence operation to serve the needs of other departments cannot be established. Unless such mechanism is provided, therefore, our future governmentwide intelligence activities will be characterized by the same compartmentation, competition, and expensive operation as present.

The various ad hoc type of interdepartmental committees used during the war have served to promote cooperation but have been unable to effect real coordination. Further, the committees so created have been more concerned with exchanging intelligence and information than in coordinating operations. It is perhaps unreasonable to expect that they should, in view of the newness of intelligence on the scale necessary in wartime and in view of the absence of any pressure or necessity to achieve results economically.

Similarly, experience with an independent agency such as the Coordinator of Information at the level of the executive office of the president indicates a corresponding inability of such mechanisms to achieve coordination of operations.

High-Level National Policy Intelligence

The conclusions discussed above relate principally to the strengthening or organizing of intelligence operations within the departments and to means of coordinating them on a governmentwide basis. The need to provide some centralized professional intelligence operation at all levels where decisions are made or action is taken has been pointed out.

Not all the decisions or actions of the government fall into categories that permit their handling by the departments alone. The president, too, should have facilities for securing access to the facts underlying possible courses of action with respect to those decisions of national policy cutting across departmental lines which he alone must make. This need extends beyond the president as a person and includes all those individuals, groups, interdepartmental or international bodies, which make decisions above the level of the departments as such.

This need is apparent to many observers of our present deficiencies. In some quarters, however, there is a tendency to view this need as being our sole or principal one, and to conclude that what is needed is the continuation on a permanent basis of some such large-scale central operation as exists now in the Office of Strategic Services. Such a conclusion fails to take into account the fact that the principal intelligence operations of the government must be organized at the point where decision is made. It does not recognize the leading role of the State Department as a staff agency to the president. It further fails to take into account the growth and improvement that has occurred in the departments and the further improvement that can be achieved.

In 1939, when the Coordinator of Information (predecessor to OSS) was first organized, its principal role was to bring some order out of the conflicting intelligence being produced in the departments in order that the president and the already envisioned combined and joint agencies would have but one place to which to turn. It was at first considered to be but a secondary responsibility of this agency to engage in intelligence operations on its own except as might "facilitate the securing of information not now available to the government" (presidential letter of July 11, 1941). The extensive program, not only of collection of information but of independent evaluation, which subsequently grew up in COI is a direct result of the inadequacy at that time of the departmental programs. Such development was therefore vital to our wartime needs, and COI (now OSS) has undoubtedly blazed new trails and raised the level of competency of our total intelligence operation. However, the war agencies in other fields than intelligence, uninhibited by past weaknesses, staffed with new personnel (many of them of the type not available to government in peacetime), and with practically unlimited funds and freedom of action, can lay claim to the same achievement. We cannot, however, continue a complete structure superimposed on top of the normal structure of government beyond the period when our war needs demand it. The problem is how to capture that which is good and to integrate it into the normal framework of the government. Had our intelligence base been strong when war came upon us, COI would not have had to build independent facilities. However, to continue such facilities in the future will tend to perpetuate the very weaknesses that must be corrected.

The improvement of intelligence operations in the departments and their coordination as one governmentwide program will provide the principal facilities through which this high-level need can be met. However, it may be desirable to anticipate the need for some additional central facilities to provide or secure the intelligence needed at the top of government. Such independent central staff as may be required, however, can be small, since it could rely very largely on the product of research and analysis in the departments and will not engage in large-scale original research and analysis itself. Its responsibilities would be to secure and harmonize intelligence, to reconcile conflicting intelligence, and as envisioned in the JIC paper already quoted to "mobilize the resources of all agencies in the fulfillment of an urgent intelligence requirement."

Centralized Operations

None of the individual intelligence agencies of the government can hope to engage, independently of the resources that exist elsewhere in the government, in all the operations which conceivably could be justified to serve its needs. Similarly in the development of central facilities, the purpose of which will be to coordinate intelligence operations, care should be taken that such facilities do not engage in operations which can be performed at the departmental level.

Even with such care, however, it appears desirable to anticipate the establishment of some operations at a central level. This report attempts only to illustrate some of the kinds of operations which might be centralized. The full development of plans for the eventual central operating program might well wait on the creation of central planning facilities to develop such plans.

Whether this country should engage in secret intelligence activities (espionage) in the postwar period is a policy decision which is beyond the scope of this report. Such activity, if undertaken, should be principally conducted centrally and where permitted in the departments should be rigidly supervised centrally.

Special intelligence, involving the interception of communications without the knowledge or consent of the sender, and the use of crypto and other forms of analysis, raises similar questions. Here the case for central direction of such activities (should they be undertaken in the postwar period) is particularly strong because of the extreme difficulty of dividing up operations, the great cost involved in duplicating services, and the potential shortage of available skilled personnel.

With regard to files and maps of common widespread use, especially of a strictly factual or data type, the evidence of extreme duplication now inherent in the present picture would seem to demand centralization at least of indexing if not of the files themselves. The theoretical advantages of·centralization are frequently offset by the practical difficulties inherent in removing the intimate working tools too far from the operation they serve. The British, however, have centralized some files with reported success, and perhaps we can too, if the proper framework is created for their operation. Here, too, the precise solution can best be developed by the central planning facilities already suggested.

Summary of Conclusions

To summarize then, there are six conclusions, of which four are of primary importance and priority for action and two are of a secondary nature on which the need for action is not yet sufficiently established and therefore can be deferred.

1. There must be a more widespread understanding of intelligence and a more widespread participation in the development and implementation of plans for improved intelligence in government.

2. The principal intelligence operations of the government should be organized at the point where decision is made or action taken, i.e., at the departmental, or lower, level rather than in any central agency.

3. The basic intelligence operation in each department should be organized apart from the operation producing security intelligence. There is a need for some interdepartmental coordinating machinery to develop an integrated governmentwide security and security intelligence program.

4. To insure optimum results from departmental intelligence operations, there is a need for some central interdepartmental coordinating machinery to develop through specific operating plans, an integrated governmentwide intelligence program.

5. It may be well to anticipate a need for central facilities to secure intelligence needed by the president. If separate facilities are found necessary, however, such intelligence can be produced principally through intelligence available in the departments. Any small central facilities subsequently found desirable or necessary should not engage in large-scale initial research and analysis.

6. There may be some need to centralize certain operations common to all agencies or which for policy reasons may best be performed centrally. The determination of the kind of central operation which will be needed must await high policy decision with respect to certain of the operations which would lend themselves to central direction ·and operation. A decision with respect to other of the operations which might fall into this category can await the study and development of plans by the central coordinating body provided for in 4.*

---

*These conclusions appeared, at the time, to be eminently reasonable; no one could quarrel with the idea of improved intelligence. However, they avoided the fundamental issue: how and under what criteria should those limited resources be matched against intelligence requirements? The individual departments were not unwilling to do the extra things implied in his operating plans, but not at the expense of their own organizations' priorities. If these conclusions and the resource

Recommendations

Many of the specific changes in internal organization that are indicated from a consideration of the conclusions are of interest or concern only to one department. Recommendations applicable to a single department are presented in broad terms only when they are of general interest or to illustrate the broad principle involved. Recommendations concerning proposed change or action of common or overall concern are, however, presented in some detail.

The greater portion of this section of the report is thus devoted to the proposed central coordinating machinery. This should not lead to the assumption that the creation of central machinery is viewed as the most important step to be taken. Of far greater importance is the creation of strong departmental organizations, particularly in the State Department, and the separation of security intelligence operations from the more basic intelligence operations, especially in the State, War, and Navy Departments.

More Widespread Understanding of Intelligence

Throughout this memorandum it has been noted how vital to a more adequate governmentwide foreign intelligence program is a more widespread understanding of what intelligence is, how it is produced and how the intelligence agency relates to and serves the action-taking or policy-determining groups. No specific recommendation is possible.

Conduct of the Intelligence Operation at the Departmental Level

Each department (and in some cases subdivisions of departments) which has important responsibilities in international matters including our national defense, or which has public responsibilities for providing foreign information, should provide for a competent foreign intelligence operation.

The kind of facilities which will be required in the various departments and their size will vary. Except in the case of departments with major responsibilities, such as the State Department, the facilities can be quite small.

In each case, however, some provision must be made for the following functions:

1. The careful determination of the department's actual requirements. This determination will require the development in each department of a planning staff. The requirements of the department will need to be expressed in accordance with a standardized terminology and classification of intelligence and will need to be stated in sufficient

---

requirements which followed from their adoption had been matched by a Smith statement calling for an expansion of the intelligence services, it is quite likely that the interdepartmental notion would have produced support rather than opposition from the intelligence leaders. Also, conclusions 5 and 6 were fatally flawed in that Smith did not comprehend or adequately consider the president's need for intelligence and the fact that this need, based on the intelligence target in question, is *usually* best met by a centralized operation. Finally, Smith's ideas about "security intelligence" were those of the intelligence neophyte who was unable to make the connection between investigatory activities—counterintelligence, counterespionage—and their interaction with secret intelligence operations. The real question about this matter then, as now, is not the separation of "security intelligence" from other intelligence activities (secret intelligence), but how in a practical way these functions can be integrated and reinforce the intelligence derived from each.

detail to guide reporting, either by activities of the department itself or of other departments on which the department may rely for information.

2. The systematic cataloging and utilization of all possible sources to supply the needed information or intelligence.

3. The thorough analysis and evaluation of information through research techniques. In this way new information is tested against the accumulated knowledge and established facts of the past and a complete and digested picture is available in which each pertinent piece of relevant information is present and in the right place with the whole so interpreted that conclusions can be drawn and trends are visible.

4. Careful dissemination of the resultant evaluated product rather than the mere distribution of incoming reports "of interest." The intelligence office must be responsive to the needs of its department and see that those needs are supplied in full and when needed. On the other hand, it must protect the department from the voluminous flood of casual, unrelated, and unevaluated reports or scraps of information. Just as a department expects its statistical office to analyze, tabulate, and summarize data and point to its significance, so in its search for knowledge of foreign nations, peoples, conditions or events it must look to its intelligence office to do a similar job on the raw material of foreign information.

Our wartime experience has shown that the need for foreign information and intelligence in any department far exceeds the ability of its intelligence office to secure or produce without the utilization of facilities that exist elsewhere. In each case, therefore, whether the intelligence facilities provided in a department are large or small, the responsibilities of such groups should include not only responsibilities to their departments but to a total government program as well. In the latter category are responsibilities such as (1) to participate in the planning of a governmentwide program, (2) to interpret the needs of their agencies to the other agencies on which they may rely for evaluated summary intelligence, (3) to review the adequacy of coverage and competency of result with respect to intelligence obtained through other agencies, (4) to serve as the liaison point between their agencies and the intelligence groups of other agencies. In general, the departmental intelligence units should only establish such independent facilities for collection, evaluation, or dissemination as are consistent with their role in a governmentwide program.

The success of our postwar intelligence operation rests on the creation within the State Department of an intelligence operation with responsibilities such as those stated above. The creation of a centralized intelligence operation in the State Department would not only provide that department with facilities it has long needed. In addition it would serve to provide the place where leadership of the governmentwide intelligence activities would be centered.

The intelligence operations of the War and Navy Departments need to be readjusted to postwar needs. The war has been responsible for an emphasis on current news as exemplified in daily situation reports and on operational intelligence as reflected in the large-scale order-of-battle operations. Neither the organizations nor the staffing have been fully developed to serve the purposes of active War and Navy Department participation in interdepartmental discussions of high future policy. In the Navy Department as an illustration, the entire intelligence mission is stated to be in support of the fleet. In neither of the two departments has sufficient emphasis been given to research and analysis nor has provision been made for all available information to be brought together at one point for evaluation. Further, as already pointed out, both still permit an overemphasis on security intelligence to interfere with the full development of more basic intelligence.

Other departments such as Commerce and Agriculture need to recast their intelligence organization so as to become participating groups in a total governmentwide foreign intelligence program.

Separation of Security Intelligence Activities

The security intelligence activities, either at home or abroad, serving internal security purposes should be separated organizationally from the more basic intelligence activities, except for the mutual exchange of highly evaluated and summarized reports of general import (not merely of "cases"). It is further recommended that an integrated security program, including the security intelligence activities that support it, be planned for the government as a whole.

The implementation of the first recommendation will require action in a number of departments, not necessarily simultaneously.

In the State Department, for example, the creation of new central intelligence facilities should not be accompanied by a transfer of activities now centered in the Office of Controls in the Division of Foreign Activities Correlation.

In the Navy Department some separation has been undertaken by the creation of new intelligence facilities in the Office of the Commander in Chief apart from the Office of Naval Intelligence, which is the principal Navy Department organization concerned with security and security intelligence. These new facilities offer the possibility of becoming the nucleus for an expanded basic intelligence operation in the postwar era when the needs for strictly operational intelligence will be greatly curtailed irrespective of whether the Office of the Commander in Chief is retained or not. The role of ONI, however, as the central staff agency for security matters is not clear, and a number of related activities, not only in the bureaus and auxiliary services but in the Office of the Chief of Naval Operations itself, are not now coordinated under a single head or staff unit.

In the War Department, too, some separation has resulted from the reactivation of the Office of the Provost Marshal General. The predilection for continuance in the field of security intelligence, however, still permits the Military Intelligence Service to become too engrossed with matters that could be further centralized outside MIS. Further, because of its organizational placement the PMG cannot be fully effective as a staff agency to coordinate all security matters.

In both the War and Navy Departments the separation of the security intelligence operation and the more basic foreign intelligence operation should be furthered and the security intelligence and the various forms of internal security operations be more closely coordinated.

The implementation of the second recommendation will require the creation of an interdepartmental coordinating committee described below.

Coordination of Intelligence and Security Operations

To insure that the intelligence and security activities of the government, carried on by a number of agencies, fulfill all the national requirements, that they are developed as a total program producing the maximum result with a minimum of duplication, overlap, and confusion and that adequate planning is accomplished for their expansion in any future emergency, it is recommended that two interdepartmental groups be organized under the leadership of the Department of State.

The one group, which would consist of the assistant secretaries of state, war, navy and commerce, would compose an Interdepartmental Intelligence Coordinating Committee. It would be concerned with developing an integrated governmentwide foreign intelligence program. It also would be concerned with planning for the future.

The other group, consisting of the assistant secretaries of state, war, navy and treasury and the assistant attorney general, would compose an Interdepartmental Security Coordinating Committee. It would be concerned with developing an integrated governmentwide internal security program and of an integrated governmentwide security intelligence program. It would also be concerned with planning for the future.

These two groups, by direction of the president and by means of planning conducted by permanent staff of their own working through subcommittees including representatives of any agency of interest either as customer or contributor, would develop a series of specific operating plans. These plans would serve as common directives for the assignment of operating responsibilities among the departmental intelligence and security agencies. The manner in which such planning would be conducted will be the same in both the security coordinating committee and in the intelligence committee, and is described below.

Except as discussed later under "Conduct of Central Operations," the committees would have no responsibilities for the production of intelligence itself nor for the conduct of operations. Rather their responsibilities would consist of the following:

1. To develop a detailed and clear statement of the national intelligence objectives and requirements and of the national security requirements, including those of all departments and agencies.

2. To determine the means in terms of actual operations for meeting the national intelligence and national security requirements.

3. To assign, through a series of specific operating plans, operating responsibilities to the various departments.

4. To review the adequacy and economy of the total intelligence program of the government and of the total security program of the government.

5. To develop plans, legislation, and other instruments in readiness for the adjustment of the intelligence and the security programs in the event of emergency or other changed conditions.

The above list of responsibilities describes in effect the steps in planning. The visible result of such planning, and, therefore, the principal concern of the committees would be the operating plan itself. Each operating plan when issued would reflect the determination of the appropriate committee under each of the first three continuing and long-range responsibilities shown above, i.e., the requirements, the means for their accomplishment, and the specific operating assignments allocated to the various departments and agencies. When issued, the specific operating plans would be directives to the departments and agencies. The departments and agencies would adjust their operations to conform to them.

Operating Plans. A typical operating plan when published should contain such material as the following: the subject, area or kind of operation covered by the plan; the specific requirement covered by the plan; the scope of the plan; provisions of the operating plan (operating requirements, assignments, etc.) as reporting, tabulation and filing, evaluation, and dissemination.

Such planning would not be accomplished overnight. Nor, if the committees were to be effective, could they wait in any broad field for the accomplishment of full planning before issuing a specific operating plan to effect an obviously needed change.

Ultimately, specific operating plans would be published by the intelligence coordinating committee in at least the following subjects or categories of intelligence: geography; economics; finance; armed forces; government, politics and national policy; transportation and communication; people and social forces; technology and scientific development.

These broad categories, however, are made up of lesser categories. Long before anything like a total governmentwide operating plan in one of these categories is complete, operating plans would have been determined upon and published in subdivisions of the category. The total operating plan for economic intelligence, for example, would require plans in such subjects as industrial plant and potential resources; trade and commerce; labor supply and employment; and others. Similarly the operating plan covering intelligence concerning people and social forces will require plans on population and characteristics; living standards; cultural standards and customs; and others.

Other types of specific operating plans would also be developed in connection with certain kinds of operations (unrelated to any category of intelligence). Thus plans would be developed as needed for such operations as the monitoring and interception of foreign radio or communications; the single or combined collection of information through sources of interest to a large number of agencies (such as the Interdepartmental Committee for the Acquisition of Foreign Publications, the Technical Industrial Intelligence Committee, the Survey of Foreign Exports, etc.); and interdepartmental procedural matters such as the standardization or joint operation of files, distribution, and liaison problems.

Similarly the operating plans of the security coordinating committee would encompass not only the various aspects of security intelligence, including the filing of such intelligence, but also the various security operations such as border and harbor patrol, port security, censorship, preventive investigation, security advisory services, etc.*

Planning staff. An essential element of these central coordinating committees is a full-time planning staff. Specialists not only in skills of administrative analysis but with a knowledge of the field to which they will be assigned would ultimately be required in each of the major subjects or categories of intelligence, including security intelligence, as well as in various kinds of intelligence and security operations. These specialists should not carry departmental responsibilities but should be assigned to reasonably permanent duty with the committees. Providing for this staff will be a special concern of the State Department but should be a responsibility of all the agencies represented on the top two committees.

*Although Smith's concept of "operating plans" appeared to be new, it wasn't. Intelligence collection plans are a time-proven device designed to systematize acquisition of intelligence information in accord with an ongoing requirement—for example, to follow the development and introduction of new military hardware such as artillery pieces or aircraft. To this extent Smith's operating plans were not a marked departure from past practice; however, the idea was badly flawed in assuming that this procedure would adequately deal with such dynamic situations as border crises, introduction of missiles into Cuba, etc., and/or that realistic intelligence contingency plans could be cast without a central analytical intelligence capability which was able to provide the kind of intelligence assessments carried out by the OSS's Research and Analysis branch during the war.

Each major subject or kind of operation in which an operating plan is necessary should be assigned as a continuing responsibility to a member of the planning staff. The member of the central planning staff would call upon each of the many agencies which has an interest in the matter assigned, either as a consumer or as a contributor, to designate one person to represent his agency in a continuing and responsible capacity in the development and implementation of an operating plan covering the matter assigned. The agencies of interest would in almost all cases include many agencies, not just those represented on the top committees themselves.

These groups would constitute the subcommittees to discharge the responsibilities for planning and for reviewing, as a continuous assignment, the adequacy and economy of all activities in the subject or kind of operation assigned. A member assigned from the central planning staff should serve as chairman of each subcommittee. The responsibility for its effectiveness and for much of its hard work would fall on him.

Current problems, including that of duplication, may not always be the most important matter for the subcommittees to concentrate on. The chairman of each subcommittee should not permit the handling of current problems to put aside the long-range responsibility of that subcommittee to develop a complete plan of operation in its subject or kind of operation.

Throughout, the ultimate goal should be kept in mind of a series of specific operating plans, prescribing a coordinated program in which all activities essential to the intelligence and security requirements are provided for, and in which the operations and facilities of all agencies are used to the maximum to serve the needs of other agencies.

Joint Secretariat. The two committees should be served by a common secretariat which would provide for orderly procedure through standard agenda and minute-keeping systems. The secretariat should take the minutes in each subcommittee and maintain the files of the committees.

Production of High-Level Intelligence

The need to provide for some facilities to serve groups at a level above the departments themselves is one which should be anticipated but action is not now recommended.

With the principal intelligence activities of the government being carried on in the departments in accordance with a planned and coordinated program, such intelligence as may be needed at the top of the government can be produced through or secured from the intelligence operations in the department. The State Department would provide the principal facilities for bringing to bear on any high-level problem the total intelligence available anywhere in the government.

Should it later be found, however, that independent facilities are desirable to serve the president in the occasional instance in which he may wish direct and immediate access to the intelligence involving a matter of high decision, these facilities, which should be organized in his own office, can be small and need not engage in large-scale initial research and analysis on original raw materials.

Conduct of Central Operations

The strengthening of intelligence activities in the departments and agencies and their coordination by a central planning staff are the principal means of providing a total operation serving the total national needs. Central facilities should not be created, therefore, to engage in operations which can be performed at the departmental level.

The planning conducted by the two coordinate committees may result in a decision that some types of operations may be found to be practicable only if operated centrally or under strong day-to-day central direction. It is recommended that any such service as is determined to require centralization, be conducted as an interdepartmental service under the appropriate coordinating committee.*

The Smith plan is cited here in its entirety because the reasonableness of such an approach which would deal with problems of common concern and would "coordinate and synthesize" the disparate functions and reconcile the intelligence community members' differences has over time been a lure and a cruel deception. In Smith's case, he was animated by an *Encyclopedia Britannica* outlook about intelligence which held that its problems could be divorced from the personalities of those involved in managing, directing, and manipulating the intelligence process for their and their organizations' interests. Similarly, Smith failed to learn the wartime lesson that, in Dean Acheson's words, "no committee can govern and no man can administer without his own people, money, and authority."

In various forms and guises, portions of the Smith plan have been adopted, tried and discarded by those in the government with an interest in the intelligence organization problem. This "committee urge" is a recurring phenomenon in government, especially among career administrators who, when faced with the fact of inept or indifferent leadership by elected and appointed officials, favor an organizational or interorganizational response to offset that leadership void. Sometimes the careerist response takes the form of persuading the appointed and elected officials to establish task forces to deal with specific problems and order the formation of interdepartmental committees, working groups, etc. Rarely do these actions achieve their intended purposes because,

---

*Smith's hopes for "coordinating committees" were those of the perennially optimistic bureaucrat who confuses the form of an agreement with its substance. Such committees rarely produce decisions and most frequently merely produce recommendations, which in turn spawn the creation of further committees to study the recommendations and so on ad infinitum. As the history of American intelligence organizations and that of the government itself amply demonstrates, one of the tragic results—although perhaps not so intended—of the committee approach is the creation of a false sense of security on the part of leaders who order a committee as a means to defer the act of decision. This sense of security, which is conveyed by public statements indicating a matter is under review by a committee, is quite dangerous because those who exude it often assume that conditions won't worsen while the review is underway. And, as shown below, while the committees spawned by Smith's plan deliberated about what they needed to do and how they should be internally organized, the worldwide situation deteriorated and America's field and analytical organizations frittered away many of the advantages they had gained during the war.

regardless of the permanent governmental bureaucracy's goodwill or tacit agreement that "something must be done," there is no substitute for direct and concerned leadership on the part of elected and appointed officials.

In those fateful months following the end of OSS, Truman's acceptance of Smith's plan produced chaos in the intelligence community not so much because of the plan's conceptual flaws (which were several and which could have been modified), but rather because of Secretary of State Byrnes's failure to comprehend and act on the importance of organization to a successful national intelligence effort. Furthermore, Byrnes did not accept the true role and leadership functions of the secretary of state under Smith's plan. To wit: in less than a month after Byrnes had been given the lead responsibility by Truman for breathing life into Smith's interdepartmental group concept and supposedly to orchestrate the flow of finished intelligence to the president, he was arguing for a central intelligence agency which would get him at least partially off the hook. As former Secretary of the Navy James Forrestal noted:

State-War-Navy Meeting
16 October 1945

2. *Central Intelligence Agency:* Mr. Byrnes next raised the question of a central intelligence agency . . . responsible to a Council of Defense which would consist of the secretaries of state, war and navy. Mr. Forrestal pointed out that this was substantially similar to the Joint Chiefs of Staff proposal. . . . Mr. Patterson did not recall having seen the Joint Chiefs of Staff proposal, nor had Mr. Byrnes seen it. All of the secretaries agreed with the principle of the proposal, that *any central intelligence agency should report to the three secretaries rather than directly to the president.* [Emphasis added].*

In a related finding, on October 31, 1945, Director Smith noted in a memorandum to President Truman: "The principal weakness has been the inadequacy of the intelligence operations of the departments concerned, indeed the lack of any intelligence operation in the State Department. Inadequate operations have resulted in failure to anticipate intelligence needs, in failure to recognize trends, in lack of perspective, and in inadequate pooling of intelligence except on the basis of mutual exchange of individual reports." Smith added, "The letters which you made public to Secretary Byrnes and General Donovan have apparently not yet made it sufficiently clear that we are not going back to our pre-1939 situation but are moving in accordance with a plan to develop a more effective program for the future." Smith's comments were an ominous straw in the wind.

Another postwar intelligence plan deserves some mention: one hatched by J. Edgar Hoover, which was forwarded to Truman by Attorney General Tom Clark, under his signature, on October 22, 1945:

*Walter Millis, ed., *The Forrestal Diaries,* New York: Viking Press, 1951, p. 101.

Memorandum for the President
A Plan for U.S. Secret Worldwide Intelligence Coverage

Secret worldwide intelligence coverage for the benefit of the United States Government must have as its primary objectives the providing to the executive branches of the government basic data on a worldwide scale upon which plans may be formulated and action taken, and the insuring of internal security from the threat of infiltrating foreign agents, ideologies, and military conquest. Intelligence coverage must be had immediately. There is no time for training and organizing a new corps.

There is in operation in the Western Hemisphere an intelligence plan based on simplicity of structure and flexibility of operations which has functioned efficiently, secretly, and economically since prior to Pearl Harbor, and has proved its adaptability to worldwide coverage by the effectiveness of its operation in the Western Hemisphere field.

It is proposed that the time-proved program in operation in the Western Hemisphere be extended on a worldwide basis with certain modification.

The Plan

The plan provides for the joint operation in every country of the world a service reporting through State Department channels composed of a member from each of the Office of Military Intelligence (military attaché), the Office of Naval Intelligence (naval attaché), and the Federal Bureau of Investigation (legal attaché), each as a specialist in its own field and able to operate without a duplication of effort but closely correlating their operations to insure complete coverage.

A committee to control basic policy would be composed of the secretaries of state, war, and navy and the attorney general. There would be an operational committee set up by the president composed of an assistant secretary of state, the directors of Military Intelligence, Naval Intelligence, and Federal Bureau of Investigation.

A unit for evaluation and analysis would be established in the State Department to which the three operating agencies would furnish intelligence data and appropriate review, analysis, and utilization in international matters.

Facility of Operation

The program proposed is somewhat similar in operation as that presently operating in the Western Hemisphere. It has proved its effectiveness, requires no elaborate superstructure and the interested agencies have available trained personnel and operating facilities for recruiting, training and dispatching additional personnel. The plan consequently can be placed in operation immediately by the president merely by setting up the policy board, creating the evaluation and analysis section in the State Department and then extending the authority heretofore given to the directors of Military and Naval Intelligence and the Federal Bureau of Investigation to operate on a worldwide basis.

This plan has produced in the Western Hemisphere a maximum amount of information with a minimum of operating personnel and expense, and has not resulted in any embarrassment whatsoever to the United States government. Its secrecy is assured through the dissemination of the operations among the already existing government agencies which have previously operated successfully for a long period in their respective fields.

Points for Consideration

Foreign and domestic civil intelligence are inseparable and constitute one field of operation. The German-American Bund and the Italian Fascist organization in the United States originated and were directed from abroad. The communist movement originated in Russia but operates in the United States. To follow these organizations access must be had to their origin and headquarters in foreign countries as well as to their activities in the United States. Every major espionage service has operated on a worldwide basis except that of Britain, which has had a separate organization for domestic and foreign intelligence. But Britain is in the process at present of consolidating the two services based on their experiences through the war period. In order to cope with the activities of various subversive agents in the United States with speed and dispatch, it is entirely evident that their activities must be followed throughout the various countries by one intelligence agency of the United States government. Valuable time, as well as efficiency and effectiveness, is lost if one agency covers their activities in Europe, another in Latin America, and another in the United States.

The theory that police work and intelligence coverage cannot be combined has been entirely dispelled. Police arrests under modern police practice is only one of the important functions of a police agency. In fact, all police work specifically involves the gathering of information in the nature of intelligence. Extensive intelligence coverage must necessarily precede the arrest of the enemy agent in the United States and it is not possible to separate the gathering of intelligence from police functions in view of the numerous criminal statutes such as those relating to espionage and sabotage which must be enforced by police action although directly concerned with intelligence. One of the major factors in the control of subversive activities in the Western Hemisphere during the war was the coordination of the various police organizations throughout the United States and Latin America through the Federal Bureau of Invetigation.

A hazard in intelligence operations is the possibility of a charge being made that the organization is a "Gestapo." Also, a police agency which engages in intelligence operations may be called a "political police." Both charges are obnoxious to American citizens. The set-up operating in the Western Hemisphere throughout the war has engaged in both police and intelligence activities and its record of protecting civil liberties has been praised even by the American Civil Liberties Union.

> Respectfully,
> Tom Clark
> Attorney General

Although it is somewhat unfashionable these days to say much in behalf of J. Edgar Hoover, the recommendations and contents of the Hoover/Clark plan were remarkably prescient—especially in terms of its implicit recognition of the need for integrated counterespionage operations which transcend national boundaries. Also, although Hoover might have come to dominate the "policy committee" envisioned, the plan itself provided a reasonable means for the president to control and direct the intelligence community if he were so inclined. Unfortunately, however, Hoover's plan was an idea whose time had not come because, in the blizzard of postwar intelligence proposals which had descended upon the White House both before and after Roosevelt's death, the question concerning the use to which intelligence was to be put in the postwar era had not been adequately considered. Most of the antagonists in this conflict (except perhaps Henry Wallace, who advocated a kind of unilateral intelligence disarmament) were agreed that the nation needed a "good" intelligence system, but beyond that point the disagreements were severe. And few of those involved were willing or able to raise the question "to what end and what purpose?" with Truman, who had few ideas of his own about how to use the intelligence community, nor displayed much inclination to direct and control its operations.

These plans, with few exceptions, reflect what little effect previous mistakes and wartime experiences actually had on the thinking of the time and those of the principals who were involved. The thinking embodied in these plans reflected much more than a simple institutional bias in favor of one organization or organizational form against another. It reflected a cultural mind-set which was unable to accommodate the logical and pragmatic conclusions which derive from acceptance of Donovan's "ultimate intelligence target": a thorough knowledge of the other great powers' capabilities and intentions, on which the strategic decisions of the United States will be based. In turn, this cultural mind-set was reinforced by such other external biases as domestic partisan political conditions, the scramble for funds, personnel, facilities, and other perks of power; it was the root cause of the flawed thinking which surrounded and often dominated the postwar intelligence deliberations.

The dismembered pieces of the OSS which Truman passed to Byrnes and Secretary of War Robert Patterson were received by them and their organizations with considerable misgivings. Like someone handed an unwanted sack of garbage, their first inclination was to look around for a convenient spot to put it down. In State, the problem of what to do with and where to put the Interim Research and Intelligence Service (which was created out of whole cloth from the OSS's Research and Analysis and Presentation branches) was particularly acute, especially because it constituted an alternative to State's desk officer, regional assistant secretary organizations and was therefore looked upon as an unsettling factor in the Foreign Service's way of carrying out its diplomatic duties. The matter was further complicated by the fact that once the OSS abolition order was announced on September 20, many of the persons in the OSS who were expected to take up positions in State's Interim Research and Intelligence Service simply "demobilized" themselves and went home. To be sure some, such as H. Stuart Hughes, Franz Neumann, Herbert Marcuse, Charles Stelle, and Allen Evans, who were among the best of the interdisciplinary research teams put together by Donovan and Langer, made the move to State. However, without Donovan and his principal lieutenants to hold the band of wartime research brothers together, many dispersed to the winds, like a troop of Confederate cavalry after Appomattox. The intact transfer of the Research and Analysis and Presentation branches was carried out on paper, but only about half of the 1,200 plus individuals who were designated in the order actually took up positions in the new organization.

Secretary of State Byrnes, who had no inclination to exploit the unique analytical intelligence capability he had been handed on a silver platter, directed Undersecretary of State Dean Acheson to take charge. Acheson in turn asked Colonel Alfred McCormack, who during the war had brought some order out of the organizational chaos surrounding analytical intelligence in the army's G-2 under the sometimes brilliant but often erratic Major General George V. Strong, to head up the Interim Research and Intelligence Service. McCormack, who prior to his wartime service had been a New York corporation lawyer and who was now waiting to be demobilized, was not easily persuaded. Nevertheless, Acheson's charm, promises of support, resources to do the job, access, etc., overcame his initial reluctance; McCormack, along with a small band of personal "brothers" from G-2 who were also lawyers, moved to State. Theirs was an impossible task. Besides the old-line Foreign Service opposition to establishing the kind of analytical intelligence envisaged and demonstrated in the OSS's performance, the vocal right-wing Cold Warriors in the press, Congress, and elsewhere jumped on McCormack and Acheson for harboring "collectivists, do-gooders and what-nots" in the State Department. As R. Harris Smith notes:

In March 1946, while McCormack and Dean Acheson struggled to secure a renewed appropriation for the research unit, the chairman of the House Military Affairs Committee charged that persons with "strong Soviet leanings" had joined the State Department intelligence group. McCormack denied the charge and demanded a retraction. Instead, Congress cut the entire appropriation for his unit. On April 23, 1946, Colonel McCormack resigned.*

Like many who were later tarred with the "soft on communism" brush, McCormack went quietly back to his law practice and the problem of what to do with the Research and Intelligence Service (now without funds of its own) was resolved by splitting it into seventeen "committees," which in an act of bureaucratic euthanasia were in turn reorganized out of existence. Besides the devastating effect these congressional wrecking tactics had on the United States' ability to carry out the analytical intelligence function, there are also several pieces of historical irony. The first is that one can date acceptance and currency of the "ten-foot tall" Russian in America's analytical intelligence circles from the final demise of the OSS's research and analysis capability. Another is that one can similarly date the beginnings of the requisite conditions and political climate which propelled Senator Joseph McCarthy from the congressional charges levied against unnamed persons in McCormack's Research and Intelligence Service. Although these charges of widespread communist sympathies and activities remained unproven at the time, in early 1947 they gained an "I told you so" kind of credibility: Carl Marzani, a former

*Smith, *op. cit.,* p. 364.

deputy chief of the OSS Presentation branch who had transferred to State upon the abolition of OSS, was indicted, convicted, and sent to prison on a charge of disloyalty and concealing his membership in the Communist Party.* One Communist in the State Department or elsewhere does not necessarily a movement make, but it did provide a convenient peg on which to hang "analyses" which saw the Soviets on the move everywhere and about to take over the United States government.

Meanwhile, the White House intelligence situation in the post-OSS period went from bad to worse. As suggested, the analytical intelligence situation in State's Research and Intelligence Service was in shambles, and Truman was being buffeted from one crisis to the next by the current "hot" intelligence reports which flowed across his desk as if propelled by some unseen sorcerer's apprentice. In official Washington, then as now, these reports, delivered by those known in the intelligence trade as "purveyors of the hot poop," achieved a remarkable currency all their own, which made Truman's task of deciding among crises extremely difficult. In essence, this uncontrolled flow of current intelligence from the military intelligence services forced Truman into the uncomfortable and personally unwanted role of being his own intelligence officer. Also, although Truman was consistently personable toward the intelligence aides who awakened him (and frequently Mrs. Truman, a light sleeper) when delivering the latest crisis report from areas where people were awake, he wondered aloud if all those nocturnal awakenings were really necessary. In a sense they were, because the intelligence community was fearful of being charged with failure to keep the president adequately informed on a timely basis. In those days no one could be entirely certain that a crisis occurring after dark in Washington might not result in an act of war before daylight. In response to intelligence pressures, which induce a sense of paranoia in even the most experienced after a period of time, Truman—after bemoaning the intelligence situation set upon him, griping to Admiral Leahy about Secretary Byrnes's failure, and being shown a bootleg copy of an internal War Department memo by his naval aide, Captain Clark Clifford**—personally con-

---

*Ibid., p. 364(n). See also the New York Times, 28 June 1947.

**The memorandum, dated November 7, 1945, read as follows:

Central Intelligence Service

It appears that the development of plans for a coordinated foreign intelligence program for all federal agencies concerned is bogged down because the War and Navy Departments believe that the problem is being worked out by the Department of State in obedience to the president's letter to the secretary of state dated 20 September 1945.

The only apparently promising prospect of getting useful action on this problem in the reasonably near future is as follows:

The president to call a conference with the secretaries of state, war and navy, and direct them to work together in the preparation of a plan for the establishment of a Central Intelligence Service that is acceptable to the three Departments of State, War and Navy.

This to be completed and submitted to the president for his approval at the earliest practicable date, and not later than 31 December 1945.

ducted a series of meetings in the White House in January 1946 with the key principals to examine the various plans suggested for a centralized intelligence authority.

Thus, although Smith had had his way, it was clear to Truman that the formula he had endorsed, which separated the functions of analytical intelligence and operations and gave them to the State and War Departments respectively, was an unmitigated disaster. Or at the very least, his secretary of state was not the man to whom he should have delegated the responsibility for managing the intelligence effort. To be sure, the flow of current intelligence was reaching Truman's desk, but examination of these streams of information merely served to point out that the American intelligence effort was providing not much more than an after-the-fact, or slightly before-the-fact, recital of enemy successes and a post-mortem report of Allied failures. The spate of current intelligence information, which was evaluated largely in terms other than source because it was soon overtaken by the next "flash report," produced a situation wherein the government was seldom forewarned in time to preempt an action.

Consequently, on January 22, 1946, Truman somewhat reluctantly turned his back on Smith's plan and in an executive letter to the secretaries of state, war, and navy directed establishment of a new National Intelligence Authority and a Central Intelligence Group:

To the Secretary of State, the Secretary of War, and the Secretary of the Navy:

1. It is my desire, and I hereby direct, that all federal foreign intelligence activities be planned, developed and coordinated so as to assure the most effective accomplishment of the intelligence mission related to the national security. I hereby designate you, together with another person to be named by me as my personal representative [Admiral Leahy], as the National Intelligence Authority to accomplish this purpose.

2. Within the limits of available appropriations, you shall each from time to time assign persons and facilities from your respective departments, which persons shall collectively form a Central Intelligence Group and shall, under the direction of a director of Central Intelligence, assist the National Intelligence Authority. The director of Central Intelligence shall be designated by me, shall be responsible to the National Intelligence Authority, and shall sit as a nonvoting member thereof.

3. Subject to the existing law, and to the direction and control of the National Intelligence Authority, the director of Central Intelligence shall:

    a. Accomplish the correlation and evaluation of intelligence relating to the national security, and the appropriate dissemination within the government of the resulting strategic and national policy intelligence. In so doing, full use shall be made of the staff and facilities of the intelligence agencies of your departments.

    b. Plan for the coordination of such of the activities of the intelligence agencies of your departments as relate to the national security and recommend to the National Intelligence Authority the establishment of such overall policies and objectives as will assure the most effective accomplishment of the national intelligence misssion.

    c. Perform, for the benefit of said intelligence agencies, such services of common concern as the National Intelligence Authority determines can be more efficiently accomplished centrally.

d. Perform such other functions and duties related to intelligence affecting the national security as the president and the National Intelligence Authority may from time to time direct.

4. No police, law-enforcement, or internal security functions shall be exercised under this directive.

5. Such intelligence received by the intelligence agencies of your departments as may be designated by the National Intelligence Authority shall be freely available to the director of Central Intelligence for correlation, evaluation, or dissemination. To the extent approved by the National Intelligence Authority, the operations of said intelligence agencies shall be open to inspection by the director of Central Intelligence in connection with planning functions.

6. The existing intelligence agencies of your departments shall continue to collect, evaluate, correlate, and disseminate departmental intelligence.

7. The director of Central Intelligence shall be advised by an Intelligence Advisory Board consisting of the heads (or their representatives) of the principal military and civilian intelligence agencies of the government having functions related to national security, as determined by the National Intelligence Authority.

8. Within the scope of existing law and presidential directives, other departments and agencies of the executive branch of the federal government shall furnish such intelligence information relating to the national security as is in their possession, and as the director of Central Intelligence may from time to time request pursuant to regulations of the National Intelligence Authority.

9. Nothing herein shall be construed to authorize the making of investigations inside the continental limits of the United States and its possessions, except as provided by law and presidential directives.

10. In the conduct of their activities the National Intelligence Authority and the director of Central Intelligence shall be responsible for fully protecting intelligence sources and methods.

Sincerely yours,
Harry S Truman

The intelligence community's reaction to the letter, formally known as "Directive on Coordination of Foreign Intelligence Activities" ranged from incredulity over the flipflop in attitude it included to more pragmatic questions about whose appropriations were going to be tapped to pay for the NIA's Central Intelligence Group, and how and by whom it was going to be staffed. Wayne Coy, Smith's deputy, recalled, "By January 1946 we were in Truman's doghouse because of what had happened in the intelligence community and as a result Smith was not invited to participate in the NIA discussions and more surprisingly was not tasked to find separate funds to support it." In spite of the directive's obvious weaknesses, which reflected a reluctance on Truman's part to think the intelligence organization control problem through to its logical conclusion, it did, in establishing the NIA and CIG, constitute begrudging acceptance of the fact that some kind of a refereeing body besides the president or secretary of state was required to regulate and coordinate the flow of intelligence information reaching the White House. Similarly, it recognized the need to orchestrate the acquisition of intelligence in accord with a sense of priorities which acknowledged that the president was the preeminent consumer of the nation's intelligence product.

Two days later, at a January 24 press conference, Truman was asked what he thought about the new approach to intelligence his actions had wrought. The exchange was as follows:

Q: Mr. President, would you care to make any observations on the new National Intelligence Authority?

A: Yes. I think it is a practical program, and that it will work for the best interests of the government. It was a necessary arrangement, in order to have all the information available for the people who need it in implementing foreign policy. It combines the intelligence services of the State, War, Navy and the president in a manner so that the information will be available to all four for the transaction of government business.

Q: . . . is it a revival of the OSS in general?

A: No it is not. *It isn't. It isn't.* [Emphasis added.]

Q: Mr. President, do you suppose if we had such a set-up back in 1940 or 1941, that there would not have been Pearl Harbor?

A: I can't say that it was . . . contributing greatly toward its not taking place. I can't say whether there would have been a Pearl Harbor or not. You can make "if" meet any situation.

A psychoanalyst might be able to draw some abstruse conclusions about Truman's sense of dread and fear revealed by these responses. At the time, as he assessed the postwar world, the crises and flash points far exceeded American capacity to respond; the intelligence system which had followed in the wake of the OSS was unable to order these conflicts in terms of their relative importance or give an accurate assessment of the time frame associated with each. China, Greece, Yugoslavia, France, Italy were all problem areas, and depending on which intelligence was last read, the tendency was to respond as if there were no tomorrow. It was a period best described as the "Chicken Little" era in American intelligence: after the Soviets' successes in establishing hegemony in Eastern Europe had finally sunk in, the actions of the Soviets at the rim of their influence provoked a much greater and opposite reaction than the evidence supported. One Navy Department document describes this period by saying, "We fell prey to Hitler's syndrome during the invasion of Russia, where regardless of defensibility or internal conditions in the marginal areas, we diluted our limited resources and failed to mount effective counterprograms in any one of these areas." In early 1946, the beleaguered intelligence community had at least done the job of identifying the major problem areas and forecasting the events should the United States chose not to intervene.

At the onset, the NIA and its operating arm, the CIG, were ill-equipped to carry out coordinated positive intelligence operations or those designed to preempt or forestall such partially predicted outcomes as the defeat of Chiang Kai-shek (the so-called loss of China) or the success of communist movements in France, Italy, and Greece. The CIG as an operational entity was a contradiction in terms. It had no money of its own, no personnel, and no real authority to compel the specific performance of either military or intelligence services. By virtue of the January 22 directive, the United States was back to a committee or "war cabinet" approach to intelligence; one which included the right players, but not necessarily the ones who could direct and control the intelligence agencies and assets ostensibly under their command. This is not to say that as members of the Joint Chiefs of Staff and Chiefs of Staff of the Army, Navy, and Air Force respectively, or the heads of the military intelligence services, would have disobeyed orders from the service secretaries and /or the secretary of state in their joint role as the NIA; but rather that their acceptance of the charge to "cooperate" with interdepartmental collectives, such as the NIA, more often than not resulted in very little real performance unless such cooperation was considered to be in their own self-interest and that of their organization.

To preside over the Central Intelligence Group as director of Central Intelligence, Truman turned to a former St. Louis businessman, Rear Admiral Sidney Souers. Souers had served in the Office of Naval Intelligence during World War II, but that service did not encumber him with much in the way of new or unique ideas concerning the meaning, capabilities, and limitations of intelligence insofar as they effected the adoption and execution of national policy, or its role in facilitating the accomplishment of operational intelligence missions on behalf of national policy.* Admiral Souers, by virtue of his ap-

---

*The essential thrust of Souers' outlook on the question of centralized intelligence was expressed by him in the chapter entitled "Intelligence" in the Eberstadt Report prepared for Secretary of the Navy Forrestal. In part, Souers wrote:

Complete merger of the intelligence services of the State, War and Navy Departments is not considered feasible since each of these departments requires operating intelligence peculiar to itself. Intimate and detailed knowledge of the objectives and problems of each service is obviously indispensable to successful operation. Although each of these departmental services must be maintained on a highly efficient basis and supplied with adequate funds, it has been demonstrated that many of their functions can be performed more effectively as joint undertakings.

In the light of the lessons learned in wartime, it is apparent that (1) further coordination of intelligence relating to national security is highly desirable; (2) such activities of common concern as can be more efficiently conducted by a common agency should be so handled; and (3) there must be synthesis of departmental intelligence on the strategic and national policy level. Manifestly these three functions can be accomplished most effectively in a common intelligence agency, provided suitable conditions of responsibility are maintained toward the departments primarily concerned with national defense.

It is, therefore, recommended:

(1) That there be established a Central Intelligence Agency to coordinate and, as far as practicable, unify all foreign intelligence activities and to synthesize all intelligence concerning military, political, economic, and technological developments abroad for the ben-

pointment as America's first director of Central Intelligence, was not in over his head; rather, because he possessed no real weight on his own, he floated on the intelligence community's sea and was blown hither and thither by winds of political change and circumstance. When asked upon first assuming his post what he wanted to do, Souers replied, "go home." Souers remained in his post until June 1946, and returned to Washington a year later, eventually assuming the position of executive secretary of the National Security Council, a job he held from September 1947 to 1950.

Although Souers had participated, along with others, in the drafting of the January 22 directive and was recommended by Secretary of the Navy James Forrestal to head the CIG, he provided little direction of how it should actually proceed under the National Intelligence Authority. As one might expect, those early days of the CIG were characterized by considerable confusion. During that time, Souers' principal role was to serve as the man out front who was expected to cajole the intelligence services' leaders into providing material support and people to run the CIG. In this role, because of the selective misperception of the intelligence leaders who thought he was one of Truman's Missouri cronies, Souers proved more successful than if he had come on strong as the director of Central Intelligence. Somewhat sardonically it should be noted that at the time Souers became DCI he and Truman were far from being cronies; however, they later became close friends, and this formed the basis of his subsequent appointment as the National Security Council's executive secretary.* Nevertheless, while Souers was out "dog robbing" to get the people and resources the CIG needed, the real work of putting together a centralized intelligence organization did go on, principally under the direction of Colonel

---

efit of those responsible for the determination and execution of governmental policy pertaining to national security.

(2) That courses of instruction in intelligence be established at appropriate levels of military education in order to indoctrinate officers with the importance of the function of intelligence to our national security.

(3) That only thoroughly trained intelligence personnel be selected for intelligence duties, including those of military and naval attachés.

(See: "Eberstadt Report," *op. cit.,* p. 163.)

*As a measure of Truman's feelings toward Souers, Margaret Truman notes that one day her father sent the following memorandum to Admiral Leahy and Rear Admiral Souers,

To My Brethren and Fellow Doghouse Denizens:

By virtue of the authority vested in me as Top Dog I require and charge that Front Admiral William D. Leahy and Rear Admiral Sidney W. Souers, receive and accept the vestments and appurtenances of their respective positions, namely as personal snooper and director of centralized snooping. . . . I charge each of you not only to seek to better our foreign relations through more intensive snooping but to also keep me informed constantly of the movements and actions of the other, for without such coordination there can be no order and no aura of mutual trust.   H.S.T.

See: Margaret Truman, *Harry S Truman.* New York: William Morrow, 1973, p. 332.

Louis J. Fortier, U.S. Army, and Captain James F. Cullen, USNR, who served as his deputy.

Colonel Fortier, who had won his spurs in Washington's high-level intelligence league as the army's senior member on the ill-fated Joint Intelligence Subcommittee, was extremely able. Similarly, Captain Cullen, who had floated between the JCS, the White House, and the chief of Naval Operations' inner staff, was a talented utility infielder who could be counted upon to head off unfavorable reactions from some of the navy's stiff-necked brass who looked askance at the CIG. Almost as their first task, Fortier and Cullen undertook a damage assessment of the intelligence community. In so doing, based upon discussions with Colonel McCormack, they wrote off State's Research and Intelligence Service as a lost cause, and instead turned their attention to the War Department's Strategic Services Unit (SSU), which had been formed out of the OSS's operational intelligence assets at the time the latter was abolished.

In the War Department, Colonel Fortier quickly determined the Smith plan had not wreaked the havoc it had in the State Department because the newly designated SSU did not have to wait on approved operating plans in order to continue with actions already underway since V-E day by OSS personnel in connection with the military occupation of Europe. Also, Assistant Secretary of War Howard C. Petersen, on whom the SSU responsibility had devolved, had established a policy designed to "preserve the assets and eliminate the liabilities." This position statement by Petersen enabled Brigadier General John Magruder, who had been Donovan's deputy director of the OSS's Intelligence Service, to hold together its band of spies and saboteurs and bring those on duty in Washington and overseas—more or less intact—under the War Department's rubric. Those who followed Magruder in running the SSU— Generals William Wyman, William Quinn, and Don Galloway—although not of the OSS, were staunch believers in the worth and necessity of secret intelligence operations. Their beliefs, coupled with Secretary Petersen's support, was flashed to the field and, unlike the situation which resulted at State, provided sufficient encouragement to many of the young "lieutenants and captains" of Donovan's secret army to stay the course, or at least stick around long enough to consolidate the gains made by the wartime organizations and establish a postwar secret intelligence service. As such, many of this group came to dominate, or vie for real control of, the CIA throughout the Cold War period.

Fortier and Cullen's initial assessment also indicated that the OSS legatees were operating, essentially in Europe, under fairly effective control and that as long as their "self-starting" penchant did not produce flaps with General Eisenhower and his subordinate field commanders there was no immediate need to alter the arrangements which had been in effect since V-E Day. On the other hand, Colonel Fortier recognized the primary necessity to complete an inventory of the OSS assets, facilities, resources, and operations which SSU had inherited.

On the surface, the idea of such an inventory appears to be a simple, straightforward task; nonetheless, as various congressional investigations have shown in recent years, the problems in finding out what secret intelligence organizations have done and are actually doing on a current basis can indeed become quite complex. In this case, the complexity was made even greater because through the Donovan years projects, programs, and operations had been initiated by people in the field, by Donovan's informal approval (he often forgot to let his staff in Washington know what he had authorized), or as a spin-off from something requested by a military field commander. As a result, what SSU was actually doing, who was doing it, and who else was involved became one of Fortier's principal concerns.

Fortier knew that the broad authority contained in the January 22 directive was insufficient to get the keepers of the keys to the SSU secret intelligence operations to open their files and tell all. Therefore, in a series of bureaucratic masterstrokes, Fortier first prevailed upon the NIA to issue a further directive calling for a "broad survey of all existing government facilities for the collection of foreign intelligence information by clandestine methods." He followed this up by issuance, under Souers' signature, of CIG Top Secret Directive #3 on March 21, 1946, which indicated that the scope of the survey would include all clandestine methods for collecting foreign intelligence information, *except the intercept of electric communication.* * [Emphasis added]. Fortier knew that he had no chance at this time to open the communications intelligence can of worms, hence the exception. Nevertheless, the survey's objectives were important and did provide the basis for the CIG's subsequent movement toward taking over the clandestine services. The objectives were as follows:

(1) To secure sound descriptions of methods used now or during the war, including details of training, administration, finance, communication, control, and all other details required for complete understanding. (2) To produce uniform terminology. (3) To secure correct estimates of the productivity and efficiency of the various methods. (4) To appraise the availability of trained and qualified personnel. (5) To appraise the facilities of separate departments or permanent agencies for conducting various phases of clandestine operations, either separately or jointly. (6) To determine whether particular phases of clandestine operations may be performed more efficiently as central services. (7) To prepare recommendations for submission to the National Intelligence Authority.

Because such a survey was likely to succeed or fail based on the attitude of J. Edgar Hoover, the directive also stated that "In addition to the permanent members of the Intelligence Advisory Board, the director of the Federal

---

*Besides the kinds of security associated with communications intelligence, as indicated in the discussion about Pearl Harbor Fortier was aware of the separate compartments one had to transit in order to get to the heart, or rather brain, of America's communication intelligence organization and which neither he nor other members of the CIG were cleared for passage. This is not to say that the CIG's upper hierarchy was not cleared to receive and handle communications intelligence, but rather that they had not been given the metaphorical "cardinal's cap," presented to those who are authorized to enter the communication intelligence community's inner inner sanctum.

Bureau of Investigation is a member for the purposes of this survey" and "will appoint a representative to serve as an expert consultant with the Central Planning Staff for the purposes of this survey." By bringing Hoover into the CIG activities at the onset and at a level and manner which acknowledged his position and power in the foreign intelligence scheme, Fortier—perhaps by playing on Hoover's curiosity and/or ambitions—was able to head off the behind-the-scenes maneuvering Hoover had used in the past to sabotage similar efforts designed to evaluate the United States' clandestine intelligence programs.

With the FBI safely on board, Fortier moved quickly to prepare the additional analytical groundwork vis-à-vis other areas of intelligence activities which were perhaps suitable candidates for centralization under the CIG. For example, CIG Directive #4 of March 28 ordered a survey of "all facilities for covering the foreign language press in the United States in order to determine:

a. The adequacy of present methods and facilities and the information obtained therefrom.
b. The desirability of centralizing the effort on foreign language press coverage.
c. What agency of the government should be charged with this press coverage.

Other surveys and assessments were initiated in rapid order to enable the CIG to "perform, for the benefit of said intelligence agencies, such services of common concern as the NIA determines can be more efficiently accomplished centrally." These included the intelligence targets of China (CIG Directive #5m, March 29, 1946), index of United States residents with foreign intelligence information (CIG Directive #10, May 31, 1946), "Biographic Intelligence," (CIG Directive #16, May 28, 1946), and the USSR (CIG Directive #9, May 9, 1946). Each of these directives was a harbinger of things to come. In particular, after the USSR was targeted, the initial directive was amended to read:

6. (a) The classification of this project shall be TOP SECRET. The greatest care will be taken to maintain the security of the *existence* of the operation. [Emphasis added.]

Also, the reference to the USSR was made less conspicuous by retitling the project as the "Strategic Intelligence Digest."

Finally, CIG Directive #15 of October 1, 1946, had the unwieldy title: "Exploitation of American Business Concerns and Scientific, Educational and Religious Organizations with Connections Abroad and American Residents Traveling Abroad as Sources of Foreign Intelligence Information." It was issued in order to multiply the assets of the CIG. The resulting CIG organization which administered the program was called the "Domestic Contacts Service," and became the precursor organization of the CIA's program for domestic intelligence. The Domestic Contacts Service also reestablished ties with American business and industry, which were once again used to provide cover for American agents abroad and for the handling, transmission, and "laundering" of secret funds.

Throughout the existence of the CIG there was no doubt in Fortier's mind and those with a similar persuasion about secret intelligence operations that they were moving toward the establishment of an autonomous CIG, or Central Intelligence Agency. Though the progress was slow and unspectacular, the groundwork was laid with exceptional care. Each of those most intimately involved had taken to heart Donovan's mistakes in trying to move too fast and in making unnecessary enemies in the process. The visible members of the CIG's professional staff in Washington never appeared to be excessive in number.* Fortier avoided the trap of appearing to be a big organization by decentralizing day-to-day control over actual operation to CIG field offices in the United States and overseas. Also, because the "soft on communism" chorus was vocal and active, Fortier preempted their position by purging CIG's personnel of those who might become targets of such criticism. This was done by CIG Directive #8, of May 9, 1946, which required that personnel assigned to it be individuals:

a. of excellent character who are native-born citizens of the United States and who have no member of their immediate family or next of kin thereof subject to a foreign power;
b. whose loyalty, integrity, discretion and trustworthiness are unquestioned;
c. whose financial status and habits are such as to render unlikely their succumbing to any temptation arising from these sources.

There was some loss to the CIG from eliminating some first-generation Americans who had family contacts abroad, but the price was considered minimal in view of the fact that there was hard evidence in hand to indicate that the Soviets were playing a family-tie "squeeze game" with CIG and SSU personnel in the United States and overseas. Besides the investigatory clearance procedure, CIG Directive #8 also established that:

All military and civilian personnel assigned to or attached for duty with the Central Intelligence Group will be required to execute a declaration of secrecy which will be administered by the director of Central Intelligence or his authorized representative.

*For example, the CIG's executive organization in Washington included only 55 key positions, which were filled by senior field-grade officers detailed from the War Department. These were distributed as follows: Office of Collection and Dissemination, 6; Office of Security, 7; Office of Reports and Estimates, 20; Office of Operations, 3; Office of Special Operations, 10; Interdepartmental Coordinating and Planning Staff, 7; Executive Staff, 2. Overall, the total CIG organization numbered approximately 2,000 persons. Proportionately, approximately one-third were overseas with OSO (see below); of the remainder stationed in Washington, approximately one-half were involved in administrative and support functions, one-third were assigned to OSO, and the rest to intelligence production activities. In essence, the CIG was an extremely lean organization by normal bureaucratic standards, given the extent of its responsibilities and activities.

And, upon termination of duties with the Central Intelligence Group all military and civilian personnel will be given an exit interview designed to impress upon them their obligation with regard to maintaining the security of all matters pertaining to Central Intelligence Group activities and provision of the laws and statutes which apply.

Inclusion of this secrecy oath imparted a special "us and them" tone to the CIG's operation which was to carry over once the CIA was formed, and which was broadly construed by those in charge as the basis for keeping the organization's activities secret from Congress and other agencies of the government, especially the Justice Department.

By the end of March 1946, although the clandestine facilities survey ordered by CIG Directive #3 had not been fully completed, it was clear to Fortier that it was necessary to liquidate the SSU and begin to turn it into an autonomous operating entity under the direction of the CIG, instead of allowing it to operate as a two-step adjunct of the NIA, requiring both NIA and departmental concurrence for operations. Consequently, on April 3, in a memo to the director of the SSU, acting Secretary of War Howard C. Petersen directed:

Effective immediately, you are directed to continue the liquidation of the Strategic Services Unit (SSU) as ordered in paragraph 3 of the executive order dated 20 September 1945, subject: "Termination of the Office of Strategic Services and Disposition of Its Functions." The liquidation will be completed not later than 30 June 1947.

The liquidation of SSU will be coordinated with the development of the permanent peacetime intelligence program. You will carry out the liquidation in accordance with instructions of the director of Central Intelligence or his designated representative. The director or his representative will deal directly with you. He will have such staff as he requires working with SSU.

During the period of liquidation you will administer and operate the SSU so as to service within your capabilities, the intelligence agencies subject to coordination by the National Intelligence Authority in accordance with directives provided by the director of Central Intelligence or his designated representative. In addition, you will make available, within your capabilities, to the director of Central Intelligence, upon his request, *any facilities and services of SSU which may be useful in the performance of an authorized function of the Central Intelligence Group.* [Emphasis added.]

Previous War Department instructions relating to this problem are amended accordingly.

Petersen's memo was followed the next day, April 4, by one from the director of Central Intelligence to the director of the Strategic Services Unit, which stated:

Pursuant to the provisions of NIA Directive #4, dated 2 April 1946, it is hereby directed that you administer and operate the Strategic Services Unit, War Department, in accordance with the initial policies set forth herein:

1. *Operations*

    a. Until otherwise directed, you will continue such operations, services and liaisons considered absolutely essential to

    (1) United States armies abroad,

    (2) The United States sections of Allied Control Commissions,

    (3) Diplomatic missions,

    (4) Departmental agencies in the United States now being served.

    b. You will perform such collecting missions, distribution, and other intelligence services as may be ordered from time to time by my representative.

    c. Nothing contained in subparagraph 1-a will be considered as an authority for any expansion of the functions and facilities now operating, nor will additional personnel be assigned to duty outside the continental limits of the United States without the approval of my senior representative.

2. *Administration*

    a. You will continue the orderly liquidation of the Strategic Services Unit.

    b. You will furnish the administrative support to operations indicated in paragraph 1.

    c. You will furnish such administrative support to the Central Intelligence Group as may be called for by my representative.

    d. You will provide the necessary administrative facilities to effect the transition of personnel, funds, and communications, records, services and facilities, with the necessary means of maintenance, from SSU to an appropriate group in the War Department or to other appropriate agencies, as subsequently determined.

3. *Command Liaison*

    Colonel Louis J. Fortier, USA, assistant director and acting chief of Operational Services, CIG, is designated my senior representative. Further directives and orders will be issued to you by me or by my senior representative. You will keep my senior representative informed of the progress of the mission outlined herein. Captain Thomas F. Cullen, USNR, will be his deputy.

    Sidney W. Souers
Director

The result of these directives was that the SSU's duties, responsibilities, and personnel were transferred to the CIG, along with SSU's seven overseas field station and communications and logistical apparatus. Once the transfer was completed the DCI reconstituted assets in a new organization called the Office of Special Operations (OSO), which was given responsibility for secret intelligence and counterespionage operations. At about the same time, the Office of Reports and Estimates (ORE) was established. "ORE's functions were manifold—the production of national current intelligence, scientific, technical, and economic intelligence as well as interagency coordination for national estimates."* With these bureaucratic tours de force safely in hand, Fortier's restructuring of CIG was fairly well completed. OSO gave CIG an indepen-

---

*Foreign and Military Intelligence, Book I, "Final Report of the Select Committee to Study Governmental Operations with Respect to Intelligence Activities." United States Senate, 94th Congress, 2nd Session, Report No. 94–755, April 26, 1976, p. 102.

dent secret intelligence capability, ORE an analytical intelligence production capability, and DCS an outreach capability in America's civilian community to support both.

Thus in June 1946, when Souers was replaced as DCI by Lieutenant General Hoyt Vandenberg (the aggressive, ambitious nephew of Arthur Vandenberg, chairman of the Senate Foreign Relations Committee), the CIG existed as an intelligence instrument capable of producing intelligence on its own and carrying out clandestine intelligence operations and activities. Vandenberg, as the new man out front, was an ideal choice. He exuded sincerity of purpose and was extremely adroit in fending off any prying congressional eyes which might have been interested in looking into how the CIG had implemented Truman's charge to the DCI to "protect intelligence sources and methods."

In commenting on the maneuverings which produced the CIG's organizational outcome in 1946, Fortier noted that success was based on two factors. One, moves were made quietly and in a manner which didn't directly threaten the military intelligence status quo; and two, that in the emerging debate concerning unification of the military services under the Department of Defense and the establishment of an independent air force, the question of a separate central intelligence agency did not attract much attention. However, organizational integrity and General Vandenberg's personality aside, the question about the subsequent actions and effectiveness of the CIG and especially of OSO is most compelling.

Although the military hierarchy was diverted from paying close attention to the CIG by their involvement in the unification debate, there were others in the intelligence community, especially J. Edgar Hoover, who realized the real significance of the CIG/OSO's secret intelligence capability. OSO's capability and apparent freedom of action represented a real threat to Hoover's secret intelligence operations in the Western Hemisphere. Hoover's estimate of the situation reflected his almost uncanny sense of bureaucratic reality and remarkably prescient grasp of the future evolution of the secret intelligence function in the United States.

In the first instance, Hoover was prepared to coexist with OSO if his suzerain over secret intelligence in the Western Hemisphere were permitted to continue. From his own sources he knew that he would face a challenge from Vandenberg, and while it might be possible to beat back such a challenge the cost would probably be prohibitive. Secondly, Hoover reasoned that since Truman issued the January 22 directive, the FBI's acquisition of worldwide secret intelligence responsibility, as embodied in the Hoover/Clark plan, was a dead issue. Thirdly, as he and his personal assistants had observed during their participation in the CIG surveys and in the deliberations of the Intelligence Advisory Board, there was a leadership void at the operational level within the SSU and OSO. Each of these conclusions formed the basis of Hoover's subsequent strategy, which was designed to keep him in a key position to influence America's secret intelligence activities and operations.

As Hoover correctly surmised, soon after Vandenberg took over as DCI he began to cast covetous eyes on the Western Hemisphere, where his OSO would probably be able to operate without the constraints imposed by military commanders in what had been the European theater of operations. Hoover remonstrated against extending the OSO charter for operations to include the Western Hemisphere; however, he did so in a manner designed as much to encourage Vandenberg as to oppose him. It was a sophisticated game of bureaucratic cat and mouse in which Vandenberg, the cat, was left unsure as to whether Hoover, the mouse, wanted to be eaten or was simply maneuvering to gain some unspecified advantage. While this drama was being played out on a more or less visible bureaucratic level, another was underway which, unknown to Vandenberg, would effectively negate his expected victory. This subsurface game involved Hoover's penetration of OSO by key FBI agents who had been part of his secret intelligence apparatus in the United States and the Western Hemisphere. Before describing this proceudre, it is also necessary to take note of the fact that Hoover was well aware of Vandenberg's future ambition (to become chief of staff of the air force) and that his tenure as DCI was likely to be brief; in fact, Vandenberg actually served in the DCI post only from June 1946 to May 1947.

Hoover's plan to penetrate the OSO, both in concept and execution, was brilliant enough to qualify as a classic example of how a counterespionage operation—one designed to manipulate another intelligence service—should be run. Hoover was personally convinced that the momentum toward creation of a separate central intelligence agency was strong enough that it would occur sometime during the next two years. He saw the CIG as a first and irreversible step in that process, especially in view of the careful preparations carried out by Fortier. He further reasoned that whatever subsequent evolutions occurred, the resultant separate organization would be derived from and include the principal elements of the CIG.

Based on Hoover's estimate of the secret intelligence situation, he acted to place FBI agents with extensive experience in this area of intelligence within the OSO. The task was made easier than one might suppose because during the SSU period and following the establishment of OSO a number of feuds and personality clashes had ensued which had resulted in the loss of some of the most able leaders available to those organizations. The feuds were multifaceted: there was a conflict between former OSS personnel and the West Pointers over how and by whom OSO should be run; there was conflict between former OSS personnel who had been involved in X-2, secret intelligence (counterespionage) and those involved in secret operations (sabotage). This latter conflict was much more fundamental to Hoover's purpose because it enabled him to unite the opposition of OSS secret intelligence personnel and the West Pointers against the OSS personnel whose stock in trade were the dirty tricks of sabotage and guerrilla operations rather than the acquisition of intelligence. One should remember that at this time (mid-1946) covert operations per se had not received a presidential or national policy imprimatur, whereas clandestine secret intelligence and counterespionage operations had routinely been authorized following the creation of the SSU in October 1945. Because each of the warring factions could not agree over how the OSO should proceed and who should direct or mediate the varying viewpoints in carrying out its missions, there was an opportunity for Hoover's men to serve as peacemakers and, in so doing, to pick up much of the power which fell from the factional conflicts.

To carry out his plan, Hoover carefully identified and selected a few key persons from among the cadre of agents he had personally recruited and trained prior to World War II and who had demonstrated remarkable skill in both operating and managing secret intelligence activities in the Western Hemisphere during the war. Some of these agents were fully "witting"—i.e., they were informed either directly or indirectly about Hoover's grand design. However, most were only partially witting in that their departure from the FBI was made to appear as an act of self-sacrifice on Hoover's part, his willingness not to stand in their way to go onward and upward in the secret intelligence field. It is not altogether clear from exit interviews Hoover had with some of these agents whether their shifting from the FBI to the OSO was intended to be permanent, or what the subsequent relationships between themselves and Hoover were to include. Nonetheless, the shifts did occur and were facilitated by the West Pointers who were looking for ways to get out of the CIG and back to duty with the army, but who were unwilling to leave the direction of OSO to the former OSS personnel.

The list of this first wave of emigrés from the FBI to America's fledgling central intelligence service was not long. There were perhaps at most twenty-five who made the shift and went on to bigger things in OSO and later in the CIA. They also prepared the way for the expanded wave of additional emigrés. Men like William H. Doyle, Robert N. Dahlgren, William King Harvey, S. Herman Horton, Raford W. Herbert, Harry G. Jacobsen, Raymond G. Leddy, Alfred A. Pease, Winston MacKinlay Scott, Horton R. Telford, William M. Wheeler, David E. Wright and others were among the first wave. Few of these names have become household words; however, each became a leading player in America's postwar intelligence community. Their contributions will be described in later chapters; in connection with the shift from the FBI to OSO, two in particular stand out as the kind of professionals who were involved. One was Winston MacKinlay Scott, who as a renowned theoretical mathematician was an unlikely secret agent, but who ended up in Mexico City and ran the CIA's Western Hemisphere clandestine services field operations for fourteen years. The other, William King Harvey, went on to head the CIA's clandestine services in its early years and later served as chief of station in Berlin and Rome during the hottest periods of the Cold War.

Harvey's shift from the FBI to OSO bears special mention. As one of Hoover's best counterespionage agents, he had a bright future ahead of him in the FBI. His wartime exploits were numerous; he was best remembered by Hoover because of his skill in capturing Nazi spy William Sebold and turning him into an effective double agent.* And Harvey had a personal penchant for the anonymity which Hoover demanded from those who worked closely with him. At the time of Harvey's shift, the OSO top job was very much up in the air. The conflicts and the lack of anyone with clear stature in the intelligence community provided Harvey with an opportunity to take over the OSO leadership, but to do so he needed to gain some allies (in addition to Hoover) and to get rid of some internal competition. His first and perhaps best ally was James J. Angleton, Jr., who at the time was the keeper of the X-2 flame which had been lighted in England several years earlier by James Murphy, Norman Holmes Pearson (who recruited Angleton to X-2), Ed Lawlor, and John Waldron. Murphy describes Angleton best by saying, "He was a natural for counterespionage. In the early days he steeped himself in its intricacies, mastering the use of counterespionage files, and while in England slept on a cot in the office in order not to waste time coming and going from his billet."

With Harvey in his corner, Angleton moved up to take over the counterespionage responsibility from Colonel Richard Hawes, and in the course of this perturbation acquired the further responsibility for liaison with the FBI on matters dealing with what would later become the Israeli intelligence service. The result of this personnel shuffling—and others, like the "retirement" to Beirut University of Steve Penrose, who had come to the SSU along with General Magruder and Whitney Shepardson—gave Harvey the opportunity to constitute OSO along the lines originally established by Donovan and Murphy when they put together the OSS's secret intelligence and counterespionage apparatus. That is, he split secret intelligence away from counterespionage and reinstituted the authority of the latter group in vetting secret intelligence sources before they were put on the payroll.

While this subsurface reordering of the OSO and its direction was underway, the unification debate was waxing in the administration and in Congress. Throughout this period (mid-1946 to mid-1947), there seemed to be tacit acceptance on the part of Truman and his principal advisors that once the unification bill was passed a new central intelligence agency would take the place of the CIG and its subordinate elements. For example, according to Truman's naval aid, Clark Clifford, "An intelligence agency was the tail of the establishment of CIA. The entire defense establishment spent 1946 and part

---

*This involved the FBI's discovery that the Nazis were operating a radio station set up by Carlos Retelsdorf (GBO in Coatepec, Vera Cruz state) at the end of 1940 which was sending its messages to an *Abwehr* station on Long Island, New York for relay to Germany by William Sebold (code name: "Tramp"). Through Harvey's efforts, Sebold was turned into a double agent who transmitted false information. When the FBI collapsed the *Abwehr* network in New York City on June 30, 1941, GBO could no longer function effectively. During this operation Harvey played Sebold liked a master, getting him not only to convey false information, but to seek out and acquire information which enabled the FBI to identify the *Abwehr*'s sources, contacts, and membership. (See Faragos, *op. cit.*, pp. 580–583.)

of 1947 arguing about the National Security Act. How should we merge the army and the navy and establish the air force and what should be the powers of the secretary of defense, and what should be the mission and the authority of each service? That was the dog. Nobody paid much attention to the intelligence part of the bill."*

During the unification debate some subrosa consideration was given to the idea of providing the about-to-be-established CIA authority for covert and unvouchered funds, but this idea was placed on hold until the other implications of the unification plan had been digested and implemented. A few diehards in Congress like Clare Hoffman of Michigan wanted to prevent the new intelligence agency from "the collection of intelligence"; this was made to appear ridiculous, and Hoffman's proposed amendment was soundly defeated.

On July 26, 1947, after two years of debate and discussions, the National Security Act of 1947 was passed. The act established an independent air force, provided for coordination by a committee of service chiefs, the Joint Chiefs of Staff, and a secretary of defense, and created the National Security Council (NSC). The CIG became an independent department and was renamed the Central Intelligence Agency. The act provided the CIA with statutory authority for its activities. Section 102(d) of the act lists the following "powers and duties" of the CIA:

(1) to advise the National Security Council in matters concerning such intelligence activities of the government departments and agencies as relate to national security;

(2) to make recommendations to the National Security Council for the coordination of such intelligence activities of the departments and agencies of the government as relate to the national security;

(3) to correlate and evaluate intelligence relating to the national security, and provide for the appropriate dissemination of such intelligence within the government, using where appropriate existing agencies and facilities: Provided, that the Agency shall have no police, subpena, law-enforcement powers, or internal security functions: Provided further, that the departments and other agencies of the government shall continue to collect, evaluate, correlate, and disseminate departmental intelligence: And provided further, that the director of Central Intelligence shall be responsible for protecting intelligence sources and methods from unauthorized disclosure;

(4) to perform, for the benefit of the existing intelligence agencies such additional services of common concern as the National Security Council determines can be more efficiently accomplished centrally;

(5) to perform such other functions and duties related to intelligence affecting the national security as the National Security Council may from time to time direct.**

Careful reading of these powers and duties shows that aside from making the CIA responsible to the direction of the new National Security Council,

*Braden, op. cit., pp. 11–12.

**Title 50 U.S. Code 403(d).

they were almost identical to those used by Truman in the January 22 directive to the secretaries of state, war, and navy. Also, the act did not change the functions previously assigned to CIG. The CIG had been given responsibility and authority for clandestine collection, overt collection, production of national current intelligence, and interagency coordination for national estimates. These functions were continued under the new statutory authority, and the CIG's personnel and internal structure were carried over into the newly designated Central Intelligence Agency.

Thus in the space of slightly more than two years, President Truman presided over a major change in America's intelligence community, which endorsed and provided legal authority for the centralization of intelligence. How the resulting CIA served Truman, how it was used by him, and how centralization of intelligence was easier said and legislated than done, is described in the following chapter.

CHAPTER 6

TRUMAN AND THE INTELLIGENCE COMMUNITY: PART II

With passage of the National Security Act of 1947, the years of pulling and hauling between those in the national security and intelligence hierarchies was ended for a while as the principals tried to digest what had been authorized. For those in the newly designated Central Intelligence Agency (CIA), the change in name from the Central Intelligence Group made little difference in actual operation. Under Rear Admiral Roscoe H. Hillenkoetter, who relieved Vandenberg as the director of Central Intelligence (DCI) in May 1947 and who assumed that the National Intelligence Authority's orders and authorizations still applied, the CIA continued with clandestine collection, secret intelligence operations, and some rather low-key covert activities (which avoided a direct American role in their control), and production of current intelligence, thus retaining the lead in the interagency intelligence coordination task. Internally, the new CIA's organizational structure was identical to the CIG's. In fact, the first CIA organization wire diagrams, issued in August 1947, merely inked out the earlier CIG designation, replacing it with "CIA," and replaced references to the National Intelligence Authority ("NIA") with the words "National Security Council" ("NSC").

As initially established in 1947, the National Security Council was an independent agency with a membership including the president, the secretaries of state, defense, army, air force, navy, and the chairman of the (now defunct) National Security Resources Board, with the option that the president might also include the heads of two other special defense units. Two years later the membership of the National Security Council, over Truman's objections, was overhauled by Congress (63 Stat. 579) to include the president, the vice-president, the secretaries of state and defense, the chairman of the National Security Resources Board, and certain other defense officials whom the president might specify as members, subject to Senate confirmation. Also, in accordance with Reorganization Plan No. 4 of 1949 (63 Stat. 1067), the council was formally located within the executive office of the president. As such, the NSC became more or less the conduit through which intelligence was passed by the DCI to the president. In general, this procedure was roughly the same as the CIG's.

The only real area of change involved personnel and the methods by which the CIA was to become permanently staffed. In the first six to twelve months of the CIA's existence this change was more real than apparent. Because this paradox is often overlooked in explaining the what, how, and why of CIA operations in its first two decades, it is important to look at the manner in which individuals were brought into the new agency on a permanent basis. The CIG and its subordinate elements had been staffed by detailees from the military services and various departments and agencies, many of whom had come to the War Department at the time the OSS was disbanded and SSU was founded. Also, during the CIG/SSU era others from the FBI and temporary wartime organizations were picked up by the War Department for duty with those groups. At the CIA's onset these persons remained in place, thereby creating the impression that the personnel in the new CIA was the same as in the CIG. To this extent there was no outward change in the CIA's personnel and personnel practices; however, with passage of the National Security Act, the director of the CIA, who also held the title DCI, was authorized "to directly employ" individuals, rather than rely solely on detailees to staff the new agency. Also, the CIG's budget for fiscal year 1947, which had been negotiated by DCI Vandenberg at approximately $47 million, was augmented by $23 million to pay the personnel costs associated with establishing permanent positions in the CIA.

All this was quite consistent with the government's past procedure in turning a temporary organization into a permanent one, with its own budget and personnel. To get CIA employees, Admiral Hillenkoetter, as director of the CIA, made use of the bureaucratic device known as lateral transfer. This enables an employee of a department or agency to transfer to another, generally with no loss in grade or rank if the job description and/or responsibilities in the former are considered to be equal. To be sure, in today's bureaucracy "agency hopping" from, say, Commerce to Labor does occur, oftentimes to gain an increased civil service grade; but these shifts are individually negotiated and are not part of an officially encouraged, ongoing effort to redistribute talent from one department to another.

Consistent with the idea of lateral transfer, Hillenkoetter's first call to potential transferees went to those already on duty with the CIA. As detailees from the military services and various departments and agencies, they were already in jobs supposedly commensurate with their rank; they therefore met the qualification criteria connected with lateral transfer and presumably their change in status could be affected quickly and easily. But there was much, much more involved than simply processing a batch of papers through the bureaucracy's personnel process.

What was involved was the future control and effective day-to-day direction of the CIA. J. Edgar Hoover had anticipated this eventuality and had acted to salt the CIG with key individuals from his personal stable of counterespionage specialists and Latin American experts. The military intelligence services' leaders had not been nearly as farsighted as Hoover, and in many cases their detailees were less than fully competent and had been assigned to the CIG more on the basis of their military rank than on relevant intelligence experience. This was based on two considerations: the military services, faced with shrinking force levels in the postwar period, used duty with interagency groups or joint organizations like the CIG to hold onto positions outside the military services per se which called for individuals of high rank; and by filling these slots in the CIG—essentially division or regional chiefs, with officers in the grade of colonel or navy captain—the military intelligence services maintained effective control over the CIG, rather than allowing it to pass to those who had previously served with OSS.

By mid-1947, the military's dominance of the CIA was fairly complete. The ex-FBI personnel had settled into various deputy positions, and because their ideological bent and outlook on procedures and practices was consistent with those of their military colleagues and superiors, there was considerable harmony at the top. At this time, most of the simulated colonels from the OSS had long since abandoned the national intelligence scene and had returned to the law practices, businesses, and universities from which they had been recruited by Donovan, Langer, et al. To be sure, some former OSS personnel were taken into the new organization, but most of them lacked the rank to be serious contenders for the top jobs. Lateral transfer, which allowed individuals to convert their wartime military ranks to equivalent civil service grades, gave the CIA's initial leadership a military outlook and later served as the basis of the agency's internal controversy between secret intelligence and covert operations.

Hillenkoetter's selective use of lateral transfer in the CIA's first year of operation resulted in the "civilianizing" of slightly more than half of its professional staff (the remainder of whom continued to be provided via the detailee process) and, with the exception of some military communications technicians and other specialists who were detailees, all of the technical, support, clerical, and administrative positions. For many of the former colonels and captains, lateral transfer was a boon, because by mid-1947 almost all were facing reversion from their inflated wartime ranks back to ones consistent with the military's postwar force levels and austere command structures.

With the ex-officers and FBI watchbirds safely in control, the CIA got on with the problems of national intelligence. In 1947 these were perceived as countering the Soviet Union's worldwide clandestine espionage and subversive activities. To be sure, the necessary routine intelligence information collection, analysis, and dissemination function received continuing attention, but underlying this task were the covert activities of the Soviets which threatened American foreign policy objectives in almost every area of the world.

Although the problems posed by Soviet covert activities were basically acknowledged by most intelligence personnel, there was a general lack of consensus in the intelligence community over how these problems should be solved. On the one hand, those who were of the secret intelligence, counterintelligence, counterespionage persuasion believed the name of the game to be defense. That is, by making use of intelligence derived from secret intelligence sources and manipulating foreign intelligence services (a counterespionage function), it would be feasible to pursue an active counterintelligence defense against the Soviets' subversive activities. This approach left something of a void in dealing with Soviet covert operations, but those who favored it believed that covert operations were best countered by exposure rather than confrontation. On the other hand, in simplified terms, those of the secret operations persuasion believed in fighting "fire with fire"; that is, if the Soviets were operating a front organization the United States should establish one of its own in competition, and so on. Subsumed in these two rather antithetical views was the American wartime disagreement over the role, purpose, and extent of psychological warfare, as well as the exceedingly more complicated postwar question of where and how, if at all, secret operations (espionage and sabotage) should be carried out. Although the Cold War had been announced, it was undeclared; consequently, there were doubts and misgivings about how far secret operations should extend. There were those who advocated stirring up unrest in the Soviet Union and the Eastern European satellite nations, but few volunteers to actually carry out such a task.

In the argument about American covert activities, it was never certain whether the Soviets intended and/or were willing to back their espionage and subversive activities with overt military force. For every offensive-oriented estimate there was another which either denigrated the Soviets' military strength, or explained their KGB's covert activities as primarily defensive. Similarly, for every analysis of the "world domination by communism" thesis there was enough disagreement over how and by what means the Soviets planned to bring this off to make the choice between secret intelligence and secret operations exceptionally difficult. In spite of these differences of opinion, there was broad agreement both in and out of the intelligence community that the threats posed by the Soviets' covert activities were quite real.

As intelligence reports proclaiming Soviet espionage and subversive successes intensified, pressure mounted to increase American covert operations and activities in those areas outside Eastern Europe which were immediately threatened. The idea was to "contain" Soviet influence while surrounding the USSR with viable Western-oriented governments.

In consequence of these tentative premises and untested conclusions about the long-range effects of Soviet covert activities, on December 9, 1947, at the National Security Council's first meeting, at the joint suggestion of Secretaries Marshall (State), Forrestal (Defense), Patterson (War) and with the encouragement of George Kennan, director of the State Department's Policy Planning Staff (and the man who conceived the theory of containment), Truman approved issuance of NSC-4, entitled "Coordination of Foreign Intelligence Information Measures":

This directive empowered the secretary of state to coordinate overseas information activities designed to counter communism. A top secret annex to NSC-4—NSC-4A— instructed the director of Central Intelligence to undertake covert psychological activities in pursuit of the aims set forth in NSC-4. The initial authority given the CIA for covert operations under NSC-4A did not establish formal procedures for either coordinating or approving these operations. It simply directed the DCI to undertake covert actions and to ensure, through liaison with State and Defense, that the resulting operations were consistent with American policy.*

Issuance of NSC-4 and NSC-4A apparently decided the covert activities question; however, in the period immediately following, Hillenkoetter dragged his heels, preferring to initiate additional covert actions on a carefully planned basis which took account of their inherent difficulties and potential damage to the CIA's secret intelligence activities. Although Hillenkoetter's go-slow approach made eminently good sense, he was pressured to speed up and expand the scope of the psychological warfare activities previously authorized for the CIG and supposedly reaffirmed by the issuance of NSC-4 and NSC-4A. Most of these were media-related, including the use of false publications, "black" radio broadcasts, and subsidies to publications.

As part of this pressure, on or about January 6, 1948, Secretary of Defense James Forrestal asked Hillenkoetter the "why not" question, "Could the CIA spend money to help defeat the Italian Communist Party (PCI) candidates in the upcoming parliamentary elections?" Forrestal prefaced his question by citing the summary of a CIA report forecasting a PCI victory. Unfortunately, the summary seen by Forrestal left out the assumptions on which the forecast was based; but because a communist victory at the Italian polls was possible, Forrestal was persuaded that it was necessary for the United States to prevent such an outcome. On this latter point Forrestal was not alone: both Marshall and Kennan shared his trepidation, but no one was exactly sure how the PCI victory could be forestalled and who should do it. Upon their and others' examination, the CIA's covert media activities in Italy were admittedly less than effective in this kind of a short-term situation.

In response, Hillekoetter promised Forrestal he would look into the matter, raising the caveat that he wasn't sure that he had authority under the National Security Act or NSC-4 and NSC-4A to spend money directly (though covertly) in order to defeat the PCI candidates. There was no question in Hillenkoetter's mind that he had authority to continue with the CIA's media propaganda activities; but direct covert action, especially that which constituted interference with a friendly power's internal affairs, was a different matter. Based on Hillenkoetter's personal experience in Germany before World War II, he knew that covert operations of this type, while potentially desirable, were extremely

---

*Foreign and Military Intelligence, Book I, "Final Report of the Select Committee to Study Governmental Operations with Respect to Intelligence Activities." United States Senate, 94th Congress, 2nd Session, Report No. 94–755, April 26, 1976, p. 49.

dangerous—particularly if they went awry. Rather than go ahead on his personally assumed authority as DCI, he asked the CIA's general counsel, Lawrence Houston, whether the National Security Act in fact conferred upon him the authority to spend money directly to obtain an American-favored outcome in the Italian elections.

Houston told Hillenkoetter he doubted the new agency had that authority. Then he went back to his office, got out the legislation, and reread it. There it was: "such other functions and duties. . . ." He thought about it, and decided that it did not constitute congressional authorization to spend money to influence an election in a foreign country. He informed Hillenkoetter that this was his opinion.*

In spite of Houston's legal opinion, Forrestal remained unconvinced that the necessary authority was lacking. Hillenkoetter was unsure, preferring a direct order from Truman before carrying out any action. Such was not to be the case, however; Truman endorsed the idea that if the National Security Council affirmed its own authority in this matter he was inclined to go along with its decision. Truman's tacit acceptance of this presidential delegation of authority to the National Security Council was strangely based. Leaving aside the president's Constitutional responsibilities and authorities in the field of foreign affairs, it was extremely dubious that any of these responsibilities or authorities were delegable to the National Security Council and hence assignable by that body to the CIA.

Under the National Security Act of 1947, which Houston reviewed, it was the CIA's duty "to perform such other functions and duties related to intelligence affecting the national security as the National Security Council may from time to time direct." In the Italian election decision, as in those which followed, the authority of the National Security Council is the key factor— not the president's. Hillenkoetter was sensitive to this distinction, recognizing that as a government official subject to the Senate's "advice and consent" powers he would have difficulty justifying actions taken by him or the CIA in response to orders from the NSC, regardless of the fact that the president was a member of that organization. Hillenkoetter was well aware of the legal and personal hazards of actions taken by intelligence personnel in the president's name rather than under his personal direct order.

Also, although the National Security Act had not been law very long, Hillenkoetter, who had been DCI at the tag end of the CIG and had struggled to keep peace between the National Intelligence Authority, CIG, and the other members of the intelligence community, knew that the National Security Council was not an action agency. Its primary function was:

To *advise* the president with respect to the integration of domestic, foreign, and military policies relating to the national security so as to enable the military services

*Braden, *op. cit.,* p. 13.

and the other departments and agencies of the government to cooperate more effectively in matters involving the national security. [Emphasis added.]*

The NSC was also given certain "additional functions," none of which gave it any more operational responsibility than its primary function. These additional functions were:

(a) to perform such other functions as the president may direct, for the purpose of more effectively *coordinating* the policies and functions of the departments and agencies of the government relating to the national security.**

(b) *to assess and appraise* the objectives, commitments and risks of the United States in relation to our actual and potential military power, in the interest of national security, for the purpose of making recommendations to the president in connection therewith.***

(c) to *consider* policies on matters of common interest to the departments and agencies of the government concerned with the national security, and to make *recommendations* to the President in connection therewith.****

(d) *to make such recommendations, and such other reports* to the president as it deems appropriate or as the president may require.[Emphasis added.]*****

From the foregoing, Hillenkoetter didn't need Lawrence Houston to tell him that nothing in the National Security Act gave the NSC power to order the CIA to conduct political operations, because it had no such power to delegate. In spite of these legal impediments, Forrestal, with Truman's tacit acquiescence, prevailed on Hillenkoetter to accept the NSC's direction as the president's own and use it as justification to order the CIA to intervene in the Italian election. In a typical response, Hillenkoetter groused to his key subordinates, especially Major General William Wyman, the director of the CIA's OSO, about the Italian election "problem" in a manner which suggested that some action was being considered at the "highest levels." As a consequence, most assumed that NSC-4A provided the CIA with authority to intervene in the Italian election, or otherwise to attempt to influence its outcome, and that a high-level sign-off for the operation—although not strictly needed—would soon be forthcoming. Reinforcing this selective misperception about NSC-4A's authority was the negative fact, known by key CIA personnel, that the NSC never met as a group to consider whether or not to intervene in the Italian election. Hence the authority or lack thereof for such an operation raised no significant questions.

*50 USC para. 402(a).

**50 USC para. 402(b).

***50 USC para 492 (b) (1).

****50 USC para 402 (b) (2).

*****50 USC para 502 (d).

Compounding this confusion in the CIA operators' minds was Hillenkoetter's nattering nature; he was slow to anger and slower to make up his mind or be unequivocal in his declarations on even mundane matters. For example, Hillenkoetter often became a bottleneck in the flow of intelligence paper from the CIA to the NSC, spending hours and sometimes days poring over lists of subversives furnished to him by the CIA's office of security and J. Edgar Hoover.

However, once the presumptive command decision to intervene in the Italian election had been announced by Hillenkoetter, those who were required to busy themselves with preparing contingency plans for the operation concluded from the admiral's remarks that Truman had given the green light to the operation. In spite of the assumed presidential order, the decision itself became a matter of considerable debate within the CIA. The secret intelligence members wanted no part of the action, preferring to keep their sources (the "agents in place") far from possible discovery if the operation should fail. No one was exactly sure how to proceed; however, when apprised of the mission statement—"to intervene in the Italian parliamentary elections in order to prevent the Italian Communist Party from gaining a role in the Italian government"—the CIA's station chief in Rome cabled Hillenkoetter that the key to success was money: at least $10 million. Without any further question this amount became the benchmark figure for all subsequent planning.

Briefly, the operation plan had two main facets. The first, based on the CIA's analysis of the strengths and weaknesses of the Christian Democratic Party and those of its PCI opponents, provided funds to pay for local campaigns, "walking around" money to get out the vote, some under-the-counter "bonuses" to voting officials, publication of anonymous pamphlets which defamed PCI candidates' sex and personal lives, as well as smearing them with the Fascist and/or anti-Church brush. In short, the operational plan involved a form of American "technology transfer" in which the corrupt political techniques perfected over the years by the Boss Tweeds were transplanted to Italy from the United States.

The intelligence on which the field operation plan was based proved to be excellent. The targeting of seats sufficient to give control of the government to the Christian Democrats, rather than going for a complete sweep, was successful in all but two of the two hundred plus seats selected. As a result, on April 18, 1948, the Christian Democrats won 307 of 574 seats, thereby effectively preventing the PCI from gaining any role in the Italian government. The targeting method also reflected the harsh realities and necessary selectivity required in buying a politician and rigging an election's outcome. Many of the Christian Democratic candidates welcomed money from any source and support which disparaged their opponents; others proved to be personally venal, and were just interested in being elected; and still others required subtle persuasion and in some cases coercion to go along with the program. One laconic remark in the CIA's "after action" assessment of the Italian election operation underscores the symbiotic effect on both sides in carrying out these kinds of activities: "Although the operation was quite successful, whether we like it or not now we're intimately involved in Italian politics and the next time the price tag will be considerably higher."

The operation's other thread involved getting the money and laundering it through appropriate conduits for transmission and subsequent distribution by CIA-controlled assets in Italy. At first, the money posed a bit of a problem; although the CIA did have some confidential funds, these were inadequate to finance the entire operation. In order to maintain "plausible denial" and avoid the danger of letting the Bureau of the Budget know about the operation if the president's confidential funds were used, it was considered necessary to get the money from another source. Later, this kind of situation would be handled by burying covert action funds in the CIA's budget; but in 1948, the problem was essentially one of getting the money in a hurry and keeping the need-to-know circle about the operation to an absolute minimum. The source finally selected was the Economic Stablization Fund, a War Powers Act creation which had been established partly out of confiscated Axis assets as an antiinflation tool designed to ameliorate swings in the value of American and other currencies. As such, the Economic Stablization Fund was operated and controlled under the discretionary authority of the secretary of treasury, who could spend its funds without reporting the details of those transactions to Congress. The choice of the Economic Stablization Fund was an inspired one because the world of international finance, especially that part which moves currencies from one country to another, is even more secretive than the intelligence community. John W. Snyder, then secretary of the treasury, was discreetly approached by Forrestal and Hillenkoetter. The secrecy of the entire operation was impressed on Snyder, an avowed Truman loyalist, who in addition to coming up with the money had to provide IRS support to prevent blowing the method by which the funds were laundered and thence transferred to the CIA's covert assets in Italy.

The method employed was basically as follows: $10 million *in cash* was withdrawn from the Economic Stablization Fund, after which it was laundered through individual bank accounts whose owners in turn "donated" the funds to a variety of front organizations which either bought Italian lira or transmitted the funds directly to the CIA's secret assets and front organizations in Italy. To cover these transactions the individuals involved were advised to place a three-letter/number code on their income tax forms alongside their claimed "charitable deduction," and to keep the amount out of their income-tax liability calculations. This apparently convoluted procedure had several justifications: it enabled the individuals who agreed to assist the CIA to do so without violating United States tax laws, and it gave the CIA (with the IRS's assistance) an internal audit procedure to provide a check on the flow and amount of money as it passed from the CIA and individuals to the front organizations and the CIA's assets in Italy. And by using many individuals to make contributions to a variety of front organizations, any connection with the CIA and, presumably, the United States government was blurred. In view of the fact that committees for one purpose or another appear and disappear in the United States like wild flowers, it was believed that the Soviets (or anyone else) would not be able to unravel their origin.

A footnote to the Italian election operation justifies the elaborate precautions which were taken in the United States and Italy. In the course of other secret intelligence operations being carried out in Italy and elsewhere in Europe, the CIA learned that Soviet intelligence leaders in Moscow disbelieved reports from their field intelligence personnel about the flow of funds into the election. This information showed, among other things, that the Soviet intelligence leadership distrusted its agents' reports, partly out of a belief that they had become "contaminated" by too close an association with the PCI; it was felt that their reports of large amounts of secret funds being channelled to Christian Democratic candidates was simply a ploy to get more rubles from Moscow for the same purpose on behalf of PCI candidates.

The response of the Soviet intelligence hierarchy was almost classic. A senior official was sent from Moscow to check out the "outrageous" claims. He returned to Moscow erroneously convinced of two things: that the amount of secret funds available to Christian Democrats was greater than $10 million, and that the source was the Vatican rather than the United States. The result of the Soviet official's misinformation or misinterpretation was, according to secret intelligence sources, that the Soviet intelligence leaders concluded they were too far behind in the spending race to catch up and that their resources for such a purpose were inadequate to compete with the Vatican's. At the time, the Soviets were spending approximately $200 million worldwide on clandestine covert activities, and in Stalin's Kremlin those who made a pitch for "supplemental appropriations" did so at the risk of spending an extended vacation in the Gulag archipelago.

Another feature of the Italian election operation deserves careful consideration because, almost by default, it established a precedent which since 1948 has plagued the CIA in its relationship with the State Department. The actual operations in Italy were carried out neatly, efficiently, and with dispatch, thereby providing a "success." Covert secret assets were recruited, used and provided no evidence of linkage to either the CIA or the United States embassy in Italy. This latter fact was due to the extreme professionalism of the CIA's station chief in Rome who, although carried on the embassy's roles, maintained an extremely low personal profile; he appeared to be no more than an analyst, hardly the person actually responsible for the CIA's operational activities. His judgment in this respect was as much based on the need for secrecy and nonattribution of the United States in covert operations as it was on the fact that American secret intelligence sources had warned him about a Soviet penetration in the United States embassy. In consequence, the station chief did not inform the United States ambassador, James Dunn, about the operation nor of its increasing prospects for success in the period prior to April 18, 1948. In fact, partially as a deception plan and partially as a hedge concerning the election's outcome, the Rome CIA station, in conjunction with the embassy's political section, produced a series of reports and analyses suggesting the possibility of a PCI success. Ironically, these reports were embodied—with no mention of the covert operation underway—in an NSC document provided to the NSC's members on March 8, 1948, entitled: "Position of the United States with Respect to Italy in the Light of the Possibility of Communist Participation in the Government by Legal Means."

Prior to this document's issuance, the flow of alarming intelligence about the PCI's possible success stimulated a substantial amount of overt activity in the United States exhorting the Italian people to reject the communists. Much of this effort was orchestrated by Francis Cardinal Spellman, who called upon Italian-Americans to write to their friends and families in Italy, urging them to defeat the PCI. Other organizations, such as the American Sympathizers for a Free Italy, picked up on Spellman's letter-writing appeal. Special radio broadcasts were beamed to Italy, echoing the theme "war can be avoided if the free peoples of the world will keep strong their democratic institutions by resisting all the sinister forces of intimidation which seek to destroy them from within." Similarly, on March 17, Truman made a speech in New York City denouncing the Italian communists. This speech constituted a bit of overkill, but it served to further the Soviet impression that the United States was talking rather than taking direct covert action with respect to the elections.

Although the reasons for deciding that Ambassador Dunn, in spite of his extensive experience in intelligence matters, did not have a need to know about the covert intervention in the Italian election were probably valid at the time, the decision established a damaging precedent, especially since the operation turned out to be successful. Consequently, those in the CIA who were buoyed by the Italian operation's results concluded that as a matter of routine the less the ambassador—any ambassador—knew about the CIA's covert activities, the better.

Theirs was a natural enough conclusion; nonetheless, it subsequently led to bad blood between the State Department and the CIA when American covert activities either failed or were exposed, thereby leaving the American ambassador and the secretary of state with egg on their faces and causing damage to United States relations with the host country. More importantly, the CIA practice of keeping the ambassador in the dark also produced a bifurcation in the intelligence reporting from overseas missions. In brief, intelligence acquired not simply from secret intelligence deep-cover sources, but also from covert activities and operations, was transmitted to Washington by separate CIA channels. Although this intelligence information was subjected to field analysis by the CIA station's personnel it was not routinely shared with such other elements of the United States mission as the embassy's political section, military and legal attachés, etc. As a result, intelligence information with preliminary analyses travelled back to the Washington intelligence community on various parallel tracks of communications, often with each track describing the same situation or circumstance. This in turn contributed to a horrendously chaotic outcome, as the Washington analysts vainly tried to reconcile the disparate analyses produced in the field, making a mockery of "interdepartmental intelligence." As President Kennedy noted in 1961 when he tried to assert the ambassador's responsibility to act as the chief of the United States mission—i.e., to take the lead in producing field analyses of all information acquired by all United States intelligence services in a given country—"These reports [CIA, State, and Military Intelligence] sound like they came from different countries."

Finally, one can also date from the Italian operation and its nonsharing of intelligence information the beginnings of a deep resentment among the other intelligence community members toward the CIA's implicit view about its greater sensitivity to the sanctity of sources and methods. A resentment, one might add, which continues unabated today, and which often produces polemics in the Washington intelligence community rather than the best possible national-level intelligence for both operational and policy purposes.

As the Italian operation moved ahead to its successful outcome, pressure to mount more covert activities elsewhere came from an unexpected source: General Lucius Clay, commander in chief, European command, who in March 1948 cabled the army's G-2, Lieutenant General Stephen J. Chamberlain: "I have felt a subtle change in Soviet attitude which I cannot define but which now gives me a feeling that it [war] may come with dramatic suddenness." The results in Washington from General Clay's cable were predictable. A major flap ensued in the overall national security complex which earned the sobriquet "war scare," and which set off a major battle of intelligence estimates. When the dust from this battle settled, a shaky "interdepartmental" conclusion emerged which held, although there was no immediate hard evidence available to indicate that the Soviets were about to start a war by attacking Western Europe or the United States, that the *possibility* of future action was real enough to justify increasing the intensity of American participation in the Cold War and to take action to remedy the sorry state of the armed forces, occasioned by the chaotic demobilization following World War II. In the course of the intelligence estimates battle, which was hidden from public view, it became obvious to Truman that the intelligence community tail was capable and perhaps willing to push his foreign policy dog into a preemptive war against the Soviet Union. Some of the estimates which made their way to the president's desk were particularly disquieting because their treatment of Soviet intentions subtly insinuated references to act sooner rather than later by citing earlier lost opportunities in countering Hitler. Truman's response to this intelligence battle was twofold. On one level, because the take from communications intelligence proved conclusive in resolving the ambiguities surrounding intelligence from "hum int" (human intelligence) sources, he ordered a study of the communications intelligence subcommunity designed to see whether it should be centralized and/or brought under his and the NSC's direct control. His second response was to agree with Secretaries Forrestal and Marshall that more covert activities were required and that these should be operated separately from the CIA and the NSC per se. Thus Truman, by virtue of the war scare provoked by Clay's cable and his awareness of Hillenkoetter's reluctance over covert activities and the CIA's internal bickering between the secret intelligence and secret operations advocates, came full circle and embraced Donovan's idea concerning the need to separate secret intelligence from secret or special operations.

Unfortunately, in the course of his latter-day conversion to the secret operations credo Truman failed to take note, nor was he adequately warned about, the OSS wartime experience, which clearly indicated that secret operations soon achieve a dynamism and ethos all their own. And, unless carefully orchestrated and controlled on a case-by-case basis as part of a total intelligence effort, they produce much more harm than benefit. Superficially, Truman assumed that this kind of control would be provided by Forrestal and Marshall. He was totally in error; not only is it practically impossible for two individuals to maintain such control, but the task is a full-time one which cannot be carried out successfully by persons with the multitude of responsibilities incumbent upon them in their service as secretary of state or defense.

Besides these historical and managerial oversights, the outcome of the Cold War crosscurrents and Truman's subsequent response was that in June 1948 a CIA component, the Office of Policy Coordination (OPC), was chartered to carry out an expanded program of covert activities. These were set forth in NSC 10/2, which superseded NSC-4A on June 18, and which added to the psychological warfare mission political warfare, economic warfare, and preventive direct action—i.e., support for guerrillas, sabotage, and front organizations. "OPC's budget and personnel were appropriated within CIA allocations, but the DCI had no authority in directing OPC's activities. Responsibility for the direction of OPC rested with the office's director, appointed by the secretary of state. Policy guidance—decisions on the need for specific activities—came to the OPC direct from State and Defense, bypassing the DCI."*

Before examining the damage done by the OPC to American interests and the abilities of the intelligence community to provide valid national intelligence for policy and operational purposes, it is necessary to comment further on the implications of OPC's creation. Unlike the circumstances which obtained at the time of NSC-4 and NSC-4A, during which the NSC members nodded mute acquiescence based on information which said that their issuance was simply

*U.S. Congress. Senate. Select Committee to Study Governmental Operations With Respect to Intelligence Activities. First Report: Books I–VI. Washington: U.S. Government Printing Office, 1976, p. 106.

a reaffirmation of actions ordered and considered necessary by the defunct National Intelligence Authority, the NSC 10/2 decision was different and the individual members knew it. The fact of going beyond psychological warfare to adopting a policy of engaging in political, economic, and guerrilla warfare was not lost on the NSC members. However, in the course of the meeting when this question was "considered," not a single serious question was raised, nor was the wisdom of extending the Cold War into these areas of dubious legality discussed. To say that the NSC's other members—Arthur M. Hill, chairman of the National Security Resources Board; Stuart W. Symington, secretary of the air force; John L. Sullivan, secretary of the navy; and Kenneth C. Royall, secretary of the army—were overcome by the logic and necessity of Forrestal and Marshall's urging is to deny these men their independent integrity and extensive experience in matters affecting national security. The point is that each of these men realized that the "fix" was in and that real decisions, in the sense of challenging the preconceptions of the White House's inner circle, were neither called for nor would be effected by what they might say or do. Any of those involved could have resigned, gone public and made a fuss over what was being contemplated, but this is not the American way of government; especially not at the top, where the notion of a circulating elite has become a way of life. Further, in the course of the NSC 10/2 discussion none of the uncommitted either acted as devil's advocate or went personally to Truman (who did not attend the NSC meeting) and say, "Harry, do you really want to do this?" Truman in later years made it clear that of those involved in the NSC 10/2 decision, none said no, nor did anyone raise serious objections that letting the covert action genie out of the bottle might prove irreversible, or produce greater problems than it was supposed to solve. To say that Hill, Symington, Sullivan, and Royall didn't know what they they were endorsing by placing their names, titles, and positions in support of NSC 10/2 is to further challenge their basic intelligence. Each of these men knew the essential difference between secret intelligence and covert operations and by their tacit —although formally recorded—acceptance of NSC 10/2 they endorsed illegal and extralegal practices and procedures as being acceptable to America's national security leadership. The intelligence community's reaction to the NSC's apparently unanimous endorsement and support of the "dirty tricks" authorizations was swift. In their view no holds were barred. The NSC 10/2 decision was broadly intepreted to mean that not only the president but *all* the guys on the top had said to put on the brass knuckles and go to work. As word about NSC 10/2 trickled down to the working staffs in the intelligence community, it was translated to mean that a declaration of war had been issued with equal if not more force than if the Congress had so decided.

The issuing of NSC 10/2 reinforced the intelligence community's perception that with respect to covert operations the NSC was a "three little monkeys" organization which wanted neither to see, hear, nor speak any evil. However, special note was taken that a "10/2 Panel," otherwise known as an Executive

Coordination Group, was established to review, but not approve, covert action proposals. To those in favor of covert operations, this was a clear signal that the name of the game was "just do it—no one in power really wants to know about it until it's over and successful." The 10/2 Panel initiated the committee approach to covert operations; an approach, one might add, which through various boards, groups, and numerically designated committees (the "40," "303," and "5412") has never been able to control or effectively limit the scope of covert activities on a consistent, rational basis. In the planning which preceded NSC 10/2, its progenitors—Forrestal, Marshall, Kennan, and to a lesser degree Truman—"did not plan to develop large-scale continuing activities. Instead they hoped to establish a small capability that could be activated where and when the need occurred—at their discretion."* In view of what followed one has to ask the question, "What went wrong and why?" Those involved were not malevolent, although they may have overreacted to the Soviet threat, nor were they dilettantes in the ways of government or intelligence. Nevertheless, almost from the onset they lost effective control over covert operations because their personal "discretion"—i.e., the exercise of their informed judgment about the risks, worth, and ultimate value of a specific covert operation—was not really delegable. Specifically, although NSC-4A, 10/2 and those which followed by necessity had to be cast in broad, mission-type terms such as "political warfare," the review and approval procedure is rendered meaningless unless that procedure also explicitly addresses the "who needs it and why" question. Since 1948 that question has scarcely been raised in connection with covert operations, being replaced by one which infrequently, in passing, questioned the feasibility of a given covert task. Sometimes the issue of exposure has been raised in the various committees' deliberations, but this, then and now, is hardly the same as examining a covert action in terms of its ends and purposes. Thus, NSC 10/2 cast the covert action procedure in an open-ended form; that is, covert actions were broadly constituted to deal with the generalized threat of Soviet communism. As covert activity became a kind of movable feast in which any operation which *might* have some deleterious effect on the Soviet Union and communists in general, no matter how far removed or indirectly carried out, was routinely "approved," or undertaken under a kind of *stare decisus* procedure which held that prior approval to establish a front organization in country X conferred without further action similar approval to do the same thing in countries A through L. The fault in this procedure was not that Forrestal, Marshall, Kennan, and Truman delegated authority to the OPC for the conduct of covert operations, nor in establishing the 10/2 Panel, nor in bypassing the DCI and the NSC; but rather in not establishing a separate organization to evaluate the results of covert activities in terms of their actual rather than intended benefits.

Periodically since 1948, largely in response to visible, egregious failures of

Ibid., p. 106.

specific covert operations, a number of special panels, commissions, and committees have reviewed the CIA's covert operations and activities. For example, in September 1954, the Doolittle Commission Report condemned the autonomous proliferation of covert action projects without significant attempts to relate them to defined prior objectives. And in December 1968, the Lindsay Report on Covert Operations of the United States Government, which took the military intelligence services as well as the CIA to task, reiterated the conclusion that covert activities had become an end unto themselves, and that when pressed, those nominally in charge lacked any real explanation and justification for their extent and purpose. In spite of these and other reports no substantive change has taken place since 1948 in the United States' covert operations procedures, nor has there been an independent, ongoing evaluation of their real benefits carried out by an element without proprietary or vested interest in the continuation of covert activities. Congress, which might be assumed to have such an interest, has been reluctant to provide such an evaluation. This has been based largely on the so-called "want to know" principle expressed in a 1956 statement made by a congressional overseer of the CIA, Senator Leverett Saltonstall, in which he said:

It is not a question of reluctance on the part of CIA officials to speak to us. Instead it is a question of our reluctance, if you will, to seek information and knowledge on subjects which I personally, as a member of Congress and as a citizen, would rather not have, unless I believed it to be my responsibility to have it because it might involve the lives of American citizens.*

To preside as director of the newly designated OPC, Secretary Marshall turned to Frank Gardner Wisner, then serving as deputy assistant secretary of state for occupied countries. Marshall's choice was not without considerable irony because Wisner, who was of the moneyed New York legal establishment and had been one of the OSS's most effective field operators, had been eased out of intelligence in the course of the CIG/SSU battle between the West Point colonels and the OSS veterans. Born in Laurel, Mississippi, in 1909, Wisner received a BA from the University of Virginia in 1931 and an LLB from the university's law school three years later. He was admitted to the New York bar in 1935, and practiced law for several years with the firm of Carter, Ledyard and Millburg. In 1941, prior to Pearl Harbor, he joined the United States Naval Reserve. When war came he found himself bogged down in the navy, which wanted him more as a lawyer than as a line naval officer. However in 1943, through the intercession of mutual acquaintances in the legal profession, Donovan brought Wisner into the OSS, and for the next three years the Balkans were his beat. He masterminded and personally participated in some of the most imaginative operations conceived by anyone in the OSS. At war's

*Ibid., p. 149.

end, Wisner held the rank of commander, and like many who tasted the OSS wartime wine he became addicted to intelligence. But the West Point colonels and others who were determined to eliminate the Donovan influence on postwar intelligence derailed Wisner's intelligence career. Undaunted by this exposure to the bureaucratic in-fighting, he briefly returned to civilian life to take care of family business and perhaps reenter an active law practice. But in 1947, in response to the initiative of Undersecretary of State Dean Acheson, Wisner was persuaded to return to government in a related intelligence assignment as the deputy assistant secretary of state for occupied countries. In this role Wisner became intimately aware of Soviet subversive activities in the peripheral countries not yet encompassed in the Soviet sphere of influence and the intelligence potential included in the thousands of displaced persons and refugees milling around Western Europe. Thus by background, temperament, experience, training, and understanding of the Soviet threat's dimension, Wisner was the right man to become director of OPC. However, although Wisner's qualifications and Acheson's endorsement commended his selection, Marshall was somewhat reluctant to name him to the post because of stated opposition from army intelligence leaders, who looked upon him as "another Donovan who'll run away with the ball." This before-the-fact criticism of Wisner was never fully silenced in the years which followed; but when Secretary of Defense Forrestal endorsèd Marshall's choice, those in military intelligence went along with the new director in order to get along in their own bailiwick.

During the two and a half months of backstage maneuvering culminating on September 1, 1948, when he was officially named director, Wisner steeped himself in what had been done with covert operations since the end of World War II, and made an assessment of the secret intelligence and secret operations networks which had been established during the war with the British secret intelligence services. While carrying out this covert operations "market analysis," Wisner made discreet inquiries through former OSS friends and associates to find out who among the Donovan band might be interested in returning to secret operations. All this was time exceptionally well spent, because once he was officially in place he had a plan for future operations, knew who he wanted to get to carry these out and, most importantly, was ready to flow into the secret operations void which had remained unfilled since October 1945. Like others of his era and experience, he required no persuasion to become an active anticommunist Cold Warrior.

In order to assess Wisner's performance (and that of the OPC, in its four-year existence from 1948 through most of 1952), it is necessary to examine what occurred prior to the outbreak of the Korean War and in its first two years. Beginning in September 1948, Wisner, based on his belief that the Cold War was destined to be a long one which would be fought in a series of guerrillalike skirmishes rather than big battles, built his organization with considerable care. Unlike Donovan, who had to select his OSS personnel largely by intuiting their future promise, Wisner was able to pick and choose from among former OSS personnel and others with intelligence backgrounds who had either been declared surplus or were in the CIA and military intelligence services' backwaters. Like Donovan, Wisner sought individuals with an added dimension who could be expected not only to run a field operation effectively and competently, but could also who be counted upon to "come in from the cold" without recriminations and serve OPC in related training, administrative, and analytical tasks. This is not to say that Wisner adopted a revolving-door personnel policy, but rather than he wanted people in OPC who were not so imbued with the field operator's ethos that they would distort what Wisner conceived as an overall system of covert operations.

To facilitate his bidding for individuals with intelligence talent, Wisner sought and received permission from Secretary Marshall to offer premium rates. Unlike Hillenkoetter, who had to make do with lateral transfer in staffing the CIA, Wisner was able to offer as many as two or three jumps in grade or rank equivalents to get the man or woman he wanted. By itself this was a powerful inducement to get someone to sign on with a new but not permanent or statutorily authorized organization. In 1952, when OPC was absorbed by the CIA's Office of Special Operations (OSO), these personnel practices produced considerable acrimony.

In a related personnel action, Wisner realized the necessity to maintain a steady flow of new recruits into the OPC in order to maintain the organization's upward promotional ability. Overt recruitment of such persons neither appealed to Wisner nor was considered practicable in view of OPC's arm's-length relationship with the CIA. To meet his needs Wisner turned to the unofficial band of former OSS brothers who had returned to their former existence as academics after World War II. The OSS wartime experience of this group of some 500 persons was almost equally divided between field operations and analytical intelligence. As a result, in most of America's major universities, ex-OSS academics were quite capable of constituting OPC "selection committees"; and in several score of such small though prestigious colleges as Reed in Oregon and Berea in Kentucky, there were one or two faculty members also available for similar service. In response to Wisner's request, these academics became the OPC's unofficial recruiting arm. As such they constituted an across-the-board interdisciplinary search committee. At Harvard or Brown University, for example, a potential CIA/OPC recruit could hardly fail to come under scrutiny by a member of Wisner's band if he were studying history, political science, economics, anthropology, linguistics, or applied mathematics. The result of this effort was an effective screening of individual students designed to measure their attitudes, mental equipment, and adaptability to the intelligence profession's vagaries as well as providing the opportunity to meet the broad mix of personal talents required in staffing a covert operations organization. In today's post-Vietnam and post-Watergate environment this recruiting activity might appear to be one more malevolent expression of America's "invisible government." However, in all fairness to Wisner and those who participated in the effort, it was a necessary and worthwhile one which was designed to get the best and most highly motivated young men and women to join America's intelligence forces. Quite often the OSS academic's final session with a potential OPC intelligence novitiate took on the appearance of those warnings given to individuals about to embark on the suicide missions so common in wartime spy fiction, rather than one which laid out the frequently boring, nitty-gritty details of intelligence work. In most cases the "secret society" sell was effective; those who accepted the OSS academics' blandishments became willing converts to the anticommunist cause.

Wisner's OPC college recruiting techniques were not materially different than those used by the United States Naval Academy's "Blue and Gold" program, which uses former products of the Naval Academy and navy and marine retirees to help identify and preselect young men to become midshipmen at Annapolis. Wisner also realized that the OSS academics were in a favored position which enabled them to evaluate potential recruits over time and often in a classroom setting, which further enabled them to probe deeply the individual student's outlook in terms of what each sought for himself and his potential to serve silently and anonymously in the intelligence world.

The OSS academic recruiting program, also known as the OPC's "P source" (professor source), was extremely effective. It produced the necessary flow of recruits to feed the OPC's expanding appetite for personnel to manage, direct, and control the almost exponential expansions of covert action projects as well as administer the organization. If Wisner had quit while he was ahead—that is, merely used his academic sources for this purpose—no criticisms of the program would be valid. But the successful recruitment led to actions of more dubious value and justification. These followed almost as a matter of course, as the screening of Americans to serve with the CIA/OPC was expanded to deal with the opportunity of similarly recruiting foreign students attending colleges and universities in the United States. For many of the OSS academics it required no great moral turn to increase their recruiting quotas to include foreign students—not necessarily to become American intelligence officers, but rather to become witting agents in place, who when they returned home and moved up in their governmental hierarchies would owe their soul to the CIA/OPC's company store.

The recruitment of foreign students for intelligence purposes was not accomplished overnight, but by late 1949–early 1950 the basic system (which still operates today, though on a much greater scale) had been established. It is worthwhile to trace the CIA/OPC foreign student recruitment story because from its beginnings to the present day the premises on which it was based have never been challenged. And like most similar clandestine practices (such as the surveillance of persons on the basis of a "class" type of category, like "war protesters"), the foreign student recruitment program has grown to such magnitude that it is now a going concern seemingly beyond the ability of anyone to really control its operation or structurally reform its overall process.

It should be noted that the idea of recruiting foreign students did not originate with Frank Wisner. Essentially it began in the period between World War I and World War II when as a matter of international amity individual students from friendly nations were admitted to West Point and Annapolis. These young men, who were sent to the United States for an education and to soak up the martial arts, were the first of the foreign student intelligence targets. As such, because they were expected to return home to the Philippines, Argentina, or Brazil, etc. and become part of their nation's military élite, they were carefully courted. Personal relationships with faculty members as well as with cadets and midshipmen at West Point and Annapolis were fostered; the foreign cadet of 1936 was targeted as the field marshall of 1966. Embodied in this effort was the view that these young men might ultimately render two services to the United States: influencing policies favoring the United States and supplying vital inside intelligence. The first was the more important from the military's point of view; but if the relationship did result in the creation of an intelligence source, so much the better.

In the OPC era, based on an evaluation of the military intelligence services' successful courting of foreign students attending West Point and Annapolis, a corollary thesis was adopted by Wisner: the flow of foreign students coming to the United States to study everything from anthropology to zoology constituted a much larger talent pool which should be systematically tapped. In 1949–50, for example, there were fewer than 8,000 foreign students in the United States. In 1955 the number was 34,323, in 1965 82,045, and by 1975 it was close to 250,000. Thus since 1948, OPC and later the CIA's clandestine services has examined, with varying degrees of intensity, more than one million foreign students with an eye toward making as many as possible of any given year's total "moles" in their nation's political, social, business, or intelligence hierarchies.

To be sure, in the early days of the program many of the foreign students who came to the United States were from families with élitist ideas and backgrounds; however, as the various cultural exchange programs of the late 1950s and '60s evolved, many of the foreign students of more modest backgrounds came to the United States under grants provided by the Agency of International Development (AID), and as such were intensively targeted because of the greater likelihood of their returning home and becoming leaders in the social ferment and political movements occurring in their native lands. Year after year, as political instability increased worldwide in connection with the "revolution of rising expectations" and the flow of foreign students coming to the United States increased dramatically, additional pressures were placed on the CIA and the intelligence services to up their quotas and get agents in place in newly liberated nations as well as previously existing ones.

In this regard, success truly spoiled Frank Wisner and those who followed in his stead. Without distorting the reality and extent of the foreign student recruitment program, in 1976 one former CIA official familiar with the program's evolution and extent said: "By 1985 we'll own 80 percent of the Iranian government's second and third level of officials." This might be something of an exaggeration, because the record of the program suggests that the once "bought," foreign students only stay bought in about one out of four cases. One might similarly question how many former foreign students carried as agents in place are truly operational. Because so many were "recruited" by blackmail and coercive techniques, one must ask if these foreign students have (a) been "doubled" by other powers and their own countries, and (b) have become worthless "paper mills" who only provide intelligence garbage.

Although the OPC's and CIA's recruitment of foreign students does not immediately raise a Constitutional question, it does raise some serious ethical as well as practical ones. Over time the questions have barely been acknowledged by the intelligence community, let alone considered by Congress. Most recently, the Senate's Select Committee to Study Governmental Operations with Respect to Intelligence Activities, popularly known as the Church Committee after its chairman, Senator Frank Church (Dem., Idaho), backed away from any such consideration by saying: "American academics are now being used for such operational purposes as making introductions for intelligence purposes." Without making a moral judgment about the inaction of Senator Church et al. to expose this abuse of human rights by America's intelligence services, one can ask what would be the reaction of American parents who sent their son or daughter to the Sorbonne to study if they knew that the French intelligence services were actively recruiting their children to spy on the United States for the French. At the least, most parents would be highly resentful about such a practice; and if they were aware of the immoral techniques often employed by intelligence practitioners in carrying out the recruitment, they would construe such actions as being consistent with a totalitarian society. Also, one might question the integrity of an educational system, or university, which would condone or look the other way if it were aware that members of its faculty were, in essence, corrupting the young minds and personalities of those who had been placed in their trust. These questions are equally as serious as those raised by warrantless wiretaps, illegal surveillance, and mail openings; however, they remain largely unasked and unanswered. The reasons for this inattention are complex and interconnected. In the first place, the recruitment of foreign students for intelligence purposes has been eminently possible and can be looked upon as a long-term investment, because those recruited are only likely to acquire real intelligence value after the passage of a substantial length of time. Secondly, of all the United States' covert activities, the recruitment of foreign students is probably the most easily hidden from public view. The students themselves, if they attempt to protest, are easily discredited. And in cases where some have sought the protection and intercession of their own nation's diplomatic representatives, they have found themselves propositioned to become double agents in place. For the youngster who came to the United States simply to get an education it produces a bewildering state of affairs, and reinforces the cultural shock he or she encounters in dealing with American society and its educational system. And finally, because America's universities and colleges have become so dependent on governmental largesse—both from intelligence and other sources—to maintain the frosting on their cakes, none of those directly and indirectly involved has been willing to blow the whistle on this insidious practice.

Today, the original band of OSS academics has been expanded tenfold, producing a situation in which some 5,000 American academics are doing the bidding of the CIA: not only identifying and recruiting American students to its service, but providing screening committees designed to select 200–300 future agents in place from among the 250,000 foreign students who come to the United States each year. Of these 5,000 "professors, administrators, and researchers" approximately 60 percent are fully aware of what they are doing and either receive compensation directly from the CIA as contract employees, or indirectly in the form of research grants or subsidies to carry out intelligence-related tasks. The other 40 percent appear to believe that they are assisting the career development of their foreign student charges by identifying those with a potential for employment by one of the United States' multinational firms. Rarely, if ever, does the unwitting academic relate to the fact that the recruiter from corporation X is other than he represents himself.

One might ask how such a large-scale activity could be carried out without any substantial public disclosure. The answer is deceptively simple: American academics are not about to advertise their role in this operation and the foreign students have no real court of open resort to present their case. This raises the further question of why those in charge of the universities and colleges in which the recruiting takes place don't act to stamp out these practices. There is no final answer to this question. Obviously the government-academic money connection plays a role. Certainly the failure of academic leaders to act is not based on a lack of information. In the spring of 1976, at a secret meeting held in Washington's Mayflower Hotel, eight presidents of America's most prestigious universities were given information describing the full extent of the CIA's foreign student recruiting and its special relationships with faculty members at their institutions. At this meeting, these men were told that the Senate was not going to expose these matters, but if they were interested in cleaning up their own institutions, complete details would be provided to help them to do so. The results were disappointingly predictable—none of the university presidents wanted to know any more, vouchsafing contentment with the status quo. It was a sobering experience for the individual who conducted the meeting, and led him to conclude that it was an absolutely futile exercise to get anyone to do anything to rectify these distortions of America's educational values and system.

Without rendering final judgment on the temerity of America's academic leaders in failing to face the relationship of their institutions and its faculty members to the intelligence community, there is a final aspect of the recruiting situation which needs mention. Since 1948, more than 40 of the agents so recruited have committed suicide in response to the fear of exposure of their relationship with America's intelligence services. These deaths have largely gone unnoticed in the United States, but in several countries—some of which are essential to the United States' international and national security—suicide notes detailing the United States' perfidy are in the hands of those countries' leaders; and unknown to presidents since Kennedy, these have been a factor in souring American relations with those countries.

Wisner made haste slowly in expanding the number of covert operations, recognizing the need to get his carefully selected staff in place first and not to attempt to do too much too rapidly. In theory the concept was sound; however, when the Soviets detonated their first atomic weapon in 1949, the pressures to intensify and expand OPC's covert activities forced an abandoning of Wisner's orderly approach. In response, several things happened: one, OPC's personnel strength, starting from its pre-1949 base of 302, doubled and doubled once again within approximately six months. The results of this inordinately rapid personnel expansion were predictable: Wisner's idea of tight management control was lost because its effective span could not keep up with the amoebalike dividing and proliferation of subelements which occurred. Thus, like Topsy, OPC "just grew." Secondly, as a corollary to OPC's personnel explosion and in consonance with the frenetic sense of urgency engendered by the Soviets' breaking the United States' nuclear monopoly, the idea of organizing covert activities in support of general programs or policy objectives was abandoned in favor of the project approach. Basically the OPC's project approach was a "hot button—don't just stand there, do something, even if it's wrong" idea which encouraged the view, for example, that if one front organization is good, ten would be better. The results of this approach to covert activities in any given country were disastrous. In the example mentioned, the ten front organizations were often controlled, or rather barely presided over, by five or six separate OPC operators; operator A or B did not know what the other was doing, or why. This kind of compartmentalization produced mass confusion. OPC front organizations ended up attacking each other rather than those sponsored by the Soviets. As the Senate's Select Committee on Intelligence noted:

An individual within OPC judged his own performance, and was judged by others, on the importance and number of projects he initiated and managed. The result was competition among individuals and among the OPC divisions to generate the maximum number of projects. Projects remained the fundamental units around which covert activities were organized, *and two generations of Agency personnel have been conditioned by this system.* [Emphasis added]*

*"Foreign and Military Intelligence: Book I," *op. cit.,* p. 107.

As with the nonintervention of the 10/2 Panel with respect to the origin of covert operations, the project approval within OPC was left basically to the initiative of individuals within the respective divisions rather than to any kind of an interdivision review board, or executive-level organization. As a result, Wisner's band of self-starters generated more projects than could be counted, let alone controlled, reviewed, or evaluated. Also, the extreme compartmentalization which characterized the OPC project system made it almost impossible for anyone except Wisner to render an accurate statement about how many operations were underway at any given moment—and he was too busy with other problems to carry out such a census.

In the battle to win the OPC project "sales contests," the operators also adopted a ploy well known to anyone who has been a parent. If some possible objection or obstacle were anticipated in connection with a potential project, the operator would play off the secretary of state's (or defense's) allegedly stated desire for the project as a means to get back-up support from one or the other organization. For example, if State's passport control or its administrative organizations balked at placing ten more OPC agents in the Economic Cooperative Administration office attached to the United States embassy in Paris, the authority of the secretary of defense would be invoked to justify the action, and vice versa when the military services were pressured to provide OPC personnel with military cover. This practice is a common enough part of bureaucratic brinksmanship; if the OPC operator encountered serious opposition, he could say "OK friend, it's on your head to tell the secretary of defense that he can't have what he and the president want."

Between the Soviet detonation of an atomic weapon in September 1949 and the North Korean invasion of South Korea on June 24, 1950, Wisner struggled mightily to bring some order out of the organizational chaos produced by the OPC's forced and hurried expansion. By early June 1950, in spite of the fact that covert operations were springing up like dandelions in some forty-seven overseas operational areas and countries in which OPC had deployed its field forces, Wisner had made some progress—although at considerable cost. Wisner, ever a "workaholic," had been compelled to exceed even his personal work norms. In an atmosphere of 17- and 18-hour days which continued without break, mistakes were bound to occur; many procedures, including the project system, would probably have been modified or scrapped altogether if there had been time to carry out careful planning. But there never was enough time. The sense of urgency was unremitting; the pressures on Forrestal and Marshall to get on with the covert tasks—which contributed to the former's suicide—were passed on to Wisner, who was compelled to drop his persuasive, friendly, "nice guy" image and crack knuckles here and there in the rest of the intelligence community to make things happen. Like Donovan before him, Wisner was mission oriented to the point of personal obsession. This kind of attitude led to immediate, direct, and bitter conflicts with Hillenkoetter, who, in response to the complaints of the OSO's hierarchy about the OPC "cowboys," tried to curb Wisner. However Hillenkoetter, though DCI and director of the CIA, was completely bypassed in the chain of authority given to Wisner as director of OPC. This was sufficient to test the patience and amity of any two persons supposedly engaged in pursuit of a common cause. However, because it was also a practical necessity in most cases to colocate OSO and OPC field personnel in the same environment—for example, in a United States embassy or with a Military Assistance and Advisory Group (MAAG)—the arguments between Wisner and Hillenkoetter went beyond those of secret intelligence versus covert operations, analytical intelligence techniques and conclusions, validity of differing sources, etc., to include the amount of office space one group got at the expense of the other as well as the extent of the perks and amenities provided their personnel. Although these kinds of creature-comfort arguments for those who were supposed to be operating as intelligence personnel in cover roles might seem trivial, they were not. Disputes between OSO and OPC field organizations over who got what and how much government-controlled housing reached back to Washington for resolution and added substantially to the difficulty Wisner and Hillenkoetter had in getting the two organizations not to work at cross purposes, let alone with some semblance of cooperation.

Thus, in the final month before the North Korean invasion, the OPC-OSO feud had reached major proportions, the other elements of the intelligence community had been effected by it, and the state of national intelligence—the intelligence derived from all sources and supposedly synthesized by the CIA —was chaotic. Intelligence community organizations held on to information acquired by their sources, or used it to discredit the actions, estimates, and analyses of one or more of the other community members. It was intelligence competition at its worst, and Hillenkoetter was caught between the rock and the hard place.

Although the number of "flash points"—areas in which hostile military action or insurrectional violence might erupt—exceeded the intelligence community's grasp to monitor on a completely coherent basis, the potential for military action in Korea had been an agenda item on various "watch committees" in the Far East and Washington since mid-1949. These so-called watch committees were charged with, among other chores, sounding the alarm if hostile military action were imminent. In all, there were more than fifteen separate watch committees looking at events in Korea. At the top of this span of observers was an interdepartmental group in Washington which was expected to reconcile, reject, or affirm the conclusions of the field watch committees on the basis of all information available in the intelligence community.

Unfortunately, the Washington interdepartmental watch committee was not fully able to carry out its basic responsibilities. Partly this was due to the "hole card" game which was played with intelligence information under the sole control of a given community member, and to the fact that the members, neither singly nor collectively, were willing to challenge General Douglas

MacArthur's revealed wisdom from his Tokyo vantage point that all was well in Korea and throughout his realm. As in the Pearl Harbor case study cited in Chapter 4, the Korean case study reveals no shortage of valid intelligence information reaching either MacArthur or the intelligence community in Washington; the question is what did the recipients make of the intelligence information they received. Beginning in June 1949, the North Koreans had staged raids across the 38th parallel against South Korean border outposts. In most cases these were hit and run attacks which suggested local probes or reconnaissance sorties. These attacks continued intermittently throughout the rest of 1949, but by early 1950 they had become large and frequent enough to warrant the conclusion that they were probes designed to test the South Korean forces and the strength of their local defenses. In connection with this increased attack activity, North Korean propaganda became more bellicose in its tone, suggesting that South Korea was about to launch an attack against North Korea. This propaganda was carefully monitored and analyzed and the results were integrated into the watch committee deliberations. Also, the movement of war materiel was detected and traced as moving in ever increasing quantities from the Soviet Union via Manchuria into North Korea. Significantly, this logistical flow provided hard intelligence showing that the Soviets were building up the North Korean supplies of ammunition and petroleum products, the basic ingredients consumed in an attack. At the time, American intelligence about North Korean forces in terms of training hours, vehicle utilization, and ammunition authorizations for training purposes was quite good, and the analysis of the build-up suggested in one example that the North Koreans had received in one three-week period the equivalent of twenty years' artillery shells (based upon the training level which had remained constant for the previous three years). No one in the watch committee system was exactly sure what all this activity meant or was willing to venture the opinion that an attack of the South was reasonably imminent. However, coming on top of these events, the intelligence community received confirmed reports that a substantial number of North Korean troops which had served with the Chinese Communists during the Chinese civil war had returned (April–May 1950) to North Korea and rejoined its army's units, which were deploying their way toward the 38th parallel. This information added fuel to the speculation that something was brewing in Korea.

Seen retrospectively, all this intelligence established a clear picture that the North Koreans had materially increased their attack capabilities. At the time, however, the intelligence community believed it did not have valid intelligence concerning the North Koreans' intentions. On the basis of what was known or confirmable by other sources, no one was willing to cry wolf to MacArthur —although the increasing North Korean attack capabilities were routinely forwarded to him and his intelligence chief, Major General Willoughby—or to recommend to Truman and/or the Joint Chiefs of Staff that they issue a Red Alert order to MacArthur.

While the watch committee and the intelligence community in general dawdled, the CIA acted somewhat unilaterally and put out an estimate on June 14 which stated that the North Korean capabilities had reached the point where its forces could invade South Korea at any time and capture Seoul in ten to twelve days. This report was disseminated to State, Defense, and the White House; in each department, because it did not address the North Korean intentions issue, the information was given short shrift by policy makers. They looked at the contents as not much more than a ploy designed to justify increased military assistance funds. When Truman was shown the CIA report he was curt in his dissatisfaction, saying that it threatened disaster but didn't provide any real answers to his and the United States' problems.*

The result of Truman's reaction to the CIA's "if this, then maybe that" report was seen several days later. On June 20, Dean Rusk, assistant secretary of state for Far Eastern affairs, testified before the House Committee on Foreign Affairs about the military situation in Korea. This was a previously scheduled appearance of Assistant Secretary Rusk; however, because in the seivelike atmosphere of official Washington reports about the CIA estimate were making the rounds of the press and "informed" circles, it was feared that administration critics in Congress might also publicly raise the issue. In consequence, a White House decision of sorts was made to brief Congress that all was well in Korea. It was the kind of mission no one in the State Department likes to get, especially when the intelligence community was raising portents of disaster. But Rusk had the title and he was designated to carry the water up to Capitol Hill.

Rusk's testimony was as follows:

On the military side our people there have been impressed with the smartness and the diligence with which the Koreans have applied themselves to their security problem. Their armed forces are able, they are being trained by an American military advisory group, they seem to be motivated by a fair amount of nationalist spirit and loyalty to the government. They certainly are devoted to the concept of Korea as a free and independent country and their activities along the 38th parallel in reducing incidents

*Even today, considerable controversy surrounds this particular CIA report. At a hearing on June 26, 1950, before the Senate's Appropriations Committee held in executive session, Hillenkoetter testified that the CIA had given warning of the impending attack. He was, he said, unable to explain why this notice had not been acted upon. However, an analysis of CIA intelligence reports undertaken in the Joint Chiefs of Staff's Joint Intelligence Group revealed that no such information had been received by the JCS. See especially: Top Secret Memo, Director of Office of Military Assistance to Secretary of Defense, "Intelligence Aspects of the Korean Situation," June 29, 1950, same file, sec 21; Top Secret Memo, Vance to Megee, "Korean Situation—Advanced Warning of Invasion by CIA," July 10, 1950, same file, sec 23; (TS) Memo, Director OMA to SecDef, "Intelligence Aspects of the Korean Situation," June 29, 1950, Combined Chiefs of Staff, 383.21 Korea (3–19–45) sec 21; (TS) Memo, Col. R.F.C. Vance, USAF, JIG, to Brigadier General Vernon E. Megee, USMC. These documents, which have recently been declassified, do not resolve the controversy over prior warning of the North Korean invasion, but they do point out that the CIA report did not reach the persons in America's military network who conceivably might have done something to prevent the total surprise the North Koreans achieved at the time of their attack.

and meeting guerrilla bands coming across the border indicates they seem to mean business about what they are doing.

They, of course, cannot expect to establish in South Korea, an army, or armed forces which would be able to meet an organized major invasion from the North but we think that they can get themselves up as a going concern if they can take care of everything short of that. Our goal here is to assist the South Koreans to establish a security force which can deal with domestic disorders, armed bands coming across the 38th parallel, and force the opposition to make the choice to fight a major war as the price for taking over southern Korea. *We see no present indication that the people across the border have any intention of fighting a major war for that purpose.* [Emphasis added.]

I should inform the committee—could I have a minute off the record on this, Mr. Chairman?*

In the off the record discussion which followed, Rusk further waffled the details of the North Korean build-up mentioned in the CIA estimate by casting it in terms of a longer range process in Asia which the administration was monitoring closely, but which in itself provided no valid evidence of North Korean hostile intentions against the South. The committee was reassured. Five days later the figurative roof fell in when North Korean tanks, which had been detected "exercising," turned south and crossed the 38th parallel, accompanied not by "guerrilla bands" but organized units of the North Korean army. The facts of the North Koreans' surprise attack and its successful drive on Seoul are well enough known not to bear repeating; however, the ramifications of what appeared to be another Pearl Harbor intelligence failure merit some mention. In the first place, Truman was furious with Hillenkoetter for failing to warn him, conveniently overlooking the fact that the admiral could hardly be classified as the master of America's intelligence house. In the second, as the discredited members of the intelligence community took a second look at what had been known before the fact of the attack, a serious omission in the estimate process was revealed. In spite of casting the North Korean capability estimate in terms of such positively observed facts as the logisitical build-up and troop unit movements, the analysts had overlooked or discounted uncorroborated information from secret intelligence sources elsewhere and had misread the North Koreans' communications deception plan. Seen later, this plan's analysis revealed that the North Koreans had made a conscious effort not to increase the volume of their radio traffic and had disguised tactical orders and instructions in innoucuous administrative messages. In essence, this produced a kind of "radio silence," but one which left confirmation of the North Koreans' intentions and timetable to human rather than communications sources. Also, in the detailed intelligence evaluation carried out, it was shown that there had been no follow-up collection require-

*U. S. House of Representatives, Committee on International Relations. Selected Executive Session Hearings of the Committee, 1943–50. Volume VII, "United States Policy in the Far East, Part 2." Washington: U.S. Government Printing Office, 1976, p. 464.

ments levied on all available intelligence sources to confirm or reject the intentions question. Partly this was due to MacArthur's control in the Far East, which denied intelligence collection to any organization but his own; more importantly, it was due to the fact that the results from secret intelligence sources and those of communications means were not integrated into an ongoing collection-question process.

In the wake of the North Korean attack, Major General Willoughby, fearing a rerun of the Pearl Harbor investigation, tried to amend MacArthur's pooh-poohing statements made in response to the watch committee and the CIA's "any time" capability estimate. Willoughby's attempt to rewrite MacArthur's comments was rejected out of hand by those in Washington. When informed, MacArthur was unperturbed, voicing the view that his on-the-record (although officially confidential) opposition to Secretary of State Acheson's omitting Korea from America's strategic periphery in the Far East, and the administration's previously denied requests for additional forces to deter such an attack, constituted an adequate defense against the charge that he had been surprised.

The outbreak of the Korean War presaged major changes in the intelligence community. By early August, secret intelligence and communications intelligence means were warning of large-scale Chinese troop movements in the direction of Korea, coming from as far south as Shanghai. By September, in spite of these reports and the capture of Chinese soldiers whose interrogation confirmed the existence of Chinese combat units in Korea, MacArthur refused to concede that this intelligence was significant. Again Hillenkoetter warned Truman, complaining that MacArthur's "drive to the Yalu" (Korea's northern boundary with China) was likely to induce a major Chinese response. Here again, neither Truman nor the Joint Chiefs was willing to interfere with MacArthur, the commander in the field, based on the valid intelligence which they believed he was ignoring. Rather than act himself, Truman gently sacked Hillenkoetter—sending him to command at sea—and replaced him with General Walter Bedell Smith, who according to Winston Churchill was "America's bulldog" and who, it was believed, would have more success in restraining MacArthur.

Thus began the Smith-MacArthur battle over intelligence which by mid-November had resulted in a major confrontation over the number of Chinese divisions located in forward combat areas. MacArthur claimed there were none, saying that the Chinese units were simply support and supply units. Smith, unlike Hillenkoetter, was not easily put off by semantic gymnastics, and responded by sending a series of messages to MacArthur which identified eleven Chinese combat divisions where none were supposed to exist. MacArthur ignored the intelligence gauntlet thrown down by Smith, pressing on toward the Yalu and perhaps beyond; however, when the Chinese poured into Korea in late November in massive force, the means were at hand to bring MacArthur to intelligence heel. This was done in early January 1951, when

Smith went to Tokyo and laid down the new intelligence law to MacArthur. Among other things, it established the fact that the CIA as well as other national intelligence organizations would operate in Korea and elsewhere in the Far Eastern command. In these meetings it was made perfectly clear to MacArthur and Willoughby that their days of intelligence monopoly were over, and that the rules for controlling the exercise of national intelligence resources in the Far East were going to be the same for MacArthur as they were for any military field commander. MacArthur was chastened, but not given to mending his ways; these ultimately led to Truman's relieving him. In the wake of Smith's ultimatum to MacArthur, a new, expanded intelligence setup was initiated in the Far East.

Almost immediately, OPC, in response to Defense Department urgings, accelerated its performance of "preventive direct action" missions which had been authorized by NSC 10/2 but which for lack of a suitable area had not been instituted on the same scale as other covert operations. The preventive direct action missions which followed ran the gamut from recruiting Koreans and Chinese (basically from Chinese Nationalist forces on Taiwan) to become line crossers or to serve in OPC commando units in attacks on North Korean rear-area installations. In all this flurry of activity was seen a renaissance of the OSS's wartime salad days. The number of preventive direct action projects proliferated at a dizzying rate, increasing from the number underway in the year prior to the Korean War by some 1600 percent between January 1951 to January 1953. This expansion of covert action was similarly matched by a second population explosion in the overall ranks of the CIA, with the OSO side of the house doubling to a size of some 1,200 persons and the OPC group reaching approximately 6,000.

Besides the CIA's physical expansion of personnel, money, and covert action projects, a similar expansion of attitudes about what was proper and necessary in the intelligence cause also occurred. For most, the Korean War signalled the return to a War Powers Act environment in which anything goes that might hinder or harm the enemy. The result was that the psychological outlook about intelligence in total war was carried over into a limited war environment with little regard for its consequences upon ours and other nations' peoples, institutions, and rights.

Although the stated diplomatic and military policy of the United States with respect to the Korean "police action" was explicit in its denial of any desire to widen the war, the national intelligence policy actually employed was one designed with little recognition or acceptance of that end. As a specific case in point, the CIA's OPC, in late summer 1950, recruited (or rather hired) a batch of Chinese Nationalist soldiers from Chiang Kai-shek. This action, carried out in the face of MacArthur's intelligence monopoly, was considered quite a coup. These mercenaries, who received only modest compensation from the Chinese Nationalist government on Taiwan for their efforts, were transported by the OPC to northern Burma, where they were expected to launch guerrilla raids into China. At the time this dubious project was initiated no consideration was given to the facts that (a) Truman had declined Chiang's offer to participate in the Korean War either as a declared United States ally or in the guise of a UN member; (b) Burmese neutrality was violated by this action; and (c) the troops provided by Chiang were utterly lacking in qualifications for such a purpose.

Fortunately, the ChiNat "Li Mi" guerrilla project did not achieve its purpose of provoking the Chinese to greater military activity. Nor did it produce a visible diplomatic incident between the American and Burmese governments. However, it did display some lessons which had to be relearned the hard way in the 1960s, during America's secret war in Laos. Among these lessons was one that showed that the anticommunist convictions of those supposedly willing to fight under American direction—although for pay—were extremely shallow. In the case of the ChiNat guerrillas, once they had been ensconced in the forward base area, their first demand was that their CIA/OPC mentors bring their dependents to join them. This was in fact done. However, after repeated pleadings, cajoling, and issuance of "either/or" orders by OPC personnel to get on with the war, the guerrillas responded by proving themselves to be lovers rather than fighters. In short order the guerrilla enclave became a curious anomaly in the OPC's scheme of preventive direct action. The guerrillas wouldn't fight and nothing could make them. Various stratagems were employed, but none was successful. The suggestion that Americans actually lead them on their forays rather than direct the operation from the splendor of Bangkok, or by one-day, in-and-out visits to the front, was rejected by OPC personnel on the grounds of "diplomatic implications." However, rather than abandon the entire operation as an exuberant mistake by the OPC leaders who didn't realize that the war outside the direct confines of Korea was much different than the one waged in those areas during World War II, it was allowed to continue, with vast plans hatched in Tokyo and Taipei by OPC personnel who knew they were engaged in a paper exercise designed to enhance their bureaucratic positions and give sustenance to the OPC's Cold Warriors' positions in the Washington intelligence community.

Meanwhile, as the bureaucratic battle over intelligence support for the forces in Korea continued, the guerrillas, peasants by background and inclination, went into business for themselves. Jumping the claims of the Burmese peasants, they took over their poppy fields and became "businessmen farmers" rather than guerrillas. During this agricultural phase of the guerrillas' existence, they played on the sympathies and egos of the Americans involved in the program by saying they had to do something to compensate for the meager pay they were receiving and that once the next crop of poppies was brought in and sold they would carry out the requested raids. In the course of this activity, the guerrillas conned the Americans into allowing the OPC's "contract" supply aircraft to carry the guerrillas' opium to market in Bangkok. Thus, what had initially been conceived as an OPC plan to sting the Chinese at their exposed, lightly defended underbelly turned into a narcotics operation of fairly significant proportions. There was a ready market for the guerrillas' opium in Bangkok, especially because its price did not include the imposition of "bandits' taxes" which were levied on other opium reaching Bangkok overland and by inland waterways. The CIA's aircraft subsidy gave the guerrillas a substantial market advantage; they and their factors (those who disposed of their product) made the most of it.

In the temper of the times, the United States' complicity in the international drug traffic—although not officially acknowledged, it was revealed in internal documents and memoranda—was viewed at the highest levels of government as a necessary cost in carrying out the mandates of covert action. This fiction, or self-imposed official blindness, about the ChiNat guerrillas' extracurricular opium activities came home to roost on the night of February 5, 1951, in Thailand's coastal province of Lopburi. The opium grown by the ChiNat guerrillas, stolen or acquired by bartering American-supplied arms, was transported by OPC contract aircraft from the forward base area to Bangkok for sale to buyers from the various "connections." The pilots who flew these bushtype aircraft and often served as agents or go-betweens with the guerrilla leaders and the opium buyers were a motley band of men. Some were ex-Nazis, others part of the band of expatriates who emerge in foreign countries following any war. Regardless of their individual backgrounds, they filled an operational need of the time; they were recruited to fly the support and supply missions for the OPC's guerrilla forces, not only in northern Burma but elsewhere in Asia as well. It should be noted that recruitment of these airmen of fortune was also based on the fact that pilots with skill and experience were in short supply, and that there was a strong reluctance on the part of the United States Air Force to detail active-rated pilots for duty with the OPC. In response, the OPC, like the OSS, took the persons it needed from those available rather than waiting for some training program to meet those needs.

In the case in question, one of the contract pilots, Jack Killam, who had been a major in the army air corps in the China-Burma-India theater during World War II and elected to remain in the Far East upon his discharge, became a casualty of the ChiNat guerrilla drug-running operation. The available evidence suggests that for reasons and by persons unknown, Killam was brutally murdered. This by itself is not unique in view of what goes on in the world of narcotics smuggling. But Killam, an American citizen at the time, had a contractual relationship with the United States government; what is unique is the still unexplained role of CIA/OPC personnel in burying him in an unmarked grave, and the fact that the CIA covered up this event for more than twenty-six years.

From information given to the Senate Select Committee on Intelligence in 1975, it was alleged that Jack Killam had been shot in the head; he was then buried by two CIA operators, Dennis Fleming and Peter Joost. There was no evidence to suggest that either Fleming or Joost was responsible for Killam's death; but some four years later the CIA's general counsel, Lawrence Houston, described the events to Attorney General Herbert Brownell without getting to the specifics which preceded the murder or of Killam's relationship to the CIA. Brownell, in response to Houston's oblique search for an opinion, deferred any Justice Department action and agreed not to press the case because of an assumed lack of United States jurisdiction. On this point the law is probably clear: murder in a foreign country, even though the victim is an American citizen, is not covered by the United States criminal code. Similarly, the law of conspiracy is far from uniform anywhere in the world. However, the question of Killam's activities and relationship to the CIA is much less clear. Several theories have been advanced by those familiar with the Killam case to suggest that the trafficking in drugs in Southeast Asia was used by the CIA as a self-financing device to pay for services and persons whose hire would not have been approved by Washington (or condoned if discovered), or that it amounted to the actions of "rogue" intelligence agents who had decided to make some money on the side in addition to the pay they received as front-line Cold Warriors. The accuracy of the various theories is less important than the lesson which holds that covert operations which stray beyond previously defined limitations acquire a dynamic of their own, which leads to more and greater excesses on the part of field agents who, in turn, will act to keep the unauthorized parts of those operations secret from those with a legal and administrative responsibility for their contents.

Coincident with General Smith's appointment as DCI, he moved on October 12, 1950, to bring OPC under his administrative control and to require that State and Defense submit their policy guidance for OPC's operations through him rather than Frank Wisner. At the time, neither Secretary of State Dean Acheson or General Marshall, who had replaced the bumbling Secretary of Defense Louis Johnson, wanted to be bothered with the Pandora's box which had been opened by the OPC's covert operations and activities. Acheson and Marshall were quite willing to turn the responsibility of orchestrating the Cold War's intelligence response over to Smith, in whom they had the highest confidence. Although most of the covert action supporters read Smith's message loud and clear, it took a face-to-face confrontation with the general before Wisner accepted the fact. Smith, who was an acknowledged master in the military's fine art of chewing ass, respected Wisner's ability and did not want to fire him; however, as in the bracing of MacArthur, Smith made it clear to Wisner that his concept of the chain of command did not allow for prima donnas or those who acted without recognition of the CIA's overall mission. As a measure of Wisner's essential integrity, he accepted Smith's beration and went on to become an exceptionally meritorious team player and good soldier in the CIA. Smith, who knew a good man when he saw one, subsequently treated Wisner as a trusted lieutenant; the two men became fast friends.

What Smith and Wisner said in Washington was not easily and effectively communicated to the field, where the rivalries between the separate OSO and OPC organizations continued unabated. By mid-1952 the CIA's internal civil war—one waged in its overseas stations—had reached a point which called for a Draconian solution. In spite of Smith's recognition of the hazards and the conceptual discrepancies in blending secret intelligence and covert activities, in August 1952 he ordered the merger of OSO and OPC into one organization, the Directorate for Plans (DDP). As further measure of Smith's confidence in Wisner's ability, he named him to head the new organization and directed him to bring order out of the admitted chaos. Smith's action was a bold bureaucratic attempt; but "the merger did not result in the dominance of one group over another; it resulted in the maximum development of clandestine operations over clandestine collection. For people in the field, rewards came more quickly through visible operational accomplishments than through the silent, long-term development of agents required for clandestine collection."*

Also, as part of Smith's overall plan for the CIA's internal reorganization:

In January 1952, CIA's intelligence functions were grouped under the Directorate for Intelligence (DDI), ORE was dissolved and its personnel were reassigned. In addition to ORE, the DDI's production components included: the Office of Research and Reports (ORR), which handled economic and geographic intelligence; the Office of Scientific Intelligence (OSI), which engaged in basic scientific research; and the Office of Current Intelligence (OCI), which provided current political research. Collection of overt information was the responsibility of the Office of Operations (OO). The Office of Collection and Dissemination (OCD) engaged in the dissemination of intelligence as well as the storage and retrieval of unevaluated intelligence.**

Finally, "to consolidate the management functions required for the burgeoning organization, Smith created the Directorate for Administration (DDA). From the outset, much of the DDA's effort supported field activities. The directorate was responsible for personnel, budget, security, and medical services Agencywide."***

The importance and persistent effect of Smith's internal reorganization of the CIA can be seen in the fact that by early 1953, when he left the post of DCI to become undersecretary of state, the CIA had achieved the basic structure it would retain for the next twenty years. To wit:

Three directorates had been established. The patterns of activity within each directorate and the directorates' relationships to one another had been developed. The DDP commanded the major share of the Agency's budget, personnel, and resources; in 1952 clandestine collection and covert action accounted for 74 percent of the Agency's total

---

*"Foreign and Military Intelligence, Book I," *op. cit.*, p. 108.

***Ibid.*, p. 104.

****Ibid.*, p. 108.

budget; its personnel constituted 60 percent of the CIA's personnel strength. While production rather than coordination dominated the DDI, operational activities rather than collection dominated the DDP. The DDI and the DDP emerged at different times out of disparate policy needs. They were, in effect, separate organizations. These fundamental distinctions and emphases were reinforced in the next decade.*

It should be noted that this basic organization of the CIA followed closely the recommendations of the Dulles-Jackson-Correa report to the NSC on the CIA and the National Organization for Intelligence (January 1949), which studied the structure and organization of the CIA, existing CIA activities, and the relationships of those activities to those of other departments and agencies. This report, in addition to giving Smith the blueprint he needed to help the CIA live up to its promise and charter, suggested to him that its principal architects**—William Jackson, a New York attorney with a wartime background in army intelligence, and Allen Dulles, with variegated careers in diplomacy and intelligence, who had served as an advisor to successive DCIs since 1947—should be asked to back their words with action and join him in the task of reforming the CIA. Jackson joined Smith almost immediately after the general's confirmation, and served in the post of deputy director, Central Intelligence (DDCI) until November 1951. Similarly, Dulles joined the CIA on a full-time basis in January 1951, serving as its deputy director of plans until Jackson's departure, when he moved up to the DDCI post. In February 1953, he was appointed DCI and director of the CIA.

Although Smith's actions in using the Dulles-Jackson-Correa report as the basis of reorganizing the CIA and in recruiting Jackson and Dulles to assist him in implementing its provisions might tend to diminish his own contribution to this effort, it does not. The truth of the matter is that without Smith in the driver's seat it is doubtful that much, if any, real change would have occurred. Smith possessed a clear vision about national intelligence and more importantly, as a result of a lifetime of leadership responsibilities, he knew how to take a man's measure and secure his best effort in accomplishing a difficult task. By virtue of being a leader of men, Walter Bedell Smith proved to be a leader in American intelligence.

On the other hand, this is not to say that under Smith the CIA and the overall operations of the American intelligence community were an unalloyed success. As suggested above, the War Powers Act psychology of intelligence field operators, which took over after the start of the Korean War, and the knee-jerk reactions of national leaders to the multiple threats of Soviet communism in the Cold War's other theaters set in motion events and actions beyond the ability of Smith and his principal lieutenants to fully control.

*Ibid., p. 109.

**Matthias Correa, a New York lawyer and a wartime assistant to Secretary Forrestal, was not an active participant in the survey.

In trying to assess the growth, effectiveness, and impact of covert operations and other clandestine activities in the Truman years, it is easy to be shocked by the sheer size and scope of what occurred. But this loses sight of the fact that each of the various streams of covert activities—psychological warfare, political warfare, economic warfare, and preventive direct action—had a way of broadening out, and a single "project," not really thought through in terms of risks, ends, purposes, and consequences, became the precedent and justification for a trickle of similar ones. From them, a torrent emerged, engulfing intelligence operators and many presumptive friends and allies. In such an intellectual and emotional environment it is not unexpected to find, for example, that the successful planting of an article in a foreign newspaper leads to the hiring of journalists to carry out that task on a regular basis, and that the propaganda conveyed abroad was fed back into the American body politic. Thus, the bottom line of the Truman era may be seen as a groping forward in further search of a centralized intelligence system, an inadequate blending of intelligence capabilities in pursuit of a coherent, consistent foreign policy, and the tacit as well as executive legitimization of clandestine intelligence activities, especially those involving covert operations.

We have not attempted to further subcategorize or otherwise specify all the covert activities contained under the rubric of psychological warfare, political warfare, economic warfare, and preventive direct action. To do so would require classification of the OPC's inventory of many thousands of projects—a task which was attempted and abandoned by several panels. However, the more important fact of the Truman era's (essentially 1948–52) waterfront of covert activities is that this is when each of the categories (except political assassination, which began in the Eisenhower years) began, and the precedents of their creation were used by successive DCIs and presidents to continue and expand their scope.

Before we turn to the Eisenhower administration, it is necessary to mention two other features of the Truman era in intelligence which, although much less visible and not immediately portentous, have had a lasting impact on the evolution of American intelligence and the intelligence community.

The first involves America's special relationship with Israeli intelligence. Although this relationship predates Truman's term in the White House—it dates back to the World War II period, when OSS representatives in England dealt with the Israeli state-to-be's "shadow government" and recruited some of its members and followers as American secret intelligence sources—it gained its greatest impetus following Truman's diplomatic recognition of Israel in May 1948. To be sure, much of the earlier wartime cooperation between the OSS and the Jewish nationalists and Zionists was based on a commonly shared belief in the necessity to destroy Hitler and Nazism. However, in the immediate postwar period, the relationship further prospered because of the American need to rely on Israeli help to solve the complex intelligence task of locating war criminals, stolen property, and assisting in the task of reestablishing the identities of DPs and other war victims. Throughout this period the personal relationships between American secret intelligence operators (first in SSU and later in the CIG and CIA's Office of Special Operations) and those in the fledgling Israeli intelligence services also facilitated the planting of deep-cover agents in place in a wide variety of countries which had become targets for Soviet espionage and subversion. In turn, this cooperation led to a sharing of intelligence information between Americans and Israelis, in some cases letting an Israeli who was better positioned actually run the source for mutual benefit. The full story of this cooperation cannot be recounted here; suffice to say that when Israel's existence was proclaimed by David Ben-Gurion and affirmed by Truman, the mutuality and common purposes of the two nations in the field of secret intelligence had been solidly established and tested many times, producing a strong bond of trust between the two.

During Truman's elected term, the American-Israeli secret intelligence relationship was expanded even further. Up to the founding of Israel, the FBI had been privy to much of what flowed between the two secret intelligence groups; however, after Israel became a sovereign state, J. Edgar Hoover severed those connections and left them to those in the OSO. Hoover's rationale was based on the view that it might embarrass the bureau if another relationship similar to that with the British Security Coordination during World War II should surface in the postwar era, and that for every supporter of the Zionist cause in the United States there were ten detractors.

Those in the OSO, most notably James Angleton, were pleased to have the Israeli relationship to themselves. And over time, not only during the Truman years, the relationship produced some remarkable results and intelligence coups. One in particular is worth mentioning briefly. It involved the identification and subsequent manipulation of three British intelligence officials who were Soviet spies. The three were David MacLean, who was in charge of the chancery at the British embassy in Washington between 1944–48, Guy Burgess, who was posted to Washington in 1950 as the second secretary in the British embassy; and Harold Adrian Russell Philby, known commonly as Kim Philby, who served as England's anti-Soviet intelligence chief and who in 1949 was the British SIS representative in Washington, working in liaison with the CIA and the FBI.*As a result of the American-Israeli secret intelligence connection, each of these three spies was identified, MacLean's identification leading to Burgess' and thence to Philby's. By itself the mere act of identifying these Soviet spies is noteworthy; but the subsequent manipulation, which included providing them with intelligence disinformation to mislead the Soviets, makes the overall operation a classic case. In the course of manipulating

---

*Philby's defection was formally reported by the British Foreign Office on 1 July 1963. See *New York Times,* 2 July 1963.

Burgess and MacLean's defections were the subject of a report. *Report on the Disappearance of Two Former Foreign Officials.* London: British Foreign Office, 23 September 1955.

them—playing on their personal, physical, and moral weaknesses and vanities —the CIA's small band of secret intelligence professionals were able to discover the identities of other Soviet agents in place in the United States and elsewhere, and to use that information to thwart Soviet subversive initiatives in a wide variety of government, business, and scientific endeavors. Although each was allowed to make his way to the Soviet Union (Burgess and MacLean in 1951, Philby in 1963) without incident, their departures were looked upon with some sadness, because they had been such good sources for the CIA as well as for the Israeli and British secret intelligence services. Ironically, Kim Philby described his career as a Soviet secret agent in a book entitled *My Silent War*, a title one might, if the full story is ever written, accurately amend to read "with words and pictures furnished by my secret intelligence opposition."

The Burgess-MacLean-Philby case illustrates two important general principles about counterespionage and secret intelligence, as well as an important ramification about how American secret intelligence was aided and abetted by the Israelis during the Truman era. The first principle is that, almost redundantly, secret intelligence must be practiced in secret to be effective; the second is that to be successful one must be patient and willing to play the game out to its full length rather than seek a quick, visible, yet incomplete victory. The important ramification is that Truman's foreign policy commitment to Israel —which was opposed by some of his top advisers—facilitated the building of the American-Israeli secret intelligence connection, without which the United States would have been deprived of intelligence assets it would have been unable to acquire on its own at any price.

The second leitmotif of the Truman era in intelligence involved his establishing in October 1952, by presidential memorandum, directions on how communications intelligence activities were to be conducted. He directed the secretary of defense to be his executive agent in these matters, directed the establishment of the National Security Agency (NSA), and authorized the missions and functions to be performed by the NSA. This presidential memorandum was issued in response to a series of investigations beginning in the wake of Pearl Harbor, followed by others in 1948, and one following the North Korean attack, which finally culminated in an intensive review in 1952 by a panel of distinguished citizens. In brief, the various investigations and reviews pointed out that the centralization of intelligence ordered in the National Security Act of 1947 had left the communications intelligence subcommunity not fully integrated, and that there was a definite need to provide a communications intelligence equivalent of the CIA. This took the form of the NSA, under whose rubric it was believed this vital stream of intelligence information could be brought more effectively to bear in meeting national intelligence needs. It was a step long overdue; however, the capacity to contain the communications intelligence genie in a bottle—no matter how carefully proscribed by a president—has proven to be an elusive, never-ending task.*

In conclusion, the Truman era in intelligence may be looked upon as a period in which some new intelligence vessels were launched and many others were taken from America's mothballed wartime intelligence fleet to do battle against the forces of many nations on the ambiguous and often turbulent seas of social and political change.

*During World War II, the military services controlled all communications intelligence. After the war, a U.S. Communications Intelligence Board (USCIB) was established to coordinate communications intelligence (comint) activities for the National Security Council and to advise the director of Central Intelligence on comint issues. However, in 1949 the secretary of defense set up a separate comint board under the Joint Chiefs of Staff to oversee the military's comint activities, and this arrangement stood for three years, despite the DCI's objections. In 1952, NSA was established with operational control over comint resources and the secretary of defense was given executive authority over all comint activities. At the same time, the USCIB was reconstituted under the chairmanship of the DCI to advise the director of NSA and the secretary of defense. In 1958, the USCIB was merged with the Intelligence Advisory Committee to form the United States Intelligence Board (see Chapter 7). The Comint Committee of the USIB was formed soon thereafter; this became the Sigint Committee in 1962, when its responsibilities were extended to include Elint (see Chapter 8).

CHAPTER 7

EISENHOWER: THE COLD WAR LEGACY

When Dwight D. Eisenhower assumed the presidency in January 1953 he faced a problem not dissimilar from that of his immediate predecessor: the bringing to an end of a foreign war fought by American forces in the twentieth century. Truman, however, had the Roosevelt policy of unconditional surrender to help him define World War II's end; Eisenhower had to define a different set of war aims which would satisfy most Americans, who had long since wearied of the Korean War, and which would not fan the fires of right-wing conservatism or induce a resurgence of "Fortress America" isolationist thinking. His subsequent definition came about almost by default. Given that the Korean War was a limited one, his aim included neither unconditional surrender nor MacArthur's view that "there is no substitute for victory." In essence, Eisenhower accepted the armistice, the justification for which was that the American and United Nations military effort had stopped aggression in Korea, strengthened the United Nations organization, and demonstrated that the Western nations were prepared and willing to meet the communists' military challenges. Communist acceptance of the armistice was not immediately forthcoming and, in the spring of 1953, Eisenhower made it clear to them "that in absence of satisfactory progress [of the armistice negotiations] we intend to move decisively without inhibition in our use of weapons, and would no longer be responsible for confining activities to the Korean peninsula."*

Eisenhower's thinly veiled nuclear threat apparently did the trick, and an armistice was finally concluded at Panmunjon on July 27, 1953. Whether Eisenhower's fanning of his nuclear card was actually the key variable in the North Koreans' decision is difficult to document. However, in early 1953, prior to Eisenhower's public remarks, the intelligence community carefully orchestrated a flow of intelligence disinformation through secret intelligence channels to indicate that A-bombs were being readied and were on their way to the Far East. Disinformation in this operation and, as a general proposition, needed to be believable, but not necessarily directly verifiable by its intended recipi-

*John M. Blum, et al., *The National Experience: a History of the United States.* New York: Harcourt Brace Jovanovich, 1973, p. 735.

ents. In order to avoid the enemy's outright rejection of the planted disinformation there was a requirement to provide some hard evidence which tended to corroborate it in an indirect manner. The form of this evidence is contained in quotes from the then chairman of the Joint Chiefs of Staff, General Omar Bradley, in testimony in a closed-door executive session of the Senate Foreign Relations Committee on February 10, 1953. In the course of this testimony, General Bradley said, among other things,

We have discussed many times the use of the atomic bomb tactically. Of course, you know there are not strategic targets worth mentioning in Korea. We have looked for a long time and studied the possible tactical uses in Korea and it is rather hard to find a target at this time that we think is sufficiently remunerative as a target for the expending out of the stockpile. . . . However, get them out in the open and I think we would have to consider it very seriously.

At this point the committee chairman, Alexander Wiley (Rep., Wis.) interjected the question, "What?" Bradley replied,

Consider very seriously the use of the A-bomb, if we found a suitable target now in Korea, and of course that might have considerable effect on operations. . . . [or] use a couple of Chinese Nationalist divisions, and the chiefs have recommended they be used from a military point of view. The Joint Chiefs have given great consideration to the possibility of bombing Manchurian airfields and rail and production centers elsewhere."*

All this was suitable grist for the intelligence disinformation mill, playing basically on the view (which it was believed Stalin held) that with Eisenhower's election the United States' military hierarchy would hold sway, and that the decision to use the A-bomb should the armistice negotiations remain deadlocked had in fact been made. Finally, the effort was further backed by the movement of additional B-29s to the Pacific area, in the course of which some preplanned "security leaks" occurred to reinforce the disinformation and corroborative information previously sold or otherwise fed to the Soviets.

Thus almost from the onset of Eisenhower's presidency a die was cast which reflected a willingness to use positive intelligence techniques to further policy objectives. This occurred largely because, unlike Truman, Eisenhower became president and assumed his role as first intelligence officer having been thoroughly prepared. His experience as chief of staff in World War II, and after the war as supreme commander of NATO, gave him an exceptional advantage in dealing with the problems of intelligence and in recognizing the limitations of its techniques to bring about a predetermined end.

In the transition period between Eisenhower's election and inauguration he was brought completely up to date on where United States intelligence matters

*U.S. Congress. Senate. Hearings Before the Foreign Relations Committee, 10 February 1953.

stood around the world. During the course of these intelligence briefings he was watched closely by the intelligence community's leaders for a clue as to which course he might direct them to follow once he became president. It was a completely unavailing exercise; Eisenhower kept his own counsel, preferring to listen rather than probe or otherwise indicate his approval or disapproval about what the intelligence community was doing.

The "morning line" forecast by the intelligence community leaders about Eisenhower's intelligence intentions ran the gamut from the military intelligence services' somewhat forlorn hope that the CIA might be reduced to simply an analytical intelligence organization and/or a glorified central intelligence reference service, to the desire of the CIA's deputy directors to see the DCI be given some real substantive authority over the other intelligence community members' activities. This latter wish was based on the fact that the departure of General Smith from his post as DCI was anticipated, not as part of the new Eisenhower administration's housecleaning and appointment of its own top officials, but for health reasons. And lacking a replacement with Smith's personal clout at the Pentagon, the CIA would have trouble in dealing with the rest of the intelligence community, especially with the military intelligence services.

Rumors abounded concerning the identity of the next DCI/director of the CIA, the most provocative being that "Wild Bill" Donovan would be brought out of retirement to fill the twin post.* Another guess, based on the fact that the president-elect had held a long private conversation with General Lucian Truscott, then military advisor to John McCloy, the United States high commissioner for Germany, held that Truscott would be named to replace Smith. What gave added substance to this rumor was Eisenhower's experience with, and personally stated favorable view about, the British method whereby the head of its SIS was a retired military officer. In addition to Truscott's distinguished combat record in World War II, the retired four-star general was thoroughly experienced in sensitive intelligence matters, especially those involving the exploitation of communications intelligence means and methods. Truscott also possessed a significant intellectual grasp of the subtleties and ironies of the Cold War and some of the fallacies on which it was based. Related to the Truscott rumor, another held that Smith had concurred in the selection of Truscott as his replacement; however, it was also alleged if—for political reasons—the post had to be filled by a civilian,

---

*As it turned out, Eisenhower appointed Donovan to serve as the United States ambassador to Thailand, and among other assignments he was given the one of rolling up the Li Mi Chinese Nationalist guerrillas, whose operation was described in Chapter 6. Donovan was reasonably successful in this task, getting about 90 percent of the guerrillas to accept repatriation back to Taiwan, thus effectively ending the CIA's Korean War idea of conducting espionage and sabotage in mainland China. While in Thailand Allen Dulles kept Donovan under close scrutiny and discouraged his grandiose schemes for creating a counterinsurgency force to combat rebels in northeast Thailand.

that Smith had recommended Frank Wisner's elevation to the post.

Somewhat surprisingly, Allen Dulles' name did not figure highly in the speculation about Eisenhower's next DCI. It was alleged that Dulles was "dead" because he was a Dewey man. Like most good rumors there was some substance to the charge that Dulles had in fact been much more than a closet supporter of Governor Dewey in his 1948 bid for the presidency, aiding him by writing speeches and providing "insider" intelligence from a wide variety of private and governmental sources. The rumor further alleged that Dewey had promised Dulles the DCI job in 1948, but following Truman's surprise victory, it was assumed that Dulles had proven himself to be a Democrat in Republican clothes by quickly shifting his allegiance to Truman's foreign policy. Thus, *ipso facto*, the rumormongers concluded that Dulles, the political chameleon, would be less than satisfactory to Eisenhower.

This kind of guessing game is more serious in the intelligence community than one might suppose. Its outcome often determines the fates of carefully nurtured projects and the careers of those involved. For example, in this situation the positions of those who were strongly identified as Smith men would be jeopardized if the new DCI were selected from another camp in the intelligence community, or from the "outside." Partly this jeopardy was due to the internal housecleaning which takes place when a new team takes over in any of the intelligence community's major components, but it was due more to the fact that these changeovers usually lead to retributive paybacks for past inter- and intra-agency factional conflicts.

In spite of all the rumored inside information surrounding Eisenhower's choice for DCI, no one was really sure who would get the top job and who in turn would emerge as the new administration's intelligence leaders. The Republicans had been out of power for twenty years, and the extent of Eisenhower's political debts incurred in his quest for the nomination and election gave scant indications about who would be rewarded and what criteria would govern cabinet appointments and such top jobs as the DCI. Although these questions were never fully answered, the designation of John Foster Dulles as secretary of state on December 20, 1952, and that of his younger brother, Allen Welsh Dulles, as DCI on February 11, 1953, led most of the intelligence community's band of Eisenhower watchers to conclude that there had been reservations in Eisenhower's inner circle about Allen Dulles' appointment. Later it was learned that these reservations were overcome when Allen Dulles, at the urging of John Foster Dulles, agreed to accept an Eisenhower-Smith-Cutler-approved deputy director rather than designating one of his own choosing.

The choice of John Foster Dulles was looked upon as a double plus by the intelligence community leaders. In the first place Dulles, whose ties to military intelligence went back to before World War I, had long been an active member of the intelligence subculture fraternity, aiding an operation here and there with his legal and business connections as well as being himself a producer and consumer of intelligence information. The second plus involved his de facto endorsement of covert operations beyond the Korean War's UNO authority. John Foster Dulles' idea that the proper goal for the United States vis-à-vis Soviet communism was not to coexist with it but to destroy it was in total harmony with the intelligence community's activist wing of Cold Warriors. These warriors drew great encouragement from Dulles' statements in the Republican party's 1952 foreign policy plank: "We will abandon the policy of containment and will actively develop hope and resistance spirit within the captive peoples," and "the United States wants and expects liberation to occur which would change, in an electrifying way, the mood of the captive peoples."

Although the nation as a whole did not necessarily endorse Dulles' ideological militancy, the intelligence community looked upon his words as an affirmative charter of practices carried out during the Korean War and justification to continue and expand them during the Eisenhower administration. Thus, John Foster Dulles' appointment was seen as giving the Cold War a legitimate and much more dramatic aim, replacing Kennan's idea of containment with "liberation."

On the choice of Allen Dulles as DCI, the intelligence community leaders were not so enthusiastic. The brother relationship was looked upon as a guarded plus because it implied some additional high-level political clout on the intelligence community's behalf. However, because relationships between the two brothers were not as close as they appeared on the surface, there was some concern that their personally based disagreements would inhibit the CIA's freedom of action. Also, in assessing Allen Dulles' potential worth as DCI, the intelligence community leaders, especially those in the military intelligence services, feared that he was "accident prone," in the sense of being administratively inept. This fear was soundly based on the military intelligence leaders' experience with Eisenhower, in which most of them had personally felt the general's wrath over sloppy staff work and improvisation rather than thorough planning for operations. Besides these reservations, there was a serious question of how his personal style would play with influential members of Congress. There was no fear that Congress would seek to reform or otherwise exercise any effective control over the intelligence community, but rather that Allen Dulles might alienate, by seeming to patronize, the small group of ranking members in the House and Senate who directed and chaired the armed services and appropriations committees and who were central to the intelligence community's unfettered existence. Each of these men—Carl Vinson and Clarence Cannon in the House and Chan Gurney, Millard Tydings, Leverett Saltonstall, and Richard Russell in the Senate—were powers in their own right and, although they were "friends of intelligence," their friendship could not be taken for granted. Nor could any DCI function effectively if he treated these key members of Congress in cavalier fashion or with obsequious respect.

President Eisenhower was neither insensitive nor unaware of these criticisms. Nevertheless, in the course of balancing all the competing interests, paying off political debts, and negotiating cabinet and high-level appointments for his administration, he concluded that Allen Dulles was the best choice of those available. The field had been narrowed considerably, primarily because Eisenhower, after consultation with Robert Cutler (see below) became convinced that it was politically desirable to place a civilian imprimatur on the CIA and the DCI rather than continue the tradition of naming a military officer for the top intelligence job. Donovan had been ruled out on the grounds of his old feud with J. Edgar Hoover, which had reemerged in nasty fashion during the period when the DCI/CIA post was under consideration. Wisner was ruled out on the rather spurious grounds that he would bring further disharmony to the continually bickering intelligence community. This "faulting" method of political selection has some merit, of course, but it frequently results in not selecting the best qualified person for the job, the one with the most relevant qualifications of experience, temperament, and capacity to do the job.

Allen Dulles' faults led ultimately to his fall from intelligence power. In 1953, Eisenhower moved to offset his weaknesses by further selecting, on Smith's recommendation, Lieutenant General Charles P. Cabell, USAF, to serve as the deputy director of Central Intelligence (DDCI) and deputy director of the CIA. Cabell, who was equally at ease in dealing with administrative and management problems as he was in dealing with the dons of the House and Senate's armed services and appropriations committees, was a perfect match for Dulles. From Eisenhower's point of view about the role of intelligence, in both its staff and positive functions, Dulles and Cabell constituted a very reassuring couple, or so it seemed at the beginning.

Under Eisenhower's modified military staff system, the White House and, especially, the National Security Council were organized to deal with intelligence matters in a more formalized manner than in previous administrations. To ride herd on the NSC, which in addition to fulfilling its national security policy advisory role was expected by Eisenhower to serve as the CIA's "corporate board of directors," the president-elect in late December 1952 advised the NSC's executive secretary, James Lay, that Robert Cutler* would be his

*Robert Cutler's career embraces all that is conveyed by the term "establishment." Born in Brookline, Massachusetts, in 1895, Cutler graduated cum laude from Harvard in 1916, was an instructor at Harvard in the 1916–17 academic year, and when World War I broke out served as a first lieutenant in France with the American Expeditionary Force from 1917–19. After World War I, Cutler returned to the Harvard Law School, was editor of the *Harvard Law Review* and received his LL.B. cum laude in 1922. Thereafter he practiced law in Massachusetts until World War II, during which period he returned to active military service and advanced to the grade of brigadier general. This wartime military service included assignments as assistant deputy director, Army Specialist Corps, 1942; chief procurement director, Officer Procurement Service, 1942–43; general staff corps, Office of the Secretary of War, 1943–45. After World War II, from 1946–53, Cutler moved into banking, serving as the president and director of the Old Colony Trust Company in Boston, from which post Eisenhower recruited him to become the president's special assistant for National Security Affairs.

administrative assistant with special responsibilities for the NSC.

In connection with his assignment, Cutler moved swiftly to restructure the National Security Council in accordance with Eisenhower's modified military staff ideas. On March 16, 1953 (four days before its due date), after a thorough-going review of the NSC's past operations, Cutler submitted a report to Eisenhower detailing significant procedural and organizational changes designed to enhance the NSC's presidential advisory function and character. Of the many reports before and since dealing with how intelligence and national security policy should be handled, the Cutler report stands without peer.

Because of its importance in understanding how intelligence was managed during the Eisenhower years and to the later discussion about the influence of intelligence on policy and policy makers, the Cutler report is described rather fully below. Significantly, Cutler concluded that no changes were required in the 1947 National Security Act's statutory statement of the functions of the council. On the subject of attendance at NSC meetings, Cutler held, as a general rule, that no more than eight persons should have the right to participate as council members; that is, to actually cast a vote and be placed on formal record in favor or against a policy statement, recommendation, or decision. In addition, he established five different categories of attendance at NSC meetings: (1) statutory members, (2) participant members, (3) advisers (statutory and others), (4) observers, and (5) staff.

Within the category of participant members a further distinction was made between those individuals who were invited on a standing-request basis to attend all council meetings until the president decided otherwise, and those who were invited to attend a meeting or a part of a meeting on an ad hoc basis. The categories generally formalized prior practice and were of value in providing a framework within which individual decisions on attendance could be made on a flexible basis in the light of the requirements of a particular council agenda. Cutler confirmed existing arrangements as to actual council attendance with two exceptions: (a) providing that the statutory membership of the Chairman, National Security Resources Board (NSRB), should be transferred to the director, Office of Defense Mobilization, and (b) the special assistant to the president for Cold War Planning became an adviser to the council, while the director, Psychological Strategy Board, was eliminated as an observer.

Thus council membership was limited to a regular group of seven participants: the president and vice-president, the Secretaries of State and Defense, the director for Mutual Security and the director, Office of Defense Mobilization (statutory members), and the Secretary of the Treasury. In recognition of Eisenhower's modified military staff concept, Cutler recommended that if the president was unable to attend a council meeting, the vice-president would preside in his stead. Only in the absence of both the president and vice-president would the secretary of state preside. It should be noted that Eisenhower presided at 306 (or 90 percent) of the 338 council meetings which were held from January 29, 1953 through June 30, 1960.

To make sure that the council would not become a theoretical debating society, Cutler explicitly rejected participation in the council by individuals who had no departmental responsibilities. Cutler envisaged a council of "operators"; however, he also recommended appointment on an ad hoc basis of consultants from outside the government who would either individually or in groups serve as informal advisers to the council.

In the back-up support for the council, Cutler recommended that the Senior Staff be renamed the Planning Board, but carry out the same basic functions. Members of the Planning Board were to include, in addition to the special assistant to the president for National Security Affairs, representatives of State, Treasury, Defense, Mutual Security, and Office of Defense Mobilization. The Joint Chiefs of Staff, CIA, and the Psychological Strategy Board (PSB) were represented by advisers. (When PSB was later abolished and the Operations Coordinating Board established, a member of the OCB staff [usually the executive officer or his deputy] became a Planning Board adviser.)

The chairmanship of the Planning Board was to be assigned to Cutler in his newly established post of special assistant to the president for National Security Affairs. This assignment reflected the view that the chairman of the council's principal policy-formulating staff body should be a person without departmental ties who "through a direct and close staff relationship with the president, was fully cognizant of the desires and requirements of the president."* Both Cutler and Eisenhower were sensitive to the hazards of allowing someone with strong parochial ties to a former organization, be it the CIA, State Department, or the military services, to become the national security policy gatekeeper through whom the options, analyses, and dissents would have to pass. Of course, Cutler and Eisenhower both recognized the tactic of "end running" national security information around the council to the president; at the time, their intent was to establish procedures which could forestall such tactics and still make sure that all views had been given a proper hearing and consideration before being brought to the council for decision.

To underscore the Planning Board's importance, Cutler recommended that its members continue to be nominated by the agency head and, after approval by the special assistant to the president for National Security Affairs, be formally appointed by the president. In this regard, each Planning Board member and adviser received a personal letter of appointment from President Eisenhower. Cutler stated that each member or adviser should have direct access to and the personal confidence of his agency head. He specified that each member or adviser should:

---

*Robert Cutler, "The Development of the National Security Council." *Foreign Affairs*, v. 34, April 1956, p. 445.

... have as his principal responsibility, which overrides all other duties and with which no other duty can interfere, his work with the board, including preparation for and attendance at meetings; yet at the same time continue to be sufficiently in the stream of activity of his department or agency so as to be capable of representing its views.*

This requirement was derived from Cutler's analysis of the NSC's operations during the Korean War, which revealed that although the Senior Staff members were persons with considerable ability and sufficient rank, their departmental responsibilities during wartime made it extremely difficult for them to devote enough time and attention to NSC tasks. The problem was not new, nor was it confined to the NSC. Cutler's solution reflected the fact that those who must deal with day-to-day operational matters are not able to simultaneously engage in long-range or strategic planning. Further, Cutler's solution and subsequent use of the special assistant's approval for Planning Board membership reflected his belief that the members must also possess the outlook of a planner as opposed to that of a line operator.

Besides Cutler's conception of an NSC "general staff" organization embodied in the Planning Board, the most important change recommended in the report was the creation of the post of special assistant to the president for National Security Affairs. This change further formalized the relationship of the president to the NSC by designating a member of the White House staff to serve as the president's principal staff officer for national security affairs. The executive secretary, who had previously performed this general role on an informal basis in the Truman administration, was reappointed head of the career staff of the council and designated to act for the special assistant in his absence.

The Cutler report further recommended that the special assistant be made responsible for determination, subject to the president's desires, of the council agenda, for briefing the president in advance of council meetings, and for presenting matters for discussion at the council meetings. Also,

As chairman of the Planning Board he was responsible for scheduling Planning Board work and for the manner of presentation and quality of such work. He was to appoint (subject where necessary to the president's approval) such ad hoc committees, such consultants from outside the government and such mixed governmental-nongovernmental committees as might be required. Finally, the special assistant was charged with bringing to the attention of the president, with recommendations for appropriate action, lack of progress by an agency in carrying out any policy assigned to it; provided it was not possible to expedite performance at the Planning Board level. The report emphasized, however, that responsibility for implementation rested with the agency

---

*U. S. Senate, Committee on Government Operations, Subcommittee on National Policy Machinery. "Organizing for National Security." 87th Congress, vol 2. Washington: U. S. Government Printing Office, 1961, p. 443.

head concerned and that the role of the special assistant was, on behalf of the president, *to inspect, not to evaluate or direct.* [Emphasis added].*

Finally, in recognition of the need to keep the Planning Board on the proper track and to provide a means to deal with and identify unforeseen problems as well as especially sensitive issues, Cutler recommended strengthening the NSC staff by establishing within it a small "Special Staff" under the supervision of the deputy executive secretary. In Cutler's terms, the Special Staff would act as a trouble-shooting organization for the NSC by carrying out the following duties:

(a) independent analysis and review of each Planning Board report before its submission to the council;

(b) continuous examination of the totality of national security policies with a view to determining if gaps existed which should be filled and if important issues or anticipated developments were sufficiently explored;

(c) continuing integrated evaluation of the capabilities of the free world versus the capabilities of the Soviet Union and satellites, and estimates of the situation, in order to bring such evaluations and estimates before the council;

(d) providing a chairman or member of, or observer with, ad hoc nongovernmental or mixed governmental-nongovernmental committees, and assistance in recruiting such committees; and

(e) keeping currently informed on the status of all national security programs and seeing that reports and pertinent information thereon were currently available.**

In essence, the Cutler report made clear the differences between the council, the Planning Board, the special assistant and the NSC staff. It provided a basic form of reference to deal with national security problems in an orderly manner, and affirmed the point that although the council and the Planning Board's membership, as well as the person designated as special assistant, would likely change in the course of the Eisenhower administration, there should be continuity in the composition and membership of the NSC staff. In Cutler's view there was an urgent requirement to professionalize and depoliticize the NSC staff in order to prevent its manipulation by council members and/or their agencies and departments. By affirming the NSC staff's permanence, Cutler hoped to cut down on and partially offset the revolving-door nature of personnel activities in the field of national security where, for example, the average assistant or deputy assistant secretary of defense served for less than a year and a half before returning to more lucrative outside practices and businesses.

On March 17, 1953, Eisenhower approved the Cutler report without modification; it served as the organizational basis on which the NSC's future activities were carried out during his administrations. However, not too long after Cutler had assumed his post as special assistant for National Security

Ibid., pp. 443–44.

**Ibid.,* p. 444.

On another level the PBCFIA did try to create a stronger institutional structure for the community. In 1957 the board recommended merging the United States Communications Intelligence Board with the Intelligence Advisory Committee (IAC). The USCIB was established in 1946 to advise and make recommendations on communications intelligence to the secretary of defense. The PBCFIA's recommendation for the IAC-USCIB merger was intended to strengthen the DCI's authority and to improve intelligence coordination by making the DCI chairman of the newly established body. The services objected to the creation of the board, since it meant that in the area of electronic intelligence they would be reduced to an advisory role vis-à-vis the DCI and would lose the representational dominance they held in USCIB. Despite the services' objections, in 1958 the United States Intelligence Board (USIB) was created to assume the duties of the IAC and USCIB.*

The PBCFIA, or as it was redesignated in 1961, the President's Foreign Intelligence Advisory Board (PFIAB), has had a long tradition of secrecy. Beginning in the Eisenhower administration it has met for at least two days in Washington every other month. Part of Eisenhower's reason in establishing the PFIAB, in addition to dealing with press revelations about the CIA's involvement in Iran and Guatemala, was to establish a vehicle to deal with the increasing importance of science and technology in intelligence matters. As can be seen from the appointment of Edwin H. Land of the Polaroid Corporation, who served on the PFIAB for fifteen years, William O. Baker of Bell Telephone Laboratories, who served for seventeen years, James R. Killian of the Massachusetts Institute of Technology, who retired from the board for health reasons in 1963 after serving for six years, as well as the appointments of nuclear scientist Edward Teller in 1971 and John S. Foster, Jr., in 1973, the PFIAB's membership gave it a significant capability to deal with fundamental scientific and technical decisions. However, it never had any real authority to resolve the jurisdictional squabbles in the intelligence community, and critics have often condemned its alleged role as an "impartial reviewing agency."** Regardless of these critics' statements, the PFIAB was not an altogether unsuitable vehicle for the president to get an informed and relatively unbiased opinion about the effectiveness of the intelligence community and its operations. According to Clark Clifford, whom John Kennedy appointed to the PFIAB, it enjoyed considerable power when the president backed it: "He let the intelligence community know that if they didn't cooperate they were definitely in peril."

The place of science and technology in the intelligence process during

*"Supplementary Detailed Staff Reports on Foreign and Military Intelligence, Book IV," *op. cit.,* pp. 62–63.

**See Deborah Shapley, "Foreign Intelligence Advisory Board: A Lesson in Citizen Oversight?" *Science,* March 12, 1976. Shapley notes: "Senator Mike Mansfield (Dem., Mont.) says that the board's value as an 'impartial reviewing agency' has been so dubious that 'it would be easier, cheaper, and more logical to abolish it.'"

Eisenhower's administrations is perhaps best revealed in the development of the U-2 and its follow-on systems. The U-2 and some other seemingly unrelated scientific and technical developments, which began in the late 1950s and early '60s, did more to change American intelligence than any of the intermittment bureaucratic centralization efforts taken since its colonial beginnings.

The U-2 story is basically that of one man's vision which could see beyond bureaucratic constraints and recognize how separate pieces of technology could be combined to produce a method able to solve the basic intelligence problem of keeping systematic, accurate track of physical changes and movements of equipment in hostile or denied territory. That man was Richard M. Bissell, whom Allen Dulles named as special assistant for Planning and Coordination in 1954, to organize a small group of Agency personnel to shepherd the U-2 project through the bureaucratic shoals of the CIA and the rest of the intelligence community.

The Senate Select Committee describes Bissell's efforts thusly:

Bissell's background was in economics, and he combined academic experience with extensive government service, first during World War II in the Department of Commerce and the War Shipping Administration and later with the Economic Cooperation Administration, among other positions. Bissell was an innovator above all, quick to seize new ideas and to sponsor their development. For the next six years he maintained virtually exclusive control over the development of the U-2 program, its management, and the initiation of follow-on reconnaissance systems.

The Agency's sponsorship and deployment of the U-2 reconnaissance aircraft was a technical achievement nothing short of spectacular. The U-2 represented dramatic advances in aircraft design and production as well as in camera and film techniques. In July 1955, only eighteen months after contracting, the U-2 became operational and a fleet of 22 airplanes was deployed at a cost of $3 million below the original cost estimate.*

Besides the "virtually exclusive control" which he maintained in developing the U-2, Bissell had the uncommon good sense not to try to be an engineer in addition to being the driving force behind the project. His instructions to the engineers at Lockheed who built the U-2 were a masterpiece of simplicity. He told them in essence: "here is the camera, it is this big, weighs this much and must be in this position relative to the surface of the earth; put it in an airplane to be piloted by one person which can fly this high and this far." The result of these instructions was the design, development, and production of a superb aircraft which was able to fulfill its function precisely and effectively. Neither Bissell nor his staff interfered with the research and development

---

*U. S. Senate, Select Committee to Study Governmental Operations with Respect to Intelligence Activities. "Supplementary Detailed Congress, 2nd Session. Report No. 94–755. Washington: U.S. Government Printing Office, April 23, 1976, pp. 58–59.

process; their function was to help, not hinder, those whose job it was to build an airplane. It was a beautiful one-of-a-kind relationship which confirmed the fact that the cost of committees to oversee the R&D of an aircraft whose function can be clearly set forth is a redundant expense. The lesson of Bissell's approach to the development of an aircraft is one which has yet to be learned by those who have meddled in the development of fighting aircraft for the United States government; witness the TFX, B-1, and others.

One should also note that there was considerable skepticism in the CIA and the military intelligence services, especially the air force's, that "Bissell's bird" or "Dulles' folly" would actually fly, or produce any valid photographic intelligence.* However, as the trickle of early U-2 photos rapidly turned into a torrent of high-resolution photos, the skeptics' voices were muted and the "bread and butter" intelligence analysts in the military intelligence services who dealt with the problem of maintaining the enemy's "order of battle" applauded Bissell for enabling them to keep up with the deployment of Soviet tanks, armored cars, artillery pieces, trucks, and so on inside the USSR and Eastern Europe. Quite literally, by the time the U-2 system was replaced by the Samos-spy-in-the-sky satellites (which perform a similar function with even greater accuracy), the volume of pictures it had taken would have filled two football stadiums. The implications of the U-2 program as a means to reduce uncertainty about an enemy's capabilities and intentions as revealed by the movement of its forces were well appreciated by Eisenhower. He, perhaps more than his predecessors, realized the necessity to establish and maintain a harmonious relationship between those who practice the intelligence craft and those who understand its science and technology.

Although the U-2 stands without peer in its effect on American intelligence, there were several other scientific and technological breakthroughs which occurred in the Eisenhower era which had and continue to have significant influence on the form of American intelligence. Not necessarily in the order of their occurrence or importance, these include: the transistor, which, by basically eliminating the heat problem, made the development of large-scale computers possible; the perfection of magnetic tape, which replaced wire in

---

*Ibid., p. 59. In 1955, to coordinate collection requirements for the U-2 program, Bissell arranged for an informal Ad Hoc Requirements Committee (ARC), comprised initially of representatives of CIA, army, navy, and air force. Subsequently, representatives of NSA, the Joint Chiefs of Staff, and the State Department were included. In 1960, after the deployment of the U-2's follow-on system, a formal USIB subcommittee, the Committee on Overhead Reconnaissance (COMOR), succeeded the ARC. COMOR was responsible for the development and operation of all overhead reconnaissance systems. The development of overhead reconnaissance systems created a need for another group of intelligence specialists: photographic interpreters. The Agency had established a photographic center in the DDI in 1953. As a result of the U-2 deployment that group formed the nucleus of a quickly expanding specialty among intelligence analysts. In 1961 the National Photographic Interpretation Center (NPIC) was established under the DCI's direction. Staffed by CIA and military personnel, NPIC was a DDI component until 1973, when it was transferred to the CIA's Directorate for Science and Technology (DS&T).

recording devices; and the transoceanic 707 jet airplane. Each of these break-throughs changed intelligence in ways which have yet to be fully mastered by the intelligence community and its leaders.

For example, transistorized computers made it possible to manipulate intelligence information more quickly than at any time in history. And the existence of magnetic tape and punch cards produced the means by which more information could be stored and retrieved than ever before. Obviously, these increased capabilities in handling intelligence information have produced their own set of problems (See Chapter 9, "The Future of American Intelligence"). It should be noted that under Eisenhower the development of these means was hastened because of his personal belief in their applications in solving intelligence problems. Eisenhower was a man of many dimensions, but above all he was a commander who understood and had no hesitation about introducing scientific and technological means to solve problems.

What Boeing's 707 contributed to the intelligence equation is a little less clear. In 1946 the CIG had a component within its organization called the Domestic Contacts Service (DCS), whose purpose was to solicit foreign intelligence information on a voluntary basis from American tourists and business-men. In the early days, the DCS's operations were minimal. It was an index-card kind of operation, with low priority; it could be handled on a fairly leisurely basis because the flow of Americans to and from overseas areas was only a trickle. Also, the number of international ports of air entry into the United States was small, and coverage of returning travellers could be handled with a limited liaison effort. However, Americans' foreign travel picked up in the first decade after World War II. This was handled without too much additional investment of time and personnel, but when the 707 began to fly in the late 1950s the DCS situation changed markedly. More airports and cities became international ports of entry, worldwide tourism increased exponentially, multinational corporations began to emerge, and American students increasingly began to vacation and study abroad. Soon the DCS people had more potential targets than they could reach; and as the mail-intercept program began to identify more and more potential counterintelligence targets, they became swamped. As a result, the DCS operation received a high priority in the total scheme of things; CIA offices in places like New Orleans, Detroit, and San Francisco were opened up to keep up with the increased flow of Americans going abroad, not simply to the conventional watering holes of Rome, Paris, and London, but also to places like Albania, Yugoslavia, Zaire, and especially the Soviet Union. The results of this technologically inspired, unprecedented foreign-travel boom on the intelligence community and especially the CIA were many. It provided an additional flow of intelligence information which, when added to the growing stack acquired from the U-2 program and other overt sources, threatened, in spite of the developing data storage and retrieval capability, to overwhelm the community's ability to digest and analyze its meaning. It also added ominous fuel to the intelligence community's paranoiac internal-security fires because American travelers, especially those going to Eastern Europe, were seen as giving the Soviet Union an opportunity to recruit them to their intelligence cause. The fears were not completely unfounded because, as the Domestic Contacts Service division and various counterintelligence organizations learned, the Soviets had, in fact, been successful in a number of cases in recruiting, blackmailing, or otherwise coercing Americans into serving the Soviet intelligence service. For many who worked in this complicated and complex area of intelligence in the Eisenhower years and thereafter, the realization that for every American they detected who had succumbed and had been put under surveillance, there were perhaps twenty or fifty more they had missed, was a deeply disturbing thought. This is cited not to justify Lyndon Johnson's illegal order to place Vietnam antiwar activists under army, CIA, and FBI surveillance, but rather as evidence of the effect of technology, in this case the jet airplane, on the problems of internal security and those associated with acquiring intelligence information from American citizens who, although they had no legal requirement to assist their government, since 1946 have overwhelmingly (approximately 90 percent of all those contacted) been willing to share their experience, observations, and opinions about the countries they visited.

Finally, no discussion of the Eisenhower years and their effect on American intelligence would be complete without mention of the human side to intelligence efforts. This, in spite of the emergence of science and technology in American intelligence, was still most important. The role of the Dulleses, Cutlers, Truscotts, Bissells, Angletons, et al. while occupying center stage scarcely reflects the problems, fears, and perceptions of the intelligence community's foot soldiers in trenches and sparsely furnished offices as they attempted to obtain and make sense out of the profession's raw material. Most took their lead and opinion from the men at the top. In the case of Allen Dulles, who carried the affectionate but unspoken nickname of "Papa," those in the CIA were content with his leadership and only a slender few took the position that "father didn't know best."

On the whole, the Eisenhower years were not a time of questioning throughout the intelligence community. The Cold War was real, but not very well articulated by its leaders; as a result demagogues were able to use its existence for their own purposes. Often those purposes produced a situation which prevented an effective consideration of genuine intelligence problems and which also produced long-term damaging results to the efforts of those who were doing their best to build a responsive, effective intelligence system. The best example of the deleterious effects of demagoguery on the intelligence community can be seen in the antics of Senator Joseph R. McCarthy, whose unwarranted attacks on the United States Army and the CIA for harboring "communists, homosexuals, and rich men" did more to enhance the Soviet cause than anything pulled off by the KGB in the 1953–61 period.

Today, some twenty years later, McCarthy is seen by many as a media-created monster of grotesque proportions, or as a prophet before his time. One can pick which characterization is most apt, or simply conclude that Joe McCarthy was a venal politician who only was interested in his reelection. But certainly McCarthy's actions, however intended, damaged the intelligence community so profoundly that one can only hope it will ultimately recover from them.

When McCarthy set off on his one-man crusade to unearth communists in the United States government wherever and whomever they might be, the real problem of maintaining American internal and national security was made infinitely more complicated. Those who had given their lives to the complex tasks of counterintelligence were completely thwarted by McCarthy's rushing hither and yon like a rutting bull elephant who had lost his way. McCarthy knew less about catching a spy than he did about catching a cold. The results of his efforts were that by accusing anyone—except J. Edgar Hoover, whom he had reason to fear deeply—he compelled the commitment of limited intelligence resources to carry out the time-consuming task of proving that those who had been capriciously accused by the senator were not communists, a task much more difficult than proving an individual *is* a communist.

In the course of McCarthy's attacks on the CIA, many in the Agency and elsewhere in the intelligence community wondered why Eisenhower didn't stand up to McCarthy and stop him. Obviously political conditions were considered more important than the effect of McCarthy's charges on CIA morale; however, according to R. Harris Smith, "Vice-President Nixon was dispatched to pressure McCarthy into dropping his plans for a public investigation. The senator suddenly became 'convinced' that it would not be in the public interest to hold public hearings on the CIA, that it perhaps could be taken care of administratively."*

In the wake of this lamentable situation, which fortunately did not produce the carnival of a McCarthy-chaired public hearing, each of the intelligence services, especially the CIA, instituted additional personnel security measures such as polygraph testing of employees, which, in turn, led to the compilation of information about the sexual habits, fears, doubts, etc., of intelligence personnel. To be sure, homosexuals were not welcome as members of the intelligence community, but the "loyalty" program produced a compendium of personal information which would have amused and interested Kinsey, Masters, and Johnson but had little to do with intelligence personnel's loyalty to the United States or the fervor of their anticommunism. Also, in the course of the intelligence "reinvestigations" (or purges, as some called them), a dangerous precedent was established in the CIA where, after the polygraph test was made a condition of employment,** a select group of approximately fifty

*Smith, *op. cit.,* p. 371.

**The CIA's reliance upon polygraphy as an almost exact science to determine the fitness and loyalty of its employees was refuted in testimony by J. Edgar Hoover on March 27, 1953, before the Senate Appropriations Committee, when he said:

or sixty persons was excused from the test. These persons, came to be known as the "above and beyond suspicion" group by those who resented the Agency's unwarranted intrusion into their private lives, but nonetheless had to submit to the test if they wanted to keep their jobs. Other effects on morale due to the McCarthy attacks were manifested in an alarming increase of alcoholism and a divorce rate about twice as high as the national rate, especially among those persons serving in overseas assignments.

On the production side of intelligence, McCarthy's excesses created an Orwellian response which made accomplishment of the analytical intelligence function much more difficult. For example, subjects such as the Sino-Soviet split had to be waffled over, leaving the impression from analyses that, like Mark Twain's death, it was rumored but not actually reported. Other topics, such as analyses reporting the improvements in the economy and living conditions in the Soviet Union and China, had to be qualified as "probably temporary," or that "in spite of the evidence it appears that the Communist regime is preparing more repressive measures," etc. Also, those involved in covert collection overseas became fearful that they might be charged with "consorting with known communists" if they sought intelligence information about the communists from the most likely source. As a result many agents used a cut-out or spurious identity of their "CAS" (Controlled American Source) if that source was an "unapproved" communist. It was a crazy situation under which, unlike the Jesuits who were given papal authority to deal with heretics, no one could be completely sure that they would not be summoned to appear

---

The name "lie detector" is a complete misnomer. The machine used is not a lie detector. It shows the variations of your blood pressure and of your emotions. The person who operates the machine is the lie detector by reason of his interpretations. The machine technically is known as the polygraph. The man operating it must be extremely skilled and must be conservative and objective. He must be able to properly interpret the recordings made. However, whenever the human element enters into an interpretation of anything, there is always a variance. I would never accept the conclusion of a lie detector as proof of innocence or guilt. All that it can be called is a psychological aid.

For instance, I have in mind defalcations in banks. There was a case where one or two defalcations had been reported. We never use the lie detector except upon agreement of the employees. Two employees immediately admitted they had committed this defalcation and eleven others admitted other defalcations which the bank did not know of and which had not been reported. That was psychological.

I saw the lie detector used in a kidnapping case which I handled some years ago in which a young man in his early twenties was picked up. He was quite a nervous and high-strung individual. The lie detector indicated that he was guilty of kidnapping and murdering a child. We were not satisfied to accept that: We tried it on another suspect. He proved to be as innocent as any man could be. Five days later I received a full confession from the second man whom the lie detector proved to be innocent and he went to the chair and paid the penalty.

That is why I have said I do not have confidence [in the polygraph] as specifically proving anything. It is a psychological aid but as you and I both know, there are many persons who are highly excitable and highly emotional, who get very nervous when they have committed no crime.

before some grand inquisitor to explain their motives and justify anew their faith in the anticommunist cause.

On looking back at the damaging effects of McCarthy's attacks on American intelligence and those who served its cause, one can derive some satisfaction that both survived—although with some deep scars and impaired efficiency—and that the intelligence community did not fight McCarthy's fire with their own. Allen Dulles, in the cases of McCarthy's 1954 attacks on William Bundy, a member of the CIA's Board of National Estimates, and on Cord Meyer, Jr., the Agency's chief of Covert Operations, used the truth and facts to expose the content of McCarthy's accusations for the nonsense they were. And out of his own love of country and the Agency, Dulles refused to beat McCarthy at his own game. There were those in the CIA and elsewhere in the intelligence community who advocated a "dirty trick" counterattack against McCarthy. But Dulles acted as a genuine director of Central Intelligence and rejected that course of action completely out of hand, even to the extent of not allowing anyone to provide some live rounds of ammunition to McCarthy's foes in the Senate, which in the often brutal but "courteous" debate would have thoroughly discredited McCarthy and driven him from office. But this was not done, and the various McCarthy files remain safely out of sight in the intelligence community's secret archives, if they have not already been shredded in the wake of recent investigations of the community's members.

There can be no final summing up of the Eisenhower legacy. Eisenhower took the American intelligence community as he found it, improved its operations, moved it into a closer relationship with science and technology, and demonstrated its capabilities and limitations in serving the president. What his successors either learned or failed to learn from his and other presidents' experiences in trying to use American intelligence as the servant of the president and his policies is described in the succeeding chapter. Many of these lessons were lost on his successors and had to be relearned at great and painful cost by them and the nation itself.

CHAPTER 8

KENNEDY TO CARTER: INTELLIGENCE AND POLICY MAKING

When President John F. Kennedy became the United States' first intelligence officer on January 20, 1961, the intelligence community's leadership had serious reservations about his future conduct of intelligence affairs. Although these reservations were diminished somewhat by Kennedy's reappointment of Allen Dulles as DCI, concern was voiced about how, if at all, he was going to use the intelligence community "to get the country moving again," how he would react to the skyrocketing costs of deploying the U-2's follow-on systems, and how he would deal with the unprecedented increased cost of research and development for communications intelligence. As intelligence community members came into contact with the "knights of the Camelot round table," they voiced fears to one another about the new team's lack of experience, youth, abrasiveness, etc. These fears constituted a normal enough reaction on their part; the inherent difficulty in effecting a change from one set of policy leaders to the next is quite real. However, the Kennedy accession presented especially difficult problems due to the ongoing nature of some projects—like the contemplated invasion of Cuba—and the thrust and direction of internal security measures which required Kennedy's early reaffirmation to prevent the intelligence system from grinding to a halt. To be sure, the nuts-and-bolts collection process was generally seen as continuing come what may; but its direction in support of positive intelligence and covert operations was one which also needed prompt presidential endorsement and approval.

Very shortly after his inauguration, Kennedy, as is the president's right, set the tone for the direction he wanted the intelligence community to take by two actions. The first week of his administration saw his uncritical acceptance of the CIA's planned Bay of Pigs invasion; next was his disestablishment of the NSC's Operations Coordinating Board (OCB) on February 11, 1961, while maintaining its "Special Group" to deal with the approval of covert actions.*
In the case of Kennedy's approval of the Bay of Pigs invasion, his decision was

---

*The etymological trace of the term "Special Group" is slightly confusing because of the way the control, initiation, and approval of covert activities, beginning in 1948, evolved. From the creation of the OPC in 1948 to the PSB on April 4, 1951, to the OCB on September 2, 1953, coordination of covert operations reverted to a smaller group identical to the 10/2 panel, without OCB staff

widely interpreted to mean that high-risk covert actions had received another presidential green light; the OCB decision showed that he saw little value in the modified military-staff concept developed by Eisenhower, which was designed to ensure that all points of view were considered in the covert operations decision-making process. Also, because of the way the Bay of Pigs decision was actually reached, the retention of the Special Group was seen as further evidence of Kennedy's intent to involve the White House more directly in the management of covert actions.

In the aftermath of the Bay of Pigs fiasco, Kennedy claimed that he had been badly misinformed prior to the invasion attempt. As a result, he was convinced that the intelligence community needed to be thoroughly overhauled—especially the CIA, which Kennedy blamed the most. Although there was some truth to Kennedy's claim, the greater truth is that he himself failed to exercise much prudence in dealing with the intelligence information provided by the CIA in support of its invasion plan. In Kennedy's defense he was new to the job, but it is not correct to say that the CIA conned him into accepting a plan that Allen Dulles, Richard Bissell, General Cabell, et al. believed to be flawed, either conceptually or practically. To be sure, the Bay of Pigs invasion plan was presented in hopeful and optimistic terms, but its certainty of success was never asserted by those who briefed Kennedy and his advisers.

Because the Bay of Pigs soured Kennedy on the intelligence community, it is worthwhile to examine how he came to affirm what he assumed had been Eisenhower's decision to make an amphibious landing on Cuban soil using a brigade of Cuban émigrés with air support supplied by émigré pilots in unmarked military planes. In early April 1960, the Special Group, which since March 26, 1957, had given the secretary of state sole operational authority for particularly sensitive projects which did not have military implications, approved a covert action plan which called for the "insertion" of company-sized

---

participation. In March 1955, NSC 5412/1 was issued, which established the Planning and Coordinating Group (PCG) as an OCB committee and directed that it serve as the channel for policy approval of covert operations. As such, the PCG (the 5412 Committee, or as it came to be known, the "Special Group") was composed of "designated representatives" of the president, secretaries of state and defense, and the DCI. In practice the Special Group's actual membership varied as ad hoc task forces were organized for different situations. These are less important than the fact that NSC 5412/1 established the rule that covert operations were subject to approval by an executive committee (Special Group), whereas in the past these operations were initiated on the authority of the DCI. In June 1964, National Security Action Memorandum NSAM 303 was issued. NSAM 303 left the composition, functions, and responsibilities of the Special Group unchanged. The effect of this directive was quite simply to change the name of the Special Group to the 303 Committee. The purpose of NSAM 303 was just as simple—the name of the Special Group had become public as a result of the publication of David Wise's *The Invisible Government* and, therefore, it was felt that the name of the covert action approval committee should be changed. These procedures and the 303 Committee designation remained in effect until February 17, 1970, on which date National Security Decision Memorandum NSDM 40 was issued. It created the "40 Committee" and made additional changes in the procedures for initiating, approving, and controlling covert actions.

(150–200) groups of trained guerrillas into each of Cuba's six provinces by September. For reasons which remain obscure even today, this plan was assumed by the Special Group not to have "military implications." The plan was premised on the belief that Castro, the recently victorious guerrilla leader, would be even more vulnerable to guerrilla attacks than his predecessor, Fulgencio Batista, because of Castro's necessity to maintain security both in the cities and the countryside. It was further assumed that the Cuban army, which had neither displayed a real inclination to fight a counterguerrilla war nor to oppose Castro's forces when they left their guerrilla sanctuaries during the conventional warfare phase of the Cuban Revolution, would be of little use to Castro. On the whole, the operation scarcely qualified as a "major" covert operation; nonetheless, it came before the Special Group and was routinely approved. The United States' involvement was minimal, and Castro's before-the-fact rhetorical attacks against counterrevolutionaries provided a highly appropriate "plausible denial" cover story. However, between April and August of 1960, the CIA's leadership and the operators who were training Cuban émigré guerrillas became convinced, largely due to the enthusiasm of the Cubans themselves, that a long drawn-out guerrilla campaign was not required to topple Castro; rather, if a major show of force could be arranged, the Cuban people would rise up in a popular revolt and drive Castro and his followers from Cuba.* The émigrés' enthusiasm was contagious. It infected most of the CIA's operators, who came to accept the fervent belief of their émigré charges about a popular uprising as valid intelligence about Cuban conditions rather than as a hypothesis which should be tested before changing the original plan. But the necessary determination by other sources of whether the conditions for a mass popular uprising in support of a military show of force existed in Cuba was not carried out. Nor was much of an effort made by the CIA to avail itself of intelligence information the Office of Naval Intelligence had acquired, both before and after Castro's victory, from its own agents and Cuban nationals who were employed at the United States Naval base at Guantanamo Bay. This information—as revealed in the Bay of Pigs post-mortem carried out at Kennedy's direction by the attorney general, Robert Kennedy; the president's military adviser, Maxwell Taylor, and former chief of naval operations, Admiral Arleigh Burke (the "Special Review Committee")—suggested that the Cuban people were more concerned with their economic circumstances than with nebulous ideas about political "freedom."**

*For a full discussion of the actual Bay of Pigs operation see especially, Karl E. Meyer and Tad Szulc, *The Cuban Invasion.* New York: Praeger, 1962.

**On April 22, 1961, following the Bay of Pigs failure, the president requested Maxwell Taylor to conduct a reevaluation of "our practices and programs in the areas of military and paramilitary, guerrilla and antiguerrilla activity which fall short of outright war." Taylor was to give special attention to Cuba and Robert Kennedy was to be his principal colleague in the effort. The resulting review concluded:

We have been struck with the general feeling that there can be no long-term living with

It is not clear why ONI's intelligence information, which suggested that a different political climate existed in Cuba than the one set forth by the émigrés, was not considered by the Special Group before they signed off in late August after changing the original plan to one which embraced the idea of an amphibious invasion. No date was given for its execution; perhaps the Special Group's intent was to leave the final decision and the setting of a target date to the next administration. Or if Nixon were elected, to serve up the changed plan for his consideration during the transition period. Also, although the records of this entire matter were not available to the Special Review Committee, those they did examine indicate that Eisenhower was aware of and at least endorsed the earlier (April) decision to insert guerrilla bands into Cuba. However, they do not show that the amphibious invasion plan was similarly given to him for review and approval. In view of the fact that after leaving office Eisenhower never publicly disavowed the Bay of Pigs invasion, it is perhaps fair to conclude that if he did see the amphibious invasion plan, he looked on it more as a contingency rather than an operation plan. Eisenhower was too well-versed in military matters to have bought the Bay of Pigs plan in a poke devoid of better intelligence than that offered by the CIA. And after the experience of Hungary he would have thought long and hard before embarking on an operation which was likely to provoke a Soviet military response.

Regardless of what Eisenhower knew, decided, or did or did not convey to Kennedy about the amphibious invasion plan during the transition period, the go-ahead decision was made by Kennedy in the first week or so of his presidency. In the course of reaching that decision it is precisely correct to note that "His top advisors—the secretaries of state and defense, the Joint Chiefs of Staff, and the CIA director—recommended he carry it out. After seeking the advice of other experts he finally gave the go-ahead."* Unfortunately, this circle of top advisers and "other experts" to whom Kennedy turned for an opinion did not include the one person who could have given him some much-needed perspective about the contemplated amphibious invasion scheme: the commandant of the United States Marine Corps, General David Monroe Shoup. Why General Shoup wasn't invited to participate in the Bay of Pigs discussion is a question whose answer is lost in the vagaries of Pentagon politics, or perhaps is more simply explained by the fact that Shoup could have

---

Castro as a neighbor. His continued presence within the hemispheric community as a dangerously effective exponent of communism and anti-Americanism constitutes a real menace capable of eventually overthrowing the elected governments in any one or more of weak Latin American republics. . . .

It is recommended that the Cuban situation be reappraised in the light of all presently known factors and new guidance be provided for political, military, economic and propaganda action against Castro.

(Report to the President, 6/13/61, Memo No 4., p. 8. Cited from the "Interim Report," *op. cit.*, p. 135.)

*Rositzke, *op. cit.*, p. 176.

been counted upon to speak his mind to the president regardless of which way the debate was leaning. In discussing this matter some years later, Shoup, without inveighing against any of those involved, remarked that "Anytime a commander finds everyone on his staff in favor of a course of action he should look elsewhere in his command until he finds someone who'll tell him no. Not as a means to justify inaction, but to help the commander identify the things that can and are likely to go wrong in the best of plans."

In the course of the post–Bay of Pigs investigation, Shoup's wisdom was further confirmed by the facts that the ONI's political intelligence did exist, and that intelligence information from the navy's Fleet Intelligence Center at Norfolk decrying the unsuitability of the landing beaches and assessing the mobility of Castro's armored defense forces had reached the Washington intelligence community but had not been considered by the CIA's planners. Kennedy had good reason to be miffed, not only at the intelligence community's failure to properly warn him about the operation's hazards, but also at himself for not making effective use of all the intelligence resources at his disposal.

The ill-fated Bay of Pigs invasion was a tragedy of epic proportions. It resulted in needless loss of lives, damaged America's international relations and standing in the United Nations, prematurely ended the intelligence careers of such extremely able persons as Allen Dulles and Richard Bissell, put America's intelligence community members, especially the CIA, under a cloud, and caused President Kennedy to suffer personal embarrassment at a critical time in his administration. But most all the failed invasion gave Castro a golden opportunity to broaden his base of popular support and consolidate his guerrilla victory. All these factors were important in effecting the post–Bay of Pigs evolution of the American intelligence community.

One of the valid conclusions derived from the review following the Bay of Pigs was that the original plan to insert guerrillas into Cuba in September 1960 was, at the time, a valid covert action which had an extremely high probability of preventing Castro from consolidating his hold on the Cuban government and people. This plan was discarded in favor of the amphibious invasion, even though the original conception and analysis of the situation were correct. However, in the course of rediscovering and examining the original plan, the Special Review Committee took its specific case validity and used that as the general basis for adopting a counterinsurgency, paramilitary strategy elsewhere in the world, most notably in Southeast Asia. (This is further described below in connection with the beginnings of United States involvement in Vietnam during Kennedy's presidency.)

To Kennedy's credit he personally took the lumps for the failed Bay of Pigs invasion. However, he failed to take all the necessary actions required to keep the intelligence community from making policy by default during the remainder of his administration. This is not to say that Kennedy's responses to the perceived intelligence failure of the Bay of Pigs operation were inappropriate, but rather that they didn't go far enough. After his death, these responses were either aborted or not considered necessary enough by President Johnson and his administration to be carried out to their logical end.

One of Kennedy's first responses, which was designed to insure a broad base of advice about intelligence matters, involved his reliance on the PFIAB to come up with recommendations designed to change the intelligence community's way of doing business. In this regard,

According to official records, between May and November 1961 the PFIAB met twenty-five times. This was more often than it had convened during its previous five years of existence. Clark Clifford estimates that of the 180 recommendations it made to Kennedy, some 170 were adopted. Among the recommendations were proposals to establish the science and technology directorate in the CIA and to consolidate some military intelligence activities in the Defense Intelligence Agency.*

The continued top secret and secret classification of the PFIAB's recommendations to Kennedy prevents an extended discussion of their contents; suffice it to say that taken together they provided a comprehensive blueprint to effect a most sensible, needed structural reform of the intelligence committee which, if fully enacted, would have enhanced the intelligence community's ability to perform its various missions as well as provided the president with the effective means to oversee its operations. It is possible to describe one major result which resulted from this review: the creation of the Defense Intelligence Agency (DIA) in August 1961.

President Kennedy's efforts and, to a lesser degree, those of Secretary of Defense Robert S. McNamara in breathing life into the DIA is an often overlooked major contribution of the Kennedy administration to the evolution of American intelligence. It was a remarkable bureaucratic tour de force which had eluded Truman and Eisenhower, both of whom recognized that the military intelligence services were largely beyond effective presidential or civilian control. But Kennedy, still smarting from the Bay of Pigs, was not about to let the military intelligence services remain outside his control. It was not an easy fight to bring them in.

At the end of World War II, the JCS had decided to continue the Joint Intelligence Committee created in 1942 as a coordinating mechanism to meet interdepartmental military intelligence requirements. Following the abolishment of the OSS in October 1945, the JCS created the Joint Intelligence Group (JIG, sometimes referred to as J-2) within the Joint Staff, which was authorized by the National Security Act of 1947. The JIG represented the military's acceptance of an armistice-type organization in which the various intelligence services would agree to discuss problems of common interest without surrendering any of their perquisites, and cooperate with each other beyond the strict

*Shapley, *op. cit.*, p. 12.

criteria of self-interest. The result of this situation was that before an individual army, navy, marine, or air force intelligence officer was posted to duty with the JIG, he was routinely informed by his mentors not to forget the color of the suit he wore and that if he did, his homecoming to his parent service after he had completed his tour would be less than cordial. These kinds of instructions produced a curious form of schizophrenia in which, for example, a navy intelligence officer on duty with the JIG had to first divine the effects of his analysis on the navy's interests before he forwarded those analyses to the JCS (and presumably to the secretary of defense) for consideration and possible use. Duty with the JIG—and to a similar extent with the CIA—amounted to very hazardous duty for the individual military intelligence officer who took an apolitical or nonparochial military service point of view.

Between the end of World War II and the appearance on October 4, 1957, of the Soviet's Sputnik I orbiting about every hour and a half over the United States, the JIG carried out this bureaucratic game of one-upsmanship without too much difficulty, nor was there much concern in the military and political hierarchies of the Department of Defense; each of the secretaries of defense was taking most of his intelligence from other tables. However, after Sputnik II was launched on November 3 to prove the first was no fluke, the question of what this significant Soviet technological feat actually meant became a matter of serious internal debate in the military intelligence services, the CIA, and the JIG.

The obvious requirement to come up with an overall estimate and explanation of the Soviet success produced a painful reexamination of the intelligence community's conventional wisdom. It was a time during which the military intelligence services and, to a lesser extent, the CIA were hoisted by their own petard for their earlier pandering to the whims of political leaders who deprecated the Russians and Chinese as illiterate barbarians. The Sputniks were irrefutable facts of the Soviet's scientific and technological capability. Once the initial shock of Sputnik had passed, the military intelligence services, individually and through their JIG surrogates, turned the situation to their services' advantage by using the Soviets' "unprecedented and incredible" accomplishment as the basis for justifying self-serving budget requests for defense weapons. These overinflated estimates of Soviet scientific prowess, like those which had described the Soviet's espionage and subversion efforts a decade earlier, produced their own equal and opposite reaction, which caused the USIB in 1959 to study the military intelligence agencies. Because the study group found, among other deficiencies, that the military intelligence services were taking their cues for analysis from American political dogma about the primitiveness of the Soviets and the Chinese, it recommended changing the military departments' status from member to observer on the USIB, and creating a coordinating DIA which would represent the armed services as a member of the USIB. The study group's conclusion calling for downgrading the individual military intelligence services was hotly debated in the Pentagon. The bureaucratic in-fighting was exceptionally severe, as each of the military intelligence services' leaders (as well as the military service chiefs) tried to hold on to their intelligence fiefdoms.

For several years prior to the study group's examination of military intelligence, the secretary of defense's special assistant for Special Operations, General Graves B. Erskine, USMC, who served as the principal aide to the secretary and deputy secretary on all matters pertaining to national intelligence, had repeatedly tried to warn the military intelligence services' leaders that their failure to provide good, valid, and thorough intelligence would result in their being reorganized out of business—but to no avail. In describing this state of affairs one of Erskine's aides, Colonel Henry A. Aplington III, USMC, noted: "They [ONI, G-2, and the air force's A-2] were all in business for themselves and didn't take seriously the needs or role of the secretary of defense in the national intelligence process. Although each was badly burned by Sputnik, each thought, like in the past, this [the JSG's recommendations] too shall pass away."

The military intelligence services were almost correct in this latter conclusion. Secretary of Defense Thomas S. Gates tabled the SG's recommendations in late October 1960 because of the political implications of making a major reorganization of military intelligence so late in the Eisenhower administration. And when Kennedy won the presidential election, the military intelligence services' leaders believed that the issue would either be placed on a back burner or that they would have an opportunity to fight the battle once again when the new administration took office in January 1961.

A second battle of sorts over the organization of military intelligence did take place following Kennedy's inauguration and the appointment of Robert S. McNamara as secretary of defense. However, it was short-lived, because when the Bay of Pigs failure was examined there was blame enough to give each of the military intelligence services its ample share. Consequently, without significantly changing the JSG recommendations, McNamara established by departmental directive (DOD 5105.21, dated August 1, 1961), the Defense Intelligence Agency (DIA), making it responsible for:

(1) the organization, direction, management, and control of all Department of Defense intelligence resources assigned to or included within the DIA;

(2) review and coordination of those Department of Defense intelligence functions retained by or assigned to the military departments. Overall guidance for the conduct and management of such functions will be developed by the director, DIA, for review, approval and promulgation by the secretary of defense;

(3) supervision of the execution of all approved plans, programs, policies, and procedures for intelligence functions not assigned to DIA;

(4) obtaining the maximum economy and efficiency in the allocation and management of Department of Defense intelligence resources. This includes analysis of those

DOD intelligence activities and facilities which can be fully integrated or collected with non-DOD intelligence organizations;

(5) responding directly to priority requests levied upon the Defense Intelligence Agency by USIB;

(6) satisfying the intelligence requirements of the major components of the Department of Defense.

This rather matter-of-fact statement of the DIA's responsibilities belies the horrendous complexity of the tasks involved. It has, since 1961, been an unremitting, oftentimes unrewarding mission for each of the DIA's directors to undertake, because in addition to fulfilling intelligence requests for policy purposes the DIA must also ensure—in conjunction with America's farflung overseas combat commands—that the nation's operational military intelligence needs are met. To give the directive some added perspective in terms of the magnitude of the tasks imposed on the DIA's director by the stroke of McNamara's pen, one should note that:

The director of DIA functions as the principal intelligence staff officer to both the secretary of defense and the Joint Chiefs of Staff, reporting to the secretary through the Joint Chiefs. The director is also commander of the Defense attaché system and chairman of the weekly meetings of the Military Intelligence Board, composed of the chiefs of the four armed services. In addition to a General Counsel office, an Inspector General unit, and a Scientific Advisory Committee, the DIA presently consists of the following components which respond directly to the director/deputy director leadership: chief of staff/deputy for Management and Plans (policy development and coordination, plans, operations management, and formulation of requirements for functional management systems); deputy director for Intelligence (including responsibility for all-source finished military intelligence but not scientific and technical intelligence, maintenance of target systems and physical vulnerability research, military capabilities, and current intelligence assessments, reporting and warning); deputy director for Collection; deputy director for Scientific and Technical Intelligence; deputy director for Estimates; deputy director for Attaché and Human Resources; deputy director for Support (support activities and administrative services); deputy director for Information Systems (intelligence information and telecommunications systems); deputy director for Personnel; Comptroller; and the Defense Intelligence School supervised by a commandant.*

Although the total number of personnel committed one way or another to the DIA is obfuscated in the federal budget, it is not inaccurate to say that there are at least four CIAs included in the total DIA effort, and that this organization does all that the CIA does and more. Critics of the DIA contend that it doesn't do any of these tasks very well, but this is unfair; since its

---

*U.S. Congress. Senate. Select Committee to Study Governmental Operations With Respect to Intelligence Activities. *Supplementary Report.* Book VI. Washington: Government Printing Office, 1976, pp. 266–67.

inception, the DIA has had to build an organization while simultaneously providing usable military intelligence to those who have had an operational responsibility to pick up the pieces of failed foreign-policy actions from Laos to Cyprus, and to place valid, up-to-date intelligence in the hands of military commanders in the several dozen potential flash points around the world.

Not unlike the CIA, the DIA was plagued from its bureaucratic breech birth with similar personnel and identity problems. The most severe of the DIA's personnel problems was the fact that the DIA had been "born old" and its personnel, both military and civilian, retained parochial ties to their individual military services. For example, the DIA, in picking up the mission of intelligence in support of targeting (missiles and aircraft bombardment), brought together under one roof the personnel of army, navy, and air force intelligence services who had been separately carrying out this task for their parent service. Thus the merged organization had three sets of chiefs, all of whom generally possessed the same seniority and rank. This produced the worst of all possible worlds in the DIA because, besides the difficulty of producing intelligence by committee, it created internal strains among the individuals involved as each struggled in a bureaucratically ordered environment which contended that all views were equal. Also, the effect of creating the DIA out of the military intelligence services' whole cloth precluded for more than a decade the upward promotional mobility of new people coming into the DIA. As a result, intelligence personnel who remained on duty with the reduced military intelligence services in assignments like counterintelligence, tactical intelligence, and special operations which were outside the DIA's initial rubric of authority were loath to accept duty with the DIA.

Another key point about the DIA's creation and the effect of the Bay of Pigs on the military intelligence services is Secretary McNamara's abolishing the Office of Special Operations. On rather flimsy grounds, the Special Review Committee concluded that OSO should bear some of the blame for not acting to stop the Bay of Pigs fiasco. It was a bum rap because, although Erskine and his staff did possess considerable military and paramilitary experience in amphibious raids, OSO did register some objections and doubts to the secretary of defense about the changed plan to invade Cuba in August 1960; it was not subsequently consulted during Kennedy's discussions either before or after the go-ahead decision had been made. Erskine, affectionately known by thousands of marines as the "Big E," was philosophical about the Bay of Pigs aftermath purges, noting: "Gentlemen, we have a secretary of defense, but we sure as hell don't have a secretary of war."

Following the abolition of Erskine's OSO, McNamara named his deputy secretary, Roswell P. Gilpatric, responsible for certain interdepartmental operational functions. Gilpatric designated Brigadier General Edward Lansdale to serve as a special assistant to carry out these functions and to represent the defense secretary and deputy on special interdepartmental boards and committees. Most of Lansdale's later responsibilities involved so-called counterinsurgency operations in Southeast Asia. In the fall of 1961, soon after his appointment, Lansdale was asked by President Kennedy to examine the administration's Cuban policy and to make recommendations for the future.

A similar examination was carried out by the president's Special Group and the NSC staff under the direction of the president's special assistant for National Security Affairs, McGeorge Bundy. On October 5, 1961, it issued National Security Action Memorandum NSAM 100, entitled "Contingency Planning for Cuba." Addressed to the secretary of state, it noted: "In confirmation of oral instructions conveyed to Assistant Secretary of State Woodward, a plan is desired for the indicated contingency."* The objective of this contingency planning was, in addition to developing an overall covert action program for Cuba, to prepare one in connection with the possible removal of Castro from the Cuban scene. The result of all this high-level concern was that on November 30, 1961, Kennedy issued a memo to the secretaries of state and defense and the DCI which set forth his decision to begin Operation MONGOOSE, "to use all available assets . . . to help Cuba overthrow the communist regime."**

To oversee Operation MONGOOSE, a new control group, the SGA (Special Group Augmented), was created. The SGA comprised the regular Special Group members—McGeorge Bundy; Alexis Johnson, undersecretary of state; Roswell Gilpatric, deputy secretary of defense; John McCone, DCI; and General Lyman Lemnitzer, chairman of the Joint Chiefs of Staff —augmented by Attorney General Robert Kennedy and Maxwell Taylor, the president's military adviser. Although Secretary of State Dean Rusk and Secretary of Defense Robert McNamara were not formal members of the Special Group or the SGA, they sometimes attended meetings.*** Kennedy appointed Lansdale to coordinate Operation MONGOOSE with the activities of the Departments of State and Defense, and named Taylor the chairman of the SGA.

Thus began the Kennedy administration's attempt to orchestrate insurrection by committee. It was a bureaucratic shambles from the start, which left the CIA and the military intelligence services' veterans of covert action shaking their collective heads in amazement at the spectacle of, for example, Richard Bissell, head of the CIA's DDP, being "chewed out in the Cabinet Room of the White House by the Brothers Kennedy for sitting on his ass and not doing anything about getting rid of Castro and the Castro regime."**** On January 18, 1962, in partial response to the Kennedy brothers' pressure, Lansdale assigned thirty-two planning tasks to the organizations participating in MONGOOSE:

---

*"Interim Report", *op. cit.,* p. 136.

**Ibid.,* p. 139.

***Ibid.,* p. 140.

****Ibid.,* p. 141.

The thirty-two tasks comprised a variety of activities, ranging from intelligence collection to planning for "use of U.S. military force to support the Cuban popular movement" and developing an "operational schedule for sabotage actions inside Cuba." In focusing on intelligence collection, propaganda, and various sabotage actions, Lansdale's tasks were consistent with the underlying strategy of MONGOOSE to build gradually toward an internal revolt of the Cuban people.*

On January 30, 1962, the SGA approved the thirty-two tasks, and on February 20 Lansdale detailed a six-phase schedule for MONGOOSE, designed to culminate in October 1962 with an "open revolt and overthrow of the communist regime." Most of these plans came to naught for a reason the Kennedy brothers were unwilling to accept: that it is not feasible to schedule espionage and sabotage operations on a rigid timetable, especially when these operations lack the wartime cover of conventional military operations. Although planned covert actions are not generally directed against "targets of opportunity" (those of a fleeting nature) it is difficult, dangerous, and foolish to proscribe the field agent's freedom of action to decide when, for example, to destroy a bridge. To be sure, some general instructions concerning the desirability of accomplishing a covert action by a certain time are suitable; however, it rarely makes sense for headquarters to dictate that the bridge over the River Kwai be blown up at high noon next Monday. To do so is to confuse intended with actual results. In connection with MONGOOSE, partly out of the recognition of the faulty planning which went into the Bay of Pigs invasion, the SGA went overboard in demanding detailed plans which as a group they were incapable of using as the basis for approving or disapproving a proposal. There is a fine line in determining how much detail should be considered at each level in the decision-making process of covert action; in the case of MONGOOSE the process was badly flawed by the SGA's demands for plans in "nauseating detail." As a result, because plans had to be submitted and resubmitted—and the operators were prohibited from initiating physical preparation before their approval—inordinate delay was built into MONGOOSE by the SGA. And as the delays continued to mount, the Kennedys' patience and tempers ran short and hot against Bissell, Harvey, and McCone for "dragging their feet."

An offshoot of the proddings to treat the overthrow of Castro as the top priority of the United States government was, according to former CIA director Richard Helms, that Castro's assassination was implicitly authorized by "higher authority." It matters little whether this was actually the case because, as the Senate Select Committee discovered, the perception (or perhaps, selective misperception) of Helms, Bissell, and others was sufficient to create a spin-off from MONGOOSE, Task Force W, organized to kill Castro. In defense of Helms, Bissell, et al. on this issue, there was sufficient precedent from

Ibid., p. 143.

the Eisenhower administration, especially in connection with the Lumumba murder, to assume that Castro's assassination had been ruled "in" by higher authority. As the Senate Select Committee learned, there can be no final answers to the question concerning how the attempts on Castro's life were authorized and who authorized them. Memories of those involved some fifteen years after the fact were hazy and often self-serving, leaving the impression that the decision to kill Castro "just happened." Regardless of the ambiguities about what the president knew and when he knew it, the fact remains that the CIA did, in fact, make at least eight separate attempts on Castro's life, of which none, obviously, was successful.

The bottom line of Operation MONGOOSE, aside from Task Force W's inability to kill Castro, is seen in the fact that its conception and execution was fatally flawed by the belief that such an operation could be carried out on the level and rate contemplated by the SGA without the Soviets taking actions to help Castro counter the threat. In the case of MONGOOSE, the objective of bringing about an "open revolt and overthrow of the communist regime," especially within a time frame of less than a year, was extremely farfetched. The difficulties and lessons learned from dealing with covert actions from a distance far removed from the objective area were ignored and overlooked by those in charge. With only a few exceptions, all of the planning tasks conceived by Lansdale and approved by the SGA required a clandestine penetration of Cuba by small teams from the CIA's "secret army" and their subsequent clandestine extraction after the assigned task was either completed, aborted, or crushed. Superficially, given the extent of the Cuban coastline, this was not a particularly difficult task; however, no significant attempt was made to insert agents, keep them in the objective area, conduct sabotage and prepare the peasants for the revolutionary day. Instead, a hit-and-run tactic was adopted which led most Cubans to conclude that the wisest course of personal valor was to stand aside and not invite personal retribution for aiding the here-today, gone-tomorrow CIA raiders. Admittedly, most of the people the raiders might have counted upon for assistance in building a support movement had left Cuba for a more tranquil existence as refugees in Florida; nevertheless, the failure to enlist the Cuban peasants under the CIA's liberation banner only underscores how weak a vehicle MONGOOSE was on which to predicate a popular uprising. In essence, the detailed plans (which were often made more complex than necessary to insure their approval by the SGA) amounted to harassing missions which expended limited covert-action human resources without much regard for the fact that the "secret war" in Cuba might not be won in one or even ten years.

Unfortunately for MONGOOSE's objective, the Kennedys cut themselves off by word and deed from any thoughtful consideration of the explicit "why not?" which should have been raised before the project was announced. MONGOOSE was a foolish and unnecessarily dangerous action on Kennedy's part. Leaving aside the illegality involved in the acts of insurrection the United

States government was aiding and abetting, it was a decision born, perhaps incorrectly, out of Joe Kennedy's advice to his son "not to get angry, but get even." No one can be certain what went through Kennedy's mind when he approved MONGOOSE, but it is not unreasonable to assume that he had some lingering doubts about the CIA's ability to create a revolution on command. These doubts must have intensified following his face-to-face meeting with Khrushchev in Vienna in the spring of 1961, which sobered him; he recognized that international politics was a much tougher league than Boston's south ward. It should be noted that none of the Camelotians opposed the revealed wisdom of Kennedy's decision to go ahead with MONGOOSE. To do so would have been a denial of an article of faith: that once the president has spoken it is improper to tell him, in effect, "Jack, cool it—your fly is un-zipped." MONGOOSE was given the full force of the president's imprimatur.

Some six weeks after the issuance of NSAM 100, which resulted in MON-GOOSE, Kennedy answered the basic "why not?" himself in a speech delivered at the University of Washington on November 16, 1961:

We cannot, as a free nation, compete with our adversaries in tactics of terror, assassination, false promises, counterfeit mobs, and crises.*

These words should have caused Kennedy to reconsider what he had decided to do about Castro, but obviously they did not. Kennedy similarly failed to take account of the fact that the Bay of Pigs fiasco had enhanced Castro's popularity as well as his hold over Cuba's social and governmental infrastructure, and that covert action by the United States, no matter how "plausibly denied," could only serve to improve Castro's situation. Although it is theoretically consistent to suppose that if Castro repressed the Cuban people in response to American-sponsored covert action he might promote discontent, it is also true that such discontent grows very slowly even in the most repressive of regimes, when the basic physical needs of the populace are met. In fact, the actual physical conditions in Cuba at the time of MONGOOSE were not bad. Castro very wisely followed his guerrilla success (which was due more to the Cuban army's neutrality than any broad-based ideological or popular support) with substantial effort to make the fruits of revolution generally available to the people. For example, following the Bay of Pigs invasion and the Kennedy administration's imposition of a total embargo of all United States trade with Cuba, Castro retaliated by expropriating all American capital in Cuba. This action enabled him to play the role of benefactor to the poor and disadvantaged in Cuba. One agent who stayed in Cuba reported that "Castro's bringing of Havana's poor into the Sears & Roebuck store to select the clothes and necessities they needed was the best political public relations

*Public Papers of the Presidents: John F. Kennedy. Washington: U.S. Government Printing Office, 1961, p. 724.

gimmick since Boss Hague commandered Christmas turkeys from the Teamsters to give to Jersey City voters." These acts of charity with nationalized property, as well as giving the pathetic Havana whores a second chance at life, commended Castro to the deeply religious Cubans who, in spite of the church's opposition to communism, ignored his communist-inspired rhetoric. To most Cubans, Castro had become, if not a popular savior at least a leader who had removed some of the shame and indignity of their previous existence. In the revolution's early days, ideological purity and dialectical materialism were muted; at the time of MONGOOSE, the yoke of communism seemed much lighter on the necks of the great bulk of the Cuban people than the one which had preceded it.

For reasons which lie outside objective analysis, these facts about Castro, his regime, and the Cuban peoples' greater concern with food than ideology were ignored by the Kennedys, who chose to believe what they wanted rather than allowing the intelligence community to challenge these beliefs with facts. And once their attitude was transmitted to the intelligence community by its "underground telegraphy" out of the White House, the analysts retreated into their shells, counted armored cars on the Autobahn, and left the field to the operators who were willing to try anything once, twice, or a dozen times so long as "higher authority" provided the appropriate approval. One further fact needs emphasis: after the Bay of Pigs, the intelligence community's leaders had been sufficiently discredited and traumatized that no one was willing to say no to the president, or challenge the faulty premises on which MONGOOSE was based.

The one person who could have challenged NSAM 100 and what followed under Operation MONGOOSE on the grounds of his personal wisdom painfully acquired in Hungary and the Bay of Pigs itself—Allen W. Dulles—was silenced when these matters were debated. In the course of the Special Review Committee's investigation, in which he cooperated fully, Dulles was left to twist slowly in the wind. Following transmittal of the Special Review Committee's report to President Kennedy on June 13, 1961, Allen Dulles was subtly pressured by the Kennedy forces to offer his resignation; he demurred. However, as presidential access was denied Dulles and as ad hoc meetings of the Special Group—to which he was not invited—were convened, the signals that Dulles was on his way out were not lost on the other intelligence community leaders, who tried to put some distance between themselves and the beleaguered chief. Thus in those fateful months between June and November 1961 there was quite literally no one to tell Kennedy that he was about to embark on an even more slippery path than the one which resulted in the Bay of Pigs disaster. Whether Dulles would have been that man is impossible to say with certainty; however, during the Special Review Committee's investigation he acknowledged and identified the flaws in his and others' thinking which led to the wrong decision. But this was not enough to save his job; Kennedy fired him in November 1961, replacing him with John A. McCone.

Dulles' passing from the national intelligence scene provoked considerable comment throughout the intelligence community. In the wake of his departure many who had complained about one feature or another of Dulles' direction of the CIA or his performance as DCI found that there was much in his performance which would be sorely missed. To many, Kennedy's firing Dulles looked like a cheap shot, especially after the president had gone to such great pains to claim personal responsibility for the Bay of Pigs fiasco.

At the time of McCone's appointment as DCI, the intelligence community's "book" on him was fairly thin. Aside from his background—private industry, where he had distinguished himself as a corporate manager, and government, where he had served as undersecretary of the air force in 1950–51 and as chairman of the Atomic Energy Commission since 1958—not much was known about McCone's ideas on intelligence and the operations of the intelligence community. Also, although McCone had served as a deputy to Secretary of Defense Forrestal in 1948, during which time he became peripherally involved in the formation and operations of the OPC, there wasn't much hard evidence to indicate that he was a Cold Warrior who believed in the efficacy of covert action. Most of the intelligence community leaders, who had grown accustomed to Dulles' easygoing way of doing business as DCI, believed that at best McCone might be able to help sort out some of the intelligence community's management problems, but that he was not likely to cut much of a swath as a policy maker in the Kennedy administration.

Kennedy moved to help McCone's assumption of power by giving him visible presidential access, but this was less important in the short run than John McCone's own actions. McCone knew he was taking over the CIA from a very popular leader with considerable personal following, whose firing had produced serious divisions within the agency. He also knew that he could never emulate his predecessor, and to try would only make worse the CIA's internal situation. He certainly could not fire all those who felt a personal sense of loss and loyalty to Dulles. In essence, McCone's problem was to send a clear signal throughout the Agency and the intelligence community at large that he was the new director and he was in charge. This is not an uncommon problem in either business or government, and no single solution exists to resolve it. In McCone's case, although it is not certain he planned it beforehand, an aprocryphal situation occurred which enabled him to assert and actually gain much more substantial control over the Agency than either he or the president could have contemplated.

As the story goes, on November 28, 1961, President Kennedy presented the National Security Medal to Allen Dulles at CIA headquarters, after which he said, "So I do want to express my appreciation to you now, and I'm confident that in the future you will continue to merit the appreciation of our country as you have in the past." Later, after a farewell luncheon in the director's dining room, Dulles was escorted to the headquarters' main entrance by McCone and some key staff members to take formal leave of the CIA he had directed for more than eight years. Dulles was still in a consultant status to the Agency to carry out some "historical research" and remain available if questions came up which required his personal knowledge. As such, a decision of sorts was made to let him temporarily keep one of the trappings of his former office, the director's car. This car, unlike the garden-variety Cadillac limousine, was capable of very high speeds, equipped with bulletproof glass, special light-weight armored panels, and communications equipment including scrambler telephones and other highly sophisticated two-way radio devices. In short, the car was the director's land-based mobile command post, which enabled him to keep in constant touch with and direct the CIA's farflung operations while travelling from CIA headquarters to the White House, "black houses," training centers, etc.

After handshakes all around and some final quips to those who had served so closely with him for many years, Dulles entered the director's car and was driven off by his "chauffeur," a very special agent. Thereupon McCone, who had directed his aide to fetch his briefcase after the luncheon had broken up, told one of the deputy directors in the farewell group that he too was ready to go home for the evening. The new director's car was summoned forth. It was a large Mercury with one telephone and the Washington status symbol —reading light in the back seat—but it clearly wasn't a land-based command post. Someone hastened to say that the new director's car was not ready. McCone replied that this car would be all right for tonight and the following morning, when he was to go to the White House for his swearing in as DCI, but that he wanted *his* car (that is, one just like Dulles') tomorrow evening at 5:30 when he had to go to a reception. With those words he got into the Mercury and was driven off, leaving his new subordinates with a major crisis.

After some flailing around, General Motors was contacted and arrangements were made to fly one of their Cadillac limousines in a special air-mission aircraft on an urgent priority basis to Washington. This was done in remarkably short order. The new director's car was delivered to the CIA's New York Avenue garage, and technicians from the Technical Services Division (TSD) labored throughout the night to turn it into a carbon copy of the Dulles vehicle. At times the work took on a feverish, almost comical quality, as the deadline approached; the final soldering and adjustment of one of the radio transceivers was completed in the director's parking space in front of the headquarters building just two minutes before he was scheduled to leave. Promptly at 5:30 PM McCone appeared at the entrance, again with some of his key deputies (although not the larger band of the day before). The director's car was summoned forth, the door opened, he said good night, got in, and was driven off.

The signal of this event went forth loud and clear throughout the Agency. In one fell swoop, John McCone let all concerned know that he meant business. By getting into the director's car without making fuss or complimenting his aides on their efficiency, he told them in so many words, "You think you're good, so don't expect pats on the head for extraordinary effort—I expect and will not accept anything less from you in your performance of duty."

Before turning back to Kennedy's problems with intelligence, it should also be noted that McCone further consolidated his control over the CIA by paying close attention to the Agency's internal analytical intelligence activities and its role in developing interdepartmental intelligence. McCone carefully read the analyses and estimates which went into the production of national intelligence for the president, and in doing so discussed their meanings with individual analysts. His recognition that the analytical side of the CIA's house was essential had a salutary effect on the analysts who, because of Dulles' preoccupations with operations and the operators, had come to think of themselves as step-children in the Agency's family.

As McCone took hold of the CIA, Operation MONGOOSE moved inexorably ahead. The number of raids was increased and, although the Cuban people tended superficially to ignore the CIA's secret army activities, Castro began to feel imperiled by their frequency and the strains on Cuba's economy occasioned by the United States' trade embargo. As a result, Castro turned to the Soviets for economic and military assistance. Both were soon forthcoming. The Soviets' rudimentary economic assistance barely kept the failing Cuban economy afloat. However, the Soviets' military assistance—in the form of guided missiles—changed the MONGOOSE equation to a substantial degree because, after the missiles were tipped with nuclear warheads, the use of American forces in anticipation of the contemplated "popular uprising" was ruled out on rather obvious grounds. A description of the dramatic events of the Cuban missile crisis of October 1962 does not require full consideration here, save for one related point: that in the course of getting the Soviets to withdraw the missiles and the warheads Kennedy became further disenchanted with the intelligence community and the military services for not having an on-the-shelf contingency plan to carry out the naval blockade of Cuba he had ordered. As a result, in the course of the president's and his executive committee's almost unilateral takeover of the military's command and control system during the crisis, more bad blood was created between the president and his national security and intelligence community leadership.

The removal of Soviet missiles did not end MONGOOSE; rather, it was reduced in scope. A greater emphasis was placed on the use of "subtle sabotage," actions designed to hinder the Cuban economy without creating visible and attributable destruction. MONGOOSE was pursued off and on in a rather desultory fashion until 1967, when with little fanfare the director of the CIA finally ordered the operation rolled up. Once the Cuban missile crisis was past Kennedy lost most apparent interest in Cuba, and looked elsewhere for more hospitable worlds to conquer and a better tactic than the one espoused by MONGOOSE's creators.

Almost in anticipation of the president's shift of emphasis following the Bay of Pigs, noninvolved wings in the CIA and the military intelligence services began to beef up their clandestine organizations and operations in the Far East. During this period, generally between May and December of 1961, it was much simpler and far safer to carry out intelligence operations in the relatively tranquil countries of Southeast Asia. The duty was pleasant, living was cheap and there was a ready supply of willing indigenous personnel to work as personal servants, clerks, and drivers. And the Asian communists, rebels, or whatever were much less adept at counterespionage and sabotage than their European counterparts.

While Kennedy fretted about the slow progress of MONGOOSE in 1962, he was pointed—partly to distract him—in the direction of the Far East and especially to South Vietnam, where it was assumed that the communist-inspired and led insurgency could be countered cheaply and easily by Americans on the ground, who would provide the South Vietnamese with "good old American know-how" in putting down the rebellion. Not unlike the earlier response to Cuba, which resulted in the creation of the Special Group (Augmented), another White House organization, the Special Group CI (counterinsurgency) was established by National Security Action Memorandum (NSAM) 124 to deal with the nebulous world of counterinsurgency.*

The effect of NSAM 124 on top of MONGOOSE on the intelligence community was devastating. Counterinsurgency as a strategy and the intelligence needs it generates was like beauty—strictly in the eyes of the beholder. As those who were trying to put some distance between themselves and their involvement with Cuba jumped on the counterinsurgency bandwagon, their folly became the administration's conventional wisdom for dealing with this extremely complex problem of unconventional warfare.

There is no way to describe adequately what went on in the intelligence community in Washington during 1962. One element of the intelligence community was busy trying to determine what kind of intelligence was needed to facilitate the ordered overthrow of Castro. Another element was equally busy trying to figure out what kind of intelligence was needed to keep Ngo Dinh Diem in power in South Vietnam and eliminate those who were trying to overthrow his regime. Superficially these two tasks might appear to be the opposite side of the same coin, but they were not. For those with one foot in the MONGOOSE camp and the other in counterinsurgency it was a hopelessly complex situation which caused one to wonder what, if any, American foreign policy objectives one was supposed to assist. In large measure, aside from the

---

*The Special Group CI was chaired by Maxwell Taylor, the president's military adviser. Members were Hugh Alexis Johnson, undersecretary of state for Political Affairs; Lyman Lemnitzer, chairman of the Joint Chiefs of Staff; Fowler Hamilton, U.S. Agency for International Development (AID) administrator; John McCone, DCI; Robert Kennedy, attorney general, and McGeorge Bundy, the president's special assistant for National Security Affairs. At the time of the Special Group CI's creation Edward R. Murrow, director of the United States Information Agency (USIA), asked to be included as a member. Several months later Murrow was added to the full group as a voting member, rather than remaining an observer.

fact that NSAM 124 embraced the notion (however vaguely) of counterinsurgency, it is not inaccurate to say that the early planning activities were more designed to distract Kennedy from his dissatisfaction with MONGOOSE's slow pace of progress than to do anything substantial in South Vietnam. The entire idea of counterinsurgency in those days was one of a solution in search of a problem. For example, NSAM 162, issued on June 19, 1962 and entitled "Development of United States and Indigenous Police Paramilitary Activity," looked upon counterinsurgency as a law-enforcement activity rather than a political and military strategy. As such NSAM 162 became the official vehicle which authorized an exponential expansion of Michigan State University's police-training program (which had begun in the mid-1950s on a limited basis) through the aegis of the USAID program in South Vietnam. NSAM 162 was premised on the rather naive hope that political dissatisfaction could be countered by police tactics, which basically involved crowd dispersal and the rounding up of demonstrators. In the wake of NSAM 162, former police personnel were sent to South Vietnam in increasing numbers to show President Diem and his brother, Ngo Dinh Nhu, how to break up a riot rather than how to deal with a politically motivated, highly controlled guerrilla campaign.

Although many of the cops who were recruited to the Michigan State police program did know that the operation was a CIA cover, many did not; this produced some ludicrous situations as the "unwitting" CIA assets were given orders they couldn't understand. One noted, "It was never like this in Boston," and was told that nothing over here is just like it was in Boston. Diem and his brother smiled throughout. Both were happy in the recognition that the expanded police program was adding necessary foreign exchange to their coffers without causing any real interference in their internal secret police activities. By the end of July 1962 the so-called police assistance programs were ridiculous, as were the Americans who were trying to advise the South Vietnamese to follow Maoist maxims in getting their lackluster army to wage a counterguerrilla war.

Kennedy, because of his preoccupation with Cuba, paid only fleeting attention to the machinations of his counterinsurgency warriors in South Vietnam. But by mid-August 1962, no matter how favorable a light was shined on the antics of the CIA and others in South Vietnam, it became clear to him that no one involved in the entire operation really had the foggiest notion about what he or she was actually doing, or why. In response to a PFIAB recommendation, on August 24, 1962, Kennedy issued NSAM 182, entitled "Counterinsurgency Doctrine." It called for developing a statement of principles to guide those who, by virtue of South Vietnam's increasing dependence on the United States, were, through their own ineptitude, doing the very things which were strengthening the communists' insurgency rather than countering it. For example, although South Vietnam's National Police (or as they were dubbed by the Vietnamese people, the "White Mice") didn't need lessons in police brutality, the approving presence of a CIA/USAID police adviser who stood by while the White Mice administered the rubber hose to a Vietnamese who displayed a lack of "political enthusiasm" for Diem's actions, was adequate to cause the individual to join the Viet Cong after he had been so "rehabilitated." In the subsequent war, these activities bore their bitter fruit as the South Vietnamese people contrasted American statements about democracy with the actions of those Americans who participated in and condoned acts of official repression.

Unfortunately, NSAM 182's requirement to come up with a suitable counterinsurgency doctrine only made matters worse, as those with no sense about the nature of insurrectional violence (other than that gleaned from a cursory reading of Mao's maxims) attempted to cast the South Vietnamese situation into comfortable, familiar terms. The search in official Washington for a counterinsurgency doctrine—a statement of principles derived from evaluated experience—took on the appearance of a game of charades. Madness was the rule and anyone who tried to question the Special Group CI's wisdom was castigated for not being a team player. The authors of one CIA/military intelligence estimate, based upon their actual experience in the South Vietnamese countryside (where the insurgency was actually being waged), and indicating the need for the United States to adopt a policy of benign neglect to compel the South Vietnamese to get off their duffs and get out of the cities, were severely rebuked for their negativism and denigration of the positive role the United States could and was expected to play in countering insurgency.

The search for a counterinsurgency doctrine proved completely unavailing. As a result, the counterinsurgency strategy and tactics which were employed by American advisers in 1962 and 1963 were dictated by the personalities and backgrounds of those on the Special Group CI rather than by evaluated experience.

In the wake of the Cuban missile crisis, the counterinsurgency emphasis was shifted from the discredited police assistance program to the resettlement of the threatened South Vietnamese rural population into "strategic hamlets" and the insertion of some 25,000 American military advisers who were expected to transform the army of the Republic of Vietnam (ARVN) into a counterguerrilla force. During this fateful period the intelligence community raised scant objections about where all this was leading, or for that matter how badly the counterinsurgency campaign was going. Again, it was not a time for nay-saying. Negative intelligence analyses and estimates were held back from the president and the Special Group CI by the intelligence community leaders because it was clear to them that intelligence challenges to the emerging program were not welcome. In spite of the intelligence community's self-imposed silence about the conditions in the Vietnamese countryside, the fact that Diem was dragging his feet in carrying out a guerrilla campaign could not be ignored. Diem became a vexatious source of frustration in Washington and Saigon to the Americans who desperately wanted to achieve a demonstrable, politically valuable success in defeating communists.

As 1963 culminated in the assassinations of Diem on November 1 and Kennedy three weeks later, the outstanding questions before the intelligence community were ones designed to determine what additional American actions might be sufficient to counter the insurgency. The intelligence community did, in the several weeks before Diem's assassination, provide Kennedy and the Special Group CI with intelligence information which clearly indicated the communist insurgency was growing and that the Viet Cong was acquiring more and not less control over the countryside and its rural population. This intelligence information was very carefully worded in order to avoid any appearance of pointing a finger of responsibility for the communists' success or making any judgment about American policy.

How Kennedy would have responded to the deteriorating situation in South Vietnam if he had lived is a question forever lost to history, but a reasonable case can be made that he would not have introduced American combat troops in South Vietnam—which, as subsequent events proved, caused an escalation of the conflict to higher and unmanageable levels. This supposition stems from Kennedy's increasing acceptance of General Shoup's views about the ineffectiveness of the military-adviser program's thrust to turn the ARVN into a counterguerrilla force, the nature and requirements of a guerrilla war, and the kinds of intelligence one must have. Shoup, who was neither bashful or reluctant about challenging prevailing conventional wisdom concerning America's actions in South Vietnam, had, by late 1963, become an important if inauspicious source of advice to Kennedy; it was speculated that Shoup would be offered the DCI post following completion of his tenure as commandant of the Marine Corps on January 1, 1965. The merit of such an appointment is not at issue here; rather, the fact that Kennedy could have counted upon Shoup to provide opposition to attempts by the Joint Chiefs of Staff to insert American combat forces in South Vietnam. But Dallas foreclosed that possibility, and just as no one can ever know what FDR would have done at Potsdam, no one knows what Kennedy would have done with South Vietnam and the intelligence community.

One other problem of the brief Kennedy period needs mention: the persistent one of internal security, with which each president has had to grapple, and turn over to his successor never fully resolved. In Kennedy's administration the internal security problem was subsumed in the case of William H. Martin and Bernon F. Mitchell, employees of the National Security Agency who defected to the Soviet Union in August 1960.

Briefly, in the somewhat lurid prose of the House Un-American Activities Committee:

There was uneasiness in the minds of millions of Americans when, on August 1, 1960, the news broke that two employees of the supersecret National Security Agency were missing and unaccounted for, having failed to return from a "vacation" trip they had taken together. Uneasiness deepened into shock as, in the days immediately following, it was learned that they had purchased one-way airline tickets to Mexico City and then to Castro's Cuba. There was no relief for the anxiety of the people of this country in the Department of Defense's statement of August 5, 1960, that "it must be assumed that there is a likelihood that they have gone behind the Iron Curtain." This statement was climaxed by the appearance of the two men at an elaborately staged press conference in Moscow on September 6, 1960. In the course of this conference, the two former NSA employees revealed that they had left a "parting statement" to the American people in a safe deposit box in a Maryland bank, and then gave their all to a Soviet propaganda attack on the United States that had worldwide repercussions.

It was hard to believe. These two men, Bernon F. Mitchell and William H. Martin, had supposedly gone through the most rigorous of loyalty and security checks prior to and during their employment with the most sensitive and secretive of all agencies established by the United States government to protect the nation's security and that of its people in a deadly cold war. Yet, they had gone over to the enemy.

The propaganda and psychological blows these men had struck against their country and in behalf of the enemy were telling and hurt deeply. But the damage done was not limited to these. There was also the question of how much they knew of our most vital secrets—because their actions indicated that whatever they knew, they would surely pass on to the rulers of the Soviet Union. That they had had access to top secret cryptologic information and knew the operations of highly specialized electronic devices used by NSA was apparent. How much more information of a dangerous nature was in their hands, no one knew, except NSA officials and a few other top security officers of the nation.

Something was obviously wrong. Was it just Mitchell and Martin? Were others involved? Was there something basically wrong with our security program and the procedures of the NSA?*

As answers to these questions were found—which revealed, among other things, that Martin and Mitchell were homosexuals and had indeed made off with many of the NSA's most closely held secrets—Kennedy became sorely troubled by the implications of these revelations. Although Martin and Mitchell were apparently self-recruited to the Soviet cause out of revulsion to the dirty espionage tricks the United States was practicing (they conveniently ignored the fact that the Soviet Union was up to the same tricks), the answers suggested severe vulnerabilities in the United States national security apparatus, Congress, and the White House to the *selective* penetration of each organization by Americans who were susceptible to recruitment by the Soviet KGB. This was particularly nettlesome to Kennedy because, in attempting to close loopholes in the internal security system, he did not want to let loose the scourge of McCarthyism, or to create the impression that there were hordes of Soviet spies in the government. It was then as now an extremely complex problem. The laxity of the NSA's hiring practices revealed in the investigation

*United States House of Representatives. House Un-American Activities Committee. "Security Practices in the National Security Agency (defection of Bernon F. Mitchell and William H. Martin)." Washington: U.S. Government Printing Office, August 13, 1962.

were corrected, and reinvestigations were carried out of personnel whose behavior was dubious and who had slipped through the NSA's screening processes much like Martin and Mitchell. But these measures by themselves were insufficient to detect deep-cover penetrations by Americans who had been taught how to beat the polygraph and lie dogo in one of the intelligence agencies as they made their way up the bureaucratic ladder. Nor could these measures be applied very effectively in dealing with possible penetrations of Congress and the White House, since use of the polygraph as a screening tool (or as in the case of the CIA and NSA, as a condition of employment) was repugnant on political grounds. Kennedy was warned that the danger of Americans becoming self-committed to Soviet ideology, as had Martin and Mitchell, was less severe than those who might be convinced to aid the Soviets by opposing American actions, or those whose interests were strictly mercenary.

Several interagency committees and task forces were constituted by Kennedy to deal with these problems, but they all floundered on the jurisdictional boundaries between the FBI, CIA, NSA, Secret Service, etc., which effectively precluded pursuing a counterintelligence investigation no matter where it might lead—especially if it led to Congress or the White House. Kennedy considered, as did Truman in 1950, initiating additional internal security legislation, but this was rejected on the grounds that to do so would set off a public furor. As a result the jurisdictional boundaries remained intact and each of the organizations was admonished to do the best possible job in detecting and eliminating security risks in their respective bailiwicks. Quite obviously it is impossible to successfully operate a "zero-defect" security risk program in either a democratic or totalitarian society. There are always bound to be defectors for one reason or another, and attempts to identify these persons before the fact are chancy at best. Kennedy accepted this fact and in so doing struck an uneasy balance between the need to count upon the essential loyalty of persons entrusted with vital secrets and the requirement to monitor their behavior to see that their loyalty remained intact. In practical terms, the interagency internal security reviews carried out at Kennedy's direction resulted in improving the individual agencies' procedures. This was all to the good, but it did little to prevent possible Soviet penetration of Congress and the White House; Kennedy backed away from his earlier desire to have the Special Group consider positive counterespionage and counterintelligence operations. He agreed that the fewer who knew about these operations the better. In evaluating how Kennedy handled this problem, it is fair to note that he didn't have too many options in dealing with the internal security problems subsumed in the Martin/Mitchell defection. It was a tricky and difficult Constitutional question, especially in terms of balancing the answer with American secret intelligence activities in "friendly" countries. In essence, Kennedy crossed his fingers, trusted the existing internal security system and vented his anger to no one in particular when, for instance, prior to the Bay of Pigs

invasion reports about that not-so-secret operation appeared in *The New York Times* and other newspapers.

Lyndon Johnson's abrupt accession to the presidency on November 22, 1963, and the bizarre events of the next several days, gave him an insight into the intelligence community's workings denied to most new presidents. In Johnson's case the tone and temper of crisis compelled the intelligence community leaders to realize that, although he might not be their personal choice, Johnson was the only president the United States had, and he needed all the help they could provide. None of the leaders was completely certain what else the Kennedy assassination signalled.

Johnson's tenure as first intelligence officer is less significant to the evolution of American intelligence than that of his predecessors and successors. In large measure he took the intelligence community as he found it, preferring generally to treat it more as a staff organization than an operational entity under his direct command; nor was he interested in playing it off against other competing power centers in the national security system.

Like Truman, Johnson wanted his intelligence in printed form. To be sure, he accepted the daily morning intelligence briefing as one of the burdens of his office, but he was extremely reluctant to sit through a long-winded exposition by one of the intelligence community's "managers." This is not to say that Johnson was indifferent to intelligence; Richard Helms, whom Johnson appointed DCI, commented that in discussion with the president about intelligence matters LBJ would often take up a report which had been provided and ask Helms deep, insightful questions (which he had written in the report's margin) about its real meaning and greater significance. As a corollary to this self-educating process, when Johnson was particularly struck by an intelligence report (as frequently happened), he would bypass the DCI, find out from one of his aides who had written the report, and give the individual analyst a call or invite him to the White House for a personal chat. This latter practice drove the intelligence community leaders quite literally up the wall, since they could not interpose their "superior" wisdom between the president's interests and the person who knew the particular topic in intimate detail.

A major consequence of Johnson's rather unorthodox investiture into the intelligence community involved his orders to tighten up the approval procedures for covert actions and operations. In so doing, the Special Group (after June 1964, the 303 Committee) made a significant effort to integrate the initiation of these activities with specific policy decisions in a coherent manner designed to facilitate policy implementation—in short, to prevent the covert action tail from wagging the policy dog. Regarding this changed approach, a CIA memorandum dated February 25, 1967, stated:

As the sophistication of the policy approval process developed, so did the participation of the external approving authority. Since establishment of the Special Group (later 303

Committee), the policy arbiters have questioned CIA presentations, amended them and, on occasion, denied them outright. The record shows that the group/committee, in some instances, has overridden objections from the DCI and instructed the Agency to carry out certain activities. . . . Objections by State have resulted in amendment or rejection of election proposals, suggestions for air proprietaries and support plans for foreign governments. . . . The committee has suggested areas where covert action is needed, has decided that another element of government should undertake a proposed action, imposed caveats and turned down specific proposals for CIA action from ambassadors in the field.*

For the first year of his presidency, Johnson was content to stick with the team of national security advisers he had inherited from Kennedy. But following his election in November 1964, he began to chafe a bit at the attitudes of the "best and the brightest" toward his security leadership.

Others have written with deep insight about Johnson's fears, frustrations, and conception of the presidency,** but psychohistory is not the concern here. The fact is that as the military-adviser and assistance program and the communist insurgency in South Vietnam expanded in symbiotic fashion, Johnson became increasingly frustrated with the military and intelligence advice he was receiving. Not incorrectly, Johnson regarded this advice like that given in a poker game in which, contrary to his advisers' opinions, every time he raised the ante the communists matched his raise and added one of their own. What became particularly bothersome to Johnson was that after one of these betting rounds—predicated on the communists' supposed inability to match the increase—he was given alibis by his advisers, who tried to pin the blame on someone else rather than accept their fair share for misreading the situation. This kind of behavior was anathema to Johnson, and one result was a distinct cooling between himself and DCI John McCone, who was cut off from the easy access he had enjoyed with Kennedy.

As events in early 1965 moved toward an unwanted consideration of the fateful decision to insert United States combat troops into South Vietnam, John McCone, whose words echoed the CIA's objections to such an action, was heard less and less in the administration's inner councils. It was a time for "positive thinking," during which those who asserted that introducing United States combat troops in South Vietnam was very much like becoming pregnant with no chance for an abortion went unheeded. In spite of the intelligence community's reservations, the decision was made in February 1965 to deploy combat troops and initiate a program of aerial bombardment of North Vietnam, which was ominously dubbed "Operation Rolling Thunder." Much has been written about that decision, the actions of Johnson's advisers in playing mute, inglorious Miltons to the fatuous comments of

---

*"Foreign and Military Intelligence, Book I," op. cit., p. 56.

**See especially Doris Kearns, Lyndon Johnson and the American Dream. New York: Harper and Row, 1976.

"bombing the North Vietnamese back to the Stone Age," and the disastrous consequences which followed.

What was the intelligence community's role in the events leading up to that decision? The most important was the reporting and subsequent interpretation of the August 1964 incidents in the Gulf of Tonkin, which initially misled Johnson and publicly committed him to a misinterpretation of what had occurred. The full story of this intelligence failure remains to be told, perhaps at a later date when emotions about American involvement in Vietnam have reached the point where mistakes can be looked upon as mistakes rather than acts of conspiracy. It is possible to state now that the Gulf of Tonkin attack and the congressional resolution which followed it were due simply to the fact that information about the attack was assumed to be *intelligence*. That is, the raw information, which was highly disjointed, ambiguous, and confused, had not been evaluated, corroborated, and analyzed before its validity as intelligence was assumed. Today, the data to determine the accuracy of this statement is in the hands of the Senate's Oversight Committee on Intelligence; probably for the reason cited above, it has not been made public. To do so might open old wounds without much gain other than to demonstrate human fallibility in carrying out the process of turning information into intelligence and the hazards of acting before the process has been completed. This is not to justify Johnson's decisions, but rather is further evidence of any president's difficulty in making an operational decision based on the intelligence information the system provides for his immediate personal consideration.

Once the United States' combat involvement in Vietnam commenced, Johnson's relations with the intelligence community changed in a variety of ways. First, he accepted John McCone's resignation as DCI in April 1965, and subsequently appointed Vice Admiral William Raborn to fill the post. The passing of McCone, the "nay sayer," was a clear signal to the intelligence community that like it or not the United States was in a war, and its role was to help the president win it. Raborn's appointment was greeted with some incredulity and hurt feelings by the CIA's sophisticates, who pooh-poohed it on the grounds that he was not a member of the intelligence brotherhood. One comment frequently heard was, "How would the navy like it if one of us was designated chief of Naval Operations!" Admittedly, Raborn lacked a background in the esoteric ways of intelligence, but Johnson's purpose in appointing him DCI was premised on the belief that his experience as a combat officer and as an administrator—most notably in the development of the Polaris missile system—would make the CIA more responsive to the combat intelligence needs of American forces. Unfortunately, such was not the case. Raborn was ravaged by the CIA, being able neither to marshall its resources in adequate support of the United States combat involvement or to prevent internecine bureaucratic conflict in the intelligence community as a whole. In spite of Raborn's obvious failures during his tenure as DCI (April 1965–June 1966), from the United States' point of view the Vietnam War went reasonably well.

During this period Johnson took his role as commander in chief seriously—some said too seriously—in terms of his demands to be informed in detail about combat operations, bombing target selections, and other military specifics. However, discontent against the war was building. At first it was a trickle of opposition, but as victory eluded the American forces (despite military successes), it began to increase.

The effect of these two streams caused Johnson to look to the intelligence community for additional help. This took initial form in the person of Richard Helms, whom Johnson appointed DCI in June 1966.* From the vantage point of the CIA and the intelligence community as a whole, Helms's appointment was viewed as a "natural." The war had reached the point where unless a doubling or tripling of the then 300,000 United States forces was authorized, not much could be done at the margin to eliminate the Viet Cong and North Vietnamese forces in South Vietnam. It was a classic dilemma: American forces had achieved a remarkable success against the enemy, but eliminating them completely and compelling the abandonment of the insurgency, given the war's political constraints, would have raised the United States' combat involvement to a totally unacceptable cost-effectiveness level. To resolve this dilemma Johnson looked to Helms, by virtue of his clandestine experience, to mobilize the CIA in pursuit of the enemy at the margin, to wage a secret war in Laos, and to fill his military personnel needs with indigenous sources rather than Americans. To assist Helms, much of the army's Special Forces resources were turned over to the CIA's operational control. Thus began the third phase of the Vietnam War, in which the level of United States combat involvement was supposed to remain at about 300,000. However, following Johnson's trip to Vietnam and the Philippines in October 1966, during which he made his "coonskin on the wall" statement, the United States force levels once again began their inexorable upward climb as the military sought to locate the elusive Viet Cong and North Vietnamese "coons."

The other stream Helms was expected to dry up was the antiwar activists in the United States. This was an even more difficult task than the mass

---

*Richard Helms became DCI following nearly twenty-five years in the clandestine service. Just as Allen Dulles had identified himself with the intelligence professions, Helms identified himself with the CIA as an institution. Having served in a succession of senior positions since the early 1950s, Helms was a first-generation product of the CIA, and he commanded the personal and professional respect of his contemporaries. Helms's international orientation began early. Most of his secondary education consisted of private schooling in Germany and Switzerland. After graduating from Williams College in 1935, he worked as a journalist. In 1942, he joined the service and was assigned to OSS. Helms remained an intelligence officer through the transitions to SSU and the Central Intelligence Group. As a member of the CIA's Office of Special Operations, he rose to become deputy assistant director for Special Operations. An excellent administrator, he served as assistant deputy director for Plans (ADDP) under both Wisner and Bissell. In 1963 Helms was named DDP and was appointed deputy director of Central Intelligence (DDCI) under Raborn. ("Supplementary and Detailed Staff Reports on Foreign and Military Intelligence, Book IV," *op. cit.*, p. 66.)

expansion of clandestine activities in Southeast Asia. Many of the CIA's domestic activities—the mail-intercept program, funding of educational and research organizations—which had begun under Eisenhower continued under Kennedy and Johnson. These activities were relatively unobtrusive, but once the search for antiwar activists and the penetration of the proliferating antiwar organizations was intensified, it was only a matter of time before the CIA's roles in these areas became exposed.

This occurred at a February 14, 1967, press briefing when the State Department publicly confirmed a statement by leaders of the National Student Association (NSA) that their organization had received covert support from the CIA since the early 1950s. "The NSA statement and disclosures in *Ramparts* magazine brought on a storm of public and congressional criticism. In response, President Johnson organized a committee composed of Undersecretary of State Nicholas Katzenbach, Secretary of Health, Education and Welfare John Gardner, and CIA Director Richard Helms to review government activities that may 'endanger the integrity and independence of the educational community.' "* The so-called Katzenbach committee, according to Katzenbach, was a damage-control exercise designed by Johnson "not only to deal with the relationship of the CIA to educational and voluntary organizations, but to head off a full-scale congressional investigation."**

In this regard the Katzenbach committee was reasonably successful. The broad-based surveillance program of antiwar activists, known as Operation CHAOS, remained undetected, as did the mail intercept, media manipulations and student recruitment efforts. And as each of these activities fed on each other, they poisoned Johnson's point of view by promoting the idea that America's growing opposition to the Vietnam War was *the* most important single factor in the American and South Vietnamese inability to bring the war to a successful conclusion. It was an unfortunate and sardonic outcome in which Johnson, the consummate politician, who indeed did understand the American people, was turned against them by the intelligence community. The distrust fostered by the reinforcing nature of the domestic surveillance programs and the administration's inability or unwillingness to admit the futility of its search for victory led to Johnson's downfall. When the Tet offensive exploded on January 30, 1968, it left the intelligence community in almost complete control of American policy in Southeast Asia. In consequence, the surveillance programs were expanded, the secret war in Laos was pressed with added vigor, the "numbers games" over body counts, captured weapons, etc. were played with increasing sophistication—making it truly impossible to know who was winning or losing and by how much—and Johnson was left with no option except renouncing his and others' past rhetoric about the war as false in order to seek a new way to lead the United States out of the Vietnam

*"Foreign and Military Intelligence, Book I," *op. cit.,* pp. 185–86.

**Ibid.,* p. 186.

quagmire. Following Johnson's announcement on March 31, 1968, that he would not seek reelection in November and his subsequent departure from office in January 1969, he was a pathetic image of his former self. His hopes for peace and the Great Society had been dashed on the rocks of Vietnam, leaving him an almost total captive of the military hierarchy and the intelligence community, whose complicity in the illegal activities to curb dissent over the war insured his silence and effectively proscribed his ability to accept the peace proposals which had been worked out in Paris by Averell Harriman and Cyrus Vance.

There is a postscript to Johnson's uneven stewardship of the intelligence community: the seizure of the U.S.S. *Pueblo* by North Koreans in the Sea of Japan on January 23, 1968. This event, coming only a week before the Tet offensive, was somewhat diminished in its importance by the obvious crisis of the offensive. Nonetheless, from the military and intelligence community's point of view, the *Pueblo* seizure was much more important because within hours after the North Koreans had brought the American spy ship into port, the Soviets were removing its highly sophisticated electronic equipment. Although much has subsequently been written about the intelligence community's bureaucratic absurdities which preceded authorization of the *Pueblo*'s mission and the ensuing events,* at the time only a handful of persons in the intelligence community actually knew how severe a loss was occasioned by the capture of the *Pueblo*'s electronic equipment. These persons advocated a "burial by fire" of the ship and its contents, but the domestic political climate —and perhaps the ability to get aircraft over the target to do the job—made this action infeasible. In the congressional investigation which followed, emphasis was placed on the layers of intelligence committees which had routinely approved the *Pueblo* mission, the faulty command and control system which was supposed to back up the mission, and the apparent indifference of American officials to the North Koreans' prior warnings about incursion into their national waters. Examination of these issues satisfied the congressional investigating urge, and public attention was diverted away from the *Pueblo* by the month-long Tet offensive, which produced a several hundred percent increase in the weekly rate of American combat deaths. Similarly, Johnson was more concerned about the Tet offensive results because they gave added impetus to the antiwar movement and clearly signalled that the advertised light at the end of the tunnel announced by General Westmoreland to Congress in the fall of 1967 was a mirage. However, within the intelligence community *Pueblo* was recognized as a major disaster because, according to one estimate, the Soviets had gained three to five years on the United States in the continuing race for communications and electronic supremacy. After *Pueblo*, the United States still remained ahead in the race, but in one fell swoop—due to the intelligence

---

*For a thorough discussion of the *Pueblo* matter see especially Trevor Armbrister, *Matter of Accountability: The True Story of the* Pueblo *Affair*. New York: Coward McCann, 1970.

community's internal organizational flaws which permitted the mission to take place—the Soviets had been able to cut substantially into the American lead.

In response, besides terminating the dubious *Pueblo* type of electronic surveillance programs, the intelligence community's leaders redoubled their efforts to gain back the advantage which had been lost as a result of the ship's seizure. As a consequence, the intelligence budget had, once again, to be increased by a substantial amount. By itself *Pueblo* did produce some internal reordering and reorganization of the communications intelligence subcommunity, but because of Johnson's preoccupations with other problems it did not result in a presidentially sponsored initiative to effect a meaningful structural reform of the entire intelligence community. The bottom line of Johnson's stewardship is that he took the intelligence community as he found it and it remained relatively unchanged or improved—but with considerably more power to decide policy—when he left office.

On January 20, 1969, when Richard Nixon assumed office as the thirty-seventh president of the United States, his immediate problems were many. Quite obviously the Vietnam War was his preeminent consideration; moreover, he was, through his personal sources in the intelligence community, quite aware of the disparity between the intelligence "facts" about the war as reported in Washington and those which actually obtained in Vietnam. Instead of challenging the intelligence community head-on with this knowledge, Nixon asked his assistant for National Security Affairs, Henry Kissinger, to play the heavy and bring about some order and truth in the intelligence being served up to the president. Kissinger relished his role as the president's hard-nosed exec. On February 1, 1969, he issued National Security Study Memorandum No.1, which required various departments and agencies to provide independent answers to a comprehensive series of questions about the Vietnam War. NSSM 1 was a masterstroke on Kissinger's part (one aide called it Henry's equivalent of a Ph.D. candidate's oral examination) because it not only provided a cross-check on the intelligence community members' actual knowledge of the situation, but also gave each an opportunity to criticize the other's performance and analytical position. Armed with the "divide and conquer" information submitted by the community, Kissinger was able to assess the strengths, weaknesses, and future usefulness of, say, the DIA in a future conflict with the CIA over the latter's acceptance of his direction and authority.

The NSSM 1 exercise, in addition to quickly establishing Kissinger's role as a key player in the intelligence community, also served to reestablish a form of competition in the community by breaking the gentleman's agreement to not criticize each other's intelligence, or seek to gain a bigger share of the overlarge intelligence pie. Although Kissinger arrogated unto himself the dominant position in the intelligence community, he made it clear that the others could fight among themselves for larger pieces of the remaining action. All this did not necessarily result in improved national intelligence, but it did serve to give Kissinger a free hand in pursuing his and Nixon's foreign policy ideas.

It took Kissinger a little more than a year to achieve substantive control over most of the intelligence community. The part remaining outside his immediate grasp was the communications intelligence subcommunity, which was under the executive-agent authority of Secretary of Defense Melvin Laird. But Kissinger was not completely thwarted, because the CIA's independent communications intelligence (comint) capability gave him the means to test the information that NSA and the military communications intelligence organizations provided the USIB and the NSC. In the world of official Washington, where intelligence information is the basis of power, Kissinger's access to the CIA's comint enabled him to treat Laird as an effective equal in the struggle for intelligence domination.

As a measure of Kissinger's power—as well as his confidence in his control of the intelligence community—on February 17, 1970, he issued National Security Decision Memorandum (NSDM) 40. According to the Senate Select Committee:

It created the 40 Committee. The directive superseded and rescinded past NSC covert action directives. It discussed both policy and procedure. With regard to policy, NSDM 40 stated that it was essential to the defense and security of the United States and its efforts for world peace that the overt foreign activities of the United States government continue to be supplemented by covert action operations.

The directive also spelled out the role of the 40 Committee. It stated that the DCI was responsible for obtaining policy approval for all major and/or politically sensitive covert action programs through the 40 Committee. In addition, NSDM 40 continued the committee's responsibility for reviewing and approving overhead reconnaissance missions, a responsibility first acquired in 1959.

A new provision, not found in previous NSC directives, required the committee to annually review covert operations previously approved.

Guidelines for the submission of covert action proposals to the 40 Committee were spelled out in an internal CIA directive. The DCI decided whether an operational program or activity should be submitted to the 40 Committee for policy approval.

The internal CIA directive also stated that before proposals were presented to the DCI for submission to the 40 Committee, they *should* be coordinated with the Department of State. Further, paramilitary action programs *should* be coordinated with the Department of Defense, and, *ordinarily,* concurrence by the ambassador to the country concerned would be required. [Emphasis added.]*

NSDM 40's significance was twofold: it delegated back to the DCI (then Richard Helms) from the secretary of state (William Rogers) coordinating authority and responsibilities for covert action proposals, and it declared that covert action was to be employed to facilitate American foreign policy objec-

*"Foreign and Military Intelligence, Book I," *op. cit.*, p. 53.

tives rather than simply to counter the threat of international communism. Quite obviously, there was some connection between these two features; the stress on promoting American policy objectives provoked explicit consideration of covert action in areas not directly threatened by the Soviets. NSDM 40 formalized the use of covert action in "friendly" as well as in hostile or threatened countries. In some ways this merely amounted to stating what had already been carried out with implicit justification (that the threat of international communism was "worldwide"); but it also served to give those involved in covert action added explicit justification to expand covert action in countries like Chile, Bolivia, and Venezuela. Also, the fact that NSDM 40 took from the secretary of state authority which had been his since 1957 was seen by intelligence community leaders as further measure of where the real power would lie in the Nixon administration.

Kissinger's intent in issuing NSDM 40 was based on his recognition that covert action was a fact of political life which needed to be routinized rather than agonized over, or endlessly debated by persons with no ultimate responsibility for policy. Nixon agreed, content in the belief that when he or Kissinger considered a truly major covert action (like the military coup d'etat in Chile) necessary, it would be ordered and carried out without the benefit or burden of the 40 Committee's approval. As a result, formal meetings of the 40 Committee became less and less frequent. "Most business was done by telephone after proposals had been circulated in advance by couriers. . . . 'Telephone concurrences,' involving quick checks, rather than intensive discussion was the rule."*

The next step in the Nixon/Kissinger attempt to gain control over the intelligence community was taken by both men as much from fear as from any grand design. Their fear was real enough. By early 1970, even avid Nixon supporters' patience had worn thin over the president's lack of a plan to get the United States out of Vietnam—a plan he had claimed to have during the 1968 presidential campaign. As a result, social tension in America was increasing. To be sure, "Vietnamization" had been announced in 1969, but this had produced no apparent difference in the way the war was being fought. And when United States forces invaded neutral Cambodia on April 30, 1970, it set off extensive and violent demonstrations and student strikes in campuses across the country. Conceivably, Nixon might have gotten away with the Cambodian "incursion"—that is, not have been compelled to cut it short and abandon the military's war-by-attrition policy—had not four students been killed by trigger-happy National Guardsmen at Kent State University on May 4, 1970. Nixon's "bleed 'em 'til they surrender" strategy went up in smoke. Kent State, like other signal events in America's long history of violence, marked a watershed in the antiwar movement in the United States. The shock of the tragedy caused a brief pause in the violence, but several days later there

*Ibid., p. 55.

were 400 bomb threats within a twenty four-hour period in New York City alone. Believing that Cambodia and Kent State signaled the beginning of really serious insurrectional violence, Nixon moved to further organize the federal government's domestic intelligence resources to meet the perceived threat. The fear uppermost in the minds of Nixon and those surrounding him was that the separate violence-prone activist groups might somehow coalesce to produce a wave of terror which could not be countered without imposing martial law on a nationwide basis.

According to Egil Krogh, John Ehrlichman's former assistant, the smell of fear in the White House in those spring days of 1970 was as pervasive as that found in a military unit about to be ordered back into an area where they had been surprised and badly mauled before escaping. It was not a time for levity in the White House, and those who tried to display some humor to break the tension were severely rebuked by the keepers of the White House "Berlin wall." In the Kent State evaluation, the valid point was made that the White House had had no reliable *a priori* intelligence to measure the potential public reaction to the Cambodian invasion. None of the intelligence community members with stated/unstated, legal/illegal responsibilities for domestic intelligence had raised any questions or warnings about the invasion's possible effects on public attitudes. This state of affairs seemed absolutely incredible to Nixon, but Kissinger carefully obscured the fact that his orders to the military authorities and the intelligence community had kept the fact of the Cambodian invasion from those people involved in counterintelligence and domestic intelligence who might have had something to add to the discussions preceding the fateful decision to invade Cambodia. Kissinger also stifled any staff objections to the decision-making process. This fact caused him to lose some very able personnel, including Morton Halperin, Anthony Lake, and Richard Holbrook, from his NSC staff. In spite of these facts Kissinger's mystique remained intact as far as Nixon was concerned.

The congruence of these events, pressures, and fears came to fruition on June 5, 1970, at a meeting arranged by Tom Charles Huston between President Nixon and the directors of the FBI (J. Edgar Hoover), CIA (Richard Helms), NSA (Admiral Noel Gaylor) and DIA (Harold Bennett). In his well known capacity to not implicate himself directly in the illegal activities of others, Nixon stressed the need for improved coordination among the agencies to strengthen their capabilities to collect intelligence about "revolutionary activism" and "the support—ideological and otherwise—of foreign powers" for these activities. Poor blind Tom Huston added to this charade by preparing a talking paper for Nixon to read at the meeting which declared, "We are now confronted with a new and grave crisis in our country—one which we know too little about."* Of course Huston did not know at the time that each

---

*U. S. Senate, Select Committee to Study Governmental Operations with Respect to Intelligence Activities. "Intelligence Activities and the Rights of Americans, Book II." 94th Congress, 2nd

principal participant was intimately aware of the illegal activities each of their organizations had been carrying out for years. Admittedly these activities had not been completely integrated or coordinated, but they had been carried out with varying degrees of cooperation. Unfortunately Huston was the last to know that Nixon was telling his intelligence leaders, in so many words, that he knew what they had been doing and that the threat at the White House gates compelled them to work together in a systematic fashion rather than to continue their activities on an individual basis. It was a time for bargaining, not unlike the way a medieval monarch brought the dukes of his realm together to seek their support against a revolutionary mob which might destroy them all. A close reading of Huston's testimony before the Watergate and the Senate Select Committee on Intelligence reveals that he was never really aware that Nixon had full and substantial knowledge about what had been going on unofficially in the intelligence community in the guise of internal security since the early 1950s.

One month after the June 5 meeting, the special report of the Interagency Committee on Intelligence (Ad Hoc), prepared jointly by representatives of the FBI, CIA, NSA, and DIA under Huston's direction, was submitted to Nixon. The report gave Nixon a series of options, and Huston recommended the president approve the following:

(1) "coverage by NSA of the communications of U.S. citizens using international facilities";

(2) "intensification of electronic surveillance and penetrations" directed at individuals and groups "who pose a major threat to the internal security" and at "foreign nationals" in the United States "of interest to the intelligence community";

(3) removal of restrictions on "legal" mail coverage and relaxation of "restrictions on covert coverage" [mail opening] on "selected targets of priority foreign intelligence and internal security interest";

(4) modification of "present restrictions" on "surreptitious entry" to allow "procurement of vitally needed foreign cryptographic material" and "to permit selective use" against "high priority internal security targets";

(5) relaxation of "present restrictions" on the development of "campus sources" to permit "expanded coverage of violence-prone and student-related groups";

(6) "increased" coverage by CIA "of American students (and others) travelling or living abroad";

(7) appointment of a "permanent committee consisting of the FBI, CIA, NSA, DIA, and the military counterintelligence agencies" to evaluate "domestic intelligence" and to "carry out the other objectives specified in the report."*

Session. Report No. 94–755. Washington: U.S. Government Printing Office, April 26, 1976, p. 113.

*Ibid., p. 113. Note: The seven recommendations were made in an attachment to a memorandum from Huston to Haldeman, July 1970.

The extent of Huston's naiveté on these matters is seen in his statements about the legality of two of these collection techniques. He wrote, "covert coverage [mail opening] is illegal, and there are serious risks involved." As for surreptitious entry, Huston stated:

Use of this technique is clearly illegal: it amounts to burglary. It is also highly risky and could result in great embarrassment if exposed. However, it is also the most fruitful tool and can produce the type of intelligence which cannot be obtained in any other fashion.*

Huston, who had not the slightest knowledge that these two techniques had been carried out for decades by the agencies at the meeting, testified that his recommendations "reflected what I understood to be the consensus of the working group of intelligence officials on the interagency committee."**

One can feel some sympathy for Huston. He had come to the Cold War late in the game and had no idea that while he was a young man studying the law, its warriors had long since declared the civil rights of "subversives" to be inoperative. There was no way Huston could have found out on his own what had actually been going on in the field of internal security. The one man who could have told him—Richard Nixon—preferred instead to use him as a tool in achieving a compact among the intelligence community's leaders to work on the president's behalf and under his direction.

On July 23, 1970, Huston informed the FBI, CIA, NSA, and DIA directors that the "president has made the following decisions—to accept all the recommendations set forth above." The result was that henceforth, with presidential authority, "the intelligence community could intercept the international communications of Americans; eavesdrop electronically on anyone deemed a 'threat to the internal security'; read the mail of American citizens; break into the homes of anyone regarded as a security threat; and monitor the activities of student political groups at home and abroad."***

In spite of Huston's memorandum citing "presidential authority," J. Edgar Hoover balked. He went to Attorney General Mitchell, who had not previously known about the Interagency Committee on Intelligence's deliberations or the president's decisions. In a memorandum to the attorney general, Hoover, the compleat bureaucrat, said he would implement the plan only with the explicit approval of the attorney general or president:

Despite my clear-cut and specific opposition to the lifting of the various investigative restraints referred to above and to the creation of a permanent interagency committee on domestic intelligence, the FBI is prepared to implement the instructions of the White

*Ibid., p. 114.

**Ibid.

***Ibid.

House at your direction. Of course, we would continue to seek your specific authorizations, where appropriate, to utilize the various sensitive investigative techniques involved in individual cases.*

Huston fussed to Haldeman at what he assumed to be Hoover's intransigence, again not knowing that Hoover had been down this slippery path once before with FDR at the time of the agreement to let the British Security Coordination organization and the FBI do many of the same things before and during World War II. All Hoover wanted was to have the authority *in writing,* with Nixon's or Mitchell's signature appended thereto. Such was not to be the case. Nixon knew that to sign the so-called Huston plan would have the practical effect of giving Hoover and the other intelligence directors incontrovertible proof of his criminal behavior, thus handing them a highly effective piece of information which could be used for blackmail. Unlike Roosevelt, who was willing to run such a risk, Nixon had had enough problems with the intelligence community not to pursue such a course of action. As a result, Mitchell advised Nixon to withdraw his approval, Huston was told to rescind his memorandum, and the White House Situation Room dispatched a message to the intelligence directors requesting that the copies be returned.

From the testimony of the intelligence directors (excepting J. Edgar Hoover) at the Watergate and Senate Select Committee hearings, the original copies of the memo were returned, but no one was able to state with certainty how many copies had been made in his organization during the five days for which it had been in effect. As the investigations revealed, Nixon's withdrawal of approval for the Huston plan did not, in fact, terminate the operations it sought to authorize. These continued, and in the case of Operation CHAOS, which included the surveillance of antiwar activists and other "security risks," it was expanded severalfold. Also, in partial response to the Huston plan,

A new group, the Intelligence Evaluation Committee (IEC), was created by Attorney General Mitchell within the Justice Department to consider such expansion [in domestic intelligence]. NSA, CIA, army counterintelligence, and the FBI each sent representatives to the IEC. NSA Director Gayler provided the IEC with a statement of NSA's capabilities and procedures for supplying domestic intelligence. Although the IEC merely evaluated raw intelligence data, over 90 percent of which came to it through the FBI and the CIA's mail-opening and CHAOS program, which was channeled to the FBI.**

The IEC added little to the overall situation other than providing a central repository for much of the surveillance information. Its ability to evaluate the raw intelligence data was limited, since the individual collection agencies held back information about the sources and methods used to obtain information.

*Ibid., pp. 114–15.

**Ibid., p. 116.

For examaple, the IEC would receive a report which said, "Subject stated that he would meet so-and-so at the meeting."*

Despite the on-again, off-again nature of the Huston plan, the agencies continued to pursue illegal domestic intelligence operations; and although these activities were not "coordinated" in the manner suggested by Huston, the White House, in the person of John Dean (who took over from the bureaucratically discredited and discouraged Huston), became responsible for directing part of the agencies' resources against special targets.

Later, on September 18, 1970 (almost two months after Nixon claimed the plan was rescinded), Dean sent a top secret memorandum to the attorney general suggesting certain procedures to "commence our domestic intelligence operation as quickly as possible." This memorandum called for the creation of an Interagency Domestic Intelligence Unit, an integral part of the Huston plan. Dean's memorandum to the attorney general observed that Hoover was strongly opposed to the creation of such a unit and that it was important to "bring the FBI fully on board." Far from indicating that the president's approval of Huston's recommendation to remove restraints on illegal intelligence gathering had been withdrawn, Dean suggested to the attorney general:

I believe we agreed that it would be inappropriate to have any blanket removal of restrictions; rather, the most appropriate procedure would be to decide on the type of intelligence we need, based on the recommendations of this unit, and then proceed *to remove the restraints as necessary to obtain such intelligence.* [Emphasis added.]**

Dean's removal of the restraints led to creation of the infamous "enemies list," a special intelligence unit in the IRS, and other actions reflecting a White

*The IEC was not established by executive order. In fact, according to minutes of the IEC meeting on February 1, 1971, Dean said he favored avoiding any written directive concerning the IEC because a directive might "create problems of congressional oversight and disclosure." Several attempts were nevertheless made to draft a charter for the committee, although none appears to have been accepted by all of the IEC members. The last draft which could be located, dated February 10, 1971, specified the authority for the IEC as "the Interdepartmental Action Plan for Civil Disturbances," something which had been issued in April 1969 as the result of an agreement between the attorney general and the secretary of defense. Dean thought it was sufficient just to say that the IEC existed by "authority of the president." The Intelligence Evaluation Committee met on only seven occasions; the last was in July 1971. The Intelligence Evaluation Staff (IES), on the other hand, met a total of 117 times between January 29, 1971 and May 4, 1973. The IES prepared an aggregate of approximately thirty studies or evaluations for dissemination. It also published a total of fifty-five summaries, called intelligence calendars, of significant events. The preparation of these calendars was directed by John Dean from the White House or by Robert Mardian, chairman of the IEC. Both the IEC and the IES were terminated in July 1973 by Assistant Attorney General Henry Petersen. (U.S. Commission on CIA Activities Within the United States, *op.cit.,* pp. 126–28.)

**U.S. Senate, Select Committee on Presidential Campaign Activity. "The Final Report. . . ." 93rd Congress, 2d Session. Report No. 93–981. Washington: U.S. Government Printing Office, 1974, pp. 4–6.

House domestic intelligence intent which went far beyond Nixon's stated concern about revolutionary activism.

Giving Nixon the benefit of a very large doubt, his not necessarily invalid attempt to gain control over the intelligence community's domestic intelligence operations and activities opened the door to even more illegal activities, and created acceptance of his stated belief that when the president does "it," "it" isn't illegal. This belief was the basic source of the poison which led to Watergate and Nixon's being driven from office. It is worth noting that Nixon expressed his belief about presidential illegal acts well before they were aired in the David Frost interviews. More than a year before, on March 9, 1976, in a notarized reply to the Senate Select Committee, which had asked him:

Interrogatory 34. Please state whether you believe that actions, otherwise "illegal," may be legally undertaken pursuant to presidential, or other high-level authorization, following a determination by the president, or some other senior government official, that the actions are necessary to protect the "national security" of the United States.

Nixon stated:

I assume that the reference to "actions, otherwise 'illegal' " in this interrogatory means actions which if undertaken by private persons would violate criminal laws. It is quite obvious that there are certain inherently governmental actions which if undertaken by the sovereign in protection of the interest of the nation's security are lawful but which if undertaken by private persons are not. In the most extreme case, for example, forceable removal of persons from their homes for the purpose of sequestering them in confined areas, if done by a person—or even by government employees under normal circumstances—would be considered kidnapping and unlawful imprisonment. Yet under the exigencies of war, President Roosevelt, acting pursuant to a broad war powers delegation from Congress, ordered such action be taken against Americans of Japanese ancestry because he believed it to be in the interest of national security. Similarly under extreme conditions but not at that point constituting a declared war, President Lincoln confiscated vessels violating a naval blockade, seized rail and telegraph lines leading to Washington, and paid troops from Treasury funds without the required congressional appropriation. In 1969, during my administration, warrantless wiretapping, even by the government, was unlawful, but if undertaken because of a presidential determination that it was in the interest of national security was lawful. Support for the legality of such action is found, for example, in the concurring opinion of Justice White in *Katz v. United States.*

This is not to say, of course, that any action a president might authorize in the interest of national security would be lawful. The Supreme Court's disapproval of President Truman's seizure of the steel mills is an example. But it is naive to attempt to categorize activities a president might authorize as "legal" or "illegal" without reference to the circumstances under which he concludes that the activity is necessary. Assassination of a foreign leader—an act I never had cause to consider and which under most circumstances would be abhorrent to any president—might have been less abhorrent and, in fact, justified during World War II as a means of preventing further Nazi atrocities and ending the slaughter. Additionally, the opening of mail sent to selected priority targets of foreign intelligence, although impinging upon individual freedom, may nevertheless serve a salutory purpose when—as it has in the past—it results in preventing the disclosure of sensitive military and state secrets to the enemies of this country.

In short, there have been—and will be in the future—circumstances in which presidents may lawfully authorize actions in the interests of the security of this country, which if undertaken by other persons, or even by the president under different circumstances, would be illegal.*

We leave this unholy omelet of historical and legal misconceptions to be unscrambled by historians and jurists; there is also room for a psychiatrist, who might be able to explain Nixon's choice of the term "sovereign" in the immediate preamble to his brief.

The next round in the Nixon/Kissinger battle to gain control over the intelligence community was much less sinister in intent and purpose than the domestic intelligence issue. It stemmed from the fact that both men were dissatisfied with the quality of national intelligence estimates, analyses, and reports which made their way to the White House. Kissinger, who seemingly possessed his own ouija board, was especially distressed by the intelligence community's analytical prognostications about the future intentions of the Soviets and Chinese. Admittedly, forecasting the future and other nations' intentions is a chancy business at best, but Kissinger had no patience with views other than his own. Consequently, he believed it was necessary to reorganize the intelligence community—ostensibly to make it more consistent with the changed world he and Nixon were orchestrating, in reality to make the Nixon/Kissinger foreign policy a self-fulfilling prophecy, and one written by the intelligence community.

To get a better handle on the intelligence community's spending habits, Nixon, in December 1970, directed Assistant Budget Director James Schlesinger to make a study of the intelligence community with an eye toward restructuring its overall management. In his report, Schlesinger concluded that,

. . . the division of labor envisaged by the National Security Act of 1947 had been rendered obsolescent and meaningless by technology and the ambitions of U.S. intelligence agencies. [The Schlesinger report] recommended nothing less than the basic reform of U.S. intelligence management, centering upon a strong DCI who could bring intelligence costs under control and bring intelligence production to an adequate level of quality and responsiveness. In addition, he pinpointed nine specific mergers or shifts of intelligence programs estimated to save nearly one billion dollars annually.**

*"Supplementary Detailed Staff Reports on Foreign and Military Intelligence, Book IV," *op. cit.*, pp. 157–58.

**"Foreign and Military Intelligence, Book I," *op. cit.*, p. 66.

Not unexpectedly, the intelligence community dug in its collective heels over the Schlesinger report because its basic thrust, which was designed to bring about centralized control over the entire intelligence budget, threatened each of the community members' individual empires. The Schlesinger report, although extremely closely held, quite literally stirred up hornet's nests of opposition throughout the intelligence community, on Capitol Hill, and in the aerospace industry, which had become highly dependent on intelligence funds spent on aerial reconnaissance programs. Nixon was personally bewildered by the furious reaction to the Schlesinger report. On the surface the report appeared to be just one more management review; however, because Schlesinger had fingered the intelligence community's genuine point of vulnerability—the cost/benefit output of the intelligence process—it provoked a violent reaction.

Although Nixon delayed taking immediate action on the Schlesinger report, the White House announced on November 5, 1971, a number of management steps to improve the efficiency and effectiveness of the United States foreign intelligence community. Stating the president's objectives to ensure: (1) continuing review of the responsiveness of the United States intelligence effort to national needs; (2) strengthened leadership of the community as a whole; (3) more efficient use of resources in the collection of intelligence information; (4) elimination of less efficient or outmoded activities; and (5) improvement in the quality, scope, and timeliness of intelligence information. The major management improvements included:

(1) An enhanced leadership role for the director of Central Intelligence in planning, reviewing, coordinating, and evaluating all intelligence programs and activities, and in the production of national intelligence.

(2) Establishment of a National Security Council Intelligence Committee, chaired by the assistant to the president for National Security Affairs. Its members to include the attorney general, the DCI, the undersecretary of state, the deputy secretary of defense, and the chairman of the Joint Chiefs of Staff. The committee will give direction and guidance on national intelligence needs and provide for a continuing evaluation of intelligence products from the viewpoint of the intelligence user.

(3) Establishment of a Net Assessment Group with the National Security Council Staff. The group will be headed by a senior staff member and will be responsible for reviewing and evaluating all intelligence products and for producing net assessments.

(4) Establishment of an Intelligence Resources Advisory Committee, chaired by the DCI, including as members a senior representative from the Department of State, the Department of Defense, the Office of Management and Budget, and the CIA. This committee will advise the DCI on the preparation of a consolidated intelligence program budget.

(5) Reconstitution of the United States Intelligence Board chaired by the DCI, including as members the deputy director of Central Intelligence (vice chairman); director of Bureau of Intelligence and Research, State Department; director of National Security Agency; director of the Defense Intelligence Agency; representatives of the secretary of the treasury and of the director of the Federal Bureau of Investigation and the Atomic Energy Commission. The board will advise and assist the DCI with respect

to the production of national intelligence, the establishment of national intelligence requirements and priorities, the supervision of the dissemination and security of intelligence material, and the protection of intelligence sources and methods.

The president's intention was that the DCI advise him on communitywide budgetary allocations by serving in a last review capacity. It was an admirable but rather foolish intention, because it assumed a power on the part of the DCI beyond what he legally possessed or could have conferred on him by the president. Significantly, Nixon could have sought legislation to expand the DCI's authority, but he chose not to because to do so would have been an invitation to Congress to investigate the intelligence community and open, among other things, the covert action and domestic intelligence boxes. Lacking additional legislative authority the DCI, Richard Helms, followed the path of least resistance in preparing the "consolidated intelligence program budget" by simply passing along to the Office of Management and Budget (OMB) and the president the agreed views and budget requests of the departmental intelligence community members. Peace was maintained in the intelligence community as a result of Helms's benign direction, and the last review of intelligence budgets stayed in the various departments where it had reposed for decades.

However, in order to placate Kissinger, who had been challenged by his former peers at Harvard over the Cambodian decision, Helms established the Intelligence Community (IC) staff as a replacement for the National Intelligence Programs Evaluation (NIPE), ostensibly to assist in community matters but realistically to eliminate any genuine before- or after-the-fact consideration of Kissinger's revealed wisdom. (Many of Kissinger's ex-colleagues had been consultants to the NIPE; when it was replaced by the IC, their relationship and access to intelligence information was terminated.) Although not stated in so many words, the IC staff's role was to provide a chorus extolling the omniscient Kissinger. It was a simple lyric for those on the IC staff to sing, and those unable to reach high K were given the sack.

Nixon, Kissinger, and the intelligence community, having gone through such battles, reeled uncertainly into 1972. Neither was completely sure what the year would bring, other than the quadrennial spectacle of a presidential election. Like a nagging backache which has settled at the base of the body politic's spine, Vietnam continued to be a source of concern; Nixon's phased withdrawals did little more than keep the antiwar activist movement from erupting violently.

An interesting sidelight to the Nixon/Kissinger battles with the intelligence community occurred during the first Nixon administration. It involved the problem of leaks emanating from Kissinger's NSC and the White House itself. Both Nixon and Kissinger fumed over their inability to prevent the administration's positions from being prematurely revealed in the *Washington Post* and *The New York Times*. Out of the increasing sense of frustration was born the "plumbers," as well as the wiretaps of former and present White House staff and "hostile" newsmen. Their obsession over the leaks was so all-consuming as to be ridiculous. Theirs was not a concern about national security per se, but rather one based on an almost paranoid view that because they possessed revealed wisdom about foreign policy, any actions designed to challenge that wisdom were treasonous.

Egil Krogh, whose control of the plumbers ultimately led to his downfall, understood the absurdity of Nixon's and Kissinger's paranoia over leaks; but he was swept up by its madness and unable to resist the urge to fund the spies in his midst. "Bud" Krogh, older and much wiser now, knows the truth of Pogo's statement, "I met the enemy and he is us." However, in Nixon's White House in 1972, to have said that the source of the leaks was the president or his national security adviser would have been an unforgivable folly.

In discussion with the author in the fall of 1971 Krogh—who was deeply troubled about the plumbers' activities—stated that leaks as a way of protesting government policy were endemic to a democratic government. The leakers' motives were not necessarily partisan, but more often based on an apolitical or idealized view of government. It was a complex discussion which concluded with the author's admonition to tell Nixon not to worry too much about Daniel Ellsberg, Morton Halperin, et al., but about the Cold War true believers, who were more of a threat to his global designs because they possessed a real power to thwart anything he might choose to do with which they disagreed. Bud was attentive and receptive to the advice, but he was a captive of the Nixon/Kissinger paranoia.

By early 1972 the concern over leaks had diminished and, among other things, the break-in of Ellsberg's psychiatrist's office had been blotted from official memory, a nonevent. These and other concerns had been replaced by the preeminent one of securing Nixon's reelection. Much, perhaps too much, has been written about the Committee to Re-elect the President (CREEP) and the actions known generically as Watergate. How did Watergate effect Nixon's relationships with the intelligence community?

The series of conflicts Nixon and Kissinger had with the intelligence community, beginning with the NSSM 1 skirmish, produced mixed results. Nixon won some of the battles and predictably lost others; and in the spring of 1972 Nixon was diverted from further conflict by the consuming problem of winning reelection. It was considered an unnecessary danger to seek any further conflict with the intelligence community as Nixon moved forward into what he considered to be a difficult, problematic presidential election. As a consequence, a basic truce was struck with the intelligence community, the terms of which indicated to all concerned that no change in the status quo would be initiated, at least until January 1973. This took form in the issuance of National Security Council Intelligence Directive (NSCID) #1 on February 17, 1972, which told the intelligence community that Nixon's and Kissinger's attacks on their ordered existence had been temporarily called off. NSCID #1, which superceded the previous directive of 1964, read as follows:

National Security Council Intelligence Directive No. 1

Basic Duties and Responsibilities
(Effective 17 February 1972)

The intelligence effort of the United States is a national responsibility and must be so organized and managed as to exploit to the maximum the available resources of the government and to satisfy the intelligence requirements of the National Security Council and of the departments and agencies of the government. For the purpose of coordinating the intelligence activities of the several government departments and agencies in the interest of national security, and pursuant to the provisions of Section 102 of the National Security Act of 1947, as amended, the National Security Council hereby authorizes and directs that:

1. Overall Coordination

The director of Central Intelligence shall coordinate the foreign intelligence activities of the United States in accordance with existing law and applicable directives. Such coordination shall include those forms of intelligence that constitute the foreign intelligence activities of the United States.

2. The National Security Council Intelligence Committee (NSCIC)

The National Security Council Intelligence Committee will be comprised of: the assistant to the president for National Security Affairs, chairman; the attorney general; the director of Central Intelligence; the undersecretary of state; the deputy secretary of defense; and the chairman of the Joint Chiefs of Staff.

The National Security Council Intelligence Committee will give direction and guidance on national substantive intelligence needs and provide for a continuing evaluation of intelligence products from the viewpoint of the intelligence consumer.

3. The Director of Central Intelligence

a. The director of Central Intelligence will discharge four major responsibilities:

(1) Planning, reviewing and evaluating all intelligence activities and the allocation of all intelligence resources.

(2) Producing national intelligence required by the president and other national consumers.

(3) Chairing and staffing all intelligence community advisory boards and committees.

(4) Establishing and reconciling intelligence requirements and priorities within budgetary constraints.

b. The director of Central Intelligence shall prepare and submit each year, through the Office of Management and Budget, a consolidated intelligence program budget as directed in the presidential memorandum of 5 November 1971. In preparing the program/budget, the director of Central Intelligence will take into account such considerations as the comparative effectiveness of collection programs and the priorities of intelligence targets.

c. The director of Central Intelligence shall act for the National Security Council to provide for detailed implementation of National Security Council intelligence directives by issuing, after appropriate consultation, such supplementary director of Central Intelligence directives as may be required. Such directives shall, as applicable, be promulgated and implemented within the normal command channels of the departments and agencies concerned.

d. The director of Central Intelligence shall formulate, as appropriate, policies with respect to arrangements with foreign governments on intelligence matters.

e. The director of Central Intelligence shall make recommendations on foreign intelligence matters to appropriate United States officials.

f. The director of Central Intelligence shall develop and review security standards and practices as they relate to the protection of intelligence and of intelligence sources and methods from unauthorized disclosure.

g. Director of Central Intelligence directives to be issued in accordance with the provisions of subparagraph c above shall include:

(1) General guidance and the establishment of specific priorities for the production of national and other intelligence and for collection and other activities in support thereof and their formal transmission to the National Security Council.

(2) Establishment of policy, procedures and practices for the maintenance, by the individual components of the intelligence community, of a continuing interchange of intelligence, intelligence information and other information with utility for intelligence purposes.

h. The director of Central Intelligence, or representatives designated by him, in consultation with the head of the intelligence or other appropriate component of the department or agency concerned, shall make such surveys of departmental intelligence activities of the various departments and agencies as he may deem necessary in connection with his duty to advise the National Security Council and to coordinate the intelligence effort of the United States.

i. In making recommendations in matters concerning such intelligence activities of the departments and agencies of the government as relate to the national security, the director of Central Intelligence shall transmit therewith a statement indicating the dissenting views of the members of the United States Intelligence Board and the Intelligence Resources Advisory Committee in matters relating to intelligence production and resource management.

4. Intelligence Resources Advisory Committee (IRAC).

An Intelligence Resources Advisory Committee is hereby established to advise the director of Central Intelligence on the preparation of the intelligence budget and the allocation of resources among programs and to ensure that they are employed in accordance with approved requirements with no unwarranted duplication. It will consist of the director of Central Intelligence, chairman, and senior representatives of the Department of State, Department of Defense, Central Intelligence Agency, and the Office of Management and Budget.

5. The United States Intelligence Board (USIB).

a. A United States Intelligence Board is hereby established under the chairmanship of the director of Central Intelligence. Subject to other established responsibilities under existing law and directives, the United States Intelligence Board will advise and assist the director of Central Intelligence with respect to:

(1) The establishment of appropriate intelligence objectives, requirements and priorities.

(2) The production of national intelligence.

(3) The supervision of the dissemination and security of intelligence material.

(4) The protection of intelligence sources and methods.

(5) As appropriate, policies with respect to arrangements with foreign governments on intelligence matters.

b. The membership of the United States Intelligence Board shall consist of the following: the director of Central Intelligence, chairman; the deputy director of Central Intelligence, vice-chairman; the director of Intelligence and Research, Department of State; the director, Defense Intelligence Agency; the director, National Security Agency; a representative of the secretary of the treasury; a representative of the Atomic Energy Commission; and a representative of the director of the Federal Bureau of Investigation.

The director of Central Intelligence, as chairman, shall invite the chief of any other department or agency having functions related to the national security to sit with the United States Intelligence Board whenever matters within the purview of his department or agency are to be discussed.

c. The board shall be provided with a secretariat staff, which shall be under the direction of an executive secretary appointed by the director of Central Intelligence. Subordinate committees and working groups shall be established, as appropriate, by the director of Central Intelligence.

6. National Intelligence

a. National intelligence is that intelligence required for the formulation of national security policy, concerning more than one department or agency, and transcending the exclusive competence of a single department or agency. The director of Central Intelligence shall produce national intelligence that will carry a statement of abstention or any substantially differing opinion of a United States Intelligence Board member or of the Intelligence Chief of a Military Department.

b. Departmental intelligence is that intelligence which any department or agency requires to execute its own mission.

c. Interdepartmental intelligence is integrated departmental intelligence required by departments and agencies of the government for the execution of their missions, but transcending the exclusive competence of a single department or agency to produce. Such subcommittee structure of the United States Intelligence Board as may be established by the director of Central Intelligence may be utilized for the production and dissemination of interdepartmental intelligence.

d. The director of Central Intelligence shall disseminate national intelligence to the president, members of the National Security Council, as appropriate, members of the United States Intelligence Board and, subject to existing statutes, such other components of the government as the National Security Council may from time to time designate or the United States Intelligence Board may recommend. He is further authorized to disseminate national intelligence and interdepartmental intelligence on a strictly controlled basis to foreign governments and international bodies upon his determination after consultation with the United States Intelligence Board that such action would substantially promote the security of the United States, provided that such dissemination is consistent with existing statutes and presidential policy, including that reflected in international agreements; and provided further that any disclosure of Federal Bureau of Investigation intelligence information shall be cleared with that agency prior to dissemination. Departmental intelligence and interdepartmental intelligence produced outside the United States Intelligence Board subcommittee structure may be disseminated in accordance with existing statutes and presidential policy, including that reflected in international agreements.

e. Whenever any member of the United States Intelligence Board obtains information that indicates an impending crisis situation that affects the security of the United States to such an extent that immediate action or decision by the president or the National Security Council may be required, he shall immediately transmit the information to the director of Central Intelligence and the other members of the United States Intelligence Board, as well as to the National Indications Center and to other officials or agencies as may be indicated by the circumstances. The director of Central Intelligence shall immediately prepare and disseminate, as appropriate, the national intelligence estimate of the situation.

7. Protection of Intelligence and of Intelligence Sources and Methods

The director of Central Intelligence, with the advice of the members of the United States Intelligence Board, shall ensure the development of policies and procedures for the protection of intelligence and of intelligence sources and methods from unauthorized disclosure. Each department and agency shall remain responsible for the protection of intelligence and of intelligence sources and methods within its own organization. Each shall also establish appropriate internal policies and procedures to prevent the unauthorized disclosure from within that agency of intelligence information or activity. The director of Central Intelligence shall call upon the departments and agencies, as appropriate, to investigate within their department or agency any unauthorized disclosure of intelligence or of intelligence sources or methods. A report of these investigations, including corrective measures taken or recommended within the departments and agencies involved, shall be transmitted to the director of Central Intelligence for review and such further action as may be appropriate, including reports to the National Security Council or the president.

a. Authorized Disclosures

The director of Central Intelligence, with the advice and assistance of the United States Intelligence Board, shall establish procedures for review by intelligence authorities of all classified intelligence information contemplated, proposed or prepared for release to the public or for use or disclosure in other unclassified activities in the course of which there is danger that intelligence sources and methods might be revealed. Intelligence information that has been authorized for unclassified disclosure shall be released, used or utilized only in the form and manner authorized under the established review procedures.

8. Community Responsibilities

a. In implementation of, and in conformity with, approved National Security Council policy, the director of Central Intelligence shall:

(1) Seek the attainment of the following objectives as essential to the efficient and effective functioning of the intelligence community:

(a) The responsiveness of the United States intelligence effort with respect to national requirements must be subject to continuing review.

(b) Authoritative and responsible leadership for the community as a whole must be assured.

(c) A more efficient use of resources by the community in the collection of intelligence information must be achieved. Utilization of the means available must be in consonance with approved requirements of United States security and national interests.

(d) Assignment of intelligence functions within the community must be reviewed and revised to eliminate inefficient, unnecessary or outmoded activities.

(e) The quality, scope and timeliness of the community's product must be improved.

(f) The provision of intelligence and its utilization must enhance the formulation of the foreign and economic policies of the United States government and the planning for and conduct of military operations by United States forces.

(2) Call upon the other departments and agencies, as appropriate, to ensure that on intelligence matters affecting the national security the intelligence community is supported by the full knowledge and technical talent available in or to the government.

(3) Ensure that the pertinence, extent and quality of the available foreign intelligence and intelligence information relating to the national security is continually reviewed as a basis for improving the quality of intelligence and the correction of deficiencies.

(4) Take appropriate measures to facilitate the coordinated development of compatible referencing systems within the departments and agencies engaged in foreign intelligence activities. Central reference facilities as a service of common concern shall be provided by the Central Intelligence Agency and/or other departments and agencies, as appropriate.

(5) Make arrangements with the departments and agencies for the assignment to, or exchange with, the Central Intelligence Agency of such experienced and qualified personnel as may be of advantage for advisory, operational or other purposes. In order to facilitate the performance of their respective intelligence missions, the departments and agencies concerned shall, by agreement, provide each other with such mutual assistance as may be within their capabilities and as may be required in the interests of the intelligence community for reasons of economy, efficiency or operational necessity. In this connection primary departmental interests shall be recognized and shall receive mutual cooperation and support.

(6) Be provided with all information required from all departments and agencies of the executive branch required for the exercise of his responsibilities.

b. Insofar as practicable, in the fulfillment of their respective responsibilities for the production of intelligence, the several departments and agencies shall not duplicate the intelligence activities and research of other departments and agencies and shall make full use of existing capabilities of the other elements of the intelligence community.

c. The departments and agencies of the government shall establish appropriate policies and procedures to control and limit undesirable publicity relating to intelligence activities.

Nixon's truce with the intelligence community, established by NSCID #1, lasted until February 1973; at which time he went back on the attack, this time against the CIA. He appointed James Schlesinger to serve as DCI and director of the CIA, replacing Helms. (It was assumed that Helms's acceptance of the ambassadorship to Iran meant his willingness to remain out of the way in the expected battle to reorganize the CIA and bring it more closely under the White House and Kissinger's wing.) Schlesinger was an inspired choice. Unlike previous DCIs who were "outsiders," Schlesinger came to his new post not only armed with some very solid experience in government,* but more importantly with a clear understanding about the Agency's operations, which he had gained in the course of his management review study. To be sure, during the conduct of that review Schlesinger had not been made totally privy to the workings of the Agency's "black" side—the clandestine services under DDP Thomas Karemessiness and those of the Counterintelligence Staff headed by James Angleton—but he did generally find out how much those operations cost in terms of people and dollars. Once he had received his "director's clearance" (which theoretically clears one for access to the Agency's most closely held secrets), Schlesinger was in a strong position to carry out a modified cost/benefit analysis of the Agency's clandestine services.

Schlesinger's subsequent analysis pointed out that although the number of approved covert actions had declined in the past five years and the Agency's paramilitary activities had been largely wound up at the end of 1972, the clandestine services still claimed a lion's share of the CIA's total budget. As a result of this analysis, in March 1973 Schlesinger launched a two-pronged attack. The first changed the name of the clandestine services' Directorate for Plans (DDP) to the Directorate of Operations (DDO), thus effectively stripping planning from the DDP organization. This change was more than simple semantics or bureaucratic face-lift; taking away its planning function gave Schlesinger the bureaucratic justification to abolish more than 1,000 "slots" in the resulting DDO organization. Most of the jobs so abolished were held by covert-action supporters who had been brought in out of the cold to become planners; in Schlesinger's view, they were merely serving out their time waiting for retirement, or for another Cold War crisis to break out in one country or another. Many of the old hands who had served the covert-action cause in cold and hot wars for many years were angered by Schlesinger's arbitrary action, which forced them into early retirement. Most looked upon Schlesinger with the kind of disdain combat soldiers show toward those who did not serve.

Schlesinger's decision to gut the Agency's clandestine services was a calculated risk. His intellectual conviction that covert actions were not, in terms of the money and personnel resources they sometimes involved, worth the cost was not widely shared at the time of his decision. Furthermore, if covert

---

*Schlesinger began his career as a member of the University of Virginia faculty. From 1963 to 1969 he served as director of Strategic Studies at the Rand Corporation. He was appointed assistant director of the Bureau of the Budget in 1969 and continued as assistant director during the transition to the Office of Management and Budget. In 1971 Nixon named him chairman of the Atomic Energy Commission, from which position he became DCI in February 1973.

actions were going to be continued (as they were), the Agency's diminished capability opened the door for those in the military intelligence services to move into the gap—which they did. The logic of Schlesinger's decision to cut the DDP back to a more appropriate size is not at issue here, but rather that the men who had served in the CIA with great loyalty and courage deserved more compassionate treatment than that meted out by Schlesinger. As a result, Agency morale was unnecessarily weakened at a critical time.

Schlesinger also became aware of the fact that many of the DDP's past and present activities were clearly illegal. This was particularly worrisome to Schlesinger because, as the events of 1973 were already showing, revelations of official wrongdoing were occurring with increasing frequency. Schlesinger, who knew in spite of his clearance he would never personally (or through the efforts of the few persons he brought to the Agency as special assistants) uncover the full extent of the Agency's dirty tricks, took a different tack and asked all employees to send information directly to him about activities which they knew, believed, or heard about that had been carried out on improper grounds. His appeal produced some remarkable results. Many of the items were reported anonymously by persons who quite obviously had a strong feeling of guilt about their involvement in illegal activities. Others reflected a "poison pen" approach designed to finger someone they disliked. Nevertheless, the overall responses indicated 693 examples of Agency activities which, if publicized, would have presented Schlesinger with a serious problem in trying to explain how and by what authority they had been undertaken in the first place. The compendium of these transgressions became known as the "Family Jewels," and subsequently served as the basis of Congress' investigation of the intelligence community.

While the perturbations from Schlesinger's dramatic moves to reorganize the CIA and consolidate his DCI authority in the production of national intelligence were being felt in the intelligence community, other events were underway which would result, in July 1973, in his dismissal as DCI and immediate appointment as secretary of defense. These events, which stemmed from the Watergate inquiry, set off a game of musical chairs in the Nixon administration's key cabinet posts. And as the Watergate plot thickened, it left the intelligence community, like the rest of the government, to run itself.

To replace Schlesinger, Kissinger, who in the second Nixon administration had become secretary of state in addition to retaining his position as the president's assistant for National Security Affairs and head of the NSC, sought and received Nixon's approval to designate William Egan Colby as DCI. Colby, who had served as the CIA's executive director under Schlesinger, was in Kissinger's eyes the right man for the job for several important reasons. One, although Colby came out of the clandestine services, he was not a charter member in the Helms CIA headquarters clique. Two, Colby could be counted upon to continue the institutional and managerial reforms initiated by Schlesinger which, regardless of the personal rivalry between Schlesinger and Kissinger, Kissinger knew were long overdue and quite necessary. Three, as the Watergate crisis moved toward its final denouement, Colby would be a team player in Kissinger's efforts to carry out the administration's foreign policy no matter what. This third reason was extremely crucial because Kissinger was well aware that with Nixon almost completely preoccupied with Watergate there was a real danger of the intelligence community's going off the reservation to oppose his conduct of foreign policy.

After his appointment, Colby moved in rapid order to initiate major management improvements in the CIA.* These included adoption of the system of Management by Objectives (MBO), which was designed to replace the project system originated in 1948 at the time of the OPC with specific program objectives against which projects were to be developed. The Senate Select Committee noted:

Under MBO, related projects are aggregated into "programs" aimed at a policy objective. As such, the system is primarily a means of evaluation to measure performance against stated objectives. Although the DDO directive establishing MBO in January 1974 ordered the elimination of the project system for purposes of planning, projects remain the basic units for approval procedures and for budgeting at the station and division levels. Thus, the internal demand created by the project system remains. MBO was not intended to rectify the incentives for the generation of projects and has not succeeded in replacing the project system administratively. The nature of DDO operations makes it difficult to quantify results and therefore limits the utility of MBO. For example, recruitment of three agents over a given period may result in little worthwhile information, while a single agent may produce valuable results.**

Colby also abolished the Office of National Estimates (ONE) and its board and established in their place the National Intelligence Officers (NIOs).

. . . the NIOs are responsible for collection and production in their designated fields. The senior NIO reports to the DCI. The NIOs serve two specific functions. First, they are the DCI's senior substantive staff officers in their designated specialties. Second, they are coordinators of the intelligence production machinery and are to make recommendations to the DCI on intelligence priorities and the allocation of resources within the community. Their access is communitywide, including the DDO. Their job is not to serve as drafters of national intelligence estimates but to force the community's

---

*It is of some interest to note that William Colby was the first DCI to appear in public hearings in connection with Senate confirmation for the post. All previous DCIs were questioned in closed hearings by the Senate's Armed Services Committee and even today its chairman, Senator Stennis, has declined to make the five pages of the transcript of Allen Dulles' 1953 executive hearings public. There is some irony in this fact because, as the Carter nomination of Theodore Sorensen to become DCI revealed, public acceptance of the president's nominee to this important post has become an important consideration.

**"Supplementary Detailed Staff Reports on Foreign and Military Intelligence, Book IV," *op. cit.*, p. 86.

intelligence machinery to make judgments by assigning the drafting of estimates to analysts. They do not collectively review estimates in the way the board did. Essentially, they are intended to serve as managers and facilitators of information.*

Finally, Colby initiated a system designed to identify specific categories of intelligence information needs. This took form in establishing Key Intelligence Questions (KIQs), which were expected to force the intelligence community to be more responsive to national intelligence production requirements rather than simply serving their departments' and agencies' self-perceived needs. Colby gave each of these efforts a good try, going so far as to call meetings of the CIA's alumni to explain that he wasn't selling out the Agency. These meetings, held at a local Holiday Inn, turned into rather acrimonious affairs as those who knew Bill Colby "when" told him in rather blunt terms that he had broken faith with the intelligence brotherhood. The intelligence fraternity's resistance was not easily overcome because most present and former active members believed that the CIA's going along with Kissinger was a bad bargain. These attitudes were not Colby's fault. They had been building for years because reorganizations and management improvements without basic structural reform—which can only be achieved by legislative change—is and was inadequate to alter the intelligence community members' essential independence to carry out their missions as they see fit. The Senate Select Committee noted in this regard:

The notion that control can be imposed from the top over an organization without some effort to alter internal patterns and incentives is ill-founded.**

Before discussing what happened in the intelligence community under President Ford, it should be noted that Kissinger's fears about the capacity of the intelligence community (or perhaps more properly of key persons in it) to thwart the accomplishment of foreign policy objectives with which they disagreed were well placed. Kissinger, more than most secretaries of state, was aware of the power of intelligence information for negative as well as positive purposes. As a result of leaks over the India-Pakistan situation, the Pentagon papers, etc., he was more than a little concerned about the possible responses of the intelligence professionals to his policy of detente with the Soviet Union and the overtures to China. He also knew that these two policy initiatives had provoked more internal criticism in the community than that directed at John Kennedy a decade earlier for pushing through the Nuclear Test Ban Treaty.

It may seem a bit strange to speak of the intelligence community's opposition to American foreign policy (or Kissinger's concept and conduct of that policy), but the community is made up of strong-willed persons not all of

*Ibid., p. 87.

**Ibid., p. 87.

whom are apolitical in the sense of a soldier who is expected to obey orders without question. This is not to say that the intelligence community is replete with dissenters, or a large number of individuals prepared to thwart policy merely for the sake of thwarting; rather, because they must implement policy which may be improperly drawn or determined, there is a temptation on their part to throw some sand in the gears. This can take several forms, such as the leak of MAGIC information to Tom Dewey in 1944 or Allen Dulles' Operation Sunrise in 1945, which negotiated the surrender of the German army in Italy and which almost upset the Allies' unconditional surrender policy by creating a major rift between the United States and the USSR. These historical examples and others in more recent times were not lost on Kissinger, who in his efforts to reestablish peace between the Arabs and Israelis after the October 1973 Mideast war found out that his views and actions were not unanimously endorsed by key persons in the intelligence community. Also, as the White House role in the Watergate cover-up was revealed in a series of stories in the *Washington Post* by Woodward and Bernstein, the suspicion that their "Deep Throat" source was somehow connected with the intelligence community someplace in the White House or the NSC became quite real. Much speculation has surrounded the question of Deep Throat's identity, or indeed his/her existence. Woodward won't tell, but from a close reading of the *Post* stories and *All the President's Men* it is possible to distill the essence of Deep Throat's information and the manner by which Woodward and the *Washington Post* were run. Because the Deep Throat operation had and presumably continues to have intelligence implications which affect the execution of foreign policy, it is significant to note the counterespionage techniques the secret source employed. Besides the examples of tradecraft employed in the meetings and information drops, these were used to manipulate Woodward et al. by giving them instructions where to look rather than providing the information directly. The entire operation bears the imprimatur of a highly skillful, organized counterespionage operation whereby another intelligence service—the *Washington Post*—was manipulated in a classic manner. Perhaps Haldeman and Kissinger will, in their forthcoming books, indicate their suspicions about Deep Throat's identity; regardless of their accuracy, Deep Throat's ability to alter national policy and bring about a change in events is a clear and important statement of the power of intelligence information.

Thus, one may conclude that in Nixon/Kissinger's last battle with the intelligence community, Nixon came away a loser and Kissinger, although initially successful in settling the 1973 Arab-Israeli war, at best achieved only a draw; the fallout from the Arab oil embargo thwarted his conduct of foreign policy throughout the rest of his tenure as secretary of state.

On August 9, 1974, the United States once again had a new president and first intelligence officer. Gerald Ford's was perhaps even more traumatic than the other abrupt accessions to the presidency in American history, coming as it did in the unprecedented wake of Nixon's resignation. Ford's problems upon assuming the presidency were many, but he had little reason at the outset to expect that the past and present activities of the intelligence community would rise up to dog his administration's efforts to stimulate the faltering economy, develop a valid response to the energy problem, etc. From what he knew and was told about the intelligence community, it was continuing to carry out its missions much as in the past, and the efforts of Colby and others to improve management in the community's operations were well advanced. Ford needed intelligence to meet his foreign policy responsibilities and these seemed to be adequately provided for by the community's system. Also, he was reassured by the presence of the principal intelligence and national security advisers he had inherited from the Nixon administration. These men—Kissinger (State and NSC), Schlesinger (Defense), Colby (CIA), General Alexander Haig (White House chief of staff), and Lieutenant General Brent Scowcroft (Kissinger's deputy at the NSC)—appeared to be totally competent and apparently untainted by Watergate. Although the Ford-Schlesinger relationship soured later on, the president was completely at home with defense questions as a result of his long service on the House Military Appropriations Subcommittee, and was in no awe of Schlesinger, whom he could treat as an intellectual equal. Although he was a bit new to foreign policy, Ford had confidence in, endorsed and understood Kissinger's foreign policy goals and objectives. These factors, coupled with the need to meet pressing domestic questions, tended to make Ford an intelligence consumer rather than a personal director of intelligence. This is not to say that Ford did not task the intelligence community with questions to help solve his problems; but because his advisers shared, appreciated and understood those problems, they were able to anticipate many of his intelligence needs.

Ford's basic approach to intelligence and the intelligence community was much like Truman's: as long as it worked reasonably well to provide him with the intelligence he needed or wanted, he left the leaders alone to do their job. For those in the intelligence community, after the turmoil of Watergate, Ford's presence in the White House was reassuring. His demeanor and attitude suggested that it would now be possible to get on with the real tasks at hand; most encouragingly, as Colby and others noted, the perennial interagency bickering had apparently been replaced by a new sense of cooperation. It took the rest of the country a little longer to get used to Ford, especially after his pardon of Nixon, but within a month of taking office the intelligence community leaders were more than content with Ford as the nation's first intelligence officer. There are those who cynically contend that the intelligence community's contentment with Ford was based on the fact that he largely left them alone to do their jobs, but this is grossly unfair. Ford went out of his way to acknowledge their efforts and to convey "well dones" to the folks at the working level. No matter one's political predispositions, it is accurate to say that Ford assumed responsibility for the nation's intelligence system with grace and humor and, without engaging in any false dramatics, let all hands know he was in command.

Ford's behavior in the first several months of his presidency inspired confidence in the intelligence community, and some internal attempts to rehabilitate the system in order to meet national intelligence needs were accomplished. However, on December 22, 1974, when Seymour Hersh's *New York Times* story alleged CIA involvement in a massive domestic surveillance program and hinted at other misdeeds, the roof fell in. This story and others which followed handed Ford a sack which had been filled by his predecessors, and as its contents were publicly spilled out it became his responsibility to explain the raison d'etre for these official acts of wrongdoing.

The analogy which comes to mind is that of a person who inherited a house from a distant relative and then found himself arrested because custom agents found contraband in a locked trunk in a hidden compartment of the house's attic. Although Hersh's original story was fairly thin in terms of actual content, it restimulated Congress' and the public's appetite for exposure of official crimes, which had been incompletely satisfied when the impeachment proceedings against Nixon were stopped. Overnight, the operations of the intelligence community were transformed from a staff function in support of the presidency into a pressing domestic problem with some serious legal and foreign policy implications.

The Hersh story caused Ford, on December 23, 1974, to order Secretary Kissinger to produce a report "within a matter of days" on the story's allegations. At the end of the month Kissinger gave the president a report from Colby which basically substantiated those allegations, but which had been carefully drawn not to raise items which had not been broached in the Hersh story. An aside to these events, perhaps more important than the story's allegations but which got somewhat lost in their onrush, was that James Angleton, the CIA's counterintelligence chief for more than twenty years, resigned from the Agency upon the request of "higher authorities." The politics surrounding Angleton's forced retirement are beyond our scope; suffice it to say that these had more to do with Kissinger's conduct of foreign policy and the premises on which it was based than with punishing Angleton for his alleged responsibility in domestic spying. The public is entitled to that story, but it is James Angleton's to tell and his alone.

The Colby report, in spite of its selectivity, was a clear signal to Ford that the allegations could not be dismissed out of hand by a presidential announcement that the activities were either curtailed or terminated. Therefore, on January 4, 1975, Ford issued Executive Order #11828, which established a "Commission on CIA Activities Within the United States" under the chairmanship of Vice-President Nelson Rockefeller to:

(a) Ascertain and evaluate any facts relating to activities conducted within the United States by the Central Intelligence Agency which give rise to questions of compliance with the provisions of 50 U.S.C. 403;

(b) Determine whether existing safeguards are adequate to prevent any activities which violate the provisions of 50 U.S.C. 403;

(c) Make such recommendations to the president and to the director of Central Intelligence as the commission deems appropriate.

Not to be outdone, on January 27 the Senate adopted by an 82 to 4 vote Senate Resolution 21, which established a Select Committee to Study Governmental Operations with Respect to Intelligence Activities, under the chairmanship of Senator Frank Church (Dem., Idaho). As a measure of how this issue grew, S.R. 21 also added the charge to determine the "extent, if any, to which illegal, improper, or unethical activities were engaged in by *any* [emphasis added] agency of the federal government." S.R. 21 listed the following specific areas of inquiry and study:

(1) Whether the Central Intelligence Agency has conducted an illegal domestic intelligence operation in the United States.

(2) The conduct of domestic intelligence or counterintelligence operations against United States citizens by the Federal Bureau of Investigation or any other federal agency.

(3) The origin and disposition of the so-called Huston plan to apply United States intelligence agency capabilities against individuals or organizations within the United States.

(4) The extent to which the Federal Bureau of Investigation, the Central Intelligence Agency, and other federal law-enforcement or intelligence agencies coordinate their respective activities, any agreements which govern that coordination, and the extent to which a lack of coordination has contributed to activities or actions which are illegal, improper, inefficient, unethical, or contrary to the intent of Congress.

(5) The extent to which the operation of domestic intelligence or counterintelligence activities and the operation of any other activities within the United States by the Central Intelligence Agency conforms to the legislative charter of that Agency and the intent of Congress.

(6) The past and present determination by the director of Central Intelligence of the responsibility to protect intelligence sources and methods as it relates to that provision of the National Security Act of 1947 which provides ". . . that the agency shall have no police, subpena, law-enforcement powers, or internal security functions. . . ."

(7) The nature and extent of executive branch oversight of all United States intelligence activities.

(8) The need for specific legislative authority to govern the operations of any intelligence agencies of the federal government now existing without that explicit statutory, including but not limited to agencies such as the Defense Intelligence Agency and the National Security Agency.

(9) The nature and extent to which federal agencies cooperate and exchange intelligence information and the adequacy of any regulations or statutes which govern such cooperation and exchange of intelligence information.

(10) The extent to which United States intelligence agencies are governed by executive orders, rules, or regulations either published or secret and the extent to which those executive orders, rules, or regulations interpret, expand, or are in conflict with specific legislative authority.

(11) The violation or suspected violation of any state or federal statute by any intelligence agency or by any person by or on behalf of any intelligence agency of the federal government including but not limited to surreptitious entry, surveillance, wiretaps, or eavesdropping, illegal opening of the United States mail, or the monitoring of United States mail.

(12) The need for improved, strengthened, or consolidated oversight of United States intelligence activities by the Congress.

(13) Whether any of the existing laws of the United States are inadequate, either in their provisions or manner of enforcement, to safeguard the rights of American citizens, to improve executive and legislative control of intelligence and related activities, and to resolve uncertainties as to the authority of United States intelligence and related agencies.

(14) Whether there is unnecessary duplication of expenditure and effort in the collection and processing of intelligence information by United States agencies.

(15) The extent and necessity of overt and covert intelligence activities in the United States and abroad.

The House produced parallel legislation on February 19, naming Congressman Lucien N. Nedzi (Dem., Mich.) to chair a ten-man Select Committee. This committee made little progress because of a dispute between Nedzi and other committee Democrats. As a result, on July 17 the House dissolved the Nedzi panel and transferred the job to a new committee with the same investigation mandate, appointed a new chairman, Congressman Otis G. Pike (Dem., N.Y.), and three additional members.

Thus as 1974 was known as the year of Watergate, 1975 became the year of intelligence investigations. Each of the investigating groups—the president's commission, the Senate Select Committee and the House Select Committee— moved in their own ways and at varying rates in order to respond to their differing mandates and perceptions of the problems. Taken together, the investigations constituted by far one of the most bizarre events in the history of the republic.

Predictably and quite properly the president's commission tried to confine its investigation in accordance with the limited mandate of Executive Order 11828, but items such as assassination plots against foreign leaders and drug-testing programs kept popping up to reveal that the CIA was only one culprit among many, and that the restrictive clause "within the United States" was relatively meaningless.

In the course of its five-month investigation, the president's commission compiled 2,900 pages of sworn testimony from fifty-one witnesses and took depositions from many others. It was the eleventh investigation of the CIA since its establishment in 1947.* The commission's 299-page report was delivered to Ford on June 6 and made public June 10, 1975. The commission stated that although "the great majority of the CIA's domestic activities comply with its statutory authority," some were "plainly unlawful and constituted improper invasions upon the rights of Americans." Some activities which "should be criticized and not permitted to happen again were initiated or ordered by presidents either directly or indirectly."

Although Senator Church claimed that the Rockefeller report only exposed the tip of the iceberg, its findings did indicate that:

• The CIA has not as a general rule received detailed scrutiny by Congress, and no executive-branch agency has the specific responsibility of overseeing the CIA to determine whether its activities are proper.

• Through a secret agreement with the Justice Department, the CIA for twenty years was able to decide for itself whether its employees or agents should be prosecuted for alleged criminal misconduct, which had the effect of involving the agency directly in forbidden law-enforcement activities, and represented an abdication by the Department of Justice of its statutory responsibilities.

• Between 1952 and 1973 the CIA intercepted mail between the United States and the Soviet Union at post offices in New York and three other cities.

• A special group within the CIA from August 1967 to March 1972, called Operation CHAOS, collected information on dissident groups within the United States, compiled

---

*The primary studies were:

(1) Dulles, Jackson, Correa report to the NSC on the CIA and National Organization for Intelligence, January 1949: A study of the structure and organization of the CIA, existing CIA activities, and the relationship of those activities to those of other departments and agencies.

(2) Jackson report (President's Committee on International Information Activities), June 1953: A survey and evaluation of the international policies and activities of the executive branch.

(3) Doolittle report, September 1954: A report on covert operations of the CIA.

(4) Clark report (Task Force on Government Intelligence Activities), May 1955: A survey of the CIA and intelligence activities of the State and Defense Departments and the National Security Council.

(5) Sprague report (President's Committee on Information Activities Abroad), December 1960: A review of the impact of international actions of the United States government on world public opinion and on other governments, with particular reference to the CIA.

(6) Kirkpatrick report (Joint Study Group Report on Foreign Intelligence Activities of the U.S. Government), December 1960: A series of recommendations to assist the director of Central Intelligence in coordinating foreign intelligence activities.

(7) Kirkpatrick, Schuyler, Coyne report, April 1962: A study of the organization and activities of the CIA and its relationship with other agencies in the intelligence community.

(8) Katzenbach report, March 1967: A review of the relationship between government agencies and educational and voluntary organizations which operate abroad.

(9) Lindsay Report on Covert Operations of the U.S. Government, December 1968: A study of supervision by Congress and within the CIA of covert operations.

(10) OMB report (Schlesinger Study of the Intelligence Community), March 1971: A study of the organization of the intelligence community and its cost effectiveness. (See: "Report to the President by the Commission on CIA Activities within the United States." Washington: U.S. Government Printing Office, 1975, pp. 79–80.)

files on 7,200 Americans, and developed a computerized index with the names of more than 300,000 persons and organizations. The CHAOS staff was insulated from review even within the CIA.

- The CIA infiltrated dissident groups in the Washington, D.C., area in the late 1960s to learn if they planned any activities against CIA or other government installations.
- The CIA used wiretaps or physical surveillance of American newsmen to discover their sources of classified information.
- A defector to the United States was unlawfully held by the CIA for three years in solitary confinement; a second defector was physically abused.
- The CIA provided alias documents, disguise material, a tape recorder and photography equipment and services to former CIA employee E. Howard Hunt, who later used some of them in his Watergate activities.
- At Nixon's request, the CIA in 1971 turned over highly classified information which "undisclosed to the CIA was to serve the president's personal political ends."
- In 1972 and 1973 the CIA monitored telephone calls between the Western Hemisphere (including the United States) and two other countries.
- The CIA conducted an illegal drug-testing program from the late 1940s until 1967.
- For two and a half years in the early 1970s the CIA, through one of its proprietaries, recruited nineteen agents for the Bureau of Narcotics and Dangerous Drugs.
- The agency conducted a training school for foreign police and security officers for over twenty years, and annually sold the officers and their departments from $6,000 to $48,000 worth of firearms and police equipment.
- At the request of the White House, the CIA in 1970 contributed over $33,000 for stationery and other costs for replies to persons who wrote to the president after the Cambodian invasion.
- The CIA indexed information contained the names of *seven million* persons of all nationalities, including 115,000 American citizens. It maintained open files on 57,000 American citizens, in addition to the 7,200 compiled by Operation CHAOS.

Predictably, the commission's report and Ford's statements that corrective measures had been and would be taken to prevent recurrences of these and other abuses did not still the public clamor. Additional news and magazine stories appeared alleging further examples of CIA and other intelligence community organizations' abuses. In view of the fact that Congress was on the trail of these other matters, Ford was persuaded that the best course of action was to stand back and let the investigation proceed. Although Ford publicly announced his willingness to cooperate with congressional investigations, as exampled by the turnover of political assassination material acquired by the Rockefeller panel, he did retain the right to veto information turnover on the grounds of national security. Thus, a rather vague set of battle lines was drawn between the White House and the congressional committees.

Under Senator Church, the Select Committee worked quietly and under tight security conditions through the first eight months of 1975. As the summer wore on, it became obvious to Senator Church and the committee staff that they would not be able to complete their work by the September 1 deadline specified in S.R. 21. Consequently the committee's life was extended to April 30, 1976.

On September 16, 1975, in its first public hearings, the Senate Select Committee demonstrated that there was much more involved in the alleged illegal actions of the intelligence community than had been revealed by the president's commission. This took form in an admission by CIA Director Colby that Agency employees had violated a 1970 presidential order requiring the destruction of two deadly poisons, one derived from shellfish and the other made from cobra venom. Senator Church noted that besides the venom and eleven grams of the shellfish toxin—which could kill "hundreds of thousands" of people if administered with "sophisticated equipment"—the secret cache (discovered by CIA officials earlier in 1975) contained quantities of strychnine, cyanide pills, and a chemical known as BZ that attacked the central nervous system. Colby testified "there was no indication that the Agency wanted to defy a presidential order"; however, there is no question that a middle-level officer violated the 1970 presidential order. Further in the course of his testimony Colby indicated that CIA Director Richard Helms, who headed the agency from 1966 to 1973, and Thomas Karemessiness, DDP in 1970, "were [both] aware of the requirement" that the chemical and biological agents be destroyed. "They recall that clear instructions were given that the CIA stockpile should be destroyed by the Agency and that, in accordance with presidential directives, the Agency should get out of the biological warfare business."

Following Colby's admissions, Helms testified on September 17 that he had given oral instructions to his deputies to carry out Nixon's order, but admitted that no follow-up check was undertaken, saying, "I thought they had been destroyed." Senator Church asked, "Who told you the toxins were destroyed?" Incredibly Helms replied, "I read it in the newspapers." The hearings transcript further revealed that Helms had passed the Nixon order to Karemessiness, who testified on September 17 that Sidney Gottlieb, former head of the Agency's Technical Services Division (TSD), "reported to me that the materials had been destroyed." Gottlieb told the committee through his lawyer that he would invoke the Fifth Amendment and refuse to answer the committee's questions.

In attempting to close the loop about who told what to whom, the committee called Nathan Gordon, who was in charge of TSD in 1970 and who testified on September 16 that he had never received any instructions from Gottlieb to destroy the material, but that he was aware of the Nixon directive. Gordon added that he did not follow the order because he felt it was directed at the Defense Department rather than the CIA, and that his decision was based on the cost and difficulty of isolating the toxin. The remainder of Gordon's exculpatory testimony confirmed that the toxin was shipped secretly from Fort Detrick, Maryland, to a CIA storage facility in Washington, and that Gordon and two colleagues agreed without telling Gottlieb to withhold the toxins from other materials that were to be destroyed.

In a rather prescient comment, Senator Charles Mathias, Jr., told Helms, "This is an illustrative case. It tells us how the CIA works and raises questions about the entire command and control structure within the CIA." In response, Colby attempted to reassure the committee by stating that the Agency's procedures "are being changed to assure accountability," conceding, "it is entirely possible that some person can do something not authorized." Colby cited an expansion of the agency's inspection and organizational changes which were expected to "break down the high degree of compartmentalization within the CIA."*

The toxin revelation is, as Senator Mathias noted, an illustrative case which indicates not only how the CIA works but also the extreme difficulty of *any* external organization, whether constituted by the president or Congress, to pierce the intelligence community's veil of secrecy and find out what its organizations are actually doing. In the toxin phase of its investigation the committee encountered extreme difficulty in locating witnessess and, in the case of Gottlieb, great reluctance on the part of the CIA to let the committee identify his role in the toxin case (as well as in the drug-testing programs and the attempt on Lumumba's life). The CIA's reason for shielding Gottlieb from the committee was based less on its concern with sources and methods as applied to the protection of agents in the field than on the painful recognition that Gottlieb, if compelled to testify, would directly establish the connection between illegal dirty tricks and who knew what and how much about them in the Agency's hierarchy. In essence, Gottlieb's testimony would have completely rent the blanket of plausible denial which successive DCIs have used to obfuscate their as well as the president's role in covert actions. The importance of Gottlieb, whose twenty-year span of service in TSD gave him a remarkable insight into the Agency's clandestine operations, was thoroughly appreciated by the Select Committee, which offered him immunity from prosecution for his full cooperation and testimony—but with no success.

Following close on the heels of the toxin revelations, the Select Committee, in a series of public hearings and through the issuance of special reports, was able to establish that intelligence abuses were widespread and not simply confined to the CIA. For example, on September 25, 1975, Senator Church disclosed that the FBI had carried out 238 break-ins against "domestic subversive targets" between 1942 and 1968, and records of the burglaries were placed in secret files kept by former FBI Assistant Director William C. Sullivan. This disclosure was followed on November 18–19 by public hearings which detailed the FBI's twenty-year history of disrupting protest groups and movements carried out in connection with its counterintelligence program (COINTEL-PRO), undercover attempts to discredit civil rights leader Martin Luther

---

*U.S. Senate, Select Committee to Study Governmental Operations with Respect to Intelligence Activities. Hearings, September 16–18, 1975. Washington: U.S. Government Printing Office, pp. 7–62 ff.

King, Jr., which involved blackmail, bugging, and intimidation, and Director Hoover's use of the FBI to collect "items with an unusual twist concerning prominent personalities" which he in turn provided to the White House on a regular basis under a project code-named "Inlet."*

On October 21–22, the Select Committee, also in public hearings, established that the CIA opened more than 200,000 pieces of mail and intercepted and photographed more than 2.7 million envelopes in its twenty-year mail-surveillance program. This despite the fact that internal CIA examination of the program in 1960 and again in 1969 had found it to be of little intelligence value.**

On October 29, 1975, the Select Committee initiated an unprecedented public investigation of the activities of the National Security Agency. This investigation, which was carried out over the strong protests of the Ford administration, indicated, according to the testimony of NSA Director Lew Allen, Jr., that beginning in 1967 such agencies as the CIA, FBI, and Secret Service supplied lists of persons to the NSA "in an effort to obtain information which was available in foreign communications as a byproduct of our normal intelligence mission." Allen said that the initial purpose of the cable and telephone monitoring was to "determine the existence of foreign influence" on civil disturbances occurring in the United States. Later, the surveillance was expanded to include names of persons suspected of drug trafficking and acts of terrorism. Allen testified, "We estimate that over this six-year period, about 2,000 reports were issued by the NSA on international narcotics trafficking and about 1,900 reports were issued covering the three areas of terrorism, executive protection, and foreign influence over U.S. groups. Their reports included some messages between U.S. citizens, but over 90 percent had at least one foreign communicant and all messages had at least one foreign terminal."***

Following Allen's appearance and over the objections of the Ford administration, the committee released its Shamrock report, which revealed that over the past thirty years three international telegraph companies—RCA Global, ITT World Communications and Western Union International—supplied the United States government with international telegrams originating in or forwarded through the United States. As the report noted, "At the outset, the purpose apparently was only to extract international telegrams relating to

*U.S. Senate, Hearings before the Select Committee to Study Governmental Operations with Respect to Intelligence Activities. Volume 6, Federal Bureau of Investigation, November 18–19, December 2, 3, 9, 10, 11, 1975.

**U.S. Senate, Hearings before the Select Committee to Study Governmental Operations with Respect to Intelligence Activities. Volume 4, Mail Opening. October 21, 22, 24, 1975.

***U.S. Senate, Hearings before the Select Committee to Study Governmental Operations with Respect to Intelligence Activities. Volume 5, National Security Agency and Fourth Amendment Rights. October 29 and November 6, 1975.

certain foreign targets, but later the government began to extract telegrams of certain U.S. citizens."*

And so it went, with each of the Select Committee's revelations preceded by protest from the Ford administration, but which, in spite of objections by Republican members on the committee, were made public. Although the Ford administration's skirts were shown to be clean as these revelations were exposed, an attempt was made to put some additional distance between himself and the actions of his predecessors. On November 3, 1975, Ford reshuffled his national security advisers. He fired Secretary of Defense Schlesinger and replaced him with White House Staff chief Donald Rumsfeld, and he replaced Kissinger as national security adviser with Kissinger's deputy, Lieutenant General Brent Scowcroft. Ford also fired CIA Director William Colby and replaced him with George Bush, then United States envoy to China.

The effect of Ford's firings on the intelligence community's morale was devastating. The CIA's personnel, already badly divided in their opinion over Colby's cooperation with Congress, looked upon the Bush appointment with serious misgivings over his ability to either lead the Agency or deal with the congressional investigations. The military intelligence services, on the other hand, although worried about whether the NSA storm cloud might not come up again, "hunkered down" safe in their belief that Rumsfeld would have his hands full with the problem of learning how to cope with the Joint Chiefs of Staff.

Granting the essential accuracy of Ford's claims that he wanted to have his own team of advisers there is, however, a curious coincidence involved in the firings, especially Colby's (who by a quirk in the law and Civil Service regulations had to be brought back to serve as DCI until Bush could be confirmed). It involves the fact that by November 1975, the Senate Select Committee's investigation was on the verge of breaking new ground in full answer to S.R. 21's fifteen questions. Both the congressional investigating committees (Church and Pike) used the Schlesinger "family jewels" report as their point of departure. To be sure, the investigations fleshed out the improprieties specified in the report, but basically its contents provided a road map for the investigations. By November, it was clear to the Senate Select Committee that much more lay below those roads than was originally thought. In essence, in spite of all that the Senate Select Committee had learned and disclosed, the really hard work still lay ahead, and due to the "compartmentalization" referred to by Colby it was going to be an infinitely more complex and difficult task than the earlier ones. In addition, many of the Select Committee members had tired of their role, feeling, especially in view of the bitter controversy revealed in the Senate's secret debate about making the committee's assassination report public, that not much more could be learned which would be of

*U.S. Senate, Select Committee to Study Governmental Operations with Respect to Intelligence Activities. Operation Shamrock. Washington, U.S. Government Printing Office, December 1975.

relevance to the legislative process. Also, senators from both parties wondered aloud "how much is enough," fearing that more and deeper revelations might actually damage the nation's intelligence system rather than help reform it. These were genuine and serious concerns, but they missed the essential point: for Congress to effect a structural reform of the intelligence community it had to know what the community was actually doing.

Senator Church and key members of his committee's staff understood this necessity and consequently pushed ahead with the task. Its accomplishment was marred by a rash of leaks of strange and mysterious origins. The leaks by themselves were not all that serious or revelatory, but their appearance added fuel to the argument that the Senate's investigation endangered national security and was in the process of turning into a witchhunt as a means to justify its continued existence. Senator Church's aides pushed on, but it became increasingly clear to them that the earlier cooperation they had received from the community and its leaders had been replaced by a posture of literal compliance with their requests for additional information. That is, it became necessary for the investigators to specify precisely what they wanted rather than simply ask for information about the funding procedures for covert actions or front organizations. Thus began the period of semantic camouflage which, given the community's use of euphemisms, acronyms, and code words to identify its activities, had the effect of sealing off the community's current operations from the committee's scrutiny. Also, hard negotiations became the order of the day before access was given to *any* information about sensitive issues such as the use of newsmen as "agents of influence" in the United States and abroad.

The Senate Select Committee's progress was acutely slow. However, by mid-December 1975, with a great deal of diligence and some luck, it was clear to the staff that they were on the right track, having learned that there were levels within levels of the iceberg which were unknown even to those presently in positions of authority. Then, on December 23, 1975, an external event occurred which effectively ended the Senate's probe: the assassination of the CIA's Athens station chief, Richard S. Welch,* in a terrorist ambush at his home. Colby acknowledged in an interview that Welch's murder was the "single most crucial" event in changing the climate of opinion toward the CIA. Welch's death tended to implicate all critics of the CIA, including the congressional investigating committees. The result was that the initiative for making

---

*Although a causal relationship between the congressional investigations and the leaks which identified Welch as the CIA's station chief in Athens was alleged, it was never proven. Like his predecessors, Welch had made no secret of his position, which was confirmed, before the leaks, by his living in the same apartment and using the same embassy office as his predecessors. Also, as the Ford administration carefully orchestrated the Welch murder's press treatment, not much was heard about the possibility that the real motive for his murder was to be found in connection with the United States' role in the Turkish invasion of Cyprus. Welch, an exceptionally gifted person, took his chances like any other intelligence officer; it is unfair to eulogize him on the improper grounds that he was killed because of leaks and congressional investigations.

meaningful changes and reforms in the intelligence community passed from Congress back to Ford.

In response to this opportunity, Ford, whose political future was on the line, announced yet another reorganization of the intelligence community. On February 18, 1976, he issued Executive Order 11905, designed "to establish policies to improve the quality of intelligence needed for national security, to clarify the authority and responsibilities of the intelligence departments and agencies." The major change was the formation of the Committee on Foreign Intelligence (CFI), chaired by the DCI and reporting directly to the NSC. Other members of the CFI included the deputy secretary of defense for Intelligence and the deputy assistant to the president for National Security Affairs. The CFI was given responsibility to: (1) "control budget preparation and resource allocation for the National Foreign Intelligence Program"; (2) "establish policy priorities for the collection and production of national intelligence"; (3) "establish policy for the management of the National Foreign Intelligence Program"; and (4) "provide guidance on the relationship between tactical and national intelligence." Ford's executive order, like Nixon's of November 5, 1971, poured old wine in new bottles by giving the DCI additional responsibilities without reducing the independent authority of other intelligence community members over their operations and activities. Most significantly, Ford's order left the control of budget preparation and resource allocations to be fought out between the DCI and the secretary of defense, such that the CIA was pitted against the military intelligence services on totally extraneous and irrelevant grounds, leaving unresolved how the comparison between tactical and national intelligence was to be made. In partial response to this loophole's effect on covert actions, the executive order designated the Office of Management and Budget director be made an observer to the Operations Advisory Group (OAG), established as the successor to the 40 Committee in an attempt to remedy the weaknesses in the "telephonic concurrences" system employed during the Nixon years. The order states in this regard:

The Operations group shall discharge the responsibilities assigned . . . only after consultation in a formal meeting attended by all members and observers; or . . . when a designated representative of the member or observer attends. [Sec 3(c) (3)].

Ford's intention was to place OMB more directly in the intelligence community's internal review and resource-allocation process. Given the fact that the DCI and the secretary of defense were left to fight their battles on irrelevant grounds, Ford's decision was not that bad; the OMB director did have some potential authority over both antagonists. However, because emissaries from Defense and the CIA had infiltrated the OMB's ranks of budget examiners, it had little practical effect on the intelligence budget process. Once again, the informal network of former intelligence community members was able to minimize the attempts of the president and executive branch leaders to bring the intelligence community under their direct and close control. For those uninitiated in the practical inner workings of the intelligence community's financial methods, this is far less sinister than it sounds. Only rarely has the intelligence community needed to misrepresent or otherwise overly obscure its budget requests, and these were designed as much to spare Congress the burden of knowing who was receiving the public monies as by the need for secrecy; an example is Howard Hughes' building of the Glomar. In reality, the Ford order only made more explicit the common practice of a call from an OMB budget examiner to a friend in the community to tell him to revise his budget request up or down based upon his insider's knowledge of what the traffic would bear. This informal process of consultation is not irrational economic theory, but it has no relevance in allocating financial resources in a manner designed to maximize the quality of intelligence obtained.

Few persons in the intelligence community quarrelled with Ford's executive order. Although it established two deputies to the DCI—one for intelligence community affairs and one for CIA operations—it maintained the status quo, quieted most of the congressional critics, and, as a result of the November 3 firings, established no one in a position of titular authority who had the foggiest notion about what was really going on in the intelligence community. One admittedly cynical former high official in the CIA, who also had held a position of similar importance in the Department of Defense, noted caustically that "the CIA and DOD will love George Bush and Don Rumsfeld more than they hated or feared Bill Colby and Jim Schlesinger because neither will make any real waves." As subsequent events demonstrated, this judgment was not completely off the mark. Although both Bush and Rumsfeld were personable and not altogether incompetent, their charge was simple: it is a presidential election year and there is a compelling necessity not to let the intelligence community become an election or partisan political issue.

Generally, Bush and Rumsfeld defused the intelligence issue by emphasizing in their public statements the changes ordered by Ford and the necessity to get on with the job of meeting the nation's intelligence needs. By the spring of 1976, public opinion polls clearly showed that the intelligence question ranked very low in the public's set of priorities.

On April 26, 1976, when the Senate Select Committee released its final 651-page report (Senate Report 94–755, Book I) about United States foreign and military operations, it created little public interest. To most Americans, the Senate Select Committee, after its spectacular revelations at the end of 1975, had little else new to say. The report pinpointed the following problem areas that it said needed "urgent" attention:

(1) Congress has failed to provide the necessary statutory guidelines to ensure that intelligence agencies carry out their missions within the framework of the Constitution. Congressional oversight procedures have not been effective, and Congress has not found effective ways to use the valuable data developed by the intelligence agencies.

(2) Presidents have made excessive and at times self-defeating use of covert action. In addition covert action has become a routine program with a bureaucratic momentum of its own.

(3) Congress' failure to monitor the intelligence agencies' expenditures had been a major element in the ineffective oversight of the intelligence community. Without the power to authorize the budgets of the agencies, an oversight committee may find itself in possession of secret information, but unable to act effectively to protect the principles, integrity, and reputation of the United States.

(4) The operation of an extensive and necessarily secret intelligence system places severe strains on the nation's Constitutional system; means must be provided for lawful disclosure of unneeded or unlawful secrets.

(5) Intelligence should not be regarded as an end in itself.

The fundamental issue the committee said it faced during the investigation was *how the requirements of American democracy could be balanced against the need for secrecy.* [Emphasis added.]

As a measure of the effect of the Welch murder on the Senate's probe, at the insistence of the intelligence agencies, information on "cover," "espionage," and "budgetary oversight" were not included in the published version of the report. Also eliminated were sections on covert action that dealt with the techniques of such operations and with the actual procedure by which they were approved. In the chapter on the State Department's intelligence activities the section dealing with the cover provided by the department to intelligence agents from other United States agencies was deleted. Further, portions of the chapter describing the CIA's use of American academic and religious institutions and the communications media were rewritten at the request of the Agency, with those portions printed in italics. The material deleted from the report, or appearing only in abridged form, was deposited with the permanent Senate Intelligence Committee. It was made available to members of the Senate, but not their staffs.

In spite of these omissions, deletions, and indications of investigations left incompleted—which tended to diminish the "urgency" of the problem areas cited above—the report did set forth some valid proposals for Congress' and the president's considerations. These included eighty-seven specific proposals divided into four categories:

(1) New laws to define the activities and organization of the intelligence community.

(2) Reviews of intelligence operations by the executive branch.

(3) Restrictions on certain intelligence activities.

(4) Congressional oversight procedures.

Without going into the specifics of all the proposals, the committee noted that the 1947 National Security Act did not provide a comprehensive charter for the CIA and that the other key intelligence agencies—the National Security Agency and the Defense Intelligence Agency—did not have charters at all.

The committee recommended legislation which would define the basic purposes of federal intelligence activities and the relationship between Congress and the executive branch on intelligence matters, establish charters for the National Security Council, the CIA, and all other elements of the intelligence community, and contain specific and clearly defined prohibitions or limitations on illegal activities, such as assassination attempts.

In response to the loose manner by which covert actions had been initiated, approved and reviewed since 1948, the committee proposed that the executive branch review and approve all covert action projects, "however small," before they are put into operation. The committee said it had "given serious consideration" to barring all forms of covert action, but this was discarded; it concluded that the United States "should maintain the capability to react through covert action when no other means will suffice to meet extraordinary circumstances involving grave threats to U.S. national security." However, the committee did not specify what circumstances might require the use of covert action projects. The committee did recommend in the control of covert action that Congress and/or the president:

(1) Prohibit by statute (a) political assassinations; (b) efforts to subvert democratic governments; and (c) U.S. government support for police or other internal security forces that engaged in systematic violation of human rights.

(2) Specify by law that the CIA was the only government agency authorized by law to conduct covert projects.

(3) Require a review by the National Security Council's Operations Advisory Group of every covert action proposal.

(4) Require that the appropriate congressional committees be notified in advance of any covert operation planned by the executive branch.

(5) Prohibit the intelligence community from using religious leaders, the media, and academic community personnel for clandestine activities without their knowledge.

(6) Prohibit the CIA from subsidizing the publication of books or magazine articles unless the material is publicly attributed to the Agency.

Importantly, the committee recognized that DCIs had been pressured by presidents and other policy makers to produce intelligence estimates that would support policy. "The DCI's responsibility over intelligence activities should be enhanced and spelled out clearly in detail by statute," and the president "should not continue to define the DCI's responsibilities through executive orders and directives." Also, the committee suggested that the DCI be separated from direct responsibility over the CIA because "the DCI's new span of control—both the entire intelligence community and the entire CIA—may be too great for him to exercise effective detailed supervision of clandestine activities."

In connection with congressional oversight, after acknowledging that its lack was a basic reason for many of the intelligence community's failures, inefficiencies, and misdeeds, the committee proposed that a new congressional oversight panel be given authority to consider and approve a "National Intelligence Budget." The total amount would then be made public. Further, the committee said oversight could be improved by requiring (1) prior notice of significant covert operations, (2) approval by Congress of the United States combatants in paramilitary activities, and (3) prompt reporting by the agencies of wrongdoing within their jurisdictions.

Facing another issue which had been allowed to drift into a serious state, the committee called for the establishment by law of a counterintelligence committee headed by the attorney general to coordinate and review foreign operations as well as the clandestine collection of foreign intelligence within the United States by both the CIA and the FBI. The report said, "The goal would be to ensure strict conformity with statutory and Constitutional requirements."

Many of the Senate Select Committee's proposals were preempted by Ford's executive order which, if it could be made to work, might obviate the full necessity for new legislation to delineate more clearly the lines of accountability and responsibility for foreign intelligence production and activities. However, by the end of Ford's presidency the intelligence community, although no longer deserving of Senator Church's pejorative appellation of "rogue elephant," was in even greater disarray because the DCI's nebulous authority was insufficient to maintain effective executive oversight, carry out the budget procedures set forth in Ford's order and respond fully to the Senate Oversight Committee on Intelligence which had been created on May 19, 1976.*

---

*Senate Resolution 400 established a permanent Select Committee on Intelligence to monitor the activities of the CIA and other federal intelligence agencies. It is composed of eight Democrats and seven Republicans selected by the Senate majority and minority leaders. It required that two members be chosen from each of four committees—Appropriations, Armed Services, Judiciary, and Foreign Relations; the remaining seven members were to be selected at large. Among its basic provisions, S.R. 400:

(1) Limited a member's term of service on the Select Committee to eight years and provided for rotation of a third of the panel members with each Congress.

(2) Gave the panel exclusive jurisdiction over legislation dealing with the CIA. But jurisdiction over the FBI, Defense Department intelligence agencies, and all other federal intelligence agencies was to be shared by the committee with the appropriate Senate standing committee.

(3) Required the Select Committee to authorize the budgets of the intelligence agencies annually. The CIA authorization would be handled exclusively by the panel and reported directly to the Senate, and authorization measures for the defense intelligence components, the FBI, and other federal intelligence agencies would be considered by both the Select Committee and the appropriate standing committee. Measures reported by one committee were to be referred to the other, with a thirty-day time limitation, for consideration.

(4) Allowed the intelligence committee to release classified material to the public if a majority voted to disclose the information and the president raised no objections within five days of the panel's decision. If the president objected in writing, the committee could take the matter to the full Senate, which could take one of three actions: (a) approve disclosure of all or any parts of the material, (b) disapprove disclosure or (c) refer the matter back to the Select Committee, which could then decide whether or not to release the information.

The House Select Intelligence Committee's stormy four-month probe of the intelligence community bears little mention here. It did not add much to what the president's commission and the Senate Select Committee discovered. The brouhaha which resulted from the House of Represenatives' action on January 29, 1976, which blocked release of its Select Committee's 338-page investigative report of the CIA and other intelligence agencies; the leaks of the report's contents which appeared in *The New York Times;* the *Village Voice*'s publishing excerpts of the panel's report in a 24-page supplement; and the role of CBS newsman Daniel Schorr in making a draft of the report available to the *Village Voice,* obscured the real issues involved in achieving a structural reform of the intelligence community. Instead, according to the *Village Voice* excerpts, the House Select Committee took an accusative stance in its investigation, condemning the community's failures in not providing the president with timely warnings of several previous international crises, for being inefficient and ineffective, and by damning Henry Kissinger for having a "passion for secrecy" and for obstructing the Select Committee's investigation.

Thus by January 20, 1977, when Jimmy Carter became president and first intelligence officer, he inherited an intelligence community which had been badly battered in the previous two years. The changes occasioned by Ford's executive order—especially the creation of the permanent Senate Select Committee on Intelligence Oversight—had induced a sense of caution on the part of the intelligence community leaders as they attempted to comply with the mandates of both. No one was quite sure what Carter's forthcoming stewardship of the intelligence community presaged. This produced a period of watchful waiting because Carter, like Nixon, gave scant indication during the transition period about his intentions for the intelligence community's role in his administration. Carter's dumping of George Bush and subsequent designation of Theodore Sorensen to serve as DCI was greeted in the community with a combination of glee and dismay. Glee by those who believed that Sorensen would, if he attempted to try, get lost in the maze of compartments which lock off covert and secret actions from one another, and dismay by those who—

---

(5) Prohibited disclosure of classified material by a member or staff assistant except by the procedure described above.

(6) Gave the Senate Select Committee on Standards and Conduct authority to investigate any alleged disclosure of intelligence information in violation of the committee's rules and to report to the Senate any allegations found to be substantiated.

(7) Stated as the sense of the Senate that the intelligence agencies should keep the committee fully and currently informed about its activities, but the panel would not have veto power over an agency's activities.

(8) Authorized the Select Committee to investigate any matter within its jurisdiction, and gave the panel subpena power.

(9) Authorized the committee to study the quality of U.S. intelligence and the desirability of changing any laws relating to intelligence matters and the need for establishing a joint Senate-House intelligence committee. The panel could also recommend whether the disclosure of secret intelligence funds was in the public interest.

for the previous eight months—had been dealing with the Senate Oversight Committee, because they knew that the intelligence community did, in fact, need a strong DCI if the setting of intelligence policy and direction of operations was not to pass by default to Congress. The withdrawal of the Sorensen nomination in the face of the Senate's opposition, and the subsequent designation and quick confirmation of Admiral Stansfield Turner as DCI, altered these perceptions to a significant degree. It changed the glee to worry that Turner would pierce the compartmentalized secrecy, and changed the dismay to fear that Turner might prove to be too strong a DCI and set off another civil war in the intelligence community.

As has been shown, each president's discharge of intelligence responsibility has been inexorably bound up in external events, both international and domestic, and in his own perceptions about the role, function, and capacity of the intelligence community. And for better or worse, the intelligence community has helped or hindered the president's response to events. In recognition of this inescapable historical fact and the need to continue to work at the task of perfecting American institutions, in this case the intelligence community, the following chapter, "The Future of American Intelligence," offers a statement of what yet remains to be done.

CHAPTER 9

THE FUTURE OF AMERICAN INTELLIGENCE

The future of American intelligence is beset with uncertainties and several as yet uncontemplated problems. Much more is at stake than the historical battles among the intelligence community members for dominance over one another; rather, it is a battle among the president, the intelligence community, and to a lesser degree the Congress over who will actually control the entire intelligence community. This battle—which, as the record shows, has been building for many years—is now upon us. It is a complex battle whose dimensions have attracted little public attention, but which go to the heart of the question concerning the ability of the intelligence community to produce the kinds and amount of intelligence the president needs to conduct national policy in a coherent and rational manner. For the intelligence community to meet those presidential needs it must be brought under genuine centralized control, held accountable for its performance, and be objectively evaluated as to the effectiveness and necessity of its varied missions, tasks, and operations.

Many unresolved and unanswered questions are subsumed in this battle over intelligence. These, in spite of the past several years of investigations and reorganizations of the intelligence community (including the most recent one ordered by Gerald Ford), involve: legislative oversight of intelligence activities; charters for each intelligence agency or department; future intelligence requirements; counterespionage and secret intelligence means and methods; the utility of covert action, secrecy, disclosure, and classification; long-range budget requests for national intelligence; and final resolution of intelligence improprieties discovered by the Church Committee in its fifteen-month investigation of intelligence abuses.

Each of these problem areas is being and has been considered by the Senate's permanent Select Committee on Intelligence since its creation on May 19, 1976; however, its progress has been slow because these are complex, interrelated problems which require new and imaginative solutions. As the Select Committee on Intelligence noted in its first annual report:

The most difficult task facing the committee was to balance the right of the public and the Senate to be informed of the government's activities with the countervailing

453

necessity to protect valid national secrets. The Constitution's design of interaction among the three separate branches of government is based on the conviction that the responsibilities for all that government does, even secret activities, must be shared by the three branches of government in their appropriate ways. This is the best protection that the public has that secret activities will not erode our freedoms.*

Since Jimmy Carter became president on January 20, 1977, he has pursued these and related issues, especially centralizing and consolidating the control of the entire intelligence community under the DCI, by issuance of Presidential Review Memorandum (PRM) #11, which calls for a study of the intelligence community's organization, development of a plan to bring it under executive branch management and control, and identification of what additional legislation is required to effect the needed changes. The PRM 11 review, carried out under the lead of the director of Central Intelligence (DCI), Admiral Stansfield Turner, was long overdue. Not that the intelligence community hasn't been studied, restudied, and reorganized almost ad nauseum in the past thirty years; but because the present review is premised on the recognition, long ignored, that the problem of intelligence production and the performance of the intelligence function is one which should be solved in terms of resource constraints. That is, the amount of money available today for intelligence purposes is no longer unlimited, and future intelligence budget requests by the president must be evaluated and authorized by Congress within the framework of the total federal budget. This situation indicates a changed approach to intelligence appropriations whereby the intelligence community's needs will have to be weighed in terms of the nation's needs for energy, clean air, social welfare, etc. For example, on June 22, 1977, the Senate authorized the intelligence community's fiscal year 1978 budget (beginning on October 1, 1977) without a roll-call vote and without amendments. According to the chairman of the Select Committee's Subcommittee on Budget Authorization, Senator William Hathaway (Dem., Maine), the subcommittee held more than 45 hours of hearings involving over 500 questions for the record, produced 1,300 pages of testimony and reviewed 2,000 pages of intelligence-program justification material provided by the executive branch. The result of the subcommittee's deliberations was a classified report which sets forth the details of the authorization bill to include the dollar figures for intelligence operations and descriptions of programs cut back or eliminated by the overall Select Committee. Besides the seventeen Select Committee senators who know concretely what the authorization bill contains, only three other senators took up the invitation of the Select Committee chairman, Senator Daniel K. Inouye (Dem., Hawaii), to read the classified report. This suggests, as Lee Lescaze of the *Washington Post* noted, either a great deal of trust toward Senator Inouye and his committee, or a lack of

---

*U.S. Senate, Annual Report to the Senate of the Select Committee on Intelligence. 95th Congress, 1st Session. Committee Print. Washington: U.S. Government Printing Office, May 1977, p. 1.

interest among noncommittee members in monitoring the intelligence community.* This situation is bound to change in the future, especially if the DCI is given actual line authority over the preparation and forwarding of future intelligence budget requests to the Senate Select Committee for its approval.

In a closely related sense, the PRM 11 review has met head-on the often obscured, avoided, or evaded question of the DCI's authority over the entire intelligence community. This issue, like the one concerning the intelligence budget, sooner or later will have to be fought out in public because its resolution is crucial to the future of American intelligence. As has been shown, each iteration since 1947 of the words "cooperation" and "coordination" used to assert or reassert the DCI's authority in dealing with the intelligence community, has been inadequate either to enhance his authority or to bring about a truly centralized, systematically controlled intelligence system. The historical record shows a curious thirty-year lag in the agreed to, but never genuinely achieved, central intelligence system. For example, in 1918, when Secretary of the Treasury William C. McAdoo proposed a central intelligence system, it was shot down by the powerful members of the intelligence community: General Van Deman, chief of the Military Intelligence Division (MID), and John Lord O'Brian of the Justice Department. At the time, the McAdoo plan made eminent good sense in that the intelligence community was still relatively small and a DCI equivalent—given presidential backing—could have presided over community affairs in terms of seeking cooperation and coordination in the production of national intelligence and in the resolution of jurisdictional disputes. This obviously wasn't done and, as a result, the subsequent evolution of American intelligence up to World War II, described in Chapters 2 and 3, was chaotic. Similarly, the World War II intelligence experience clearly indicated the necessity and worth of a centralized intelligence system as the United States struggled with the problems of producing the kinds of intelligence required in a total war. However, like McAdoo's plan, the World War II experience was ignored and, in essence, the National Security Act of 1947 merely codified what had been suitable in 1918 but which was out of keeping with the reality that the intelligence community had grown to an unprecedented size, acquired substantial independent power, and was no longer amenable to direction by "friendly persuasion." Thus today, some thirty years later, the United States is now about to confront the most crucial question concerning the establishment of a central intelligence system: who will run it and under what authority? Make no mistake about the crucial nature of this question; once open to public debate, it will provoke more controversy than the armed services unification conflict, the creation of the Joint Chiefs of Staff, and designation of a secretary of defense did thirty years ago.

Because the role and authority of the DCI is so important to the future of American intelligence, the arguments both for and against changing that role

*The *Washington Post,* June 24, 1977.

and enhancing the DCI's authority deserve extended mention here. Without preempting the results of the PRM 11 review, or anticipating President Carter's decision, the arguments against giving the DCI additional powers and statutory authorities fall into two general categories: (1) dissent in the intelligence-estimating process, and (2) the dangers of intelligence "czardom."

The dissent argument is not without some precedent, but its relevance to the centralization issue and the authority of the DCI is not all that clear. As the historical record shows, the existence and/or encouragement of dissent in the intelligence-estimating process is more a question of the attitudes of a president toward intelligence and his style or method of making policy than of the intelligence community's organization. For example, if those in charge of the intelligence-estimating process are directed by the president to provide justification for policy rather than to measure its effectiveness or its before-the-fact adoption suitability, dissent per se is not the issue; dissent cannot exist when the intelligence-estimating process is not permitted to operate in an independent manner. This has happened in the past with predictably devastating results during the Johnson administration in connection with spurious "estimates" about the numbers of enemy forces in Vietnam, and during the Nixon administration over the Cambodian invasion.

Implicit in the dissent argument is the view that somehow in a centrally controlled, single-authority intelligence system, as an intelligence estimate made its way to the president it would be purged of dissenting analyses and opinions in order to present a uniform view in support or opposition to a policy question. This is certainly a hazard because, whether the intelligence community is organized vertically or horizontally, there are levels in both forms of organization and the tendency is strong to broaden the consensus in support of any idea as it works its way to the organization's decision point. Nevertheless, this tendency can be overcome without destroying the intelligence-estimating process if sensible leadership is employed which deals with dissenting opinions and analyses at each level on their own terms rather than by arbitrarily eliminating them from the process.

Defense Secretary Harold Brown has addressed the dissent argument in slightly changed terms, citing the need to have differing opinions and analyses heard at the "highest levels." Presumably Secretary Brown's reference to the highest levels means the president and/or the NSC; if so, this argument still hinges on the question of leadership, because single-authority DCI or no, the president of the United States can if he chooses require the inclusion of dissent in the preparation of written intelligence estimates, or invite the testimony of the proponents and dissenters when an estimate is being considered for acceptance as the basis for a policy decision at the highest levels. Although cynical sophisticates may contend that the president's tapping opinions of the Armies of Ignorance's foot soldiers and company-grade officers is a naive and foolish suggestion, the actions of Presidents Eisenhower and Johnson in trying to find out the opinions and ideas of those who were totally immersed and expert in one special area suggest that this can be done without too much difficulty. Also, if the president makes it clear to his DCI and cabinet officers that he wants to receive opinions reached without fear or favor and that he will not tolerate bureaucratic reprisals against those who provide opinions which go against the conventional wisdom, the quality and diversity of the opinions and intelligence provided the president will improve in marked degree. Secretary Brown, better than any member of the Carter cabinet, is well aware of the disaster which results from proscribing the dissenters who, for example, during the Vietnam War kept their silence and did or said nothing to prevent President Johnson from entering a morass—and who did not use their talents to develop a way for him to get out of the morass once the original policy went awry. Witness the spate of books by officials at the "highest levels" in the Johnson administration who later claimed to have been "closet" antiwar supporters, but who nodded assent to intelligence estimates which they knew amounted to sheer fantasy.

Most presidents, either directly or indirectly, have endorsed the view that they did not want to be surrounded by yes-men. It is hardly a unique notion; however, most presidents who have endorsed it have found that in times of crisis it is most difficult to abide or invite the opinions—no matter how well reasoned—of the dissenter.

One might contend that dissent in the overall intelligence-estimating process at the highest levels is a phony issue. Its phoniness stems from the fact that in the modern history of the United States there is not one significant example of a cabinet officer or high presidential adviser resigning his post based upon his belief that a policy decision was made based on a flawed intelligence estimate. The opportunities and provocations have been many, if one believes the memoirs of those who have served presidents in war and peace, but the record also shows that none has been willing to say with Martin Luther, "Here I stand, I cannot do otherwise." This also suggests that those who have continued to support a presidential policy they believed to be flawed have little to add to the question of dissent in the intelligence-estimating process. Admittedly, dissent in the intelligence-estimating process can be stilled or bureaucratically suppressed, as Admiral Turner well knows; however, as a former commander of men, he also knows that to carry one or several policy decisions on the basis of suppressing dissent can only lead to an irreversible mistake, as it renders *all* intelligence estimates suspect.

In addition to the kinds of presidential actions suggested above, another would enhance the integrity and utility of intelligence estimating in the determination of national policy: the hitherto unique provision of sharing with the Congress, in this case the Senate Select Committee on Intelligence and/or a Joint Committee or a House Select Committee on Intelligence (should these latter organizations be established), the intelligence estimates which are the presumptive basis on which presidential foreign policy decisions are based. This has never been done before and would serve several valid purposes. First, it would, before the fact, make clear to the Congress the ambiguities inherent in the intelligence estimating process concerning the capabilities and intentions of potential and actual opponents in impending crises. Second, it would provide a sound basis for what has euphemistically been referred to in the past as "prior consultations with the Congress." And third, it could conceivably dampen Congress' carping criticisms of presidential foreign policy decisions by giving the Senate Select Committee members a much better appreciation of what is known and not known about the consequences of a presidential decision. There are those who will contend that this kind of congressional participation in the intelligence-estimating decision process invites chaos, interferes with the president's right to make foreign policy, injects partisan politics into foreign policy, etc.—but I think not. Wisdom and concern about the United States' foreign policy role is not the monopoly of the executive branch, and for the president to share the intelligence community's understandings and insights with Congress seems to be an important step in establishing a truly nonpartisan foreign policy. Although formal, regularized precedent for this idea is lacking, there is partial precedent in the actions of Truman, who not only provided Senator Vandenberg with hard-copy intelligence estimates (contrary to the ideas of his advisers), but more importantly ordered—outside of customary channels—a number of individual (and in some cases, supposedly low-level) analysts to explain to Senator Vandenberg the intelligence "take" on which the estimates were based. Today such an approach has even greater relevance, since trust in the president has been sorely eroded, and there exists a pressing necessity for Congress to know what the presidential decisions designed to keep peace in the Middle East, Korea, and elsewhere are actually based upon. A current intelligence estimate, complete with dissenting views, based upon what is known and not known about the Soviet Union's capabilities and intentions, if explained and discussed with the Senate Select Committee on Intelligence, could have the effect of giving President Carter and Secretary of State Vance the kind of congressional support they need to achieve the goals which eluded Henry Kissinger for so many years in the Middle East.

The arguments against giving the DCI increased statutory powers which fall under the czardom rubric are more complicated than those dealing with dissent. Basically, the arguments stem from a widespread belief of the American body politic in Lord Acton's dictum that "power corrupts and absolute power corrupts absolutely." Although there is some theoretical truth and historical evidence in support of Acton's remark, the American system of government, laws, and judicial review is such that absolute power cannot be conveyed to any individual or organization. To be sure, the United States has as a nation conferred a great deal of power and authority on government organizations, the president, etc.—but this has been given to carry out the laws, not to be exercised in an arbitrary or self-perceived manner. And, as with the various war powers acts, these have been circumscribed in their scope and duration.

Nonetheless, the czardom question gives one pause; the quasiautonomous, independent power of the intelligence community members is such that if its components are aggregated under a DCI it would, as a whole, possibly create a new power center with total authority greater than the sum of its parts. Although possible, this outcome provides inadequate justification for not giving the DCI increased statutory power over the community because, like the logic used to justify the creation of a Department of Energy under a single secretary, there is an overriding necessity to bring some order into the loosely confederated intelligence community and to turn it into a truly national intelligence system. To deal with the large and complicated questions of national intelligence there must be sufficient power and authority to focus the intelligence community's solution of those questions.

A related argument already being heard on the intelligence czardom issue involves the potential for intelligence abuses such an arrangement might produce. In its simplest terms, the argument contends that an unscrupulous president and an equally unscrupulous, more powerful DCI could use the intelligence community for their own nefarious or partisan ends and order it to carry out intelligence abuses which would infringe on the rights of Americans. Certainly this is possible; however, those who advance this argument overlook the fact that the intelligence abuses carried out in the last several decades took place while the intelligence community was decentralized and that successive presidents, either directly or indirectly, permitted, condoned or directed such abuses. Thus the argument cuts both ways; while the DCI might use increased statutory powers to commit intelligence abuses, those powers can also be used by the DCI to reject a president's call to engage in such activities. Quite obviously there are no ironclad, foolproof means to prevent intelligence abuses from being initiated by a president and a DCI operating in concert; but the force of law, especially law which precisely sets forth the DCI's powers and authorities and *effective* congressional oversight, would provide a realistic deterrent in almost all conceivable situations. Similarly, the force and specificity of law would also bolster the willingness and ability of individuals in the intelligence community to resist or reject unlawful and illegal orders, no matter their highest authority source.

One can expect, after the principle of granting the DCI increased statutory powers and authorities is acknowledged, that the argument will shift rapidly into a consideration of the question, "how much?" The first public proposal in this regard has been made by the Senate Select Committee's Subcommittee on Charters and Guidelines, which said:

The director's responsibilities would be detailed in any legislation in order to avoid the ambiguity of the National Security Act of 1947 and more recent executive orders. He would be given a clear right and a duty to review all ongoing and proposed intelligence activities, including military intelligence activities, to insure that they are properly and effectively directed, regulated, coordinated and administered, that they are providing the necessary information and analyses to the executive and legislative branches, and that they safeguard Constitutional and legal rights. This would assure an effective overview of all the intelligence activities of the United States.

Among the responsibilities the DCI could be given are:

- Serving as the president's and Congress' chief intelligence officer;
- Controlling the annual budgets for national intelligence activities, thereby increasing his role in resource allocation, replacing the committee-based system of Executive Order 11905;
- Producing intelligence estimates for the president and the Congress, making sure, however, that representative views and disagreements are considered and indicated. In order to have "competing centers of analysis," any entity of the intelligence community would be given authority to produce its own analyses of national intelligence, but these would have to be supplied to the director;
- Establishing and implementing review procedures for clandestine intelligence activities based on their potential impact on the national security, national defense, or foreign relations of the United States;
- Coordinating all clandestine collection of intelligence by human sources;
- Maintaining relations between U.S. intelligence agencies and intelligence or security services of foreign governments, and providing any agreements to the appropriate committees of Congress;
- Developing security standards for the management and handling of information relating to intelligence activities.*

On the surface, the subcommittee's suggestions appear quite reasonable and almost benign in their effect, but in reality they signify a major break with the past; by virtue of their extent, they explicitly confirm the fact that American intelligence is almost a separate branch of government. Also, explicit and implicit in these suggestions is the hope that the DCI and the intelligence community operating under his direction can and would serve two masters: the president and Congress. This indicates a partnership between the executive and legislative branches perhaps not fully intended by the Constitution and certainly not one which has hitherto been accomplished, even when the president and the congressional majorities were of the same political party.

Consider, for example, the implications of the DCI serving as the president's and Congress' chief intelligence officer. This suggests, in addition to keeping the president and Congress informed, that the DCI would respond to orders from both. This flies in the face of the time-honored principle of "unity of command"; however, it bespeaks Congress' recognition of the need for oversight of the intelligence community *and* its independent needs for intelligence which only the community itself can provide. The first recognition was clearly established by the Church Committee's investigation, which showed that many of the abuses committed by the community were due to the lack of

*Annual Report of the Senate Select Committee on Intelligence. *op. cit.,* pp. 28–29.

congressional oversight. The second is more subtly derived from the fact that since World War II, Congress has authorized the expenditure of ever-increasing amounts of public funds for such operational activities as wars, foreign aid, and the intelligence community based on less and less information, or on information with insufficient relevance to making those decisions.

Whether tasking the DCI to serve two masters can actually be made to work is a serious question for which there is no easy answer. It suggests the necessity for the president to be willing to share or give up, on a continuing basis, some of his power over executive branch resources to meet Congress' needs for intelligence. This goes far beyond such presidential offers as Ford's to make the full resources of the FBI available to former Speaker of the House Carl Albert to find the source who leaked the Pike Committee report to *The New York Times* and newsman Daniel Schorr—an offer, one might note, which was turned down by Speaker Albert. It includes giving Congress authority over executive branch intelligence resources which conceivably could be used to gather information to challenge the president's positions and decisions. No matter how this question is ultimately resolved, it is correct to note in advance of the public debate that it will require a great deal of trust on the part of the president to share his authority over the intelligence community with Congress. We hope that the president will agree to this sharing not only on the grounds of meeting Congress' independent needs for intelligence, but also because for him to do so would go a long way toward eliminating the "us and them" sense of confrontation between the intelligence community and Congress which has dominated that relationship for decades. For example, if the intelligence acquired by the community in connection with the Gulf of Tonkin incident had been fully shared with Senator Fulbright and the Senate Foreign Relations Committee, a reasoned and measured response to events in Vietnam could have been developed by Johnson and Congress operating together, instead of allowing personalities in the White House and the intelligence community to define Johnson's decisions.

The subcommittee's suggestion to give the DCI line authority over the intelligence community's budget is fraught with hidden implications. In 1977, under Senate Resolution 400, the Senate Select Committee on Intelligence for the first time dealt with the national intelligence budget in a single authorization bill. It was an interesting and educational exercise which revealed that a national intelligence budget was possible, that these authorizations could be assembled in one place before being split up and buried in parts of the total federal budget, and that it was perhaps amenable to the control of a DCI in its preparation and execution. This years' national intelligence budget request did not stir much controversy in the intelligence community because it was, as in the past, based on a committee approach which allowed each element of the intelligence community to review its requests internally and deal with its own leaders before submitting them to the committee. Similarly, the budget "marks" given the community members by the director of OMB—that is, a predetermined, tentative amount or percentage of the overall total for each agency and department—provided for an increase over the previous year and retained the members' authority to shift or reprogram funds from prior fundings as they saw fit. Thus in one sense, the fiscal 1978 national intelligence budget authorization is the benchmark from which all future changes in intelligence spending will be measured. As such its total is a tidy figure which is a simple summing of the monies authorized, for example, to the National Security Agency, the National Reconnaissance Office (NRO), and the CIA to carry out their various programs. So much for tidiness. But what is implied by the suggestion to give the DCI the power to control future annual budgets for intelligence activities? On an immediate and practical level it doesn't change the internal budget review procedures in the agencies and departments; however, it does imply a DCI final review and approval of these budget requests in place of that provided by the directors and secretaries of the agencies and departments. In short, it forces the executive branch, under the DCI, to set priorities for all intelligence budget requests in terms of the DCI's judgment, rather than one based upon the director of OMB's budget marks, which say "you have X million dollars to spend, and how you spend it is up to you." All this may appear simple, straightforward, eminently sensible and long overdue, but appearances are misleading. Once the DCI is given the budget authority it will become necessary for him to judge the effectiveness and quality of intelligence programs in terms of their total cost and that of the entire national intelligence budget. This means, for example, choosing between the CIA, DIA, and NSA to carry out a specific program rather than allowing all three to do the same thing. And also to deal with the paradox that there frequently is no correlation between the size and cost of an intelligence program and the quality or usefulness of the intelligence it produces. It will require the DCI to decide the worth of "contingency" intelligence information collection programs, such as those directed toward energy sources, against that of current needs for diplomatic and military intelligence. Because intelligence resources and money are equally limited, this implies difficult choices and considerable controversy; the advocates of each intelligence program can be expected to make a strong case that without their program the nation will be placed in grave and serious peril.

But beyond these predictable internecine budget quarrels and the attempt of the intelligence community leaders to hold on to the budgetary control of their organizations, there is an even bigger time bomb involved in giving the DCI control over the annual budget for national intelligence activities: if such control is given, the national intelligence budget will probably increase by two to three times its present size.

To explain: in 1977, the Senate Select Committee on Intelligence was pleasantly surprised by the size of the national intelligence budget. For some members it was a bit higher than previously supposed and for others less than they had been led to believe by educated guesses which had appeared in the press.

In short, the national intelligence budget was high, but not too high; that explains why it passed the full Senate without a roll call and without amendments. In this respect, one has to remember that while perhaps only one or two members of the Senate and the House had a fairly precise idea of the intelligence community's total budget in years past, this was the first time it was embodied in a single package. As such, the intelligence authorization bill is like a framed picture, easy to read and easy to accept by men used to dealing in hundreds of billions of dollars. However, coincident with this framing of the intelligence authorization bill, the Senate, somewhat in advance of the DCI budget authority decision, has also, in effect, "fenced in" the various line items and program authorizations for the different agencies and departments. Fencing in means that within the overall authorization bill there is no concomittant authority given to the directors and secretaries of the departments to reprogram funds from one activity to another. If the money authorized to support a given program runs out, it will be necessary for the DCI, if given budgetary authority and responsibility, to go back to the Senate for a supplemental appropriation. This is certainly not without precedent; however, Congress' present budget procedures, which require the preparation of its own budget and approval of a Congressional Budget Resolution expected to bind committee chairmen to its total, makes it more difficult and invites extremely close scrutiny of supplemental budget requests. Under present congressional procedures the intelligence community is expected, like other elements of the government, to accept its budget and live within it. Furthermore the House, in connection with its passage of the intelligence authorization bill, voted to restrict the size of the CIA director's "contingency fund" to $35 million; said fund can be used by the director to pay the unanticipated costs of various programs without going back to Congress for more money.

So much for theory and the intentions of the Congress. The intelligence community is different, and this difference will become apparent to the members of Congress once the DCI is given the kind of budgetary authority envisaged by the Select Committee's Subcommittee. To wit: the present national intelligence budget does not reflect the support costs borne by the various agencies which play host to the intelligence community components and their assigned personnel. For example, during the shrinking military budgets of the late 1950s the army, navy, air force and marines sorely resented the rather extensive costs associated with detailing members of the armed services for duty with the CIA, and providing physical cover, facilities, etc. for the Agency's use. Although these support costs were included in the Defense Department's authorization bill, their justification was rarely attributed to the back-up costs of supporting the intelligence community. To have done so would have surely forced a congressional consideration of the actual costs of intelligence much earlier than 1977.

Estimates vary concerning the size of support costs associated with line-item intelligence operations; however, from the author's experience evaluating a variety of CIA and Defense line intelligence operations (both labor and/or technologically intensive), it is clear that their support costs range anywhere from three to twenty times larger than the line item itself. For example, one such study—not prepared by the author—indicated a line-item cost of a project designed to get reports of a foreign political leader's medical examinations, treatments, etc. of $20,000; however, the support cost calculation revealed that the total cost was in excess of $500,000 annually. This is noted here not because it might seem a bit strange to want that kind of information in the first place, but to point out that if its acquisition price tag were set at $500,000 instead of $20,000, a very hard second look would have been taken at the project's necessity.

To assume, as some intelligence leaders do, that the support-cost issue will not become a part of the DCI budgetary authority debate seems most unlikely. Both of the principal departments—Defense and State—have their own problems with Congress in getting funds to carry out their assigned missions and in competing with the other executive departments for their share of the budget pie. This suggests that although intelligence is expected to serve all, the justification of the total cost of rendering that service is going to fall to the DCI, who will not only have to justify the total cost but also the quality and necessity of the service. This doesn't constitute an impossible task for the DCI, but it clearly indicates that the "selling of intelligence" is going to be infinitely more difficult in the future. In plain terms, the DCI will, for example, have to justify the total cost of satellite programs which produce more intelligence information than the intelligence community can absorb, digest, evaluate, and turn into the valid intelligence on which, as William Donovan hoped, "the strategic decisions of this nation will be based."

Related to the intelligence budget issue and the future partnership of Congress, the president, and the intelligence community is the possible conflict between the Constitution and the CIA Act of 1949. Article I, Section 9 of the Constitution states, "No money shall be drawn from the Treasury, but in consequence of appropriations made by law, and a regular statement and account of the receipts and expenditures of all public money shall be published from time to time." This contrasts with Section 8(b) of the CIA Act, which states:

The sums made available to the Agency may be expended without regard to the provisions of law and regulations relating to the expenditure of government funds; and for objects of a confidential or extraordinary nature, such expenditures to be accounted for solely on the certificate of the director and every such certificate shall be deemed a sufficient voucher for the amount therein certified.*

---

*50 USC 403 (b).

According to the Church Committee, "The language contained in Section 8(b) is adequate authority to exclude the operation of proprietary corporations from the law governing government corporations in 31 U.S.C. 841 et. seq."* However, under the kind of future partnership and budgetary review envisioned by the present Select Committee on Intelligence, it also seems necessary that the Congress' General Accounting Office (GAO) will have to be allowed to audit the CIA's secret operations. This kind of audit involves much more than examining the books of the CIA's proprietaries—those business entities, wholly owned by the CIA, which either actually do business as private firms, or appear to do business under commercial guise. It includes, for example, a GAO audit of the CIA's Glomar Explorer Project, which involved the attempt to raise a sunken Soviet submarine from the Pacific floor. Such an audit, concerning the financing of the Glomar Project by the CIA through Howard Hughes' Summa Corporation, could be expected to provide Congress with the kind of information needed to evaluate the merit, worth, and cost-effectiveness of similar high-priced secret intelligence collection operations. It also would make clear what statutory changes are needed in any future CIA act or charter to insure that the United States government received fair value for public monies expended on secret projects.

The question of proprietaries per se is not an issue here. The continued existence and usefulness of the CIA's proprietaries, although a matter of some debate, is a question which Congress can treat on its merits by providing for changes in the CIA's charter which would establish review procedures to prevent abuses of proprietary profits, violation of commercial statutes, and United States tax laws. What is at issue in a future congressional partnership with the intelligence community over its budget are the broader questions involved in the CIA's overall investment policy. The Church Committee posed these questions by asking:

(1) Should the CIA engage in investments which could accumulate funds outside the budget process and thus be available for operations that have no public scrutiny outside the CIA?
(2) Is CIA investment policy too restrictive in regard to bank deposits? Specifically, should the CIA place large amounts of money in commercial banks without drawing interest?**

The answer to question (1) seems fairly straightforward: such funds should not be used to bankroll operations not subject to congressional oversight. Whether they should be returned as a profit on intelligence operations or be retained by the CIA to help finance *approved* operations is again a question for Congress decide on its merits. Since February 1975, the CIA policy was

---

*Foreign and Military Intelligence, Book I, "Final Report," *op. cit.,* p. 234.
**Ibid.,* p. 254.

changed to require proprietaries' profits and proceeds of liquidation to be returned to the Treasury as miscellaneous receipts; they cannot be used to augment the Contingency Reserve (Director's Fund) or otherwise be applied to operations. This overturned past practice which on occasion included the transfer of proprietaries' net proceeds to the Contingency Reserve for later release to operations.* There is a loose parallel here between the operations of the Federal Reserve System and the CIA in that both organizations' investment policies are not subject to a GAO audit; however, the Federal Reserve is an autonomous organization and the CIA is not.

It may sound a bit bizarre to speak of the CIA's investment policy. A government agency, especially an intelligence agency, is generally thought of as spending money rather than engaging in activities designed to make money. In the case of the CIA's functional proprietaries like Air America and Southern Air Transport, the purpose was to provide the Agency with a nonattributable service, not to make a profit. Although both organizations did make a profit, this was not the Agency's intent. However, the CIA's insurance complex had different purposes which made profit a necessary part of the operation. These purposes included provision of the following services:

(i) Handling of risks ostensibly covered under commercially issued policies;
(ii) extending term life insurance, annuities, trusts and workmen's compensation to Agency employees who are not entitled to United States government benefits;
(iii) handling escrow accounts for agents (escrow accounts are established when an agent cannot receive his full payment from the CIA without attracting suspicion; the funds not paid to the agent go into escrow accounts and are invested under the complex); and,
(iv) limited operational support and investment activities.**

The insurance complex was created in 1962, initially to provide death and disability benefits to agents and beneficiaries when security considerations precluded attribution to the United States government:

The complex was originally capitalized in 1962 with $4 million. Most of the assets are held outside the United States and the companies do not write insurance in the United States. Each of the United States companies pays little tax and is audited by a proprietary firm. This method of self-insurance enables the Agency to funnel money where needed in any of its project categories. Currently, 60 percent of the investments are in long-term interest-bearing securities abroad, 20 percent in off-shore time deposits in United States banks, and the balance is in common stocks, debentures, and commercial paper of various types. In the past twelve years the sale of stocks has resulted in profits in excess of $500,000 accruing to the CIA. The combined total assets of the complex

*Ibid., p. 253.
**Ibid., p. 215.

are in excess of $30 million, including its retained net earnings of approximately $9 million.*

By itself the CIA's insurance complex fulfills needed purposes. These are not at question here; however, the fact that Congress was never informed of the existence or extent of the insurance complex until the Senate's investigation of the intelligence community in 1975 suggests the need for a GAO audit to determine whether the CIA's internal procedures have been adequate to prevent personal profit-taking by CIA analysts who have access to clandestinely collected economic analysis.

We agree with the Church Committee's recommendation "that the intelligence oversight committee(s) of Congress require at least an annual report on all proprietaries. The report should include a statement of each proprietary's nature and function, the results of internal annual CIA audits, a list of all CIA intercessions on behalf of its proprietaries with any other United States government departments, agencies, or bureaus, and such other information as the oversight committee deems appropriate."** If adopted, this recommendation would be sufficient to detect and prevent abuses by the CIA's insurance complex as well as by its functional proprietaries, but it would prove inadequate to deal with the investment activities and decisions of the CIA's quasiproprietary, the Northwest Federal Credit Union.

The Northwest Federal Credit Union (NWFCU) was originally chartered as the CIA Federal Credit Union on November 4, 1947, under Charter #5603. On March 14, 1955, its name was changed to NWFCU. For purposes of deception NWFCU statistics within the Bureau of Federal Credit Unions (presently known as the National Credit Union Administration [NCUA]) were filed under the name Arlington Federal Employees Federal Credit Union, Charter #5500. Apparently the idea for a CIA credit union derived in part from the World War II experience with the OSS's credit union, which was organized to provide its employees whose jobs involved cover roles to have access to some form of personal credit. Although a similar justification exists in part for the NWFCU, the secrecy of its operations and connection with the CIA causes one to raise the question whether the protection of its members' identity is simply a smokescreen for using the credit union for other purposes.

Today, for example, Article II, Section 5 of the NWFCU's charter reads:

The field of membership shall be limited to those having the following bond: civilian employees of the Central Intelligence Agency; military personnel of the Department of Defense who are assigned to and under the control of the Central Intelligence Agency; widows and widowers of such persons who were joint owners at time of member's death; employees of this credit union; persons retired as pensioners or annui-

* *Ibid.*, p. 216.
** *Ibid.*, p. 458.

tants from the Central Intelligence Agency; *and organizations of such persons.* [Emphasis added.]

This statement of membership appears harmless; however, in its thirty-years' existence the NCUA's examiners have been unsuccessful in receiving any information from the NWFCU concerning the number of members, let alone their names or that of "organizations of such persons." It also should be noted that all NCUA examiners have been cleared by the CIA before being given access to NWFCU financial data, and the results of their audits have been kept locked in a separate safe within the NCUA. The NCUA's annual audits of the NWFCU also reveal some very curious anomalies. For example, in 1973, payment of a 6.25 percent dividend rate was authorized for NWFCU shareholders at a time when the going rate of other federal credit unions was approximately 5.5 percent, and this payment was authorized at a time when the NWFCU was experiencing a delinquency loan rate several times higher than the national average. Also, the NWFCU's "selected loan accounts" to directors and other anonymous individuals, which reflected interest rates below the going rate, suggests a very curious way of doing business.

But what is most surprising about the NWFCU is the rapid rise in its assets —from $47 million in 1973 to more than $100 million by the end of 1976. According to national credit union statistics, a credit union with assets in excess of $100 million suggests a total membership of between 80,000 and 100,000 members. Similarly surprising is the large amount of cash, more than $1 million, which the NWFCU holds in its office. This large cash balance is at least partially due, according to NCUA examiners, to the practice of giving members cash rather than a check for share withdrawals.

We don't question here the necessity for the CIA to have its own credit union. There is some justification in providing a secret organization with means to meet the needs of its employees whose identity and relationship to the CIA is secret. However, from a careful review of the NCUA's records it is obvious that there exists an opportunity for the CIA to use the NWFCU for other than its stated legal purposes. Because, as shown in the NCUA's record, the NWFCU has substantial real-estate holdings throughout the United States it is necessary to know whether these are legal investments or blinds for CIA activities. It also seems necessary to determine whether the NWFCU is being used as an auxiliary to the Director's Contingency Fund whereby profits from proprietaries are being squirreled away for operational purposes or laundering operations.

The Church Committee did not probe very deeply into the NWFCU, apparently content in the belief that the NCUA's audits were sufficient to make sure that its relationship to the CIA was nonoperational, or not in conflict with government statutes dealing with the operation of government corporations. Nonetheless, the facts suggest that congressional oversight of the NWFCU as a quasiproprietary is in order to resolve these and other questions.

The Church Committee's second financial question was whether CIA investment policy is too restrictive in regard to bank deposits; specifically, should the CIA place large amounts of money in commercial banks without drawing interest? This is much more complex than the problem by proprietary investments and the treatment of their profits. As the Church Committee noted:

A sizable percentage of the Agency's annual appropriated and advanced funds are deposited here and abroad in commercial accounts on an incremental basis to fund operational needs. If accounts are maintained at levels above the minimum balance necessary for offset costs to the bank, the banks selected earn an interest or investment bonus. The selection of these institutions is noncompetitive, rooted in historic circumstance, albeit in institutions that have shown themselves flexible and responsive in providing the Agency services. Further investigation of this area is needed, and we encourage the new oversight committee to study this issue in greater detail than we have been able. This is one area where the exclusion of the General Accounting Office from CIA audits has had an unfortunate effect: there is no outside reviewer of a complex set of financial records and, consequently, confidence in the Agency's role in this area may have been eroded.*

Besides the immediate questions posed above, between the lines of this quote lies an enigma without parallel in the history of American intelligence. It involves the riddle of how to finance secret projects and operations through overt means and insure that the means do not draw attention to, or are inconsistent with, the directions of those in charge of secret operations. In this regard the CIA's "banking connections" are crucial if Congress is to understand what the Agency is actually doing. These connections remain very obscure because the "historic circumstances" mentioned above refer to relationships and activities many of which predate the CIA's with financial institutions in the United States and abroad.

The full story of the intelligence community's financial connections cannot be told at this time, but a suitable beginning exists with the relationship of Allen W. Dulles to the J. Henry Schroder Banking Corporation and the Schroder Trust Company. Dulles was appointed a director of the two organizations in 1937 and remained in both posts until 1943. During this period Dulles was also a partner in the New York law firm of Sullivan and Cromwell. Schroder's relationship with Dulles and the OSS during World War II is quite murky; another Schroder director, Valerian Lada-Mocarski, who served from 1930 to 1968, also served with Dulles in the OSS during 1943 in secret intelligence operations in Italy.

By way of background, the J. Henry Schroder Banking Corporation was incorporated in New York on September 22, 1923, and the Schroder Trust Company was organized under the laws of the state of New York in April 1929. Since that time, both organizations have continued to operate general

---

*"Foreign and Military Intelligence, Book I," op. cit, p. 254.

banking and trust organizations under United States domestic control. However, on September 18, 1959, their capital was acquired by Schroders Limited (London) and control of both organizations was vested in England. Schroders Limited was initially established in 1804 as J. Henry Schroder and Company, and on April 12, 1954, it was incorporated in England as a private company under the title of Schroder Successor's Limited. On April 30, 1957, it became J. Henry Schroder and Company Limited. In June 1960 J. Henry Schroder and Company Limited acquired 70 percent of the issued capital of Helbert Wagg Holdings Limited (which in turn owned the capital of Helbert Wagg and Company Limited), and on March 1962, the remaining 30 percent. On April 16, 1962, J. Henry Schroder and Company Limited merged with Helbert Wagg and Company Limited, and its name was changed to J. Henry Schroder, Wagg & Co., Limited. It is a private company engaged in international finance and investment banking.

Another thread to the Schroder puzzle involves the German banking house of Schroder Gerbruder and Company, which was established in 1846 and which merged in 1969 with the Bankhaus Fredrich Hengst and Company (established in 1832) and is now known as Schroder Munchmeyer Hengst and Company. Its only apparent connection to Schroder Limited is a correspondent banking relationship; however, the earlier version (Schroder Gerbruder and Company) had an interesting relationship with Hitler and the International Telephone and Telegraph (ITT) company's subsidiaries in Germany. This, in the 1930s, was manifested by the actions of the Schroder Gerbruder and Company president, Kurt von Schroder, who later became the Gestapo's treasurer and a general in the Waffen SS security service, while continuing (until World War II) as a director of ITT's German subsidiaries. In this latter role Kurt von Schroder came into contact with John Foster Dulles, who was respresenting ITT. Their relationship is still not clear; but it should be noted that ITT, which was founded in the United States by Colonel Sosthenes Behn, did provide cover to United States intelligence personnel who were posted to Germany as part of a secret intelligence operation designed to get information about the Nazi's code and cipher equipment. Presumably, John Foster and Allen Dulles, who were close to the United States intelligence effort even at this early stage, were aware of the ITT overseas penetration operation, but it is impossible to state this with certainty.

This rather complicated organizational evolution of the Schroders Limited operation and the early involvement of Allen Dulles provides a frame of reference by which the CIA moves sizable amounts of money around for its worldwide purposes. There is no question that Schroder Trust has a financial relationship with the CIA. This was established in open court in connection with the payment of $38,902.31 to Edwin Moore, a former CIA employee, on the order of Director Richard Helms (see below). That relationship is not at question, nor is using commercial banks for such a purpose; rather, the issue is the further extent of the CIA's involvement with Schroder and/or other banks in terms of monitoring their accounts and participating in their operations.

In this latter regard, what is clear is that the interests of the United States government and presumably those of the CIA are not left to chance or the tender mercies of anonymous bankers who merely discharge their part of the bargain by keeping their CIA accounts and connection secret. For example, as part of a long monitoring line, former Secretary of War Robert Patterson served on the board of the J. Henry Schroder Banking Corporation and Schroder Trust Company in 1949–50. In more recent times, the board of the English-based Schroders Limited—which controls Schroders' American entities—has been graced by a former deputy secretary of defense, Paul H. Nitze, and the present secretary of defense, Harold Brown, who served from 1970 through 1976 and for which in 1976 he received compensation totalling $5,712. It should be noted that Secretary Brown resigned his Schroders Limited directorship upon his appointment by President Carter to his present post. Nonetheless, while Brown has resolved any apparent conflict of interest, one might ask why a nuclear physicist should be called upon to serve on the board of directors of an international investment bank. Similarly, examination of the New York-based J. Henry Schroder Banking Corporation's board of directors reveal a curious thread of persons whose relationship to the intelligence community, although not immediate and direct except for their wartime service in the OSS or other intelligence organizations, is one of "friendly" assistance by the organizations which they represent.

We offer no final explanation of where the Schroder-CIA connection may lead. As the Church Committee noted: "Further investigation of this area is needed, and we urge the new oversight committee to study this issue in greater detail than we have been able." Interestingly, in the course of the Church Committee's fifteen-month investigation of the intelligence agencies, no mention was made, according to key staff persons, by the CIA of the Schroder connection, nor did the committee staff discover any. It is beyond our scope and purpose here to unravel the entire Schroder story; to do so involves an analytical effort akin to that of explaining a complex world of interlocking directorates, holding companies on top of holding companies, a worldwide system of international banking outlets and subsidiaries, real-estate trusts, computer services organizations, and most importantly the personal and professional relationships between those who preside over that entire system and the United States intelligence community. Having said this, there is one other reason for the GAO to audit the CIA-Schroder connection. Based on our investigation to date, it is clear that the "comingling" of Agency funds in commercial banks and attempts to monitor the use of these funds may lead to intolerable conflicts of interest between the CIA and a variety of unwitting institutions in the private business sectors around the world. It is far from a simple problem to resolve, but clearly the first step involves an outside review by the GAO to assure that no American or foreign laws have been violated by the CIA and Agency personnel.

The subcommittee's recommendations that the DCI be given authority and responsibility for "establishing and implementing review procedures for clandestine intelligence activities based on their potential impact to the national security, national defense, or foreign relations of the United States" and "coordinating all clandestine collection of intelligence by human sources" are a natural corollary to the one giving the DCI budget authority over the entire intelligence community. As we have shown, control over the intelligence community's purse strings confers a de facto control over its operations because of the necessity to allocate limited financial resources among competing claims. Similarly, the subcommittee, by specifying further DCI control over clandestine activities and operations, is in effect saying that Congress wants to establish a clear line of authority and responsibility for those activities and operations among themselves, the president, and the intelligence community instead of the vague committee approach used in the past.

This suggests a congressional intent not simply to take a continuing look at covert activities and operations under present Select Committee procedures,* but also to reconsider the question of whether these actions should be authorized or prohibited in the future. This question, although thoroughly examined by the Church Committee, deserves further consideration because the actual as opposed to intended effects and utility of clandestine activities and operations remain unclear. Too often in the past covert actions have been approved

---

*1. Notification.

When the CIA is informed of a presidential finding, the committee is notified prior to implementation per S.R. 400. The Select Committee receives a full report shortly after presidential approval. CIA reports on covert action projects have included such information as:

- A summary of the proposal and what it is expected to accomplish;
- The origin of the proposal: whether CIA, U.S. ambassador, host country, etc.;
- Policy considerations citing applicable policy documents;
- Justification for a covert effort and how it will supplement overt U.S. action;
- Timing and duration of the operation;
- The relationship of the project to decisions of any previous NSC committee;
- The risks involved and the possible consequences of disclosure of the operation;
- A plan of action which appropriate U.S. government elements would take in the event of a disclosure; and
- The estimated cost level, the availability of CIA funds, and the need, if any, for new money allocations.

Briefings are given to the committee by CIA, State, and any other relevant agency. Additional documentation, if required, is provided by relevant agencies or the committee staff. Actions by the committee, if any, can include the following:

- Comment to the executive branch;
- Referral of information to other committees, if appropriate;
- Disclosure under provisions of S.R. 400, Sec. 8; and
- Funding restrictions.

(See: "Annual Report of the Senate Select Committee on Intelligence," op. cit., pp. 17–18.)

on the grounds that they were possible, not too costly, deniable, etc., and *might* aid some general purpose, or contribute to a more favorable sequence of events than those ensuing if nothing was done. This is a totally inadequate methodology with which to approach the question of covert action in the future. What is now at issue is to determine whether there exists an alternative to covert action as a means to protect national security and meet national intelligence needs. We believe this alternative exists in the form of secret intelligence and counterespionage tactics which do not rely on positive intelligence techniques such as espionage and sabotage, but which are carried out covertly and can be tied into overt actions taken by the president, Congress, and the State Department.

We advocate this approach on several very practical grounds. First, the objective results of *active* clandestine operations—those designed to alter the sequence of events—are at best transitory. Second, once done they alert the warning and defensive systems of a government or other organizations, thereby complicating the task of getting further intelligence information. And third, the present array of power centers in the world plus the lack of a shooting war's objectives makes the task of targeting an active clandestine operation infinitely more complex. Grounds (1) and (2) are clearly visible, for example, in the several years' effort to assassinate Fidel Castro, which resulted in his being able to consolidate his political hold and severely limit American ability to acquire valid intelligence information about the social and economic conditions in Cuba. The third ground is not immediately obvious to those conditioned to think in terms of the East-West conflict. Nevertheless, today's political realities are such that from an intelligence point of view we are living in a polycentric world made up of competing centers not conceived by those who drew up the Cold War's battle lines thirty years ago. This is not to minimize the Soviet threat or the impact of its KGB. These are very real; however, there is an equally compelling reason to be concerned by threats to American security posed by the conflict between the developed and under-developed countries, the oil cartel, the multinationals (which in many cases have become nation-states unto themselves), international organizations (which now number over 2,000), and finally the revolutionary content of worldwide rising expectations, which has a very elusive ideological base.

This situation suggests the need for intelligence, much of which can only be acquired by secret intelligence means involving guile, deception, and patience and avoidance of covert actions which could precipitate a chain of unfortunate and unpredictable events. For example, a very real possibility exists that if a covert action project was approved to "destabilize" one of the Third World countries leaning toward the Soviet Union, its unintended effect might likely be one which destabilized, if not actually produced a collapse, of the world's international financial system. Today, as a result of the relending by United States and Western European banks of Arab oil money to Third World countries to meet their current consumption needs, there is a potential liquidity crisis which threatens lender and borrower alike. This by itself is sufficient to warrant adoption of a no–covert action policy. The added intelligence requirements posed by polycentrism suggests the need not to waste limited intelligence resources on covert action projects of dubious value. The plain fact is that the need for intelligence information clearly obviates any attempt to alter the sequence of events by covert action.

For those not in the ideological camp which contends that the United States needs no intelligence other than that acquired by satellites and overt sources, a further word about our suggestion of secret intelligence and counterespionage as an alternative to covert action is in order. The two ideas may look alike and sound alike, but they are much different in concept, execution, and purpose. Conceptually, secret intelligence is based upon the fact that besides attempting to acquire intelligence information of obvious national security interest (such as defense secrets) it is also targeted against areas of economic, social, and political intelligence not discernible or available from open sources. This is a very subtle process which requires an understanding of a nation's or organization's infrastructure beyond what can be specified completely in advance of a collection plan. It requires a very careful creation of a clandestine network—the so-called plumbing—of "assets" other than those hitherto recruited on the grounds of their ability to influence the behavior of governments. Today, the kinds of assets—witting and otherwise—required may include microbiologists, behavioral scientists, and agronomists rather than journalists, trade-union leaders, and politicians. However, to recruit and maintain such agents in place is time consuming, costly, and much more difficult if the waters are muddied by covert actions.

In execution, secret intelligence requires avoiding the highly visible cover one associates with the attachment of a CIA station to a United States embassy or military installation abroad. This practice has little utility in supporting secret intelligence operations which require truly deep cover to maintain their effectiveness and secrecy. Also, because of the diminished and altered role of the United States government abroad, it seems equally prudent not to associate a secret intelligence effort with the government. Such a change obviously poses problems to those who have become accustomed to the CIA's overseas "good life," but these are not insurmountable if agreement can be reached on the requirement to pursue secret intelligence objectives. These objectives include acquisition of a wide variety of intelligence information outside the usual categories of military and diplomatic as a means of providing the United States with forewarning, rather than for use in a covert action designed to alter the outcome of events. To be sure, such information could be used to preempt or to attempt to alter events, but this action would be taken overtly or through diplomatic procedures. In essence, secret intelligence information would have as its proper purpose and justification giving diplomacy a better chance to succeed, instead of being used to set in motion covert actions which create more problems than they solve.

To make the dichotomy between secret intelligence and covert action clear, consider the example of President Carter's stated policy in support of human rights. From a secret intelligence point of view support of that policy would be confined to the gathering of information about the status of human rights and their violations in a target country. Such information would be used by the president or secretary of state as they see fit, either to justify withholding military or economic aid or simply to assist in negotiations with a given country. On the other hand, from a covert action point of view—like that which dominated during the "captive peoples' liberation" era—support of the human rights policy would include plans and operations to stir up trouble, attempt jailbreaks of political prisoners, etc. There is no logical inconsistency in using covert action for such purposes, but common sense suggests that such actions, if taken, are more likely to worsen the human rights of all persons in a given country than if the policy is promoted overtly through diplomatic procedures. The intelligence community, in its role of implementing policy, has many capabilities at its disposal and, if lacking precise instructions about what to do and not to do, can be expected to do what it thinks is called for by policy statements.

Closely related to secret intelligence as an alternative to covert action is the field of counterespionage, a distinct and independent intelligence function. As the War Report notes:

It embraces not only the protection of the intelligence interests of the government it serves, but, by control and manipulation of the intelligence operations of other nations, it performs a dynamic function in discerning their plans and intentions, as well as in deceiving them. An effective counterespionage organization is therefore an intelligence instrument of vital importance to national security. The development of a secret intelligence organization makes protective counterintelligence inevitable. However, to confine such activity to its protective aspects would be to eschew the development of the affirmative phases of counterespionage which give it its unique and distinct value.*

These words have more relevance today to the future of American intelligence than they did when written more than thirty years ago. A whole new dimension has been added to the intelligence equation by the creation and expansion of an unprecedented number of active intelligence organizations and networks whose interests are inimical to those of the United States. If the counterespionage problem of countering the KGB were the only one, it would be difficult enough; but the field has been expanded to include the Korean CIA, Iran's SAVAK, the Chilean DINA, as well as those of the multinational corporations. As the Korean bribe probe demonstrates, foreign intelligence organizations that the United States breathed life into during the Cold War years have taken the tactics, techniques, and even the equipment the United

*War Report, op. cit., p. 188.

States provided and turned them against the United States. This is a serious problem for which there is no simple solution; it is made more complex by the still unresolved jurisdictional boundaries between the CIA, FBI, Secret Service, Treasury, and the Bureau of Narcotics and Dangerous Drugs (BNDD).

Theoretically, for example, if the CIA detects an intelligence agent abroad who is targeted against the United States and that agent comes to the United States, the Agency is expected to turn the case over to the FBI, and vice versa if the agent leaves the United States. It is an awkward procedure to say the least, which assumes quite erroneously that both agencies are interchangeable entities with similar attitudes, interests, skills, etc. This is not meant to slight either organization, but rather to draw attention to the fact that this procedure is and has been proven to be inadequate to counter the penetration of foreign intelligence organizations, or provide an organization base to manipulate the intelligence operations of other nations.

The Church Committee concluded:

(1) A Subcomittee on Counterintelligence should be established within the framework of the National Security Council. Its purpose would be to monitor CI activities, authorize important counterespionage operations, and adjudicate interagency disagreements over CI policies, coordination, defector bona fidesm, suspected hostile penetrations, and related matters.

(2) The president, in consultation with the oversight committee(s) of Congress, should undertake a top secret review of current issues in the realm of counterintelligence. This review, which should form the basis for an internal presidential statement on national counterintelligence policy and objectives, should include close attention to the following issues; compartmentalization, operations, security, research, accountability, training, internal review, deception, liaison and coordination, and manpower.*

In the main we support these conclusions and recommendations, but would go a bit further and establish a separate Counterespionage Corps (CEC) under the line authority of the DCI. Such a corps would be more than a pouring of old wine into new organizational bottles. It would be premised on the recognition that counterespionage is a special form of intelligence activity, separate and distinct from other disciplines, which requires autonomy and integrity of organization if it is to be pursued successfully. To staff such a corps would require opportunities for transfer of personnel with suitable skills and experience from existing intelligence agencies and departments. Thereafter, its personnel needs could be met by normal recruiting methods and by a more limited transfer program of counterintelligence personnel from the intelligence agencies and departments who displayed an inclination and motivation to deal with counterespionage problems. We believe that such a corps should be statutorily chartered to deal with counterespionage problems not only as an intelligence organization, but also in the sense of a law-enforcement agency. Although

---

*"Foreign and Military Intelligence, Book I," *op. cit.,* p. 177.

there is some apparent conflict here between the role of the CEC and that of the FBI, it is less significant than it appears, because counterespionage problems are sufficiently discreet to split them off from the FBI's other law-enforcement functions. Also, in view of the subcommittee's recommendation that the DCI be made Congress' chief intelligence officer, such a corps operating under his authority would be empowered to deal with attempted foreign intelligence penetrations of Congress and its members. Today, as a result of the lack of such authority, a convoluted procedure exists whereby foreign intelligence operations like the KCIA have been able to ply their trade on Capitol Hill free from much worry of discovery by either the FBI or the CIA.

Obviously, a CEC constitutes a major break with the past, but it is an idea whose time has come. To adopt it, however, requires a recognition that the threats posed by foreign intelligence penetrations against the United States require an integrated worldwide response if they are to be effectively countered. Although government committees are rarely the best means to create a new organization—especially one to deal with unprecedented problems— there seems a necessity to constitute a committee for this purpose which would reconcile the conflicts over counterintelligence and counterespionage manifested by the approaches of the former CIA counterintelligence chief, James Angleton, and the former CIA director, William Colby. As the Church Committee noted:

These differences in viewpoint raise several important questions concerning how best to protect the United States, including the proper degree of compartmentation of CI information, methods of operation, approaches to security, research priorities, extent of liaison cooperation, and emphasis on deception activities, among other things. A high-level executive branch review of the classified issues which have surfaced in this disagreement is of considerable importance. Included in this review should be an examination of the approval procedures for certain counterespionage operations.*

Similarly, because counterespionage involves working with friendly intelligence organizations and maintaining security thereunder as well as in one's own organization, such a review could serve the added purpose of providing specific guidance to the DCI in carrying out the subcommittee's suggestion that he also be made responsible for "maintaining relations between United States intelligence agencies and intelligence or security services of foreign governments" and "developing security standards for the management and handling of information relating to intelligence activities."

Indirectly implied in the subcommittee's recommendation about security is the question concerning the justification and need for an Official Secrets Act. Former CIA director Colby has advocated such an act as a means to protect national secrets from disclosure. Others have argued against such an act on

*Ibid., p. 172.

the grounds that it would enable the government to cover up its mistakes, executive branch illegalities, and intelligence abuses. We may assume that an Official Secrets Act will become an item on the intelligence debate agenda; it is the author's opinion that such an act would not only be Constitutionally inappropriate, but that its passage is entirely unnecessary. To be sure, present espionage statutes need to be brought up to date, but this can be done by amending the law, not by substituting an Official Secrets Act in its place.

Recent espionage cases clearly demonstrate that individuals can be successfully prosecuted under existing law, and that no damage was done to the republic by CIA officials testifying in open court in connection with the government's prosecution. For example, on December 21, 1976, Edwin G. Moore II threw a package of classified Central Intelligence documents over the fence at the Soviet residence on Tunlaw Road in Washington, D.C. An employee mistook the package for a bomb and summoned Executive Protection Service officers, who turned the papers over to the FBI. Moore was arrested the following day as he awaited payment for the documents outside his home in a Washington suburb, and was accused of trying to sell classified documents to a foreign power.*

Moore's trial opened on April 12, 1977. His defense centered on a mysterious man named "Joe," whom Moore claimed had asked him to sell the documents to the Soviets as part of a CIA clandestine operation. The Agency denied the allegation; Moore was found guilty (after several psychiatrists argued over his legal sanity), but not before a number of interesting details had been revealed in the three-and-a-half-week trial.

The papers which had been offered to the Soviets and others found in Moore's home included numerous reports marked "secret" and "confidential," as well as copies of the CIA's secret telephone directory. Apparently Moore had gathered the documents during his twenty-two-year career as a CIA employee. Interestingly enough many of these classified documents were never discovered to have been missing by the CIA until Moore's trial.

Although a long-term CIA employee, Moore had only received one promotion. He was fired under the signature of DCI John McCone in 1961, after having been accused of arson; a home he owned in North Carolina had been burned down. For the next six years he fought the charge and was ultimately acquitted. Then, despite his unsatisfactory employment record, he was rehired by the Agency under the signature of Richard Helms. In addition, Moore was given $38,902.31 in back pay for the 1961–67 period, even though he was not supposed to have done any work for the CIA during that period. The back pay was provided Moore in the form of a treasurer's check dated December 22, 1967, and drawn on the Schroder Trust Company of New York City. It should be noted that most CIA employees are paid with U.S. Treasury checks.

Perhaps Moore was more than a low-level CIA clerk, but the strange check for services unrendered and the reasons for the rehiring of a man with a poor

---

*Moore was convicted of espionage on 5 May 1977. See the *Washington Post*, 6 May 1977.

work record became lost in the course of the trial. Another strange fact emerged: that six weeks before Moore threw the documents into the Soviet compound, his $2,057.68 debt at the CIA's Northwest Federal Credit Union was mysteriously paid off by an unknown source. This transaction was never satisfactorily explained. Moore claimed the Agency did it, in effect giving him the money as compensation for planting the documents at Tunlaw Road, but a CIA credit union official denied the charge without explaining how the debt was cancelled.

Another major espionage trial of 1977 was that of Christopher J. Boyce, 25, and Andrew Daulton Lee, 25. Boyce was a documents clerk with a top secret clearance at TRW Systems, Inc. in Los Angeles. He stole papers which Lee sold to a KGB agent named Boris A. Grishin. Boyce and Lee had grown up in California together. Boyce is the son of an ex-FBI agent who now works for an aerospace firm, and Lee is the son of a wealthy physician.

They were arrested in January 1977: Lee in Mexico City, where he was trying to pass the documents, and Boyce in Riverside, California. Both have since been convicted. Unlike Moore, whose motive for espionage was apparently that of a disgruntled employee, Boyce's motive was tied to his friendship with Lee and the fact that he had learned from his work that the CIA was cheating on an intelligence agreement with Australia. Lee was rebelling in response to his dislike of an American government which had arrested him on drug charges, and a desire for wealth and adventure.*

Almost all testimony during the Moore trial, including that of CIA officials, was made public, but much of the Boyce trial was withheld because it dealt with TRW's secret contracts with the CIA for intelligence satellites. Traditionally, the CIA has been reluctant to pursue public trials for fear of having its secrets revealed; but in these two trials, the only secret information which came up involved the CIA's finances through the Schroder and Northwest Federal Credit Union connections, an area which the Church Committee had largely neglected. If these two trials succeed in punishing three spies and beginning a thorough illumination of the CIA's questionable financial arrangements, then both American justice and intelligence will have been well served.**

Finally, one might add in argument against an Official Secrets Act, which would have the practical effect of allowing the intelligence community to operate outside the law, that no agent, intelligence officer or source deserves additional protection bought at the expense of the civil rights and liberties of 220 million Americans. The United States does not provide that kind of protection to law-enforcement officials and military personnel, who are expected to risk their lives for their country; none should be given to those in the Armies of Ignorance.

Taken together, the subcommittee's suggestions for an enhanced set of

*For more on Boyce and Lee, see: Robert Lindsey. "To Be Young, Rich—and a Spy." *New York Times Magazine,* May 22, 1977.

**Boyce and Lee were convicted on 29 April 1977. See the *New York Times* 30 April 1977.

statutory power, authorities, and responsibilities for the DCI—or in their terminology, a national intelligence director—causes one to pause and consider not the czardom question but one concerning whether any one man could conceivably handle such an awesome job. It is a question certain to be raised in the public debate over the future of American intelligence. Based on the subcommittee's recommendations and all that they imply, its answer is a simple yes. Nevertheless, these suggestions need to be augmented by two more which are more procedural than substantive: namely, the splitting away of the CIA director's tasks from those of the DCI. This involves appointment of a separate director for the CIA, and the DCI's treating the CIA as one intelligence member of the community with its own role and missions. This has been advocated from time to time but never acted upon; however, if the DCI is going to be given the added tasks set forth in the subcommittee's suggestions, it is absolutely essential that he not be encumbered with direct responsibility for the CIA.

Looking ahead, it is now time to deal with the intelligence community on a functional basis whereby intelligence tasks are assigned on a rational basis, taking account of national intelligence needs as well as those of the departments. To be sure, some overlap and duplication will exist under the best ordered distribution of functions and tasks; that is all to the good if they occur as a result of a genuine effort to find the best mix rather than because of politicking, scare tactics, and false bureaucratic pride. Fortunately, there is a considerable body of organizational theory and models on which such an effort can be properly based.

We don't minimize the controversy explicit in giving the DCI added statutory power over the intelligence community. This will be serious enough, for in some cases it will have to be taken from the secretary of defense, the secretary of state and the president himself. But the subsequent controversies likely to occur when the DCI attempts to assert and implement his new power and authority need not and should not be fought out in a manner designed to pit one intelligence community member against another. The United States neither deserves nor wants such an outcome. It wants a good intelligence system in whose leaders and the effectiveness, propriety, and economy of its activities it can have confidence. This should go without saying, but alas, because considerable power over men and money is at stake, there is a real danger that the debate over the future of American intelligence will be waged on the spurious grounds of personalities and irrelevant issues.

Looking beyond the DCI and intelligence community organizational debates, the future of American intelligence is tied to other features only dimly perceived at this time. It is a different world today than only a few years ago. The Cold War's East-West conflict is only one of many the United States must confront. This requires a broadened intelligence outlook on the part of American intelligence personnel, one designed to take account of a multiplicity of threats to the world order and the United States' interests besides those of nuclear war, military invasions, espionage, and subversion. To be sure, the old threats will still be there in the future and will require continued attention, but they must not be pursued at the expense of ignoring the more subtle ones of food, energy, poverty, etc. This suggests, to me, the necessity to rethink the entire American approach to "human intelligence"—to the kinds, qualifications, and motivations of those who will make up the future Armies of Ignorance. Today, and in the future, the United States requires much more from its intelligence personnel than in the past. They must possess an added dimension—an ability to deal with the new, the uncomfortable, and the unfamiliar, and to master the use of technology in carrying out their manifold and complex tasks. This doesn't mean "every intelligence officer a computer programmer"; rather, that whether one is assigned to operations or analysis, he or she needs to be able to operate a computer terminal to call up the intelligence information available to help carry out the job.

A matter of further serious concern is how and by what means will the intelligence services be able to attract and recruit the men and women they need to carry out these expanded and complex tasks. Although the CIA has said that it is experiencing no present difficulty in recruiting the kinds of persons the Agency needs and wants, one can't be certain that such will be the case in the future. Perhaps a career in intelligence will prove sufficiently attractive to fill the intelligence community's ranks with highly motivated and skilled men and women, but such an outcome cannot be taken for granted any more than the all-volunteer armed forces will be successful in getting the mix of people it needs to maintain, operate, and repair its increasingly complex weapons systems. Many things aside from the provision of creature comforts and pay increases can be done to make a career in intelligence attractive to American men and women. These include "selling" a career in intelligence not in terms of its hazards, cloak-and-dagger romance, and intelligence hijinks, but rather in terms of the genuine intellectual challenge posed in pursuit of answers to such valid intelligence questions as, for example, what are the actual intentions of the Soviets vis-à-vis Africa, Western Europe, and the United States. Similarly, secret intelligence and counterespionage problems pose a significant intellectual challenge as well as a personal one in trying to unravel truth from myth and using the former to promote American interests and protect its security. However, for these kinds of arguments to be effective there is a requirement on the part of the president—to paraphrase William Donovan's dictum about the "ultimate intelligence target"—to take the thorough knowledge of the other great powers' capabilities and intentions acquired by the intelligence community and genuinely use that knowledge as the basis of America's strategic decisions.

In connection with the need for greater emphasis on "hum int" in the future, scientific and technological advances in intelligence have reached a very curious state. Today, for example, satellites make it possible to detect well in advance any massing of conventional armies in preparation for a military invasion. Similarly, other devices operated in conjunction with satellites can detect the readying of missiles, arming of warheads, etc. To be sure, none of these methods is totally foolproof—a surprise limited nuclear attack could be initiated without much chance of prior detection—but together they do provide a substantial early warning capability of a massive attack which did not exist just a few years ago. The science and technology of communications intelligence has reached the point where the use of advanced computers makes a nation's codes and ciphers virtually invulnerable to attempts by another to break them. The goal of communications security has been one pursued for centuries; today it is a reality. Even the defection of another Martin and Mitchell would cause little difficulty. Research in fiber optics promises a further revolution in communication; electronic transmission by fiber-optical techniques and methods cannot be intercepted. The fact of these scientific procedures are not secret; they are known to the other great powers. However, what remains and should remain secret are the details of the research and the progress in bringing the new technology and equipment on line. These are the intelligence targets of the future and unfortunately they can't be pursued simply with other machines and devices. They require "hum int" sources who are capable of knowing, for example, the meaning and significance of equations written on a blackboard, and not sources who only know how to blow up a bridge or are adept at "silent killing." This suggests to me that the intelligence agent of the future is going to have to be a person with skills not hitherto demanded of those who must actually go and get the intelligence information the United States requires. Hopefully, these persons will be as equally well-motivated by their love of country as have those mentioned previously in this book. If they are, the fate of the United States and the future of American intelligence will be in good hands.

One last point concerns the Armies of Ignorance themselves: as we have shown, their ranks have been filled with Americans from all walks of life who have served the cause of intelligence in both war and peace. Their efforts are without parallel in the world's history. Certainly the United States has made intelligence mistakes and been responsible for failures; these are expected in any human endeavor, and those involved are well aware of their own human frailty. This is not cause to castigate or depreciate the efforts which led to the mistakes and failures. We have tried to point out the good and the bad in order to give the reader perspective in answering the question, "How do we get a *good* intelligence system?" and all that the question implies. Part of the answer is found in improper organization, which has dogged the best efforts of many persons for decades. Another part is found in the weaknesses of leadership both inside and outside the intelligence community. But Senator Joseph Biden (Dem., Delaware) put his finger on the part of the answer which is most important to the future of American intelligence:

At the heart of what is wrong with the intelligence community and what indeed has caused many of the abuses we have seen is the fact that most officials of the intelligence community do not know what they should and should not be doing. The watchword of intelligence officials is that they are not and do not want to be policy makers. And most of all, they resent being castigated for activities which are now labelled abusive but in which they engaged in good faith upon orders of some policy maker.

I soon learned that a serious threat to our national security today is the intelligence official, faced with a real threat, for example, a real case of espionage, who is traumatized by the exposure of recent years and in the absence of precise orders from his superiors is afraid to act. We will not solve that problem by restating the obvious, that the Soviets operate a very effective intelligence service, unfettered by the restrictions of a vibrant constitution. We solve that problem by putting our time and energy to seeking a workable balance between a strong and effective intelligence community, and the countervailing values of our country that make us the light of the world, our civil liberties and a foreign policy based on honor and a fundamental respect for humanity and peace.*

To that, Senator Biden, we say "amen."

*Select Committee on Intelligence, "Annual Report," *op. cit.*, pp. 2–3 of additional views.

CHAPTER 10

AFTERWORD

This chapter details the exploits of some of America's many thousands of patriotic spies from the Revolutionary War up to World War I. Their performance is an essential element of America's intelligence heritage. In the reports of their activities can be seen the human drama behind today's intelligence problems. These men and women were individuals who bound themselves to the intelligence cause out of a strong patriotic sense of personal duty, and in so doing helped the republic survive some of its darkest hours. In their careers can be seen how the individual intelligence practitioner confronted and resolved the legal and moral dilemmas associated with spying as well as those involving the ineptitude and often improper actions of elected and appointed officials who abused the public trust. Theirs is a proud, although little known, part of American history.

Before examining the colonial contribution to America's intelligence heritage, it is first important to take note of the status of spying elsewhere in the world at the time of the American Revolution. By the late eighteenth century, Europe had long been crisscrossed by the agents of many nations, and espionage was an accepted fact of political life and military strategy. It was tolerated, if not accepted, by Europe's leaders, who traditionally looked upon the spies in their service as not much more than common crooks. As members of a mutual club, Europe's spies shared the view held by their ostensible masters and played the intelligence game according to the criminal's rules. These rules provided that intelligence was gathered and sold to the highest bidder. This practice encouraged many nations' leaders to suspend the death penalty for captured spies and recruit them to become double agents. Changing sides, or rather employers, was commonplace. Some of Europe's most notable spies either avoided capture or successfully plea-bargained their discovery; they became information brokers, using their contacts in different camps to spread information in both directions, creating the illusion of allegiance to both.

Most spies became agents first, and citizens of specific nations second. Their national allegiances were as flexible as the morality of their profession. It is no coincidence that the great spies—Bancroft, De Batz, Schulmeister, and

Montgalliard—all speculated heavily in European stock markets.* In this sense they were the first insiders. But essentially they were gamblers who put their lives up for collateral and hoped that their talents for gathering bits and pieces of information and distributing them to the right person at the proper time would keep their necks from the noose and earn them an ample reward. As veteran gamblers, these spies operated on the rule "the greater the risk on an investment, the greater the potential return." Spying in those days represented the highest risk. The returns were often the equivalent of fortunes today, plus the ability to influence the world's most powerful men and women. The other half of the risk rule, the side which the addicted gambler suppresses in his own mind, says "the greater the risk, the greater the potential loss." Spying's great risk and reward turned on the fact that the slightest error in personal judgment meant death if one was unable to convince his captors that he was worth more to them alive than dead. Because many of the decisions to accept the captured spy who was willing to be turned around were made on the capricious whims of national leaders, it was a chancy business.

The brotherhood of European spies, then, was motivated by the gambler's desire to achieve profit and power. For the colonial spies in America, the incentives were not always the same. The fledgling United States did not wield the power of England or France, nor were its coffers spilling over with gold to pay agents. Thus, the American spy developed into a new breed; not because his methods were new or unique, or because he was less of a gambler, but because he was willing to play for different stakes. America's leaders discovered that their spies' desire to work for their best self-interest and that of their country could be fulfilled other than by influence and money. The changes in American society which motivated the colonies to revolt also lent a new motivation to American espionage.

The settlers who arrived in America in the 150 years preceding the Revolutionary War worked long and hard to establish a new social order for themselves. This new order sought the exclusion of the arbitrariness which characterized England's social hierarchy founded on birth and tradition. The colonists did not abandon the English idea that class distinctions should exist, but colonial distinction followed achievement in property, education, and religion, whereas the English relied on past achievements, leading to an identification of merit more with blood than deed.

As the British attempted to reassert their system through the imposition of taxes, royal governors, and various "intolerable" acts, the colonists rebelled

---

*Richard Wilmer Rowan, *The Story of Secret Service.* New York: Literary Guild of America, 1937, pp. 323–354. The American spy Benjamin Tallmadge made his fortune by speculating in a joint-stock company after the Revolutionary War. (See: Charles Swain Hall, *Benjamin Tallmadge.* New York: Appleton and Company, 1899, pp. 81 ff.) Another spy with gambler's problems was Edward Bancroft, Benjamin Franklin's companion in Paris and a British spy. When George III learned that Bancroft was speculating in securities which dealt with American colonial developments, he dismissed him from Britain's Secret Service. (See: Allison Ind, *A Short History of Espionage.* New York: David McKay, 1963, p. 63.)

because England threatened to wipe out their newly won social position by reaffirming the traditional English values of king, church, and aristocracy. The people with the most to lose were those who had risen to the top of colonial society: large landowners, merchants, scholars, politicians, and clergy. To secure their positions it was necessary to achieve genuine independence from the English system. As a minority, these people could not fight the war alone. They convinced the other colonists that the preservation of the liberties which had allowed the upper-class colonists to develop would leave the door open for others to follow. The English offered a proven system, but one which largely closed off individual passages to positions of power.

It should be emphasized that despite the obvious differences, leaders in both America and England held much in common. Both groups had "made it" in their respective settings. They shared the fine clothes, parties, religious ceremonies, and erudite conversations to which the lower orders in both societies were denied because of their lack of wealth and education. The two sides fought over the standards used to define position, but the final positions differed more in degree than in kind.

As war became more and more inevitable, the wealthy merchants of Boston and the wealthy landowners of Virginia were the first to raise their voices in support of defending the colonies (and their means of wealth). Thomas Jefferson and Thomas Paine penned rhetoric for a revolution, while Paul Revere, Sam Adams, and other Boston merchants set up a spy network to patrol their city and keep one step ahead of British efforts to squelch rebellion. When Lexington and Concord occurred, the colonists rallied to whichever side held the most promise for preserving their position. Some wealthy colonial merchants perceived more advantages in trusting their friends in the British aristocracy, but many others saw that English tariffs and other restrictions would quickly erode their wealth and gambled for all or nothing by supporting the revolution. Those who had attained their positions by virtue of religious and educational freedom in the colonies quickly moved to support the principles which had created their opportunities. Colonial leaders in peace became leaders in war.

A Tradition is Begun: Nathan Hale, The First Patriotic Spy

By September 1776, the British were threatening the Continental Army in New York City, and General Washington sat with his vastly outnumbered troops wondering where the British would attack. He wrote to General Heath:

As everything, in a manner, depends upon obtaining intelligence of the enemy's motions, I do most earnestly entreat you and General Clinton to exert yourselves to accomplish this most desirable end.*

*Morton Pennypacker, *The Two Spies: Hale and Townsend.* Boston: Houghton Mifflin, 1930, p. 6.

Clinton managed to send a few men into areas where they could speak with American sympathizers living in British-controlled territory, but the informal and haphazard reports of untrained observers did little to ease Washington's anxieties. His next move was to contact Lieutenant-Colonel Knowlton, the commander of Knowlton's Rangers, an elite corps of the Continental Army's best soldiers organized for reconnaissance between American and British lines. Washington asked Knowlton to find a volunteer to enter British territory as a spy. Knowlton approached his officers for the general, but doubted he would find a volunteer. After no one responded to Knowlton's first appeal, Captain Nathan Hale stepped forward to answer the colonel's second and seemingly hopeless attempt.

An overwhelming stigma was attached to spying at this point in history. Admittedly, espionage is still not viewed as the most honorable of professions, but honor was a more valued quality in the eighteenth century, in war as in romance. The risk existed then, as it does today, that a disguised agent behind enemy lines during wartime would face immediate death, rather than the prisoner-of-war status accorded to a uniformed man. (Actually, during peace-time today it's more likely that an agent would merely have to return home because of a blown cover, or be imprisoned by one country in order to use him or her to barter for a captured spy in the first agent's homeland.) For this reason, Washington could not order a man to serve as a spy; he could only solicit volunteers. In addition, one must remember that the officers of the Continental Army were gentlemen. They considered loss of honor through ignoble action and public discovery of that action as a fate akin to death. William Hull (Yale 1772), a friend of Hale's and member of his regiment, stated: "The very death assigned him [the spy] is expressive of the estimation in which he is held."* This sentiment was echoed by Benson J. Lossing in his book on spies written in 1886: "A man of honor . . . ever declines serving as a spy."** Washington, however, recognized the importance of spies, and indicated so by requesting volunteers (especially because he needed one of his best gentleman soldiers) to become agents.

As a member of a respected family of strong Puritan traditions, it was surprising that Nathan Hale was willing to risk his future. His father, Richard Hale, was a church deacon and a substantial farmer. His mother, Elizabeth Strong, came from a family closely tied to the church, and both her parents wanted Nathan to enter the ministry. In his youth he studied with a minister, and became quite accomplished in the classics; he took special interest in two ancient leaders, Cyrus the Great and Philip of Macedon. While giving enough attention to his studies to be remembered as one of the foremost scholars in his class at Yale (1773), Hale still found time to distinguish himself as a leader

*George Dudley Seymour, *Documentary Life of Nathan Hale.* New Haven: Private printing, 1941, p. 308.

**Benson J. Lossing, *The Two Spies: Hale and André.* New York: Appleton and Company, 1899, p. iii.

of the Linonian Society, a group which emphasized discussion and oratory. He was also known for his athletic prowess. There were no formal teams, but records show that Hale was fined for enjoying the campus sport of shattering window panes.*

Hale's classmates at Yale included his older brother, Enoch; Benjamin Tallmadge, who would later distinguish himself in Washington's secret service; and William Townsend, a brother of Robert Townsend of Tallmadge's spy ring. Hale and Tallmadge were very close friends. At graduation in 1773 they supported the affirmative in a debate on the contention that women should be educated. Hale had already demonstrated his ability to turn a fine phrase and think on his feet. In addition to his debates in the Linonian Society he played in one of Yale's first dramatic productions and was praised for his talents.

Upon graduation, Hale and Tallmadge both became schoolmasters. Hale's school was in New London, Connecticut, where he taught twenty girls early each morning and fifty boys during regular hours. He enjoyed his work and was a favorite in the community, but his teaching was interrupted by the outbreak of hostilities at Lexington and Concord. Three of Hale's brothers engaged in the battle. When news of war reached New London, much of the town gathered around the messenger bearing the news. Caught up in the emotion of the moment, Hale returned to the spirit of his Linonian Society days and made an extemporaneous speech stirring the assemblage to the cause of liberty. Shortly thereafter he resigned his teaching post and accepted a position in the Continental Army.

Hale's army diary shows that most of his career was routine. He includes much discussion of the quotidienne, and also mentions sundry wrestling matches and checker games. Lieutenant Elisha Bostwick remembered Hale as an active and pious man.** Hale's mother disliked card playing and Bostwick relates an incident showing that Hale never forgot the lesson: when he caught several of his men at cards he seized the deck and cut it to pieces. Hale's greatest exploit as a soldier demonstrated his leadership and bravery. He commanded a small group of men in a rowboat up to a British supply ship, surprised its crew, and sailed it away. The capture was especially daring given that the ship was anchored next to an English man-of-war.

Hale was an intelligent, religious, and patriotic man with a propensity for action. He had disappointed his parents in electing not to study for the ministry, but such a calm existence was not for him. He noted in his diary:

A man ought never to lose a moments [sic] time. If he put off a thing for one minute to the next, his reluctance is but increas'd. . . .***

---

*Seymour, *op. cit.*, pp. 95–107.

**Ibid.*, p. 324.

***Ibid.*, p. 181.

William Hull, one of Knowlton's Rangers and Hale's friend at Yale, tried to dissuade him from undertaking his spy mission, but Hale replied:

I am fully sensible of the consequences of discovery in such a situation. But for a year I have been attached to the army, and have not rendered any material service, while receiving a compensation, for which I make no return. Yet, I am not influenced by the expectation of promotion or pecuniary reward; I wish to be useful, and every kind of service, necessary to the public good, becomes honorable by being necessary. If the exigencies of my country demand a peculiar service, its claims to perform that service are imperious.*

This blind devotion to duty led Hale to accept an unpopular assignment, but blindness also characterized his performance. His mistakes cost him his life. A British lieutenant described Hale's hanging:

He behaved with great composure and resolution, saying he thought it the duty of every good officer to obey the orders given him by his commander in chief and desired the spectators to be at all times prepared to meet death in whatever shape it might appear.**

The other British officer to comment on Hale was Captain John Montresor. Montresor was an engineer with alleged interest in the drawings Hale had made of British positions. He invited Hale to his tent, and the two officers had an amicable discussion prior to Hale's trip to the gallows. Montresor was highly impressed with Hale, and is credited with recording Hale's last words: "I only regret that I have but one life to lose for my country." Historian Charles Dudley Seymour points out that these words closely parallel those in a dramatic piece of the period with which Hale was familiar—Addison's *Cato:* "What pity is it that we can die but once to serve our country."*** Montresor's ready friendship and admiration for Hale illustrates the similar character of both armies' officers. The same phenomenon occurred between Tallmadge and the British spy, Major André, later in the war. The ability to mix on easy social terms with the British was used by Robert Townsend as the basis for his espionage efforts.

Hale was the kind of man Richard Rowan referred to when he called "sacrificial ardor the very bloodstream of patriotic secret service."**** Although he was a failure as a spy, Hale's readiness to sacrifice himself despite the taboo against espionage provided an example which others would follow, providing Washington with the intelligence his situation demanded.

*Ibid., p. 309.

**Ibid., p. 292.

***Ibid., p. 376–82.

****Rowan, op. cit., p. 150.

Tallmadge and Company

Whereas Hale was clearly motivated to serve by his devotion to patriotism, honesty, adventure, and Puritan morality, Benjamin Tallmadge helps demonstrate the broader character of most American spies. Like Hale, Tallmadge grew up in a religious family. His father was Rev. Benjamin Tallmadge, who attended Yale College in 1747. His mother, Susannah Smith, was the daughter of Rev. John Smith. Tallmadge studied the classics in his early education, being such a devoted scholar that he was offered a place at Yale at the age of thirteen. Instead, he waited and enrolled with the Hales in the class of 1773. While at college he and Nathan became close friends. Their graduation debate has already been mentioned; they also assumed the affected literary aliases of Damon and Pythias when addressing each other. Even after graduation, when both were instructors at different schools, the two men corresponded under their nicknames.

Tallmadge entered the army before Hale, and accepted a lieutenant's commission on July 20, 1776. On that date he wrote:

Believing myself influenced by the most patriotic principles. . . . My ambition was almost boundless, I felt ready to do or undergo almost any service that might be assigned to me.*

On July 4, 1775, Tallmadge expressed his philosophy in a letter to Hale:

Private interest must be far removed, and the community, with the good thereunto accruing by your present choice, must sway your mind. . . . Our country, a land flowing as it were with milk and honey, holding open her arms, and demanding assistance from all who can assist her in a sore distress . . . we all should be ready to step forth in the common cause.**

Tallmadge's enthusiasm soon waned. By the end of 1776 he was discouraged by the sorry state of the army and shocked by the death of General Woodhull after his capture by the British. (Woodhull was a second cousin of Abraham Woodhull, later a key link in Tallmadge's spy chain.)

The campaign of 1777 revived Tallmadge's spirit. He was promoted to captain of a dragoon regiment. Ever the gentleman, he took a keen interest in the color of his horses and the cut of the troop's uniforms, and "fired with military ambition and panting for glory"*** he was appointed major on April 7, 1777.

Having proven himself a good officer, Tallmadge came to the attention of

---

*Benjamin Tallmadge, *Memoir of Colonel Benjamin Tallmadge.* New York: Gillis Press, 1904, pp. 7–8.

**Seymour, *op. cit.,* pp. 37–39.

***Tallmadge, *op. cit.,* p. 26.

General Washington, and found himself assigned to patrol the area between the American and British lines near Philadelphia. At this point, Tallmadge was not actually spying, but he was dealing with spies. Numerous colonists would pass through Tallmadge's zone, either on business from Philadelphia or specifically to inform on the British. All such civilians were questioned by Tallmadge's troop. In this manner, Washington began to gain intelligence.

After his experience in New Jersey, Tallmadge returned to Connecticut. Washington still desired the information from Long Island which Nathan Hale's mission had failed to accomplish, and Washington asked Tallmadge to pursue the project. A native of Long Island, Tallmadge had family and friends there with whom he had kept in touch. It was easy for him to use these contacts to establish the famous Culper spy ring, the most tightly organized espionage operation of the Revolutionary War.

Tallmadge started one end of the chain from his Connecticut headquarters, and reported his information directly to Washington. The other end of the chain was in New York City in the person of Robert Townsend, better known as Samuel Culper, Jr. Tallmadge's alias was John Bolton, and Abraham Woodhull was Samuel Culper, Sr.* Tallmadge developed an extensive code during the course of the war, copies of which were held only by him, Woodhull, and Washington. The spy ring also used invisible ink perfected in London by James Jay, John Jay's brother. Jay provided this ink to Washington, and he passed it on to Tallmadge for distribution to the Culpers. One of the couriers for Townsend's trading company, Austin Roe, carried his employer's messages out of the city and across the island to the coastal home of Abraham Woodhull. The messages were picked up near Woodhull's home whenever Woodhull signalled Caleb Brewster, and were then taken in Brewster's whaleboat across Long Island Sound to Tallmadge.

As the most significant espionage effort made by the Americans during the war, the Culper chain was forged by a fortunate combination of influences. These combined differently in each man, but included patriotic spirit, loyalty to family and class, desire for secure economic position, and trust in Washington's leadership. The Woodhull, Tallmadge, and Brewster families were all neighbors on Long Island, and many were blood relatives. Benjamin Tallmadge was romantically inclined toward Townsend's sister for a time, but finally married the niece of General Nathaniel Woodhull, a cousin of Abraham's father. One of Abraham Woodhull's sons married a Brewster, and General Woodhull's grandson married Robert Townsend's niece.

The Woodhulls were a wealthy family of farmers, soldiers, and statesmen. Caleb Brewster gained his experience with boats as a whaling merchant. Robert Townsend inherited and expanded his father's retail business in New York. Tallmadge abandoned his intentions to study law when the war was over and became a businessman and member of Congress. Austin Roe appears to

*Ibid., p. 38.

be the only member of the chain without significant social status. He was joined in his patriotic ardor for spying by his brothers Nathaniel and Philip, both of whom operated in the Long Island area. Another indirect member of the chain was James Rivington, an alleged Tory printer and coffeehouse owner. Rivington's true identity as an American sympathizer and spy was unknown even to Tallmadge. Rivington operated out of New York as a direct confidant to Washington. His identity was probably known by Townsend, but there is no clear evidence for this.

As gamblers for lives, each of these men required a special motivation to push him into active espionage, especially with the shadow of Nathan Hale swinging before them. Not only did they have to rely on their own abilities to avoid capture in the act of spying, but they needed total confidence in the reliability of their fellow agents not to reveal the operation either intentionally or through error. The fact that most of the chain was composed of personal acquaintances helped ease the fear of disclosure. Significantly, the only member who became uneasy about secrecy was Townsend, who was the only non–Long Island native. The Roes seem to have operated largely from Haleian motives: they were strong patriots, eager to protect their land and family on Long Island. Perhaps Austin realized that his job with Townsend hung in the balance, and this added a little incentive. Caleb Brewster knew that life under the British would mean more taxes, but he was a wealthy and highly successful whaling merchant who would have held a powerful position in North America even in the event of British victory. Brewster seems to have been drawn into his new vocation out of a love for adventure, and in support of his Long Island community. After the war, many American agents secreted their identities as spies, but Brewster was proud to speak about his journeys across the sound in high seas and black nights. Abraham Woodhull's involvement reflected the patriotic heritage of his family and a desire to preserve their hardworked farmland. General Nathaniel Woodhull had been one of the first Americans killed in the war, and the family felt his loss acutely. Abraham's uncle, Captain Nathan Woodhull, also served in the Continental Army.

Robert Townsend's motivation is a less clear-cut case. His father, Samuel, had been commissioned to British service in 1741. With this background, and as a well-educated, successful Quaker merchant under the British, he was slow to warm to the revolutionary cause. When he finally decided to embrace the movement, he took a large role. He became a member of the New York provincial congress and the Committee of Safety. Along with General Woodhull, he worked to preserve the livestock of Long Island for the Continental Army. He was to serve on the committee for the first New York state constitution, but when the British occupied the city he signed an oath of allegiance to the king rather than abandon his business and property.

Prior to the British occupation, Robert had taken an interest in his father's business, and was appointed commissary officer to General Woodhull's brigade. He chose to stay with the business rather than leave New York, and hence was available to Washington. Even as a spy, however, Townsend refused to give up his business so that he could devote more time to espionage. In the end, his occupation proved to be a valuable cover, providing an ample number of excuses to sneak messages out of the city in regular merchandise shipments. By paying strict attention to the secrecy of his role, Townsend also ensured that his business could continue to operate whether the British or Americans were victorious. The ambivalence that his father's heritage showed accrued to the son. Both men demonstrated distinct patriotic leanings (there is no evidence that Robert Townsend spied for the British), but neither was willing to abandon his wealth or social position. Possibly, the Townsends were playing the European spy's gambit of coexisting with both sides. Robert was very friendly with the British officers occupying New York. He took the job of social editor with James Rivington's Tory newspaper. This association made him a sure contact for any officer who wanted to see his name in print. As a man with taste and status similar to the British, it was easy for Townsend to mix in their banter at Rivington's coffeehouse and other local taverns.

Townsend's fear of exposure was heightened when Benjamin Tallmadge helped to expose Benedict Arnold through the capture of Major André. Townsend had known André, who was frequently entertained at the home of Townsend's niece, who was married to a British officer. (In fact, Townsend's sister, Sarah, observed André's suspicious actions at this house, and, through her brother, forwarded Tallmadge the information which incriminated André. This is one more example of how often spying was a family operation.) Townsend was concerned that Arnold might know his identity as an American spy, but Washington's strict rules of secrecy in espionage meant that not even the highest-ranking officers knew who his agents were. (Had Townsend not been so paranoid, he would have realized that Arnold would have long ago exposed him had the traitor known of it.) Even though safe, Townsend used large sums of his own money to reinforce the silence of his confederates. He also suspended his espionage activities for several months until assurances were forwarded from Washington that Arnold could not possibly implicate him. As a measure of Townsend's care and Washington's protection of his agents, it should be noted that Robert Townsend's identity was not discovered until 1930.

Townsend's motivation appears more purely selfish and mercenary than the other members of the Culper ring; the role of James Rivington is perhaps the most interesting. Little is known about the man. He was a New York printer who published an avidly pro-Tory newspaper and was well liked by the occupying British troops who frequented Rivington's other business, a coffeehouse. Rivington knew George Washington, and communicated with him by binding messages written on tissue paper into the covers of schoolbooks.* He also gave Townsend the social reporter's job, enabling him to gather much of his intelli-

---

*Ind, *op. cit.*, p. 65.

gence. One would logically assume that two men working together would know each other's true colors, but Townsend may not have known that Rivington was also a spy. Perhaps Rivington was used by Washington to keep a check on Townsend's motives and the reliability of his reports. Since Rivington stole a copy of the British navy's signal book and passed it on to Washington, it is clear that he had a pipeline to the general other than through the Culper chain.* When the war ended and Washington marched into New York, one of the first places he visited was Rivington's, where he personally paid the spy with a bag of gold.** As Rivington prospered during the war, it stands to reason that he would have prospered after a British victory, but his patriotism and friendship with Washington moved him to become a valuable spy.

Tallmadge, as ringleader, showed dedication along the lines of his friend Nathan Hale, without showing Hale's fatal lack of talent for espionage. It required great courage and imagination for Tallmadge to develop his chain of communication and also to take the time and risk to personally meet with his spies on Long Island during the war. On one occasion Tallmadge had a British fort on Long Island scouted out, and then he and Brewster led a small group of men to surprise the fort, using their intelligence information to determine when and where to strike. They were so successful in their experiment with offensive espionage that they didn't lose a man.

The issue of Tallmadge's mercantile investments did not raise the same doubts as Townsend's. Tallmadge had intended to study law, but as the war continued and he grew older, he decided to risk investment in privateering stock companies. These were companies formed to raise capital to finance shipbuilding. The ships were centered in Connecticut River ports safe from British naval power. They would sneak out and rob British ships and then return to port. Stockholders earned a percentage of profit from each successful venture, but if the ship sank, so did the investor. Certainly, this was a patriotic kind of knavery. Not only could Tallmadge draw on Hale's memory to cement his devotion to the cause, but he also had the example of his brother William, who was starved to death in a British prison on Long Island.

Tallmadge had numerous communications with Washington because of the Culper chain, and late in the war became a part-time personal secretary of Washington's handling some of the general's paper work. In later life Tallmadge served for seventeen years in Congress and fought to preserve the consensus which Washington had created in his military victory. Clearly, Tallmadge's personal admiration and affection for Washington played a major role in his ardor for espionage. When Washington died, Tallmadge prepared a eulogy calling him "first of Patriots and best of

*John Bakeless, *Turncoats, Traitors and Heroes.* Philadelphia: J. B. Lippincott, 1959, p. 228.

**Ibid.*, p. 358.

Men," and urged that black armbands be worn at public occasions for the six months following.*

Other Patriotic Spies Who Also Served

One cannot detail the thousands of colonists who spied for either the Americans or British in one way or another. However, a few individuals were successful enough in their endeavors to attract notice in the form of written accounts, and a few more left behind personal correspondence or narratives with the War Department's pension board. A look at some documented cases can be used to extrapolate the character of other spies, since they might well reflect these individuals to a greater or lesser degree.

One of the earliest converts to American spying was a shoemaker named Enoch Crosby. Crosby had just reached the age of 21 when the shots were fired at Lexington and Concord. He immediately enlisted in the Continental Army and served out one term of duty. He returned to his trade, but finding life too dull, he reenlisted. He was on his way to report at his new post when he met a Tory sympathizer who mistook Crosby for one of his own. Using some of the spur-of-the-moment ingenuity which characterized the neophyte American spy corps, Crosby played along with his new acquaintance, attended a Tory meeting, and then created an excuse to depart. He proceeded directly to John Jay's home. Jay, together with Nathaniel Sackett, had been instructed to gather intelligence in the New York area. Their methods generally consisted of picking up casual information from friendly farmers, merchants, itinerant artisans, their wives and daughters, and the like. Jay immediately perceived Crosby's potential for uncovering networks of Tory supporters in the region and signed him up as a paid spy, complete with aliases. For the next few months, Crosby moved around the area, joining Tory groups, being "captured" by the Americans when these groups were arrested, and "escaping" to finger other Tory bands. His cover did not last long in this limited region, so Sackett sent him up to Albany, where he was unknown. Crosby retired in 1777, returning to his brother's home. While there he was shot at several times, and finally was given a severe beating when a gang of Tories broke into the house. They left Crosby for dead, but he recovered from his injuries and demonstrated his patriotic spirit by reenlisting for two more terms of duty with the Continental Army. Crosby retired to a life as a farmer, justice of the peace, sheriff, and deacon of the Presbyterian church. He was finally paid only $250 for his efforts, a sum hardly commensurate with his risks. In some respects, Crosby is fortunate to have been paid at all. Unlike the European spy business where money flowed freely, Washington operated on a tight budget. Many spies used vast quantities of their own funds for which they were never repaid. Americans gave up their time and their money as well as risking their lives for the new nation.

---

*Benjamin Tallmadge, "Address to the Society of Cincinnatus," December 30, 1789.

Family ties often formed the basis for espionage involvement. Participation by several members of the Woodhull, Hale, Townsend, and Roe families in the war have already been mentioned. Robert Townsend also used his brother James's assistance on one occasion, but James stumbled into the hands of some overzealous patriots while carrying a message directly from his brother to Washington. James ran into a man whom he took to be a Tory, and assumed a Tory role for himself in an effort to prevent the man from discovering his true mission. Unfortunately for James, he guessed wrong. He and his alleged Tory friend were both on the same side. James was trapped in a conversation with the farmer and his two daughters, was accused as a spy, and saw the messages he carried taken and conveyed to General Washington. Washington immediately perceived the truth of the incident and had Townsend secretly returned to New York, but the new communication route was never again attempted by the Culpers.

That Townsend was so quickly identified and revealed to authorities demonstrated the surprising effectiveness of common people infused with patriotic spirit as amateur agents of espionage, and especially counterespionage. Americans tended to be reluctant to become offensive agents, but their aversion to active spying made them especially willing to uncover the distasteful espionage activity of their opponents. This "eternal vigilance" in relation to the presence of spies in America became paranoia following the Revolutionary War, more than a hundred years later during the Red Scare, and in the 1950s during the McCarthy hearings.

Another family involved in the American cause was the Darraghs of Philadelphia. William and Lydia Darragh kept a Quaker household across the street from British headquarters. The British officers were becoming cramped in their building and requisitioned the Darragh house. Mrs. Darragh protested, and the officers compromised by agreeing only to use the parlor as a council chamber. Mr. Darragh was a schoolmaster who tutored some of the British, so the redcoats trusted the family. Perhaps they were not aware that the Darragh's son, Charles, was a lieutenant serving in Washington's army. Mrs. Darragh, like so many other colonial citizens, took the initiative to spy on her own. She used her proximity to the British officers to gain information about their military plans. She sent her intelligence to Washington by way of young Lt. Darragh. In order to get messages from Philadelphia to her son, she used her younger boy, 14-year-old John. Because of his age, John easily passed unsuspected in and out of British lines. Mrs. Darragh sent messages in this manner for several months before she discovered the information which made her famous. On the night of December 2, 1777, the British informed Mrs. Darragh that they would be using her parlor for a special meeting and that all members of the family would have to remain above the main floor of the house. Lydia immediately knew that something important was afoot. She waited until the meeting had started and the house was quiet, and then crept down to the keyhole at the parlor door. She discovered a planned British attack to surprise the Americans on the night of December 4, using about 6,000 men.

The next morning she grabbed a flour sack and headed out of town on the pretext of going to buy flour at a mill. She reached the mill, left the sack to be filled, and proceeded to the Rising Sun tavern.

The Rising Sun was established by Washington's intelligence operation in Pennsylvania as a rendezvous for patriot informers. Although the Pennsylvania operation was never as sophisticated as the Culper ring, there was an effort at organization made by Colonel Elias Boudinot, Washington's chief of intelligence. Boudinot, who went on to become president of Congress after the war, created a loose confederacy of local farmers, artisans, peddlers, country girls selling produce, etc. to keep informed of British plans. The main points for collecting information were two taverns, the Red Lion and the Rising Sun. Boudinot presided over the Rising Sun, and delegated the Red Lion operation to Major John Clark, Jr. From these two inns they both received casual reports and dispatched agents on specific missions.*

As Lydia Darragh approached the Rising Sun on December 3, she met Col. Boudinot on horseback. He listened to her story and quickly rode off to inform headquarters of the impending attack. Lydia proceeded to the tavern, repeated her message, and then returned home via the mill. There she picked up her flour sack which she lugged home to preserve her cover story. In his *Memoir,* Benjamin Tallmadge mentions that he too visited the Rising Sun that day. He and a farm girl bearing information both arrived at the tavern just as the British started to raid the area in preparation for their attack. Tallmadge explains how he gallantly swept up the young lady and rode away with her. Fortunately, he also describes the ensuing "surprise" attack by the British. Washington was totally prepared by his intelligence staff. After a brief skirmish followed by several days of staring at each other across a battlefield, the British retreated to Philadelphia and the Continental Army obtained a peaceful winter in which to regroup.

Lydia Darragh's patriotism and bravery were undoubtedly encouraged by her son's presence among Washington's troops. Although other spies in the area were beginning to report troop movements, it was only because of Mrs. Darragh's concrete information that Washington knew what the other reports were pointing toward. As is so often the case in intelligence, it is not one but a series of reports which must be interpreted to obtain an accurate picture. Mrs. Darragh's expedition may literally have saved the war for the Americans. Historians have speculated that if the British had attacked an unprepared Continental Army at this stage, the blow could have been fatal.

Another American in the British confidence was Captain David Gray, a double spy to rival Enoch Crosby. Gray was a 19-year old in Lenox, Massachusetts, when the war started. He enlisted twice with battle regiments, serving with Ethan Allen at Ticonderoga and at the siege of St. John's in Canada, before being assigned to the Quartermaster Corps upon his third enlistment in 1777. This duty required Gray to travel throughout New England, where

*A. A. Hoehling, *Women Who Spied.* New York: David McKay, pp. 5–6.

he discovered a line of Tory communications running from New London, Connecticut, into Canada. While in New London in 1777, Gray met Captain William Beckwith, the chief of British intelligence who operated out of New York. Gray fooled Beckwith by adopting the role of deserter, and soon he was running Tory messages into New England and Canada from New York. Gray's routine was to deliver his messages via Washington's headquarters. The general would read the letters and then Gray would deliver them as assigned. In addition, Washington helped to assure Gray's disguised reputation by having him listed as a deserter, and feeding him both obvious and false pieces of information to give General Clinton. In this way Clinton believed Gray to be a valuable spy, when Gray actually imparted nothing of import. The British believed in Gray until the end of the war. He went back to regular service in 1782, but the British never dreamed that he had returned to the Americans. They assumed that another of their loyal agents had given up the trade by flight or death, as spies were wont to do.

Like other American spies, Gray differentiated between legitimate service as a soldier and illegitimate service as a spy. In 1781 he reached New London on the day that Benedict Arnold was planning his attack; he was able to provide the town with a few hours of warning. Rather than return to his spying after delivering the message, Gray made a spur-of-the-moment decision to return to war's overt side and assumed command of some of the troops during the battle. Gray's warning had not been in time, and as Arnold entered the town the Americans were forced to retreat. Gray the soldier left behind the coat of Gray the spy, containing his passes and messages; fortunately, it found its way to Washington. Gray was saved to serve out the war and then retire to Vermont, where he farmed and wrote his memoirs.*

Hercules Mulligan was another of Washington's spies in New York. Mulligan and his brother were partners in a West Indian trading company. After serving in the early battles of the war, Mulligan fled New York when the British entered. He was captured by a band of Tories and returned to New York, where Washington contacted him and requested that he keep his eyes and ears open. The Mulligan company handled finances for Alexander Hamilton when he was away at school, and Hamilton lived for a time with the Mulligans; when Hamilton became an aide to Washington it was natural that he would mention his brave friend Hercules as a candidate for secret service. Mulligan never spoke about his exploits after the war, exhibiting the same embarrassment that Robert Townsend showed when his children discovered a British officer's uniform in the Townsend attic. Despite his uneasy conscience, Mulligan was the first man to entertain George Washington when the Americans returned to New York. Washington breakfasted at Mulligan's home before going to pay James Rivington his bag of gold.**

The Mersereau clan, like the Roes, embraced espionage as a family business.

*Pension statement of David Gray, National Archives, Record Group 15A, File s/38/776.

**Bakeless, op. cit., pp. 240–41; 364.

They were originally from Staten Island, where they had been shipbuilders. Washington contacted Joshua Mersereau in 1777 when he needed information in the New Brunswick, New Jersey, area, because the Mersereaus had provided information about Staten Island prior to the British advance. Joshua spoke to his family, and his son John (not to be confused with Joshua's brother of the same name) agreed to stay in New Brunswick after the Americans evacuated. For the next eighteen months, John repeatedly crossed the river to Staten Island on a raft, bringing information when his family signalled. (John carried his messages in a bottle with a string tied around the neck. If stopped he could let go of the string and any incriminating evidence would drop to the river bottom.) When the British began to suspect him, John called on his younger brother, 16-year-old Paul, to carry on the operation. John had wanted to enlist for regular military service, but his right arm was crippled and he could not carry a musket. Instead he made himself useful tending to the troops. Although his disability initially helped keep the British from suspecting him, it took incredible courage for John to spy among them and make his daring river crossings under such a handicap.

The Mersereaus were part of a New Jersey spy network established by Colonel Elias Dayton at Washington's request. The group included Joshua, his two sons, and his brother John. It appears that this John coordinated many of the actual espionage missions. There were at least a dozen other agents involved. One of Washington's letters speaks of asking Dayton to dispatch twenty agents at one time. Another member of this ring, John Vanderhovan, mentioned contacting Caleb Brewster of the Culper ring, and John Mersereau corresponded with Elias Boidinot of Philadelphia intelligence fame. Like many other American spies, Vanderhovan used his own funds to finance his spying. He was finally forced to give up espionage when the expenses became too great and he was unable to obtain funding from the Continental Congress. The Mersereaus went back to their earlier business after the war. Joshua also became a surrogate in two New York counties. His brother John boasted in his old age that "there was none in our army that run so many risks and underwent so many hardships and fatigues as I did."*

Charles Morgan offered a more modest interpretation to counter Mersereau's boast. Morgan was a private in the army who was asked by Lafayette to go over to the British as a deserter to spread false information and survey troop strengths prior to Yorktown. Morgan reluctantly agreed, with the stipulation that Lafayette would clear his name should anything happen to him. Trusting Lafayette's assurance he "deserted," was taken to Cornwallis, and convinced the British general that Lafayette had the capability to transfer all his troops across the James River and pursue any movement by the British. Morgan went on to observe British fortifications, and returned to Lafayette

*Bakeless, *op. cit.,* pp. 177–81; George S. Bryan, *The Spy in America.* Philadelphia: J. B. Lippincott, 1943, pp. 88–89.

with five Redcoats he had convinced to desert with him and a captured Hessian. Lafayette offered Morgan a promotion, but Morgan thought he made a better private than he would a sergeant. Lafayette's offer of payment was also refused. All Morgan wanted was his musket back. Someone had stolen his favorite rifle while he was away.*

Sergeant Daniel Bissell reflected Morgan's feelings when he refused his government pension when he was unsure the government could afford it. Bissell had been enlisted to determine the strength of Henry Clinton's army in New York during the last months of the war. Bissell succeeded in gathering the information, and also managed to use several daring moves in his escape from British lines. As a result of his efforts, Bissell was awarded the first Purple Heart ever given to a spy.** (Bissell was extremely proud of his award. He lost it when his house burned down, but had memorized Washington's citation.)

Not all spies, whether British or American, operated from totally altruistic motives. William Heron, a member of the Connecticut assembly, was more interested in the financial aspects of spying. Heron spied for both the British and the Americans at the same time, although most of his efforts benefitted the British, since they had more money with which to reward him. He not only passed military information, but also news from the Continental Congress, to which he had access as a member of the Connecticut Assembly. At one point he received permission to sneak a cargo ship through the British blockade to Ireland. When he returned, a group of loyalists captured his ship and threw him in a New York prison, little realizing that they held a British agent. This incident eventually stood Heron well in the eyes of his countrymen. When the war was over this was viewed as a sacrifice he had made to the new nation, not a result of his own greed. He was elected to the General Assembly, and at his death in 1819 no one knew the truth about his role in the war. Fortunately for Heron, he was smart enough to play his greedy game, but if the British or Americans had discovered him, either would have been justified in hanging him.

The Father of American Espionage

The performance of the persons mentioned here and the many others not described served to establish the patriotic tradition in American espionage, and is also noteworthy in terms of how it was orchestrated and controlled by America's first "spy master," George Washington, who wrote:

. . . everything, in a manner, depends upon obtaining intelligence. Single men in the night will be more likely to ascertain facts than the best glasses in the day. Secrecy and despatch may prove the soul of success to an enterprise.

*Bryan, op. cit., pp. 87–88; Bakeless, op. cit., pp. 337–38.

**Bakeless, op. cit., pp. 346–58.

Many have criticized George Washington's apparent temerity as a military leader; however, when he accepted appointment as commander-in-chief of the Continental Army, he realized that he faced an uphill struggle. An experienced soldier, Washington knew the requirements for success. As he surveyed his army's preparedness in comparison with the British, he saw weaknesses in numbers, training, experience, and equipment. The commander needed an edge with which to hold off British strength until the Americans could grow into an effective army. He turned to intelligence.

Like most Americans in the eighteenth century, Washington had little experience in espionage. As a soldier in the French and Indian Wars, he had observed the ways Indian scouts and guides had been used to great advantage. A few well-placed Indians watching silently could inform their employers of enemy troop movements and battle preparations. Washington remembered the experience of General Edward Braddock, who was ambushed when he marched into a wooded ravine. Braddock had spurned the use of Indians to scout ahead of his advance. Meanwhile, Indian scouts in French employ had given their employers warning of Braddock's movement and enabled the smaller French force to triumph.

The key to success in this attack had been surprise, achieved on the basis of accurate prior intelligence about the enemy and absolute secrecy. This strategy became the foundation for American victory during the Revolutionary War. Washington had already learned the lessons of his earlier experience well. As early as 1775, he wrote of deploying men to collect "intelligence." Letters from this period show that he dispatched numerous scouting expeditions, using both Americans and Indians, during the French and Indian Wars. The young officer was also beginning to understand the nuances of counterespionage. On November 9, 1756, he captured an enemy spy and ordered the man hanged.

The rationale for espionage success was not foreign to George Washington. A business leader and military officer, Washington's achievements were founded on an ability to observe and understand his associates and he planned his operations on the basis of analysis. In a letter to Benjamin Tallmadge, he outlined his analytical approach in relation to battle preparedness:

. . . obtain the minutest intelligence of the strength of the Corps, the situation and position where you can make the stroke, and [at] the same time to estimate and consider well the number of men that will be necessary to insure success, and above all the number of boats that will be wanted and the practicability of obtaining them in time and with secrecy. You will after making yourself as perfectly master of the subject as possible, and calculating the chances of succeeding or miscarrying in the execution of the Project, (if you should think it eligible to prosecute the affair) give me your sentiments there on. . . .*

*Each of the quotes cited here below attributed to George Washington are to be found in John C. Fitzpatrick, editor, *The Writings of George Washington from the Original Manuscript Sources 1745-1799.* Washington: U.S. Government Printing Office, 1944.

To read between these lines into Washington's logic, the true role of intelligence becomes to perceive strengths and weaknesses in others and oneself. With this knowledge one can hide one's weak points and exploit the enemy's. Accurate intelligence provided Washington with the means to surprise his enemy, counterintelligence enabled him to give the British false information which masked the Continental Army's weaknesses. But only Washington could act on the basis of the intelligence available to him; in this regard he was intelligence officer and commander combined.

With his first lessons in espionage learned, Washington began organizing a spy network for his army even before Nathan Hale's ill-fated mission. There were plenty of men like Hale willing to risk the taboo against espionage to spy for the revolutionary cause, but it took a man like Washington to coordinate their efforts and exploit the intelligence they acquired. Recognizing the social and physical risks of espionage for the individual agents in their dangerous pursuits, he insisted on paying all his operatives, and supported them with his personal faith and the power of his national position. This enduring commitment by the Continental Army's commanding general encouraged outstanding individuals such as the Culpers and Tallmadge to volunteer for secret service.

As his own chief of intelligence, Washington's emphasis was on accurate information swiftly and secretly received. To achieve this goal he stressed close communication with his agents, double checking of all reports, and scrupulous attention to expenditures, including careful accounting for all disbursed funds. An examination of the general's writings during the war years reveals almost daily communication with agents in the field, and charts the growth of America's first espionage organization.

On July 15, 1775, Washington noted the following in his account book:

. . . 333 1/3 Dollars given to —— to induce him to go into the town of Boston; to establish a secret correspondence for the purpose of conveying intelligence of the Enemys [sic] movements and designs.

This entry showed that Washington was already keeping careful track of his expenses, a policy to which he adhered throughout the war, but whose precedent was lost amidst the vast secret expenditures of succeeding American espionage groups. The absence of a name in the record shows the general's early concern with protecting his agents by revealing their names to as few others as possible. He encouraged his agents to refrain from signing their messages to headquarters, preferring to identify the sender by his handwriting or by having him use invisible ink.

Although agents like the anonymous man dispatched to Boston were the backbone of Washington's intelligence operation, he soon began exploiting other sources of information. In September 1775, he wrote Governor Nicholas Gage with special instructions:

I need not mention to you the vast Importance of gaining Intelligence of the Enemy's Motions and Designs as early as possible; The great saving to the Continent both of Blood and Money; a Detection of our secret and most Dangerous Enemies, with inumerable other Advantages, would result from the Interception of their correspondence at this Juncture: I have therefore thought proper to propose to you the seizing [of] the mail by the next Packet.

Reading the enemy's mail was not a new device, but Washington's purpose was astute. At this early stage of the war he hoped to use the mail from England to discover citizens of the colonies sympathetic with the British cause. This counterespionage move identified agents of the Crown who might have undermined Washington's plans to deceive and surprise the Redcoats.

In establishing his espionage network, Washington tried to leave nothing to chance when charting enemy motions and disguising the numbers and maneuvers of his own forces. The first means to this end was the swift accumulation of intelligence; the second was the establishment of a corroborative system so that all intelligence was verified by more than one source. Washington also personally screened the character of his agents through his network of multiple sources. If one agent in a locality consistently forwarded false information or conducted himself suspiciously, a second agent in the area, known to Washington but not to the other operative, would report on the first man's trespasses. Although Washington briefly expounded on this intelligence strategy in his communications throughout the war, he found time to express it in more detail during the conflict's last months:

. . . it is my earnest wish that you would impress upon the persons in whom you seem to place confidence, urging them to be pointed, regular and accurate in all their communications. No service can be greater than this, if it is well performed; these with an account of the nature and progress of their public works is of infinite more consequence than all the chit-chat of the Streets and the idle conjecture of the Inhabitants.
[GW to Colonel Matthias Ogden, April 2, 1782]

Washington's insistence on reliable information as opposed to rumor allowed him to draw accurate pictures of British strategy:

It is by comparing a variety of information we are frequently enabled to investigate facts, which were so intricate or hidden that no single clue could have led to the knowledge of them. In this point of view, intelligence becomes interesting which but from its connection and collateral circumstances, would not be important.
[GW to James Lovell, April 1, 1782]

Because Washington depended upon a variety of inputs to make his intelligence judgments, silence made him nervous. When regular communication with an agent was interrupted, he quickly inquired into the situation. His concern was threefold: to keep an unbroken chain of information concerning

British activities in the area so that he could not be surprised; to be sure that his agent had not been captured or injured; to ascertain whether the British had used the agent to gain information which could reveal American strategy. The general's sentiment was best expressed in a letter to one of his officers:

It is now 3 days since I have received any intelligence from your Lordship; this makes me the more uneasy as my movements depend altogether upon the indications you give me of those of the enemy. It is of so much importance to me to be regularly informed that I must request you will send expresses daily, acquainting me precisely with the enemy's position and communicating such intelligence as you may collect from spies, deserters and ca. It is often a satisfaction to know that nothing new has happened altho' it may not appear very interesting to make a report of; it will always be in your Lordship's power to compensate the dearth of events by favoring me with your conjectures.
[GW to Lord Stirling, October 4, 1778]

These quotations reveal an important part of Washington's success as a leader and organizer. He was very specific in instructing his agents about the basics of the craft of espionage and in giving them specific questions about the enemy, but when he trusted a man he delegated the authority to conduct specific operations. This attitude insured that the general would receive the information he needed, but also freed him from tedious operational details and made his operatives feel that they were important enough to have earned the trust of the commander in chief. Although Washington was careful to pay his agents whenever possible, many were happy to serve in the secret service and spend their own funds just for the opportunity of associating with their leader. During his lifetime, Washington was much more than a general. The public perceived him as what would today be a combination of war hero, politician, movie actor, and sports star. Washington could generate a crowd just by walking down a street. He enhanced his reputation by refusing to put on airs and by steadfastly supporting his troops. In the grim early days of the war, as his army was routed from New York City, Washington stayed behind on the island to supervise the withdrawal until the last of his troops had been evacuated. During the bitter winter at Valley Forge, Washington was constantly engaged in securing supplies for the beleagured Continental Army. When the Contintental Congress was strapped for funds, Washington appealed privately to friends like financier Robert Morris. The commander in chief's presence on the battlefield provided the impetus to rally colonial troops. During the battle of Monmouth, Colonel Harry Lee was in the process of retreat despite superior forces. Washington rode onto the field of battle and assumed command, lifting the spirit of the army and producing a notable American victory.

The influence of Washington's personality was clear throughout the war, and he did not abandon his men when the war ended. Although he had never met Culper, Jr., he informed Benjamin Tallmadge that on the basis of Culper's work:

I shall be ready to recommend him to the public if public employ shall be his aim and if not that I shall think myself bound to represent his conduct in the light it deserves and provide him with compensation of another kind.
[GW to Benjamin Tallmadge, September 16, 1780]

Washington earlier offered to speak personally with Culper, Jr., to assuage any doubts the agent had about beginning his espionage activities. The general was so sure of his methods that he wrote Tallmadge, "I could put the mode of corresponding upon such a footing that even if his letters were to fall into enemy hands, he would have nothing to fear, on that account." On April 30, 1781, Washington informed Tallmadge that he had carried through on his promise of reward:

I am engaging, in behalf of the United States, a liberal reward for the services of the C[ulper]s, (of whose fidelity and ability I entertain a high opinion) it is certainly but reasonable, from patriotism and every other high principle, that reward for their exertions should be proportionately great, to subserve essentially the interest of the Public.
[GW to Benjamin Tallmadge April 30, 1781]

The clearest example of Washington's concern for his agents came when he had Tallmadge enter New York City prior to the Continental Army's occupation so that American agents could be protected against British retaliation. Washington's early visits to the homes of spies such as Mulligan and Rivington after the occupation demonstrated his close relationship with the agents. (A full ten years later, then President Washington wrote to Mulligan to request a special fabric with which to make breeches such as those Hercules had given Washington.) A last measure of Washington's respect for the work of his agents was shown when he awarded a special certificate to Daniel Bissell, one of the first of the awards now known as Purple Hearts.

That Washington appealed to the patriotism of his agents is clear from his recruitment requests as well as recorded praise after the war. Washington soothed the doubts of those who saw espionage as contrary to the spirit of the new nation by equating spying during wartime with patriotism:

. . . you cannot more effectually serve your country at this time than by deligence [sic] in this line of duty; while we remark Your Reputation will be much concerned (from your advantageous situation) in giving the earliest, most particular and authentic intelligence of any person whatever.
[GW to Captain John Pray, August 14, 1782]

Although intensely spy conscious, Washington treated the problem of internal security with more moderation and legality than have many of his successors. As an expert manipulator of many spies, Washington recognized the presence of much British espionage activity during the Revolutionary War. This recognition led him to request passage of a resolution dealing with treatment of enemies during time of war. He summarized the legislation in a letter to New Jersey's Governor Livingston:

A resolve of Congress gave me the power of trying all persons taken within thirty miles of the Head Quarters of the Army, carrying Provision to the Enemy, acting as Spies or Pilots for them, or any ways assisting them . . . I have just received yours of the 11th respecting Moss. I would only mean to shield him from harm, upon a supposition that he had been no further concerned in going to the Enemy than to serve us; But if he has been playing the double part and his villainy can be proved, he ought not to be screened.
[GW to Governor Livingston April 15, 1778]

As with Washington's common-sense attitude in respect to careful accounting for espionage expenditures, the language of this resolution, and the general's attitude toward the suspected double agent Moss, show a concern for security combined with justice.

The meticulous leadership which Washington employed in positive intelligence was applied equally to counterespionage and deception. In his opinion there was no excuse for an American officer's being surprised, given the expertise of the Continental Army's intelligence system. Sloppy espionage and counterespionage greatly upset the commander in chief:

While the safety of the Army often rests on their vigilance, they [some officers] neglect the most ordinary precautions for their own security, and risk their own honor, the lives or liberty of their soldiers, and open an avenue for some more extensive operation of the enemy. If any Officer regardless of his own reputation and the important duty he owes the public, suffers himself to be surprised, he cannot expect, if taken, that interest should be made for his exchange, or if he saves his person, to escape the Sentence of a Court Martial.
[GW to Brigadier General Charles Scott, October 8, 1778]

Washington's foremost defenses against British infiltration were threats such as the above, secrecy whenever possible, and careful checking of all American agents. In assigning two untried agents to the same region, Washington sent these instructions:

The less they are acquainted with the end, and design of their mission the better; and if they had no knowledge of the business entrusted to each other the better chance would there be to come at the truth by comparing their Acts.
[GW to Colonel William Patterson, March 1, 1779]

When such operations revealed an untrustworthy agent, Washington either fired the man or earmarked him for another purpose. The general expressed special concern about agents with a weakness for money. Anyone known to be using his position in secret service to improve his private financial holdings was immediately suspended. Washington recognized that if it came to a question of bribery, "the enemy can purchase their fidelity at a higher price than we can." [GW to Major General Alexander McDougall, March 25, 1779.]

In dealing with double agents, Washington combined elements of military strategy, law, and propaganda in deciding upon a course of action. A typical case was that of Captain Gifford:

If there are good reasons for suspecting Captain Gifford's fidelity, I would by no means give him a discharge from the Army, because he might go off to the enemy, and we should not have it in our power to treat him as a deserter should he fall into our hands again. I would at any rate bring him to trial on his arrest; something may, in the course of it, turn up, which may give sufficient grounds for securing him afterwards, if the sentence of the Court should not find him guilty in a military point of light. Should he be cashiered, and then go off, the enemy will not have much to boast of, from the acquisition of such a character.
[GW to Lt. Col. Francis Barber, December 13, 1780]

Had Captain Gifford been found guilty, Washington would have had him carefully interrogated before his dismissal. It was the general's policy to obtain all possible information from spies and deserters, and, if possible, to use them as double agents to work against the British:

Both the persons apprehended by you come I think under the denomination of spies, perhaps by holding this Idea up to them strongly, and threatening them with the consequences except they confess, something material may be got out of them (by examining them apart from each other). . . . Do you think they might be kept and used as Guides, if they were to be told, that instant death would be the certain consequences of treachery[?]
[GW to Brigadier General Edward Hand, March 24, 1779]

Washington's methods of interrogation were not always above board. When faced with a pair of uncooperative British spies, the commander in chief wrote to Reverend Alexander McWhorter requesting the church's assistance:

There are now under sentence of death, in the provost, a Farnsworth and Blair, convicted of being spies from the enemy, and of publishing counterfeit Continental currency. It is hardly to be doubted but that these unfortunate men are acquainted with many facts representing the enemy's affairs, and their intentions which we have not been able to bring them to acknowledge. Besides the opportunity of affording them the benefit of your profession, it may in the conduct of a man of sense answer another valuable purpose. And while it serves to prepare them for the other world, it will

naturally lead to the intelligence we want in your inquiries into the condition of their spiritual concerns. You will therefore be pleased to take the charge of this matter upon yourself, and when you have collected in the course of your attendance such information as they can give, you will transmit the whole to me.
[GW to Rev. Alexander McWhorter, October 12, 1778]

Although unorthodox, such conspiracy between church and state proved most beneficial in the intelligence it produced. The technique was used successfully by the Confederates during the Civil War to obtain evidence which convicted Timothy Webster, one of the Union's most capable spies.

Despite his reputation for personal honesty, Washington was willing to use deception to further his espionage goals. In most cases he was able to dupe the British, but Benedict Arnold succeeded in defeating Washington's espionage operation where most others failed. Indeed, Benjamin Tallmadge nearly exposed Arnold before the traitorous general could flee to the British; but Arnold did escape, and exposed Washington's zeal against traitors, which rivalled his zeal for patriotism. Arnold's actions affronted Washington on a personal level as well, since he had been a trusted fellow officer.

Tallmadge's exposure of Arnold thwarted the traitor's plot, but Washington was not satisfied merely to be rid of Arnold. He wished to deal with his former friend before a court martial, and plotted a kidnapping scheme to bring the now British general back to Continental hands alive:

My aim is to make a public example of him, and this should be strongly impressed upon those who are employed to bring him off.
[GW to Major Henry Lee, October 20, 1780]

Washington did not want other officers to believe that a traitor could succeed in duping him. Also, some of the Continental spies were uneasy after Arnold's defection, and feared that he would be able to reveal their identities to the British. Theirs was a groundless fear, as Washington kept the identities of his agents secret even from the highest-ranking officers for security reasons (even Washington knew some of the agents only by their aliases); but many refused to rest secure in the commander-in-chief's assurances. As Washington told Lafayette, "Arnold's flight seems to have frightened all my intelligencers out of their senses." [GW to Marquis de Lafayette, October 30, 1780.]

Due to remarkable luck on Benedict Arnold's part, none of the American kidnapping plots proved successful in capturing him. However, the many intelligence schemes conceived by Washington helped to win the war for the United States. Faced from the outset with the enemy's superior troop strength, Washington used his intelligence operation to discover weak points in British defense where his small forces could bring their full power to bear and gain advantage. He also planted misleading information which led the cautious British commanders to believe there were masses of Continentals where, in reality, none existed.

Deception played an important role in the early decisive victory at Princeton. Recognizing that British agents would be watching his camp,

General Washington caused the fires of his encampment to be kept up, and suitable sentinels and patrols to be on duty through the night, while, with the main body of his troops, he filed off to the right, and the next morning at daybreak was at Princeton.*

Along with such physical deceptions, Washington often conspired to send false information to the British commanders. Sometimes the information would be provided by American agents planted at British headquarters; but with experience, Washington achieved greater effect by allowing British spies to "discover" misleading Continental Army documents. A classic example of this technique took place in early 1777, as the American army rested for the winter at Morristown. Knowing that he had fewer than 4,000 troops, Washington feared that the Redcoats would seize the opportunity to attack with their superior numbers and attempt to win the war. As the first part of the ruse to keep his meager troop strength secret, Washington circulated a rumor that the army's true strength was 24,000. Next he arranged to billet his troops in groups of two or three to a house throughout the Morristown area, thereby misrepresenting the army's need for accommodations.

Such a simple scheme might soon have been discovered, had not the first British spy to arrive on the scene been identified by American officers before he could begin his investigations. On Washington's order, the agent was befriended by American officers, who lodged him with the adjutant general rather than arrest him. Washington next instructed each brigadier to file a greatly inflated report of his brigade's numbers. The false documents were forwarded to the adjutant general, who conspired to leave them in an unguarded room with the suspected agent. The next day the Britisher disappeared, carrying the false impression that there were 12,000 members of the Continental Army at Morristown. Washington saw that the information was corroborated for his adversaries by having one of his regular double agents deliver a similar report to British headquarters. The plot worked so well that when a British agent finally learned the truth and took it to his superiors, they disbelieved him and had him arrested as an American spy.

Similar tricks continued throughout the war, but Washington's masterpiece came in preparation for Yorktown. Positioning his troops on the New Jersey coast across from New York City, Washington made it appear that he was gearing up for the assault on New York which the British had been anticipating. The crafty general gathered all the small boats his men could find on the beach, and had them begin the construction of permanent camps, including large brick ovens for the baking of bread, which were clearly visible from the

*Tallmadge, *op. cit.,* p. 23.

city. It appeared that Washington intended to mass his troops and move across to New York. Just to make sure the British had no doubts, he prepared inaccurate documents under official signature and handed them to a messenger who was instructed to ride through an area known to be patrolled by British troops. As planned, the messenger's dispatches were stolen, leaving the recipients secure in their misconception. The program had the British so completely deceived that when they received accurate reports that Washington and his army were moving south through New Jersey they dismissed the movement as an attempted diversion, sure that the American commander would double back to the North. By the time they discovered their error, it was too late to send Cornwallis reinforcements. Yorktown was soon in the hands of the Continental Army.

Washington's effectiveness as intelligence chief was a combination of his natural flair for military espionage and counterespionage, and his secrecy and meticulous attention to detail. The program was held together by the general's personality. He clearly commanded the devotion of his subordinates. Toward the end of the war, when many officers were upset by a published rumor that promised rewards would not be enacted by Congress, and felt that they should, therefore, revolt, Washington

. . . assured them that they might depend upon his exertions to obtain remuneration from the United States for their services. To this the officers responded most respectfully and affectionately, and assured their great leader and commander that they abhorred the measure proposed by the anonymous writer, and would not dishonor themselves by adopting the course by him suggested.*

Washington's commanding yet humble character helped him avoid public scandal over the the Society of Cincinnatus. The society was proposed as a brotherhood of former Revolutionary War officers, and they selected Washington as president of the general society to preside over the thirteen state societies. The societies became investment clubs for the ex-officers, wherein they contributed funds with which each state society then purchased public securities. Having just won independence from a British aristocracy, many citizens felt the officers were trying to establish themselves as a superior class, and opposed the society. An observer commented:

. . . there seemed to be a jealousy in the minds of some that it [the Society of Cincinnatus] would be like encouraging a sort of self-erected aristocracy.

About this time, General Washington, our President-General, feeling unwilling to do anything to excite a popular ferment, especially toward the officers of the revolutionary army, proposed to the State Societies to abolish the Institution.**

*Tallmadge, *op. cit.,* p. 81.

**Tallmadge, *op. cit.,* pp. 85–86.

The state societies readily accepted their leader's proposal, demonstrating their respect for his judgment.

Washington's inspired espionage program set high standards which took many years for his intelligence descendants to equal. After the war, he argued at length for the creation of a peacetime military force, and as president saw that one was established according to his careful plans, but he made no similar arguments for the continuation of an espionage organization. In his "Sentiments on a Peace Establishment," Washington argued for

. . . the necessity of the proposed institution [a standing army] unless we intend to let the Science become extinct, and to depend entirely upon the Foreigners for their friendly aid, if ever we should again be involved in Hostility.
[GW to Alexander Hamilton, May 2, 1783]

During the Revolutionary War, Washington's emphasis had been on military intelligence in support of military operations. There were some minor intrigues among the members of United States delegations abroad, and the Americans parlayed their understanding of Anglo-French relations into decisive military support from France, whereas Washington's intelligence concerns had been principally domestic. With the nation secure, there seemed to be little need for continued espionage. This feeling was reinforced by the sentiments of the new Bill of Rights, which in insuring individual liberties precluded domestic espionage, and by a concern against the possibility of special powers being used to create an aristocracy, as demonstrated by popular opposition to the Society of Cincinnatus. Therefore, instead of reaffirming the value of espionage demonstrated during the war by arguing for the founding of an ongoing government intelligence organization, Washington bowed to public opinion and insured that the foreign dependence he had feared in military defense would become the rule in American foreign intelligence activity for decades thereafter. To this aspect of Washington's intelligence legacy one must add that, as well as bowing to public opinion, he made it, by saying in his inaugural address that:

Nothing is more essential than that permanent, inveterate antipathies against particular nations and passionate attachments for others should be excluded. . . . The great rule for us in regard to foreign nations is, in extending our commercial relations to have with them as little political connection as possible.

From Washington to Lincoln

The history of American intelligence from the dispersal of Washington's Revolutionary War espionage organization to Lincoln and the Civil War followed an irregular path as the new nation and succeeding presidents found themselves embroiled in international diplomacy and its domestic fallout. Like many new nations founded in the fire of successful revolutionary battle, threats to America from without and within preoccupied much of the national leaders' time and attention in the first half of the nineteenth century. Some of the external threats were real and others were imagined; however, faced with disputes involving the French and pressures from the British and Spanish, the dangers of depending upon foreign countries or United States ambassadors abroad for intelligence soon became apparent to successive presidents. But little was done by any of them to remedy the deficiency, and their reliance on questionable, often contradictory information planted by foreign envoys in Washington and New York made the situation worse. Fortunately, the buffer provided by the Atlantic Ocean prevented most of these disputes from degenerating into war, although the rumored threats of "invasion" which drifted across the ocean set off the first of America's many spy scares. The immediate response of the press and Congress to these rumors was to spew forth a paranoid babble about spies being everywhere, which spread like wildfire by word of mouth throughout the states. When no sabotage was reported and no armadas materialized on the horizon, the public furor began to subside.

The Federalist party, however, in the great American spirit of political opportunism, refused to let the spy threat die. Since there had been no American intelligence activity at home (aside from mapping expeditions), there was no accurate knowledge of foreign espionage activity in the United States. Rushing into the intelligence void, the Federalists created their own evidence, turning placid immigrants into enemy spies through rabid oratory and diatribes in journals sympathetic to their cause.

In Europe, in response to the republican revolution in France, the conservative European monarchies had been made acutely aware of their vulnerability to domestic subversion and took steps to keep such activities under strict control. The American Federalists sympathized and thoroughly embraced the monarchial view. They felt that war between France and the United States was imminent and argued that aliens were working within the United States to prepare America for French conquest. This concern with alien enemy spies went hand in hand with the Federalists' political fears of the Republican Party. Indeed, the Jeffersonian philosophy of the rights of man had many points of agreement with the feelings which led to the French revolt; but when the Federalists started calling Jefferson a French agent, they carried their spy paranoia too far. The passage of the Federalist-supported Alien and Sedition Acts in 1798 was an extreme political move which directly precipitated the demise of the Federalist party. The aristocratic Federalists found their elite minority swallowed up by an emerging popular majority which included many of the aliens whom they had sought to exclude. In the election of 1800, Thomas Jefferson was elected the third president of the United States.

The three alien laws were aimed at French and Irish immigrants, most of whom supported the Jeffersonian Republicans. The laws raised the waiting period for naturalization from five to fourteen years, thereby delaying immigrants' from obtaining the vote. They also provided for the detention of any alien without cause and authorized the president to expel any alien. Although President John Adams perceived the evils in this proferred arbitrary power and never exercised it, the mere presence of the law on the books scared many Frenchmen out of America.

The Sedition Act was aimed at the Republican press, which was critical of the Federalists. It prohibited publication of "false or malicious" writing against the government, or the inciting of opposition to acts of Congress or the president. Enforcement of the Sedition Act against the Republican press was widespread, although usually only through threat. Whereas no one was prosecuted under the alien acts, twenty-five persons were brought to trial under the Sedition Act and then were convicted. As popular opposition to the Sedition Act increased, including Jefferson and Madison's Virginia and Kentucky resolutions citing violation of the First Amendment, prosecution and harassment diminished. Forty years later, Congress refunded most of the fines collected under the Sedition Act to the families of those convicted. The Alien and Sedition Acts expired or were repealed between 1800 and 1802.

This spy scare was the first in American history, and set an example for its successors by quickly making espionage an excuse for battles involving national party politics. Free speech, the right to privacy, voting rights, xenophobia, and popular versus aristocratic rule were the real issues at stake, but the unknown, fearful consequences of espionage were used by partisan politicians to confuse and mislead the American people. It is a measure of the character of both Hamilton and Adams that despite their vanity and avid Federalism, they declined to battle for the Alien and Sedition Acts—with the exception of the Alien Enemies Act. This act received bipartisan support, in that it would only apply in time of war, at which point both Federalists and Republicans saw the need for counterespionage defenses. In the course of the debate preceding passage of the Alien and Sedition Acts, the Federalist leaders often invented facts, such as the threat of French espionage based on alleged French spying in other countries having lead to the defeat of those nations. In fact, these countries were undermined by natives who sympathized with the French, but not by agents from France.

The Federalists were fighting for their life as a political party. Representative Harrison Gray Otis summed up the Federalist position during the debates when he said, "to punish licentiousness and sedition is not a restraint or abridgment of the freedom of speech or of the press." The only problem was that the Federalists demonstrated their unreasoning fear by equating dissent with sedition. They failed to differentiate between a threat to the union by subversion of the Constitution and a threat to their party by criticism in the press.

If the Federalists had a valid fear, it was best expressed by John Adams, who really did believe that factions ameliorated by foreign intervention could destroy the nation. Adams did not believe in the extreme measures of the Alien and Sedition Acts, but he did state:

. . . divisions are generally harmless, often salutary and seldom very hurtful, except when foreign nations interfere and by their acts and agents excite and ferment them into parties and factions; such interference and influence must be resisted and exterminated or it will end in America as it did anciently in Greece, and in our own time in Europe, in our total destruction, as a republican government and independent power.

In the wake of the Alien and Sedition spy scare things began to return to a somewhat normal routine. However, in 1811—based upon ambiguous intelligence information derived from foreign envoys and American ambassadors—President James Madison became convinced that war with England was inevitable. In connection with his almost Rooseveltian clandestine preparations for war, which he kept secret even from his secretary of state, James Monroe, Madison acted to keep England from using Florida, then under Spanish rule, as a base of operations in the expected war. In consequence, President Madison, in his role as first intelligence officer, sent George Mathews into Florida in 1811 on a double mission. Madison ordered Mathews to proceed secretly to Florida and "assume" the role of American commissioner. In that capacity Mathews was further instructed to accept Florida for the United States if he could influence Spain to give up the territory. In the event that negotiation failed, Mathews was to take Florida and set up a provisional government.*

Mathews, like other special presidential agents in the United States' checkered intelligence history, had an interesting past to qualify him for Madison's mission. He was 72 years old, having been born the son of an Irish immigrant in 1739. At the age of 22, he led a volunteer company against the Indians. He entered the Continental Army in March of 1776, and was a colonel when captured at Germantown after the regiment he commanded plunged too far behind enemy lines. He is said to have received nine baoynet wounds in the action. In December of 1781 he was exchanged, and by the next year had been breveted to the rank of brigadier general after the Virginia campaign.

In 1785, Mathews moved from his home in Virginia to Georgia. A contemporary described him as brave, strong-minded, and almost illiterate. Despite that last characteristic, by 1787 he had been elected governor of his new home state. From 1789 to 1791 he represented Georgia in Congress, and was again governor from 1793 to 1796. In 1798, President Adams wanted Mathews to become the first governor of the Mississippi Territory, but the nomination was withdrawn after Mathews was accused of playing a dubious role in a land speculation scandal.

By 1811 it was time for the Mathews' experience to pay off. Spain refused to cede Florida, but this proved but a small obstacle. Mathews returned to

*Rowan, *op. cit.*, p. 252.

Georgia and assembled a band of sharpshooting frontiersmen and Indian fighters. With these men in support he returned to Florida. He first tried to stir up an insurrection of the English-speaking natives who, at his instigation, declared their independence from Spain on March 17, 1812. The next day Mathews and his men moved in and captured their first city. The sharpshooters, aided by "volunteer" reinforcements from the regular army, moved easily through Florida. They were about to take St. Augustine in June when the secret insurrection began to attract too much attention in Washington. Secretary of State Monroe, who had been informed about the mission by Madison only after it had come to public attention, ordered Mathews to suspend operations.

A gentleman and patriot to the core, Mathews left his troops and went to Washington in an attempt to clear his name. Monroe announced publicly that Mathews had "misunderstood" his instructions. In reality, he had carried them out too well. Unfortunately, the 73-year-old leader never had a chance to set the record straight; he died en route to the capital. His troops were still in Florida in 1813; Andrew Jackson absorbed them under his command when he moved against the British outpost there, which had indeed, as Madison surmised, been established after Mathews was called off. In response to public criticism about American operations in Florida, Congress redirected Jackson toward New Orleans, and some of Mathews' special forces were still serving with him at that city's famous battle.

The War of 1812

American espionage and intelligence activities were minimal for this war. There was certainly no organized American effort, and the British were equally remiss. Some of the only documented espionage was by the "Blue Light Federalists," so named because they signalled British ships along the New England coast with blue lights when it was safe to land their forces.

The prelude to the war revealed a few spy scandals as the British made some half-baked efforts at playing on the Federalists' anglophilic sentiments to divide the nation. Of these, the Burr intrigue probably came closest to success. Burr had visions of a "Western Empire," but he was discovered and forced to flee for his life. He had been employed along with one Charles Williamson to scout American geography, population, political beliefs, and military preparedness. Although the two men made detailed reports, there does not appear to have been any comparable British efforts after the war began to exploit the intelligence they acquired.

Andrew Jackson apparently was the only commander among the American leaders to use agents to good effect in his campaigns. One of his detailed letters transmits information from a "confidential source" about enemy supplies, troop strengths, and battle plans. Jackson was also aided by pirate Jean Lafitte, who engaged his men to scout, spy, and fight for the American general in Louisiana.

The espionage effort which had the greatest effect on the war took place before battle ever started. A man named James Henry was employed with London's knowledge by Sir James Craig, the ex-governor of Canada. Craig ordered Henry to spy in New England and determine the possibilities for a Northeastern secession.

... obtain the most accurate information of the true state of affairs in that part of the Union [New England], which from its wealth, number of inhabitants, and known intelligence and ability of its leading men must naturally possess a very considerable influence over, and will probably lead, the other Eastern States of America in the part that they may take in this important crisis.*

Henry's reward was to be a patronage position in Canada worth a thousand pounds a year. The British reneged on their promise and Henry responded by squealing to Secretary of State Monroe in February of 1812. Monroe reported to Madison, and in March the president passed Henry's revelations on to Congress. The Henry documents played a catalytic role in securing congressional and public approval for the upcoming war. As Madison stated to a Joint Session of Congress on March 9, 1812:

In addition to the effect which the discovery of such a procedure ought to have on the public councils, it will not fail to render more dear to the hearts of all good citizens that happy union of these states which, under Divine Providence, is the guaranty of their liberties, their safety, their tranquility and their prosperity.

The situation was similar to the XYZ Affair at the the turn of the century, before the quasiwar with France. In both cases, a bungled espionage operation was revealed to the American public, raising moral indignation in support of what might otherwise have been a luke-warmly supported war. (President Adams averted war with France in 1800 through negotiation, despite public sentiment for combat.) Other manipulations of public opinion took place during other nineteenth-century wars. For example, during the Seminole War (1835), Chief Osceola was taken prisoner by a band of American soldiers who obtained audience with him under a flag of truce, but the public never got the true story. A hundred years later, in 1935, Secretary of Interior Harold Ickes finally trekked into the Everglades to sign a treaty formally ending hostilities and to apologize for the United States government's lack of ethics.

*Ind, *op. cit.,* "Most Secret and Confidential Letter of Sir James Craig to James Henry," (1809), p. 73.

The Mexican War (1846–1848)

United States intelligence operations during the Mexican War were slight. However, they bear some mention because they reflect the first attempt by the government to use indigenous agents in a "foreign" war, and reveal the attitudes of military commanders toward such a practice. In addition, the Mexican War offers the second assertion of "executive privilege" by a president in connection with the funding and accounting of secret intelligence activities.

The start of the Mexican War, like others before and since, was misrepresented to the American people. The Polk administration reported that Mexico had attacked first when, in fact, Polk had hard evidence in hand which showed that the United States had previously committed direct aggression in Mexican territory. The misrepresentation worked well: public opinion rallied behind the war, especially when it was also made clear that the fighting would be handled by the regular forces, and that no financial sacrifice would be required on the public's part.

Command of United States forces was in the hands of General Zachary Taylor and his deputy, General Winfield Scott. If Taylor had been the sole commander, the war would have been fought without any intelligence not observed through his binonculars. Secretary of War Marcy had instructed Taylor to use natives as scouts, but the general had refused on the grounds that such persons were untrustworthy. Fortunately General Scott, on whom the real responsibility for seeking out and destroying the Mexican forces devolved, recognized the need for intelligence information when fighting in an unfamiliar country where the enemy was likelier to be a peasant than a Mexican soldier in dress uniform.

Scott urged Taylor to authorize the hiring of the "*contrabandistas,*" who were ruffians—or in today's parlance, "insurgents"—opposed to the Paredes regime. Scott even assured Taylor that he held hostages who would guarantee the *contrabandistas'* fidelity, but the offer was nonetheless refused by the stubborn soon-to-be president.

Faced with Taylor's intransigence, Scott, with "back channel" approval from Secretary Marcy and President Polk, set up his own "spy company." At the time, Polk was aware of Taylor's personal popularity and political ambitions, and decided against relieving him on the admittedly difficult grounds of failing to heed the neccessities for intelligence prior to being surprised by the enemy.

To run his spy company, General Scott selected the able Lieutenant Colonel Ethan Allen Hitchcock, the grandson and namesake of the original Green Mountain Boy of the Revolutionary War. Born in Vermont in 1798 and a West Point graduate, Hitchcock served in the Florida War and on Indian patrol in the Northwest. He learned the value of intelligence from Indian scouts first hand, as had George Washington before setting up Revolutionary War intelligence.

In 1855, Hitchcock resigned his commission after an argument with Secretary of War Jefferson Davis, and went to live in St. Louis, where he wrote on general literature and philosophy. Later, General Scott coaxed him back to serve with the Union in the Civil War; Hitchcock became a close friend of both Secretary of War Stanton and President Lincoln.

Hitchcock perceptively determined that his spy network was largely preconstructed. There was no time to recruit agents one by one; therefore, he took over a band of outlaws led by one Dominquez, whom Hitchkock described in his journal as a man with a keen eye, bold as a lion, and with knowledge of the whole country and all his men. The men under Dominquez's leadership meshed perfectly with the standards for spies prescribed by Marcy and Scott, both of whom were reluctant on practical grounds to employ American spies against a non-English-speaking opponent. They wanted agents indigenous to the land and not of American ancestry. Money and excitement were all the motivation they needed to obtain these men's services.

Displaying the instincts of a veteran spymaster, Hitchcock tested Dominquez's reliability by sending him on a minor reconnaissance mission. After the test was passed, the two made an agreement whereby:

. . . for a sum of money yet to be determined, the robbers shall let our people pass without molestation and that they shall, for extra compensation, furnish us with guides, couriers and spies.*

Out of secret funds provided for that purpose, Hitchcock gave Dominquez money and instructed him to enlist professional bandits at $2 a day. Dominquez agreed, but straight out warned Hitchcock that he could not insure their loyalty. Nonetheless, two hundred bandits were recruited and formed into companies which operated under Hitckcock's and Scott's direction. Hitchcock also had prisoners released from Mexican jails to serve in the spy companies, thereby gaining their allegiance through the liberations. As he noted on June 28, 1847, ". . . they find everything. Each man counts, if fact, for two of us, for if we did not employ them they [Santa Anna's forces] would."** Dominquez's unorthodox tactics included the recruitment of other guerrilla bands. If they refused to assist him he would capture their leaders and force their capitulation. Santa Anna tried to induce Dominquez to switch sides, but even when bought he and his men remained loyal to Hitchcock.

Unfortunately, the American government was not as loyal to the Mexican spies after the war as they had been to America. Despite the fact that Polk had Congress appropriate funds to pay the Mexican agents who had to flee Mexico after the war, few ever received their intended reward. Similarly, American

*Journal of Lieutenant Colonel E.A. Hitchcock. Library of Congress, Original Manuscript Division. Entry of June 30, 1847.

**Ibid. Entry of June 28, 1847.

officers who paid Mexicans out of their own pockets were not remunerated by the government. Many loyal men were either abused or forced to return to Mexico, where they faced hostile authorities. Hitchcock commented on the final disposition of his troops in his journal entry of June 5, 1848:

> . . . got here [Orizaba] this morning under the escort of the Spy Company. The Spy Company I am to discharge, with their own consent, by paying them $20 per man at Vera Cruz—except the chief, Dominquez, who will go to New Orleans. He says he would be killed if he remained here. The remainder of the company expect to go to Campeach on an expedition proposed by General Lane on his own hook.

Beyond the failure to provide compensation overtly (though after the fact) to those who had been involved in essentially a covert intelligence operation, the Mexican War also reveals the beginnings of the conflict between the president and Congress over unvouched or secret funds for intelligence purposes. As suggested above, Congress and President Polk fought out the second round in this long-running conflict; the first took place in March 1796, when the House of Representatives requested from the executive branch all documents related to Jay's Treaty. President Washington responded to the request by noting that diplomatic negotiations depend "on secrecy; and even when brought to a conclusion a full disclosure of all the measures, demands or eventual concessions which may have been proposed or contemplated would be extremely impolitic."* Although "all measures" was never satisfactorily defined in the minds of Washington's opponents in the House of Representatives, it was broadly construed to mean the payment of bribes, etc., to insure the support of foreign leaders.

During the Polk administration the question of secret funds and activities surfaced once again.** Disregarding the precedent implied in Washington's earlier refusal, Charles J. Ingersoll, Democrat of Pennsylvania and chairman of the House Foreign Affairs Committee, raised a furor in 1846 over the alleged misuse of foreign intercourse funds by Daniel Webster while he served as secretary of state in previous Whig administrations. Portions of these funds, known as Secret Service Funds, were available for unvouchered use by the secretary of state on the certificate of the president that their expenditure had been for confidential purposes. On April 9, 1846, a resolution of the House of

---

-*George Washington to House of Representatives, March 30, 1796.

**By act of Congress on July 1, 1790, the president was authorized to make payments without specifying the purpose or the recipient if he deemed it essential to the nation's interest. Starting in 1806, a contingency fund was voted each year by Congress as a separate item from the regular diplomatic budget to be used at the discretion of the president or his designated agent to pursue foreign policy. Some legislators later argued that the fund was used because the president wanted to appoint executive agents without seeking Senate approval. Indeed, these funds could allow a president to appoint special envoys, but more Congressmen were upset because of the secrecy involved in such operations.

Representatives introduced by Ingersoll requested Polk to furnish the House
with all records of expenditures of these confidential Secret Service Funds
during Webster's tenure as secretary of state under Presidents Harrison and
Tyler. Although Webster was Polk's political foe, the president, in denying the
House's request on April 20, 1846, wrote:

> The experience of every nation on earth has demonstrated that emergencies may arise
> in which it becomes absolutely necessary for the public safety or the public good to
> make expenditures the very object of which would be defeated by publicity. . . . In no
> nation is the application of such sums made public. In time of war or impending danger
> the situation of the country may make it necessary to employ individuals for the
> purpose of obtaining information or rendering other important services who could
> never be prevailed upon to act if they entertained the least apprehension that their
> names or their agency would in any contingency be divulged. So it may often become
> necessary to incur an expenditure for an object highly useful to the country; . . . But
> this object might be altogether defeated by the intrigues of other powers if our purposes
> were to be made known by the exhibition of the original papers and vouchers to the
> accounting officers of the Treasury. It would be easy to specify other cases which may
> occur in the history of a great nation, in its intercourse of other nations, wherein it
> might become absolutely necessary to incur expenditures for objects which could never
> be accomplished if it were suspected in advance that the items of expenditure and the
> agencies employed would be made public.

Further confrontation on this matter was avoided when Polk subsequently
told the House the total amount of money Webster had spent for confidential
purposes, "but he did not reveal to whom the money had been given or for
what end. The House accepted his judgment."*

Although Polk's action temporarily ended the controversy, out of it was
born the recurring impasse between the executive branch and Congress' (representing the public's) "need to know" about the uses to which unvouchered
funds may be put, and the need for secrecy in such activities. And which today,
some one hundred and thirty years later, continues to bedevil and generate
controversy over the legality and propriety of secret intelligence activities
authorized by the president and carried out in his behalf.

The Heritage Expands: The Civil War Intelligence Experience

As did the Revolutionary War, the Civil War demonstrated that the early
development of American espionage was more dependent on the economic,
political, and social climate of the nation than on any specific decision to
develop an organized intelligence operation. Instead of molding their personalities to the historical character of espionage, American agents forced the

---

*See especially Richard W. Leopold, *The Growth of American Foreign Policy.* New York: Knopf,
1962, pp.32ff.

pursuit of espionage in this brutal war to conform to their search for national ideals. Espionage evolved with the growth of America; it was founded upon individual analysis and ingenuity and original actions rather than on textbook lessons about how and why to practice espionage in the European tradition.

This is not to say that American espionage during the Civil War was totally divorced from the seamier aspects which had long led to its being taboo within the United States. Copying the Revolutionary War experience, certain individuals instinctively followed the European heritage and traded information for money and special privileges which enabled them to run contraband to enemies and play both sides against each other. In fact, the confusion in espionage which allowed such immoral activities to succeed greatly surpassed the confusion of 1776. Lack of centralized intelligence establishments by both North and South created a hodgepodge of independent and overlapping espionage efforts and programs, in the midst of which counterespionage operations became almost totally ineffective; profiteering in contraband and the peddling of false and misleading information flourished. Nor was there a single unifying figure equal to George Washington, although there were several to earn the sobriquet "master spy." From Polk through Buchanan, the growth of the American nation had increased both the size of the army and the government as well as the physical territory which comprised the republic. Washington and the Continental Congress were still hammering out the basic limits of civilian and military power in 1776, with Washington winning the lion's share because of his heritage as both general and statesman. But by 1860, government officials in the executive and legislative branches had carved out their own positions of power; since Andrew Jackson there had been no preeminent individual in the presidency. Consequently, when the Civil War began, the power struggle over how to conduct the war, which involved senators, cabinet members, generals, and Lincoln himself, extended to espionage, where overlapping and not always cooperative operations were established by the various factions. These political power squabbles insured a high degree of ineptitude in espionage operations and organization, and foredoomed the prospects for an ongoing espionage operation after the Civil War. In the face of such official confusion, the few individuals who could ignore or rise above internecine conflict scored the greatest espionage successes. By war's end this group included the leading generals of both sides, a self-righteous ex-vigilante, and an aging spinster in Richmond, each of whom became, for better of worse, a part of America's intelligence heritage.

The Pinkerton Era

On the Union side, espionage's incompatibility with the idealized morality of the federal government—as well as the weaknesses of presidents from Polk through Buchanan—had effectively precluded the formation of an operating intelligence agency prior to the Civil War. At first the War, Navy, and State

Departments each pursued individual ideas for intelligence programs. The War Department was hamstrung by the inept and corrupt secretaryship of Simon Cameron (whom Lincoln dispatched as the American minister to Russia in short order, thereby clearing the way for the appointment of Edwin M. Stanton); both Lincoln and Commanding General Winfield Scott turned to Secretary of State Seward for direction. Seward ordered detectives into the South and Canada. They agreed that Scott should instruct all department commanders to appoint their own chiefs of secret service. These chiefs in turn assembled mixed groups of soldiers and civilian agents. District and post provost marshals also appointed their own secret service chiefs. This proliferation of intelligence organizations started Union intelligence off on a confused course from which it never fully recovered.

What little intelligence activity the Union did achieve in the first two years of the war (along with most of its major blunders) may be credited to the work of Allan Pinkerton. The son of a policeman, Pinkerton was born in Scotland in 1819. His father's failing health, the result of an attack while on duty, led the future detective to apprentice himself to a cooper at an early age. His experience as a laborer led him to become active in England's Chartist movement, which sought to limit privilege and promote the rights of working people. From all accounts, the young Pinkerton was a ready participant in Chartist plotting, protesting, and rioting.

At the age of 23, Pinkerton decided to marry and leave the Chartist conflicts for others to resolve. He and his wife boarded a ship for Canada, and arrived belatedly but safely, having been separated after their ship ran aground off the coast of Nova Scotia. Pinkerton decided not to settle in Canada, opting first for Detroit, and soon after for Chicago. They arrived penniless, but Allan found a tinker for whom to work, and they saved enough money to move to the nearby Scottish immigrant settlement of Dundee, Illinois. Here Pinkerton established a successful cooper's business and began dabbling in detective work for his neighbors. Pinkerton also revived his interest in individual rights as a foreman on the underground railway, which transported slaves from the South to freedom in the North. Through this period, Pinkerton supported abolition with a fervor equal to that he had previously demonstrated in support of the Chartist cause.

News of Pinkerton's early successes as a detective reached Cook County, and he was hired by that area's police chief. From there he went on to become one of the founders of Chicago's police force and its only detective. Soon Pinkerton's reputation came to the attention of the local railroad moguls, and they prevailed upon him to set up a private detective agency specializing in railway security. In 1850, the Pinkerton Detective Service opened with an ever-vigilant gazing eye as its symbol, underscribed by the motto "We Never Sleep." In addition to its railroad work, the agency handled local mysteries and became famous for solving cases whose resolution depended on attention to obscure details. Pinkerton also handled counterfeiting and fraud investigations for the Treasury Department in Washington and developed the most up-to-date criminal files then in America.

Pinkerton's first espionage work for the United States involved an accidental discovery in the period just prior to the outbreak of the Civil War. While infiltrating bands of rebel sympathizers in Baltimore who had threatened to blow up the railway bridges of a Pinkerton client, the agency's detectives uncovered a plot to assassinate the newly elected Abraham Lincoln as he stopped in Baltimore enroute to Washington for his inauguration. When Pinkerton contacted Lincoln, the president-elect was reluctant to believe in the conspiracy; however, Pinkerton succeeded in obtaining Lincoln's acquiescence to a counterplot to avert the assassination attempt. On the night before Lincoln was scheduled to reach Baltimore, Pinkerton arranged for a special train to speed the new president through the trap. All went smoothly until the early hours of the morning, when the train reached Baltimore; there it was necessary to transfer aboard the regular train to Washington, which used a set of tracks on the opposite side of the city. Pinkerton and Lincoln hopped in a coach with drawn shades and navigated a prearranged route guarded by Pinkerton agents, who waved lanterns to indicate that all was clear at designated checkpoints. The secret party reached the station without difficulty, but the Washington train was delayed. The president and the detective spent two uneasy hours inside the coach. Fortunately, Lincoln was not as worried as Pinkerton, and filled the time telling anecdotes from his youth to the assembled agents. Just before dawn, the Washington train arrived and safely sped Lincoln to the capital.

When the war began, Lincoln remembered Pinkerton and summoned him to Washington to examine the Union's security situation. Pinkerton conducted a brief investigation and rightfully warned the president of the widespread spying, sabotage, and corruption in Washington being sponsored by the Confederacy. Lincoln listened attentively, but chose not to have Pinkerton organize a detective force for the government. Instead the Scotsman returned home, where his old friend George McClellan, formerly of the Illinois Central Railroad, had been placed in command of the Ohio Volunteers. McClellan put the detective in charge of his secret service subject to Scott's orders, and when McClellan assumed command of the Army of the Potomac, Pinkerton followed him to Washington and received his chance to found the first national secret service organization. It was not a very successful effort. Pinkerton's problems were a combination of the government's lack of organization, his inexperience in espionage, and his blind devotion to McClellan. As a first-rate detective, Pinkerton related most easily to counterespionage work, using a small and efficient team of agents to round up Confederate operatives in Washington. Unfortunately, he never developed the required manpower to conduct a thorough cleansing of the capital, but notable successes were scored, including the arrest of Rose O'Neale Greenhow, one of the South's ablest spies.

When it came to positive intelligence, Pinkerton was out of his field. A superior judge of counterfeit notes, the detective could not estimate the size of an enemy army to save his life. Indeed, if he had been able to, and if his hero McClellan had not been so reluctant to attack the outnumbered Confederate troops, many Union lives would have been saved. One man who paid the ultimate price was Pinkerton's most outstanding agent, Timothy Webster.

Webster was an Englishman, born in New Haven in 1818. He came to America with his family and worked as a machinist in Princeton, New Jersey. Pinkerton met him in 1853 at the New York World's Fair, where Webster was working as a police sergeant. The detective immediately admired the policeman for his intelligence as well as his physical size and strength; he hired Webster on the spot for his fledgling detective agency. Over time, Webster proved to be a remarkable actor, a crack shot, and a man of amazing endurance. As a spy, he was far superior to his employer.

Baltimore was Webster's first Civil War assignment. In early 1861, Pinkerton sent "Big Tim" to infilitrate a group of known Rebel conspirators in that city. Webster soon established himself as one of the more rabid Southern sympathizers around town, and uncovered plots to blow up bridges and assassinate Lincoln. His was one of the lanterns marking the escape route as Pinkerton and the president-elect traversed Baltimore in February. He also discovered caches of rifles for Confederate troops, and exposed the practice of smuggling contraband to the South under the hoopskirts worn by Baltimore women. Large quantities of quinine and other medical supplies had been reaching Richmond through this method.

Webster left Baltimore in March, journeying South to study Southern fortifications for McClellan's Ohio Volunteers. When McClellan and Pinkerton moved to Washington, they asked Webster to join them. They requested the star agent to return to Baltimore, where he was welcomed by his conspiratorial friends as a hero of the Confederacy.

For the next ten months, Webster proved himself the most effective double agent of the Civil War. He quickly rose in prominence among Baltimore's rebel underground, and was elected to the secret Knights of Liberty. This subversive group worked directly with the Southern army to organize anti-Union conspiracy and sabotage in Baltimore. Webster tipped off Pinkerton about the location of one of the group's meetings, and federal troops engineered a raid which captured much of Baltimore's rebel leadership. Webster managed to be one of the few men who "escaped" the meeting. This alleged act of resource and valor augmented the agent's already substantial reputation for quick-wittedness, strength, and marksmanship among Baltimore's Confederate community.

In October 1861, shortly after the raid, Webster announced that he planned a trip to Richmond in order to escape the pressure of Union detectives trailing him in Maryland. Friends wrote notes of introduction to Confederate leaders in Richmond, and many individuals gave Webster letters to friends and relatives in the South. He stopped in Washington to allow inspection of the mail by Pinkerton, and then arrived in Richmond, where he delivered his mail and volunteered his services to the Richmond *Examiner*. He ran messages for the newspaper, and provided them with inconsequential information from the North. While carrying his messages, Webster took the opportunity to survey the military installations surrounding Richmond. He paid a call on Confederate Secretary of War Judah P. Benjamin, giving him military information about the North which he had been instructed to plant by Pinkerton and McClellan. In turn, Benjamin provided him with a pass to Manassas and back across the Potomac. From there, Webster delivered information to Washington and returned to Baltimore.

In Baltimore, Tim Webster rested long enough to enjoy his hero's welcome, distribute letters he had picked up in the South for Northern citizens, and collect letters with which to return across the Potomac. By this time he was so well known as a Baltimore Confederate that he was arrested by two Pinkerton agents unaware of his true identity. When they turned Webster over to Pinkerton, the chief of detectives quickly arranged for his agent to once again escape. This time the break was made as he was being transferred to a federal prison. This story, coupled with the earlier escapes, enhanced Webster's reputation even more in Rebel opinion.

For his next journey South, Webster was joined by another Pinkerton agent, John Scobell. Scobell had been the Mississippi slave of a Scotsman who educated and freed him. As part of his education Scobell had learned a wealth of Scottish ballads, which enabled him to spy throughout the South posing as a wandering minstrel. He also assumed roles as a servant, roustabout, and fisherman to fool the Confederates, who would hardly suspect a black of being intelligent enough to be a Union spy.

The return of Webster and Scobell to Richmond was delayed when the boat on which they were travelling sank in the Potomac. The two spies spent hours in the icy water helping other passengers to escape. As a result Webster developed a severe case of inflammatory rheumatism which plagued him for the next several months and indirectly caused his death.

When Webster finally reached Richmond, he was hailed by both Benjamin and President Jefferson Davis. He delivered his mail, checked in at the *Examiner*, and then obtained a pass from Benjamin to tour the South. Webster made extensive observations, fulfilled his duties as mail carrier, and received special messages from both Benjamin and Davis to carry to conspirators in the North. Webster again allowed Pinkerton and McClellan to read his letters before delivering them in Baltimore. His information gave an accurate picture of Southern military strength and led to the capture of several more conspirators, but with the dawdling McClellan in command, the information was never effectively utilized.

Webster made his mail delivery and pick-up in Baltimore, and then embarked on yet another trip to Richmond. This time he travelled with Hattie Lawton, another Pinkerton agent. It rained throughout their journey to the Rebel capital, and by the time they reached Richmond, Webster's rheumatism had flared up so badly that he became bedridden. Mrs. Lawton stayed by his side and nursed him, but she failed to apprise Pinkerton of the situation. The chief of detectives panicked when no word was received from his leading agent, and decided to take drastic action.

From Washington, Pinkerton dispatched two agents, Pryce Lewis and John Scully, to find Webster. The decision was a risky one, given that Lewis and Scully had both been used for counterespionage work; their faces and identities were familiar to individuals since deported south of the Potomac. The use of a small number of agents to conduct both positive and counterintelligence showed a limitation of scope and effectiveness in Pinkerton's espionage operation, even though he believed that his minimal number of agents improved security.

Realizing that Scully or Lewis might be recognized, Pinkerton checked his intelligence reports for the whereabouts of Southerners whom the two detectives had arrested in their counterespionage duties. Discovering that none was reported living in Richmond, Pinkerton sent the men South. The question of how he could be so certain that there were no witnesses in Richmond when he was not even certain that Webster was in the city casts one more shadow over Pinkerton's qualifications to manage an espionage operation.

To his credit, Pinkerton selected excellent agents. Scully had travelled in disguise to Richmond during one of Webster's previous journeys, and Lewis had carried out one of the more gutsy and successful spy roles of all time. Pinkerton had Lewis, a native of England, disguise himself as a young British noble looking for cotton investments. Equipping him with a fancy coach, expensive clothes, champagne, and a servant in the person of Sam Bridgman, another agent originally from Mississippi, Pinkerton sent Lewis southward shortly after the outbreak of war. Befriending Rebel troops and officers with their wine and charming alibi, they were guided through many military installations and told of others. Bridgman's love of rum, and his habit of speaking too freely when he drank it, eventually revealed their mission. Fortunately, a friendly Southerner drew them a map which allowed them to escape via back roads to Pinkerton and McClellan in Ohio.

On the 1862 trip, there were no disguises for Scully and Lewis to use when they reached Richmond. They visited the ailing Webster and Lawton, but were soon identified by several of the individuals whom Pinkerton has assured them would not be in Richmond. Webster risked his own life and cover story by vouching for the men during the subsequent trial, but both were convicted and sentenced to death. The two spies were separated in different jails, and Lewis almost succeeded in a daring escape, but was recaptured on the outskirts of the city. Meanwhile, a wily Confederate counterespionage man sent an alleged priest into Scullly's cell to convince the spy that a full confession would be the best thing for his soul. A good Catholic, Scully accommodated the request, including a revelation of the true identities of Timothy Webster and Hattie Lawton. As a result, Lewis' and Scully's death sentences were commuted, but

Webster, the ailing friend of the Confederacy, was quickly tried and sentenced to hang. Pinkerton received word of his bungled operation, and ran to Lincoln with the news. Even direct appeals by Lincolon and Secretary Stanton after a hastily convened cabinet meeting failed to save Webster's life. Lawton was apparently lost in the shuffle, and benefitted from the reluctance of Victorian gentlemen to prosecute women. This chauvinistic error allowed women to perform some of the most valuable espionage of the Civil War.

Although he served only for a short time, Webster must be counted a great double agent. Without Pinkerton's mistake his value to the Union would have been inestimable (not to mention his potential worth to Pinkerton's private agency after the war). Webster's death was only one of Pinkerton's failings. Unfamiliar with military intelligence, Pinkerton consistently misinterpreted his agents' accurate field reports of troop strengths. The resulting inflated estimates helped scare McClellan, already a reluctant warrior, from pressing attacks which might have brought the war to an earlier resolution. Pinkerton also failed to communicate well with other government branches and other army officers. "Little Mac" was his hero, and anyone who did not support the general became an instant enemy. When McClellan felt threatened by criticism from government officials, he assigned Pinkerton to spy on his critics in Washington, thereby hurting the Union's overall intelligence program. Pinkerton left headquarters when McClellan was relieved of command. The detective served his country for the remainder of the war, but concentrated on cotton-fraud claims in newly captured territory of the South. Pinkerton was a loyal Unionist, a staunch abolitionist, and earned some intelligence victories for the causes in which he so firmly believed. His recognition of the importance of exhaustive data files to detail intelligence was a first for America. If he had been better able to adapt his detective skills to those of espionage and see beyond McClellan to coordinate a broad range of espionage activities, his contribution could have been far greater.

Lafayette Charles Baker: Spymaster Extraordinaire

While Pinkerton and McClellan were making their awkward exit from official Washington, a new star was rapidly rising in the Union's espionage ranks. The man was Lafayette Charles Baker, another of America's self-educated spies. By the end of the war he was the most controversial figure in the capital; hated by many, loved by few, and misunderstood by all, due to the cloak of secrecy his job required. The full scope of his wartime activities may never be realized, but he left behind clues which allow an examination of his character and effectiveness.

Baker's contribution to America's intelligence heritage reached back to the spirit which produced the United States. He was born on October 13, 1825, in Stafford, New York, the seventh child of Cynthia and Remember Baker. Remember was a veteran of the War of 1812 and had served under General

Winfield Scott in the Mexican War, but spent most of his life as a farmer and outdoorsman. Lafayette's father took his military experience seriously, and ran his family like a pack of recruits. A strict Puritan, he made up for the religious prohibition of work on Sunday by ordering chores from dawn to dusk on the remaining days of the week. No blasphemy or drinking was permitted in the Baker family, and since education did not rank highly on Remember Baker's list of objectives, the children were forced to teach themselves. Young Lafe learned the basics of reading and writing, and cultivated talents for horsemanship and shooting which would later save his life as a spy. In 1838, the family began moving West, finally settling in the rugged Michigan territory. It was there that Remember Baker died after his return from Mexico, and whence Lafayette ran off as a teenager to assume the life of a wandering adventurer in the cities of the Northeast.

Both the severity of his father's character and his capacity to survive under adverse circumstances revealed themselves during Lafe's career as a secret agent. But perhaps the most influential events of his childhood were those which he never directly experienced. These events were contained in his father's tales of Lafayette's great-grandfather, the original Remember Baker, who lived prior to the Revolutionary War.

Captain Remember Baker was one of the three original leaders of the legendary Green Mountain Boys, along with his first cousins Ethan Allen and Seth Warner. Lafayette's father would regale his children with true though sometimes embellished accounts of how Captain Baker killed a bear using only a short-bladed knife, and how he killed scores of men during the battle of Fort Ticonderoga. The tradition of the righteous outlaw, which the young Baker preserved in his lifetime, had been cultivated by his great-grandfather with the Green Mountain Boys. The Warner, Baker, and Allen families had claimed land for themselves in the wilds of Vermont contrary to the wishes of New York colony land speculators. Border disputes followed, leading the Green Mountain Boys to become vigilantes of the forest. Settlers who attempted to claim land in Vermont on the basis of certificates from New York were terrorized and often burned out of their cabins. New York constables responded by placing a bounty on the heads of Baker and Allen. The pair countered by offering double the reward for the capture of any New York constable, thereby showing the same sense of sangfroid and audaciousness which Lafayette Baker later demonstrated in dealing with the threats of government officials.

This same spirit of daring led directly to Remember Baker's death, and was passed on to plague his great-grandson a century later. While leading a patrol to spy on British outposts near Montreal, Captain Baker stumbled upon a group of Indian scouts allied with the British. Baker recognized that the colonists had no quarrel with the Indians, and hoped to talk his way out of the confrontation. He positioned his men in the underbrush and walked out alone to negotiate with the Indian leader. As he walked into the clearing an

Indian shot and killed him, precipitating a battle during which several braves carried off Remember Baker's body. They decapitated Baker and paraded into Montreal with his head on a stick. Word of the incident quickly reached General Schuyler, Baker's superior officer, but the British had been sickened by the display and buried the body. On Schuyler's word that Captain Baker had merely been attempting another of his daring and unorthodox ploys, Commanding General Washington decided it more valuable to preserve stable relations with the Indians than to protect Baker's good name.

Armed with this special education from his childhood and the experience of several years on the road, Lafayette Baker reached Philadelphia in 1852, and shortly thereafter married Jennie Curry. The couple settled down and tried to have children; when none arrived Lafe began to grow restless with the city. His sharp mind perceived many prospects for successful business ventures among the local confusion and political corruption, but his brother Milo's letters painted enticing pictures of the gold fever in California. In 1856, he left to join him.

En route to the west coast, the first of Lafayette Baker's many recorded incidents of violence occurred. According to Baker, while crossing the Panama isthmus in a small boat, a Panamanian attacked one of the passengers. Baker shot the man and jumped overboard into the shallow swamp, evading several pursuers who soon gave him up for lost. A fugitive, Baker reached the American consulate and hid there for several days. He shaved off his red beard, disguised his 5'10" frame in native guise and escaped on a boat bound for San Francisco. Throughout his career, Baker used numerous disguises, including many variations of beards, moustaches and sideburns of various colors, to confuse his enemies.

Once in San Francisco, it took Baker little time to blend in with the city's rough and tumble lifestyle. The product of his Puritan heritage—including a membership in the Sons of Temperance, which he had acquired in 1848—he fell in with the law enforcers rather than the outlaws, although in early San Francisco the distinction between the two was not always clear. In 1856, he joined the local vigilance committee, and swore the Vigilante Creed:

No thief, burglar, incendiary, assassin, ballot box stuffer, or other disturber of the peace shall escape punishment, either by quibbles of the law, the insecurity of the prisons, the carelessness or corruption of the police, or the laxity of those who pretend to administer the justice.*

In carrying out this oath, Lafayette participated in the night raids, exhaustive and brutal investigative sessions, entrapments, evidence framings, and recruitment of crooks and prostitutes as spies and informers which would later become his modus operandi as the Union's secret service chief. Baker enjoyed

*Jacob Mogelever, *Death to Traitors.* New York: Doubleday, 1960, p. 34.

his work and performed well. When he left for the East on New Year's Day of 1861, a group of San Francisco bankers gave him $250 and a cane of manzanita wood with a gold and quartz head to commemorate his efforts.

By this time, Lafayette Baker was ever ready for violence, having adopted the practice of wearing his twin pistols wherever he travelled. In addition, he had discovered a new hero to join his great-grandfather in his personal pantheon. The man was François Vidocq, a French criminal turned detective. Vidocq helped to introduce "brainwashing," entrapment, and manufactured evidence into law enforcement on a systematic—almost scientific—basis, and believed it better to wrong a hundred innocents rather than allow one guilty person to escape punishment. He was a master of disguises, adopting the role of spy in the French underworld to solve most of his cases, just as Baker would later pose as a Rebel to apprehend the Union's enemies.

Vidocq's career set an interesting example which Baker's roughly paralleled. The Frenchman served in the army, then left to pursue a life of crime. He was arrested, but escaped; he later turned informer. His informant's role began to include detective work, and Vidocq was soon appointed chief of detectives, staffing his department largely with ex-convicts. He retired to start a paper mill, again using convict laborers, but the business failed and he reentered police work. Unwilling to submit himself to the day-to-day order of a superior (Baker also demanded such freedom), Vidocq plotted to regain his position as detective chief. He planned and executed a daring theft which he then solved. Unfortunately, he was discovered, fired and discredited; he died in obscurity.

Like Vidocq, Baker had familiarized himself with both sides of the law; he ended his eastward journey in a confused national capital preparing itself for war. Lafayette's patriotism began to stimulate his itch for activity. Mirroring the spirit of equality which his great-grandfather had shown in dealing with the Indians, Baker was a violent opponent of slavery. He would later call it the "soul of the rebellion" and criticize the Union for not opposing slavery at the beginning of the Civil War. Baker decided the best hope of achieving his ideals lay in support of the government. His arrogance prevented him from enlisting like other men; instead, he gained entrée to Commanding General Winfield Scott, under whose orders he hoped to apply the experience of his travels and the lessons of Vidocq.

General Scott was himself one of the Union's problems. At 74, Scott embodied a lifetime of military knowledge, but his 6'7" frame was so bloated that he was incapable of mounting a horse on which to lead his troops into battle. One of the general's chief concerns in 1861 was to obtain intelligence of Virginia's "Black Horse" Cavalry. From his experience with Colonel Hitchcock and intelligence during the Mexican War, Scott knew that effective espionage and swift, accurate reporting was essential to military victory. Baker was sized up as a good potential agent. The general gave him ten $20 gold pieces and sent him toward Virginia with instructions not to carry a weapon, since the civilian Baker was to impersonate would not ordinarily be armed. Although this kind of informal recruiting of a spy might appear to be a historical phenomenon associated with an earlier and simpler time, it is not. Even today, the most sophisticated intelligence organizations have precise procedures to handle "walk-ins," and while these may not involve giving the would-be spy some pieces of gold they often do include preliminary field tests before a spy is actually processed and placed on their secret rolls.

The imaginative but inexperienced new operative left Scott's suite at the Willard Hotel and proceeded to a photography salon, where he purchased a camera and tripod. Baker knew that at this early stage of the photographic art, every soldier wanted a picture to send home; he believed his equipment would be a passport into the military camps. He marched to Alexandria, where he met up with the Second Maine Regiment and asked to see the colonel. The officer welcomed the photographer and requested a panoramic shot of the camp. Baker arranged the regiment on a knoll and perched himself on a nearby hill. As the soldiers posed, Baker backed up, pretending to frame his shot; he soon backed into a nearby wood and ran away. Two hours later he was stopped by a Union patrol and returned to the angry colonel from Maine. He was referred to the provost marshal, General Heintzelman, who punished Baker by sending him all the way back to General Scott. Scott accepted the prisoner, laughed at the neophyte spy, and instructed him to try again.

This time Baker chose a new tack. He watched an extended string of soldiers filing across Long Bridge and fell in at the end of one of the last regiments. He was noticed and arrested, but pleaded an innocent photographer's role and was released. At that point Baker abandoned his camera and selected a more imaginative route for his third attempt. He walked for miles through southern Maryland until he arrived, exhausted, at Port Tobacco. There he slept in a field and awoke to find a Negro working close by. The man agreed to row Baker across the Potomac near Dumfries in return for one of Scott's gold pieces. Once across the river, Baker was soon picked up by a Confederate patrol. He had a cover story and letters to substantiate the legitimacy of his presence in the South, but the soldiers followed orders and led their prisoner toward camp. In a few miles Baker spied a tavern, and had little trouble convincing his captors to join him for a round of drinks to escape the July heat. Normally a teetotaler, Baker used his poison for a purpose in this case—before long the soliders had dozed off under the generous lubrication provided by their prisoner.

Back on the road toward Manassas, Baker was again taken by a Confederate patrol. He explained that he was Sam Munson, the son of a Tennessee judge whom Baker had once known, and that he had business in Richmond. He showed them the contrived letters of introduction which he had prepared in Washington. The soldiers were once again not to be fooled and took Baker to General Bonham. The spy-conscious Bonham sent Baker on to General Beauregard, and although the Creole general wanted to hang Baker on the spot, he had the agent thrown in the stockade pending further investigation.

Exhausted and with his life hanging in the balance, Baker quickly made friends with his young guard and gave him a gold piece to bring back a meal. The soldier came back with a large supper, including a bottle of wine which the abstemious inmate cheerfully passed on to his captor. After supper, Baker bribed the officer in charge of the stockade and began a tour of the vicinity with his guard as escort. After a brief stop at a hotel where Lafe further fortified his companion with drink, Baker undertook a systematic reconnaissance of the camp, noting commanders, numbers, and names of brigades. When he inquired after the Black Horse Cavalry, the guard promptly directed him to those notorious troops. Soon his companion wandered off, and Baker played the obedient prisoner by returning to his cell unescorted.

Once there, Baker found that Beauregard had prepared a couple of tests. First, two men came up to Baker and tried to get him to carry messages to Washington for them. Baker reported them to Beauregard as traitors. Next, a young woman entered his cell posing as a purveyor of religious tracts. She told Baker that she knew he was a Union agent and that his secret would be safe with her. Again following his instincts to avoid a trap, the novice spy played dumb and avoided incriminating himself. The woman turned out to be Belle Boyd, a Rebel spy who was to be Baker's captive in later years.

That evening Baker was put on a train and sent under guard to Richmond. He surveyed cities, camps, and troops as he went, making mental notes of Southern troop strength. In Richmond, Baker was taken straight to the top. At the time, Confederate intelligence organizations suffered from the same confusion as Northern ones, and President Jefferson Davis was left to handle much of the war's early espionage and counterespionage by himself. The first time Davis interrogated the alleged Mr. Munson, Baker played the outraged innocent and stuck to his cover story. Later Davis summoned Baker to a session where the Rebel president questioned him about Union forces around Washington. Baker made plausible answers, but avoided revealing anything he believed would hamper the Union effort. Finally, Davis abandoned his questioning and had an orderly fetch another guest: a man from Knoxville, Munson's home town.

At this point Baker seemed to have run out of rope, but he had noticed that each time someone was brought into Davis' presence the visitor's name was printed on a card which was handed to the president before the visitor's entrance. When the card for the Knoxville guest was presented, Baker sneaked a look at the name. The surprised citizen entered to a warm greeting from Baker: "Why, Brock! Good to see you! Remember me? Sam Munson, Judge Munson's son from California." Brock thought he recognized Baker, and Davis dismissed both men. The president was not easily deceived, however. The next day he sent Brock to visit Baker and check his identity. They had a long conversation, during which Brock showed a strong propensity for storytelling; Baker let him run on, interrupting only to laugh with his companion and encourage him at appropriate places. The bluff succeeded and Brock assured Davis that Baker was indeed Sam Munson.

Several days later, Davis had Baker released and gave him the run of Richmond, but forbade him to leave the city without a pass. Baker spent his time touring the Rebel capital, making a few acquaintances and creating an extensive mental file on the city. When he determined that he had risked enough time in the South, he obtained a temporary pass to Fredericksburg and from there hired a Negro to row him across the Rappahannock. He planned to make a swift trip to the Potomac and cross to Washington, but, as on his original journey, a Rebel patrol found him. The officer-in-charge informed Baker that his pass was only good to Fredericksburg and that he would have to return there with the patrol. Baker again improvised and acquired a pronounced limp which would have retarded the officer's journey. As a result, the officer left Baker with a guard and rode toward Fredericksburg with Lafe's pass, planning to check on his identity.

Once again the fledgling Union spy was left in the care of a Rebel guard with a weakness. This time the soldier was tired from having been on duty throughout the previous night. He sat down with Baker in the shade of a tree and quickly dozed off, assuming the lame man posed little threat. The prisoner stealthily slipped the revolver from his slumbering keeper's holster and rode away on his horse. Unable to travel the main roads, Baker lost himself in a thick wood. He stumbled upon a farm in a clearing and received a meal and directions to the Potomac.

Lafe left the farm on horseback, but the trees were so thick that he was forced to double back to the clearing just at nightfall. He got rid of the horse and burrowed into a haystack to spend the night. Near dawn a Confederate search party arrived looking for him. Baker moved into the middle of the haystack and readied his revolver. As the Rebels searched the farm, swords pierced his haystack several times, but each thrust missed Baker, and the patrol departed.

Baker scrambled out of the haystack and ran toward the Potomac. When he reached the river, he spied a tent and a rowboat pulled up on shore. He approached the two Confederates in the tent, joined them for some fried trout, and asked to purchase their boat. They replied that the vessel was not for sale at any price since the Yankees were breaking up all small craft along the river. Baker decided to steal the boat after his hosts fell asleep. One of the soldiers was suspicious of the visitor, however, and refused to retire until Baker joined them in the tent. Baker acquiesced, and feigned sleep until his companions were snoring; but each time he tried to leave, one of them stirred. The older soldier reached out several times to assure himself that Baker was still asleep.

Near dawn, Baker finally slipped out and ran for the boat. With its one available broken oar, he began rowing toward the middle of the river. The soldiers awakened and pursued him along the shore. Baker killed one and the other proved a poor shot. The shooting awakened nearby Confederates, and shortly many rifles opened up on the fleeing spy; but the Potomac's friendly current swiftly carried Baker to its northern shore. He rested there briefly, and then reported to General Scott. He referred Baker to Secretary of State Seward, who was then coordinating Union espionage and counterespionage activity.

Seward's task was an impossible one. In addition to his duties as secretary of state, he was expected to cover for Simon Cameron's incompetence by handling intelligence operations for the Union. Pinkerton was of some assistance when Seward's plans coincided with McClellan's. The secretary had dispatched a handful of agents to Canada and into the South, but the most immediate problem involved attempts to rid Washington of its multitude of traitors and enemy agents. As the nation had been preparing for war prior to overt secession, those planning Southern strategy had been able to use the capital as a target in which to position the Confederacy's spies. This gave the South distinct intelligence advantage, since the Union did not know where the Confederate capital would be located, and therefore could plant no advance agents. Lincoln's suspension of habeas corpus had already allowed Seward to arrest more than 1,000 persons and send them to the Old Capitol prison, but Washington was still crawling with spies.

One congressman decided to help Seward in his counterespionage efforts, but because of his disorganized techniques his success was diminished by the added confusion it brought; even more room was left for Confederate espionage activity. The legislator was John P. Potter. He was a rabid anti-Southerner who used influence to have himself appointed chairman of the House Committee to Investigate Government Employees. In actions at least as unlawful as those used by another elected official from Wisconsin ninety years later, Potter attacked officials who retained disloyal employees, and accused hundreds of individuals. He finally arrested over 300 secessionists, but in the process untold innocent employees were slandered by secret informers. Potter's method was to strike without warning; firing first and filing charges later. Informers were taken at their word and the accused were not allowed an appearance to answer charges made against them. The necessity for loyalty transcended civil rights in the minds of Potter and his followers. Lincoln added to Potter's cause by approving stronger loyalty oaths for government employees. Although it may be difficult to excuse such blatantly unjust acts from a modern perspective, Lafayette Baker later expressed the accepted rationale of the time in defending the actions of his National Detective Bureau.

The Detective Bureau, although contrary to the spirit of our republican institutions in time of peace, is indispensable in time of war. . . . There is nothing in the secret service that demands a violation of honor, or a sacrifice of principle, beyond the ordinary rules of warfare.*

---

*Lafayette Charles Baker, *History of the United States Secret Service.* Private Printing, Philadelphia, 1867, p. 34.

Given his shortage of manpower, Seward immediately put Baker to work. In his first assignment he posed as a Confederate arms purchaser and cooperated with Philadelphia police chief Benjamin Franklin to entrap a group of contrabanders. In November, the secretary sent him into southern Maryland. There Baker discovered an extensive network of Rebel communication points, many of which were government post offices. Lafayette mapped out the territory and returned with 300 Indiana cavalrymen of whom he was placed in command, although at the time he held no official rank. The ensuing raid captured many spies and included the terrorizing of the populace and the burning of buildings. This style, similar to that of the Green Mountain Boys, would characterize the operations of the National Detective Bureau's private cavalry later in the war.

As Lafayette was earning his spurs, Abraham Lincoln unloaded the burden of Simon Cameron. The former Pennsylvania political boss turned secretary of war had been so busy accepting bribes from his cronies seeking army supply contracts that he had little time for the important duties of his office. The president shipped Cameron off to Russia as a minister in an effort to keep him as far away from important decisions as possible. Edwin M. Stanton was the replacement. Stanton was a straightforward, hardworking individual who believed in results and did not always achieve them through the most circumspect methods. He took over Seward's intelligence operations, and on February 15, 1862, the transfer of secret service operations was formally made to the War Department.

Baker's successes under Seward made him the prime candidate for secret service chief. The secretary of war called the ex-vigilante into his office and appointed him director of the newly created National Detective Police, telling him:

Your job is going to be the dirtiest of this dirty war, Mr. Baker. You will be hated as no man ever was hated, but you will perform a service no man ever had the chance to perform for our great country. Furthermore, Mr. Baker, you will never be permitted to disclose the authority for your actions. You will choose your own men. You will receive secret funds from me. You will account to me and only me.*

Armed with Stanton's commission, Baker established the National Detective Bureau at 217 Pennsylvania Avenue. He began recruiting agents from all over the country, including his brother Stan and cousin Byron. Stan's journals record that his brother was a nervous and restless daredevil. By the end of 1862, Lafe was beginning to show wrinkles and had acquired a bit of a stoop, but his stamina and skill with guns and horses remained undiminished. Stan commented on his brother's personality:

*Mogelever, *op. cit.,* p. 86.

He was exceedingly egotistical, fond of doing remarkable daredevil, and often foolish things, to excite surprise and astonishment in others. His propensity to exaggerate, especially through self-laudation was rather pronounced; this characteristic caused some slight shadows of doubt to be cast over his tales of personal adventures.*

In the early stages of the bureau, Baker concentrated his efforts on trying to clean up corruption in Washington. One of his first campaigns was against the Quartermaster Corps. Under Cameron's corrupt leadership all levels of command in the Quartermaster Corps had become tainted with the same avarice which had motivated the secretary. Supply officers in the field falsified their records to reduce contractors' payments, and sent captured materials back to their families in the North. Confederate agents were paying employees of the Washington supply depot to divert military equipment to Rebel troops. This behavior sounds too familiar in light of America's recent experiences elsewhere in the world; but in 1862, when the troops were singing "We're Coming Father Abraham" and politicians were exhorting people to sacrifice themselves for "Union Forever!" it induced a cold rage in Lafayette Baker. He was determined to stamp out the corruption and destroy those responsible for it.

Another focus of the bureau's early activity resulted from Baker's personal abhorrence of alcohol and prostitution. A teetotaler and a man so busy he rarely visited his wife in Philadelphia, Baker believed that the evils of loose women and drink could only interfere with the Union's war effort. He raised the ire of Union officers by preventing "ladies" from attending the officers' 'tent parties' in the field, but Stanton backed his secret service chief. Lafe also confiscated liquor shipments bound for Union generals.

Stan and Byron Baker had misgivings about their commander's preoccupation with the army's morality. They already questioned the propriety of agents Lafe was assembling. Many were criminals and vigilantes, both men and women, and since Lafayette Baker was a master of the art of secrecy, his relatives had no idea how many agents he controlled nor their true identities. As Stan noted, both he and Byron prayed that no ill would come from his brother's evil associations. They preferred the more conventional activities of scouting, watching enemy troops, or trailing blockade runners. Although these were more dangerous than accompanying Lafe when he marched into a saloon frequented by Union troops and chopped it up with his axe, the more traditional espionage duties impressed them, given their Puritan backgrounds, as more moral.

As Baker's raids began sweeping Washington, the secret service chief came in for the first salvo of what would become constant public criticism. Because he applied the rules of war in a city which its inhabitants believed to be at peace, and because he refused to set double standards for important individuals

*Ibid., p. 112.

in power-conscious Washington, Baker was viewed as arrogant and ruthless. This was so; and the secrecy imposed on Lafe by Stanton prevented him from explaining many of his actions. Baker accepted this reality of the intelligence profession, secure in his self-image, his loyalty, and the rightness of the Union cause. His description of the requirements and characteristics of a secret agent provide a clear insight into how Baker saw himself:

The detective must possess ability, shrewdness, great self-reliance and self-control, discretion, courage and integrity. He will have important measures to carry forward, requiring no ordinary amount of mental power, and he will have plans and plots to unravel which demand keen discernment and a profound knowledge of men; critical moments when vacillation, or even hesitation would be fatal; secrets without which a complete mastery over feeling and all its forms of expression would be disastrous; delicate questions of procedure and duty to decide which the nicest prudence will be necessary; dangers to meet, requiring a fearless spirit nothing can alarm or intimidate; and to crown all, as the servant of the government in matters of gravest responsibility, he must have reliability of character to win and to hold the unclouded confidence of its officers in his revelations, on which the most momentous operations depend.*

Personally, Baker interpreted the "servant of the government" aspect of his role as servant to the president. In the midst of the Washington hierarchy's confusion, corruption, and self-aggrandizement, Lincoln was the only man Baker completely trusted, and, along with Stanton, the only man to whom he reported. Baker was not alone among America's patriotic spies in having a mentor for whom to direct his espionage efforts. As noted, Benjamin Tallmadge clearly idolized Washington, and the effectiveness of the Revolutionary War's entire intelligence operation hinged on the relationship between Washington and his agents. Men like Rivington and Mulligan who lived in occupied territory where they benefitted greatly from friendship with the British had only their admiration for Washington and patriotism as reasons to pursue espionage for the revolutionary cause. Washington's name became synonymous with patriotism.

For Baker and many Americans, Lincoln's name was synonymous with Union and emancipation. Like Tallmadge and Washington, the bureau chief and the president had a close personal relationship. The two men shared similar opinions about slavery, union, and the importance of morality within the army as a requirement for effective conduct of the war. And both were lonely men. Lincoln suffered from the isolation imposed by his office as well as more personal problems. Baker had always been a loner, and his job now prevented his dropping his facade in front of anyone except Lincoln and Stanton. In addition, Lincoln's friendliness and frontier heritage substituted for Baker's absent family—he saw his wife only occasionally and had never been able to relax with his martinet father. Baker leaned back and swapped

*_Ibid._, p. 90.

stories with Lincoln. Lincoln, whose stories pacified Pinkerton and his agents during the lonely wait in Baltimore early in 1861, now won Baker's confidence and undying fealty with the same jovial style. Lincoln also enjoyed hearing Lafe's romantic accounts of espionage in the active world from which the president was sequestered.

The importance of a powerful mentor to a spy's effectiveness reaches beyond personal matters. The mentor's influence insures a secret power base which works behind the scenes to legitimize what might otherwise be questionable activities. It also provides a psychological crutch, or the motivation to continue with the spy's lonely work. Baker's career ended after Lincoln's assassination, when President Andrew Johnson failed to provide his personal and emotional support. Other Civil War spies had similar personal relationships with generals of both armies, and suffered the consequences of their general's success or failure. In the twentieth century, William J. Donovan saw his dream of directing a peacetime intelligence operation evaporate with the death of his friend and supporter, Franklin D. Roosevelt.

Lafayette Baker's raids netted thousands of suspects to join Seward's captives in the Old Capitol prison. Suspected Confederates were awakened by a knock on the door and dragged off to jail in the middle of the night; some had been discovered by National Detective Bureau agents, others were accused by any of the hundreds of volunteer informers who flocked to 217 Pennsylvania Avenue. Although the only operational records he kept were in his head, Baker compiled meticulous dossiers on suspected Confederates and obtained their photographs for his files whenever possible. Using Stanton's resources, Baker established a secret fund to provide for the feeding and housing of informers and agents. (Such practices were common. The Confederacy reserved several hotel rooms in Washington for its agents throughout the Civil War, and George Washington paid to have a horse stabled in New York for use by his agents there during the Revolutionary War.)

By experience, Baker discovered that taking prisoners at night lowered their resistance to interrogation and minimized the possibility of escape. As soon as he had his suspect in custody, Baker would take him to one of the rooms at the Old Capitol. There he would interrogate the prisoner, sometimes brutally. If the captive would not crack, Baker would leave and William P. Wood, the prison superintendent, would arrive. He played the role of the friendly confidant and tried to cajole the prisoner into a confession to avoid more of Baker's methods. With especially taciturn prisoners, this team interrogation might continue intermittently for days. The prisoner was allowed only brief and irregular sleep, and fed only bread and water. As the captive became more confused, the guardians would demand a confession or statement, which would then be transcribed. In the process, they inserted incriminating statements which the prisoner had never made, and then took it to the man for his signature. Often the prisoner would be so confused that he would be unsure of what he had actually stated, and would sign the falsified document in order to escape from his nightmare. Another technique of Baker's was to bring one of his detectives in as an accusing "witness" and attempt to scare the captive into a confession.

The disgrace that was the Old Capitol prison knew all varieties of prisoners, from prostitutes to government officials. General George Custer, Winfield Scott's nephew, and the brother of Postmaster General Blair all spent time there as Baker's guests. Ever the organizer, Baker kept different types of prisoners in separate rooms. Room 16 was for political prisoners, often men of good standing in their communities: doctors, lawyers, editors, and ministers who were suspected of discouraging enlistments and/or encouraging desertion. Room 17 housed Union officers who were suspected of treason or thievery, as well as those with weaknesses for gambling and women. Anyone heard uttering even mild disapproval of the war or of Lincoln's administration might find himself in one of these rooms with no rights to trial, nor the privilege of correspondence with his family. In addition, Baker scattered his own men throughout the prison to pose as captives and eavesdrop on prisoners' conversations. The prison's courtyard was used as an execution site; both gallows and firing squads were used.

Conditions in the overcrowded prison were so miserable that 500 died during its first year of operation. These conditions, coupled with Baker's arbitrary arrests, provoked several congressional attempts at inquiry, but with Stanton backing him and Lincoln urging specific spying on Union generals to make sure of their loyalty, Baker declined to cooperate with Congress. Lincoln's attitude toward Baker can be summed up by two vignettes of the period. The first occurred after Baker captured a shipment of pornography en route to Union troops; he burned the contraband outside a smiling Lincoln's office window. The second involved a man who complained to the president about the racket made by an organ player. Lincoln put his tongue in his cheek and directed the citizen to carry his complaint to 217 Pennsylvania Avenue. "Baker will steal the organ and throw its owner in the Old Capitol, and you'll never be troubled by the noise again," remarked Lincoln.

The issue of Baker's authority to play policeman, judge, and jury came to a head in the Brinsmade case. Mrs. Brinsmade was Postmaster General Blair's niece. Baker arrested her for smuggling quinine to the South, and sent her to police chief John Kennedy in New York for imprisonment. The arrest of the social and popular Mrs. Brinsmade precipitated a public furor, and Chief Kennedy was called into court to defend his actions. Baker was asked to testify during the trial, and was requested to justify Mrs. Brinsmade's arrest by defining the scope of his duties. Baker replied:

My duties would be hard to define. There is a military law for the creation of the office under Army regulations, which are there defined. The duties are to obey the Secretary of War in looking after the interests of the Government, arresting disloyal persons and deserters, seizing contraband goods, investigating frauds against the government, and other duties which I cannot enumerate. I hold a confidential position in the Government. If I am asked to reveal how I operate, I will positively decline.*

The result of the trial was that Kennedy received a public reprimand and Mrs. Brinsmade was deported to New Orleans. Baker's testimony clearly showed that he believed his powers to be limited only by instruction of Stanton and Lincoln, not Congress or the courts. Although he remained silent at this time concerning his techniques, he did comment on their propriety after the war:

It may be said that the deceptions and misstatements resorted to and inseperable from the detective service, are demoralizing and prove unsoundness of character in its officers. But it must be borne in mind that, in war, no commander fails to deceive the enemy when possible, to secure the least advantage. Spies, scouts, intercepted correspondence, feints in army movements, misrepresentations in military strength and position, are regarded as honorable means of securing victory over the foe. The work of the detectives is simply deception reduced to a science or profession; and whatever objection, on ethical grounds, may lie against the secret service, lies with equal force against the strategy and tactics of Washington, Scott, Grant, and the host of their illustrious associates in the wars of the world. War is a last and terrible resort in the defense of even a righteous cause and sets at defiance all the ordinary laws and customs of society, overriding the rights of property and the sanctity of the Sabbath. And not until the Nation learns war no more, will the work of deception and waste of morals, men and treasures, cease.**

In expressing these views, Lafayette Baker fell into the traditional lines of American thought which viewed espionage and its illegal practices as permissible only in wartime. Baker's principal conflicts in carrying out the secret agent's ethos arose because he viewed the espionage war and the war to preserve morality as being of equal importance to the military battles of the Civil War. From his point of view this made the city of Washington and the Potomac region a battleground although, at the time, most residents perceived it as a city beyond the battle and did not understand how crucial the area's security was to the Union's success. Baker's methods proved distasteful to Washington society because that society did not wish to accept the reality of the war's extension beyond the battlefield, or to allow it to touch their lives through less direct but equally destructive means. The resistance Baker encountered adds credence to the view that in spite of postwar support of American military activities and the phony chauvinism which applauds its historical military victories, there never has been a popular American war— one which actually produced widespread support and sacrifice on the part of the American populace. One can only speculate on how Baker was affected by the realization that most persons didn't give an essential damn whether the

*Mogelever, op. cit., p. 158.

**Ibid., p. 91.

Union survived or not. He did, and this may partially account for the zeal with which he approached his task.

Traditional espionage activity has always included spying and counterspying operations, and had Baker confined the bureau's activities to those fields he would have avoided much of the criticism which ultimately resulted in his ostracism and dismissal from government service. Baker's sense of moral self-righteousness led him to use the power granted by the National Detective Bureau to enforce his morality on government officials and army officers, and on the citizens of Washington as well. There was no conflict between his sense of morality and that of Stanton and Lincoln; however, in pursuit of temperance, honesty, and sexual restraint, Baker condoned, permitted and encouraged excesses in the violent methods he and his men used to eradicate the evils defined by Stanton and Lincoln. Baker was no latter-day Torquemada, but he and his informers and agents were sometimes little more principled than the sinners and heretics they prosecuted and destroyed. Stan Baker described those who joined Baker in his various crusades as:

. . . a very promiscuous lot, coming from all parts of the country, from all classes of society, and as widely varying in their ethical standards. In newspaper comment and in popular conception they were, of course, classified together and often described by adjectives far from complimentary, but as always the case where men are closely associated, the few bad ones bring the whole body into disrepute.*

Baker, who would have hired the devil himself if it would have helped the Union cause, did not help his men's public reputation by clarifying the bureau's position. As chief of the organization, Lafe accepted his duty to maintain the utmost secrecy to protect his agents and the interests of the Union. As long as he had the power of Lincoln and Stanton to support his activities, Baker saw no need to explain his actions other than by citing his executive sanction. He was so secretive that most of his agents did not know each other, nor did he confide any more of an operation to an agent than the man needed to know to act effectively. Although very demanding of his operatives, he obtained the trust of the bureau's agents by keeping their identities secret and generously rewarding them for their successes. Just as Baker trusted Lincoln and Stanton implicitly to support the bureau's actions, so each agent trusted Baker to use his power to protect each individual's operation. The secrecy which ultimately destroyed Baker's public reputation was instrumental to the continued success of his programs. Postwar revelations told of a Confederate agent who had served on Baker's staff throughout the war and reported to the South, but since Baker confided little to his men, the agent had little useful intelligence to pass on to Richmond.

Although Baker stated "It was my purpose to establish a character above

*Ibid., p. 132.

just reproach in the national department of this service," as he investigated an increasing number of Union officers and government officials for corrupt practices, these persons began to question the utility of the National Detective Bureau and the qualifications of its zealous leader. Politicians, soldiers, and citizens appealed to the secretary of war to call Baker off, but Stanton and Lincoln stood behind their man. In response, the army refused to cooperate with Baker's investigations. The army leaders involved could tolerate his interference when he confiscated their whores, liquor, cards, and pornography, but when his men began breaking up the Quartermaster Corps' nefarious kickback schemes, the military drew the line to protect its illicit livelihood.

Undaunted by this opposition, Baker discovered an old congressional act which called for the creation of a unit of District of Columbia cavalry. He convinced Lincoln and Stanton to empower him to raise a battalion. In June 1863, Stanton commissioned Baker as a colonel and authorized him to select a force of "intelligent, moral, and worthy" men to police the capital and its surrounding area. The battalion became known as Baker's Rangers. Although their legal sanction only extended to the city, Stanton allowed them to operate throughout the Potomac region. They spent much time checking up on the military, whose ire had been aggravated already by Baker's commission. A few generals believed that they would be able to give the new colonel orders because they outranked him, but they soon learned the new title had given the secret service chief a foothold in their world without giving them a voice in his bureau's activities. Colonel Baker pulled his rank only when it could be effective; when outranked he relied on his role as the secretary of war's special agent. Although the army began to train its own scouts and spies, Lincoln and Stanton increasingly turned to Baker because of his men's proven reliability.

Baker gave his cousin Stan command of the bureau's new troops. With the enlarged manpower provided by the rangers to handle the mundane but necessary details of policing corruption and immorality, Baker and his agents were freed for more interesting pursuits. The bureau's ace agent was the mysterious M. Traill, a man who rivalled Timothy Webster. Baker always saved the toughest assignments for this slightly built, swarthy Virginian with a prominently scarred face and a past so mysterious that no one ever learned his first name. Traill was intensely devoted to his friend Lafe, and was respected by the other agents on the force as the bureau's acknowledged expert. Unlike most of Baker's agents, who were assigned to either the day or night squads, Traill's value was such that he worked both on special assignments. A native of the Potomac region, Traill had a thorough knowledge of the Maryland and Virginia countrysides, and he applied this expertise to cross and recross Rebel lines on innumerable occasions.

The taciturn Traill never discussed his missions, and Baker's mania for secrecy kept most of them off the record. However, one special project occupied the two men on and off for much of the war. This was the pursuit of Walter Bowie, a notorious Rebel spy. Bowie was born in Upper Marlboro in

Prince Georges County, Maryland, in 1831. Prior to the war, this handsome young man with a droopy mustache had been a popular and successful lawyer in his home town. Always a man who loved to drink and cause a little trouble, Bowie seized the opportunity of war to apply his swashbuckling spirit as a Rebel nightrider. He and his companions ran messages, burned bridges, raided Union horses and supplies and ambushed Union troops. In these activities Bowie followed the example of Colonel John Singleton Mosby, who refined the art of nightriding as leader of Mosby's Rangers.

When Bowie's notoriety made it impossible to operate independently, he signed up with Colonel Mosby. The Union characterized Mosby's Rangers as a lawless band of cutthroats and pillagers, and although their reputation was somewhat exaggerated, they did follow the bold, adventurous life which Bowie preferred. Colonel Mosby was a wiry, clean-shaven cavalry fighter. Like Bowie, he had led a quiet early life as a lawyer and pillar of his Virginia community. He learned from Stonewall Jackson never to reveal his plans in advance. Frequently even his closest officers were not told of their final destination until an expedition was underway. His advance intelligence allowed him to strike quickly at weak points in the Union defense and then disappear into the countryside. His troops and informers were so dominant in the Virginia counties of Fairfax, Loudon, and Fauquier that the region was nicknamed "Mosby's Confederacy."

In one audacious raid, Mosby slipped into the city of Fairfax and raided the headquarters of Union General Edwin H. Staughton. The Rebel guerrilla and his men descended on the town, cut the telegraph lines, captured federal sentries, and stole all available horses. Next Mosby entered Staughton's house, when the general was sleeping off the effects of too many bottles of champagne after a night of revelry. Mosby slapped the sleeping Staughton on his rear end, woke him up and carted him off to Rebel headquarters.

This expedition made the Union look foolish, which in turn made Lafayette Baker angry. Although such escapades put Mosby at the top of Baker's most wanted list, he never succeeded in capturing the Confederate raider. Even after Appomattox, Mosby did not give up; he sent a spy into Richmond to ask Lee for orders. Mosby did not want to concede defeat, but Lee advised him to go home and "help build up the shattered fortunes of our old state." Ulysses S. Grant respected Mosby so much that the two men became close friends after the war. Grant used his influence to insure financial security for Mosby, and the ex-Rebel became a Southern Republican, the United States consul at Hong Kong, a government land agent in Colorado, and finally an assistant United States attorney for the Department of Justice. Mosby died peacefully in 1916.

Although Bowie and Mosby were very similar, Mosby sometimes had trouble controlling his subordinate's zeal. Mosby was the kind of man who ambushed a train at a position where the passengers would be least likely to suffer injury, and who refused to receive any spoils from his men's looting of the riders and cargo. Bowie, on the other hand, enjoyed making his risks as large as possible and then basking in the glory of his successes.

One of Bowie's risks which failed to succeed was his repeated visits to the house of John H. Waring. Waring was a wealthy Maryland planter who aided Confederates by allowing them to hide in his mansion and use it as a Rebel post office. He also had a young daughter with whom Bowie was in love. Traill discovered Bowie's habit of visiting the Warings, and on October 14, 1862, he had men surround the house to capture the elusive Rebel spy. Bowie was taken to the Old Capitol prison, and withstood a fierce interrogation by Baker before escaping on November 17. The escape added fuel to Baker's and Traill's hatred of Bowie, and Bowie made matters worse by returning to Washington in full Rebel uniform and having his picture taken by Baker's photographer in a studio only seven blocks from the National Detective Bureau's headquarters.

Such narrow escapes helped develop the legend that Bowie led a charmed life. Slave mystics prophesied that Bowie could only be killed by his own gun. Stan and Lafayette Baker both claimed that Traill finally shot Bowie using one of the Rebel's pistols which had been confiscated while he was in the Old Capitol. In their version, an informer led Traill to Bowie's campfire, where Traill surprised the spy and used the captured gun to kill him, thereby fulfilling the oracle.

Another version of Bowie's death depended upon his wildness rather than on occult arts. Allegedly, Bowie approached Mosby in the fall of 1864 with a plan to raid the federal governor's mansion in Annapolis and kidnap the governor. Mosby thought the plan too far-fetched, but eventually gave in to Bowie's persistence and assigned twenty-five men to his command. Upon reaching Annapolis, Bowie and his companions discovered the town to be heavily infested with Union troops. They reluctantly abandoned their mission and rode toward the Potomac, stopping at a country store which they raided for supplies. Local citizens pursued the vandals into their wooded campground, and as Bowie fled from the ensuing battle one of the townsmen is said to have shot him in the head. Whichever account is true, Bowie clearly added to the romantic aura surrounding espionage in the Civil War. He followed in the tradition of other educated and respected members of American communities who opted to serve their country through espionage. Perhaps the outdoorsman side of his family (typified by his uncle, who invented the Bowie knife) gave him blood that was a bit overeager for adventure. In any case, the same zeal which led to his death had made him a valuable spy for the Confederacy.

Not content to deal only with Confederate spies like Mosby and Bowie, Baker expanded his pursuit of those undermining the Union cause in the North, especially those in the army and government. Men like the drunken General Staughton outraged Baker. Like Lincoln, the detective chief saw them as worthless and detrimental to the federal victory. As the president said when told that Mosby stole sixty good horses along with Staughton, "I'm sorry for that. I can make generals, but I can't make horses."*

By the summer of 1863, the European press was comparing Lafayette Baker

*Harnett T. Kane, *Spies for the Blue and Grey*. New York: Hanover House, 1954, p. 174.

to Joseph Fouche, Napoleon's chief of secret service. The National Detective Bureau opened a New York office and expanded its operations in Canada. (By war's end, Baker had agents in Richmond, New York, Chicago, St. Louis, Montreal, Halifax, Havana, Nassau, Philadelphia, Britain, and France, in addition to a full regiment of rangers.) In the fall, Baker filed a report with Lincoln citing 136 gaming houses within sight of the White House and 3,600 saloons and 457 brothels in Washington. He was especially upset by the large number of congressmen and federal officers frequenting the gambling establishments and using public funds to pay off their debts. Baker and his men raided these houses at 2 A.M. one morning, arresting proprietors and effectively eradicating much of the district's gambling. Raids followed against illegal liquor trafficking by the army; Baker describes one midnight raid on a brothel in his memoirs:

. . . . The scenes which transpired at the hour of midnight, in these dens of corruption, beggar language. . . . At an hour appointed, and with a concerted plan, similar in all its details which was sprung on the gamblers, with my force I made a raid upon the disreputable houses. . . . The moment came, the signal was given, doors were opened, the windows raised, and scenes of confusion and comico-tragic nature followed, which must have been witnessed to have been appreciated. Faces quite covered to avoid recognition, gas turned off, and a general stampede of gentlemen sporting martial emblems, were some of the incidents attending the onset upon the intrenchments of vice in the midnight quiet of the nation's capital. Between sixty and seventy officers and men were arrested and locked up in the guard house, for reflection upon their suddenly interrupted debauchery.*

Baker relates an interview with Lincoln the morning after Baker's raid on Washington's gambling houses which sheds light on Lincoln's views on gambling and Lafayette Baker:

Mr. Lincoln sent for me, and I repaired to the White House, to find him carelessly sitting in shirt-sleeves and slippers ready to receive me. He said:

"Well Baker, what is the trouble between you and the gamblers?" I told my story. He laughed and said:

"I used to play penny ante when I ran a flat boat out West, but for many years have not touched a card."

I stated to him the havoc gambling was making with the Army, alluded to before, when he approved my course, but reminded me of the difficulties in the way of reform.

I replied: "I cannot fight the gamblers and the Government both."

The President replied: "You won't have to fight me."

I added: "It is a fight, and all I ask is fair play: that the Government will let me alone, and I will break up this business."

And, with this perfect understanding, we parted for the time.**

*Baker, op. cit., p. 252.

**Ibid., pp. 242–243.

Illicit sex in Washington during the Civil War was not confined to brothels. As Baker soon discovered, the Treasury Department was a haven of loose money, loose women, and loose administration. In his investigation of the Treasury, Baker broke new and significant ground, which paved the way for the later creation of the FBI, the Secret Service, and federal grand jury prosecutors.

Lincoln's cabinet was staffed by some very large and power-hungry egos. One of the foremost was Secretary of the Treasury Salmon P. Chase, who had designs on the presidency. Concerned that rumors of graft and debauchery in his department would ruin his reputation, Chase called on Secretary Stanton to borrow Baker's services for an investigation which he hoped would clear his and the Treasury's reputations. Postmaster General Blair had mixed emotions about the investigation. He also had visions of living at 1600 Pennsylvania Avenue, and hated Chase as a rival; but Baker had arrested his niece early in the war, so Blair had no love for the secret service chief. The equally ambitious Secretary of State Seward kept an eye on developments via special Treasury agent Hanson A. Risley, "Jack of all under-the-table trades."* Seward had adopted one of Risley's daughters and had tried to make her his wife after the first Mrs. Seward died. They never married, "but he made her the executor of his will with all the privileges of a wife."** Her father played his role in this quasi-incestuous relationship by spying in the Treasury Department for Seward.

Baker was already familiar with the charges against the Treasury Department. He had arrested several of the department's young female employees in his raids on gaming houses, and once had made the show-stopping move of halting a funeral cortege to seize the corpse of a one such employee for an autopsy to determine whether her death had resulted from an abortion. He set up headquarters in the basement of the Treasury building and interviewed many of the young women. He asked about alleged parties in the Treasury offices at night, how they spent their afternoons, who their boyfriends were, how they obtained expensive wardrobes on $50 monthly salaries, and whether their employers made improper advances.

In addition to the status of the Treasury women, Baker investigated charges that newly printed sheets of money were being stolen and that counterfeiters were stealing real plates from the department with which to make bogus certificates. Edward Jordan, the Treasury solicitor, was to aid Baker in his investigations. Jordan hoped to satisfy Baker by sacrificing a lower-echelon employee to cover up larger crimes. The victim was James Cornwall, the man in charge of burning mutilated bonds and notes. He was discovered with $2,000 in his pocket and marched off to the Old Capitol. Baker held Cornwall for several months for interrogation before he was formally charged. After

*Mogelever, *op. cit.*, p. 249.

**Ibid.*, p. 249.

serving two years on his sentence, Cornwall was released to come to the aid of his wife and children, whose penniless state had been amplified in the Washington press.

Undeceived by Jordan's assurances concerning the Treasury Department's integrity, Baker began checking into the new Department of Printing and Engraving. Traditionally, all United States currency had been produced by private banknote companies in New York. The Treasury had recently been convinced that it could economize by printing its own currency. The scheme was the brainchild of Spencer M. Clark, head of the new Department of Printing and Engraving, and Stuart Gwynn, an inventor who claimed to have invented new presses and paper with which to cut costs and foil counterfeiters.

Solicitor Jordan was upset when he learned of Baker's new focus, and called the detective to his office. Baker silenced Jordan's protests by explaining that Gwynn and Clark were defrauding the government with worthless presses and processes. The weight and vibrations of the new presses, which had foolishly been placed in the attic of the new Treasury building, were damaging its structure.

To prove his points, Baker took Jordan on a tour of the new department. Clark tried to dissuade them from examining the room where Gwynn manufactured his paper, citing security reasons. At Baker's insistence they went to the 80'-by-100' room and discovered that most of its doors were locked; but by entering through an adjoining furnace room they walked into Gwynn's lab via a wide open connecting door. Inside they found maintenance personnel moving freely through a room cluttered with broken-down hydraulic presses and stacks of the new paper. The man in the room had no idea how much paper there was, and explained that the only real security measure taken was to count the sheets each evening.

Baker had the room secured and proceeded to Gwynn's laboratory, where he arrested the inventor. Jordan disappeared, so Baker held Gwynn at 217 Pennsylvania Avenue until the next morning. He interrogated Gwynn throughout the night, and with new evidence which Gwynn revealed, Baker convinced the reluctant Jordan to sign an order committing the fraudulent inventor to the Old Capitol prison.

Baker's further explorations of the Treasury Building disclosed that Gwynn had destroyed federal property along with defrauding the government. Gwynn persuaded Treasury officials that he had developed a new membrane paper which could not be duplicated by counterfeiters and then purchased seventy-eight new hydraulic presses to use with the special paper. The 200 tons of presses were placed in the attic, where they bent the floor's cast-iron support girders. In order for his dry printing process to work, Gwynn needed more pressure for the hydraulic presses. To achieve this, he tore apart pieces of the Treasury building and installed oil-filled tubes running the height of the structure in which pistons were supposed to move. These "receivers," as Baker called them, were tested; they exploded. Gwynn had succeeded in defacing the

Treasury building, but his presses still failed to operate.

In theory, the Gwynn process could have succeeded; but if he had ever managed to get enough power to his presses they would have broken from the attendant stress, since Gwynn had manufactured them out of inferior materials. As Baker learned, whether the process worked or not, it was a foolish venture because of the expense. Each of Gwynn's hydraulic presses cost $1,-700; the roller press it replaced had cost $120. One roller press could do the work of six or seven hydraulic presses per day. Baker calculated that the Treasury Department was committing itself to spend at least $10,200 on machinery for work which could be produced at a $120 machinery cost. In addition, Gwynn's process required more expensive paper, more expensive ink, and the cost of the nonfunctional receiver. Despite these facts, Spencer Clark, who had set up the inventor with a laboratory in the Treasury Department and had authorized him to charge thousands of dollars worth of machinery to the government (although Gwynn was not an official Treasury employee) continued to tear down walls, build receivers, and order presses even after Gwynn had been jailed.

Salmon Chase had originally approved Gwynn's scheme after the inventor convinced Generals Irwin McDowell and Harman Haupt to introduce him to the secretary. When Baker filed his report showing that both Clark and Jordan had conspired with Gwynn to defraud the government, Chase was implicated through his own stupidity. The investigation he had hoped would clear his name signaled the end of his rising political career.

Having uncovered one part of the Treasury Department's sin, Baker then zeroed in on the accusations concerning the department's women employees. The Treasury employed more women than any other government agency; the presence of the young women added a novel touch to the predominantly male atmosphere of the Washington bureaucracy. All Washington talked about the women at the Treasury Department, and people lined up in the morning to watch them walk to work in their bright dresses. Baker discovered several women willing to testify about their relationships with their superiors. At the bottom of these allegations was the gray, fiftyish, respectable-looking Spencer Clark, Gwynn's ally and the head of the department in the treasury which employed most of the women. Clark had been forcing impoverished young women to have sex in order to gain jobs in his Department of Printing and Engraving. Baker established evidence that Clark and a friend of his named Philip Henderson were paying their employees for sexual favors using stolen Treasury funds. He also documented that Clark had fired women who refused to attend his after-hours "parties." In many instances the employees were only 17 or 18 years old. Other young employees outside of Clark's personal circle sometimes supplemented their $12.50 weekly salaries by working as prostitutes in Washington's numerous bars.*

*Baker, *op. cit.*, pp. 293–307.

Chase was ruined by Baker's revelations, but there still remained individuals eager to get political mileage out of the investigation by attacking Baker. Foremost among these was the former Union war hero, now Congressman James A. Garfield. He had already publicly questioned Lincoln's extensive war powers and imposition of martial law on the city of Washington. Garfield maneuvered his way into the chairmanship of the Select Committee to Investigate Treasury Conditions. He hoped to use the committee to strike at Lincoln's policies by attacking Lafayette Baker, while enhancing his own political reputation. In a pattern which would become all too familiar by the twentieth century, internecine politics subverted the true issues of national security.

Garfield showed little interest in the gross mismanagement of funds, conspiracy, defacement of government property, or the lewd and lascivious behavior being practiced in the Treasury Department. Even when Baker documented an instance where a cleaning woman and her lover had stolen a federal engraving plate to counterfeit bills, Garfield focused on Baker and politics rather than on security and corruption. The congressman accused Baker of working for the Copperheads to shake confidence in the government and foment public sentiment·for compromise with the Confederacy. The charge was ludicrous in light of Baker's fervent Unionism, intense anti-slavery stance, and harsh treatment of Copperheads, but the public judged on the basis of Garfield's allegations, not facts. The espionage taboo was on trial during the Select Committee's hearings: Garfield, the glorified war hero and vocal opponent of injustice, versus Baker, the secretive espionage chief who was known to the public mainly through his fanatical zeal for harsh justice as characterized by the oppressive and overcrowded Old Capitol prison. Baker became a prisoner of the secrecy which his job demanded. The public, oblivious through traditional ignorance to any formal relationship between secret espionage and good ends, assumed all secrets to be evil. Here was a community which failed to understand George Washington's productive use of tactical espionage; which did not recognize that drunken generals lose battles and cause the needless loss of untold thousands of human lives; which did not recognize that the Confederacy's military commander, General Robert E. Lee, was reading its words in captured Northern newspapers each day and using his agents in Washington to eavesdrop on conversations. By calling attention to espionage only by scaring the public with threats of foreign spies during the Alien and Sedition Acts controversy, the government had bred a negative feeling about espionage and the necessity for secrecy. In this case, the people had no historical precedent for trusting Baker. They responded to Garfield's appeal to their emotions and condemned the detective chief's actions out of hand, without recognizing the true severity of the Treasury's corruption.

The investigation ended without a prosecution in the Treasury Department. Clark returned to his young women, and although Gwynn's operation was suspended, the Treasury was stuck with the bill for his follies. Garfield won his place in the political spotlight, which he later exploited during his successful bid for the presidency. But Baker was not a total loser. Baker's faith in justice and in Garfield the political "patriot" had been shaken, but his secrecy was largely preserved, even though his reputation was greater as a result of the publicity surrounding the hearings. Surprisingly, some members of the press seized on Baker as a hero. Frank Leslie's *Illustrated Newspaper* ran a picture of Baker and commented:

Though we are pleased at having the opportunity of giving the roguish contractors and public speculators, of whom the Colonel has been the unremitting scourge, such an inviolate opportunity of studying the lineaments of the man whom it is their interest to avoid, art, however, can have no scruples as to notoriety. So the Secret Service Agent must take his place in our gallery, among other celebrities of history.*

After this ill-fated expedition into the tangled powers and vanities of Congress, Baker's next major operation returned to the world of spies and criminals which he understood best. He moved to stop the Northwest Conspiracy, a plot organized by the Confederacy with the aid of Northern Copperheads.** Judah P. Benjamin was the plan's architect. He envisioned an economic attack carried out by Canadian-based Confederates to isolate the Northwestern states from the rest of the Union. Three million pounds were obtained in London to finance the project.

Jacob Thompson, former secretary of the interior under President Buchanan, and Clement C. Clay, a former Alabama senator, were Benjamin's principal agents in Canada. They found a wealth of volunteers among the thousands of Northerners in Indiana, Illinois, Kentucky, Ohio, Missouri, and New York who were members of various pro-Copperhead or pro-South secret societies. The Copperheads were strongest in Ohio, Indiana, and Illinois. They advocated Union by negotiation and denounced the Lincoln administration's policies of arbitrary arrest and emancipation. Their chief spokesman was Clement C. Vallandigham of Ohio, a moderate who counselled against treason and violence. He was largely responsible for the Copperhead's merger with the Knights of the Golden Circle, and the widespread adoption of that name by anti-Lincoln groups.

The Knights of the Golden Circle was a secret order first formed in 1855 by a Cincinnati physician named George W.L. Bickley. He recruited members largely in the South with the expressed motives of supporting slavery and conquering Mexico. During the Civil War the organization spread into Indiana as an offshoot of local Democrat Copperheads who opposed Lincoln's

*Mogelever, *op. cit.,* p. 278.

**For complete accounts of the Northwest Conspiracy, see especially: Felix A. Stidger, *A Treason History of the Order of Sons of Liberty, Succeeded by Knights of the Golden Circle, Afterward, Order of American Knights.* Private Printing, Chicago, 1903; and James D. Horan, *Confederate Agent.* New York: Crown, 1954.

war policy. The Knights met secretly, guarded their membership, vowed assorted sacred oaths, committed minor crimes of violence, and spoke out against the government, in the conspiratorial tradition of most subversive organizations. In 1863, they were reorganized as the Order of American Knights, and in 1864 into the Sons of Liberty, with Vallandigham as supreme commander. The Sons of Liberty numbered 300,000 members sworn to oppose unconstitutional acts of the federal government and to support states rights. They opposed the draft and discouraged enlistments.

Thompson and Clay had been hard at work attempting to subvert the Union prior to the time they enlisted the Sons of Liberty to aid them in the Northwest Conspiracy. In one of their schemes they enlisted Godfrey Joseph Hyams to go to Washington to infect Lincoln with yellow fever. They also wanted Hyams to use the disease to start an epidemic among soldiers in the District of Columbia. Hyams was to be paid $70,000 for his efforts, but the Confederates reneged on the bargain and Hyams sought out Baker to inform on his employers and gain revenge. He told Baker of an organized plot hatched by Benjamin, Thompson, and Clay to burn New York City, free the 9,000 Rebel prisoners at Camp Douglas in Chicago and use the prisoners to capture, Chicago, Buffalo, and Indianapolis.

After extensive interrogation, Baker decided to believe Hyams and send him back to Canada as a double agent. Baker dispatched agents to New York and the Midwest to guard against the planned insurrection. Thompson hoped that the upshot of the plot would be the creation of a new nation along the Canadian border sympathetic to the Confederacy. To help organize his revolt, Thompson acquired the services of Captain Thomas Hines, formerly of Morgan's Raiders. Hines was joined by Lieutenant John W. Headley, Colonel Robert M. Martin, and Captain John B. Castleman. They infiltrated the North as civilians and acted as agents provocateurs to contact local Sons of Liberty groups and secure support for the Northwest Conspiracy.

The leaders of the conspiracy met in Toronto during the summer of 1864 to plot their nefarious strategy. They decided on Chicago as their first target. Captain Hines, a slight man in his 20s noted for his courageous reputation gained in service with Morgan, was placed in command. Another ex-Morgan Raider, Leger Grenfel, a British soldier of fortune and veteran of Algiers and the Crimean War, was also a leader. Colonel Vincent Marmaduke detached 300 soldiers from the Confederate army and took them North for guerrilla training. Hyams attended the planning sessions and reported back to Baker. The secret service chief then alerted Camp Douglas, Rock Island, Indianapolis, Columbus, and Johnson's Island in Lake Erie, where another 30,000 Rebel prisoners were being held by a small staff of federal guards.

The insurrectionists planned to strike during the Democratic convention, to be held in Chicago during August. Hines was present, in command of 2,000 civilian-clothed soldiers, but the plans to start fires, looting, and revolt at the climax of the convention were cancelled because the Copperheads gained control of the proceedings. Leaders feared that violence would hurt the chances of General McClellan, who had been nominated for president as a Copperhead peace candidate. The conspirators reassembled in Toronto and decided to reschedule their attack for election day.

When the moment for attack arrived, advanced warning found the Union prepared. General Benjamin Butler and 10,000 troops marched into New York to scare away any saboteurs. Grenfel and Marmaduke were captured in the home of Charles Walsh, a wealthy Sons of Liberty supporter, although Hines escaped. An attempt to capture the gunboat *Michigan* on Lake Erie and effect the escape of the Johnson's Island prisoners also failed because of an informer. In late November, Felix Stidger, an undercover agent, talked his way into the confidence of the Indiana Sons of Liberty hierarchy and had them arrested. One of these men, Lambdin P. Milligan, became the subject of an important court case.

In the Milligan case of 1886, the Supreme Court invalidated Milligan's trial and conviction by the military in 1864. He had been arrested under martial law and charged with conspiring against the United States, giving aid and comfort to the enemy, and inciting insurrection and disloyal practices. He was tried before a court-martial established by presidential authority and sentenced to be hanged. Milligan instituted suit in federal circuit court questioning the legality of the military trial and contending that he had been deprived of his Constitutional right to trial by jury.

The Supreme Court held that neither the president nor Congress had the power to set up military tribunals except in the actual theater of war where civil courts were not functioning, and that elsewhere court-martials held jurisdiction only over military personnel. The decision was decried by many Radical Republicans since it called into question the military governments established by Lincoln and Congress in rebellious states. It also confronted Baker's pursuit of martial law and detention without charge in the Old Capitol.

The total failure of the Northwest Conspiracy may be credited in part to effective espionage which informed the Union, but there were other important factors. The average Copperhead member of the Sons of Liberty was not comfortable with the large-scale violent raiding which the Confederate leaders favored. Vallandigham refused to cooperate with the violent conspirators, thereby dividing support among the Sons of Liberty. As peace Democrats, the Copperheads were reluctant to take arms against the federal government. They preferred to attack through political channels, and feared that an overt uprising would hurt their chances in the 1864 election.

An interesting aspect of the National Detective Bureau's handling of the Northwest Conspiracy was its use of female agents. As will be seen later, women played a decisive role in Civil War espionage. Baker included many women among his operatives, and a number of the capital's prostitutes and barflies became his paid informants. In cracking the Treasury scandal, he used the testimony and diaries of three women who were influenced to aid the prosecution because one of the bureau's female agents moved into their boarding house and befriended them. Female prisoners in the Old Capitol could be sure that at least one of their number was an agent planted by Baker and Wood to spy on them. Whenever Baker exchanged prisoners with the South, he sent several of his own men and women along to become spies in the Confederacy.

The woman who played the largest role in the Northwest Conspiracy was Loretta Janeta Velazquez, one of the bureau's best female agents. Velazquez was an attractive young Cuban woman who had chosen the role of *espionne*. Baker discovered her on one of his frequent journies through Washington's bars; she was disguised as a Union soldier, hoping to pick up information to sell to the South. She had a brother under arrest in New York charged with spying for the Confederacy, and though she too leaned toward the Rebels, she was more interested in money. Baker arrested Velazquez, but he admired her ability at disguise and recognized the value of her beauty for trapping Rebel soldiers. He had her released, and brought her into his secret service.

Velazquez served Baker effectively, but also decided to serve another master by sending reports to Richmond. Whether Baker was aware of Velazquez's double agentry is unclear, but by the time of the Northwest Conspiracy he appeared doubtful enough to send her only to places where he had other agents to watch her. He noticed that Velazquez was jealous of Frankie Abel, a thoroughly loyal woman eager to serve Baker and the Union. Abel could drink and swear with the best of the bureau's male agents, but her attractiveness gave her the capacity to play the coquette and entrap Confederate sympathizers.

Velazquez's role in the Northwest Conspiracy was to serve as a courier. Using identification and money provided by Baker, she journeyed to Richmond and made contact with Judah P. Benjamin's staff. There was no clear need for Baker to send her South; he already had several agents in Richmond, including one on the staff of General Winder, the Confederate secret service chief. While in Richmond, Velazquez obtained money and information to carry to conspirators in Montreal. She went to Canada without telling Baker and then returned to Washington. Baker received her report from Richmond, and then provided her with identification papers with which to enter Johnson's Island, to which she had requested assignment. There she delivered money and told the prisoners when to anticipate the Confederate raid.

When the conspiracy failed, Velazquez assumed Baker knew her true mission and never returned to Washington. From her account of the incident her motivation is not clear; but her alliance with the Confederacy may have grown from a desire to see Cuba become part of the United States. Most sentiment for the annexation of Cuba existed among representatives of the South, Northern opposition blocked the move. Although love of money and adventure certainly played a part in her decision to spy, hope to see her nation adopted by the United States may also have influenced her actions.

Upon disposing of the Northwest Conspiracy, Baker turned his attention to fraud in the cotton market. As with the Treasury Department investigation, he discovered extensive corruption reaching into the executive branch. A group of politicians including Thurlow Weed of New York, New York City customs collector Leonard Swett, United States Commissioner of Indian Affairs George W. Dole, and Hanson A. Risley, Seward's friend in the Treasury Department, conspired with a group of army officers, most notably General Benjamin F. Butler, to provide food for Lee's army in exchange for cotton from the South. The cotton was sold using illegally predated trading licenses manufactured by Risley in the Treasury Department. Risley also sometimes assigned Treasury agents to escort the goods being transferred by the smuggling ring. Union army officers received bribes up to $40,000 for their cooperation in the scheme.

Finding himself once more in the arena of politicians more concerned with money and influence than with war, Baker came in for high-level opposition to his revelations. He had tactfully withheld news of the scandal until after the election of 1864, to protect his friend Abraham Lincoln from embarrassment. Baker felt it was important to the war effort and the security of his position with the National Detective Bureau that Lincoln remain in power, but once that end was secured he moved to prosecute the violators though many were political allies of the president. General Grant helped Baker's case by believing the bureau's extensive evidence and setting up a military tribunal to investigate the army officers implicated in the case. As a result, Grant forced his friend Butler to resign.

Baker's overall concern for the condition of the Union army included the state of the public conscription program. He spent many hours attempting to insure the effectiveness and equity of the draft. It was again a lonely and unpopular cause. The Civil War draft functioned on a quota per region system. Men who enlisted were usually paid a cash bounty at the time they joined the army. Confusion in recruiting practices and the lure of bounty money led to frequent abuses. Baker conducted an extensive study of the draft's problems, especially in the New York area.

His study showed that only twenty-five percent of the number of men recorded as enlisted reached the front as soldiers. The attrition began when the enlistment rolls were falsified. Bounty hunters enlisted repeatedly, collecting a bounty each time and kicking back a portion to the local recruiting officers who doctored the records. Other men worked as brokers. It was legitimate for one area to fill its quota with men from another. Many representatives from outlying towns travelled to New York to buy enlistment papers from brokers. These papers, notarized by an army enlistment officer, could be turned into the army in lieu of bodies for the draft. Brokers bribed officers to forge these papers, using fictitious names or the names of invalids, mental patients, immigrants, and adolescents. The phony papers were then purchased by the community representatives. Regions were credited by the army with having filled their quotas when their papers represented only ghosts and misfits. The draft problem was further exacerbated when Congress passed the Draft Bill of 1863, which allowed exemption if an individual found an alternate or paid $300. The law discriminated against the poor, who could not afford to pay the money or buy an alternate. This bill was a fundamental cause of the New York draft riots, although the riots were assisted after they began by Confederate agents planted in New York to encourage the havoc.

In the face of this situation, Baker forced confessions, impounded military records, examined the bank accounts of recruitment officers, and checked the identities of names which appeared on recruiting papers. At various times he posed as a recruit and a bounty broker to entrap draft-law violators and study their techniques. Although Baker only made a small dent in the widespread corruption, he did extend law enforcement into an area where civilian justice officials had feared to tread, and which Provost Marshal General James B. Fry ignored. Baker's investigation also focused attention on the large number of men who deserted the army after enlistment but before reaching battle. He pointed out that since offenders were rarely prosecuted the law was violated with impudence.

In his *History of Secret Service,* Baker states, "However censurable, unjustifiable, or illegal my course may have been, my only desire was to serve the President and the Government."* As he worked back and forth in the regions of politics and law, both civil and military, he tried to uphold the statutes the legislators had enacted and sworn to defend, but he soon and consistently discovered that politicians did not always desire to have their laws obeyed or enforced. Along with Lincoln, Baker believed it was sometimes necessary to break the law to preserve the Union. He concurred with the president's opinion that without the Union there would not be a Constitution. Baker, however, did not believe in breaking the law to promote his or others' personal gain. This flew in the face of congressmen who both enacted and violated laws to gain power and money. Baker was especially vulnerable to these men because he had violated the law to promote the goal of winning the war and preserving the Union. Baker's illegal actions were sanctioned by Lincoln, and this afforded the secret service chief a measure of protection; but in an era prior to the broad extension of executive privilege, Baker was more subject to Congressional scrutiny than the president. Baker had hinted at the concept of executive privilege when he refused to be specific about his duties in testimony before the Garfield committee; but though he drew his legal power from the president, he was not Lincoln's equal in political power, nor could the president's be used as an absolute shield to protect him.

The vulnerability of Lafayette Baker and the National Detective Bureau to political attack became clear during the Congressional hearings on the Lincoln assassination. The army had taken initial responsibility for the chase of the president's killer, but Stanton called Baker in on the case. Baker dug into his files (which included information on civilian criminals, corrupt army officers,

*Baker, *op. cit.,* p. 593.

and even members of Congress, presaging later Military Intelligence Division and FBI dossiers) and found a picture of John Wilkes Booth. Using the picture, he issued the first handbill of reward for criminal capture to be circulated nationally. Baker was tipped off as to Booth's location. He dispatched Stan Baker and some army officers to arrest the assassin.

Booth was killed during the capture, but his coconspirators stood trial and were hanged by an executioner aptly named Christian Rath. A squabble ensued over the right to the reward offered for the conspirators' capture. Stan and Lafayette put in their claim, as did several of the soldiers who had been present at Booth's capture. A congressional committee was convened to dispose of the money, and stung the Bakers by cutting them out of most of the reward purse.

Baker was grieved by Lincoln's death and angered by Congress' slight of his detective efforts and Stan's arrest of Booth. Nevertheless, he vowed to maintain his pledge to "serve the President and the Government." Andrew Johnson was the new president, and the end of the war brought new problems of law enforcement to the nation's capital. Former Rebels streamed back into the city, and war differences were buried as Washington's residents scrambled to reestablish the nation's economy and make money.

For many former Confederates the first step in rebuilding was to obtain a pardon, which would enable them to join the federal government without being punished for their crimes against the Union during the war. The ease with which pardons were obtained and with which Rebels gained the ear of the new president upset Baker. He was outraged that those who had so recently been killing Union soldiers should now go unpunished and be welcomed into the White House, the center of federal power.

One of the favorite techniques used to obtain pardons was to employ the services of a pardon broker. The broker was usually someone closely acquainted with a powerful government official. The broker would present his client's case to the influential political friend and usually obtain the pardon. Sometimes the brokers obtained blank pardons which could be filled in with any name. Many of these brokers were women who approached the politicians with more than verbal arguments. Baker centered his attack on two of them: Lucy Cobb and Ella Bassett Washington. Mrs. Cobb was a beautiful woman of easy virtue. She was friendly with the president's dissolute son Robert, and parlayed their relationship into a friendship with the president. Ella Bassett Washington was an aristocratic descendant of George Washington, with a Rebel heritage and a wide circle of political acquaintances throughout Washington, D.C.

Baker was amazed to find Cobb visiting the White House at all hours and interrupting President Johnson with pardon requests. On one occasion Baker physically removed her from the president's reception area. He explained Cobb's true profession to Johnson, but the president defended her reputation. At the time, Johnson was more interested in reuniting the country than paying strict attention to the punishment of Confederates. He also believed Baker was involved in a plot with Stanton to undermine him.

Without support from the president's office, Baker lost his power and effectiveness. He tried to convince Johnson of Cobb's danger by describing her attempts at seduction:

"You have never seen my legs." [Cobb said.] She then raised her clothes and showed me her fine legs some distance above her knees; on another occasion she told me she could have any employee of the White House dismissed that she desired; her general conduct while at the White House has been extremely unlady-like, so much so that she became a subject of general remark among the employees.*

Johnson stood adamant against Baker and reprimanded him for interfering with Cobb. Baker responded:

Mr. President, when such vile characters as Mrs. Cobb can visit the White House at all times of the day and night, when she can procure pardons . . . and deliver them in person incompleted or without being recorded, when she boasts publicly in the streets, hotels and saloons of this city that she is a pardon broker and that the President dare not refuse any of her applications, but she has the President of the United States in her power, I think it is high time somebody interfered.**

This speech was Baker's last to the president. He resigned from the secret service, the Old Capitol was closed, and Stanton never mentioned Baker or the National Detective Bureau in the War Department's official report on the Civil War.

Baker's opponents had one last chance to attack him when he was brought to trial for the false arrest and imprisonment of Mrs. Cobb. He was lambasted in the press and refused to testify in his own behalf in order to protect the bureau's secrets and to prevent his enemies from gaining the opportunity to bait him publicly, face to face. With Lincoln dead and Stanton's power waning, no one came forward as a character witness to support Baker. He was found guilty of false imprisonment and sentenced on March 28, 1866. The judge's opinion was as follows:

The case presents itself to me in the aspect of one where an officer of the Government, in a zealous effort to discharge his duty, may have been led by his zeal to go a hair's breadth too far, and done an act which, though it cannot be justified in law, yet which, in a moral point of view, has much to mitigate the punishment.***

Ibid., p. 602.

**Ibid.,* p. 604.

***Mogelever, *op. cit.,* p. 412.

Baker was reasonably pleased with the judge's opinion and his decision to impose a fine of $1 plus court costs (a total of $36), but his disillusionment with the government was deep. He left Washington to rejoin his wife, Jennie, in Philadelphia. There he wrote his memoirs of secret service before dying on July 3, 1868, at only 42. His intense devotion to his profession had used him up.

The judge's opinion spoke well for Baker's career. Baker was certainly overzealous, and sometimes more than a "hair's breadth too far" on the wrong side of the letter of the law, but his spirit was always with the president and the nation. The work of his bureau set precedents for the creation of both foreign and domestic intelligence and law-enforcement agencies. The Secret Service was created in the Treasury Department to follow up Baker's investigations as soon as the National Detective Bureau was disbanded. Baker's old companion and coworker, William P. Wood, was appointed the Secret Service's first chief.

Lafayette Baker's patriotic zeal was not suited to the coming age of bureaucratization in intelligence. As espionage became the responsibility of agencies more than of individuals, politics played a stronger and stronger role, and politics was not Baker's game. His excesses of independent action could be lived with during the extraordinary circumstances of wartime, but not in the day-to-day compromises of government. His departure from intelligence work presaged the fight between effective intelligence and political maneuvering which continues into the present.

Besides Baker's organizational contributions to America's intelligence heritage, others' intelligence experience during the Civil War reinforced the image of the patriotic spy. Many hundreds labored, for both the Union and the Confederacy, in hazardous espionage vineyards out of genuine patriotic motives and deep belief in their respective side's cause. Unfortunately, the great bulk of their names and individual exploits are lost to history. This is due as much to the secrecy of their activities as to the penchant of military and political leaders of the period who, when writing their memoirs, tended to highlight their own genius and to downplay or ignore the critical insights often provided to them by secret (and often immoral and/or illegal) activities. Also, due to the great physical devastation wreaked in the South by the war, many Confederate records were lost or burned; and because it was the losing side, many who served in its intelligence organizations preferred not to draw attention to their wartime exploits against the Union.

The records of two women are particularly noteworthy because they give the tradition of the patriotic spy added meaning; they prove that espionage is not simply a man's world. To be sure, the thirty-three-century history of espionage is replete with stories of women spies—courtesans and femme fatales —who gained intelligence information. However, as the Revolutionary War showed, American women more often made use of their wits than their charms in carrying out the manifold and complex duties of the spy. In the Civil War the tradition was further upheld as more women were used (on both sides) than during the Revolution. Without slighting the admirable records of Pauline Cushman, Emma Edmonds, Sarah Thompson, Belle Boyd, Antonia Ford, and a host of others, those of Rose Greenhow and Elizabeth Van Lew best illustrate the female contribution to the patriotic spy tradition during the Civil War. A contribution, one might add, which continued to be made up through World War II, but which since the advent of the Cold War has been rejected by those in charge of America's intelligence community on the grounds of "chivalry" and male chauvinism.

Rose O'Neale Greenhow

Rose Greenhow was a pillar of capital society. She moved freely among the leaders of the federal government, and such license made her privy to many secrets of value to the Confederacy. By birth she was a Maryland aristocrat, born in 1817 in Rockville, Montgomery County, not twenty miles from Washington. She was related to the Lee, Randolph, and Calvert families, clans which had helped settle the original colonies. Her father's family, the O'Neales, had a long history as warriors in Ireland, the Revolutionary War, and the War of 1812. The family motto was *Semper Paratus Patriae Servire* —Always Ready to Serve the Country. They were devout Catholics, following the religion of Maryland's founder, Lord Baltimore.

Rose's father died before she was eight years old, and she went to live with her aunt, Mary Hill, who ran the boarding house in the Old Capitol Building in Washington. Rose was tutored in music, literature, and French by Catholic sisters, and received a special education from the many senators and representatives who frequented the boarding house. She was especially close to John C. Calhoun, the senator from South Carolina. In 1833, her sister Ellen married James Madison Cutts, the son of a representative and nephew of Dolly Madison, thus giving the O'Neale family another contact with official Washington. Rose later commented on her early years: "I am a Southern woman, born with revolutionary blood in my veins, and my first crude ideas on State and Federal matters received consistency and shape from the best and wisest man of this century [Calhoun]."*

When she grew old enough to enter the Washington social scene, Rose's first suitor was Representative Cave Johnson of Tennessee, who later became postmaster general. However, she decided to marry a State Department official, Robert Greenhow, fifteen years her senior, a scion of an old Richmond family. He was a brilliant scholar, having been educated at the College of William and Mary, Columbia University Medical School, the University of Edinburgh, and granted a law degree from the Sorbonne. French, Spanish, Italian, and German

*Kane, *op. cit.*, p. 18.

were languages Greenhow spoke fluently, and he wrote numerous translations for the Department of State.

By virtue of their aristocratic heritage, sharp minds and political contacts, the Greenhows became leading figures in the capital. In addition to Calhoun, a close personal friend was Senator James Buchanan of Pennsylvania. Although Rose took time out from her entertaining to rear four children, her first love was politics. In 1842, the family left Washington to help Calhoun in Petersburg, Virginia. Robert Greenhow went to work on a pro–states' rights newspaper; when Calhoun became secretary of state under Tyler in 1844, he called them back to Washington.

As part of the ruling faction in the State Department, the Greenhows met many foreign dignitaries. Rose enjoyed gossping about secret intelligence with the British envoys, and also became involved in American schemes to annex Cuba. Secretary Calhoun was a frequent visitor at the Greenhows, and a substitute grandfather to their four daughters.

When Calhoun died, Rose was at his bedside. In addition to her deep personal loss, she recognized that without their foremost political patron the Greenhow family would likely be moved elsewhere. Robert travelled to Mexico and made an extensive study of land grants in California and the Southwest. In 1850, after leaving government service, the rest of the family joined him in San Francisco, where he opened a law firm specializing in property claims. Mrs. Greenhow felt out of place at first, especially since fierce debates over slavery and sectionalism were raging back in Washington, and she yearned to make a contribution. She soon discovered a community of Southern partisans in California, however, and she was quick to become active in their circle.

James Buchanan, the Greenhows' old friend, joined the race for the presidential nomination as the election of 1852 approached. Ever the political warrior, Rose returned to Washington, worked for his campaign, and gave birth to another daughter—Rose, named after her mother. Although he lost the election, Buchanan used his influence to have Robert Greenhow appointed assistant land agent for the California Land Commission. Rose remained in Washington with her young baby rather than risk the trip westward. In 1854 she learned that her husband had died in San Francisco; in short order she was in California to settle his business. There Rose discovered that Robert's death occurred because of a fall from one of the elevated municipal walkways. Never one to miss an opportunity, she sued the city for several thousand dollars in compensation for the accident.

Robert's death left Rose with new freedom, and she used it to plunge back into political activity with more vigor than ever before. A Washington resident described her as:

. . . a leader, famous for her beauty, the brilliance of her conversation, her aptitude for intrigue, the royal dignity of her manners, the unscrupulous perseverance with which she accomplished whatever she sets her heart upon.*

Greenhow moved into a house on Sixteenth Street across Lafayette Square from the White House. She reinvolved herself with plans to take over Cuba, and cultivated a warm friendship with Secretary of War Jefferson Davis.

Buchanan pursued the presidency again in 1856, and Rose ran his campaign in California by calling on her old allies for support. He carried the state and won the election. Capital gossips noted that Greenhow was the only woman with whom the president, a bachelor, danced twice at the Inaugural Ball. Buchanan spent much time with her after he became president. His carriage could be observed frequently parked in front of the Greenhow home, and many Washingtonians commented on the late hours at which he departed Rose's for his own house across the square.

Washington was an exciting city as the country rushed toward open conflict, and Rose was in the thick of it. She had close firends on both sides of the slavery issue, and her dinner parties sometimes brought the opposing factions together. Mr. and Mrs. Jefferson Davis, William Seward, Senator Henry Wilson, and Mrs. Charles Francis Adams were all present at Sixteenth Street one night to hear Rose denounce John Brown and the abolitionists. Her ability to bring even the most radical Republicans to her home proved valuable after the war began, when these contacts and their dinner conversations provided valuable information which Greenhow passed on to the Rebels. She achieved yet another political conduit when her niece married Stephen Douglas, Lincoln's unsuccessful opponent in the 1860 presidential election. One of Rose's daughters married a Union soldier in 1861.

Rose was present with President Buchanan when he learned of South Carolina's secession. She heard Jefferson Davis' farewell speech to the Senate, and watched with interest as Congress formed a committee "to inquire whether any secret organization hostile to the government of the United States exists in the District of Columbia and if so whether any employee or officers of the federal government in the executive or judicial departments are members thereof."** She knew there were Confederates still in government service. Some of them had told her of various plots to kill Abraham Lincoln, including the Baltimore conspiracy. Rose also knew Robert E. Lee, and spoke with him on April 16, 1861, just before he left Washington.

Despite her numerous contacts with Southern sympathizers, Greenhow's best sources of information were Northern government officials who were so infatuated with the stylish widow that she charmed them out of their secrets.

Ibid., p. 21.

**Nash K. Burger, *Confederate Spy: Rose O'Neale Greenhow.* New York: Franklin Watts, 1967, p. 55.

These men included the anti-slavery Senator Wilson of Massachusetts (who wrote love notes to Rose on the floor of the Senate during debates), Senator Joseph Lane of Oregon, and Colonel Erasmus D. Keyes. Keyes was particularly valuable as an old friend from California and military aide to General Winfield Scott, the Union commander. Colonel Keyes called Rose:

The most persuasive woman that was ever known in Washington. [I am] convinced that few men could have boasted of their ability to withstand the blandishments of those Southern ladies. It would have been idle to deny that in society they were the most attractive women in the world.*

Armed with her charming personality and numerous contacts, Rose was a logical choice for the Confederate army to use for information. She could be especially valuable as a secret agent because her position in Washington would protect her from all but the most concrete evidence of treason. A young Rebel colonel approached Rose to become part of his plan to leave a spy network in Washington as Southern leaders left to pursue the war from the other side of the Potomac.

The colonel was Thomas Jordan. He was a 42-year-old native of Virginia who had graduated in 1840 from West Point, where he had been the roommate of William Tecumseh Sherman. Jordan fought in the Seminole War, becoming a staff officer to Winfield Scott. He was still under federal commission when he organized the spy ring which he turned over to Greenhow. When he resigned in May 1861, he became adjutant general under Beauregard; he served in that capacity at Manassas, and again under General A.S. Johnston at Shiloh. In July 1862 he became Bragg's chief of staff, and was brigadier general in command of the Third Military District of South Carolina when the Civil War ended.

Jordan had done some work as a journalist prior to the war, and in 1866 became editor of the Memphis *Appeal.* He supported insurrection in Cuba, and in 1869 he travelled to the island to become chief of staff and later commander of the Cuban revolutionaries. Spain placed a price of $100,000 on his head, but Jordan had learned how to sneak through enemy lines during the Civil War, and he escaped to the mainland after the rebellion failed. He resumed his literary interests, becoming editor of the *Financial and Mining Record* of New York, which championed free silver. He died in New York on November 27, 1895.

Colonel Jordan visited Greenhow early in 1861. He was about to leave for the South and needed someone to take command of his spies in the federal government. His agents reached into the top ranks of the army and senior officials of the executive branch. Rose agreed to take the assignment. She was impressed with Jordan's emphasis on secrecy. He gave her a substitution

Ibid., pp. 60–61.

cipher, warned her of Pinkerton's presence, and taught her how to use her window shades to broadcast Morse code. Jordan, in turn, was impressed by the strong recommendations in support of Mrs. Greehow he had received from such leading Confederates as Davis, Lee, and Beauregard.

Rose was especially eager to help Jordan because of her concern for her native Maryland. She urged her friends in the state to secede, but Union power controlled the state government, if not its people. As Rose saw the situation:

I knew that every genuine child of Maryland cherished in their souls but one feeling —one burning desire to share the destiny of their section, and to perish if need be, in the glorious struggle; and could well imagine how so proud and refined a people would suffer and chafe to see themsevles treated as vassals and serfs by a race they had always despised.*

Many of Rose's neighbors fled into Virginia, but she elected to remain and play her secret role in Washington.

As preparations for the first major battle of the war began, Rose sent constant messages to Jordan at Beauregard's headquarters. She saw a copy of the Union Army's marching orders in Washington, and sent a copy to General Beauregard, thereby preparing the Rebels for Bull Run. Jordan wrote back asking for precise information as to the number of troops and artillery. Greenhow contacted army friends and received quick answers in reply. Beauregard applauded her "most accurate information, of which politicians high in council, as well as war department clerks, were the unconsious ducts."** On July 23, 1861, after the Confederate success at the first battle of Manassas, Jordan wrote Greenhow:

Our President and our General direct me to thank you. We rely upon you for further information. The Confederacy owes you a debt.***

Greenhow continued to report her informants' data daily to Jordan. Sometimes the Confederate colonel would sneak into the capital and meet with her personally. She visited Rebel prisoners at the Old Capitol, taking them medication, food, clothing, and bedding. Rose asked the soldiers to give her military information to pass South, and helped their morale by counselling them against taking the oath of allegiance to the Union. She was certain of Confederate triumph. The Knights of the Golden Circle were also in contact with Rose. She agreed with their contention that the Civil War was the product of Lincoln's acting outside the Constitution without the assent of either the legislative or judicial branches of the government.

*Ibid., p. 67.
**Ibid., p. 78.
***Ibid., p. 89.

The Greenhow ring's sources of information were widespread. She consulted British and French envoys to learn new facts, and forwarded some of her reports to Richmond via those nation's diplomatic pouches. Her Washington agents included bankers, doctors, and housewives, many of whom had relatives and friends serving in the Confederate army. As Rose described her efforts:

I employed every capacity which God had endowed me, and the result was far more successful than my hopes would have flattered me to expect.

After Bull Run, Pinkerton put Greenhow and her home under surveillance. On August 23, 1861, the detective placed her under house arrest after he had caught her reviewing army maps with an officer from Union headquarters. Despite the presence of Pinkerton's guards, she continued to pass information out of her home to Jordan. She was soon taken to the Old Capitol for greater security, but was not formally charged with an offense. Rose wrote many letters protesting her illegal arrest and affirming her belief in the Confederacy and the teachings of Calhoun. The following letter went to Secretary of State Seward:

Sir—
For nearly three months I have been confined a close prisoner, shut out from air and exercise, and denied all communication with family and friends.

On Friday, August 23rd, without warrant or other show of authority, I was arrested by the detective police, and my house taken in charge by them; all my private letters and papers of a lifetime were read and examined by them; every law of decency was violated in the search of my house and person, and by the surveillance over me.

In the careful analysis of my papers I deny the existence of a line that I had not a perfect right to have written or to have received. Freedom of speech and of opinion is the birthright of Americans, guaranteed to us by our charter of liberty—the Constitution of the United States. I have exercised my prerogatives and have openly avowed my sentiments.

During the political struggle I opposed your Republican Party with every instinct of self-preservation. I believed your success a virtual nullification of the Constitution, and that it would entail upon us all the direful consequences which have ensued. These sentiments have doubtless been found recorded among my papers, and I hold them as rather a proud record of my sagacity.

Freedom of speech, freedom of thought, every right pertaining to the citizen, has been suspended by what I suppose the President calls a "military necessity." A blow has been struck by this total disregard of all civil rights against the present system of government far greater in its effects than the severance of the Southern states. The people have been taught to condemn the supremacy of the law . . . and to look to the military power. . . . A military spirit has been developed which will only subordinate to a military dictatorship.

Read history, and you will find that the causes which bring about a revolution rarely predominate at its close, and no people have ever returned from the point from which they started. Even should the Southern States be subdued, and forced back into the Union . . . a different form of government will be needful to meet the new developments of national character.

My object is to call your attention to the fact, that during this long imprisonment I am yet ignorant of the causes of my arrest; that my house has been seized and converted into a prison by the government, that the valuable furniture it contained has been abused and destroyed; that during some period of my imprisonment I have suffered greatly for want of proper and sufficient food.

I could easily have escaped arrest, having had timely warning. I thought it possible that your statesmanship might prevent such a proclamation of weakness to the world as even the fragment of a once great government turning its arms against the breasts of women and children. You have the power, sir, and may still abuse it. You may prostrate the physical strength by confinement in close rooms and insufficient food. You may subject me to harsher ruder treatment than I have already received; but you cannot imprison the soul.

Every cause worthy of success has had its martyrs. . . . My sufferings will afford a significant lesson to the women of the South . . . the iron heel of power may keep down but it cannot crush out, the spirit of resistance in a people armed for the defense of their rights.*

Greenhow continued her correspondence with Washington officials, sometimes sneaking copies of her letters into Richmond newspapers. Such actions enraged the federal government, and in an attempt to end her martyrdom sent her South on May 31, 1862, in return for her word not to leave the Confederacy. Rose arrived in Richmond five days later to a hero's welcome. President Davis said, "But for you there would have been no battle of Bull Run," and paid her $2,500. Greenhow responded by calling the occasion "the proudest moment of my whole life; to have received the tribute of praise from him who stands as the apostle of our country's liberty in the eyes of the civilized world."

The Confederacy had elaborate plans to exploit Greenhow's propaganda value. They encouraged her to publish the story of her imprisonment and arranged for her to make an expedition to Europe. Meanwhile she worked in Richmond hospitals and toured several of the Rebel armies, forwarding morale reports to President Davis. She told Davis that the South's mission was a "holy cause."

Rose left for England on August 4, 1863, and arrived a month later. She was well received in London, charming official Britain just as she had American politicians. Her book, *My Imprisonment and the First Year of Abolitionist Rule at Washington,* ** was published, and favorable reviews in Europe added to her fame. Despite the kind attention of European society, Rose longed to return home. Her mission to win the financial and physical support of the English and

---

Ibid., p. 127.

**Rose O'Neale Greenhow, *My Imprisonment and the First Year of Abolition Rule at Washington.* London: R. Bentley, 1863.

French governments for the Confederacy had failed. English officials saw a swing in the course of the war toward the Union and politely maintained a position of official neutrality. Although Rose was received warmly by Napoleon III at Versailles, she learned that France would not act without England.

Disappointed by the failure of her diplomatic mission, Greenhow assembled letters for the Confederate government praising its cause (but which carefully refrained from the commitment of funds and/or equipment), tied a bag of bullion from the sale of her book around her waist, and boarded a ship for North Carolina in August 1864. The blockade runner arrived outside Wilmington on October 1. Seas were rough. A Union patrol boat spotted the Rebel ship and gave chase. In the midst of the darkness and waves, Rose's vessel ran up on a sandbar. Greenhow convinced the captain, against his better judgment, to let her take a small boat and attempt to row to the nearby shore. High winds and waves capsized the boat, and Rose was pulled to the bottom by her heavy bag of bullion.

Rose Greenhow's body was recovered the next day. The city of Wilmington provided her with a lavish funeral and burial. She had been a patriot to the end, fulfilling her debt to the O'Neale family motto. Rose was ever ready to serve her country, secretly or above board, even at the risk of her life. And in death she was used as a symbol to rally others with much less dedication to the Confederacy's cause.

Elizabeth Van Lew

One of the Civil War's most effective spies, in terms of both length of service and accuracy of intelligence acquired, was Elizabeth Van Lew of Richmond, Virginia. Yet Van Lew hated the label "spy" and viewed herself as a patriot to both her region and the nation. Her diary notes:

Notes on Being Called a Spy [1887?]   *Personal*
There are very many now who wish they had been loyal—They have found out their mistake in the War . . .

I do not know how they can call me a spy serving my own country within its recognized borders—

A person cannot be called a spy [for] sticking with their country and serving within its borders—

For my loyalty am I now to be branded as a spy—by my own country—for which I was willing to lay down my life—is that honorable is that honest?

God knows

—there is not a vocation more ennobling more immorable [immortal?]—and even the disgraceful word cannot stain my record.

I do not think a person should be branded as a spy—because within its border they rise to their country and aid it all they can deserve.

I am in a pretty position, called a traitor here a spy north—
I now [ask] north and south—are you not ashamed to give me these names—*

Elizabeth Van Lew's life provides a deep insight into the commitment to
religion, family, country, and philosophy which motivated the self-sacrifice of
American spies throughout the early history of United States espionage. Elizabeth was the daughter of a prominent Richmond hardware merchant, John
Van Lew. His family was of Dutch and German descent and had lived in
America before the Revolutionary War. John Van Lew was born in Jamaica,
Long Island. His parents saw that he received a strong education, and had
hoped that he would become a professor of Latin, but John Van Lew had
independent ideas. He wandered to Richmond, Virginia, there making the
acquaintance of John Adams, a son of one of Richmond's first families. He and
Adams exercised the American entrepreneurial spirit and set up a small business which quickly ran up a $100,000 debt. Van Lew parted company with
Adams and established a hardware business with a man named Taylor. In
short order he repaid his enormous debt and began to prosper. Finding his
friend Adams still on hard times, John Van Lew purchased the Adams family
mansion, which soon became known as the Van Lew Mansion. In time he
became one of Richmond's wealthiest citizens. Richmond townspeople were
awed by the coach and four white horses which awaited the family in front
of the home which Van Lew had redecorated from top to bottom with the
finest antiques and materials available in America and Europe.

Elizabeth's mother was also from the North. She was a daughter of Hil-
lary Baker, one of the framers of the Pennsylvania State Constitution in
1789, and later mayor of Philadelphia. Mrs. Van Lew's grandmother had
come from France, and Elizabeth credited her with inculcating the love of
books which she remembered in both her parents. Mayor Baker died in
1798, when yellow fever swept through Philadelphia. He sent his family
out of the city for their protection, and in staying behind to help the sick,
he contracted the disease himself. His wife survived until 1818, the year
Elizabeth was born.

Young Elizabeth's childhood was a happy one, and she writes especially
fondly of her father. She felt her parents had a good marriage, and they were
successful in the Richmond community, although Elizabeth felt her Northern
ancestry early on:

From the time I knew right from wrong it was my sad knowledge to differ in many
things from the opinions and principles of my locality. This has made my life intensely
sad and earnest and if I may say it tolerant and uncompromising but liberal quick in

---

*Elizabeth Van Lew Papers; The New York Public Library, The Research Libraries, Manuscripts
and Archives Division.

feeling and ready to [protest] what seemed to me wrong—Quick and passionate but not bad tempered or vicious.*

Elizabeth's parents reinforced her Northern ties by sending her to school in Philadelphia. She returned to Richmond with a good education, a sharp wit, and a soul-felt abhorrence of slavery. Her father had died in her absence, and as the now dominant member of the family, her first act upon her return was to influence her mother to release the family slaves. This action caused some raised eyebrows among the Van Lew neighbors, but since most of the former slaves remained in the household and Elizabeth continued to move among the Richmond socialites as one of the brightest and most eligible young ladies, the city gossips wrote off Elizabeth's abolitionism as a small aberration in an otherwise solid character. Who could question a family with the Van Lews' wealth, which entertained world notables ranging from Jenny Lind to Edgar Allan Poe to Senator and Mrs. Jefferson Davis? Most people never knew that Elizabeth's eccentricity went so far as to include the purchase of the relatives and children of former Van Lew slaves so that families could be united in freedom. Small wonder that the Van Lew's former slaves willingly risked their lives to run secret messages for "Miss Lizzie" during the Civil War.

Despite her active social life as a young woman, Van Lew chose never to marry. Her early attractiveness faded with age into the rough-hewn angles of a witchlike woman. Slight in stature with a prominent nose and chin, Van Lew's most appealing feature was the piercing blue gaze of her active eyes. The extraordinary energy focused through her eyes gave the only clue to the furnace of her internal activity. It was as if the body had been reduced to a frail cinder by the fury of her spirit and the demands of her espionage activities.

What reward did Van Lew require to carry on her secret wartime activities in the face of her community's spite and the physical hazard associated with being a spy? Seemingly, only the eradication of slavery, the preservation of the Union, the love of her family, and a religious self-recognition that she had fought the good fight for these causes. It was only in her later years, after she had been deserted by her region and her nation, that Elizabeth complained about her fate.

Like most American spies prior to World War II, Van Lew was a self-starter. The spirit that had pushed her father to start his own business against the odds of a $100,000 debt motivated Elizabeth to open her own espionage operation for the Union in hostile Richmond. Even before the first battle of Manassas, she undertook as a private citizen of the United States to write letters to the War Department reporting on events in the Rebel capital, including any information she could gather from surrounding regions and her friends within the Confederate government. These reports were ignored at first, but Elizabeth's instinctive recognition of the importance of intelligence to the

*Van Lew Papers, op. cit., "Notes on My Ancestry."

success of the Union's cause kept her at her labors. Unfortunately there was no intelligence organization in Washington ready to use her information at the beginning of the Civil War; but the federal government soon caught up with Van Lew's initiative.

After open fighting began, the Confederacy began housing Union captives in Richmond's Libby Prison. Elizabeth and her mother flew in the face of the Richmond mob's calling for the murder of the prisoners by carrying food, bedding, and medicine to the prison. Soon Confederate authorities declared the prison off-limits to the Van Lews, but Elizabeth, like Rose Greenhow in Washington, knew men in positions of power, and obtained entry passes from Provost Marshal Winder.*

Not only was Van Lew taking material into the prison, she was also taking back information from the soldiers for delivery to Washington. Soldiers fresh from the front gave her first-hand accounts of every battle, including estimates of casualties, the strength of Rebel forces and artillery, and their locations. She remembered what she was told and swiftly transported the news to Union headquarters. When forbidden to speak with prisoners she gave them books to read in which they made pin pricks and underlined words to convey information before returning the books to Elizabeth.

*Brigadier General John Henry Winder was born on February 21, 1800, in Somerset County, Maryland. The stern-faced General Winder lacked the youthful enthusiasm of a Lafayette Baker, although the two men were faced with many of the same responsibilities for their respective governments. Winder graduated from West Point in 1820 and spent the next three years as an instructor in tactics at the Military Academy, resigning in 1823. By 1827 he had grown weary of civilian life and asked for reappointment. During the Mexican War he was brevetted major and then lieutenant colonel for gallant and meritorious conduct. As the Civil War approached, he elected to side with the South. He resigned his commission on April 27, 1861, and on June 21 became Provost Marshal of Richmond. As a career military man, Winder approached intelligence and security with a methodical attitude which mitigated his effectiveness. In fairness, much of the general's time was occupied with administering grossly overcrowded prison camps. He was also responsible for the capture and return of deserters, and the maintenance of order in a city which doubled in population during the war. At the end of 1864, President Davis added to Winder's duties by appointing him commissary general for all prisoners east of the Mississippi River. The Union accused Winder of deliberately starving prisoners, but such an act would have been out of character, and it is denied by the record: "Winder adopted every means at his command to assure that the prisoners received the same ration as did Confederate soldiers in the field, scanty as that allotment was. His task was rendered almost impossible by the refusal of the federal government to effect an exchange." (See especially Ezra J. Warner, *Generals in Gray*, Baton Rouge: Louisiana State University Press, 1959, p. 341.) Between the overcrowding and popular sentiment in Richmond that the Union prisoners be sacrificed to free supplies for poorly provisioned Confederate soldiers, it speaks to Winder's honor that he cared for the prisoners as well as he did. In the midst of his many tasks, Winder had little time to coordinate intelligence activities for the Confederacy. Winder's difficulties were compounded by a lack of cooperation on the part of Richmond's citizens. Ironically, one of the citizens who supported Winder was Elizabeth Van Lew, who appealed to her old firend for passes into the prisons and to other cities. A few words of flattery were all she needed to charm the necessary papers out of "Old Winder." Such lax security on Winder's part upset his subordinates. They tried to minimize the number of people authorized to pass through Richmond, but General Winder and Secretary of War Judah P. Benjamin wrote passes for almost anyone.

In addition to her positive military intelligence efforts, Van Lew helped captive soldiers whenever possible. She smuggled personal letters into and out of the Libby Prison for the men and aided their escape plans. In appreciation of her efforts in their behalf, Libby prisoners used bones left over from the meals to fashion her a ring and a set of studs engraved with American flags.

With all their activity around the prison, the Van Lews soon became objects of hatred in the Richmond community. Despite their obvious allegiance to the Union, however, the ladies and their household servants were never arrested. Confederate officials ordered the Van Lew mansion searched and tried to fool Elizabeth into betraying herself, but she was always one step ahead of them. All her messages were written in cipher using invisible ink. She kept the key to the cipher on her person at all times, hidden behind her mother's picture in a lavolier watch. When she went to bed, Elizabeth kept all incriminating letters and dispatches next to her so that they could be destroyed in the event of a surprise search. Often her friends in the Confederate government would warn her before a search party arrived, but even with the warnings the constant harassment began to wear on her nerves and the health of her aged mother. (Like Greenhow, Van Lew was in her 40s during the war.) To provide protection from the searches, she conceived a master stroke. The commandant of the Libby Prison was scheduled to leave and a new man and his wife were arriving in replacement. Elizabeth offered them lodging in her own mansion. With a Confederate officer living under her roof, she was spared the inconvenience of further searches.

Despite the officer's presence, Elizabeth was still attacked by the community; a group of ruffians left a note threatening to burn down her house. The resourceful Van Lew devised a plan to defuse Richmond's outrage. Already considered eccentric, she began to elaborate on the community's opinion. With her small frame, craggy features, and piercing eyes, she already appeared a bit strange. She stopped paying attention to the tidiness of her hair, and allowed her wardrobe to become older and shabbier as all her energy, money, and material goods went to the men in the Libby prison. (By the end of the Civil War, Elizabeth had spent almost all of the Van Lew family fortune on pro-Union projects.) She also cultivated the habit of mumbling to herself as she went about her business in the city, and soon everyone was calling her "Crazy Van Lew" or "Crazy Bet." If she had been a man, even this pose probably would not have saved her from arrest; but Southern gentlemen were not about to throw a lady in prison without clear-cut evidence of her treason. Elizabeth was also protected by her family's social standing in Richmond. These three factors—her sex, her feigned madness, and her prominent social position—coupled with her secrecy and cleverness, allowed Van Lew to maintain her espionage activities throughout the Civil War.

A few notable incidents demonstrate the scope of Van Lew's wartime occupation. In the course of her espionage she often donned farmer's clothes and rode at night to deliver messages to Union agents on Richmond's outskirts.

Her horse was essential to the preservation of her network, but the Confederate government ordered that all livestock be confiscated for use by the army. A clerk warned Elizabeth of the order. Elizabeth hid her horse in the smokehouse behind the mansion, but a neighbor betrayed the animal's location to the authorities. Not to be outflanked, Miss Van Lew was again warned of the confiscation party and led her animal into the mansion and up the steps to the library, where she had prepared the floor with straw. For the remainder of the war, save when she made her midnight rides, the horse remained in the same house with the commandant of the Libby Prison, who never suspected. As Elizabeth later noted, the horse never snorted, whinnied, or stamped about; "He was a very patriotic horse."

To aid escapees and Union agents sent into Richmond to carry messages, Van Lew constructed a secret chamber in the mansion's attic. No matter how thoroughly the Rebels searched her home, they never found the Van Lews' special guests.

One of the most important members of the Van Lew spy network was Mary Elizabeth Bowser. Bowser had been a Van Lew slave. Elizabeth noted her unusual intelligence, freed her and sent her North to college. Mary was living in Philadelphia at the beginning of the war when Elizabeth asked her to return to Richmond. Using her acquaintance with the Jefferson Davises, and knowing they had just moved to Richmond and would need servants for the Confederate White House, Van Lew had her friend installed as a serving maid in the Davis home. From this position within the Rebel president's home Bowser passed messages throughout the war.

In the midst of her already frantic schedule, Van Lew directed one of the most bizarre incidents of the entire war. In 1864, young Major Ulric Dahlgren led an ill-fated Union raid on Richmond. He and his small force were routed, and the major was killed. Dahlgren was one of the most promising officers in the Union army. He had lost a leg in combat, yet rode a horse better than most and held the complete confidence of his men. His father was a Union admiral. After his son's death was reported, Admiral Dahlgren asked that the body be shipped North. President Davis acceded to the request, but when Confederate soldiers went to unearth the body, it was not to be found. The mystery went unsolved until after the war. Elizabeth Van Lew knew the answer.

By 1864, the Confederates were becoming desperate, and Van Lew feared that inhumane treatment of Union dead and prisoners would result. A Negro whom Elizabeth knew saw Confederate soldiers bury Dahlgren in an unmarked grave, and told Van Lew. She decided to move the body so it could rest peacefully and be returned to Admiral Dahlgren after the war. Together with a local farmer, she dug up the body and hid it in the farmer's wagon under some closely packed peach trees. The next day the farmer drove out of Richmond, but was stopped at a Confederate check point. Fortunately the farmer knew the soldier in charge and was passed through without a rigorous search. Dahlgren's body was reburied the next night and returned to his father in 1865.

As the war reached its closing days, Union generals discovered that Van Lew's espionage network was not only accurate, but had been refined to a surprising swiftness. Her own inventiveness had led Van Lew to accomplish these two criteria required by any espionage text for an effective intelligence operation. She set up a series of stations like pony express stops between her mansion in Richmond and Union headquarters. In the first leg, Van Lew or one of her servants would carry concealed information from her home to the Van Lew farm on the outskirts of the city. From there a rider or another courier would speed the message to another way station from which it would proceed in assigned segments to its destination. When Grant camped outside Richmond, flowers from the Van Lew garden reached his breakfast table each morning along with the latest intelligence from Richmond.

Elizabeth received her reward for her five years of loyal service to the Union when Grant marched into Richmond. The general arrived only hours after Elizabeth had raised the first Stars and Stripes in the recaptured city above her mansion. When Grant dispatched an advance guard to protect Van Lew they found her, an agent to the end, hunting for records in the smoldering ruins of the Confederate capital building. Grant need not have worried about Van Lew. When she raised her Union flag, an angry crowd surrounded the house, demanding her life. The raging woman charged out to face the crowd, and calling many of them by name, threatened the wrath of General Grant should any harm come to her home or person. The mob curbed its fury and dispersed.

Elizabeth considered the visit of General Grant and his wife to the Van Lew mansion the high point of her illustrious career in espionage. Her fondness for Grant continued after the Civil War, and when he became president he appointed her postmaster of Richmond. Other generals attested to her valiant service, which was equated to the value of 25,000 troops. In recognition of the personal and financial sacrifice endured by Elizabeth, Grant proposed a $15,-000 award as partial reimbursement for the vast sums she had spent in the Union cause during the war. Congress, however, decided against the payment, although much greater sums were given others for far less. General Sharpe, the Union Army's chief intelligence officer, had special praise for Elizabeth. In a speech supporting the $15,000 payment he called her "one of the shrewdest and smartest women of the present age." He noted that the Van Lews'

position, character, and charities gave them a commanding influence, and many families of plain people were decided and encouraged by them to remain true to the flag, and were subsequently able during the war to receive our agents. . . . For a long, long time she represented all that was left of the power of the United States government in the city of Richmond. . . . The greater portion [of our intelligence of 1864–1865] in its collection and in good measure in its transmission, we owed to the intelligence and devotion of Miss Van Lew.*

*Van Lew Papers, *op. cit.*, letter from General Sharpe to EVL w/copy of Speech.

General Benjamin Butler wrote to Secretary Stanton about Van Lew's efforts, and called her "my secret correspondent in Richmond."* The troops also remembered Van Lew. The 79th Regiment Highlanders sent a resolution to Grant thanking him for appointing her postmaster.**

Elizabeth's tenure as postmaster was marked by outspokenness and strict discipline. On one occasion a large number of carriers protested one of her regulations and threatened to resign. Van Lew responded by firing all of them. They appealed to Washington, but the government refused to interfere and she continued to dominate her agency. On February 26, 1877, President Grant penned a letter in support of his former secret agent's continued service:

Miss Van Lew was appointed by me as Postmaster of Richmond, Va. soon after my entrance upon the duties of President from a knowledge of her entire loyalty during the rebellion and her services to the cause. She has filled the office since with capacity and fidelity and is very deserving of continued confidence by a Republican administration.***

Despite Grant's support, she was replaced by President Hayes with Colonel W.W. Forbes, a man whom Elizabeth characterized as a "Confederate Colonel of loose character."****

Elizabeth travelled to Washington in hopes of meeting with President Hayes and returning to work, but she was denied admission to the White House. In addition to her new-found financial problems, Van Lew had long suffered public ostracism in Richmond for her role in the war. She complained of slander, her own poor health from worry over the problem, and an inability to find enough friends to be pallbearers at her mother's funeral in 1875. In a letter to Grant she wrote, "I am in so much trouble that I scarcely know how to make my situation known to you."***** On October 27, 1876, she also wrote:

I was born and brought up in this city; I was ever faithful to the United States Government, and did all that I could to serve it, though I never compromised myself by any betrayal of trust or honor. I live—and have lived for years—as entirely distinct from the citizens

AS IF I WERE PLAGUE STRICKEN******

---

*Ibid., copy of April 5, 1865 letter from Butler and letter from Butler to Stanton, February 5, 1867. Official Records of the War of the Rebellion, Volume XXXIII, Series I, p. 520.

**Ibid., copy of 79th Regiment letter to President Grant.

***Ibid., letter of President Grant to President Hayes, EVL personal copy.

****Ibid., EVL letter to Howland, June 16, 1877.

*****Ibid., EVL letter to President Grant, February 1, 1881.

******Ibid., EVL letter to President Grant, October 27, 1876.

Van Lew's position in the community was not helped by her opinionated stances. She attacked the South for its closed-mindedness and noted, "When a people all think and speak one way, you may be sure there is not much liberty left amongst them."* She blamed the Confederacy's loss in part on the fact that "Our Southern leaders firmly believed in the power of cotton to rule the world."** Harking back to the Revolutionary War, she refused to pay her taxes, arguing that reconstruction government was a farce, and that therefore the liens were taxation without representation. Elizabeth was especially critical of her fellow women:

The doctrine of seccession semed to gratify an innate feeling of pride. The women became its strongest advocates, unknowing, and unreflecting. "Ah ladies, when you see your husbands, brothers, and fathers brought home dead, you'll think on this" was said to them on every opportunity by a loyal statesman, only to fall as idle words on deaf ears.

I have never yet comprehended the almost universal want of National patriotism among the women—I know very few ladies who were for their country very very few.***

Yet, reaffirming her ardor for liberty and patriotism, she pleaded for the right to be represented as a woman in a public letter addressed to the North:

As a woman I have no power, but through your vote. A vote is a tremendous power. You not only protect yourself with it, but provide for the wants and miseries, or add to the wickedness of your fellow beings. Remember the ballot is the moral lever by which you put in place and power your officials.****

Little wonder with these sentiments that the Richmond *News* could write, "Her attitudes in a man would have been death to anyone that uttered them."*****

Van Lew's righteous and often self-serving attitudes in the midst of what she deemed the immoral climate of the secessionist South and reconstruction America is traceable in part to a religious theme which underlies her writings. Before the war it was expressed in her opinion of John Brown's raid:

What struck me most painfully in all this was the universal want of humanity toward the raiders. I hold that one spark of the Divine Love of Christ in our hearts gives us a feeling of oneness, of sympathy with all his creatures, however sunken, however

*Ibid.

**Ibid.

***Ibid., Diary entry, pp. 6–7.

****Ibid., EVL letter to President Grant, October 27, 1876.

*****Richmond *News,* September 25, 1900, p. 1.

sinning. I never thought John Brown right, I have always thought him one who suffered so deeply from sense of the wrongs of the slave that his strong head faited [sic] him under.*

Later, religion appeared as solace amidst her setbacks:

I will not tell you of constant and repeated gross personal insults; they have long since ceased to move me: there is no one in this community to whom I would not render a service if in my power; NO SOCIAL OR POLITICAL ACT FOR WHICH BLUSH.

Others before me have passed through the furnace, and I have found a consolation in Matthew v.10th, 11th and 12th Luke vi 22nd and 23d, which the whole world can neither gainsay nor take away from me.**

Yet a few years before her death, Elizabeth protested strongly, "I am not a spiritualist."

Whatever her final position vis-à-vis her religion, Van Lew was a proud and independent spirit: self-righteous in her devotion to patriotism, abolitionism, her family, and her community. Although she fought against labels all her life, she did apply one to her role in Civil War Richmond: "Among the Union people of the city I was the recognized head, the leader—my word was law."*** Perhaps this is her best characterization. Like Washington, Baker, Hale, Tallmadge, and others who preceded her in American espionage she displayed the profound leadership of a pioneer in areas where others feared to tread, and added significantly to America's intelligence heritage.

The Struggle for Control Begins: Civil War Communications Intelligence

A discussion of the Civil War's contribution to America's intelligence heritage would not be complete without noting the first major intrusion of science and technology into the intelligence process, and the political struggle which underlies and accompanies that process. The basic craft of the spy hasn't really changed much in thirty-three centuries; invisible inks, poisons, codes and ciphers, silent killing devices have been improved over the ages, but these and related techniques remain basically the same as in biblical times. However, during the Civil War a quantum leap was made in solving George Washington's—and his intellectual and practical predecessors'—problem of communicating intelligence swiftly to maintain its fleeting value: Samuel Morse's invention of the telegraph.

Once Morse had demonstrated the telegraph's feasibility in transmitting

---

*Van Lew Papers, Diary entry, p. 1.

**Ibid., EVL letter to President Grant, October 27, 1876.

***Ibid., Diary, post-1885.

information via wire, it became the center of a political struggle within America's political, military, and early intelligence hierarchies. At the time, the potential commercial value of Morse's invention was less important to America's leaders than its utilization in the seemingly never-ending battle to meet national security needs.

As with the creation of other ongoing American intelligence organizations which have been spawned by scientific or technological breakthroughs, the United States Army Signal Corps, which followed in the wake of Morse's invention, was the brain child of a perceptive and imaginative individual who saw and argued for the necessity of its existence to support military operations and to deal with the problems of processing and disseminating an increasing flow of intelligence information. In this case the far-sighted man was General Albert J. Myer.

Myer was born in New York in 1827, and worked as an apprentice telegrapher through high school. He graduated from Hobart College and received an M.D. in 1851, which was followed by three years of private practice. He then decided to enter the army, and was commissioned an assistant surgeon in the New Mexico territory. While there Myer studied Commanche signal techniques and addressed a letter to the War Department to inquire whether there was interest in applying these signal techniques, along with the use of the telegraph, to the military. The request was reviewed by a committee chaired by Robert E. Lee. Because Myer's letter reflected his experience with the telegraph and the Commanche's skills, the Lee Committee's report approved telegraph field testing. In response, Congress passed an appropriation in 1860 authorizing one signal officer with the rank of major and $2,000 for telegraph equipment.

Like other applications of science and technology for military purposes—for example, rocketry in the 1930s—telegraphy would have died on the vine. However, after the outbreak of the Civil War, Myer was sent to Fort Monroe, where General Benjamin F. Butler ordered him to train a group of soldiers as signal operators. These men formed the core of the Union's Signal Corps for the rest of the war. Their efforts were used mainly to communicate information between posts and to direct gunfire in support of troop engagements. Before the end of the war, over 110 officers were commissioned in the Signal Corps. In addition, nearly 300 men left their regular army posts to serve as acting signal officers. Approximately 2,500 enlisted men saw service with the corps. This expansion was officially sanctioned by an act of Congress on March 3, 1863.

As the Singal Corps grew, Myer sought to expand his own responsibilities. He had the corps' role enlarged to include the coordination of intelligence reports for the Union. Any refugee, deserter, or other person who entered a military post was interrogated and a report filed with the Signal Corps; thus began the paper intelligence explosion. Myer had correctly determined that a record from which to cross-check information would be useful, but his intelligence collection went largely unused because there was little coordination between his department and the officers in the field, nor any recognition of the interconnected nature of intelligence information. In contrast, Lafayette Baker's National Detective Bureau maintained a similar file which was useful because the bureau both collected the intelligence and applied it in its military and other actions.

The problems of coordinating the Signal Corps with other military units were further aggravated by the presence of the United States Military Telegraph. The Military Telegraph had been created in 1861 when Lincoln ordered all civilian telegraph lines to be taken over by the army. Myer believed that his Signal Corps should have been given jurisdiction over all telegraphy, and this led him into direct conflict with the Military Telegraph. In addition, security required that all messages be censored to remove all military information, detailed facts of government operations, diplomatic messages, and criticism of the government or the armed forces. This censorship was at various times during the war under the control of the Treasury, State, and War Departments. This brought the secretaries of each department into the fight over Union telegraphy; and was a precursor of the World War II fight over control of propaganda.

Myer's immediate opponent in this bureaucratic struggle was Anson Stager, his opposite number in the Military Telegraph organization. Stager, a former Western Union official, had originally advised Lincoln to seize all telegraph lines. Secretary of War Stanton had borrowed four operators from the Pennsylvania Railroad to man the lines, with Andrew Carnegie as their supervisor. Stager thereafter became head of an expanded unit numbering over 1,200 operators and linemen, and Carnegie gained the distinction of being a Civil War "veteran."

Both Myer and Stager were forced to minimize cooperation with field officers because of the need for secrecy. Lest codes and ciphers be compromised, most of Stager's men were denied military status so that officers could not order them to reveal their codes. If this sounds a bit bizarre, it should be remembered that in the Civil War the Union forces had to face the fact that at the time of Fort Sumter almost half the officers on duty opted to fight for the Confederacy, and there was never any real assurance that those who remained behind were not Confederate sympathizers. It was not, contrary to motion picture history of the period, a popular war with either those who fought it or paid for it.

To compound the confusion, Myer's men had only limited telegraph responsibility during the war because Stanton controlled Stager and rejected all Myer's efforts to have the military telegraph incorporated under the Signal Corps. From November 1863 until the end of the war Stager's organization controlled all Union telegraphy, a fact which in later years led to the view that Stanton made use of Military Telegraph "secret lines" to hatch the scheme to assassinate Lincoln.

On November 30, 1865, all telegraph lines, except those specifically for military use, were returned to civilian control. The Military Telegraph was disbanded and all communications came under the Signal Corps' control. This should have been a triumph for Myer, but Stanton maneuvered to have him removed as head of the corps. After a protracted legal battle and with an assist from Stanton's loss of political power, Myer won reinstatement as chief signal officer on October 30, 1866, and the Armed Forces Act formally granted the Signal Corps sole responsibility for telegraphy in war zones. For the next fourteen years, until his death, Myer labored to establish telegraphy as an integral part of military training. He set up communication schools at West Point and Annapolis. Myer's recognition of the need to coordinate communications with positive and counterespionage was an important contribution to the growth of America's intelligence organizations. But like the idea of intelligence centralization, it is one whose time never fully seems to come.

Among Myer's early telegraphy trainees were J.E.B. Stuart and E.P. Alexander, two Confederate generals who later were noted for their use of the wires to conduct espionage and direct gunfire. The Confederate Signal Corps became an important part of the Southern war effort, especially for raiders like Morgan and Mosby, who depended upon surprise and deception to score their military successes.

At the beginning of the Civil War, the Confederate Signal Service was headed by Major William Norris. It operated flag, torch, and telegraphic signals, and became the main part of the Confederate Signal Corps when it was formally established in 1862. The corps operated under the central government in Richmond and was charged with espionage and secret communications by messenger as well as by flag and wire.

The Confederate Signal Corps was especially effective in the Potomac region. John Lancaster, a Union signal operator whose father and brother were in the Confederate army, read all the messages which passed through his office and forwarded them South until his arrest by Baker's agents in 1863. One signal corps officer kept a permanent post on the lower Potomac which served as a safehouse for Rebel agents and a relay point for messages. He kept the waters around his home mined and boasted of being able to get any message between Washington and Richmond in twenty-four hours through his networks. E. Pliny Bryan, a Confederate telegrapher, lived in Washington. Each day he read the Northern papers for arrivals and assignments of brigades and divisions, summarized news items, and sent a report south via secret wire.

The star wiretapper of the Civil War was George A. Ellsworth, a Confederate telegrapher born in Canada. In the early months of the conflict he retained his job as assistant superintendent of the Texas Telegraph Company, but in June 1862 he enlisted in Company A of the 2nd Kentucky Cavalry of Chattanooga. In recognition of his special skills he was detached as a signal officer a month later and promoted to captain.

On recommendation of General Beauregard, Ellsworth signed on with Confederate raider John Hunt Morgan. He played a decisive role in Morgan's famous month of raiding, during which Morgan lost only 100 of his 800-man force while travelling 1,000 miles and taking 1,200 prisoners. Ellsworth prepared the way for Morgan's attacks by tapping into Union lines and sending false messages to alarm, confuse, and delay Union forces. By listening to the North's wires he also warned Morgan in advance of enemy movements.

Ellsworth's and Morgan's use of the telegraph included transmission of fraudulent Union dispatches and taunting personal messages of disdain to federal generals. They raided Union telegraph offices and stole copies of their signal traffic messages. During some periods Ellsworth was on the Union wire so frequently that federal operators were unsure whether to trust their own transmissions.

Ellsworth and Morgan were finally captured by Union forces. Morgan escaped and Ellsworth was later exchanged, but they never worked together again. When Ellsworth returned to Confederate service, he became Beauregard's chief of telegraphy. Ironically, he occasionally discovered Union operators tapping his lines. Ellsworth continued in telegraphy and other forms of electrical experimentation after the war as a partner of Thomas Alva Edison.

During the Civil War, lax security and sloppy message enciphering accounted for extensive signal theft by both North and South. It also gave each side an opportunity to plant false information, and in this can be seen the forerunner of today's modern communications intelligence deception plans. For example, when Lee knew that his code had been broken he usually used it to plant misleading plans with Washington before changing the code. Flag alphabets were extremely insecure and frequently broken. One Confederate officer commented, "We always had the Federal alphabet, and I suppose they had ours."* The telegraph was less susceptible to codebreaking, but codes were sometimes sold for large sums of money.

Although officially more disjointed because of power squabbles in Lincoln's cabinet, Union communications services were more coordinated than Confederate efforts. In theory, the Rebel services were to coordinate espionage under the Southern executive branch, but because that branch was disorganized and held little central power, Confederate signal services were splintered under the power spheres of individual generals. The result was confusion and poor communications intelligence security on both sides.

Notwithstanding the crudeness of the Civil War's communications intelligence activities, they display the ingenuity of Americans in exploiting technology in pursuit of intelligence objectives. As was seen in the discussion of the National Security Agency, the basic functions of communications intelligence —deception plans, traffic analysis, code breaking and attempts to acquire enemy codebooks—have become immensely more complicated and sophisticated since the Civil War. Nevertheless, America's Union and Rebel forerun-

---

*John Bakeless, *Spies of the Confederacy*. Philadelphia: J.B. Lippincott, 1970, p. 302.

ners in the fields of communications intelligence pointed the way, and quite early on served to define these functions and establish their role in the overall intelligence process. And perhaps even more importantly, like the sorcerer's apprentice they expanded the flow of intelligence information from the field to an extent which called into question the previous methods used to evaluate, collate, synthesize, and disseminate intelligence to interested parties.

The Civil War's Intelligence Survivor: The Secret Service

Besides the Signal Corps, not much of the wartime intelligence organizations were carried over into the post-Civil War era. Although the military intelligence services continued to exist on paper, they too went into partial eclipse and only began to reemerge as organizations in the 1880s. On the other hand, one quasiorganization which predated the Civil War and which for all practical purposes disappeared in the face of the National Detective Bureau rose like a phoenix out of the war's ashes: the Secret Service.

This thread of the American intelligence heritage is fairly obscure because, over time—essentially in the last half century—the Secret Service's earlier intelligence responsibilities have been taken over by other members of America's intelligence community. As Stuart Knight, the present director of the Secret Service said, "Today, we're really not a member of the intelligence community, basically we are consumers of the intelligence others produce." To be sure, the Secret Service provides the intelligence information it acquires in connection with its principal activities—detecting counterfeiting, protecting the president and foreign dignitaries—to the other intelligence agencies; but its responsibilities are sufficiently unique that it is more correct to think of the present-day Secret Service as a specialized law-enforcement agency rather than an intelligence organization per se. However, from 1865 through World War I the Secret Service was an intelligence as well as an investigative agency, and in these dual roles served as a progenitor and catalyst in the evolution of later intelligence organizations.

Although Lafayette Baker entitled his memoirs *History of the United States Secret Service,* his National Detective Bureau was not the direct forbearer of the Treasury Department's group. Its origins began in 1860, when Congress appropriated $10,000 for use by the Secretary of the Treasury to stop counterfeiting. Aside from wartime, this was the first formal institutionalization of intelligence activities within the executive branch. In 1863, Congress further authorized the Treasury Secretary to "appoint, not exceeding three revenue agents . . . to aid in the prevention, detection and punishment of frauds upon the revenue." By 1864, the budget to halt counterfeiting had grown to $100,-000. These funds were most often paid to investigators from outside the Treasury Department on a case-by-case basis.

When the National Detective Bureau (which under Baker had concerned itself with some of these matters) was dissolved following Baker's falling out with President Andrew Johnson, the federal government was left without an investigative body. Responding to the counterfeiting and fraud which were still widespread despite Baker's investigations, the Secret Service Division was established within the Treasury Department in 1865. William P. Wood was sworn in as the division's first chief. He had gained his investigative experience as a spy for both Baker and Stanton during the Civil War. As commandant of the Old Capitol prison, he had teamed with Baker in making numerous arbitrary arrests, and was Baker's partner in interrogating prisoners. (Interestingly, the present day Secret Service is loath to claim any connection with Baker's National Detective Bureau, but its spokesmen freely laud Wood as their first chief.) Wood was closely tied to Baker and the National Detective Bureau's sometimes illegal methods of operation. Before the Civil War, Wood had been an expert patent model maker. He altered the model on which the rights to the McCormick reaper were based, and by this trick won a court case for McCormick and Stanton, who was then McCormick's lawyer. Stanton owed Wood a favor, which he paid by putting him in charge of the Old Capitol.

Wood's original Secret Service Division included approximately thirty men. Some of these had been trained as private detectives, but most were close friends who had spied with Wood and the National Detective Bureau during the war. They each swore allegiance to a code of conduct which included commitments to be on twenty-four-hour call; report wherever assigned by the chief; keep expenses to the minimum; demonstrate high levels of fitness, investigative ability and honesty; and provide for expenses between paydays out of their own pockets. Wood hired both full-time and temporary operatives. Secret Service offices were opened in eleven major cities. Agents used their letters of appointment for identification, and received willing cooperation from local law-enforcement agencies. By the end of the new service's first year of operation, it had logged over 200 arrests for counterfeiting.

Just as the National Detective Bureau had swiftly filled the government's investigative vacuum and widened its jurisdiction to include areas outside military intelligence and counterintelligence, the Secret Service soon found itself involved in more than the pursuit of counterfeiters. As the government's only standing investigative body, it looked into gambling, organized crime, alcohol revenue violations, and the Ku Klux Klan, as well as Treasury Department internal abuses. The president and heads of executive branch agencies often requisitioned Secret Service operatives to conduct special investigations, but control of the division remained vested in the Treasury. In 1870, the Secret Service was physically transferred to the Justice Department, but direct supervision remained with the Treasury Solicitor's Office. A change in 1879 made the Assistant Secretary of the Treasury the Secret Service supervisor.

Appropriations bills for the Secret Service sought to limit its authority to cases involving pay and bounty laws, but the division continued to expand and assume more extensive powers. Chief John S. Bell wrote:

Restricted as we are by the form in which the appropriations are made, if agents were content to abide merely by the letter of the law, they would never be able to bring a criminal to justice. To their honor be it said, however, that they interpret their duty by the spirit and not the letter, and often in the pursuit of frauds spend money from their own slender purses to protect the government from robbery, when they realize that the statute of appropriation cannot be stretched to embrace the outlay, and have no hope of reimbursement.

Such candor on the part of an intelligence leader in the late nineteenth century about his organization's illegal activities is noteworthy not simply because he said it, but because none of the public officials in the executive and legislative branches who read Chief Bell's report raised a word in protest. This report and the lack of reaction to it offer concrete evidence of the long-standing "official" view of tacitly accepting illegal intelligence activities carried out for a "good purpose." The Secret Service's other activities included investigations into thefts of timber from government lands, moonshining, violation of naturalization laws, illegal voting, and the ghoulish conspiracy to steal Lincoln's remains. From 1902 on, the Secret Service was also given responsibility for the protection of the president, a function which it has retained exclusively to the present time.

During the Spanish-American War the Secret Service became the United States' counterintelligence arm. To this end, the president placed a special fund at the disposal of the Secretary of the Treasury for use in pursuing suspected enemies. This fund was used to support hundreds of investigations during the Spanish-American War, all of which came to naught. Such activities established a precedent for the use of the Secret Service in counterespionage during World War I.

As frauds and corruption continued to plague many government bureaus, the Secret Service lent them more agents. Successful Secret Service investigations provoked Congress to further limit the division's powers. The issue of Secret Service jurisdiction came to a head in 1908 after the Roosevelt administration's attorney general, Charles Bonaparte, directed several agents to investigate a land fraud involving members of Congress. As a result of the investigation a representative and a senator were convicted. Congress, in the kind of solidarity displayed in these kinds of matters, showed its ire at being investigated by agents of the executive branch by passing a law in 1908 which forbade the Justice Department to use Secret Service agents to invesitage Congressional transgressions of the law, or to create an independent investigative bureau which could circumvent Congress's power of the purse. In 1910, Congress extended these restrictions by allowing the Secretary of the Treasury to use only four Secret Service operatives in the enforcement of Treasury regulations. These restrictions led the president, William Howard Taft, to order the formation of the Bureau of Investigation in the Justice Department, thereby expanding the American intelligence community and, in passing, serving notice on

Congress that the national security would be best served by seeking out the nation's enemies no matter who or where they were.

To put Taft's action in perspective it should be noted that the attorney general was an original cabinet officer in the United States government, but it was not until June 1870 that he was given a Justice Department to head. The following year Congress appropriated $50,000 for the "detection and prosecution of crimes against the United States." Although the money was there, the Justice Department in the first several years employed only one special agent for investigations. The lack of manpower and investigative expertise prompted the Justice Department to employ outsiders. These included private detectives, agents borrowed from the Treasury Department's Secret Service, and United States attorneys and marshals.

This system was modified in 1875 by the appointment of four regional special detectives with direct responsibility to the attorney general. These men oversaw the Justice Department investigations, which were carried out largely by private investigators hired on a case-by-case basis. In 1878, a group of examiners was added to review paper records involved in investigations, but they undertook no field work. Their effectiveness was compromised because the examiner positions soon became patronage posts, with the occupants owing their jobs to political benefactors rather than to their competence or honesty.

In 1881, with the appointment of Attorney General Benjamin H. Brewster, Justice Department chiefs began speaking out against the use of private detectives for departmental investigations, but manpower shortages forced the attorney general to continue his reliance on outside investigators. These private agents came largely from the Pinkerton Agency, a firm with a respected reputation stemming from the Civil War exploits of its founder, Allan Pinkerton. However, when Pinkerton agents were found responsible for the Homestead Massacre in 1892—Pinkerton strikebreakers at a Carnegie Steel Company factory opened fire on peaceful strikers—an outraged Congress ordered government agencies to stop using private detectives.

The Congressional prohibition on private operatives confined the Justice Department to its own meager investigative forces and to borrowing Secret Service men to keep up with official and unofficial wrongdoing. By 1906 as many as thirty-two Secret Service agents were detailed to the Department of Justice. To Attorney General Bonaparte this statistic signalled his department's need for its own large team of special agents. In 1907 he approached Congress for funding of a larger staff, and was refused. In denying Bonaparte's request, Congress was responding to both personal and public sentiment. There was widespread distrust of detectives because many were former criminals, because they operated secretly, and because of the Homestead Massacre. In the tradition of Vidocq and Baker, rough criminal types had become mainstays of the investigative profession. Congress also objected to giving the executive branch broader powers of investigation. President Theodore Roosevelt had already successfully challenged Congress on this score in 1905, following the land fraud investigation in the Northwest. When Senator John Mitchell and Representative John Williamson of Oregon were implicated in the scheme, Roosevelt issued an open threat to investigate any member of Congress suspected of criminal activities. Congress, in its "old school tie" tradition, wanted to do its best to keep funds for such investigations out of the hands of the executive branch.

In 1908, at a time when the larcenous activities of several leading members of Congress were about to be exposed by Bonaparte's small band of investigators, Congress in its collective wisdom moved to block the Justice Department's investigative powers almost completely when it voted to deny appropriations for Secret Service agents on loan from the Treasury to the Justice Department. The attorney general responded by hiring nine Secret Servicemen to serve permanently in the Justice Department. The action was financed by discretionary funds and was undertaken with the knowledge and encouragement of President Roosevelt and Henry Stimson (then United States Attorney for New York). Once again the chief executive had shown that he could circumvent Congressional power to get his way with the intelligence community.

The Secret Service agents were formally separated from the Treasury Department on June 30, 1908, and the next day were organized along with all Justice Department special agents and examiners into a twenty-three-man bureau under the direction of Chief Examiner Stanley W. Finch. On July 26, a presidential order made this new Bureau of Investigation a permanent division of the Justice Department. The order was reluctantly accepted by Congress, which feared that TR might go public with all he knew about its members' transgressions and after-hours immoral activities.

Prior to World War I, the Bureau of Investigation (B of I) dealt mainly with interstate commerce violations, investigations of labor unrest, and perceived threats from revolutionaries. Outside the Justice Department, most government investigations were still carried out by detailed Secret Servicemen, who were felt to be more expert investigators—even though the core of the B of I was composed of ex-Secret Service agents.*

By 1915, despite the existence of the Bureau of Investigation, historical experience favored the Secret Service as the organization with the best qualification to conduct government investigations. At the time, the Secret Service's boss, Secretary of the Treasury William McAdoo, favored an intensive inquiry into the widespread allegations of German espionage in the United States. Attorney General Thomas Watt Gregory was reluctant to use his men in the B of I without the legal sanctions which federal law failed to provide. With its hands thus tied, the Justice Department was powerless to prosecute its cases against German spies and saboteurs, but it could encourage their prosecution

* In general, see: Harry and Bonaro Overstreet, *The FBI in Our Open Society*. New York: W.W. Norton, 1969, pp. 1–27.

under some local laws. In addition, both Attorney General Gregory and President Woodrow Wilson requested federal security legislation, but Congress balked, fearing that any bill they passed would be used by Wilson to stifle criticism of his policies. Blocked in Congress, the president eagerly gave Secretary of State William Jennings Bryan permission to use Secret Service agents from the Treasury Department to investigate alleged espionage by German diplomats. After Bryan's request to the Treasury for help, Secret Servicemen began cooperating with New York police to watch various diplomatic offices. Shortly thereafter Bryan, an admitted pacifist, resigned and was replaced by Robert Lansing. Lansing immediately released reports of "German intrigues" to the press, and his revelations were followed in August 1915 by publication of German propaganda plans taken from the briefcase of German commercial attaché Heinrich Albert.

Albert's briefcase had been stolen by Secret Service agent Frank Burke, and the captured papers combined with Secretary Lansing's accusations gave official support to the rumors of German espionage circulating among American citizens. The Secret Service triumph awakened old jealousies on the part of Bureau of Investigation agents over the division of the government's intelligence-gathering authority. Without informing Attorney General Gregory they began competing with their Treasury Department counterparts to expose spies. By July 1916, in the wake of several major sabotage and espionage efforts (including the massive munitions explosion at Black Tom, New Jersey), the bureau received official permission to continue its investigations for the State Department. By year's end, the B of I had expanded to 300 men under Chief Bruce Bielaski. In February 1917, Gregory capitulated to the zeal of his agents and his own personal desire to control the government's intelligence activities: he gave blanket permission for his men to investigate all acts of sabotage and espionage despite the absence of federal law to sanction his actions. This decision intensified the battle within the executive branch for jurisdiction over spy investigations.

In the same month Albert M. Briggs, a vice-president with Outdoor Advertising Incorporated, walked into the office of Chicago Bureau of Investigation superintendent Hinton D. Clabaugh. Briggs explained that he had volunteered to go to Cuba in 1898, and now that it was time to fight Germany he was physically unable to serve in the army. Instead, he offered to fund a group of citizen volunteers to assist the bureau in investigating espionage at home. Clabaugh knew Briggs as a respected businessman, and had already accepted the services of several of Briggs' friends who had volunteered to chauffeur bureau agents around Chicago. The absence of bureau funds for automobiles had left his men to pursue their wealthier suspects via streetcar prior to the local offer of volunteer transportation. Clabaugh recognized that his office needed assistance. He had only fifteen agents with which to cover the states of Illinois, Wisconsin, and Minnesota. Congress' reluctance to fund the domestic internal security agency meant that Clabaugh had almost no budget.

After sleeping on Briggs' proposition, Clabaugh awoke on the morning of February 3, 1917, to read that President Wilson had suspended diplomatic relations with Germany. He called Briggs and encouraged the billboard manufacturer to contact Chief Bielaski in Washington. Bielaski received Briggs warmly on Clabaugh's recommendation and immediately accepted an introductory offer of seventy-five automobiles from Briggs and other Chicago businessmen for use by the Bureau of Investigation. Bielaski asked Briggs to write down his full civilian assistance proposal for formal consideration. Wilson's announcement had added to the rising tide of spy hysteria in America. The B of I was receiving hundreds of unsolicited reports daily from common citizens, greatly overtaxing its small staff and 400 invesitgative agents in the field. Bielaski indicated that he had high hopes for the future of Briggs' organization in coping with the bureau's manpower shortage.

As March opened, the antiespionage bill which Gregory so desperately wanted was again killed by the House of Representatives after having been approved by the Senate. The Secret Service and Bureau of Investigation could run down acts of espionage, but they still had to rely on local law-enforcement officials to prosecute under state statutes. The defeat was especially unfortunate since March also saw the publication of the famed Zimmerman telegram, which further exacerbated the spy hysteria with its revelation of planned Mexican-German espionage cooperation against the United States.

On March 14, Albert Briggs delivered his plan for an investigative auxiliary to Bielaski. The organization was to be self-financed, but totally under the control of the Justice Department. On March 20, Bielaski approved the plan and told Briggs to begin assembling his men, cautioning him that they would not have the power to arrest, only to investigate. The plan held special attractiveness for Bielaski because it would not be of any cost to the financially strapped Bureau of Investigation, and the volunteers could be used as a large source of manpower to outflank the Secret Service and establish B of I preeminence in counterespionage.

Bielaski appointed Briggs general superintendent of the new organization, which chose the name American Protective League. Briggs picked a friend, Thomas B. Crockett, to be his chief assistant because of his disciplined military background. (Crockett, a descendant of the famed Davy Crockett, later left the APL and joined the army's Military Intelligence Division to serve on its domestic counterintelligence staff, thereby creating a strong bond between the two groups.) Briggs got on the telephone and contacted associates throughout the country, asking them to establish branch APL offices in their cities. A young lawyer accepted leadership of the New York chapter, and businessmen like Briggs headed most of the other offices in cities from New Jersey to California. In Wisconsin the APL started the policy of taking over other civilian antiespionage groups. The Wisconsin Defense League was absorbed into the APL and its leader, John Stover, was named state APL chief. This policy of absorption was encouraged by Bielaski and later by the head of the

War Emergency Division in the Department of Justice, John Lord O'Brian, as a means of centralizing control of domestic counterintelligence groups under the Justice Department and extending the department's dominance in the struggle with Treasury Secretary McAdoo and later with Colonel Ralph Van Deman, Head of the army's Military Intelligence Division.

The various APL branches were organized on a quasimilitary basis, emphasizing "Secret Service Divisions" in industries and public utilities. The APL's goal was to have operatives in every bank, business, and industrial concern who were sworn to report any disloyalty, industrial disturbance, or other matter "likely to injure or embarrass" the United States government. Officers in the APL were also required to swear an oath to support the Constitution and were given badges resembling police shields. The officers then recruited other members who were told little of the organization and were assigned only numbers for identification. Typically, the captains knew each other and all lieutenants; lieutenants knew only other lieutenants and their captain; and operatives knew only the lieutenant who was their immediate superior. APL branch chiefs contacted local police officers to arrange a coordination of efforts against espionage.

American Protective League branches spread rapidly as the fear of spies swept the country. Sensational journalism combined with comments about German schemes uttered by government officials from President Wilson down encouraged the public to see spies on every corner. In April the War Department issued an order to "sternly repress acts committed with seditious intent" and to "protect public utilities." The War Department also requested newspapers to exercise "voluntary" censorship relative to spy stories. Rather than putting a damper on public paranoia, the press' sudden silence increased people's fears. Without the press to confirm or deny the thousands of spy rumors floating about, citizens assumed most of them to be true. Rumors that labor unions were fronts for enemy propaganda and sabotage gave business leaders an excuse to call in APL members to help put down the efforts of fledgling unions to organize and strike.

On March 27, Secretary of War Newton D. Baker offered a voice of reason to overzealous spy-hunters when he cautioned that no enemy alien should be detained or arrested except for the actual commission of a crime. Countering this proposal, Charlie Warren, an aide to Gregory at the Justice Department, suggested a revival of the 1798 Alien Enemies Act since Congress refused to pass new antiespionage legislation. At the Cabinet meeting of March 30, Wilson and his top advisers succumbed to the national panic and accepted as true the presence of a vast alien conspiracy. Having had no ongoing intelligence operation with the capability to make an objective estimate of the situation, the executive branch reached a false conclusion. Attorney General Gregory, in a letter to the solicitor general, wrote the next day:

There are a very large number of German citizens in this country who are dangerous and who are plotting trouble, men from whom we must necessarily expect trouble promptly of a sinister sort.

As the confusion continued, Bielaski warned Briggs on April 2 that one of the APL's duties should be to protect enemy aliens from potential mob violence as well as investigating their loyalty; but such small pleas running against the tide of panic were scarcely heeded.

Four days later war was declared. At this time there were over 100 APL branches in operation, and although most of their work was legal and in support of the Justice Department, there were already reported abuses. In one instance, American Protective League and Bureau of Investigation agents wanted to arrest a German immigrant who worked at the Ford Motor plant in Highland Park, Michigan. The German, a union organizer, was found with photos and drawings of the plant in his possession. The agents took their case to the United States attorney, who explained that the man had violated no law and therefore the agents had no case. The agents ignored his instructions and badgered the state sheriff into arresting the German on trumped-up charges. On May 6, after APL agents discovered plans for a strike at the St. Louis Aluminum Ore Corporation, the company and the agents influenced the St. Louis district attorney to request federal troops to put down the strike. There was no evidence of espionage or sabotage, and federal troops could legally only be dispatched at the president's order after a request from the state governor. Fortunately General Berry, commander of federal troops in the Midwest, had a cool head. Instead of sending troops, he wrote to Attorney General Gregory:

I believe the preventive throwing of United States troops into such strike situations will do more harm than good as nothing is calculated to agitate strikers more than premature use of United States troops.

This early attempt to use the APL to subvert labor unions rather than investigate spies was a mild precursor of the league's later excesses.

By mid-May, President Wilson had signed the Selective Service Act, and the Bureau of Investigations–Secret Service feud was heating up again as McAdoo and Gregory continued their struggle for political power. On the basis of Justice Department advice, Wilson invoked the Alien Enemies Act of 1798 to authorize the arrest of over sixty enemy aliens on presidential warrants. The attorney general convinced the president to sign an order giving the Justice Department sole jurisdiction to enforce the warrants. At the same time, McAdoo was working on his own plan to regain control of internal security operations. Under his scheme, all Secret Service and Bureau of Investigation personnel would be pooled under the direction of one of his cronies. As he waited for Wilson to act on the recommendation, McAdoo encouraged the Secret Service to fight the Bureau of Investigation. They withheld information from the bureau's agents and issued press releases claiming jurisdiction in Bureau of Investigation affairs.

When Gregory formally notified McAdoo of Wilson's order granting control of the alien enemies investigation to the Justice Department, McAdoo called his men off the case and abandoned his requests for a combined agency. Gregory had scored a clear triumph in this battle. His use of the APL to achieve power was aided by Wilson's desire to create a volunteer bureaucracy which would deal with the expanded duties created in the executive branch by the war. Wilson wanted to maintain civilian control and have a structure easy to dismantle at the war's end rather than adopt the strategy Lincoln had used in expanding the executive branch's paid staff. The volunteer American Protective League complimented this philosophy, while McAdoo's combined central intelligence concept pointed toward a new permanent and expensive agency.

William Flynn, chief of Secret Service, struck the next blow in the intelligence competition. He protested to Wilson over the confusion caused by the APL's use of the name "Secret Service" on its badges. Indeed, the reference was confusing not only to the citizenry at large but also to some members of the APL, who were uncertain whether they were responsible to the Secret Service or the Bureau of Investigation. McAdoo stepped into the new dispute by forwarding a letter to the president which stated:

[It is unfortunate] that a miscellaneous horde of so-called Secret Service operatives be loose upon the country to pry into the business of peaceful citizens. . . . I greatly fear that if this new organization of volunteer detectives and Secret Service operatives is allowed to continue to exist, suspicion will be engendered among our people, smoldering race antagonisms will burst into flame, and the melting pot of America will be a melting pot no longer, but a crucible out of which will flash the molten lead of suspicion and dissension.

The secretary closed his letter by renewing his request for a central body to coordinate espionage intelligence.

Wilson chose to duck both issues, leaving his secretaries to fight out what he properly perceived as a politically based argument. McAdoo launched a quick probe of the APL which uncovered many abuses. He warned that the government would be held responsible for APL actions because the league's agents used the words "Secret Service" on their badges. When Wilson read McAdoo's report he began to realize the seriousness of the situation. The president wrote Gregory, "I wonder if there is any way in which we could stop it [the APL]?"

Gregory's response was delayed because he and the APL were preparing for the first registration under the new Selective Service Act, scheduled to take place on June 5. The APL expected that registration would be a prime occasion for demonstrations by subversives. Even before the draft officially started they had arrested over thirty men on suspicion of opposing conscription. Although Briggs delivered a promised 80,000 plainclothesmen at registration centers to protect against demonstrations, no opposition materialized. Those who opposed the draft protested by staying home. The APL toughs spent the day explaining the confusing registration form to patriotic aliens without a good command of English who were eager to comply with the conscription regulations.

In the wake of McAdoo's allegations, the APL found itself more confused and confusing than ever. Members were not only uncertain whether they worked for the Secret Service or the Bureau of Investigation, but some elected to operate on their own. Many members were local policemen and former policemen, and many more were the absorbed members of preexisting parapolice and business security organizations. In addition, APL chapters usually cooperated with local as well as federal authorities. As a Briggs memo noted, they drew funds from "influential individuals or corporations in the community who usually are the ones most benefitted in a property sense by the protection afforded by our organization." Individual members' loyalties were splintered. Even when the federal authorities did not want APL members to carry weapons, make arrests, or interfere with labor unions, local police and businessmen often encouraged such activities. Abuses of power were frequent. Badges were used to gain free admittance for APL officers to theaters, subways, and parking lots. Local chiefs bought badges at 75¢ a piece from the government and sold them at inflated prices to members. APL agents often carried illegal weapons, made illegal arrests, posed as Secret Service agents, planned entrapments and committed crimes to secure evidence, bugged rooms, tapped telephones, and conducted interrogations without the required presence of a federal agent. Briggs and Bielaski issued orders warning against such tactics, but without a complete membership list they had no way of knowing if all league members were informed and had no effective means of enforcement. The APL was out of control. They had created a monster.

Despite the known APL violations, both Bielaski and Gregory protected their stake in the war for control of the intelligence community by supporting the APL. In the absence of any public outcry to stop the organization, Wilson decided the league was necessary. McAdoo's voice was too small and smacked of political opportunism. Even such liberal vehicles as the *New Republic* failed to warn Wilson that Americans' civil liberties were taking a severe beating. In fact, the magazine wrote in 1917, "When a democracy goes to war it is compelled for the emergency to lay aside much of its own character."

Armed with Wilson's sanction, Bielaski moved to strengthen the APL by naming it an officially sponsored organ of the Justice Department and the Bureau of Investigation. He appointed chiefs for the major cities, required full membership lists, emphasized that there was no Secret Service connection and that that name should not be used, and required that all field reports be processed through Bureau of Investigations offices. He standardized procedures for all APL branches and increased secrecy by physically separating APL offices from federal buildings. The legal sanction for league investigations was improved on June 15, when Congress approved the Espionage Act and Wilson signed it into law. Its censorship provision was so general that anyone could be arrested for merely criticising a government policy while speaking with a friend. With several hundred thousand APL agents allegedly at work by the end of 1917, one had to watch one's words everywhere.

In a last effort to regain control of American counterespionage, Secretary McAdoo used Congressional passage of a new Secret Service bill to press for his coordinated intelligence agency. The bill authorized the president to use the Secret Service "without reference to existing limitations" if "an emergency exists which requires such action." Given these new powers, McAdoo urged that Secret Service Chief Flynn should lead an intelligence clearing house including the Bureau of Investigation, Army Intelligence, Naval Intelligence and postal security. He charged that there were spies in the State Department who had gone undetected under the Bureau of Investigation's administration of counterespionage. Public panic was soon raging again as several Congressmen followed McAdoo's lead and accused the government of being infested with spies. Bielaski countered McAdoo's plan and the charges of subversion by noting that he communicated daily with the Army, Navy, and State Department intelligence forces and shared their information. Further he asserted there were secret agents of the B of I in every arsenal holding war contracts. McAdoo's plan died its final death, and by the end of July the American Protective League was a fixture in wartime America. Unfortunately, there were few genuine German spies and saboteurs for the over 900 APL units to catch, so they began to unleash their paranoid energy against largely innocent groups, especially labor unions, the IWW, and other enemies of the APL's benefactor, American business.

Military Intelligence: Post–Civil War to 1916

From the Revolutionary War to the Civil War, military intelligence had been a sometimes child, becoming a full-fledged member of the nation's security family when hostilities commenced and, much like the armed forces themselves, relegated to neglected status at war's end. However, once military leaders had solved the immediate operational and intelligence problems of the Reconstruction (or so they thought), senior officers in both the army and the navy began to turn their attention to America's possible future military role in the international theater, and in so doing discovered they possessed scant information with which to prepare for engagements in foreign territory. The resulting struggles roughly parallel the Treasury (Secret Service) and Justice Department (Bureau of Investigation) conflicts over control of investigations, counterintelligence and counterespionage until a year or so before the start of World War I, whereafter military intelligence became heavily embroiled in the internal security and intelligence control controversy.

The navy was the first to respond to the dearth of intelligence in the post–Civil War era. In looking back at American history, naval leaders perceived that the advent of crises had stimulated frantic periods of mobilization to overcome the lack of standing effective battle strength. To compensate for this, the navy's conventional wisdom held that their marine forces would have to maintain constant battle readiness and maintain a tenable position until the army was ready for war. To this end, the Secretary of the Navy on March 23, 1882, issued General Order 292, which established an Office of Intelligence within the Bureau of Navigation "to collect and record such naval information as may be useful to the Department in wartime as well as peace." Further, the Naval Library was combined with the new Office of Naval Intelligence (ONI) so that all information collected would be coordinated under a central authority.

In its formative years, ONI concentrated on technical military information, but political details occasionally arrived from naval representatives abroad. In the past, almost as the military's response to the "grand tour," American officers had visited foreign countries to observe their military forces, but the creation of the military attaché system provided for full-time, ongoing observation by United States military representatives with freedom to associate with both military and diplomatic circles. The first naval attaché was dispatched to London in 1882. He was followed by an officer in Paris (1885) with responsibilities in Berlin and St. Petersburg, and Rome (1888) with additional responsibilities in Vienna. After the Spanish-American War, the naval attaché network was expanded to Tokyo (1895), Madrid (1897), Caracas (1903), Buenos Aires (1910), and the Hague (1911). These early attachés tended to be unqualified as intelligence officers, but in establishing regular channels of communication they paved the way for the more extensive use of attaché posts for intelligence purposes in later years.

Not to be outflanked by the navy, the War Department created a Bureau of Military Intelligence in autumn 1885. The birth was triggered when the Secretary of War requested background information concerning a European power from the adjutant general's office. When the secretary discovered there was no information to be had, he created the new bureau to "gather and file information concerning the military organizations of foreign countries in which, for one reason or another, the United States might become interested." In spite of the almost unlimited global implications of the secretary's dictum, the original order called for only one officer and one clerk to carry it out. This was similar to the situation in ONI, which in carrying out its worldwide assignments was dependent on detailees from other offices.

Major William J. Volkmar was the War Department's first intelligence chief, and worked with a staff of civilian clerks who at best can be described as the sick, lame, lazy, and politically well-connected. Volkmar, who from all reports took his newly designated responsibilities quite seriously, requested intelligence reports from all other subordinate elements in the War Department and the army's field commands in an ambitious effort to coordinate the army's information files. Volkmar's efforts at establishing a collecting program were of little avail; no one in a position to do something thought Volkmar's request made much sense. In reaction to this indifference, on April 12, 1889, the War Department's adjutant general issued a separate order which established a branch of military intelligence specifically charged with the "purpose of obtaining and collating such military data as may be deemed useful and beneficial to the Army at large." This order served notice on the reluctant collectors; the new section was placed under the direction of Captain Daniel M. Taylor and three civilians.

The army also borrowed the navy's idea of military attachés. On September 22, 1888, Congress appropriated money for permanent attachés, and in War Department General Order 19, February 25, 1890, the Secretary of War established spending allowances and information-acquisition guidelines for its military attachés. It was not until October 1902, however, that the secretary accepted clear responsibility for the attaché operation. This acceptance merely amounted to reaffirming the attaché's duties, which were to:

Examine and report upon all matters of a military or technical character that may be of interest and value to any branch of the War Department and to the service at large. Keep informed through the Legation, public press and such other channels as your official position may secure for you from foreign governments. . . . Examine the military libraries, bookstores and publishers' lists . . . also give notice of such drawings, plans, etc; which may be of importance and within your power to procure. Also perform such special duties as the Secretary of War may, from time to time, assign you.*

The Bureau of Military Intelligence (BMI) was made responsible for approving military attaché selections. The BMI forwarded all requests for information within the War Department to the attachés and received the reports from abroad, which were processed and filed by the military intelligence staff.

In 1898, Major Arthur L. Wagner was in charge of BMI. His staff included eleven officers in Washington and forty additional officers reporting from around the country. Wagner was also in charge of the War Department's sixteen military attaché posts in Europe, Japan, and Latin America. He, his officers, and twelve civilians occupied four rooms in the nation's capital and were provided with $3,640 with which to operate all intelligence offices, including those of the attachés.

Like Lafayette Baker, Colonel Wagner came under attack from a superior for delivering accurate intelligence which conflicted with the superior's opinions. Wagner's confrontation took place as America's leadership prepared for

* Lieutenant Commander William C. Endicott to Major J.C. Post, March 2, 1889. War Department Records, National Archives.

war with Spain. At a Cabinet meeting, Wagner was asked for his opinion of a proposed invasion of Cuba by United States forces. He replied that a land invasion would be foolish given the raininess of the season and the strong threat of disease on the island, including a recent high incidence of yellow fever. The colonel's position was well-reasoned, but it angered Secretary of War Russell A. Alger, who had hoped for a successful land campaign to assert the army's superiority. Alger fired Wagner from his post and blocked any promotion for him. Not until many years later, while he lay on his deathbed, was Wagner promoted to brigadier general.

Wagner's valuable counsel made one more contribution to the Spanish-American War. Before leaving the Military Intelligence Bureau, Wagner selected Andrew Summers Rowan for an expedition to discover the disposition of Cuban and Spanish troops in Cuba. Rowan was a West Point graduate who had headed the BMI's map section and later served as military attaché in Cuba. In connection with his map research he published a book, *The Island of Cuba,* a scholarly report on the island's topography and climate.

Colonel Wagner briefed Rowan on his mission. He was to smuggle himself into Cuba and make contact with General Calixto Garcia Iniquez, the leader of Cuban forces. Garcia was expected to answer questions about the strength and location of the Spanish forces and tell Rowan what supplies the native forces required. The expedition took Rowan a bit over a month in April and May of 1898. He returned to popular acclaim, and was a guest at a Cabinet meeting where he reported on his adventures sneaking through the Cuban swamps and forests to deliver his "message to Garcia." Rowan went on to serve in the Philippines, where he was awarded the Silver Star for combat bravery. In 1922, he was belatedly awarded the Distinguished Service Cross for his secret expedition. He died in San Francisco in 1943, at the age of 85.

Another American officer who travelled behind the Spanish lines in Cuba was navy Lieutenant Victor Blue. He went on three missions to make contact with Cuban partisans, determine their supply needs, and ascertain the position of Spanish ships moored at inland harbors. After the Spanish-American War he rapidly advanced through the navy ranks. By 1919 he was a rear admiral and chief of staff of the Pacific Fleet. He was later chief of the Bureau of Navigation. During World War I he commanded the U.S.S. *Texas* in the North Sea, and was awarded the Distinguished Service Medal. He died at the age of 63 in North Carolina in 1928.

In the secret world of espionage some men preserve their covers so effectively that their true identities never become known. Such a man was "Fernandez del Campo." All that is known definitely about del Campo is that he was a Texan of Spanish ancestry and a West Point graduate. The United States government sent him to Madrid in an effort to determine the destination of Spanish Admiral Camara's fleet. The navy was especially concerned that these ships might be bound for the Philippines rather than Cuba. Del Campo posed as a wealthy Mexican with Spanish sympathies. He lived lavishly and was quickly befriended by influential members of Spanish government and society who admired the manner in which he freely lost his money to them at cards. After establishing his playboy reputation in Madrid, the agent journeyed to the home of the Spanish fleet at Cadiz. Finding himself at a party with Admiral Camara, del Campo plied the admiral with flattery and drink and learned the date on which the fleet would sail and that its destination was not the Philippines. He shortly returned to Washington, where he was privately honored by the Cabinet and then drifted into obscurity, leaving only his story and fictional name.

The Signal Corps was another important component in the assault on Spanish territories. It maintained submerged as well as overland lines, and operated a fleet of balloons for airborne reconnaissance. The corps' full-time personnel numbered 150, but in May 1898, Congress appropriated funds for a 1,300-man auxiliary to serve during the war. Of greatest benefit during the Spanish-American War was the Signal Corps' use of submerged cables. In June 1898, the corps severed Cuba's cable ties with Spain, thereby isolating the island. The corps also monitored all transmissions from the United States to other parts of the world. The chief signal officer was the government's chief censor. Throughout, Signal Corps transmissions kept the army and navy advised swiftly and accurately on troop and fleet arrivals to Cuba.

One other secret mission took place in the Caribbean during this period. Lieutenant Henry H. Whitney:

signed on as a crew member of a British tramp steamer. Despite an intensive search of the ship by Spanish authorities upon its arrival, resulting from newspaper articles published in America which discussed his secret mission at great length, he landed and reconnoitered the island.

Whitney's mission was important because the island in question was Puerto Rico, not Cuba. BMI was already preparing for the possible expansion of conflict in the Caribbean before the formal declaration of war with Spain.

These and other intelligence activities contributed greatly to the Spanish-American war's successful outcome. However, with the Cuban situation relatively secure following the ratification of the treaty ending the war on February 6, 1899, the United States turned its attention to the Philippines:

. . . commencing in February 1899, the American forces were called upon to conduct a long pacification campaign throughout the archipelago, first to quell insurgents under the leadership of Aguinaldo and then later to subdue the fanatical Moros.

In conjunction with this effort an insurgent records office was created in the islands to translate and file captured documents. This office expanded, and by 1901 was formally designated the Military Intelligence Division, Adjutant General's Office, Division of the Philippines. Thus began America's experience with the problems of intelligence in a counterinsurgency environment. The three officers in charge were Lieutenant Colonel Joseph T. Dickman, Captain John R.M. Taylor, and Captain Ralph H. Van Deman.

A fourth officer, Frederick Funston, was also involved in the Philippines intelligence operation. Unlike most intelligence officers of the period, Funston was not a West Point graduate. He was a volunteer for the Spanish-American War from Kansas. He first saw duty with the Cuban insurrection forces. Although captured, Funston was released in a prisoner exchange and debriefed by intelligence chief Wagner. Wagner admired the young officer's resourcefulness and leadership qualities. In short order Funston was recruited for military intelligence and sent to San Isidro, on Luzon Island in the Philippines.

Working with the Philippines MID in 1901, Funston discovered the strong likelihood that General Emilio Aguinaldo, leader of the native guerrillas, was headquartered in northern Luzon. Despite his flaming red hair, Funston used disguise techniques he had learned in Cuba and began a journey into the jungle. There he recruited approximately 100 pro-American natives as his personal expeditionary force and set out to capture Aguinaldo. So as not to attract undue suspicion and scare Aguinaldo away, Funston and the few Americans who accompanied him posed as captives of their Filipino comrades. Using forged communiqués for Aguinaldo, the party cleared the guerrilla leader's guard post and reached his hidden headquarters. They captured Aguinaldo and transported him back to the American base. This bold expedition broke the back of guerrilla resistance in the archipelago and hastened the consolidation of a secure American position.*

The Philippines MID continued as an independent operation until June 18, 1902, when it was absorbed by the Military Intelligence Division of the Adjutant General's Office in Washington. This tied the Philippines bureau into a recent agreement between MID and the Office of Naval Intelligence to share information and resources. With United States combat forces inactive, MID and ONI concentrated on mapping expeditions and studies of foreign people.

Part of the government's new interest in foreign nations included a secret mission ordered by President Theodore Roosevelt in March 1903. He instructed Secretary of State John Milton Hay to dispatch several army officers to travel as civilians in order to gather information in South American countries which might play a role should the United States involve itself in conflict within the Gulf of Mexico or the Caribbean. Hay selected two men fresh out of West Point, one of whom was Second Lieutenant Grayson M.P. Murphy.

---

* After leaving the Philippines, Funston rose rapidly through the army's ranks. By 1916 he was Major General Funston on duty at the Mexican border. He was killed there in a skirmish; otherwise he would have been the commander of the AEF in World War I. If he had been the nation's ranking officer, intelligence might have caught on much earlier than it did. Not only did Funston have a strong intelligence background, but he was also acquainted with Captain Van Deman from their mutual service in the Philippines, and would have supported Van Deman's proposals for ongoing military intelligence.

Murphy went to Venezuela as a military attaché and consulate assistant, but spent most of his time travelling incognito as a civilian while surveying the Central American region. He returned to brief President Roosevelt on October 16. Murphy resigned from the army in 1907 and went on to become a successful New York financier. After World War I he was head of the American Red Cross in Europe. He also served on Pershing's general staff and was an aviation officer with the AEF in Great Britain from November 1918. After the war he became a close friend of William J. Donovan, the future chief of the Office of Strategic Services. In 1920, Murphy and Donovan toured Europe together to make their own intelligence estimates and establish a private intelligence network to keep them and like-minded members of America's "peacetime" intelligence subculture advised of changes in Europe. Murphy died in 1937.

On February 14, 1903, the General Staff Corps was created with military intelligence designated its second division, or G-2. The chief of staff was Lieutenant General S.B.M. Young. He requested expanded personnel to assist MID in translating documents from field agents. All MID documents were gathered centrally under G-2 in Washington.

As envisioned at the time of reorganization, G-2 was divided into two large areas: military information, and the military attachés who provided an information service used mainly within the War Department rather than through the Office of the Chief of Staff.* The Washington headquarters housed six officers, whose sections were under Major W.D. Beach. The sections were:

1) Military Attaché and Manila Office Section
2) Classification, Card Indexing, and Library Section
3) Map and Photographic Section
4) Historical Section
5) Monograph Section
6) Publication Section**

Between 1903 and 1908 MID activities of note included: extensive mapping expeditions in the United States and China; the detailing of fifteen observers (including Pershing) to the Russo-Japanese War; and the detachment of four intelligence officers to Japan for the study of that nation's language and culture. (MID's early awareness of Japan was rewarded in 1915 when squads of Japanese soldiers landed in Baja California and conducted covert desert-survival training maneuvers in Arizona. These missions were discovered by Colonel Sidney Mashbir, who later served with General MacArthur's Allied Translator and Interpreter Section in World War II.***

The Military Intelligence Division developed a close working relationship with the Army War College (G-3 of the General Staff). At first both divisions

---

* Memo OCS, February 3, 1904. AWC 639–22, WDGS, National Archives.

** Memo Ch. MID to Sec. GS, August 27, 1903. AWC 639–20, WDGS, National Archives.

*** Ind, *op. cit.,* 1963, pp. 131–32.

were housed next to each other and the sharing of materials was a simple matter of loading up a cart and pushing it to the next building; later the War College expanded and moved to new and distant quarters. Shortly after this relocation, the head of the War College asked that G-2 be transferred to his building so that materials could again be centralized. General Franklin Bell, then Army Chief of Staff, approved the request. By late June 1908 he also approved a request that G-2 and G-3 be merged into one division headed by the War College. For all intents and purposes G-2 lost its autonomy and thus America lost a formalized central military intelligence organization. The small MID staff was further reduced and all intelligence reports were redirected through the adjutant general's office rather than through the General Staff. A Military Information Committee was appointed within the War College to replace G-2, but the six members devolved into assistants to the War College planners and lacked independent authority to process raw data from the field. As ex-intelligence officer and espionage historian Colonel Allison Ind has noted, the Military Information Committee consisted of "personnel with no knowledge of the intelligence unit's aims and functions and no interest in learning them."* It was these men who officially ruled American military intelligence until 1917 and the advent of World War I.

To understand why General Bell agreed to such a thorough emasculation of military intelligence one must look back to the Philippines MID and its successor organization, the Manila office of G-2. Bell had been in the Philippines and had argued against the need for extensive intelligence. He considered it a frivolous expense and the topic left a bad taste in his mouth; he had once publicly debated its merits with a young captain, only to see General MacArthur side with the captain and embarrass Bell, the senior officer. In abolishing G-2, Bell had retaliated indirectly for the disgrace. Thus again, as in so many other cases, the personal factor affected the evolution of American intelligence.

There is much to ponder in the record set forth above. On the one hand, it suggests the importance of the individual in solving intelligence problems. On the other, it suggests that these problems, essentially when the human and Constitutional rights of individuals are involved, are not much different today than in generations past. One can draw encouragement from the personal sacrifices made by the Tallmadges, Van Lews, and Bakers; their intelligence careers prove that the pursuit of America's intelligence aims by properly motivated persons is the best safeguard in keeping intelligence from being used against Americans as a people. The record is clear; no matter what laws or administrative safeguards are designed, the ultimate use of intelligence for good or evil is still in the hands and minds of those who go forth and find it.

* *Ibid.*, p. 130.

SOURCE NOTES

In addition to the sources cited in the bibliography and identified in footnotes, information throughout this book has been derived from presently available unclassified documents, memoranda, reports etc. These materials, most of which were previously classified, have in recent years been declassified as a result of inter-agency reviews, in response to Freedom of Information Act requests, or by Congressional disclosure of their contents. This ongoing declassification process has produced an unprecedented volume of original source materials dealing with American intelligence. Also, from discussions with officials at the National Archives, the National Security Council, Presidential libraries and those in charge of the military services' oral history programs it is clear that within the next several years the amount of intelligence-related information available to researchers and scholars will be doubled, if not trebled.

Chapter 1
CHANGING THE INTELLIGENCE GUARD

Reports and Minutes in Combined Chiefs of Staff and Joint Chiefs files, Modern Military Records, National Archives; Reports and Minutes of the 55th-60th meetings of the Combined Chiefs of Staff, Modern Military Records, National Archives; Joint Chiefs of Staff, draft history, *The War Against Germany*, Part 3, "Casablanca through Trident," Record Group 218, Records of the United States Joint Chiefs of Staff, Modern Military Records, National Archives. Selected files from the "Leahy Papers" (Fleet Admiral William Leahy), Modern Military Records, National Archives. Information concerning presidential assumptions of intelligence authority was derived in part from discussions and interviews with intelligence community personnel.

Chapter 2
AMERICA'S INTELLIGENCE HERITAGE

Reports of the Director of Military Intelligence to the Chief of Staff of the U.S. Army, Old Military Records, National Archives; Records of the Office of the Chief of Naval Operations, Old Military Records, National Archives; U.S. Treasury and Department of Justice files, National Archives.

Chapter 3
COUNTDOWN TO PEARL HARBOR

"The Friedman Lectures", Modern Military Records, National Archives; selected documents in The Goodfellow Papers, an OSS collection, Hoover Institution on War, Revolution and Peace, Stanford California; relevant papers of ONI and U.S. Naval Attache at London, Modern Military Records, National Archives; Counter Intelligence Corps (US) School, History and Mission of the CIC in World War II, Modern Military Records, National Archives.

Chapter 4
THE WORLD WAR II STRUGGLE FOR INTELLIGENCE CONTROL

Records of the United States Joint Chiefs of Staff, Combined Chiefs of Staff and Joint Security Control, Modern Military Records, National Archives; The Goodfellow Papers, an OSS collection, Hoover Institution on War, Revolution and Peace, Stanford California; interviews with former OSS personnel and members of the military intelligence services.

Chapter 5
TRUMAN AND THE INTELLIGENCE COMMUNITY: Part I

Chapter 6
TRUMAN AND THE INTELLIGENCE COMMUNITY: PART II

Records of the United States Joint Chiefs of Staff, Combined Chiefs of Staff and Joint Security Control, Modern Military Records, National Archives; "The Leahy Papers," Modern Military Records, National Archives. Interviews with former CIA personnel, members of the Truman administration, State Department officials and members of the military intelligence services.

Chapter 7
EISENHOWER: THE COLD WAR LEGACY

National Security Council files, documents and memoranda, Modern Military Records, National Archives; other de-classified NSC materials not held by the National Archives provided the author in response to a Freedom of Information request.

Chapter 8
KENNEDY TO CARTER: INTELLIGENCE AND POLICY MAKING

In addition to the reports of the Senate's Select Committee to Study Governmental Operations with Respect to Intelligence Activities cited in the Bibliography, information concerning the workings of the Washington intelligence bureauracy was derived from the author's personal experience and by discussions with present and former members of the intelligence community and staff personnel of the Senate's Select Committee.

Chapter 9
THE FUTURE OF AMERICAN INTELLIGENCE

Sources
Besides sources cited in this chapter, information concerning the CIA's Northwest Federal Credit Union was provided to the author by the National Credit Union Administration in response to a Freedom of Information request.

Chapter 10
AFTERWORD

Sources
Center for Military Studies, U.S. Army, Washington, D.C. Shuster Collection, Modern Military Records, National Archives, Operational Archives Branch, U.S. Navy Washington, D.C.; State Department Division of Libraries and Reference Services, Washington, D.C. Records of the Office of Chief of Naval Operations, Old Military Records, National Archives.

BIBLIOGRAPHY

American Protective League. *American Protective League: The Minute Man Division.* Seattle: American Protective League, 1918.

Armbrister, Trevor. *A Matter of Accountability: The True Story of the Pueblo Affair.* New York: Coward-McCann, 1970.

Bakeless, John. *Spies of the Confederacy.* Philadelphia: J.B. Lippincott Company, 1970.

Bakeless, John. *Turncoats, Traitors, and Heroes.* Philadelphia: J.B. Lippincott Company, 1959.

Baker, General Lafayette Charles. *History of the United States Secret Service.* Philadelphia: private printing, 1867.

Barber, Major Henry A., Jr. *ONI Funding Memorandum to Army Chief of Staff G-2, 26 August 1939.* National Archives. Record Group 165, 2610–2–38CD, #5750, Box 1956.

Basler, Roy P., editor. *The Collected Works of Abraham Lincoln* New Brunswick: Rutgers University Press, 1953.

Bates, David H., *Lincoln in the Telegraph Office.* New York: The Century Company, 1907.

Bidwell, Bruce W. *History of the Military Intelligence Division.* Washington: Department of the Army, General Staff, 1961.

Blum, John M., et al. *The National Experience.* New York: Harcourt Brace Jovanovich, Inc., 1973

Bowen, Walter S. and Harry Edward Neal. *The United States Secret Service.* Philadelphia: Chilton Company, 1960.

Braden, Thomas. "The Birth of the CIA," *American Heritage* February 1977, Vol. 28, Number 2.

Brown, Anthony Cave. *Bodyguard of Lies.* New York: Harper & Row, 1975.

Brown, Anthony Cave, editor. *The Secret War Report of the OSS.* New York: Berkeley Publishing Corporation, 1976.

Brown, J. Willard. *The Signal Corps U.S.A. in the War of the Rebellion.* Boston: U.S. Veteran Signal Corps Association, 1896.

Bryan, George S. *The Spy in America.* New York: J.B. Lippincott Company, 1943.

Bulloch, James D. *The Secret Service of the Confederate States in Europe.* New York: Thomas Yoseloff, 1959. (Reprint of 1884 edition)

605

Burger, Nash . *Confederate Spy: Rose O'Neale Greenhow.* New York: Franklin Watts, Inc., 1953.

Burns, James MacGregor. *Roosevelt: The Soldier of Freedom.* New York: Harcourt Brace Jovanovich, 1970.

Cash, W. J. *The Mind of the South.* New York: Alfred A. Knopf, 1941.

Central Intelligence Agency. *Presidents of the United States on Intelligence.* Washington: Central Intelligence Agency, 1976.

Chafee, Zechariah, *Free Speech in the United States.* Cambridge: Harvard University Press, 1941.

Churchill, Marlborough. "The Military Intelligence Division General Staff." *Journal of the United States Artillery,* v. 52. April, 1920. Pp. 293–316.

Churchill, Sir Winston S. *The Second World War* (6 Volumes). Boston: Houghton Mifflin, 1948–53.

Coben, Stanley. *J. Mitchell Palmer: Politician.* New York: Columbia University Press, 1963.

Conn, Stetson and Byron Fairchild. *The Western Hemisphere: The Framework of Hemisphere Defense.* United States Army in World War II Series. Washington: U.S. Army, 1960.

Cutler, Robert. "The Development of the National Security Council." *Foreign Affairs,* v. 34. April 1956.

Davis, Curtis Carroll, editor. *Belle Boyd in Camp and Prison, by herself.* New York: Thomas Yoseloff, 1968.

DeConde, Alexander. *The Quasi-War.* New York: Charles Scribners' Sons, 1966.

Department of State. *Postwar Foreign Policy Preparations.* Washington: U.S. Department of State. (General Foreign Policy Series #15)

Dulles, Allen. *The Craft of Intelligence.* New York: Harper and Row, 1963.

Edmonds, S. Emma. *Nurse and Spy in the Union Army.* Hartford: W.S. Williams, 1865.

Eisenhower, Dwight D. *Crusade in Europe.* New York: Doubleday and Company, 1948.

Farago, Ladislas. *Burn After Reading.* New York: Walker, 1961.

Farago, Ladislas. *The Game of the Foxes.* New York: David McKay, 1971.

Feurlicht, Roberta Strauss. *America's Reign of Terror.* New York: Random House, 1971.

Fitzpatrick, John C., editor. *The Writings of George Washington from the Original Manuscript Sources 1745–1799.* Washington: U.S. Government Printing Office, 1944.

Ford, Corey. *Donovan of OSS.* Boston: Little Brown, 1970.

Furer, Julius Augustus. *Administration of the Navy Department in World War II.* Washington: U.S. Government Printing Office, 1959.

General Services Administration. National Archives and Records Service. The National Archives. *Federal Records of World War II: Military Agencies (Volume 2).* Washington: U.S. Government Printing Office, 1951.

Gowenlock, Thomas. *Soldiers of Darkness.* Garden City: Doubleday, 1937.

Greenhow, Rose O'Neale. *My Imprisonment and the First Year of Abolition Rule at Washington.* London: R. Bentley, 1863.

Hall, Charles Swain. *Benjamin Tallmadge.* New York: Columbia University Press, 1943.

Headley, John W. *Confederate Operations in Canada and New York.* New York: The Neale Publishing Company, 1906.

Hirshson, Stanley P. *Grenville M. Dodge: Soldier, Politician, Railroad Pioneer.* Bloomington: Indiana University Press, 1967.

Hitchcock, Lt. Col. E. A. *Journal of Lt. Col. E. A. Hitchcock.* Library of Congress, Original Manuscript Division.

Hoehling, A. A. *Women Who Spied.* New York: Dodd, Mead and Company, 1967.

Hoover, John Edgar. *Reports concerning Nazi Agents in Argentina.* National Archives. Record Group 319, Box 176, File 383.2 Argentina through 2–16–43.

Horan, James D. *Confederate Agent.* New York: Crown Publishers, Inc., 1954.

Horan, James D. and Howard Swiggett. *The Pinkerton Story.* New York: G.P. Putnam's Sons, 1951.

Hough, Emerson. *The Web.* Chicago: The Reilly and Lee Company, 1919.

Hyde, H. Montgomery. *Room 3603.* New York: Farrar, Straus and Giroux, 1962.

Ind, Colonel Allison. *Allied Intelligence Bureau.* New York: David McKay Company, 1958.

Ind, Colonel Allison. *A Short History of Espionage.* New York: David McKay and Company, Inc., 1963

Jensen, Joan M. *The Price of Vigilance.* New York: Rand McNally and Company, 1968.

Johns, George S. *Philip Henson, the Southern Union Spy.* St. Louis: private printing, 1887.

Kahn, David. *The Codebreakers, History of Secret Communication.* New York: Macmillan, 1967

Kane, Harnett T. *Spies for the Blue and Gray.* Garden City: Hanover House, 1954.

Kearns, Doris. *Lyndon Johnson and the American Dream.* New York: Harper & Row, 1976.

Kennedy, John F. *Public Papers of the Presidents: John F. Kennedy.* Washington: U.S. Government Printing Office, 1962.

Leopold, Richard W. *The Growth of American Foreign Policy.* New York: Alfred A. Knopf, 1962.

Lindsey, Robert. "To Be Young, Rich—and a Spy." *New York Times Magazine,* May 22, 1977.

Lisio, Donald J. *The President and Protest: Hoover, Conspiracy, and the Bonus Riot.* Columbia: University of Missouri Press, 1974.

Lossing, Benson J. *The Two Spies: Hale and Andre.* New York: D. Appleton and Company, 1899.

McGarvey, Patrick J. *CIA: The Myth and the Madness.* New York: Saturday Review Press, 1972.

McLachlan, Donald. *Room 39.* New York: Atheneum, 1968.

March, Peyton C. *The Nation at War.* New York: Doubleday, 1932.

Meyer, Karl E. and Tad Szulc. *The Cuban Invasion.* New York: Praeger, 1962

Miles, Milton. *A Different Kind of War.* New York: Doubleday, 1967

Millis, Walter, editor. *The Forrestal Diaries.* New York: The Viking Press, 1951.

Milton, George Fort. *Abraham Lincoln and the Fifth Column.* New York: The Vanguard Press, 1942.

Mogelever, Jacob. *Death to Traitors.* Garden City: Doubleday, 1960.

Mosk, Richard. *History of the Secret Service.* Unpublished, 1964.

Ottenberg, Miriam. *The Federal Investigators.* Englewood Cliffs: Prentice-Hall, 1962.

Overstreet, Harry and Bonaro. *The FBI in Our Open Society.* New York: W. W. Norton, 1969.

Pennypacker, Morton. *The Two Spies: Hale and Townsend.* Boston: Houghton Mifflin, 1930.

Philby, Kim. *My Silent War.* New York: Grove Press, 1968.

Pinkerton, Allan. *The Spy of the Rebellion.* New York: G. W. Carleton, 1883.

Plum, William R. *The Military Telegraph During the Civil War in the United States.* Chicago: Jansen, McClurg, 1882.

Preston, William. *Aliens and Dissenters.* Cambridge: Harvard University Press, 1963.

Roosevelt, Kermit, editor. *The War Report of the OSS.* New York: Walker, 1976.

Rositzke, Harry. *The CIA's Secret Operations.* New York: Reader's Digest Press, 1977.

Ross, Ishbel. *Rebel Rose.* New York: Harper and Brothers, 1954.

Rowan, Richard Wilmer. *The Pinkertons.* Boston: Little Brown, 1931.

Rowan, Richard Wilmer. *The Story of Secret Service.* New York: The Literary Guild of America, 1937.

Sarmiento, F. L. *Life of Pauline Cushman.* Philadelphia: J. E. Potter, 1865.

Seymour, George Dudley. *Documentary Life of Nathan Hale.* New Haven: private printing, 1941.

Seymour, George Dudley. *Hale and Wyllys.* New Haven: private printing, 1933.

Shapley, Deborah. "Foreign Intelligence Advisory Board: A Lesson in Civilian Oversight?" *Science.* March 12, 1976.

Smith, George Gardner. *Spencer Kellogg Brown.* New York: D. Appleton, 1903.

Smith, James Morton. *Freedom's Fetters.* Ithaca: Cornell University Press, 1956.

Smith, R. Harris. *OSS.* New York: Dell, 1973.

Stern, Philip VanDoren. *Secret Missions of the Civil War.* New York: Rand McNally, 1959.

Steven, Stewart. *Operation Splinter Factor.* New York: J. B. Lippincott, 1974.

Stevenson, William. *A Man Called Intrepid.* New York: Harcourt Brace Jovanovich, 1976.

Stidger, Felix A. *A Treason History of the Order of Sons of Liberty, Succeeded by Knights of the Golden Circle, Afterward, Order of American Knights.* Chicago: private printing, 1903.

Strategic Services Unit, Office of the Assistant Secretary of War, War Department, History Project. *War Report of the Office of Strategic Services.* Washington: War Department, 1949.

Tallmadge, Benjamin. *Memoir of Col. Benjamin Tallmadge.* New York: Thomas Holman, 1858.

Tallmadge, Benjamin. *Memoir of Colonel Benjamin Tallmadge.* New York: Gilliss Press, 1904. (Reprint of 1858 edition with additional notes and pictures.)

Truman, Harry S. *Memoirs* (2 Volumes). Garden City: Doubleday, 1955.

Truman, Harry S. *Public Papers of the President of the United States: Harry S Truman.* Washington: U.S. Government Printing Office, 1961.

Truman, Margaret. *Harry S Truman.* New York: William Morrow, 1973.

Tuchman, Barbara W. *The Zimmerman Telegram.* New York: Dell, 1958.

Turrou, Leon G. *Where My Shadow Falls: Two Decades of Crime Detection.* Garden City: Doubleday, 1949.

U.S. Army. *The Founding of the Army's First Counter Intelligence Organizations.* Washington: U.S. Army Intelligence Command (unpublished), 1967.

U.S. Army. Military Intelligence Division. *A History of the Military Intelligence Division, 7 December 1941–2 September 1945.* Washington: U.S. Army (unpublished), 1946.

U.S. Commission on CIA Activities Within the United States. *Report to the President.* Washington: U.S. Government Printing Office, 1975.

U.S. Congress. House. Committee on Un-American Activities. *Security Practices in the National Security Agency (defection of Bernon F. Mitchell and William H. Martin).* Washington: U.S. Government Printing Office, 1962.

U.S. Congress. Joint Committee on the Investigation of the Pearl Harbor Attack. *Final Report.* Washington: U.S. Government Printing Office, 1946.

U.S. Congress. *Joint Committee on the Investigation of the Pearl Harbor Attack.* (39 Volumes) Hearings, 79th Congress, 2nd session. Washington: U.S. Government Printing Office, 1946.

U.S. Congress. Senate. Committee on Government Operations. Subcommittee on National Policy Machinery. *Organizing for National Security.* Volumes 2 and 3. Washington: U.S. Government Printing Office, 1961.

U.S. Congress. Senate. Committee on International Relations. *United States Policy in the Far East: Part 2.* Volumes VII and VVII. Selected Executive Session Hearings of the International Relations Committee, 1943–50. Washington: U.S. Government Printing Office, 1976.

U.S. Congress. Senate. Committee on Naval Affairs. *Unification of the War and Navy Departments and Postwar Organization for National Security.* Washington: U.S. Government Printing Office, 1945.

U.S. Congress. Senate. Committee on Presidential Campaign Activity. *The Final Report of the Committee on Presidential Campaign Activity.* Washington: U.S. Government Printing Office, 1974.

U.S. Congress. Senate. Select Committee to Study Governmental Operations With Respect to Intelligence Activities. *Alleged Assassination Plots Involving Foreign Leaders.* Washington: U.S. Government Printing Office, 1975.

U.S. Congress. Senate. Select Committee to Study Governmental Operations With Respect to Intelligence Activities. *Covert Action.* Hearings, 94th Congress, 1st session. December 4 and 5, 1975. Washington: U.S. Government Printing Office, 1976.

U.S. Congress. Senate. Select Committee to Study Governmental Operations With Respect to Intelligence Activities. *Final Report:* Books I–VI. Washington: U.S. Government Printing Office, 1976.

U.S. Congress. Senate. *Hearings before the Select Committee to Study Governmental Operations with Respect to Intelligence Activities. Volume 6. Federal Bureau of Investigation.* November 18, 19, December 2, 3, 9, 10, 11, 1975. Washington: U.S. Government Printing Office, 1976.

U.S. Congress. Senate. Select Committee to Study Governmental Operations with Respect to Intelligence Activities. Hearings. *Volume 4: Mail Opening.* October 21, 22, and 24, 1975. Washington: U.S. Government Printing Office, 1976.

U.S. Congress. Senate. Select Committee to Study Governmental Operations with Respect to Intelligence Activities. *The National Security Agency and Fourth Amendment Rights.* Hearings, 94th Congress, 1st Session. October 29 and November 6, 1975. Washington: U.S. Government Printing Office, 1976.

U.S. Congress. Senate. Select Committee to Study Governmental Operations with Respect to Intelligence Activities. *Operation Shamrock.* Washington: U.S. Government Printing Office, 1975.

U.S. Government. *Government Manual 1974–75.* Washington: U.S. Government Printing Office, 1974.

U.S. Joint Chiefs of Staff. *Records of the U.S. Joint Chiefs of Staff.* National Archives. Record Group 218, CCS 334, 3–11–42.

United States Office of the United States Chief Counsel for Prosecution of Nazi Criminality. *Nazi Conspiracy and Aggression* (11 Volumes). Washington: U.S. Government Printing Office, 1946–48.

Van Deman, Ralph H. *Memoirs.* Unpublished manuscript.

Van Lew, Elizabeth. *Papers of Elizabeth Van Lew.* Manuscript and Archives Division, New York Public Library.

Warner, Ezra J. *Generals in Gray.* Baton Rouge: Louisiana State University Press, 1959.

Willoughby, Charles A. and John Chamberlain. *MacArthur 1941–1951.* New York: McGraw-Hill, 1954.

Winterbotham, F. W. *The Ultra Secret.* New York: Harper & Row, 1974.

Wohlstetter, Roberta. *Pearl Harbor, Warning and Decision.* Stanford: Stanford University Press, 1962.

Worthington, C. J. *The Woman in Battle, By Madame Loreta Jareta Velasquez.* Richmond: private printing, 1876.

Yardley, Herbert O. *The American Black Chamber.* London: Faber & Faber, 1931.

Zacharias, Captain Ellis M. *Secret Missions.* New York: G. P. Putnam's Sons, 1946.

GLOSSARY

A-2	Air Force Intelligence General Staff
Abwehr	World War II German military foreign intelligence service
ACDA	Arms Control and Disarmament Agency
ACS(I)	Army Chief of Staff for Intelligence
ADDP	Assistant Deputy Director for Plans (CIA)
ADS	American Defense Society
AFOSI	Air Force Office of Special Investigations
AFSA	Armed Forces Security Agency
AGO	Adjutant General's Office
AIB	Allied Intelligence Bureau
AID	Agency for International Development
APL	American Protective League
ARC	Ad Hoc Requirements Committee
ARMISH	U.S. Army Mission Headquarters
ARPA	Advanced Research Projects Agency
ASA	Army Security Agency
ASD/I	Assistant Secretary of Defense for Intelligence
ASD/PA&E	Assistant Secretary of Defense for Program Analysis and Evaluation
ASW	Antisubmarine Warfare
BBC	British Broadcasting Corporation
BEW	Board of Economic Warfare
BI	Background investigation
BMI	Bureau of Military Intelligence
BNDD	Bureau of Narcotics and Dangerous Drugs
BNE	Board of National Estimates
B of I	Bureau of Investigation

CAA	Civil Aeronautics Administration
CAS	Controlled American Source
CAT	Civil Air Transport
CCS	Combined Chiefs of Staff
CD	OSS branch for camouflage, censorship, and documentation intelligence
CDIB	Consolidated Defense Intelligence Budget
CDIP	Consolidated Defense Intelligence Program
CE	Counterespionage
CFI	Committee on Foreign Intelligence
CFR	Council on Foreign Relations
CI	Counterintelligence
CIA	Central Intelligence Agency
CIAA	Coordinator of InterAmerican Affairs
CIC	Counterintelligence Corps
CIC	Commander-in-Chief
CID	Central Information Division (OSS)
CIG	Central Intelligence Group
CI & IA	Counterintelligence and Investigative Activity
CIRL	Current Intelligence Reporting List
CIS	Current Intelligence Staff (OSS)
CJCS	Chairman, Joint Chiefs of Staff
COI	Coordinator of Information
COINTELPRO	Counterintelligence Program (FBI)
COMINT	Communications Intelligence
COMIREX	Committee on Imaginary Requirements and Exploitation
COMOR	Committee on Overhead Reconaissance
COMSEC	Communications Security
CONUS	Continental United States
CROWCASS	Central Repository of War Criminals and Security Suspects
CSS	Central Security Service
DAS	Defense Attache System
DCI	Director of Central Intelligence
DCID	Director of Central Intelligence Directive
DCII	Defense Central Index of Investigations
DCS	Domestic Contacts Service
DCS/I	Deputy Chief of Staff for Intelligence

DDA   Deputy Director for Administration or Directorate for Administration (CIA)

DDCI   Deputy Director of Central Intelligence

DDI   Deputy Director for Intelligence or Directorate for Intelligence (CIA)

DDO   Deputy Director for Operations or Directorate for Operations (CIA)

DDP   Deputy Director for Plans or Directorate for Plans (CIA)

DDR   Deputy Director for Research (CIA)

DDS&T   Deputy Director for Science and Technology or Directorate for Science and Technology (CIA)

DDS   Deputy Director for Support (CIA)

DEA   Drug Enforcement Administration

Deuxieme Bureau   French intelligence

DIA   Defense Intelligence Agency

DIOP   Defense Intelligence Objectives and Priorities

DIPO   Defense Intelligence Program Office

DIRC   Defense Investigative Review Council

DIRDIA   Director of the Defense Intelligence Agency

DIRNSA   Director, National Security Agency

DIS   Defense Investigative Service

DKIQ   Defense Key Intelligence Question

DMA   Defense Mapping Agency

DOD   Department of Defense

DOJ   Department of Justice

DP   Displaced Person

ECA   Economic Cooperation Administration

ECG   Executive Coordination Group—covert operation review (1948)

ELINT   Electronic Intelligence

ERDA   Energy Research and Development Administration

ETO   European Theater of Operations

EWD   Economic Warfare Division

EXCOM   Executive Committee

FBI   Federal Bureau of Investigation

FBIS   Foreign Broadcast Information Service

FCC   Federal Communications Commission

FEA	Foreign Economic Administration
5412 Committee	Committee to review covert operations (1955)
FIS	Foreign Information Service (COI propaganda branch)
"Flutter"	Polygraph Test
40 Committee	Committee to review covert operations (1970)
FSO	Foreign Service Officer
FYDP	Fiscal Year Defense Plan
G-2	Army Intelligence General Staff
GDIP	General Defense Intelligence Program
GID	General Intelligence Division
GRU	Soviet Military Intelligence Service
HUAC	House UnAmerican Activities Committee
HUMINT	Human Intelligence
IAC	Intelligence Advisory Committee
IC	Intelligence Community
ICS	Intelligence Community Staff
IEC	Intelligence Evaluation Committee
IES	Intelligence Evaluation Staff
INR	Bureau of Intelligence Research (State Department)
IRA	Irish Republican Army
IRAC	Intelligence Resources Advisory Committee
IR&DC	Intelligence Research and Development Council
IRS	Internal Revenue Service
ISA	International Security Affairs (DOD)
ITT	International Telephone and Telegraph
IWW	International Workers of the World
J-2	Joint Staff Director for Intelligence (DOD)
JANIS	Joint Army Navy Intelligence Studies
JCS	Joint Chiefs of Staff
JIG	Joint Intelligence Group
JPS	Joint Planning Staff
JPWAC	Joint Psychological Warfare Advisory Committee
JPWC	Joint Psychological Warfare Committee

JRC	Joint Reconnaissance Center
JSOP	Joint Strategic Objectives Plan
JSP	Joint Staff Planners
KGB	Soviet national intelligence organization
KIQ	Key Intelligence Question
MAAG	Military Assistance and Advisory Group
MBFR	Mutual and Balanced Force Reduction
MBO	Management By Objectives
MI-5	British Military Intelligence for domestic counterintelligence
MI-6(v)	British Military Intelligence for Foreign Counterespionage
MI-8	War Department Cipher Bureau
MID	Military Intelligence Division
MIS	Military Intelligence Service
MO	Morale Operations Branch (OSS)
"Mole"	an agent in place
MONGOOSE	covert operation "to help Cuba overthrow the Communist regime"
MTO	Mediterranean Theater of Operations
MU	Maritime Unit (OSS)
NAG	Net Assessments Group
NDRC	National Defense Research Committee
NFIP	National Foreign Intelligence Program
NIA	National Intelligence Agency
NIA	National Intelligence Authority
NIB	National Intelligence Bulletin
NID	National Intelligence Daily
NIE	National Intelligence Estimate
NIO	National Intelligence Officer
NIPE	National Intelligence Programs Evaluation
NIRB	National Intelligence Resources Board
NIS	Naval Investigative Service
NKVD	predecessor of KGB
NPIC	National Photographic Interpretation Center
NSA	National Security Agency
NSA/CSS	National Security Agency/Central Security Service

NSAM National Security Action Memorandum
NSC National Security Council
NSCIC National Security Council Intelligence Committee
NSCID National Security Council Intelligence Directive
NSDM National Security Decision Memorandum
NSRB National Security Resources Board
NSSM National Security Study Memorandum

OCB Operations Coordinating Board
OCD Office of Civilian Defense
OCD Office of Collection and Dissemination (CIA)
OCI Office of Current Intelligence (CIA)
OEW Office of Economic Warfare
OG Operational Groups Branch (OSS)
OMA Office of Military Assistance
OMB Office of Management and Budget
ONE Office of National Estimates
ONI Office of Naval Intelligence
OO Office of Operations (CIA)
OPA Office of Price Administration
OPC Office of Policy Coordination
OPD Operations and Plans Division (War Department General Staff)
ORE Office of Reports and Estimates
ORR Office of Research and Reports (CIA)
OSD Office of the Secretary of Defense
OSI Office of Scientific Intelligence (CIA)
OSO Office of Special Operations (CIA)
OSO Office of Special Operations (DOD)
OSRD Office of Scientific Research and Development
OSS Office of Strategic Services
OWI Office of War Information

PB Program Branch
PBCFIA President's Board of Consultants on Foreign Intelligence Activities
PB/SUCCESS code name of CIA Guatemala Operation (1954)
PCG Planning and Coordination Group (NSC)
PFIAB President's Foreign Intelligence Advisory Board

PMIB	Philippine Military Information Bureau
PNIO	Priority National Intelligence Objective
PPB	Personnel Procurement Branch (OSS)
PSB	Psychological Strategy Board (NSC)
P Source	Professor Source—OSS academic recruiting
PW	psychological warfare
PWB	Psychological Warfare Board
PWD	Psychological Warfare Division
R&D	Research and Development
RDT&E	Research Development Testing and Evaluation
RFE	Radio Free Europe
RL	Radio Liberty
SA	Special Activities Branch (COI)
SA/B	Special Activities/Bruce (OSS)
SA/G	Special Activities/Goodfellow (OSS)
SACO	Sino-American Cooperation Organization
SALT	Strategic Arms Limitation Talks
SCA	Service Cryptologic Agency
SGA	Special Group Augmented
SI	Special Intelligence Branch
SIGINT	Signal Intelligence
SIS	Secret Intelligence Service (British)
SNIE	Special National Intelligence Estimate
SO	Special Operations Branch (OSS)
SOD	Special Operations Division (Ft. Dietrick, Maryland)
SOE	Special Operations Executive (British)
Special Group	Committee to review covert action proposals (1955)
Special Group-CI	Special Group for counterintelligence
SRC	Special Review Committee
SSI	Secret Security Intelligence
SSO	Strategic Services Operation
SSU	Strategic Services Unit
S&T	Schools and Training Branch (OSS)
SWNCC	State War Navy Coordinating Committee

TELINT   Telemetry Intelligence

303 Committee   committee to review covert operations (1964)

TOA   Total Obligational Authority

TSD   Technical Services Division (CIA)

UNRRA   United Nations Relief and Rehabilitation Administration

USAINTA   United States Army Intelligence Agency

USCIB   United States Communications Intelligence Board

USIA   United States Information Agency

USIB   United States Intelligence Board

USNR   United States Naval Reserve

WDGS   War Department General Staff

WSAG   Washington Special Action Group

X-2   counterespionage

INDEX